Martha's Vine

A Novel by
Sheree Zielke

Creeping Ivy Publishing House
Suite 329, 9768-170 Street
Edmonton, Alberta T5T5L4

COVER ART BY FRED SANFILIPO

ISBN: 978-0-9866437-0-5

Dec 2010

To Austin,

Kindest regards for a life filled with joy & success!

Sheree, '10

*"With willing hearts and skillful hands, the difficult we do at once;
the impossible takes a bit longer." - Author unknown*

*"The Lord is a shelter for the oppressed,
A refuge in times of trouble." — King David, Psalm 9:9,
New Living Translation Bible*

*For my son, Ryan, who (even at a very young age)
understood the writer side of me. When he saw me at the
typewriter, he would inform his friends that,
"Mom is on the moon."*

—◇—

*And for Andrew.
Not of my blood, but forever in my heart.
May God watch over you, wherever you may be.*

ACKNOWLEDGMENTS

FOR SOME writers, I suppose, the penning of a novel is a solo journey—but not for me. Several people joined me on this adventure—as I fought my way through the chapters. They cheered me on as I battled paralyzing fears of incompletion, indecision, and of self-doubt. Some took the trip with me more than once (thanks Rob). One person joined me only in memory; however, it is because of Professor Duncan that I fancied I was even capable of writing a novel.

To CHESTER DUNCAN (1913-2002), my English professor in my first year at the University of Manitoba. If you are a teacher reading this and you have doubts that a teacher can change a life—then know this: Professor Duncan gave a naive Manitoba farm girl a reason to believe in herself. He made me feel worthy, capable, and smart. With just a few simple words, in an English class, back in 1975, he affirmed my natural propensity to speak out, and single-handedly applauded my need to stand on my own beliefs—against any wave of majority consensus. In addition, he said that all of us had one great novel in us, and I believed him. However, in keeping with my tradition for disagreement, I believe some of us have two—perhaps even three—great novels in us, since it will take more than one book to tell Martha's story.

To DAVID THIEL, my beloved husband of nearly a quarter century and my best friend. David's brilliant mind, his sense of storytelling, and his intimate understanding of the way my brain works, makes him the perfect editor. Much of David's creative spirit runs through the veins of Martha's Vine, and I am glad of it. His insight helped to bring about massive revisions in pursuit of a more believable tale, and a more gripping adventure. In addition, he stood with me as I wrestled with the sexuality in the book; not an easy feat, I assure you.

To AARON WINTERS. I became friends with Aaron through the photo-sharing site, *Flickr*. I had shelved Martha's Vine repeatedly for 15 years, before I turned to him. He agreed to be a reader while I churned the chapters out, but only if I could keep him interested; that meant tighter writing, and constant action. And, in response to one of his constructive complaints, I was compelled to create a literary device I call an, "Under Chapter." Without Aaron's presence in my life, Martha's Vine, the finished novel, would simply not exist.

To ROB CHRISTMAN. Some friends bless you just by sharing the planet. But when they prove to have editing talents, too—then, as a writer—you are doubly blessed. While I was writing, I would regularly get lost in a jungle of indecision and despair, becoming very despondent; Rob would hike in and guide me back into the light, with great edits, encouraging words, and most importantly—prayers. In spite of serious hardships in his own life, Rob stayed with me for the entire birth of Martha's Vine, and ALL its subsequent rewritten versions. How we became friends, I will never know; that we are—is all that matters.

To FRED SANFILIPO. This incredibly talented visual artist did the cover for Martha's Vine. He has his own page at the back of this book.

To SUSAN ESTES SMITH AND WILLIAM (BILL) G. SMITH. Some people, by their very existence, bring you joy. Such is the case of Susan and her husband, Bill. I met Susan through *Flickr*, too. She expressed interest in my novel, so I asked her to be a reader. Before long, Bill was reading, too. Their enthusiasm, questions, and observations made Martha's Vine a much better book.

To JOE. Just Joe. Just because. He knows why.

To SEAN STEWART. This long ago acquaintance of mine, a fellow Canadian writer, summed up my being in one sentence: "Sheree, you drive more like a man... than a man." Thank you, Sean. Some things stay with you, no matter how many years go by.

To JOHN DENVER (1943-1997), one of the finest musicians and poets in history. I thank you for the music that made my life livable at times when there was nothing to live for, and for penning my most favorite song of all time, "Sunshine On My Shoulders": Words and music by John Denver; Copyright © 1971 by Cherry Lane Music.

To BOB DYLAN, for making such great music memories for the Boomer generation, and for creating another of my most favorite songs, "Just Like a Woman": Words and music by Bob Dylan; Copyright © 1966 by Dwarf Music; renewed 1994 by Dwarf Music.

To JOHN KAY, of Steppenwolf, for producing an iconic tune embracing rebels everywhere, both on and off motorcycles. And for being one of the best musician interviews, I have ever had. "Born to be Wild": Words and music by Mars Bonfire; Copyright © 1967-2007, John Kay & Steppenwolf.

To METEOR (yes, I am thanking a fictional character) for writing himself into the book. He was just another guy with a gunshot wound, until he turned those blue eyes on Martha. After that, well—there was no turning back. Many times when my writer's energies had fled, all I had to do was hang out with Meteor for a few paragraphs, and like magic—the creative juices would flow again, proving that adults can have make believe friends, too. Thank God.

To GOD. I have saved the best for the last. I have known God my whole life. I can't fathom an existence without Him, without feeling His presence, and knowing He is watching. And that He cares. I don't just worship God; I like him. Amen.

Table of Contents

Prologue

The Change

"TAKE IT, Martha!"

The woman winced as her husband shoved the small gun into her hand. The Browning pistol lay across her right palm—a vile thing, evil in its silence. Her chest squeezed tight as a memory bubbled up. She struggled to take a breath. She fought the rising emotions, but still her hand shook. Engines roared in the distance. She glanced over her shoulder and then she looked up at her husband.

He didn't know. He couldn't know. He would never know.

"Josef—I can't." Martha rid herself of the gun by placing it gingerly on their tiny kitchen table. Her ice blue eyes pleaded for him to understand. "I just can't."

"This is ridiculous," Josef said. "They'll kill us if we don't fight back."

"We can't fight them," Martha said. "We're too few." She waved her arm toward the living room where people sat on bench seats. It was an assortment of men, women, and children—some old, some young, some very young. "What're you thinking, Josef? We're not an army."

The growl of engines droned in the distance.

Josef shifted his gaze. Martha followed his lead and looked out the window of their RV. She couldn't see the motorcycles yet, but she knew they would be there soon. She knew who was riding. She knew why they were coming. And she knew what would happen if they were caught.

"We could die here," she said. She took Josef's face in her hands and turned it towards her. "Or we could run. And live."

Josef's eyes darted past his wife's head to the window.

"I'll drive fast," Martha promised. She dropped her hands from Josef's face.

"Drive where?" Josef asked. He was looking at her again. "Drive to where?" He held his hands up in frustration.

"To the place we heard about," Martha said quickly. "That camp outside Edmonton. Near the Hutterites' colony."

"That place?" Josef asked, as his voice rose in disbelief. "That place is an armed camp. What makes you think they'll want us showing up? What makes you think they won't shoot us on sight?"

"Josef—it's our only chance." Martha grabbed her own face, her fingers splayed across her cheeks. The rest of the family watched the exchange and waited in silence. The engines got louder. Martha raised her hands into the air, fingers fanned. Her eyes were wide. "We can't do this on our own anymore. We need to join with other people." She took a breath. "We've got to go. Now!"

Josef stood silent and then he nodded.

Martha raced to the front of the RV and settled in behind the steering wheel. The family members took their usual seats. They knew the routine. They had been following it for over a year—ever since *the Change*.

The Change is what people called the phenomenon that had altered their world. The power grid went down. It just disappeared. Without warning. It just happened. In an instant. Overnight. They went to bed with electricity; when they woke up, there was none.

Nobody understood what had happened. They simply adapted. Or died; millions had died. But not Martha. And not her family members. She had made the decision to survive—and to keep her children, and her grandchildren safe, too. They had learned to trust her. They trusted her now. No one spoke.

Martha glanced back, smiled, and turned the key in the ignition. The unit fired up. She shoved it into gear. She glanced at Josef. He stared straight ahead.

Martha swung the huge vehicle onto the pavement. A shower of dead, rust-colored leaves burst into the air and danced in the RV's jet stream. She pressed down on the gas pedal.

God, please, she prayed. *Please.*

Out of the corner of her eye, she could see Josef mumbling and she knew he was praying, too.

Only fifteen kilometers. Just fifteen.

She stepped down harder on the accelerator and the RV picked up speed. Motorcycles droned on the highway behind them.

I can do this.

God help me.

I can do this.

The speedometer needle leapt to the right as the RV roared up the highway.

Josef continued to pray.

☐☐☐

THE MAN'S message arrived by "hog." Not the fat-bellied, curly-tailed, pink, rooting-around-in-the-mud type of hog, but rather the kind built of steel and rubber, complete with two wheels, handlebars, a muffler, and... an attitude. The Man's message rolled from the Pacific to the Atlantic, and then dipped south toward the Gulf of Mexico in a relay that ran day and night, rain or shine. From hog rider to hog rider, the message passed; it took months, but thousands of bikers soon heard the news, and they embraced it—for doing so meant survival. But more than that, it meant—domination. And so, they came...

Like birds of prey, they flew to The Man, to be near him, and to follow his commands. He was The Man. His message was clear. The Man was rallying the clubs together. He was building an army. They would move north to Canada where border resistance, since the Change, had collapsed.

Motorcycles—thousands of bikes—rumbled across the US-Canada border through the Sweet Grass-Coutts border crossing: Harley-Davidson, Honda, Triumph, Yamaha, Kawasaki, Suzuki, Ducati, and vintage Indians—all shapes, all engine sizes, all colors—as colorful as the wild flowers carpeting the fields and the ditches. The bikes cruised by like a motorcade or a parade, but no watchers stood on the sidelines, welcoming them or cheering them on.

Nobody stopped the bikers—there was nobody to stop them. The Canadian border guards, the RCMP, and the military had long since deserted their posts because staying would have meant death: starvation or being shot. Now, the border between the two countries was a wide avenue leading into the Alberta heartland, a land rich with resources:

*beef, grain, honey, fresh mountain water, and—more importantly—oil.
And, guns—Albertans loved their guns. And their ammunition. For the
bikers, it was like riding into a province-sized Walmart. Currency?
Bullets, hot from a gun barrel. But only if an owner wouldn't see reason—
The Man's reason—and comply. They had the choice. However, most
people didn't resist The Man. Because he made things happen.*

*The Man was unmovable, unshakeable, and unstoppable. Small
biker gangs, small car gangs, and even small towns rose up before him,
but they were soon converted to his way of thinking: acquiesce or die. His
northern route through the province was easy to trace—a smeared trail
of blood. But it wasn't to be all smooth sailing because The Man hadn't
reckoned on the one they called, 'the Gatekeeper.'*

☐☐☐

JUST OUTSIDE Edmonton, the Gatekeeper had been strategizing and
implementing his plans for many years. Matthew was ready when the
Change hit.

When the electricity disappeared, Matthew switched over to
generators. His survival compound had been designed intelligently—more
like a fortress. They had everything necessary: guns, ammunition, food,
shelter, manpower, and a powerful alliance with one of the largest
Hutterite colonies in the province.

Matthew and his longtime hunter buddies—six of them—had turned
survival into an art form. It had taken them years to complete their
compound and amass the goods in their storehouses and bunkers, but they
had done it. They were comfortable, except for one thing—so many others
wanted what they had. So many were willing to kill for what they had.
Especially the "Crazies."

The Crazies, biker bands, modern day pirates with no law to control
them, embraced and flaunted their freedom—their freedom to take, to
destroy, and to kill. Word-of-mouth about Matthew's compound had
reached the bikers. The attack came quickly. Without warning. And it had
been deadly; Matthew's friends had died in the ambush.

However, the Crazies were just that—crazy—an eclectic mix of men
and their motorcycles. Wild and willful, but poorly organized; their lack of
leadership made them weak. And they knew it. So, when they got wind of
The Man and his plan, they were intrigued. They, too, like their American
counterparts, flocked to him. Some out of a sense of survival. Some out of a
desperate need to belong. Some out of curiosity. Some out of a carnivorous

craving for confrontation, and with an eagerness to test the supremacy of the self-proclaimed biker king. Whatever their reason, they arrived—by the thousands. All were headed for a small Alberta town called Vulcan, situated halfway between Lethbridge and Calgary.

Meanwhile, Matthew endured the memory of his friends' deaths, but his resolve was clear: The Gatekeeper would never be beaten by the Crazies again.

It would take a woman to do that.

And she was on her way.

Chapter One

The Gatekeeper

"STOP PUSHING me, *Martha*!" the young woman said as the older woman shoved her toward a man seated behind a wide desk. The Gatekeeper studied the pair. His mouth twisted as he stifled a grin.

"Breeder—she's a breeder," Martha said.

The Gatekeeper's eyes questioned her briefly. Then he grunted his understanding.

Life was much simpler since the Change. The loss of the power grid happened so quickly, very few had time to prepare for a world without instant-on electricity. In this new world, a thirsty person didn't select from an array of pops, juices, and sparkling waters—he asked for water. The best he could hope for was that the water would be clean—disease-free—and with nothing floating in it. Women who were successful in bringing forth children were known simply as, 'breeders'.

"She's already had two children with a midwife," Martha continued. "Homebirths, with no complications." The younger woman nodded her agreement. "She could probably help deliver a baby herself. Or at least coach," Martha added.

The Gatekeeper made a checkmark in the hardbound journal in front of him. Martha wondered where he had gotten his stationery supplies. She coveted the handsome marbleized blue pen he held. A spurt of anger jabbed her as she reminded herself about her own lack of foresight in not packing away enough pens and pencils—items that had become nearly as valuable as gold.

"What's your name?" the Gatekeeper asked as he butted his chin in the direction of the young woman.

"Ruth."

"How old are you?"

"Twenty-five."

"Where are your children?"

"Uh, outside with our cl— group." Ruth had nearly used the word, *clan*, but remembered that Martha had vetoed the word saying that clan sounded foolish—too much like in-bred cousins with missing front teeth.

"Are they healthy?"

"Yes. As far as I know."

"And you? Are you healthy?" He leaned closer and studied Ruth.

"Yes, sir, I am. A plantar wart now and then. But usually fine. I don't get sick very often."

The Gatekeeper continued to make notes. The two women studied his bent head with its spiky grayed hair. No nonsense haircuts were the fashion now. Fewer problems with lice that way. Even the women tended to keep their hair very short. Some, like Ruth, however, chose to run the risk and keep their hair long. They would carefully check their heads regularly though, especially after spending any time with newcomers. Lice medication was very hard to find. The alternate treatment—coal oil—was even harder to get. Just one more thing Martha regretted not having added to her heavily stocked medical kit.

"How long have you been traveling?" the Gatekeeper asked, without looking up.

"We left our acreage about a year and a half ago. We've been on the move ever since," Martha answered. She cast her eyes down as their recent narrow escape came back to her. *No sense telling this man about that*, she thought. At least—not yet.

"Do you have identification?"

"Yes, of course. We're Canadians. All of us have valid passports. Here's mine." Martha flipped the dark blue cover open to her picture. Intense blue eyes stared out from under a mop of silver hair.

"Doesn't look much like you," he observed.

"I know. I've lost a little weight. Maybe gained a little age," Martha said. "But it's me." She would not relinquish the book, even when the man tried to take it from her. Feeling her resistance, he let it go.

"How many in your group?"

"Fourteen of us," Martha answered. "Nine adults and five kids. Two children are not our family—they're both boys." Martha hesitated as she waited for the man's reaction. There was none. She continued, "We found one of the boys on the road near Beaumont. We adopted him. He's not— um—mentally up to speed."

The Gatekeeper put his pen down and folded his hands beneath his chin. "We'll be happy to take some of your group into our compound, but not all. Especially mental defectives. We have food for the fit only—those who can offer something of value to our community—like healthy babies," he said, motioning to Ruth. "I think you can understand that."

Martha lowered her hands to her sides. She spoke in a level no-nonsense tone. "If someone from my group is not accepted here, then count me out, too. And— if I go, the others go with me. That means you lose healthy adults—adults who can produce. And who can fight." She returned his stare. "I think *you* can understand *that*."

As if he had not heard her, the Gatekeeper continued, "I'll see the rest of your members now." He looked over at a tall man standing near the door; the guard's arms were crossed over his chest; he held a pistol in his right hand. The man straightened and listened as the Gatekeeper spoke: "Have them come in."

The guard turned, opened the door, and indicated to those waiting outside that they were to come forward. A little girl ran into the room, her blue eyes sparkling. She wrapped her arms around Martha's hips. Her soft brown hair hung in messy braids down her back.

"This is Mary, my granddaughter," Martha said with a wide smile.

"Hello, Mary," the Gatekeeper said. He studied the child for a moment as she peered at him from behind Martha's leg. He smiled, but Mary did not smile back. He returned his gaze to the door and watched as the rest of the family walked into the room.

A large man joined Martha. He was deeply tanned. His black hair was thin, but shiny with a slight curl. Silver streaked his temples and splashed through his thick black beard and mustache. His ample belly, apple cheeks, and bright green eyes made him look like an up-and-coming Santa Claus. A few more years, and he would be sitting in a big chair in some mall, promising some kid that Santa would 'consider' his wish list.

However, that was before. Now he was just a man trying to survive— and Christmas was merely another day on the calendar. His name was Josef. A grey canvas bag hung low across his chest.

"Open that," the Gatekeeper demanded.

Josef gave the sitting man a quick curious look, and then he opened the bag. He showed its interior to him.

"No weapons," Josef said. "Just my Bible."

Martha watched as Josef pulled out a narrow blue book. She knew that Josef always kept his Bible handy—road-weary and all covered in small lengths of grey duct tape. To another's eye, it might have looked like junk, but to Josef's eye, it was a precious jewel. Martha knew its pages were filled with colored pencil marks, scrawled thoughts, and observations. The writing was far too tiny to read, so only Josef—and God—understood Josef's notations.

Martha motioned to him. "This is my husband, Josef," she said.

The man at the desk rose, and extended his hand. "Good to meet you, Josef. My name is Matthew. They call me the Gatekeeper." The two men shook hands. The societal gesture was terse and guarded.

Josef eyed Matthew suspiciously. "I was against coming here," he said. "But Martha insisted. She's been right in the past, so here we are. Tell me, Matthew—were we right in coming here?"

Matthew gave a small smile as he settled down into the padded office chair beneath him. "That remains to be seen. As I have explained to *your woman*, we can't take everyone who comes to the compound. We're very selective. If you bring value to us—food... seeds... fuel... talents... then we're happy to have you. But we can't accept everyone."

"Understood," Josef said. "So, where do we stand?"

"Not so fast," Matthew said, holding up his hand. "Tell me something—why is a woman leading your group?"

"Because she's a leader," Josef said with a quick lift of his shoulders. "Her foresight and instincts have kept us alive and her talent for organization has kept us comfortable—in spite of the mess the world is in now.

"Two years ago, she began nagging me to buy an RV and to get educated about being a survivalist. I didn't want to listen, but she didn't give up. And now, here we are."

Josef reached out to Martha in a protective way, but she shrugged away from him. Josef dropped his arm to his side. He had long since learned not to be hurt by her rejection. Martha was in her 'general' mode where emotions and loving actions came second—or even third in priority. Getting it done was what mattered.

"So, you people are Christians then?" Matthew gave nothing away as to what his response would be to either a 'yes' or a 'no' answer.

Josef spoke. "Yes, most of us believe in Jesus. What about you?"

"Some of us are, and some of us aren't. Most of us believe in God, and His commandments, but we have our own laws, too—our own type of commandments. What was okay once upon a time in the old world—is NOT okay here."

"I'm glad to hear that, but what would you have said if I had said we weren't Christians? That we were Jews? Or Muslims? Or Wiccans?"

Matthew answered with a shrug. "Same difference. We don't care what religion you are, as long as you live by our laws. And, as long as you bring something of value to our community—we don't really care who you worship. But break our laws, and you'll be disciplined—or cast out. Same thing applies to Christians—live by the laws or get out. It's that simple."

Josef took a long breath. As he exhaled, he asked, "So, what now?"

"I'll review each member of your group and decide who'll be allowed to stay. First of all, I need the names, ages, and marital status of every person."

Josef backed away as Martha stepped up to the desk once again. "Let's start with me and Josef."

She gave Matthew the details: married, forty-seven and forty-five, respectively. Then there was Hannah, fifty-two, unmarried with one dependant, baby Moses. A young mother they found dying in a small southern Alberta town had given her baby to Hannah. Hannah, who had never had a child of her own, was totally devoted to the little boy, and had named him after the Bible hero.

Matthew wrote his notes quickly.

Next was Ruth; her husband, Peter, twenty-seven; daughter Mary, aged four, who still clung to Martha's leg; and son Samuel, nine.

Matthew's pen stopped moving. He looked up and regarded Ruth once more. "Samuel is nine?"

"Yes."

"You were sixteen when he was born?"

"Yes."

"Hmm," Matthew said. "Okay, who's next?" Another young woman stepped forward.

"I'm Elizabeth, Ruth's sister," she said. "Twenty-three. Not married. Don't want to be. This is my friend, Jonah." Matthew regarded the tall skinny man standing beside Elizabeth. Jonah stared back.

"Hello," Jonah said. He didn't smile.

"He's twenty-four." Elizabeth continued. "And that's my brother, Nehemiah. He's twenty-seven. That's his wife, Velma." Elizabeth was pointing to a tiny woman with short dark hair and pretty features. "She's twenty-five. And this—this is their son, Jacob."

A boy in dirty blue jeans, with unevenly cut blond hair, ran to the desk. "Hi," he said, as he held out a tiny hand to Matthew. Matthew shook it and smiled.

"Hi, kid," he said.

"I'm eight," Jacob said. "Do you have any video games here?"

"Um, no," Matthew said. "We don't."

"Oh, that's too bad," Jacob said. "I miss playing Mario and Luigi. My Nintendo ran out of power." Then he brightened, and added, "I bet you have a generator. Ours got taken away, you know?"

"No, I didn't know that," Matthew said with a grin. "We'll see what we can do about your Nintendo."

Jacob rewarded Matthew with a huge smile as he walked around the desk toward the man. Matthew put his hand on Jacob's shoulder and pushed him back to the other side of the desk. He looked past the boy to Martha. She had pulled another little boy next to her.

"This is Reggie," Martha said. "We think he's retarded or autistic. We don't know anything about Reggie other than his age—at least we think we know his age because he always shows us eight fingers."

Matthew watched the boy for a moment. The child muttered softly, his eyes darting around the room, never coming to rest on the eyes of the man staring at him. Matthew looked down and made another note in his book.

The group stood quietly while Matthew continued to write. He noted the newcomers into a family tree of sorts with blank lines beneath each of their names. He looked up. "Now..." he said, "...value—the children, providing they're healthy—will be admitted. Strong additions to the gene pool. And since there's no telling how long the world will remain in its present state, re-population is an important consideration." Matthew looked at Josef for a response, but Martha answered.

"Obviously, both Ruth and Velma are proven breeders. Both are happily married and their husbands are strong. All four have proven themselves many times over the past year."

"And we all got bikes," Jacob piped in. "If you ride a bike, you can burn 378 calories an hour," he added, with a self-important raise of his eyebrows.

Matthew burst out laughing. "Really," he said. He looked back to Martha as she continued to speak.

"Elizabeth and Jonah are strong and smart. Elizabeth takes after me in her problem solving and Jonah is very dedicated to accomplishing his goals. And all of them are trained with firearms."

"And you—do you use a gun?"

Martha suppressed a sarcastic response. She wanted to say, "Duh," but she thought better of it. "Yes, of course," she said. She went on with her introductions, swinging her arm toward the tall older woman holding a baby; the baby had begun to squirm.

"Hannah is incredibly healthy and happy and is one of the most reliable, hard-working members of our group. As you can see, she still looks quite young in spite of her age and she's interested in marriage—"

"—Hannah likes long walks on the beach, prefers a non-smoker, and has all her own teeth," quipped the guard at the door. Several people laughed at the unexpected comment. Matthew laughed, too. Martha didn't. She turned and silenced the guard with her glare. The guard smirked. Martha turned back to Matthew, and continued.

"Hannah can't have kids although she would adopt dozens if given the chance. She has a very practical background—and she can cook and sew." Martha paused and put her arm around the little boy next to her. "And then—there's Reggie. It's not his real name, but that's what we call him."

The room grew very quiet except for Reggie's softly repeated whisper of his own name. Matthew studied the boy's delicate elfin features. Reggie fiddled with a small wooden train imprinted with faded black mouse ears—Mickey Mouse was barely recognizable. Matthew peered at the boy and shook his head. "We don't want him here."

Martha leaned forward, her tanned hands planted firmly on the pockmarked desk separating her from Matthew. "Then you don't want me," she said. She knew she was running a risk, but she had to take it. "And I'd be a big loss to you."

Matthew pulled back. "What makes you think that?"

"First of all, I'm a leader. I can organize even the most rag-taggle crew and make them listen to me. Secondly, I can do anything from planting a garden to milking a cow. I'm trained in herbology, naturopathy, and I've trained myself in triage medicine. Tell me *that's* not of value to you, *Gatekeeper.*"

Matthew smiled. "If you're so good, why are you here, Martha?" It was the first time he had used her name.

Martha stepped back from the desk. She took a breath. "I'm no fool, *Matthew.* Winter's coming. We'll do much better in a larger group, be it this one or some other group—rather than going it alone for the next five months."

Martha held Matthew's eyes. He had to believe her. She hoped he couldn't see her nervousness. There was no sense in him knowing they had just outrun a pack of Crazies.

It hadn't been lost on her that within a couple of kilometers of Matthew's camp the bikers had given up their chase. She knew her family needed this man—needed the protection his camp afforded. However, he needed her, too. Of this, she was certain. He had to take them in. *All* of them. She waited for his reply.

Everyone else stood silently save for Reggie's soft mumbling.

Matthew glanced toward the guard near the door. He laid his pen down and folded his hands on the desk. He began to shake his head. "I can't—"

Martha turned abruptly and strode to the door. The guard came to attention and looked to Matthew for orders. Martha reached the door and yanked it open. She wasn't halfway through it before the rest of the group began to follow her.

"Wait!" Matthew said. It was a command, not a request.

Every member stopped in their tracks, but did not turn back to Matthew—their eyes were on Martha, instead. She stopped and turned. A moment's pause, and then she pushed past the others as she made her way back to his desk.

"Look, I haven't brought us here to change your life or interfere with your system of government. I have to do what's right for my people. And I believe uniting with you would be a good thing for us—*all of us!*" Her arm swept back, her finger pointing in Reggie's direction.

Matthew's face softened, and his eyebrows dipped in puzzlement. "There's no doubt you know what you're doing. But I'm confused. Why take on a mental defective? If worse came to worse, you know you'd have to dump him."

Martha smiled. "Have you ever heard the saying, 'Entertaining angels unawares'?"

Ruth grimaced and said, "That's not quite right, Mom."

"Never mind—it's close enough," Martha said quickly. "Anyway, the point is that we were meant to have him. And have him, we shall—even if that means we aren't welcome here."

"I understand that Martha—as long as you understand that you are entirely responsible for this boy—for his well-being and his behavior. Is that clear?"

"No problem."

"One more thing—do you have any relationship with the Crazies?"

"You mean other than fighting them off?" Martha said with a wry laugh. Her voice rose in pitch and she knew she had answered far too quickly, but she hoped he hadn't noticed. "No," she said, shaking her head solemnly. "No relationship."

Matthew stood up and held out his hand. Martha hid her relief as she took his hand and shook it firmly. It was hard and warm, and it closed completely over her smaller hand. Martha stopped shaking first and pulled her hand away. Matthew sat back down.

"One more thing, Martha." Matthew's eyes were dark and serious. "This is not a matriarchal society. Can you live with that? Women's lib doesn't cut it here. We appreciate who you are and what you'll bring to us, but *men* run this establishment."

Martha dismissed his concerns with a quick wave of her hand. "Matthew, you'll have no trouble from me. It was my job to get us here. I now bow to my husband's headship. I trust you need a good man on your board of elders? You do have a board of elders, don't you?"

"Yes, we do," Matthew said with a glance in Josef's direction. Then, "Would you remain behind for a minute, Josef?"

Josef and Martha exchanged glances before Martha turned and led her group out the door and into the compound. Josef waited for the room to clear before he looked back at Matthew. For a moment, the two men studied each other. Matthew spoke first.

"Is she going to be trouble?"

"Martha's good at what she does," Josef confided. "But you can't expect her to be a general and a shrinking violet at the same time."

"You'll have to keep her from interfering here, Josef. This isn't her camp. It's mine. What I say—goes. If she can't live with that, then she's out. Is that clear?"

"Sure," Josef said. "Anything else?"

Matthew shook his head. The two men regarded each other once more. Josef held out his hand and the two exchanged a firm but brief handshake. Then Matthew picked up his pen, and returned to his journal entries. Josef made his way out the door.

JOSEF CAUGHT up with Martha. She was snooping around the main yard. She turned to him.

"So? What did he want?"

"He wants you to behave yourself."

"To what?" Her eyes blazed. "What kind of crap is that?"

"C'mon, Martha." He took her hand in his, but she wrenched it away.

"I don't think I'm going to like him very much."

Josef sighed.

□□□

The Man

MOTORCYCLES ROARED *in the distance—the sound echoed through the darkened city streets. Headlights got brighter. The bikes came around the corner of the clubhouse. They eased to a stop. The two men onboard killed the engines, leaned the bikes onto their kickstands, and jumped off.*

"They call this guy, 'The Man'?"

"Yes."

The younger biker grunted. "Is that like in 'the man upstairs'?"

"Sure. Now shut up."

They walked to the clubhouse, nodding to the guards standing out front.

"This a new guy?" one of the guards asked.

"Yep."

"Okay. Go ahead."

They were ushered down a hallway to another door, closed. The biker leading the way stopped and knocked. Someone grunted from within. The biker turned the knob and pushed the door open.

A man stood behind a large wooden desk. Maps lay spread out in front of him. Handguns sat in a neat row down the right side. Stacked boxes of ammunition rested nearby. A battered Bible with a thick black cover speckled in crusty crimson patches rested near the man's left hand. Next to that, lay a spreading collection of brass knuckles, switchblade knives, and handcuffs. A box of Kleenex and a lidded glass jar with colored candies anchored the top middle of his desk. A brown beer bottle holding one wild rose sat atop a pile of papers. An ashtray filled with ashes and cigar stubs sat next to that.

Music blared from another room—"Smoke on the Water."

The Man looked up. Craggy face. Sharp nose, slightly bent to the right. Pronounced cheekbones. Firm wide mouth. Scar down his jaw. Larger scar across a high forehead. Mid-length, curly hair, inky dark with silver grey threads, parted down the middle. Copper eyes, wolf eyes, under thick wiry eyebrows. Sinewy neck. Broad shoulders. Rippled forearms. Large hands crisscrossed with scars and dotted with age spots. Square-tipped fingers pressed down on a map of Alberta, somewhere between the British Columbia and Saskatchewan border. The Man studied the two men. Then he spoke:

"I haven't got all night."

"He's got the information you want." The biker nodded toward his companion.

"Good," The Man said. He sat down in a large leather chair, clasped his hands behind his head, and swung his booted feet, one by one, up onto the desk. He crossed his legs at the ankles. "Make it worth my while," he said, "and I won't kill you."

He paused.

"Either of you."

Chapter Two

Morals and Ethics Committee

MARTHA SNIFFED the air. Acrid wood smoke mingled with the scent of the morning's fried meat and the perfume of the surrounding autumn woods—rich with pungent tree saps. She stopped walking. The place had the smell of, well—civilization. It looked normal. Very ordered. Sort of Small Town, Anywhere.

Make that Small Campsite, Anywhere, she thought.

"Was this place a trailer park before?" she asked the young man she was following.

He was tall and lanky, in his early twenties, with a military brush cut. He was dressed in fatigues; a canteen was slung across his chest; a black leather gun holster hung on his hip. He was acting upon orders from Matthew to take the newcomers across the courtyard to the Meeting House. The kid turned to look at Martha for a moment, grunted something non-committal, and then continued on his way. Martha smiled. He was similar to Jonah, someone she loved as deeply as her own blood children.

Jonah was a street kid who had come to stay with them in their Alberta home. Very serious—very military—and sometimes very naive. She smiled at a memory of him ensconced beneath a camouflage blanket in hip-deep snow. He was playing survivalist and he was making tea from snow. The attempt had been only a minor success, but it had made him beam. And Martha's heart glad. She turned her attention back to the compound.

Small wooden cabins, not much bigger than single car garages, sat gathered into clusters of about four to six units. The buildings were grouped around a large dusty courtyard. Massive RV trailers were set back near the tree line, arranged parallel to one another in perfectly measured rows.

Matthew's planning, Martha thought.

Trucks, many trucks, of all sizes, filled a graveled area near the Gatehouse. A mix of motorcycles and ATVs were parked in neat rows near the fence that ran the length of the compound, extending as far as Martha could see. In the distance, she saw gas tanks raised on tall metal stands. A high chain-link fence surrounded them.

A low rectangular wooden building, surrounded by a few smaller buildings, sat near the tree line, alongside a huge garden. She saw wooden stakes secured with binder twine lying near the garden's edge. Wheelbarrows, spades, and other gardening tools sat inside a long shed— an open building with an overhang. Rototillers—several of them—sat against the shed's far wall, well out of the elements.

Generators, of varying sizes and colors, dotted the compound. Many sat next to tall lamp poles, upon which large construction work lamps had been secured. *Light at night*. The thought produced a deep calm in Martha's spirit.

Martha saw people moving about, hanging clothes, chopping wood, washing dishes, and chatting. Small fire pits smoked lazily, while others blazed with orange flames. Children dressed in blue jeans, sweatshirts, and hiking boots played on dirt hills near the middle of the compound. They ran and shrieked in their play, chasing and tumbling into the dirt. Dogs ran alongside, jumping and barking at the children. A woman stood close by, her long blond hair caught up in a thick ponytail. She wore blue jeans, a sweatshirt, and hiking boots, too. She admonished 'Adam' to "slow down before he hurt himself."

Normal, perfectly normal, Martha thought.

"Thanks," Martha said aloud to no one in particular. Suddenly she turned to Ruth. "Remember the day I came home from the grocery store and I was upset?" Martha paused for breath. "Remember I told you that I was waiting at the checkout and I saw one of those trash newspapers—the Daily News or something stupid like that. And on the front cover was the word, 'PANIC,' in big letters. And the words, 'Please take the time to read this?' I would never have picked up that kind of paper or even given it a second look. But the rest of the words on the front page almost made me throw up. Remember?"

Ruth nodded, but didn't speak. Martha went on.

"The paper said there would be another Great Depression. And then it said that rich people were storing food and water and that everyone else should be, too. I thought, *Oh no—we're not prepared*. It made me panic—it was an awful feeling—something I'd never felt before."

Martha tripped, caught herself, and continued. Tears shone in her eyes now. "Because of that moment, we're here. We're safe."

She fought back the tears because she hated crying in front of people—especially strangers. But she could feel the weight of the past year crawl down off her shoulders. She turned her face away, and in a choked voice said, "Thank-you, God."

The others never noticed, but Josef came to Martha's side. He wrapped both arms around her in a firm embrace. It was short-lived; Martha pushed him away and kept on walking. Josef smiled and shrugged, as they continued to follow the young man in the army fatigues.

The children tripped along behind, but their real interest lay in the dirt piles and the laughter of the other kids. Samuel stopped walking, turned toward the children, glanced back at his mother, and then ran to the hill. Mary began to follow her older brother. Both were stopped short by Ruth.

"What have you been told about leaving us?" Ruth walked over and yanked both of them back by their arms. "You know you're not supposed to go anywhere without permission. That means here, too."

Mary began to cry. Samuel furrowed his brows and glared at his angry mother.

"You'll be able to play later. Right now, you stay with us. So, c'mon."

The group moved on. Samuel lagged behind, his feet moving only in accordance with his mother's command.

The group paused as the young man leading them stopped. He held up his hand. In the distance came the faint sound of motorcycle engines. He turned his ear toward the sound, listened, and then began to walk again. Jonah caught up to him. Martha could overhear their conversation.

"They come by night mostly," the young man explained. "But sometimes they come in broad daylight, too." He motioned to the gravel road winding its way away from the compound. "Lots of fighting just up there."

Jonah nodded with great interest.

"They're really nuts. They drive expensive motorcycles. Their mufflers are pretty loud so we can hear them coming. They're like—you know—like Hell's Angels, or something. And they're really crazy. That's what we call them: *Crazies*."

"Yeah, we know. We call them that, too. Did you ever have to kill any?" Jonah asked, his desperation to hear more as undisguised as the intense light in his eyes.

"Yeah... and they got lots of us, too." The young man indicated a fenced-in patch of yard situated just outside the compound. Dozens of wooden crosses covered the brown earth. "But they know we're pretty well armed and that we can hold our ground, so they don't bother us as much anymore."

"What's your name?" Jonah asked.

"Simon. What's yours again?" Jonah told him and the two shook hands with enthusiasm. "Glad to have some new faces," Simon said. "Some of the refugees that show up are not so great. We turn a lot away. I'm surprised Matthew took your whole group."

Jonah smiled and hooked a thumb over his shoulder in Martha's direction. "She's pretty pushy. She usually gets what she wants."

"Sort of like my Aunt Delilah," Simon said. "She can really make you hate her some days." He twisted both hands together out in front of himself as though throttling a chicken's neck. The boys laughed.

"Here's the Meeting House," Simon said as he led them across a small patch of grass dotted with piles of rocks the size of a man's fists.

"What are all the rocks for?" Jonah asked.

"A rock can hurt," Simon replied. "Even a kid can throw a rock. So, we keep them around just in case."

"But guns are better, right?" asked Jonah, as he eyed the butt of the .357 Smith and Wesson in Simon's holster.

"Right," Simon replied. The group followed him up wooden stairs into the simple rectangular building.

Martha paused at the doorway. She saw the shapes of people inside the room's dim interior. A catch in her spirit made her step back, but Josef's hand on her elbow drew her forward. She stepped inside.

MARTHA FROZE just inside the doorway at the sound of a man's voice.

"I don't care what you think," the man said. "She should be punished."

Punished? What had she gotten them into?

Martha saw several long tables, some of the folding leg variety, while others were made of thick rough wood. Piles of folding chairs sat near a wall. Several figures were silhouetted in the gloom. As her eyes adjusted to the light, she could see two men, three women, and a young girl. The girl was slumped at a table, her head in her hands. She was crying.

Martha slowed her pace. The sound of their group coming into the room made the men at the front stop their shouting and arguing, and turn toward them.

"What do you want?" called out one of the men.

"New members," Simon said. "Matthew just processed them." Then, as though in warning, "He'll be here in a couple of minutes."

The men glanced toward the door. Two of the women stood near the weeping girl, their hands on her shoulders. A third woman stood in front of the two men. Martha could barely make out what they were saying because their voices had dropped to angry whispers.

"She's guilty and you know it," one man said.

The woman shook her finger in the man's face. "You have no right to tell me how to discipline my own daughter," she said.

"Yes, we do," the other man said. "We are on the Morals and Ethics Committee. We make the rules."

"And we enforce them," said the other man. His hands were on his hips, and his chest thrust forward. *Looks like a bratty kid*, Martha thought. But his words chilled her. "We have the authority to tell people when they've broken the rules, and we have the power to punish them."

"Within reason," said a voice from the doorway. Martha jumped and turned to see Matthew silhouetted there.

"Matthew—" the chest man said with a quick grin. "We've got a bit of an issue here." He motioned toward the girl at the table. "She was caught again—"

Matthew held up his hand. "That can wait," he said.

"But, you said we should—" said the other man.

"It can wait," Matthew repeated. "We have new members. They'll need to know the rules." He now stood directly in front of the two men. The woman walked back to her daughter at the table. She tugged at the girl's arm, trying to lift her from the chair.

Martha stared at the girl. Everything inside her wanted to run to her, and find out what the girl had done to merit punishment. She watched as the women escorted the girl past her. *I'll ask them later*, she thought.

Martha turned back to Matthew who was in a whispered conversation with the two angry men. Try as she might, she could not overhear his words. Finally, the pair seemed to calm down.

"Okay," Matthew said to Martha's group. "This is Brad, and this is Vince." He pointed to the two men. "They'll bring you up to speed on what is allowed, and what is not allowed here." He glanced at Simon. "Thanks, Simon. I think you have work to do."

Simon tipped his head in agreement, nodded to Jonah, and marched out the door.

Like a trained dog, Martha thought. In an instant, a feeling refined itself in her heart. *Gatekeeper, huh? Gates swing both ways, Matthew.*

"Take a seat," Brad called to them. "We're gonna be here for awhile." Martha chose a seat about three tables back from the front. Vince noticed her choice.

"Sit here," he said as he pointed to a table directly in front of him.

"I'm good here, thanks," Martha said. Ruth and Josef gave her a warning look and waved her forward. Martha did not move.

"Sit HERE," Vince repeated. "I don't want to have to shout."

"You were doing a fine job of shouting when we got here," Martha said, her voice thick with creeping anger.

Vince took a step toward Martha, but Matthew placed a hand on his chest.

"I'm sure she can hear you just fine from there," Matthew said, nodding in Martha's direction "Just get on with it."

Brad and Vince exchanged glances as Matthew walked away. He stopped near Martha.

"I'd be careful around those two if I were you," Matthew said, leaning down. His breath was warm in her ear.

"They're a couple of assholes," she said.

"Maybe so, but remember you're new here. Guess who I'll have to side with if you get into an argument?" His tone was formal and hard. Martha glanced at him in surprise.

"You don't need to talk to me like that," Martha whispered back.

"I think I do," Matthew said. "Pay attention."

Martha turned in her chair and stared at Matthew as he walked away. Her anger was back, crisper and stronger than it had been before. And along with it came a new feeling—a tiny thrill had coursed through her, crashing into the pit of her stomach, as Matthew leaned in, his words slipping into her ear. Martha tried to dislodge the strange, unwelcome sensation. But it stuck.

She glanced toward the front of the room where her husband sat at a table. His canvas satchel lay on the table near him. He was listening attentively to Brad. Martha picked up her bag, walked to the front, and sat down beside Josef. He smiled.

Vince and Brad did not.

▢▢▢

The Plan

"WE GOT WORD from our riders that more clubs are coming up from the States." The biker stood a few feet from The Man's desk. The Man's back was to him. The biker waited.

The room was dusky. Low autumn light streamed in through a side window. Dust motes danced in the soft yellow rays. Empty liquor bottles—all shapes, sizes, and colors—adorning the window ledge, caught the sunlight and sprayed patches of colored light over a large map of Canada tacked to the far wall. Pushpins—red, green, blue, yellow—dotted the map. Alberta was heavily clustered with tacks; there were fewer in British Columbia and Saskatchewan.

The Man turned and sat forward in his chair, his weathered hands clasped together, resting on his desk. He didn't look up.

"They know about you," the biker said. "They got your message."

The Man brushed away a fly that had settled on his knuckles. He looked up as the biker continued to speak.

"All of them have agreed to meet you in Vulcan. In two days."

"And?"

"We need more guys, but we've started executing the plan. We're about halfway across the province now."

"Setting up chapters as we go?"

"Yes." The biker paused. "Drumheller is nearly fifty men. Red Deer is well over a hundred. They've taken over some of the private holdouts—farms and small towns." He scratched his head. "There are some big groups, though—well armed. One of the private compounds near here is allied with the Hutterites. We can't get near them. They're armed. To the teeth."

"Who runs it?"

"A guy called 'the Gatekeeper'. Name's Matthew. Sounds like he got hit pretty hard a while back... lost some men... and now no one gets near his compound."

"Insider?"

"Not yet. But we're working on it. We've got a prospect."

"Good." The Man leaned back and put his hands behind his head. *"Any word on the guy found executed near the church?"*

"No. But one of our street snitches says he saw a bunch of broads on scooters around that time."

The Man leaned forward again. He picked up a discolored and dried rose petal from his desk. It had fallen from a withered wild rose sitting in a beer bottle. The rose's head hung, but most of its petals were still intact. The Man crumbled the petal between his thumb and forefinger. He didn't look up, as he spoke.

"Find them. Kill them."

Chapter Three
The Discipline Committee

A NOISE coming from outside the window made Martha jump.

God, why am I so nervous?

But she knew the answer. This was his space. She crossed the room to his desk, laden with a pile of seemingly disheveled papers, and yet somehow they looked very orderly. She picked up one of the hard-covered books sitting close at hand. It was an old-fashioned accounting book, the kind used in the '40s and '50s. She smiled. *We've come a long way.* She giggled softly. She ran her fingers along the edge of his desk, and sidled around to the chair. It was a handsome chair—a high quality 'manager's' chair—burgundy leather—with a high back. She swung it toward her, and sat down. Sun streamed in through the room's only window. It cast golden rays across the desk, the papers, and her body. It was warm. She relaxed into the chair, cozying into its depths, and closed her eyes. A soft sigh escaped her lips. She let her mind drift.

She wondered how Josef was doing with the positioning of their RV. Matthew had assigned her and Josef a small cabin on the compound; their RV was joining the rest of the trailers in the back lot—it now belonged to Ruth and her family. *Matthew's decision.* A vision of Matthew rolled into her mind, and she felt her anger rise. Yesterday had been an eye-opener. Especially the Discipline Committee. The memory came into sharp focus.

"YOU WHIP people?" Martha had asked. Her eyes widened in disbelief. "With a whip?" She glanced at Josef to judge his reaction, but his face was impassive.

"Yes," Brad said. "We use both corporal and capital punishment here."

"For what offenses?" Josef asked.

"Um—similar to those offenses in the Ten Commandments, I guess, is the best way to put it. Stealing, cheating, lying, disobedience—those are all punishable by whip."

"Flagellation," Vince added, officiously.

"Murder—that's punishable by death," Brad added.

"I see," said Josef. "And who decides on innocence or guilt?"

"We do," Vince added. "Well, we—and members of the committee."

"What committee?" Martha asked.

"The Discipline Committee. Usually about a dozen members," Brad said. Then with a nod toward Josef, he added, "You might want to be a member."

"I think I'd like to be—yes," Josef replied.

"I'd like to be on that committee, too," Martha said.

"No women," Brad said gruffly.

"No women," Vince echoed. "Just men," he added, nodding toward Brad.

"Women get too emotional. They muddy the issue," Brad said. "Men get it done faster. More efficiently."

"I see," said Josef.

"Well, I *don't see*," Martha replied. Josef pressed his hand down on her arm. Martha shook it off and began to rise. Josef reached up, grasped her shoulder, and pushed her back into her chair. "Women should—"

"Might I remind you, Martha, I told you men run this show," Matthew said. He had been standing quietly off to the side, allowing Brad and Vince to do the talking. He now motioned to Josef as he spoke. "You'll have to trust that your man will represent your feelings."

Martha had begun to rise again. "I can represent—" Josef pulled her back down, this time roughly, clipping off her words.

"We understand," Josef said, his tone level, his face revealing nothing. "What other rules do we need to be aware of?"

Martha eyed Matthew, willing him to speak again. If he was looking for a fight, he would get one. But he remained silent, with his arms crossed. His attention was on Brad and Vince.

Brad droned on, but Martha's anger buzzed in her ears and she stopped hearing him.

□□□

"WOMEN WILL 'muddy' the issue? What kind of crap is that?" Martha turned as she spoke. Josef was sitting at a small table. He was cleaning one of his pistols. "Well?"

Josef didn't answer.

They were alone in their new home, a tiny wooden cabin with two rooms: a kitchen and a bedroom. Martha stood near a small propane stove. She was preparing vegetables for their supper. A pot of rice boiled on the burner, making the lid lift rhythmically, gushing steam and white foam over the edge of the pot. The sound drew Martha's attention and she turned back to the stove. She lifted the lid and set it slightly akimbo on the pot, allowing a bit of the steam to escape. She turned a knob, lowering the burner's heat, and then she looked back at Joseph. He was examining the barrel of his gun, as he pushed an oiled rag in and out of the slender chamber.

"Well?"

"Martha, stop it," Josef said.

"It's not right. Who do they think they are?"

"Martha—"

"No, Josef. It's just not right. Somebody has to—"

"Martha! Cut it out!"

Her rant stopped short. "So, you're taking their side?"

"It's not about sides, Martha," Josef said, his tone softening. "But it's their camp. *Their camp.* Not yours."

"I don't care whose camp it is. It's still wrong." She stopped and drew back slightly. "Or maybe you are liking this archaic attitude. Is that it?"

It was Josef's turn to pull back. His face showed surprise. "What are you talking about?"

"You know what I mean."

"No. Actually, I don't." He rubbed a grimy cloth over the barrel of the gun in his hand, examined it once more, and pushed it into the holster on his hip. He picked up his grey bag, went to a chest against the far wall, opened it, and pulled out a box of ammunition.

"Where are you going?"

"I'm on patrol," he said simply as he turned and opened the cabin door. "See you later." He paused. "Sometimes, Martha, for all your brains, you really can be very stupid."

"Wh— what?" she stammered. "What about supper?" But the door slammed shut on her words.

Martha stood, her mouth hanging open in frustration and in shock, her heart sagging with hurt. She walked to the kitchen window and watched as Josef made his way across the compound.

He had taken sides. He had never taken sides against her before. Why now? Why... now?

Martha watched as Josef chatted with an armed guard near the Gatehouse. The guard deferred to another man who had just come out of the small building. The man turned. *Matthew.* Her hands clenched as a fresh shot of anger suffused her, reddening her face. *Matthew.* Then a young man bounded up to the men; it was Jonah.

Et tu, Brutus? Et tu?

Martha slammed a frying pan down on a burner.

□□□

"COMFORTABLE, ARE WE?"

The deep voice startled Martha, and she jumped from the chair.

"Uh, sorry. I was... uh... just waiting... to talk to you." Heat crept through her body, burning her face. She hoped Matthew hadn't seen the sudden blush of embarrassment.

He passed in front of her, his flannelled torso brushing her arm as he did. She sucked in a quick breath and scurried to the other side of his desk. A smaller waiting-room chair caught her eye, and she sat down. The room suddenly felt very small. Blood pounded in her ears in quick hard beats.

For God's sakes, get it together.

She gripped the chair arms with a strength that hurt her palms, and forced her breathing to slow as she willed her heart to stop its rampage. She looked up.

Matthew was staring at her, a small smile pulling at the corner of his mouth. He could have been a model for a man's fashion magazine. Except for the scars. It was the first time she had noticed the scars and she studied them.

"How did you get those?"

"Those what?"

"The scars around your mouth?"

"A fight."

"That's it? A fight? No details?"

"What do you want, Martha?"

She raised her eyebrows, and then with a small laugh, "You ashamed? Did you lose?"

Matthew reached across the desk and rotated the book that Martha had been examining earlier. "What do you want, Martha?"

"Uh... I wanted to talk to you about your Discipline Committee."

"What about it?"

"I want to be on it."

Matthew looked up. Their eyes met.

"We don't need a woman on the committee," Matthew said. He paused. "Is that everything? Because if we're done, I have work to do."

Martha drove her top molars down, setting her jaw in tight anticipation of the fight she was about to enter.

"Kind of barbaric, don't you think? This male-only club you're running?"

Matthew moved slowly, like a cat. His eyes hardened, as he leaned into the desk, toward her, his hands folded in quiet resolve. Martha felt his meaning before she heard his words.

"Did I not make it clear when we accepted your group that this is a male-run society?" A short pause. "Funny, because I thought I had."

Martha backed into her chair; her rebel heart beat wildly against her ribs. She swallowed and then spoke: "Change is good. And I think a woman's perspective on the Discipline Committee would be a good change. A welcome change."

"No." The word was ejected dismissively and with finality.

Matthew moved back and picked up a thick fountain pen, a different one from the one she had seen him use during their initial meeting; this one was hunter green with a gold band. It caught the sunlight, sending sunbursts glinting off the metal. "I have work to do. Good-bye, Martha."

Martha's mouth hung open. She felt her eyes widen in indignation.

He's dismissed me? Dismissed me? Me?

Anger bloomed in her chest. She rose from the chair, but she willed herself to move slowly. She reached the door, twisted the handle, and then turned back to Matthew. His head was bent over a long sheet of paper; the pen flicked light as he wrote.

"We'll speak on this again, Matthew." She strode out the door, not waiting for a reply.

Martha pulled the door shut behind her—gently, not with her usual pissed-off bang. The morning sun made her squint, as she fought for a calming breath. She leaned against the door and waited. The sun lay warm upon her face, her neck, her shoulders.

Sunshine on my shoulders... The lyrics of the John Denver song echoed in her mind. She closed her hands into fists, and breathed deeply again.

I will get on that committee, Matthew. Just you wait and see.

□□□

The Informant

"SOMEONE HERE to see you," the biker said. He pulled a black woolen toque from his head as he spoke; it crackled with static electricity, causing his dirty blond hair to stick up at all angles.

"Who?"

"Says he has information on the Gatekeeper."

"Really."

"Yeah. You want to meet him?"

The Man looked away and continued to pat a cat lying atop a pile of books. The dark Persian's hair was sleek and the cat looked amply fed. Its green eyes regarded The Man as he drew his hand down the cat's silken back. The cat lost interest and began to wash its face with a curved paw. The Man looked up. The biker motioned over his shoulder.

"He's waiting. Should I bring him in?"

"Taken his weapons, have you?"

"Yes. For sure." The biker twisted the dark hat in his hand.

"Then show him in."

Chapter Four

The Crazies Dump Their Used Junk

"YOU GOTTA rein her in," Matthew said.

He and Josef were patrolling the outreaches of the camp. The day was warm. Gilded, multi-veined leaves lay scattered or delicately mounded into small wind-blown piles. Canada geese honked their triumphal exit, a self-righteous sound, as they turned tail feather and headed for warmer climes to the South. The camp dwellers welcomed the respite of the Indian summer, knowing cold temperatures were just a morning's frost away. Fruit had hung heavily on the apple trees, and the low bush shrubs had been unusually burdened with berries. A long and merciless winter was on its way.

"Why?" Josef asked as he repositioned the strap of his canvas bag across his shoulder. He carried a shotgun in his left hand; his Smith and Wesson revolver jounced in a holster on his right hip.

"Why?" Matthew said. "You know why, Josef. She's driving everyone nuts."

"Oh, that." Josef grinned, and then he turned his attention to the flutter of wings in the woods. The pair watched as two prairie chickens rose into the air. Neither man took a shot. They had plenty of meat in the compound.

"You know the folks here are more laid-back," Matthew replied.

"You mean it's a bad thing that Martha wants to teach them things they need to know?" asked Josef.

"No—but she's so damn pushy. The women are complaining. And the young guys—" Matthew paused and gave a short laugh, "—they hate her."

Josef laughed, too. "Not all the young guys. Jonah thinks the sun rises and sets on her."

"He's different."

Matthew stumbled on a tree root embedded in the hardened dirt on the path, and pitched forward. Josef made a move to assist him, but stopped himself. A couple of weeks as this man's partner had taught him that the gesture would be rejected.

☐☐☐

MARTHA HAD laughed the day Josef told her he was to be Matthew's patrol partner.

"Oh, that oughta be fun," she had said. "I can just see the two of you now. Bosom buddies." Her sarcasm hadn't changed Josef's mind, and he met up with Matthew the next day.

Their first patrol was uneventful, but a patrol later in the week cemented their trust in one another.

They had come out onto a hidden back road. Weeds and shrubbery choked the dirt road, turning it into a rutted pathway. The first shot came as a surprise. Both men had taken cover, but they couldn't tell where the bullet had come from. Or who was doing the shooting.

"Split up," Matthew had whispered. He moved to the left. Josef moved right. Both crept through the brush, keeping low. Another shot, and they fell to the ground, flattening themselves. Another shot. Then came a voice—shrill and sing-songy.

"I'll get you sons-of-bitches!"

Josef was unable to see from his vantage point, so he clambered through the brush near the road. He stayed hidden in the weeds, but he could see up the road in both directions. An old man came into view. He was dressed all in black. He wore a long oilskin coat with thick leather boots. Long grey hair hung in greasy hanks around his face and down his back. He was peering down the barrel of a rifle. Something was in his sights.

Josef looked in the direction the barrel was pointed. It was the last place he had seen Matthew. He glanced back. The old man was muttering. He was shaky and seemed unable to draw a bead on his quarry. And then he grew quiet. Josef saw faint movement to his left. It had to be Matthew.

Josef pulled his revolver. He grasped it in combat position, raised it, sighted on the man before him, and fired. The bullet hit the man's shoulder and he fell back, dropping his rifle to the ground.

Josef leapt from his hiding place, raced over, and picked up the old man's gun. The man kicked at him, knocking him off balance. Josef dropped the rifle and tried to bring his pistol up for another shot, but the man rushed him.

Josef struggled, but his assailant was powerful, even with a bullet wound in his shoulder. Josef felt the sharp sting of something across his chest. He realized he had been cut long before he saw the blade. He pushed at the man and tried to free himself, but the man was too quick. The long silver blade flashed in the sunlight as the man raised it for another strike. In that instant came the sound of a gun, and the man slumped down, his knife clattering to the hard ground.

Josef pushed the man's body aside and sat up. Blood poured from the slash wound on his chest. Matthew ran up.

"You're bleeding. Let's get back to camp." Matthew made no move to assist Josef to his feet. Instead, he had stood and waited.

Like Josef was waiting today.

JOSEF WATCHED as Matthew got back to his feet, brushing the dirt from his knees. Josef smiled at his friend. Ever since that day, trust between them was not a question.

Martha, on the other hand...

They walked a few feet together, and then Josef spoke:

"Martha's valuable to this colony." He stopped and turned to face Matthew. "And you know it. So, give her a break."

Matthew stopped walking. He reached down and rubbed his left knee.

"*I* need the break, Josef. I have to keep peace in this camp. I can't have people carping at me on a daily basis. Complaining about... Martha did this... Martha said that..."

"You really need to weigh the benefits here," Josef advised. "She's smart. She's now the camp medic. And the midwife." Josef paused, and then added, "She calls 'em like she sees 'em. If someone is screwing up, she tells them. What's wrong with that?"

Matthew shook his head. "Josef, you know what's wrong with that. I can't have her constantly interfering with my authority."

"Why? Cause Vince and Brad don't like it?"

Matthew scowled. "I can't have my men questioning my ability to lead." He leaned into Josef's face. He was Matthew, the Gatekeeper; not Matthew, the friend. "Do something about her, Josef. Tell her to back off. Let the people live their own lives. It's not her job to teach everyone."

Josef returned Matthew's stare. The men stood in silence, and then Josef spoke. Softly. Carefully.

"I won't do that."

In the distance, the droning sound of engines—many engines—made both men turn their heads. The engines were loud, and they were getting louder. The two men tucked their shotguns beneath their arms, and reached for their pistols.

Josef pulled his revolver, popped opened the cylinder, checked the load, and then pushed the cylinder closed with his thumb. When he looked up, Matthew was already running down the path. Josef followed.

"It's broad daylight," Matthew said. "Damn them!"

The sound of the motors had drawn closer to the camp. Suddenly, the sounds of acceleration slowed, as engines geared down.

Josef and Matthew quickened their pace. They were breathing heavily when they reached the first row of RVs parked along the back lot. The sound of idling engines grew louder.

The two men kept to the rear of the cabins as they advanced on the common area of the compound. They strained to hear what was going on near the Gatehouse. As they neared the cabins, they realized the motorcycles weren't as close as they had suspected earlier. They raced between the cabins, and sprinted across the courtyard. Several of Matthew's men were on the ready, guns drawn.

"What's going on?" Matthew asked one of the men.

"We don't know," came the reply from one of the guards. "We heard the motorcycles and we got ready to meet them. But they stopped— somewhere up the road." The man pointed over his shoulder.

Matthew and Josef strode up to another man, tall and dark-haired; Matthew had left him in charge of the gate. The man had just given an order to a small group of armed boys waiting behind him. He stiffened when he saw Matthew.

"Sir," he said with a quick bob of his head in Matthew's direction. "We were just going to send out a team."

"Wait," Matthew said. "Listen."

The men bent their ears toward the sound of the idling motors. Voices could be heard above the deep rumbling. But just barely. Some of the men were on one knee, their weapons aimed past the gate. A few had gone farther down the road.

"Wait!" Matthew said in a clear, deep voice. The men stopped. They turned and regarded Matthew. The sound of voices came again, this time louder, nearer. The men waited.

The voices became more distinct.

The men looked at one another, but no one spoke. The sound of motorcycle engines revving came again, but this time the motorcycles were heading away. Soon, there was no sound of engines at all, just the distant honk of a fleeing Canada goose. And the chattering of...

Females.

As the men gazed forward, a bevy of women, very young women, came into view. They were attired in everything from party dresses to fatigue pants and t-shirts. Their hair color ranged from blond to bright red, and to deep, inky black. Some were tall, some were short, some were pretty, and some were plain. But all had one thing in common.

Matthew shook his head. "What the hell?" He watched as the girls continued up the road to the gate. They drew to a stop, and huddled together.

"Wow—" Josef said. "They're all pregnant."

"Yeah," Matthew agreed. Then, under his breath, "I wonder who the daddies are."

"I think we know that," Josef added.

"This can't be good," Matthew muttered as he walked through the gate toward the girls.

"We aren't armed," one of them called. It was a tall brunette in a white gauze cotton shirt and red pants. She held out her empty hands in proof.

"Show your hands. All of you," one of the armed men yelled.

The girls obliged and soon fifteen pairs of hands pointed skyward in submission. Matthew strode forward; Josef was at his side.

"Just wait till Martha gets a load of this lot." Josef elbowed his friend. "You're gonna be glad she's around."

Matthew turned to Josef. His eyes were dark. He did not smile.

Josef stepped back, and cocked his head.

"This can't be good," Matthew repeated.

Josef laughed at the wry understatement.

Matthew strode forward.

The Meet-Up

"STAR TREK CENTRAL," some called it. Vulcan was the perfect meet-up place because of its central location in southern Alberta. And—because many bikers were also Star Trek fans—they had heard of the tiny town.

The bikers arrived—a few dozen at a time, and then in thick buzzing waves. Like a mini Sturgis, South Dakota bike rally, the streets were soon clogged with motorcycles and their riders. Their jackets and vests sported a rainbow of motorcycle club patches: Warlocks and Pagans out of the eastern United States; Vagos out of California; Rock Machine out of Quebec; Free Souls out of Oregon; Sons of Silence out of Colorado; Outlaws from across the United States, but mostly from Florida; Highwaymen out of Detroit; Bandidos out of Texas; Mongols from Canada; and the notorious 81—the Hells Angels, from all over North America.

Some men—motorcycle men, they called themselves—wore no colors at all.

The atmosphere was celebratory. Men sauntered around the streets, recognizing old friends and making new ones, joining up into small groups, talking, laughing, arguing, and getting into the odd fistfight. Leonard Nimoy and Star Trek jokes were told first by one man, and then another.

The air was heavily scented with the sweet fragrance of freshly cooked meat. Huge barbecue ovens were set up on a grocery store parking lot, and firewood sat in thigh-high piles nearby. Fires blazed in temporary fire pits dug into the lawn along one side of the lot. Huge aluminum tubs sat on iron grating. Water boiled. Freshly husked ears of corn lay in a yellow mountain off to the side.

Women bustled about with cooking utensils, plates, and small buckets of butter. They called back and forth to one another. Men lined up, and then left—their plates laden with barbecued steak, corn dripping in butter, and slices of bread. People helped themselves to salt and pepper by pinching small amounts of each from large ceramic bowls sitting on a small camp table. At another table, women served up cinnamon buns, carrot cake, chocolate brownies, apple pie, and peanut butter cookies. A generator rumbled near a table bearing huge urns of coffee.

Newcomers eyed the cooking area, but they didn't just go over; they knew better. Everyone knew the rules: Men had to trade foodstuffs, his woman's time, or both. Then he would be welcome to partake in the meal. Newcomers went to a receiving table to drop off their food donations: chickens, eggs, salt, flour, rice, oatmeal, sugar, cooking oil, condiments, honey, baked goods, vegetables, bags of potatoes, salted meats, canned goods, bags of candies, boxes of pasta—all were deposited on the table. The food was sorted and loaded into cargo trucks lined with metal shelving. The women were put to work.

A meeting area had been set up with a stage and a speaker system. Somebody had rigged up an iPod to the system and Led Zeppelin poured from the speakers, over the sound of the generators, adding to the festive feeling. When it grew darker, a group of men went into a schoolyard and set off fireworks. The chemicals burst into a kaleidoscope of colors, making the people screech and applaud in delight.

The Man watched from his perch atop a large semi-trailer parked behind the stage. His men had done a count—nearly two thousand riders. He nodded.

It was a good start.

Chapter Five

So Many Babies; So Little Room

THE PAIR of men reached the girls. Josef hung back slightly. Matthew stopped, one hand gripping his shotgun, the other resting on the butt of the pistol on his hip. Josef smiled, but said nothing.

"Who are you?" Matthew asked.

The tall brunette spoke, "Just some people who need a place to have our babies."

"What made you think you could come here?"

The girl shrugged. "There's a midwife here, isn't there?" The brunette took a small step forward, locking eyes with Matthew.

Matthew regarded her coolly before speaking:

"We have a full camp. We aren't looking for new members. Especially members of... your sort."

With a slight lift of her chin, the brunette responded.

"What *sort* is that?"

"Who brought you here?"

"Some guys... our boyfriends."

"Uh-huh. And... when are they picking you up again?"

"They won't be."

"Really?" Matthew reached up and pulled the ball cap from his head. He swept sweat from his brow and then repositioned the cap back on his head. "I suspect otherwise."

"Whatever."

"Yes... *whatever*," Matthew echoed. A soft disturbance from behind him drew his attention.

"She's here," said a young man.

Martha strode up the small alleyway that had been made for her through the crowd. She stopped at Josef's side.

"What's this?" she asked, with a nod of her head in the direction of the girls. She looked over to Matthew as she spoke.

Matthew stood, feet apart, arms now folded across his chest, with his shotgun caught in the crook of one arm.

"I was hoping you'd tell me," Matthew replied.

Martha raised her eyebrows.

Had this motley crew thrown the unshakable Matthew?

She resisted a tugging smile, but from the scowl on Matthew's face, she knew she hadn't been successful. She walked over to the girls, regarding them with great interest, and judging the state of their pregnancies.

"Are you *all* pregnant?" Martha asked.

A redhead to Martha's right, her belly poking out from beneath a too-short t-shirt, responded. "Gee, what was your first clue?"

Martha turned her head toward the girl and appraised her. "Don't be so smart with me, miss. You might need me some day."

Mumbling erupted from amongst the girls. There was a hurried consensus that this woman must be the midwife. A tiny blonde pushed forward. Heavy breasts filled a low scoop-necked shirt, their soft flesh pushing hard against the fabric, and mashed into a fleshy crevasse. Martha heard the boys murmur their appreciation.

"Please help us. I don't want to have my baby alone." Tears spilled down the girl's cheeks, and her bottom lip quivered. Other girls chimed in, adding their pleas to hers. "Please?"

Martha held up her hand, and then she turned back to Matthew.

"So? What do you need from me? Help making your decision?"

Matthew stood silently. He passed his shotgun to an armed man standing near him. He crooked a finger in Martha's direction.

"C'mere."

Martha stepped toward Matthew. She followed him as he led her away from the gathered people. She sucked in her breath when he stopped abruptly and faced her. Martha read the dark look he wore, a look she had grown to despise. She steadied herself and spoke:

"So?"

"I was going to send them away."

"So?"

"So, I decided to give my decision a little more thought."

"Uh-huh."

"What's your take on them? Do they look healthy?"

"You want a diagnosis at a glance?" She donned a mock look of concern. "Shall I consult my magic mirror?"

Matthew stood quietly. Martha hated when he did that. She wanted to speak, but remembered the words of a wise salesman she knew back in her car sales days: "He—who speaks first—loses." She held her tongue.

"I asked you a question," he asked, finally.

"At a glance—yes, Matthew. They look healthy. But I wouldn't stake my life on it."

"Can you—?" Martha cut him off.

"Can I deliver their babies? I suspect so."

"Do you see any potential problems in keeping the girls?"

Martha burst out laughing.

"Do you mean with their pregnancies? Or with the effect they'll have on the boys in the camp?"

Matthew pursed his lips, but a grin emerged.

"If I tell them they can stay, you'll be completely responsible for them."

"We'll need extra housing. We don't have room for fifteen single girls. And then fifteen babies."

"I know." Matthew looked over Martha's shoulder toward the girls. "But that's the least of our worries."

"What do you mean? Pregnancy and delivery complications?"

"No." He looked back at Martha. "I mean a return of the daddies."

Martha grunted her understanding.

"Why take them in then? Why run the risk? That you are even considering taking them in is kind of surprising—"

"Okay, Martha, I'll tell them to go—"

"You can't do that, Matthew," Martha interjected. "They have nowhere to go."

Matthew grinned. "There are worse things—I guess—than a bunch of bikers coming back for their girlfriends," he said.

"Like what?"

"Arguing with you."

"I'M NOT SURE what God has in mind," Martha said. "I suppose it's a good thing to have more breeders in the group."

She rubbed the skin on her forehead above her eyes, her signature sign of stress. She was in a meeting with Matthew and a few of the other elders. Decisions had to be made about the girls.

"Where did you get the term, 'breeder'?" Matthew asked.

The question was so unexpected that Martha snapped her head up and stared at Matthew. A few moments of silence passed before she answered.

"I had a business associate once, a lesbian—that was her term for women who bore children. She called me that once. I guess the term just stuck with me." Martha shrugged. "It fits." She shrugged again. "Besides, I have heard other people use the term since the Change, too."

Matthew made a small grunting sound in his throat. "So, now we've got them. What do we do with them?"

"I think Ruth and I can handle the births," Martha said. "She's had two children by midwife and I've studied midwifery. And our medical textbooks are fairly comprehensive. As long as I've got a sterile field to work in, I think I could even do a C-section. If absolutely necessary."

"So, you're saying we should keep the girls here and not try to get them into a major centre?" Matthew asked.

"Well, unless you know where to take them, do we really have a choice? You already said that most of the nearby towns have no working hospitals and no medical staff."

Martha got up and stretched, her fists pressed into her hips and her back arched. She yawned and rubbed her neck. A lack of sleep was catching up with her. Hot flashes and an ovulation backache—*it was so good to be a woman*, she thought. She yawned again.

"Sorry. I've got to get to bed." Martha turned and walked to the door.

"Goodnight, Martha," Matthew said. He watched her leave and then he turned to the men sitting around the table.

"Come on, guys. Get some rest. We've got lots of work to do tomorrow. We'll have to add a new wing to the Women's Bunkhouse to make room for those girls and their babies."

Matthew watched as the men filed out. He leaned his forehead into his hands. A loud sigh echoed in the empty room.

A moment later, Matthew gave his head a slow shake. He rubbed his work-roughened hands across his face. He sighed loudly again. In his mind's eye, he reviewed the faces of the new girls.

Had he recognized one of them? A brunette standing toward the back of the group?

Matthew wasn't sure, but he hoped she wasn't the girl he was remembering.

That would make things far too complicated.

□□□

The Unity

"GUNS... GASOLINE... gold... groceries," The Man said. "These things we must have. These things have value."

The bikers, the motorcycle men, and their women murmured their assent; a variety of headgear—red neckerchiefs, woolen toques, ball caps, wide-brimmed Stetsons, knitted wool tams, leather helmets—all dipped in unison.

"Until the world gets its act together—these things have priority. They'll be in short supply soon. Now is the time for us to act. To get what we want—what we need... we'll take... by force. But..." The Man held up his hand, turned it palm up and swept it in an arc across the group. "We're split right now. Unfocused."

The Man stepped to the side. He motioned to the two dozen vested and leather-jacketed men standing on the stage behind him. The club captains eyed him. They stood, elbow to elbow, a sampling of the meanest, the toughest, and the proudest of the biker gangs. Nobody spoke. The Man turned back to the crowd.

"Some of you are sworn enemies. Some of you have no alliance with any club. Some of you don't see the big picture." Pause.

A huge bonfire not far from the stage filled the silence with snaps and pops and flares of ruby flames. The Man continued:

"Let me make it clear. We MUST unite. All of us. As brothers-in-arms. Only in unity, can we rise up and take control. Modern day royalty. That's what we'll be." His voice rose steadily in volume as he spoke. "Lords of our domains."

The bikers roared with enthusiasm; their shouts of solidarity echoed against the night sky. The men rose to their feet, and applauded. They stomped the earth, leather boots beating out a wild tattoo of consent and exhilaration. The Man turned back to the captains. They were nodding their assent, too.

The Man held up his hand.

The multitude quieted—eager faces looking up in anticipation.

"Unity," The Man said, with a slow, wide smile, which maybe wasn't a smile at all, but only a trick of the light. "Some of you are 'One-percenters.' Used to going your own way—doing your own thing. That will not be tolerated."

Before the Change, it was believed that ninety-nine percent of all motorcycle owners were good and honest, law-abiding citizens; only one percent were wild and undisciplined lawbreakers. But The Man made the laws now—and in his mind, any biker or club who defied his directives— these defined the new one-percent.

"There will be ZERO tolerance of 'One-percenters.' No questions asked. Hear me, you Crazies—we will find you—and we will kill you."

A murmur went through the crowd. The Man continued:

"There's work to be done. An army to be built. Chains of command to be established. Troops to be deployed. We will become a great military force. More powerful than any army the world has ever seen. More formidable than any force in history."

The Man stopped.

He cast his eyes slowly over the crowd. He observed the upturned faces. He saw the firelight reflected in their eyes. He took a deep breath.

"Are you with me?" Pause. Then he yelled... "Are you ready to unite as brothers?"

Fists punched the air, and shouts of, "We're with you, brother!" rose up in a cacophony of voices, a sound as thick and as deafening as a fog of flying bats.

"Then, brothers—the time has come." The Man turned to his side and stared at the back of the stage. "I give to you... our colors."

Two of the club captains began to unfurl a flag attached to poles erected at the back of the stage. As the image came into view, The Man spoke again:

"One color... The color of blood."

The crowd gasped at The Man's vision: the Deathhead, eagle wings, a double-edged sword, a coiled snake. Rich crimson on black.

"Brothers," The Man said, as he raised his arms high, "Stand and unite! We... are... the Apocalypse Archangels!"

The crowd roared. Applause, piercing whistles and cat-calls, and cries of, "Yeah," thundered into the night.

The Man motioned for the captains to leave the stage. They walked in single file to the bonfire. The crowd quieted and watched.

Men stationed near the fire held out several long-handled metal serving spoons and spatulas. The handles were wrapped in towels, and duct-taped. The captains removed their vests and their jackets. They ripped at their color patches. Once torn free, threads dangling, the captains threw them into the fire. The crowd gasped. Then each man took a spoon and placed it into the fire. The Man spoke again:

"Time to show our true colors."

He turned back to the men at the fire.

One captain took a step forward—a burly man with a manicured beard and moustache. He held out his bare arm. Two other men grasped it. Another man removed a spoon from the fire, glowing hot; he hesitated, and then he pressed it down on the captain's upper arm. The captain screamed and yanked his arm to safety. The spoon came away and with it—shards of roasted skin. Where another club tattoo had been, now there was raw bleeding flesh.

Crimson.

A brand new tattoo.

The next captain stepped up. A strangled scream. Another captain stepped up. The Man smiled as a line of bikers began to form. Men's voices melded into a symphony of screams and muffled groans—guttural and primal. The line grew longer.

Now the breeze carried a new scent—no longer was it the sweet, sticky aroma of barbecue—now it was the cloying stink of burnt flesh.

Women sat on the ground near the stage, their eyes filled with horror, their mouths open. Some of the unlucky ones screamed and fought and cried as their men dragged them to the fire; many of the women had tattoos, too. Some of the women fainted before it was their turn to undergo the color cleansing. Some of the men did, too.

The Man watched as the line moved forward—man by man, woman by woman, scream by scream. A smile curved the corners of his mouth.

The Man closed his eyes.

Chapter Six

An Old Acquaintance

JOSEF GRABBED a faded jean shirt from the hook on the wall. He pulled it over his t-shirt—a brown shirt emblazoned with an image of the Alamo. He had purchased the shirt on a tourist whim when he and Martha had visited San Antonio, years before. He turned to the young man waiting near the door.

"Jonah, you and I are on the building crew today."

"I'd rather be with the guards working the Hutterites' perimeter."

"It's not for you to choose, Jonah. You know that." Josef slung his canvas bag across his chest, and checked the pistol on his hip. He glanced at Jonah whose face hung long with disappointment. Josef waited. Expectantly.

Jonah grunted—his compliance; not his acceptance. He turned and opened the door.

Josef grabbed his tool belt and headed out. He flung his arm around Jonah's shoulders. "C'mon, kid."

Jonah smiled and kept pace with the big man.

"Besides," Josef said, "Just think how happy those new girls are gonna be when they see how hard you're working to build them a place to live."

Jonah blushed. Josef laughed. Jonah kept his face turned away as he spoke. "Did you forget they're all pregnant, Josef?"

"Of course I didn't forget. But what's that got to do with the price of tea in China?"

Jonah turned to Josef and laughed. "Hey, that's Martha's saying!"

"Bottom line, kid... those girls are going to need a man in their life. Might as well be you. One of them just might like your ugly mug." Josef paused, and then added, "Maybe even that little blonde. The one with..."

Jonah laughed. He punched Josef in the shoulder. "Lay off."

"Don't tell me you weren't interested," Josef said with a wide smile. The pair headed in the direction of the sound of pounding hammers.

And giggling girls.

□□□

THE WOMEN'S Bunkhouse was one of the few common buildings on the compound built from scratch—like the Men's Bunkhouse, the Medical Building, and the Meeting House. All other buildings, like the residential units, were small wooden pre-fab cabins; they were two-room affairs, with barely enough room for a married couple—let alone an entire family. But people made do. It was better than the alternative.

Those who were unable to build a shelter and fortify it against a northern winter, and those who could not or would not find and maintain an RV, had only one option: travel south across the US-Canada border (or what was left of it) and take up residency in one of the warmer American states. Many people had done that, and many people had paid a terrible price.

The 'runners', those brave Rhett Butler types, who traveled back and forth with news from afar, shared horror stories of riots, starvation, and murder. Hunger and thirst drove hundreds of thousands into an unquenchable madness—a madness filled with murderous urges, urges that were acted upon in an instant, leaving a trail of dead bodies, big and small, across the mid- and southern States.

Mexico was even more horrifying. Very few crossed the Mexican border after the Change, and those that managed to do so—the ones who survived the ordeal—wished they hadn't. The rural Mexicans knew they could survive; they had survived for centuries on their more simplistic, technology-free culture, and they weren't about to share. Especially with those who had been reluctant to share with them not so many years prior. Foreign interlopers and their families were dealt with quickly—in the most bloody of ways. People learned from the mistakes of others that Mexico was no picnic—that it was better to stay put. Building simple shacks in the

Alberta countryside was more of a sure thing. Or at least, a way to live longer.

JONAH AND JOSEF reached the building. Several of the pregnant girls were there, chattering, pointing, and giggling. Jonah straightened and walked through their midst. Josef smiled. He watched as Jonah hitched the tool belt on his waist into a more comfortable, more masculine position. Josef began to laugh. Jonah did not turn. Instead, he bent, and picked up two of the two-by-fours crisscrossed on the ground at his feet. He looked up at three men straddling a crossbeam in the rafters of the new wing. "Where do you want these?" One of the men pointed.

Josef squinted. He didn't recognize the builders on the beam. With so many people joining the camp nearly every day, it was hard to keep track. But with sleeping spaces at a premium, he was glad to see the number of unfamiliar men at work on the new wing. He would get to know them soon enough. He turned. He saw Martha off in the distance. She was at their cabin's front door, shaking something.

The little cabins were cozy. But it took work to make them habitable. Matthew traded protection services with the Hutterites for the basic four-walled wooden structures. Although the cabins had walls, a floor, a window, a door and a roof, they were too basic to provide comfort, especially in the winter. That meant the installation of heating units, countertops, cupboards, and insulation.

It didn't take long to turn a cabin into a home when there were many hands on the job. As a result, all able-bodied men, women, and teens were expected, not just encouraged, to pitch in and lend assistance wherever their energies were needed. Or they would have to answer to Matthew. Or worse—to the Discipline Committee.

Josef glanced over to Jonah. He had proven to be a great addition to the camp. He responded well to strong authority, and he worshiped Matthew.

"Good morning, Jonah! Hey, Josef."

Josef turned in the direction of the voice. He waved a greeting and smiled as he watched Jonah sprint toward Matthew.

"Hi, Matthew," Jonah called. He joined the tall man and the pair walked toward the bunkhouse. The girls made way as Matthew strolled into the group.

"Hi, Matthew." It was one of the girls, a brunette, with a protruding stomach that made her look like she'd swallowed a beach ball. Matthew swiveled around.

"Hello," Matthew said. His gaze dropped from the girl's dark eyes to her belly, which pushed hard against her shirt, a man's flannel shirt, causing gaps between the buttonholes. "You've been busy, I see."

The girl stood there, her shiny hair pulled into a thick ponytail—a few stray wisps hugged the sides of her face. She blushed and looked away.

"It's not what you might think," she said very softly. She fiddled with the buttons on her shirt, and stared at her feet. She looked up. "Do you even remember my name?"

Matthew nodded. "Anna." His tone was curt. He hooked a thumb over his shoulder. "I have to get to work."

"Sure," Anna replied quickly. She paused. "Can I see you later?"

Matthew didn't answer her. He turned and bumped into Jonah who was standing directly behind him—eyes wide open and mouth gaping. He gave Jonah a glance that made the young man lower his eyes.

"Work. Let's go." Matthew pointed to the building. Jonah nodded. The pair walked toward the bunkhouse.

"You know her?" Jonah asked.

"Sort of," Matthew said. "Her name is Anna."

"I know. I heard. But you know her? How?"

"An old acquaintance. Nothing special."

"But how do you know her?"

"Long story," Matthew said.

"Well—uh, I'd like to hear it," Jonah replied, brightly.

"I don't feel like telling it." Matthew said. He pulled out a pair of tattered leather gloves and pulled them onto his hands. "Work."

Jonah pulled on his own gloves, but his eyes were trained on Matthew's face. Matthew pointed to the building again.

□□□

"I CAN PUT them to work."

Matthew looked up from the board he held in place with one hand; a hammer was in his other hand. "What?'

"I can give them some work. Get them out of your way," Martha said, with a crooked grin. She had wandered over and had seen the exchange between Matthew and the girl. She hadn't been able to hear their conversation, however. Curiosity burned inside her, but now wasn't the time for questions.

"Um, sure," Matthew said. "Whatever you think is best."

Martha spoke softly. "Really." She desperately wanted to ask him about the girl, but she stopped herself. Besides, she would have the girl all to herself. She was sure she could get her to talk.

"Gardening then," she said.

"Sure. Fine," Matthew said. He banged in the nail, and then bent over and picked up a sheet of plywood. He made his way to the far side of the building.

"Oh, my..." Martha muttered.

She turned her attention to the girls. They were teasing some of the boys, and giggling at the boys' responses—some awkward and shy, some brazen and bawdy, with no disguised meanings behind their words. "Okay, young ladies, it's time to earn your keep."

"What?" It was the tall brunette, the same girl who acted as spokesperson for the group when they had first arrived.

"I *said*," Martha repeated levelly, "it's time to earn your keep."

"What did you have in mind?"

"Picking potatoes," Martha replied. And then with a wave of her arm, "C'mon girls, if you want to eat this winter, you'll have to pick potatoes today." The girls grumbled, but they followed Martha.

The garden was located on the left side of the compound; it was a huge half-acre plot. A long row of freshly dug holes, with dirty red potatoes scattered near them, stretched several hundred feet beyond. The girls began to complain.

"All those?" cried one of the girls. Martha turned to face her. It was the little blonde.

"Yes, all those," Martha replied. Burlap gunny sacks sat folded in a tall pile near the edge of the garden. She picked up one of the sacks and handed it to the girl nearest her. "Let me show you how it's done." She bent, picked up a potato, rubbed at the mud adhered to the skin, and then dropped it into the bag. "Don't keep any with green sections. Like this one," Martha said. She showed the rejected potato to the girls and then tossed it into a pile to her right. "Too bitter."

"But there must be hundreds," cried the blonde.

"Thousands," corrected Martha. "Now get to work."

"Excuse me, ma'am." Martha turned. It was the girl to which Matthew had been speaking.

"Yes?"

"We're pregnant. Won't this hurt our backs? Maybe even our babies?"

"Young lady, one hundred years ago, women just like you worked in the field right up to the time they gave birth. Some of them even gave birth in the field. And then kept on working."

"They did?"

"They did." Martha paused. "What's your name?"

"Anna."

Good, Martha thought. *Now I have a name.*

"Well, Anna. You are all young and healthy and strong. Pregnancy is not an affliction. Your bodies were designed to be both pregnant and able. You'll be fine."

Martha grabbed a steel digging fork that had been impaled into the ground near the potato row. "Start picking, girls." Martha looked toward the sky where heavy dark clouds had gathered. "You don't want to be doing this in the rain. Or in the snow."

She walked halfway down the potato row, bent, grasped a potato plant near to the ground, and pulled. It came free from the earth, and she shook the potatoes from its roots. Eyeing the spot where the plant had been, she carefully aimed the fork, and stepped down on the tines. A moment later, she was twisting up earth and shaking potatoes free. She looked back at the girls.

"Get your asses moving. Now!"

Anna was the first to move. She picked up a bag and stooped down. Martha watched as the girl teetered on her haunches, steadied herself, and reached for a potato. She fastidiously cleaned off the dried mud, examined the potato, and then dropped it into her sack. She glanced up at Martha, and took another potato.

Martha scowled, and stabbed the fork back into the soil. Thunder rolled in the distance.

□□□

"MARTHA!"

Martha couldn't see who was calling her, but the female voice sounded alarmed. She had been digging, off and on, for much of the day, and sweat poured down her face. She stabbed the fork into the earth, and looked at the sky. The sun was low; it would be dark soon. She ran her shirted arm across her eyes to collect the sweat. In a moment, one of the young mothers appeared. She was flustered and on the verge of tears.

"What's wrong?" Martha asked.

"It's my little boy. He's really hot. And he's got spots." Tears spilled from the woman's eyes.

"Okay. Stop crying. I'll have a look at him." Martha looked back at the girls. Anna was watching her.

"Keep picking, girls. The sun will be down soon. I'll send some of the guys to pick up the full sacks and get them into storage."

The girls groaned.

Anna nodded.

☐☐☐

The Weapons

THE MAN TURNED to the assembled bikers. "Some of you are ex-military. I want access to the Namao army base. Some of you are munitions experts. Yes?"

The men stood silently.

"Yes?" The Man asked again. "Are you?"

"Some of us are," said a short man, his overly developed muscles bubbling out of his t-shirt sleeves. "We know where the supplies are. But the base is still guarded."

The Man walked over to the one who spoke. "Nothing is impossible," he said. "As long as one has the right amount of interest, determination, imagination, and inclination."

"And force," the short man added.

"Yes," The Man said, "there is that." He folded his arms across his chest. "So?"

"So—do you mean can we break into the army base?"

"Yes, that's precisely what I mean. Can we?"

"I suppose."

"You're beginning to tire me," The Man said. "If you can't come up with more specific answers than 'I suppose,' then I 'suppose' I will have to pass you by and start talking to one of your friends."

The Man pulled his pistol from its holster on his hip. "And if I do that, I won't need you." He pointed the pistol at the short man's left eye. "Will I?"

The short man gasped and took a step backwards. "Y-Y-Yes! We know some of the soldiers who stay on the base—we can talk our way by them." The words continued to tumble out of his mouth like oranges from a paper sack. "We can get to the weapons. Even the big guns. The rocket launchers. And all the ammunition."

The Man tilted his pistol away from the short man's face; he examined it, and then he blew imaginary dust from the barrel. He re-holstered it. "That's what I thought," he said. "Now, the only other question is—how soon can I expect delivery?"

"Wait a minute," said a redheaded man toward the rear of the group. He was dressed in full military fatigues. His bright hair was a mass of short spiky bristles. "What do we need you for? If we're getting the weapons? We're taking all the risks? What's in it for us?"

"Now there you go thinking—military intelligence." The Man laughed. He pulled his pistol out of its holster again, and aimed it across the room. The other men hustled to the side, leaving a clear path to the redheaded man. "Don't think," The Man said, as he pulled the trigger.

The redheaded man's face turned white as the bullet whined by his ear, crashing into the wallboards behind him. He ducked to the side, his hands instinctively covering his face.

"Get up!"

The redheaded man rose slowly.

"Any more questions?"

The redheaded man shook his head. "No, sir."

"Good. Now, who is going to tell me how you are going to get those weapons?"

"The best way is to bring some women onto the base," said a tall man.

"Really. Why is that?"

"No women there—well, except for lesbians. Women would make a great distraction," he blurted.

"Women—as decoys. Now why didn't I think of that?"

The Man threw back his head and gave a hearty laugh. The rest of the bikers joined in.

Chapter Seven

Measles and a Hooded Man

"HE'S SO HOT," Martha said. She peered under the child's t-shirt; red spots were just beginning to show. She checked behind his ears—more spots.

Why had this woman waited so long to say something?

"I'm pretty sure it's measles."

"Measles?" The mother reached up and tentatively touched her little boy's head. "I thought we were immune to measles?"

"Sure, before—but not now. It makes sense that the old diseases are reappearing, especially in the children born after everything fell apart. They haven't been vaccinated." Martha returned the child to its mother and went to her bookshelf.

A long wooden board stretched across the wall at eye level. It held a number of books about medical topics that ranged from herbal remedies to childhood diseases. Martha selected a book, quickly checked the index, and flipped to a page. Measles. Rubeola. She began to read as she ran her finger along the words.

"Did he seem to have a cold?"

"Yes. His nose was runny and he had a little cough. I just gave him some cough syrup."

"When was that *exactly*?"

The woman thought a moment. "Sunday, I think. Yeah, about three days ago."

Martha put down the book. She gently pried open the child's mouth. Inside, was the confirmation she was seeking: 'Koplik,' tiny red spots with white centers that appeared on the cheek walls in the first stages.

"It's measles," she said softly, almost too softly for the woman to hear.

"Oh..." the woman faltered and raised a hand to her open mouth.

"It's highly contagious. We have to get all the kids quarantined into their own homes." Martha shook her head and added, "If this goes through camp... "

There was a knock on the door. "What?" Martha called.

Ruth walked in. "Mom?"

Martha held up a hand to stop her. "No farther," she said. "This kid has measles."

Ruth looked shocked. "Really?"

"Find Matthew. Tell him to order the parents to keep their kids at home. For the next thirteen days. And tell him we have to set aside another building *away* from the Medical Building so we can keep the kids with measles in isolation."

"Okay," Ruth said and turned to leave. She paused, and looked back at Martha. "Have I had measles?"

"Yes. But I don't want you taking them back to your kids." Martha continued to study the book. "I want you to find out which of the adults have already had measles. We'll need them to help with the sick kids. The other adults will have to stay quarantined—measles in adults sounds pretty bad." Martha read on. Then turning her head slightly, she said, "And keep those pregnant girls away from all the kids."

Ruth left the room, slamming the cabin door shut behind her. Martha turned back to the mother holding the fevered child. "Okay, now listen carefully."

Martha tried to remember what she had done when her own children had had measles. She remembered that the biggest issue was protecting the eyes and keeping the child warm. The book confirmed that. "You'll have to be very careful to make sure he doesn't get a draft. Keep him warm. And you must keep his room dark to protect his eyes from the light." Martha stopped to read some more.

She reached for a thermometer, the old-fashioned kind with mercury and lines and numbers. She placed the thermometer in the pit of the child's arm. "Hold his arm like this," Martha said to his mother. Martha returned to the book.

"Uh, you haven't given him aspirin, have you?"

"Yes, a little baby aspirin. Why?"

Reye's Syndrome. Oh great. That's all we need.

Martha gave no explanation. "From here on in, ask me first before you administer any kind of medicine, okay?"

At that moment, she realized that all the parents needed to be spoken to—right away. Many of them were so used to doctoring their own children and most gave shelf medicines without ever reading the warning labels. *How many children had been given aspirin in the past few days?*

"Okay, first, his eyes." Martha peered into the child's face. Some gooey seepage was appearing at the corners. "I have a chickweed rinse that I'll give you for cleaning the guck out of his eyes. You just warm a little, dip in a cotton swab, squeeze the liquid onto his eyes, and wipe the gunk off."

Martha studied the book again. "You must keep him quiet and in bed. And keep him warm. Make him drink all the liquids you can. It says he should be peeing every two hours."

The woman looked a little sheepish as she asked, "Is breast milk okay? He still nurses once in a while."

Martha turned and looked at the toddler whom she knew to be almost two years old. She went to the young mother and put both hands on either side of the woman's face.

"Listen to me. Breast milk is God-given. It's the perfect food. Don't ever feel guilty because your child still wants to nurse. Right now, it's a blessing. Let him nurse as often as he wants. It'll give him all the nutrients he needs. And it'll comfort him."

The woman sighed with relief. "Some of the other mothers were making fun of me for still nursing him. So, I thought there was something wrong with it."

"Tell the other mothers to stick it up their asses," Martha said.

The young woman winced at hearing the swear word and then nodded her agreement. Martha smiled softly in the realization that this woman would never be able to quote her, verbatim.

"Now about the fever. Bathe him in tepid water. NOT cold water. Not HOT water. Warm water. Sit him in the tub and keep pouring the water over him. As it evaporates, it'll cool his skin. When the water gets too cool, take him out. Don't let him get chilled."

"Yes, Martha. Can we go home now?"

Martha removed the thermometer from the boy's armpit. It read: 104°F. "He'll need a cooling bath right away." The woman began to stand. Martha shook her head and said, "No, let's give him one right now."

Martha grabbed a large plastic tub from under the sink. She cleared the kitchen table, and set the tub down. She took hot water from the stove, poured it into the tub, and then added cool water, dipper by dipper. She showed the woman how to test the water on her wrist. "If you can't feel the water," she said, "then it's the right temperature."

They quickly undressed the little boy, who had begun to shiver. Martha set the child into the tub and took a thick washcloth, soaked it and gently wrung it out over his head and chest. Someone knocked on the door. She motioned for the mother to take over. The door opened.

It was Matthew.

"Hang on. Have you had measles?" Martha called out.

"Yeah, I'm fine." Matthew came into the cabin. Martha glanced his way and then turned her attentions back to the mother.

"Martha... you—"

Martha ignored him, and grabbed a small wicker basket. She packed it with a Ziploc bag filled with cotton balls and a small jar of chickweed rinse. She dropped in a tube of calamine lotion. "Later. For the itching," she said. The little boy was whining weakly, leaning up against his mother's arm. He was shuddering.

Martha turned. "Close the damn door, Matthew." He did.

Martha reached beneath a shelf and pulled a thick white towel from atop of a pile of towels. She held the towel open. "Okay, get him out of there."

They wrapped the now crying child, snugly. Martha stopped. "Have you had measles?" she asked the woman.

"I don't know," she replied.

"I'll need to check you, too." Martha turned to Matthew. The child was howling now.

"Make yourself useful. Here, hold the kid." Matthew's arms jerked up in surprise as Martha dumped the little boy into them. Matthew held the screaming child, gingerly. He grimaced.

Martha turned back to the mother. "Okay, shirt up." The woman blushed and hesitated. Martha looked back at Matthew. "Turn around." Matthew did so. The woman raised her shirt. She wasn't wearing a bra. Martha scanned the woman's back, and then her chest. "Hold out your arms." She checked the soft flesh on the inside of her elbows. Martha grunted. "Okay, now your mouth." Martha took a small flashlight from the shelf and examined the woman's mouth.

"So?" the woman asked.

"You look fine." They both looked toward Matthew and the screaming child.

"Why don't you nurse him before you go," Martha said with a conspiratorial wink. The mother smiled. She lowered her shirt back over her belly, and walked to Matthew. Matthew thrust the child into his mother's arms. He scowled and brushed at the front of his shirt.

The woman settled into the chair she had occupied earlier and pulled up her shirt once more. The child latched on to her naked breast immediately. He was still snuffling, his breath hitching as he nursed.

Martha smiled, remembering her days as a nursing mother. She never wore a bra either. Too annoying. She would nurse her girls anywhere. Just shove up her t-shirt and go for it. Middle of a department store, at Josef's workplace. Anywhere. *Just as it should be*, she thought. Martha stood for a moment longer, arms folded, and watched. Then she turned back to Matthew. He was watching the nursing pair with great interest.

"Did you get my message?" Martha leaned into Matthew's face to get his attention.

"Yeah. So—is this as much an emergency as you're making it out to be?"

"Measles?" She huffed. "Uh, yeah, Matthew." Martha collected the little boy's clothing and folded them as she spoke. "One of the biggest problems is that measles can result in pneumonia. If they die from the disease, it's because of pneumonia."

"Die?" the boy's mother cried out. Her face was stricken. "Die?"

"Yes, die," Martha confirmed. "As modern day people, we've forgotten about childhood diseases. But many people used to die from them. So just do exactly what I tell you to do."

The woman began to cry.

"Stop crying. He's not dead yet. And he won't die if you do as I tell you."

The woman shoved her balled fist against her mouth to stifle her cries, but the sobbing only got worse. Martha handed her a box of Kleenex. The woman struggled with the child in her arms as she attempted to accept the box. The child's mouth pulled from her breast, making a small sucking pop. Martha noticed and took the boy; he was still very hot.

"You'll have to bathe him again, every couple of hours, to bring that fever down. Oh, and by the way, add some baking soda to his bath water, too. It'll help when the itching starts."

The woman blew her nose. Martha handed the boy back to her. He lay back in her lap, secured her breast, and began to nurse again. Martha walked over to another cupboard and took down a jar filled with shiny colored objects. She dumped several into her hand and added them to the basket. The mother noticed and looked at her quizzically.

"They're for you. You'll need a little extra energy," Martha said with a smile. She held up a miniature foil-wrapped chocolate Easter egg.

The woman's eyes glistened with tears as she spoke, "Thank you, Martha."

"No problem," Martha said. She placed her hand on the child's head, and closed her eyes. She mumbled softly. Then she helped the woman to her feet and ushered the pair to the cabin door. Matthew held it open. He closed the door behind them, and turned to face Martha.

"What do you need?"

Martha stopped, bit her lip, and answered. "What I really need is to tell all those parents not to give their kids aspirin."

"Why?"

"Reye's Syndrome." Martha watched as Matthew's interest increased. He said nothing. Martha continued:

"It's caused by giving sick kids aspirin. It can affect the internal organs. The liver, the heart, the lungs. And it can make the brain swell up." She paused, "There's no cure."

"Okay." Matthew turned, and grabbed the door handle.

"Damn," Martha said, "I forgot to tell her about plantain."

"Tell her tomorrow. You still haven't told me if you'll need any supplies."

"Baking soda. And calamine lotion." She looked at Matthew. He was rubbing his forehead, having pulled off his cap. He looked tired. And old. "What's the matter, Matthew?"

"Nothing. Good night, Martha." He went out the door.

□□□

MARTHA STARED OUT the window. The night had gotten very dark. She checked her watch.

Where was Josef? Wasn't he supposed to have come home hours ago? She saw a light on in the Gatehouse. *I'll go and ask,* she thought. *Might as well pick some plantain, too.*

Martha grabbed her jacket and a small basket, and left the cabin.

The construction lights illuminated parts of the compound. The rest lay in pitch darkness.

Plantain. Plantain.

Lots of the low-lying heart-shaped foliage dotted the campground, so it was easy to find. She plucked some wide leaves from a patch growing near the cabin, and stuffed them into the basket. She headed off toward the young mother's trailer. Lightning flashed across the sky and rain began to fall. Martha hurried. A huge roll of thunder caught her off guard and she gave a little jump.

A movement off to her left caught her eye, and she froze. There were no lampposts set up in the RV area and she had forgotten her flashlight, so she had to rely on the moon and flashes of lightning to see clearly. She squinted and watched as shadowy figures sprinted in between the trailers. They were hunkered down. Martha stopped in surprise.

Why were people sneaking around? Kids? Playing hide-and-seek? Too big to be kids.

Martha hung back in the shadows.

How many? Four? Six?

Icy darts pricked her arms, and she held her breath.

What the heck?

"Over here," she heard one of the figures speak. It was a man's voice—a voice she had never heard before. Martha looked across the compound. There was still a light on in the Gatehouse.

Should she yell? Should she run?

Panic constricted her chest, but she forced herself to breathe. She wanted to cry out, but she couldn't force her tongue to move, her throat to open. She dropped her basket to the ground, and began creeping through the shadows in the direction of the dark figures. Suddenly, she felt a presence near her and she stopped.

"Don't move," a male voice growled into her right ear.

Fear exploded in Martha's stomach as a gun barrel pressed to her cheek. She instinctively raised her arm to protect herself, but it was grabbed and wrenched up behind her back.

"Owww… "

A hand reached around and clamped itself over her mouth. A man's hand. A massive hand that smelled of cigarettes. And of beer. The first man still held his gun against her face. Martha struggled and clawed at the fingers clamped over her mouth. Her assailant released his hold on her mouth and grabbed her wrist. In a quick gesture, he yanked her arm down and twisted it up behind her back, too. Martha screamed. She didn't see the fist coming.

Martha saw stars as the man's fist connected with the side of her head. The blow threw her off balance, but she didn't black out. She staggered and fell. The man holding her arms went down with her. They both landed heavily on the dirt pathway. But her arms were now free. She rolled and kicked at the man who was crouching before her. She heard the sounds of voices off to her right. She kicked again. This time her foot connected. With softness. She heard the man grunt, and watched as he grabbed himself. His face was contorted in pain.

Good, she thought. *Serves you right. Asshole.*

She had forgotten about the man with the gun. She turned her head and saw him level the pistol at her.

What was he wearing? A hood?

She rolled to her left, as a shot rang out.

A moving target. I've gotta keep moving.

Another shot, and a bullet whizzed by her ear. Martha looked back. The hooded man was coming after her. Something cool, like silken steel, replaced the fear that had paralyzed her earlier. She turned back. The man noticed and he hesitated. A moment too long. Martha launched herself at him, a super-charged barrel of energy.

Uhhh!" The sound erupted from him in a quick grunt as he went flying backwards. His pistol spiraled into the shadows.

"You son-of-a-bitch!" Martha's hands were balled in fury. She marched over to where the man lay, struggling to catch his breath. She drew back a booted foot and kicked him in the ribs. Another grunt, this one pain-filled and much louder than the first. She drew back again.

"Martha!"

She barely heard the distant call. The fury in her brain made her ears ring, and her world skidded into slow motion. She kicked the man again.

"Stop!" he yelled, and rolled away.

Martha walked after him. She stooped down. "Who in hell are you?" She reached for the man's hood. He slapped at her hand. Only it wasn't a slap.

Martha lifted her left hand to her face. It stung, and a thin crease across her palm was filling. Dark droplets fell to her feet, glistening silver in the moonlight. The blade came again. Martha watched it glint before it buried itself in her leg. She fell back.

"Martha!" the call came again, this time closer.

Martha watched, frozen in place, as the man scrambled to his feet. She could see his eyes burning bright through the holes in his hood.

"It's not over between us, bitch," he said. He turned and ran. Martha stared at the knife in her thigh.

She struggled to stay alert. She heard sounds around her, but she could not rise. She sat slumped over, her head swirling with clouded thoughts. Unconsciousness pulled at her; she fought the urge and forced her eyes to flicker open. She tried to focus but her vision would not clear. The effort was exhausting, so she closed her eyes and yielded to the pull of that soft, deep place.

"Martha!" Someone was calling her name again.

Martha turned toward the sound, but the vortex was sucking her down and she began to sway. A sheet of lightning lit the sky. A few seconds later, thunder growled. Through the haze, she recognized the caller.

"Hi, Matthew." She managed a tiny smile. "I'm in a little trouble here." She tilted to her right. Matthew leapt forward to catch her, but he was too late.

For the third time that night, Martha hit the ground, with a solid thud.

This time, she was unconscious.

□□□

The Woman

THE MAN TURNED and stared at the dark-haired biker shifting from foot to foot, at the other side of his desk. The Man's mouth was tight with constrained anger. "I told you—'One-percenters' either join us—or they die."

"I know," the biker countered. "But these are Outlaws. From Daytona. Tough. Thought you might want to talk to their chapter president first."

"Has he agreed to lay down his colors?"

"No."

"Kill them."

The biker nodded and left the room. The Man sat down in his chair, and lifted a bottle of scotch from his desk drawer. He pulled a crystal tumbler toward him, poured a few inches of the amber liquid into the glass, re-capped the bottle, and returned it to the drawer. He picked up the glass, and leaned back in his chair. He waited.

Sounds came from outside the door. He smiled. He was looking for a new one—new spice in his life. He was always looking. He said nothing as the women were ushered into the room. Like mixed nuts they stood— tall, small, short, fat, skinny, pretty, plain, buxom, flat-chested, some beautiful. One very beautiful—a brunette, dressed in an oversized black, leather jacket.

"Here they are," the armed biker said. He waved his gun toward the assembled women. "See anything you like?"

The Man remained relaxed, leaning back in his chair. He lifted his tumbler to his lips, and drank. His eyes flickered over the women, appraising one and then another. Most of them took a quick look at the man staring at them, but then their gaze dropped to the floor. Except for one woman—the small brunette whose eyes remained focused on The Man.

"Turn around," he said.

"Screw you," the brunette said. "We're not cattle."

The armed biker made a move for her, but The Man stopped him. "Get the other ones out of here. Leave her."

The biker nodded and herded the women out of the room, leaving the outspoken woman to face The Man. The door closed with a bang; the woman gave a little jump.

The Man leaned forward. He studied her. The woman's gaze never wavered—velvet brown eyes beneath smoky dark lashes. The Man rose from his chair.

"Come here," he said.

The woman did not move.

"Now!"

Chapter Eight

The Veterinarian's Assistant

MARTHA WAS dreaming. In her dream, she heard dogs barking.

But how could they be barking when they were dead? And on her kitchen table.

She watched as people—family members and those she didn't recognize—rip at the flesh, pulling raw, bleeding chunks away from the carcass, still covered in dog fur, and shove it into their mouths. She watched as though she were floating up on the ceiling. She wondered how the meat tasted. She grimaced at the idea of all that hair in her mouth. Prickly, dirty hair. The dogs kept barking. Someone was calling her name.

Martha moved, half in and half out of her dream state. She felt a pain in her thigh.

Had one of the dogs bitten her?

The pain came in sharp excruciating stabs. Rhythmic stabs.

Which dog was biting her?

She tried to brush the animal away only to find her hands would not move. They were stuck, held in place by some invisible force. She struggled up through the haze. She could hear moans. Soft voices. More sharp stabs. More barks. Martha slipped away.

"Martha?" A voice far in the distance. "Martha?"

Martha stirred and tried to open her eyes. A dull throb in her thigh caught her attention. She moaned. She reached to touch the source of her pain, and then noticed another pain—this one in the palm of her left hand.

"Ow..."

"It's okay," said a soft female voice. Martha tried again to open her eyes, and to focus, but her world kept shifting. The effort made her nauseous.

"You had a rough night," the voice said. "But you should be okay. It'll take time for this wound to heal. But you should be fine."

Martha tried to place the voice. A faint memory stirred.

Anna?

She fought to open her eyes. This time, she succeeded.

The girl was standing near her bed, belly protruding out from under her t-shirt. A grey cardigan sweater hung loosely from her shoulders; it was belted just under her belly. Martha stared and tried to speak, but her tongue was woolen and the words wouldn't come.

"Here," Anna said. She reached behind Martha's head and lifted her slightly. With her other hand she offered a glass of water. A paper straw moved in and out of Martha's focus. Anna used a finger to push the straw into position. Martha took a sip.

"It's the Demerol," Anna said.

"What?" Martha said, spitting water as she spoke. "Who the hell gave me Demerol?"

"I did." Anna eased Martha's head back to the pillow, and placed the glass of water back on a small side table.

Martha grabbed the girl's arm with her good right hand. "What the hell do you know about giving somebody drugs?"

Anna pulled her arm out of Martha's clutch. "You kept coming to while I was stitching you up. I thought it was a good idea."

"You? You stitched me up?" Martha shook her head to keep her eyes from glazing over and her brain from relaxing back into its earlier drugged state. "What are you talking about?"

Anna stood near the bed, her arms at her sides. "I learned how to do things like stitching flesh. My dad taught me."

"Your dad?"

"Yes, he was a vet. He practiced out of our farmhouse. I used to help him." Anna shrugged. "He said my eyesight was better than his, so when animals needed stitching up, he got me to do it."

Martha's mouth gaped in surprise.

"He taught me about drugs, too."

"I have been stitched up by a veterinarian's assistant?"

"Yes." Anna smiled a tiny smile. "It's better than bleeding to death, isn't it?"

Martha was too flabbergasted to answer. Sounds came from outside the room, and the pair turned their attentions toward the doorway. Matthew poked his head in.

"So, how's it going in here?" He stepped into the room.

Anna blushed and smiled. "I think our patient is doing well."

Martha glowered at the girl. She fixed her gaze on Matthew.

"I'm fine. A little dizzy. Did you catch those guys last night?" She eased upright, and winced at the pain that shot through her thigh. Anna was at her side in an instant.

"Do you want more Demerol?" Anna asked. She touched Martha's arm—a tiny, soft gesture.

Martha shook off the tentative fingers. "No, thanks. And what the hell do you know about morphine-based drugs, anyway?"

Anna took a step back. "Well, pain-killer drugs for dogs, like Rimadyl and Deramaxx, are morphine drugs that came from human drugs. So, I know— "

Martha was livid. "You had no right—"

"She took good care of you," Matthew admonished Martha. "You owe her one." Martha glared at him. Matthew shrugged his shoulders, "I couldn't have done it, Martha. All I did was hold your hands."

Anna had stepped away from the bed, making room for Matthew. He stood nearby and motioned with his head. "You won't be standing for a while. It was a pretty deep cut."

"I'll be fine," Martha said. Then with a quick tilt of her chin. "How did she get into the picture?"

"I sent out a call to find out if somebody else could doctor you. Ruth wanted to, but when it came to sticking a sewing needle into your leg, she backed out. Then Anna came by. She said she could do it. So I said, go ahead." Matthew smiled.

"What?" Martha's eyes blazed. "You let this kid—a complete stranger, operate on me?"

"Yep." Matthew shrugged again. "She sounded like she knew what she was talking about." He gazed down at Martha's leg. "And—it looks to me like she did."

"I think that was highly irresponsible of you," Martha said. "And— I... " She stopped. "Where's Josef?"

Anna and Matthew exchanged glances. Anna mumbled something, and made her way out of the bedroom. Martha watched the girl leave and then she fixed her stare on Matthew.

"Where—is—Josef?" she repeated.

"He's in the Medical Building."

Martha's face grew white. "What?"

Matthew held up his hands. "Slow down, Martha. He's doing okay."

"What?" Martha struggled to rise and get off the bed. She tried to move her legs, but the pain in her thigh made her cry out again. She fell back against the pillows.

"Wait," Matthew said, gently. "It's okay. He's going to be okay."

"What the hell are you talking about?" Martha's voice was shrill with fear.

"The same guys who attacked you last night? They must have attacked him, too. We found him and Jonah lying just inside the west perimeter. They were beaten. But they were still alive."

"Beaten?"

"Yeah, he's got a few bad bruises. Cuts, scrapes, but he wasn't stabbed or shot. Neither of them were. So, that's good."

"What's he doing in the hospital then? Why isn't he here?"

Matthew paused. "Uh," he said, with a small grimace, "we think he might have had a heart attack."

"What?" Martha sat upright, and this time she did swing her legs over the edge of the bed. She squeezed her eyes tight against the wave of pain. "Take me to him."

"Martha... we've got it under control."

"Now!"

☐☐☐

A SHORT WHILE later, Martha, leaning on Matthew's arm, hobbled into the Medical Building. Sweat streamed down her face from the ordeal of climbing the small set of wooden steps. She was breathing heavily by the time she reached Josef's bedside.

"Josef?" Martha touched her husband's cheek. She brushed back soft grey curls from his forehead. His face was ashen, almost grey. Raw scrapes covered the left side of his face; dried blood still clung to his lips. "Josef?" she whispered. He didn't stir.

"Get me one of my reference books!" Martha made the demand of no one, and of everyone. "What's been done for him?" She turned and eyed two women who stood near the bed. She switched her gaze to Matthew. It was accusatory.

"Nitroglycerin pills," said the taller woman. "It's all we could think of." Martha glared back at the woman. The woman's face and tone hardened in defense. "His heart had stopped, Martha. One of the guys who found him performed CPR." She nodded in Josef's direction. "We have no idea how long he was without blood flow."

"And now?" Martha demanded. "What are you doing now?"

"Just trying to keep him alive. We have *superaspirins* to stop any clotting."

Martha winced as she brushed her thigh up against the bed. She laid the back of her hand on Josef's forehead. "He's so cold and clammy." The room sank into silence.

The door banged and Anna rushed in. She had gone for the medical textbook immediately upon Martha's request.

"Is this the book you wanted?" Anna asked, shoving a grey hard-backed book into Martha's hands. Martha winced when the book hit her bandaged palm.

"Oh, sorry."

Martha stared at the girl, opened her mouth to speak, and then closed it again. She looked down at the book, and then behind her for a chair. Anna anticipated her need and grabbed a collapsible camp chair from the corner. She struggled with opening it. Matthew strode over. With a simple, firm push on the arms, the chair was open. He placed the chair near Josef's bed, and then took Martha's elbow. He guided her gently down into the chair. Martha grimaced as pain shot up her leg.

"I can get more Demerol," Anna offered.

Martha gave the girl a stare that needed no words. Anna stepped back. Martha flipped to the book's index, she ran her finger through the listed words, and then opened the book to a section on heart attacks. She looked up at the people gazing at her.

"Just let me alone for a while."

□□□

HOURS LATER, Martha awoke. Her neck was stiff, and the textbook had slipped from her hands. It lay splayed open on the dusty floor. Martha reached one hand to her neck. Her head throbbed mightily, and she groaned.

She looked up at the bed where Josef lay. He hadn't moved. He was still very pale, his chest rising and falling, rhythmically, but his breathing was shallow. Martha made a move to get out of the chair and cried out as she attempted to stand on her injured leg. In a moment, a hand was at her elbow. She turned. It was Anna.

"Let me help you."

"I'm fine," Martha growled.

"No, you're not. Let me help you." Martha shook off the girl's small hand.

"I said... I'm fine."

"Okay." Anna took a step back. "Can I get you something to drink?"

Martha thought a moment. She was very thirsty. "Sure."

"Okay. I'll be right back."

Martha struggled over to the bedside and clung to the edge, allowing a fresh wave of pain to wash over her. Sweat beaded on her forehead, and she grew dizzy.

Damn! I'm going to faint.

Martha fought her way back to the chair, and screamed out when she banged her injured thigh on the chair's arm. Nausea swept through her; she closed her eyes, and bowed her head into her hands. Her face was as cold and as clammy as Josef's. She waited for the wave to pass. However, it wasn't passing.

I need to lie down.

Her world shifted, and she pitched forward to the floor.

"Martha?" A voice called from far away. "Martha?" Martha stirred. Her body screamed in agony. Her thigh and her head throbbed with a fresh vigor.

"I need help," the voice said. Sounds of metal scraping across the floor. More voices. "Right here, is good."

Anna?

Martha moaned. Hands were lifting her. Many hands. She felt the waistband of her pajamas pulled down, and then a sharp pinch.

"Hang on, Martha. You'll feel much better in a few minutes."

Anna?

The world spun away, and Martha's mind tumbled like a die—a big fuzzy die—the kind that cool guys once hung from their rearview mirrors. She made a sound, a sound she thought was a laugh. The downward spiral felt so good, and the dreamy place was so welcome. She embraced her new universe and slipped into the mist.

MARTHA AWOKE with a start. The light was low. Camp lanterns had been turned up and they illuminated the walls of the room.

Where am I?

She forced her eyes to focus in the dim light. She was lying in a bed. A few feet away she saw another bed; she could just make out the form of her husband. Then she remembered—she was in the Medical Building. And Josef had suffered a heart attack.

Is he alive? Is he breathing?

She struggled upward to get a better look. Anna was instantly at her side.

"You had a long sleep. Do you feel any better?"

Martha studied the girl. The camp lights cast deep shadows under Anna's eyes.

"You've been here the whole time?" A small wave of sympathy struck her. "You look tired."

"I am tired, but I'll be okay." The girl smiled. "I'm kind of used to staying up with sick animals all through the night. So, this isn't so bad."

Martha gave a small grin, and motioned toward Josef. "How's he doing?"

"It's hard to tell," Anna replied. "He hasn't really moved. For hours. He's cried out every so often." Anna shrugged her shoulders. "He's sort of just been lying there—mostly."

"Help me up," Martha said. Anna extended her right arm to Martha, and gripped Martha's upper arm in a firm grasp, allowing Martha to grip her upper arm in return. "Hey, how do you know this grip?" Martha asked, surprise lighting her eyes.

"I've been to doctors."

"Oh," Martha said. She gingerly swung her legs over the edge of the bed, and tried to step down. She gritted her teeth as pain blazed up her leg. "Oh, shit."

"What?"

"I think it's infected. Help me look." She eased back on the bed. Between them, they managed to get Martha out of her pajama bottoms.

Martha reached for the bandage; she did not like the look of the gauze. The white mesh was dark with a gooey substance. She pulled at the tape, but the gauze was glued to the wound, and she had to tug it free. "Oh, shit."

Martha eyed the angry reddish color that now surrounded the cut. The stitches were all neat and orderly—no complaints there, but the wound was weeping with infection. "Shit," she said again. She did not relish the next step. Martha looked up and met Anna's eyes. "You gotta do exactly what I tell you now."

"What do I do?"

"The only way to fight this infection is to clean it with hot salt water." Martha grimaced. "Very hot salt water. And since I can't figure out a way to soak the cut like I can soak the cut on my hand, you're going to have to baste it." Martha paused. "So, we need hot water, coarse salt, and— a turkey baster." Anna turned and headed toward the door. "And towels," Martha added.

The door closed. Martha looked over at Josef; his chest rose and sank almost imperceptibly in the low light.

Please, God. Please. Don't take him from me. Please.

She ignored her lack of pajama bottoms and hobbled over to his bed. She clung to the edge as she stood there, half-naked, and stared at her husband's bearded face.

Please.

Martha heard the door open, but she didn't turn around. She waited for Anna to speak. She jumped when she heard her name.

"Martha?" It was Matthew. "Should I come back?"

Martha glanced down at her state of undress, and blushed. "No. Never mind. It's okay." She was grateful for the denim shirt she wore; it did little to cover her, but it was better than nothing. Matthew came over.

She watched as he eyed her thigh. She caught a flicker of concern as he stared at the wound. "It looks infected."

"It is."

"Are you going to open it? Drain it?"

"Hell, no. But I'm going to do something about it. I sent Anna off to get the stuff I need."

"What are you going to do?"

"Hot salt water."

Matthew gave a small grunt of understanding. "That's gonna hurt. Who's gonna hold you down?"

Martha caught his eyes. "I was hoping you would."

"Um, sure," Matthew said. He glanced away. "You gonna put some pants on first?"

"No."

They looked at each other and laughed.

The door banged shut. Anna came over to the bed. She held a steaming kettle in one hand, while the other hand held a box of salt, a turkey baster, and fresh bandages. White towels were slung over one shoulder.

"Okay," Anna said. "I got everything." She glanced at Matthew. "Are you staying?"

"Oh, yeah," Matthew said, with a small laugh. "I wouldn't miss the chance to cause Martha pain. I get to hold her down again."

Anna glanced back to Martha, puzzlement showing in her eyes. She gave a tiny nervous laugh. "Oh, okay."

Matthew gave Martha a hand as she limped back to the bed, and settled back against the pillows. Martha looked up at Anna who stood quietly by, eagerness on her face, as she awaited instructions.

□□□

SEVERAL HOURS later, Martha sat propped on the bed. She was still out of her pajamas; the area of her leg surrounding the wound was puffy and red. It was going to take many more applications of salt water to draw out the poisons, but she knew it would work. Martha checked the gauze. The plantain leaf poultice that she had had Anna scald with boiling water and then apply to the wound was firmly in place. She nodded her satisfaction.

Martha turned and picked up the medical textbook lying near her; the news wasn't good. There wasn't much anyone could do for a heart attack victim. Except pray. No one could perform open-heart surgery, and even if someone could, they would have no idea what it was they should be fixing. They would just have to watch, and wait.

"I brought you some tea," Anna said, as she placed a thick, white mug of steaming tea on the small table next to the bed.

"Thanks." Martha took the cup, blew against the steam, and sipped. "Um, good, thanks." She returned the cup to the table. Anna hadn't moved. "Shouldn't you be getting some rest?"

"Uh, I'm okay. I sort of slept on and off while you were sleeping."

"Oh." Martha glanced down to the girl's belly. "How are you doing?"

"Good—the baby's pretty active. Lots of kicking. Sometimes—he crawls up under my ribcage. That hurts."

"I remember. I would push my son back down when he did that. He was my first, and he was so big." She paused. "You said *he.*"

"Yeah, I think it's a boy."

"Have you got a name yet?"

"Probably my Dad's name... Gordon."

"Hmm. Nice name." Martha set the book aside. She reached her arms up behind her head and clasped her hands together. "So, how did you come to be pregnant?"

Anna fidgeted with a button on her sweater. She looked up. "I—uh— I was raped."

"By who?"

"Bikers." Anna glanced away. "They came to my Dad's clinic. They were after drugs. They found me... " Anna's voice trailed off.

"What about your Dad? Where's your Dad?"

Anna stared out the window, and answered as if from a far distance. "He's dead. They killed him."

Martha sat quietly, and then said, "I'm sorry, Anna. That must have been a terrible, terrible experience for you."

"Yes."

Martha waited, cocked her head, and then asked, "Are you okay with having this baby?"

"Oh, yes." Anna looked back. Her eyes were shining. "He hasn't got anything to do with what those guys did. I love him already." She smiled. "I'm looking forward to meeting him."

Martha smiled back at the girl. "Then I'm looking forward to helping you meet him." Martha squirmed her way down the bed into a flatter position. "I have to sleep. Would you give me that other blanket?"

Anna picked up the soft flannel sheet sitting on the end of the bed. She unfolded it, and then flung it over Martha. "Have a good sleep," she said.

Martha lifted her head, "You get sleep, too, missy. You're going to need all your strength. Fairly soon, I suspect."

Anna moved soundlessly around the room. She turned down the propane-fuelled lamps. She made her way to a tiny camp cot nestled in a corner of the room. She lay down, pulled an unzipped green sleeping bag over her, and snuggled down. Tears glistened on her cheeks, but she made no sound.

□□□

THE CHOKING sounds roused both of them from their sleep. Anna was already at Josef's side, while Martha was still struggling to rise.

Anna turned to Martha, her eyes filled with fear, "What should I do?"

The Report

"WE GOT INTO the compound. No problem. We had to take down a couple of perimeter guards, but we didn't kill them. Just messed them up."

The Man crossed to the window, pushed up one of the venetian blind slats, and squinted into the darkness. "So, the new prospect did as he promised?"

"Yeah, we got a good look around. We ran into a woman. He knew her. She put up a fight, but he stabbed her." The man lifted his shoulders. "Don't know if she died."

"A woman? You want to report to me about a woman?"

"She really fought. He said she's the camp's medical officer. Says she's a real discipline problem."

"A woman?" The Man held up his hand. "And just what is this problematic woman's name? Did he tell you that?"

"Martha."

Chapter Nine

The New Law

MARTHA GAZED through the window. She was still in the Medical Building. Her thigh hurt, but the pain was deadened again. She touched the tender spot high on her butt where the Demerol shots had been administered. At Anna's constant insistence, Martha had finally consented to another injection. It was good to escape the pain, if only for a few hours.

A light dusting of snow covered the compound. An early winter. Exactly what they had expected. Nature had given them fair warning. Martha pulled the flannel sheet tighter around her shoulders. The room's little wood stove had been stoked with logs and it was radiating a thick, perfumed, and cozy warmth. However, near the window, Martha felt the chill of winter wind gusting outside. It was only mid-September.

She watched as children slipped, and scooped, and laughed. Snow, their natural plaything. Martha smiled. Then she remembered something.

"Dammit!"

What were those kids doing outside? Hadn't she ordered a quarantine?

"Anna!"

"Yes?" Anna called out from across the room. Martha watched as the girl struggled up from her bed. She pushed her feet into her boots, and waddled over, her hands supporting the small of her back.

"Find out why those kids are outside. And remind their mothers that I said all kids were to be quarantined." Martha's face was flushed.

"Dammit. What in hell is wrong with them?" She turned. "Wait a minute. Have you had measles?"

"Yes, when I was three." Anna left the cabin.

Martha heard a soft sigh behind her and she turned back to see Josef stirring. Her yelling had awoken him. She hitched her way over to his bedside.

"Hi," she said softly. Josef's eyes were open, intense and questioning.

"Hi," he mumbled his voice thick and low.

The coughing and choking last night had proven to be a good thing. In the midst of the choking fit, Josef came out of his dead sleep. He had opened his eyes. And he had spoken: "I gotta go to the can."

Martha had breathed a huge sigh of relief. *No brain damage.* Anna had fetched a bed pan. Josef used the pan, and then sank immediately back into sleep. That was several hours ago. The man staring at her now looked brighter, and a whole lot better.

"Hey, you've got a little color back in your cheeks." Martha reached over and stroked his stubbled face. "Want a sip of water?"

"Yeah. But I need that piss pot, first."

Martha provided the bedpan. After he was done, she tucked it under the bed. She helped her husband into a reclining position, plumped the pillows behind his head, and held a glass of water up to him. He took a long drink through the plastic straw, and then allowed his head to fall back against the pillows.

"Ah," he said, "I feel terrible."

"I know. It'll take a while to recover your strength, but you'll do it."

Martha pulled a camp chair closer to the bed, and seated herself, taking extra care not to bang her sore leg. Josef still didn't know about the attack on her, and Martha intended to keep it that way. At least for the time being. He asked about her bandaged hand, but she had put him off with a story about a slip with a kitchen knife.

"Will you take some soup?"

Josef groaned. "I'll try."

Martha smiled. She took his chin and turned his face toward her. "I want a little more enthusiasm than that, mister."

Josef smiled back. "Bring on the damn soup!"

A half bowl of beef broth later, Josef indicated his need for sleep. As Martha settled him down, the door opened. Matthew walked in, stomping his boots on the doormat as he closed the door. The breeze made Martha shiver. She reached across Josef and pulled the covers up under his chin. His eyes were already closed, and he was snoring softly.

"Hi, Martha. How's he doing?" asked Matthew.

"Not bad. He just ate." Martha set the bowl on a small tray. She faced Matthew. "So, what's with the kids running around outside? I thought you ordered a quarantine."

"I did," Matthew said. "Some of the mothers said the kids had already had measles. I guess those are the ones playing out there." He jabbed his thumb toward the window.

"Oh." Martha hop-stepped over to a table near the door, and set the tray down. "So, where are the sick ones?"

"We're using a cabin near the east side. We put in some bunks, and an extra furnace. There are four kids in there now. Sylvie and Wanda are in charge."

"I see," Martha said as she thought about the ex-nurses who had earlier been caring for Josef. She picked up a pitcher and poured herself a glass of water. She drank deeply. "Want some?"

Matthew came over and accepted the glass. It was the same one she had drunk from. He didn't question it. He just drank. He set the glass down on the table. "Let's talk about last night."

"Okay. But I want to make sure Josef is asleep first." She looked over; Josef was still snoring softly.

The pair pulled their chairs near the wood stove, several beds away from Josef. Matthew took a gun out of his belt and laid it on a nearby table. It was Josef's beloved Smith and Wesson. Martha looked at it, but didn't touch it.

"The guys who rescued him took the gun from his holster. For safe-keeping." Mathew said. His voice was low and soft.

"So, who did this to us, Matthew? Have you figured it out yet?"

"Are you sure you didn't recognize any of the voices of the guys who attacked you?"

Martha shook her head slowly. "I don't think so. But maybe the hood... that the one guy was wearing... disguised his voice."

"Maybe." Matthew leaned back in his chair. One hand reached up and rubbed his chin, while the other rested peacefully on the armrest. Martha stared at his hand. It still bore a summer tan, several scars, wiry dark hairs, and neatly trimmed, albeit, dirty fingernails. *Manicured*, she thought. She looked up when Matthew spoke:

"Jonah has an interesting take on all of this."

"He's really okay, is he?"

"Yep. Cuts, bruises, scrapes... " Matthew assured her. "Some pretty BIG bruises, but no broken bones. The kid's tough."

"So, what's his take on this?"

"He says they overheard the guys talking before they were attacked. Says there were maybe four of them. He says he's sure he recognized two of the voices."

"Who?"

"Vince and Brad."

"What?" Martha spoke loudly. She glanced over at Josef to make sure he hadn't been disturbed, and then she lowered her voice. "What?" she repeated. "They're hugely loyal to you."

"I'm just telling you what he said."

"That's crazy. He's got to be wrong."

"Well, for now, we'll keep an eye on them." Matthew glanced out the window. "The snow will quiet things down for a bit. At least until people get hungry and start looking for handouts."

"Does that happen a lot?"

"Oh, yeah. We turned away lots of people last winter. We have only so much food." Matthew opened his hand and drew it down over his face in a smooth massage. "That's when they go after the Hutterites. And that's when our job gets even harder." He paused, and then added, "Even in the snow, they'll come. No motorcycles, but plenty of snowmobiles."

Martha nodded. She remembered Matthew explaining their relationship with the neighboring Hutterite colony to Josef when they first arrived...

"WE'RE TIGHT with the colony of Hutterites up the road," Matthew had explained as he and Josef met over coffee during their first week on the compound. "They're devout pacifists. Something to do with a quote from the Bible. Anyway, we provide protection. They provide food and other things like shoes and clothing. Our pre-fab cabins, doors, and windows."

Matthew went on to explain that starving city folks searched further afield in their quest to stay alive. The smart ones realized that farmers knew how to grow food. So, Hutterite farm colonies were among the first to be attacked.

The worst were the Crazies; they would arrive in the night, bearing guns, knives, bats, and swinging chains. The unsuspecting pacifistic Hutterites didn't stand a chance. Many were murdered as they slept;

others were clubbed down as they tried to run. Then their murderers would take what they had come for: food. But not this colony; this colony was under the Gatekeeper's protection.

"We send a group of our men every day and every night to patrol the colony's perimeter," Matthew continued to explain. "The Hutterites have a lot of land, so most of us are riding ATVs all night. It's hard work, but the guys are up to it. And they share in the rewards."

"Sounds like you know exactly what you're doing, Matthew," Josef had said. "How can I help?"

"You can join the colony patrols, or you can stay here and guard our perimeters. The younger guys like barreling around on the quads in the middle of the night. More than the older guys do. So, I give the older guys the choice." He stared pointedly at Josef. "What do you want to do?"

Josef thought a moment, folded his hands, and said, "I think I'll stay here. If it's all the same to you, thanks."

Matthew grunted again. "Can you use a gun?"

Josef had reached under his jacket and pulled out a handsome Smith and Wesson. Some of the boys, sitting near the pair, gasped at the sight of the pistol with its black rubber grip, and long steel barrel.

".357 Magnum," Josef said. "Want to test me?" he asked.

Matthew shook his head. "No sense wasting ammunition. I'll take your word for it." He looked down at his notes, "And speaking of ammunition, how much do you have?"

"I've got several boxes," Josef advised. "I've got a reloader, too."

"Okay," Matthew said. "Good."

Josef smiled, a small self-congratulatory smirk, and returned the pistol to its holster.

Matthew studied Josef and then said, "Okay, it's settled. You stay here. And from the looks of that gun, we'll all be the better for it." He gave Josef a full smile, and a warm handshake.

□□□

MARTHA LOOKED across at her husband lying injured and quiet in the bed.

Why hadn't he pulled his gun? He had it on him. He always carried it. Why hadn't he used it?

Matthew read her mind. "Jonah says it happened so fast, they never got a chance to draw. The men went straight to beating on them. Almost like a vengeance thing."

A vengeance thing? *Brad and Vince? But why? What was there to gain? And who were the other two men?*

Matthew continued, "We've tightened up that western perimeter. Since we can't build solid walls around the compound, we'll string more razor wire where the trees are spaced farther apart." He leaned forward. "And no more two-men patrols. Three men now. Not enough guys, so we'll be using women, too."

Martha sat back in her chair. She said nothing.

"They'll have to be ready to shoot to kill. Whether they like it or not," Matthew said.

Martha continued to sit quietly. She knew Matthew was waiting for her to speak. But he knew how she felt about shooting a human. She had been over that with him before. And even more times before with Josef. She remembered one of their last conversations...

"I WILL NEVER shoot another human," Martha said firmly. They were having the argument again, for the umpteenth time. This time it was in their cabin on the compound. "I can hardly bear to shoot an animal. I can't shoot a person." She had repeated the lie so many times, that it came easily. It helped to keep the memories away. She walked past Josef with a large cooking pot, its bottom blackened from having been used on open flames.

"But Martha, don't rule out the possibility," said Josef. "You might have to. To save your life. Or someone else's life."

"I hate guns. You know that. Stop trying to convince me." She turned to her husband, "I haven't shot a long gun since I was twelve years old. And you know that story."

"I know," Josef said gently, but then he added firmly, "You'll have to get over that. And move on. It could mean the difference between your survival or... " He paused and added, "... my survival."

Martha busied herself at the sink with the vegetables she was preparing for their dinner. The potatoes sat in a pile, neatly pared and sectioned, the carrots were peeled and sliced, the onions chopped, and the garlic minced. She reached for the heavy skillet hanging over the sink when Josef stopped her.

"That can wait. C'mon. Let's go through this again."

Josef motioned to a large steamer trunk against the wall. It was old, but it was sturdy. It was made of blue metal, and banded in black metal straps. He opened the clasp and raised the lid.

84

Inside, Martha saw the collection he had amassed over the past several months since the Change. A variety of guns: pistols, long guns—rifles and shotguns. She knew she wouldn't find ammunition here; Josef kept that hidden in another chest. "No sense making it easy for somebody else," he had told her.

Josef reached in and retrieved the top guns. He laid them carefully on the floor at his feet. He reached a bottom layer of protective clothing: camouflage shirts and pants, sweat-wicking undershirts, gas masks, and Kevlar vests. A scavenger raid on a police station several months back had netted them a bunch of the police-issue vests. Josef made sure every member—every adult member of their group that would be handling guns—had one. Especially Martha. He picked up one of the vests and handed it to her.

"Here," he said. "Try it on. Make sure it still fits. Make sure you still know how to do it up properly."

Martha obliged. The vest was fine, just so long as he wasn't going to take her outside for gun practice. A memory made her squeeze her eyes shut. The sound of the blast had been so loud. *And the blood*—she grimaced. She pushed the disturbing thoughts aside.

"Josef, I have to make supper."

"You haven't practiced with a gun in a long while," he said, picking up one of the rifles.

"Josef," her temper was short. "I've told you before—I won't shoot the rifles—I hate the recoil."

She was twelve when she first learned about shotgun kickback. Recoil was such a sweet word for such a nasty shock. It had nearly knocked her flat; her shoulder and underarm had been badly bruised and in pain for days afterward. She hated the man who had given her the gun, the man who hadn't even warned her about kickback: her favorite uncle. She had taken the massive gun, on his say so, shouldered it, aimed, and fired. The gun was too long for her, and she couldn't pocket the butt properly, so the kick had been fierce. When the butt jumped, it hit her in the face, loosening two teeth. She hadn't fired a long gun since. And she vowed never to fire one again.

However, Josef had convinced her to fire semi-automatic handguns. He took her to the shooting range and insisted she learn how to load, unload, and how to un-jam a jammed gun. She hated that part, too. Her small Browning pistol nearly always jammed if it was loaded with the wrong brand of ammunition. She held her pistol too tentatively, too far from her, making it nearly impossible to work the slide. Josef watched the pitiful maneuver and shook his head. That's when he introduced the revolver.

The big Smith and Wesson was far more intimidating than Martha's lady-like Browning. It was heavy, too. She had taken the gun, and with Josef's encouragement, she had fired it. But once the cylinder was empty, she laid the gun gently on the small shelf in front of her. It was littered with spent shells, still hot from the gun. She turned. She didn't even retrieve the target to see if she had made her shot. Josef did that. He ran after her exclaiming what a good shot she was. Her bullet had been sure. A neat hole in the kill zone on the paper man's chest had been proof of that. But Martha had removed her protective earmuffs and had gone back to their van. As far as Josef knew, she had never fired a handgun again.

But she had.

A memory surfaced. Panic stole her breath, and she struggled for control. But the scene was so vivid. She shook her head, grabbed the vest, and pulled it on, securing the snaps as she had done several times before. Josef insisted on wearing their vests when scavenging, in spite of how heavy they were. The vests didn't seem as necessary now in the safety of the compound, but they were ready, nevertheless.

She watched as Joseph pulled out small rectangular pads. "Don't forget this," he said as he handed one of the pads to Martha. The blunt trauma plates were extra protection for the chest. While a vest could stop a bullet, it couldn't stop the injury of impact: cracked bones, and wicked bruising. The plate, made of steel and about the size of a small notepad, helped. That is, if the bullet hit the pad, and not an unprotected area of the chest. Martha slipped the heavy plate into the pocket on the front of her vest. The body armor never made her feel protected; it made her feel afraid.

"I hate this stuff, almost as much as I hate guns," Martha said.

Josef nodded his understanding. He reached over and took Martha's chin in his warm fingers. "I know. But humor me anyway."

"Don't I always?" she asked, her eyes flashing with mischief.

Josef laughed. His fingers stroked her cheek. He bent his head and kissed her. Softly at first. And then with vigor.

In a few moments, the vest—the plates—the guns—all were abandoned.

MARTHA SMILED at the memory. She wondered if Josef would be able to make love again. She looked up. Matthew was staring intently at her.

"So, you know what that means, Martha. Gun lessons for all the women. Twice a day. That includes... you."

"Matthew... you know my feelings on guns. Besides, I don't think having a gun would have saved me the other night. There was no time to use it."

"Sometimes, just the sight of a gun is enough to make an attacker back down."

Martha turned her face away. "No, Matthew."

"I'm making it law," he said. "All women will be trained to shoot to kill. And all women *will* carry a gun."

Martha turned back to face him. Her eyes met his. "You of course mean after the measles quarantine is up, don't you Matthew?"

"Yes, I mean after the quarantine."

"Do what you will, Matthew, but I will never shoot a human. Never!"

"Then I hope my life, or—" he motioned toward Josef, "—his never depends on you."

Martha pushed herself to her feet. She stood a little unsteadily. "I've got things to do, Matthew."

"Gun practice, Martha," he repeated. "As soon as you can walk a little better."

She eyed him. "Wow, Matthew. Where were you and all your guns when I was getting stabbed, and Josef and Jonah were getting beaten?"

"That's not the point, Martha—"

"That is precisely the point. Matthew. You are going to have people running around thinking that everything can be solved with a gun."

"Martha, don't test me on this. I'm warning you." He stood up and leaned over her, his eyes holding hers in an invisible grip. "You will do as I say."

"Or what, Matthew?"

"Or, you can find somewhere else to live. Every adult on this compound has the responsibility to protect his or her neighbor."

Martha tottered back a step. Matthew advanced. She was pinned between the man and the table; she had nowhere to go.

"Do you understand me?"

Martha's eyes glittered in anger. She placed both hands against his chest and shoved. "Back OFF, pal!" However, push as she might, Matthew didn't budge.

Strange emotions raced through Martha. Anger and something else collided in the pit of her stomach, and she felt dizziness overtake her. Matthew noticed. He grabbed her elbow and guided her down into the chair she had occupied earlier. She sat down. Hard. She winced as pain shot up her leg.

"Anna!" Matthew called out. "Anna?"

Anna trotted over from the far side of the room. She was wearing a fleece-lined blue vest over her cardigan sweater and t-shirt. She had come back into the cabin in the middle of Matthew and Martha's discussion but had wisely avoided the pair. "I'm here," she said.

"Martha's feeling a little faint. Maybe she needs another shot. Or maybe it's time for more hot salt water." Matthew turned his back on the women, and moved toward the door.

Martha glowered after him. She said nothing, her lips tight. Her mind bubbled with angry thoughts. But her gritted teeth kept the thoughts from becoming words and slipping through her lips.

You will not tell ME what to do!

"Do you want another shot?" Anna asked.

"Oh, for God's sakes. NO!"

Anna jumped back at the ferocity of Martha's response. "Okay. I just thought—"

"Get more plantain. And bring boiling water," Martha said, as she hobbled toward her bed. "Don't forget the salt."

Anna grabbed a parka from a hook near the door; she pulled it on. She struggled with the zipper as she tried to close the coat over her bulging stomach.

"Will you be needing my services then?" Matthew asked, a saccharin lilt coloring his voice.

Martha turned and fixed him with a glare. "No."

"Good. Gun practices will be held every morning at ten and every night at seven." Matthew pulled on his heavy hunter's jacket.

"We'll see, Matthew."

Matthew said nothing as he buttoned his coat. Anna stood nearby. She was still fighting with her zipper. Matthew reached over, brushed the girl's fingers aside, and eased the zipper closed. Anna blushed.

A sharp cry from one of the beds set against the far wall drew Martha's attention. An elderly woman was motioning to her. Martha waved Anna over. "Go see what she wants," Martha said. Anna obeyed.

Martha waited till Anna was gone and then said, "Oh, by the way, Matthew. I sure would be interested in knowing how you know Anna. Care to share?"

Matthew's eyes grew dark. He wrenched the door open, and then said over his shoulder, "I'll expect to see you at practices, Martha." He walked out, closing the door behind him.

Martha went to the table, and picked up Josef's gun. She turned it over in her hand. She opened the cylinder. *No bullets.* She knew where to find bullets. She knew how to load the gun. She knew how to fire it.

And she knew how it felt to fire a gun at a human.

Matthew didn't need to know.

Josef certainly didn't.

□□□

The Clubhouse

"I WANT TWO new locations prepped. As soon as possible."

"Where?"

"North side, for sure. And a second one here on the west side."

"Are we in a rush?"

"Yeah. We're in a rush."

"Okay. Are we setting them up with their own captains?"

"Not yet."

"What about the new crop of women coming in?"

"Where are they coming out of?"

"Estevan."

"Saskatchewan. Young?"

"Yes."

"How young?

"Mid-teens. Some are early twenties."

"We'll need to house them."

"A motel?"

"No. Someplace we can lock to keep them contained, but where they can have their own rooms."

"I've got an idea. How about a senior citizens home?"

"Who's going to drag out the rotting bodies?"

"I don't mean a nursing home. I mean the homes where they had their own apartments and took care of themselves. There are lots of those kinds of places."

"Okay. Sounds good." The biker turned to go. He turned back when The Man spoke again.

"How is our insider from the Gatekeeper's camp working out?"

"He's been feeding us information. Seems trustworthy to me. I don't have a problem with him. He's a little weird with the broads, but the guys get along with him just fine."

"Time for his induction, I think."

The biker placed a hand on his own forearm and rubbed. The sleeve of his shirt moved up, revealing an ugly scar. *"I'll let him know."*

"You do that."

Chapter Ten

Broken Laws

MARTHA CRADLED her head in the palm of her hand. Sweaty strands of silver hair stuck to her cheek. She longed for the feel of a hot shower, a decadent bliss that—before the Change—occurred by the mere turning of a tap. She wasn't sure she had the energy today to draw a bath—to haul the buckets of water, to heat them pail by pail, and then to fill a washtub—just so she could squat in it. No, that wasn't the kind of thing she had in mind. Besides, her hand still hurt, and while she could walk okay, the cut on her thigh still made her wince. She sighed, and let her mind wander. The far-off drone of an engine caught her attention. She stiffened, and then relaxed. Just a quad.

There had been no new attacks in two weeks. Not on them, or on the Hutterites. The camp had returned to normal, almost peacefully—as if a world with violent attackers and crazy bikers didn't exist. Had never existed. But the girls' pregnant bellies were constant reminders that the Crazies were real.

To the Crazies, the world had become a giant amusement park, one that never closed. Fun and food were usually just around the corner. And in this new world, most things could be had for a simple currency—a currency that existed in abundance and needed no manufacturing: force and brutality. The Crazies had an ample supply.

The Crazies had no real leader, at least none that Matthew's group had identified. The only thing for sure was that the Crazies traveled in packs, like the motorcycle gangs of the '60s, or the pirates of the eighteenth century. Since there was no law keeping them in check, they ran wild and free. What they wanted, they took. What they didn't like, they disposed of, like the pregnant girls they had dumped outside the compound.

The girls, Martha thought. Many of them were so far along that Martha worried about the impending births. She wondered if she had enough supplies. Not much was required, but the girls needed to learn how to *give* birth. That lesson was on today's agenda.

Martha rose and went to the sink. She dippered some water from a crock into her hand and splashed its coolness onto her face. The girls would be waiting for her. All fifteen of them. All needy. And most of them– mouthy. Oh, how good a hot shower would feel.

Martha dried her face, pulled on her boots, secured the Velcro straps, grabbed her jacket from its hook, and left the cabin.

The compound was filled with the daily noises to which Martha had become accustomed: children laughing, crying, screaming; mothers laughing and screaming at children; men calling out; cattle lowing; horses neighing; ATVs buzzing in the distance, and dogs barking near the perimeter of the compound. She stopped and sniffed the breeze, crisp and clean, and slightly warmed by the late autumn sun.

The girls are waiting.

She turned and headed toward the Meeting House.

A commotion just outside the building drew Martha's attention. Two girls were in a loud argument with Brad. Vince was nearby, lending his advice when he could slide a word into the conversation.

"Don't tell us what to do, you jerk!" said a feisty redhead, her eyes blazing with contempt. "We don't take orders from the likes of you." She indicated Vince, and added, "Or from your little friend over there."

Martha watched Brad curl his hands into fists. She hurried over to stop the conflict before it became an all-out brawl. She suspected many of the girls were no strangers to fist fights.

"What's going on?" she asked.

"We told Brad that we're heading to a meeting with you, but he says we're supposed to be at gun practice."

Martha rolled her eyes and shook her head. "Oh, for crying out loud," she said. She turned to Brad. "The girls are excused from this morning's practice. We have something more important to attend to."

"Really?" Brad asked. "On whose say-so?"

"On my say-so," Martha replied.

She clapped her hands to get the girls' attention. "Okay," she said. "The misunderstanding is over. Let's go." She made herding motions with her arms; the girls turned and climbed the wooden steps into the Meeting House. Martha moved to follow them. Her forearm was grabbed in a vice-like grip causing her to whirl around.

"Get your hand off me," Martha said. "Now!"

Brad released her arm. "Look, I'm just doing my job."

"The hell you are," Martha said, as her eyes bore into his. "You are a petty asshole who likes pushing people around. Especially women." She took a breath. "I'm warning you—don't try your tricks on me. Or you WILL be sorry," she growled.

Vince walked over to Brad. The men stood shoulder-to-shoulder and glared at Martha.

Martha watched as two more pregnant girls walked up the steps, their heads turned to catch the interaction between Martha and the men. She pointed at the door. "Get," she said.

That should be all of them, she thought. She turned to follow the girls. This time it was Vince who grabbed her arm. Martha spun around again, her eyes flashing with fury.

"Touch me again, you son-of-a-bitch, and I will personally make you hurt."

Vince took a quick step back toward Brad.

Martha walked forward, and planted her legs apart. She crossed her arms, and looked up at the two men—both were taller than she was. "If you have a beef with me, then take it up with Matthew. In the meantime, I'm warning you, don't ever touch me or one of the other women on this compound—*again*." Her eyes glinted with a promise of danger. "Have I made myself clear?"

Brad and Vince said nothing.

Martha turned and limped up the steps. She looked over her shoulder to see the pair in an animated, whispered discussion—hands flying and heads nodding. Martha swung open the door.

Assholes!

□□□

MARTHA'S HEAD throbbed. Despite the headache, she launched into her lessons: signs of impending birth, breathing during delivery, resting in between contractions, vaginal care, and choosing a birthing buddy. Ruth and Martha partnered with the less popular girls who couldn't find a buddy; Anna was one of them. She sat quietly beside Ruth for most of the meeting. The only time she piped up was when one of the girls asked about drugs.

"You don't take drugs during delivery," Anna said. "It's stupid. The drugs mess up your ability to give birth. They get into your baby's system, too. The babies come out drugged." She stopped speaking and glanced around at the eyes staring at her.

"Go on," Martha said gently.

"The drugs interfere with normal maternal and infant bonding." Anna took a breath. "They did a study with lambs... " Martha held up her hand.

"That's great info, Anna," Martha said. And then to the rest of the girls, "Forget the old ways. You won't be put to sleep. You won't be given any drugs. You'll have nature to help you get your baby birthed. That'll mean pain. Lots of pain. Get used to the idea."

The girls groaned and began to natter back and forth. Martha held up her hand again, but she was interrupted.

"I don't want to be in pain," said the little blonde. She gave Martha a petulant look.

Martha eyed the girl and her heavy bosom. Martha knew the girl's pain was going to be as large as her breasts. Especially once her milk came in. Martha spoke again, "Besides the pain of childbirth, there will also be the pain of nursing."

"What?" several of the girls cried in unison.

"Yes," Martha said. She nodded to Ruth. "Do you want to tell them?" Ruth stood and joined Martha at the front of the room.

"If you want less pain when your baby starts nursing," Ruth said, "then you have to toughen up your nipples. Now."

"What the heck are you talking about?" asked the tall redhead.

Ruth continued. "Just brush them with something rough. Like a toothbrush. It sort of hardens them in preparation for the baby's sucking." Some of the girls began to laugh. Ruth looked helplessly at Martha.

"Do it—or don't," Martha said. "They'll get toughened up sooner or later." Martha breathed out heavily. "And it will be a painful experience. Especially for a couple of days after your milk comes in."

The girls groaned again. They had grown up in a different world. They didn't know about the realities of birth, or nursing a new baby, or recovering from giving birth. But they would be veterans soon enough. And for some of them—very soon.

"Okay, we need your expected delivery dates. Ruth will list them on a calendar."

The girls rose slowly, and one by one, they ambled to the front, and gave their due dates. Martha eyed the blonde again. She was huge.

Twins? Oh, God, don't let them come breech.

Martha didn't relish the idea of reaching in and turning a breeched baby. She resolved to keep a close eye on the girl. She had read about turning a breeched baby before labor started. She wasn't sure how that would work, but it would be worth a try. She shook her head. *Childbirth.* She was going to learn as much as these girls were going to learn. Maybe even more.

The door to the Meeting House opened. The backlighting made it difficult to see faces, but Martha knew that four men had entered the room. They walked up the aisle between the chairs.

Brad. Vince. Matthew. Josef.

"Hello," Martha said.

Matthew reached the table where Martha was standing. He looked at his watch. "It's almost 12:30."

"I can tell time, Matthew. What's your point?"

"These girls were supposed to be at gun practice at 10. Why weren't they there?"

Martha's face flushed. She glanced at Josef who was standing silently.

He knew. Why wasn't he standing up for her?

Her brain buzzed with anger. Martha placed her hands on her hips, lips pursed, and chin lifted slightly in defiance.

"If you hadn't already noticed, Matthew, these girls are *pregnant.* There are more important things for them to learn than how to use a gun."

Matthew turned to the girls. "It's time to go. The range officers are waiting for you." The girls stood, their eyes flicking between Matthew and Martha. "I said... GO!" The girls tumbled over each other as they made their way to the door. "Straight to the range."

Martha hadn't moved. Matthew turned to Ruth, Josef, Brad, and Vince. "If you'll excuse us, I would like to have a private word with Martha." He nodded to Josef. "That is if it's okay with you, Josef." Josef nodded and turned.

Martha held her stance. She bit the inside of her mouth to keep herself from speaking. Matthew waited for the last person to leave and then he turned to face her.

"I have told you repeatedly not to question my authority on this compound."

"I wasn't—" Martha protested.

Matthew stopped her. "I wanted those girls down at the range. If you wanted to change those plans, then you should have asked me first."

"I couldn't find you. And besides, don't you want to know why they were here?" Martha's voice had become shrill.

"No," Matthew said. His voice was lower than normal and he spoke slowly, enunciating each word. "I realize that you are still recovering from your injuries. I appreciate that. But you disobeyed me—willfully—again."

"Disobeyed? I'm not a child," Martha sputtered. Tears of rage had begun to form in her eyes. "Don't talk to me that way!"

Matthew came around the table. He grabbed Martha by the shoulders. "Listen to me. And listen to me good. Have you noticed that we are having this conversation in private? *In private*, Martha. So YOU don't lose face."

Martha took a step back. Her heart was beating a steady tattoo inside her chest, and she sucked in her breath. She tried to pull free from Matthew's grasp. "Let go of me."

He didn't.

"I'm asking you to afford me the same courtesy. If you have a beef with me, or you want to make a change to compound laws, then talk to *me—first!*" He took a breath. "*In private.*" He gave her a small shake and then released her shoulders.

Tears spilled from Martha's eyes. She lowered her head so Matthew wouldn't see them. "Sure," she said, her voice a dull monotone. And then she added, "I was prepping them for birth."

Matthew stepped back. "I told you I don't care how valid your reason was—I want to be consulted next time. Is that clear?"

"Sure."

"I don't think you quite get it, Martha. If my men lose respect for me, they won't follow me. And if they won't follow me, I won't have an army. Without an army—we won't have a compound."

Matthew turned and walked toward the door. He stopped and turned back to her. "You have such trouble following me, how would you like to have a Crazy as your leader?"

A memory roared to the front of her brain—a dirty biker and blood spray.

"Can you imagine life then?" Matthew turned and left the building.

Martha collapsed into a nearby chair. She put her head into her hands. She let the tears flow. Exhaustion overtook her, and she laid her head on the table. The door opened. She looked up. It was Josef. He motioned with his head.

"C'mon. You're supposed to be at that practice, too."

□□□

MARTHA STOOD quietly at Josef's side. He had prepared the Smith and Wesson, and now the pistol lay in front of her. Loaded and ready to fire.

"Go on," he said. "Take it."

Martha looked up at her husband. The color was back in his cheeks; he had recovered slowly from his recent heart attack. She didn't want to upset him. She reached for the gun, her fingers brushed the grip, but the memory came back, a memory she could never forget, never erase. It erupted in full color. Crimson. "I can't."

Josef stared at his wife. "What is it with you? It's just like shooting at the indoor range. Take the damn gun." His arms were folded across his chest. Martha looked past him.

The pregnant girls were each at a gun station near their male coaches. They were accepting the tutoring and the correcting; they were handling the guns given to them; and they were firing on command. Gunshots echoed, and girls screeched—sometimes in alarm, sometimes in exhilaration of having hit their target. Martha listened, but it was the sound of her own heart drumming inside her head, pulsing inside her ears—that made the loudest sound.

"Josef, I'm still not feeling very well. Can I just sit for a bit?" Martha risked a quick look at him. He was staring down at her, his eyes filled with a mixture of irritation and worry. She desperately hoped she looked piteous enough. She needed him to consent. To let her step away—from the gun. She needed to be inside her own head. For just a little while.

"The knife wound?" Josef asked.

Martha nodded. He had been outraged at the news of the attack on her when she first told him about it, and although it was now old news, she knew any reminder would elicit his sympathy.

"Okay," Josef said. He motioned to a picnic table set back and off to the side of the gun stations. "Take a few minutes. I'll coach one of the other women for a while." He picked up the revolver, and pushed it back into his holster. "I'll tell Matthew you needed a rest." He gave her cheek a gentle touch, and then he walked away.

Martha breathed a sigh of relief. She limped over to the table and sat down. The afternoon was cool, but the sun was warm. She welcomed its warmth on her back. More shots, more screeches, and then the memory came again—this time with a mocking ferocity and extreme clarity. Martha groaned.

No, not again. Don't make me see that again.

She grabbed her head in her hands and leaned forward, rocking slightly. Martha curled her fingers and squeezed her hands into tight fists. She dug her nails into her palms in a vicious attempt to force the memories away. But they would not retreat. She squirmed as the images burst inside her brain like ripe pus-filled wounds. The blood. There had been so much blood. And the smell—the acrid scent of the gunpowder—proof of her terrible act. Martha stifled another groan.

Make it go away. Make it stop, she pleaded.

But like an old reel-to-reel silent film, the images slid through her mind, frame by frame, detail by detail. The memory of what she had done was once again acute—as sharp and as horrific as the day it had happened...

□□□

THEY HAD been out scavenging—Martha, Ruth, and Martha's close friend, Amanda. It was late in the spring of the first year after the Change. Edmonton was a ghost town because so many people had either died or had left in search of food. The looting and the violence had calmed down, making the streets *seem* safer, but the threat of being attacked by strangers always existed, so they were always armed. Josef had made sure of that.

Reggie, the adopted autistic boy, was with them, too. He rode behind Ruth on her scooter. Martha and Amanda each had their own machines. They laughed as they zipped along the deserted street. It was good to feel light and free. If only for a few moments.

A huge gray church came into view. Its glass doors had been smashed and its front façade was covered in vile graffiti, but it looked abandoned. The women stopped, hid their scooters behind some bushes, and went up to the entrance.

"Can we go inside?" Ruth asked.

"Sure," Martha said. "I guess so. Are you game, Amanda?"

Amanda shrugged. "It's just another place to scavenge."

The women stepped carefully through the demolished doors, and picked their way through shards of broken glass. The inside of the church bore signs that it had once served as a temporary home—for many people. Sleeping bags, discarded empty pop bottles, candy wrappers, crushed potato chip bags, and dirty clothing lay strewn about the foyer. She peered into the sanctuary. Litter was strewn around there, too, on the pews and around the altar. Foul words had been spray-painted across the long stage drapes. Martha turned away.

The women made their way down a long hallway. Martha didn't really have a goal in mind; exploration was enough of a goal, but she found the bookstore. Oddly, the store looked intact, barely touched. Bibles and Christian literature lined the shelves. Greeting cards wishing "Happy Birthday" and "Happy Mother's Day" sat neatly in their packs on tiered shelving. Martha grabbed a few of the birthday cards after carefully reading their verses. She retrieved their matching envelopes.

A sound to Martha's left drew her attention. It was Reggie, and he was terribly excited about something. He had a DVD in one hand; his other hand was patting its front cover.

"*Weggie, weggie,*" he said, again and again.

Ruth watched him for a moment and then she began to laugh. "Oh, I get it," she shouted, "His name isn't Reggie." She held up a DVD showing Bob the Tomato and Larry the Cucumber as cowboys in a tale called, *The Ballad of Little Joe.* "He was talking about *Veggie Tales.*"

Reggie continued patting the box, his eyes bright with recognition and delight.

"I guess we'll never know what your real name is," Martha said as she stooped down in front of the boy. She tried to take the DVD, but he clung fast. "We can't play this," she said, "but we'll never be able to make you understand that, will we?" Martha let Reggie keep the DVD. She ruffled the little boy's hair.

She looked around and spotted a pile of Veggie Tales coloring books, sticker books, puzzles, a Pirate play set, and some tiny Veggie Tales finger puppets. She grabbed a couple of canvas sacks bearing Psalm verses, and stuffed them full with the Veggie Tales booty. A couple of Bibles caught her eye and she stuffed those into the bag, too.

"Because it's a church store, it feels like stealing," Ruth said.

"From whom?" Martha replied. "If things ever get back to normal, I'll be sure to come back here and put a little extra into the offering plate."

"Oh," Ruth said, as she helped herself to a few romance novels. "That sounds okay then."

"Let's go," Martha said. She held out her hand to Reggie who immediately tucked the Veggie Tale DVD in close to his chest with a grunt of resistance. "It's okay," she said. "I'm not going to take it away." Martha smiled.

It takes so little to make this child happy.

Since Reggie's hands were full, Martha grabbed him by the shoulder and steered him out of the store, and down the hallway toward the foyer. The rumble of motorcycles outside in the parking lot made her stop, and her eyes grew wide. "Crazies!" She motioned to Ruth and Amanda. "C'mon, let's find the back door."

Finding the back door was easy. Making it past the bikers would be much harder. Martha shushed Reggie as the foursome made their way outside.

"We can get to the scooters," she whispered, "but we'll have to push them for a while."

Amanda and Ruth nodded. Reggie patted his DVD. As they made their way around the side of the church, they heard loud masculine voices from somewhere up ahead.

"So?" said one voice. "Where should we do 'em?"

Martha tried to close her ears. She didn't want to hear any more.

"In the church," said another voice.

Martha heard a girl's soft scream. Sounds of scuffling.

"Get your asses in there," said the first voice. "You want the blonde or the brunette?"

"I don't care. I'll grab the beer."

The women waited till the voices had died away, and then they ran for their scooters. They had known better than to leave them out in the open. They were relieved to see they hadn't been found. They pulled them out, and began pushing them toward the street. A low voice stopped them in their tracks.

"Hey, hot Momma."

The women turned to see a large man dressed in blue jeans and a black leather jacket. He had a thick long beard, and his dark hair was pulled back into a greasy ponytail. He wore a small woolen cap. Martha froze. Her stomach knotted and she slipped her hand inside her coat. Her Browning handgun was there. It was loaded. She didn't withdraw it. Instead, she turned back to the man, motioning for the others to go ahead without her. However, Amanda had turned, too, and now stood alongside her friend. Both of them let their scooters fall to their sides.

"What's up with you, buddy?" Amanda asked. "We're just a couple of old ladies. What would you want with the likes of us?"

"I wasn't looking at you," the man said, walking closer. "I was talking about her." The man pointed at Ruth who was pushing her scooter and tugging Reggie's hand at the same time.

The man reached the women. They could smell his beery breath and the stench of many days—maybe even weeks—of no baths. Martha held up her hand to stop his advance. His meaty fist slammed into it. Martha winced and grabbed her throbbing wrist.

Not my gun-hand, she thought.

The man pushed past them and cornered Ruth. "Come here," he growled. Ruth cried out and backed toward the bushes. She dropped her scooter, too. And Reggie's hand. Reggie whimpered, clutching his new DVD to his chest. Martha moved toward the boy.

Out of the corner of her eye, Martha saw Amanda move. In an instant, the tiny older woman spun around and was now marching after the man—her shoulder bag swinging from her clenched fist.

The biker had both hands on Ruth's forearms, pulling her to him. Ruth struggled, but he still managed to shove his bearded mouth over hers. Reggie let out a high-pitched wail.

Oh dear God, Martha thought. *They'll hear.*

Martha pushed Reggie behind her. She reached for her gun, retrieved it, but her hand hurt so much that she couldn't release the safety. It was then that Amanda struck.

Martha's mouth hung open. Ruth's mouth hung open, too. The big man lay on the ground. He was out cold and blood was oozing from the side of his head.

"What did you do?" Martha asked in a strained whisper.

"I hit the bastard," Amanda said. "With this." She held up her shoulder bag and opened it. She pulled out a big smooth rock about the size of a fireplace brick. "It's sort of like swinging a slingshot," she added. "You know—like David and Goliath."

Crazy laughter burst from Martha and Ruth. They clapped their hands to their mouths to stifle the sound. Martha walked to Amanda and pulled her into a bear hug. "David, indeed," she said. "C'mon, let's drag this guy into those bushes before his friends find us."

"Do you think he's dead?" Ruth asked. Martha felt for his pulse. It was sluggish, but he was still alive.

"He's fine," she said, tucking her gun back into its holster. "Amanda set her weapon to *stun*—not *kill*." She bent down. "He'll just have a very big headache."

The three grabbed the big biker by his boots. Laughter burst from them again when they dragged him down a curb and his head bonked on the pavement.

"A really big headache," Ruth said drily. The women sniggered as they struggled not to laugh. Tears were pouring from their eyes by the time they had planted the biker behind the bushes. Their giggles continued as they hog-tied his wrists and ankles together. They stepped back, surveyed their work, saw that it was good, and ran back to their scooters. Reggie was obediently waiting and patting his DVD.

Martha slowed. "You guys go ahead of me. I want to make sure he's tied up tightly." Both women gave her a perplexed stare. "Really, it'll be okay. Go ahead. I'll catch up in a minute."

She watched as Amanda and Ruth pushed their scooters past the bushes and across the parking lot, not daring to start the machines. She waited, and in a minute, both women were out on the main street. They started their scooters and with a quick backwards glance, they headed down the street.

Martha ran back to the biker. He was still there. Still tied up. She stared at him. He moved slightly, and he moaned. Martha jumped back. He didn't open his eyes, however. She stared down at him.

This man is going to wake up. He is going to be mad. He is going to tell his friends. They are going to hunt us down. And when they find us...

Martha shuddered.

This man must not wake up. Must never wake up.

Something icy overtook her as she reached into her jacket and felt for the textured grip of her pistol. She pulled it from its holster. She held the gun and turned it over in her hand, studying it.

So small. Maybe too small.

She thought about the .22 caliber bullets in the magazine.

Too small. He'll recover.

Then another thought crept into her mind; like dark mist through a swamp, it curled itself around her thoughts.

But not if I fire up close. Point blank. Into his temple.

The blood pounded in Martha's ears, and her hand shook.

What am I thinking? Am I really going to do this?

Her palms grew slick with sweat. This was the very thing she had told Josef she could never—would never do. She felt like she was observing herself from a distance.

"I can't do this," she said, finally. She dropped her arm to her side.

She turned and walked toward her scooter. Then a memory came— of the man's hands on her daughter's shoulders. She licked her lips. She looked behind her, and to the side—no one was around.

It had to be done. She had to do it. Now.

She looked upward. She took a breath, and turned around.

Martha knelt beside the man. She raised the pistol, and pressed the barrel to his temple. Her heart hammered in her chest. She could barely breathe as cold horror washed over her. Her stomach twisted with revulsion.

Can I do this thing?

I must. I must.

God, forgive me.

She closed her eyes. Tears rolled down her cheeks.

She held her breath.

She squeezed.

□□□

The Red Deer Meeting

THE MAN had called for the central meeting in Red Deer. The motorcycle messengers drove off with news of the compulsory meeting. The Man sent them in all four directions; they were to reach captains as far away as Regina in Saskatchewan, Fort McMurray in Alberta, and Kelowna in British Columbia.

The light dusting of early snow made the Queen Elizabeth II highway slick and dangerous. The Man glanced out the window and observed the vehicles littering the ditches on both sides. The truck hit black ice and the driver fought the skid. The Man pulled a notebook from his shirt pocket. He jotted a quick note: snowmobiles, snowmobile suits, snow boots, hand warmer packs, small engine oil.

"What are our food stores like?" The Man asked.

"What?" The driver pulled the truck out of another skid.

"Why don't you slow down?" The Man asked. "We've got lots of time to get there. Do you know which exit to take to reach the Westerner?"

"You mean that big exhibition building?"

"Yes."

"Yeah, I know it."

"Good. Now about the food stores. What about our supplies for the winter?"

The driver pursed his lips. "Last I heard, we were in good shape. Lots of supplies coming up from southern Alberta. Some of the camps near the US border have been scavenging deep into Montana and they've been coming back with truckloads." He turned the wheel to avoid a jack-knifed big rig blocking the road, skidded slightly, and continued forward. "The farms are putting out. We've got guards on them. A few attacks from lone bikers, and small car gangs—but our guys knock them down pretty quick."

The Man looked out the window. "Snowmobiles," he said. "Let's start stockpiling snowmobiles."

"Any kind in particular?"

"No. Just get them. I wish I'd thought of it sooner. It might be too late."

"I'll organize an acquisitions team as soon as all the guys arrive."

"Good." He turned back to the driver. "And engine oil. That's going to be a bitch to come by if we don't start amassing it now."

"You got it." The driver slowed the truck. "We may as well start right now."

He pulled off to the right and skidded into a Shell gas station. The doors were smashed, and abandoned vehicles checkered the yard; the area around the pump was crammed tight with cars and trucks.

Both men stared—they knew the gas tanks had been emptied long ago. However, a rack of Castrol oilcans sat enticingly near the entrance.

"Hmm—I wonder why those are still there." The Man nodded to the driver. "What are you waiting for? Go get 'em." The driver jumped out of the truck; The Man did the same. "I'll see if there is anything left inside the store."

Within minutes, The Man returned—a couple of photo magazines in one hand, and a dark cloth over his mouth. He pulled it aside as he spoke, "Bunch of rotting corpses. Stinks like hell in there."

The driver nodded. He started the truck.

"Wish I had my camera."

The driver gave The Man a quick glance, and then he pulled the truck onto the highway.

"Never took shots of corpses before." The Man stared out the window. *"Well, except one. Sort of."* He glanced up and caught the driver staring at him. *"He doesn't count because he wasn't quite dead. I should have waited a few more minutes."*

The driver nodded.

Chapter Eleven

The Marriage Advice

"NO," RUTH SAID. "Not today." She gave her wiggling daughter's second braid a final twist and then secured it with a hair elastic. "I think Peter has other plans."

Martha looked up. "What?" She held out Mary's parka. The little girl gave her a wide grin as she shoved her arms into the sleeves. Martha returned the smile. It was mid-November. No new snow had fallen, but the temperatures had plummeted—mittens and heavy coats were necessary. Martha looked up. "What plans?"

"Not today," Ruth repeated. She patted Mary's behind. "Go and play." Mary skipped to the door, her braids bobbing off her shoulders.

"Here're your mitts, sweetie," Martha said, as she opened the door. She watched as Mary ran toward the center of the compound. *Taller*, Martha thought. *And bigger*. So much had changed since a few months ago. So much. She closed the door.

Martha turned back to Ruth. A sliver of hurt sliced through her as she contemplated her eldest daughter.

Again, Martha thought. *Again*.

Their family meetings, now that her family members were residents of Matthew's camp, had dwindled from every day, to every other day, to just on Sundays, and now—to not at all. Comfort and relative safety within the large group had eroded any need for family unity. Regular Bible studies—lead by Josef, had been replaced by more pressing commitments on the parts of her children—like hunting, gun practice, spending time with new friends, or working around the compound. Other than Ruth, Martha barely saw her other children anymore.

Ruth brushed past Martha and opened the door. "See you later." She walked outside.

"Okay," Martha called after her. "Maybe next week then."

She followed Ruth out the door. Brilliant morning sun fell upon her face—its intensity and her tears blinded her.

Maybe the kids didn't need her anymore, didn't want her anymore, but she still had Josef. Martha smiled. *He likes me.* And they always had their special evenings together.

The two of them would sit side-by-side, heads bent in the light of a lantern, and they would pour over his Bible. Much of it, like the Old Testament books of *Numbers* and *Deuteronomy*, bored Martha senseless— she could never understand how Josef could read these books repeatedly. However, there were some good parts in the Bible—like *Revelation*—not *Revelations*, as Josef had corrected her, time and time again.

Martha loved the fantastical world of the New Testament's final book—the Four Horsemen of the Apocalypse, Armageddon, the seven seals and the seven vials and all their accompanying woes and, of course, the Antichrist. Martha sniggered aloud as a mental picture of Matthew emerged in tandem with the last thought.

Some days, she thought. *Some days.*

Martha looked up. A young woman wearing a skirt, a peasant blouse, a parka, and lace-up winter boots—unlaced—was coming across the compound. She waved and headed straight toward Martha.

"Can I talk to you?" the girl asked.

"Yes, of course." Martha motioned to her cabin door. "Come in."

The girl glanced over her shoulder as if looking for someone who might be in pursuit. She ducked into the cabin.

Martha showed the girl to a chair. "Sit. Do you want some tea?"

"No," the girl shook her head. "Are we alone?"

"Yes. Josef is on patrol all day."

"Good."

"What's up?"

"I don't know who else to ask about this," the girl said. She fidgeted with the edge of her blouse. "But everyone says you're smart. So, I thought I'd ask you."

Smart?

Martha toyed with the word.

Smart? Everyone says so?

Her spirits lifted.

"You won't tell anyone will you?" the girl asked, an intensity lighting her brown eyes.

"No. As long as what you tell me has nothing to do with the safety of the camp."

"No—it's private."

"Okay, then. Fire away," Martha said, seating herself across from the girl.

"It's my husband. When we are in bed... sometimes he acts so... " The girl searched for the right word—she didn't find one. "... and he gets upset because I—well, 'cause I... don't... want to make love." She took a breath and groaned. "Because he's being so... so... " She made a face, and then added, "—weak."

"Oh," Martha said. She reached for a white plastic bucket filled with apples that was sitting on the floor and pulled it toward her. "Help me peel these."

Martha handed the girl a paring knife. Then she rose, filled a large metal pot with cold water, and placed the pot between them on the table. "Save the parings," she said. "The horses love them."

The girl nodded. She held the knife gingerly, and eyed Martha. Martha took a firm round apple from the top of the pail and began to peel it in smooth experienced strokes, sending thin parings to the tabletop. The apple was soon naked, but the girl hadn't yet begun on her own apple.

"Don't you know how to peel an apple?" Martha asked.

"Not really," the girl replied.

"Here—like this." Martha showed her, and the girl mimicked her moves. It took a few minutes, but she soon had a naked apple, huge chunks of its white flesh were missing, but it was peeled. The girl smiled and plopped the apple into the water.

Martha smiled her approval and nodded toward the full pail. The girl selected another apple, and began anew.

"Okay," Martha said, without looking up. "Keep talking."

"Sometimes—he acts so wimpy and that makes me mad. So, I want to make him mad." She shifted in her chair. "You know... to... " she faltered.

"To incite some passion in him?" Martha queried. She looked up from her apple.

"Yeah," the girl said, bending her head in an unsuccessful attempt to hide the blush suffusing her face. "Sometimes, I want him to make love to me... " She paused and blushed even redder. "—Rough! You know—just to do it."

Martha laughed lightly. "I understand. Many women feel that way. I'm the same way with Josef."

The girl looked up, relief shone on her face. "You don't think I'm weird—or bad for thinking that?"

"Nope. I just think you're female." Martha gave the girl a wide smile, and then she continued. "Some days I feel insecure. Sometimes, I need to know Josef loves me. And wants me. I mean, *really* wants me. But sometimes he's so preoccupied with other things. So, I try to make him mad." She shrugged her shoulders. "It gets his attention." She plopped a bare apple into the water, selected another, and continued to peel.

"Really?" asked the girl.

"Yes," Martha assured her. "Those are usually the days when I just want to... have sex." Martha wanted to use another term, but she thought better of it. "And I don't care about foreplay. It actually has the opposite effect. Just bloody annoying."

"Me, too," the girl cried out. Her face beamed with the knowledge that she could share her most intimate secret without shame. Without guilt.

"Makes me so annoyed sometimes... " Martha shook her head. "I just want to slap him." She stopped peeling and looked up. "I feel that way at least once a month—when I'm ovulating."

"Oh, exactly," the girl said, her head nodding in eager agreement.

The two women grew silent as they mentally tiptoed through their private memories of lovemaking. Martha smiled. Josef understood—he knew when only roughness would do. He had to be reminded now and then, but he knew. Martha gave a tiny gasp as a memory sent a small shock through her belly. She looked up.

"I believe there is something in all women—well, most women—a need that can only be met by hard and fast lovemaking." Martha said. "I think it's totally natural. Not rape—but force." She shrugged again. "It works for me."

The girl smiled broadly.

Martha paused and looked into the girl's eyes. She reached across the table and squeezed the girl's hand. "You aren't a freak—okay?"

The girl breathed a huge sigh.

The two women smiled and continued peeling the apples. Martha broke the silence.

"It's a sad thing," she said, "but our old world emasculated our men. They were hit over the head with the need to be sensitive, to be more caring. And that foreplay hype—well, that got completely ridiculous. Men's natural, more aggressive instincts were being educated right out of them." Martha reached for another apple. "So, I think it's our job to remind them of who they are." She smiled. "By being who we are."

"Good," the girl said. "I feel better now. I thought it was bad. I heard a woman once say it was bad to even talk about sex. That was in my old church. She'd get mad if we ever mentioned sex. She'd freak right out if she heard this conversation." The girl giggled.

"Oh, pooh," Martha said. "God made females and males. And he created sex. We are supposed to enjoy sex. We're engineered that way. And we're supposed to enjoy the differences between men and women. Men are naturally more aggressive. Why shouldn't we invite them to be more aggressive—especially in bed?"

"Oh, yes." The girl bobbed her head. Her face was very flushed.

"Are you ovulating?" Martha asked.

"Oh, yeah," the girl answered.

Martha smiled. "Where's your husband?"

"Doing some engine work on one of the vehicles, I think."

Martha reached across the table. She closed her hand over the apple and the paring knife stopping the girl's clumsy handiwork. "Perhaps you should go and find him then."

The girl released the apple. She dipped her sticky hands into the bowl of water, rinsed, and then wiped her hands on her skirt. She rose.

Martha scooped up four unpeeled apples and offered them to the girl. "For later," she said, with a conspiratorial grin. "You'll be hungry."

The girl smiled and took the apples, stuffing them into her skirt pockets. She looked up, and with a mischievous grin she said, "Give me a couple more. He's going to need all the energy he can get."

Martha laughed, as she handed the extra apples to her.

The girl headed to the door. Martha stood behind her. The girl twisted suddenly, planting a quick kiss on Martha's cheek. "Thanks." She ran out the door and across the compound—toward the vehicles.

Martha glanced at her wristwatch, and smiled a secret smile.

When is Josef getting back?

She was ovulating, too.

SIMON SHUFFLED the cards. "Ante up, guys." He dealt a round to the five young men sitting at the picnic table. The 'pot' held a variety of goods from hunting knives, to cigars, to chocolate bars, and notepapers promising favors like "Good for ONE night off patrol duty."

"Your bet," Jonah said to the blond man next to him. The poker hand continued with a final call. The players revealed their hands. The blond man gave a victorious yell as he dropped his own hand to the table: he had three aces.

"It's my lucky day!" The young man encircled the pot with his arms and pulled the assorted winnings to him.

Simon gathered the cards and began shuffling them again. He stopped and nodded toward the man who had won the hand.

"Hey, where did you go this afternoon?"

The young man looked up from his booty. "Home."

"Home?" Simon asked. "Why? It wasn't lunchtime."

The man smiled.

Simon began to deal the cards. He stopped. "Oh, wait a minute. That was after your wife showed up." Simon smiled broadly. "Now, I get it."

The men hooted their bawdy congratulations. The young man smiled again. A blush crept up his neck, making his face pop from under his mop of blond hair.

"Okay. Okay. Never mind."

"Hey," Jonah said. "The rest of us don't have women coming to get us before lunchtime." He clapped the man on the back. "What's your secret?"

The blond man straightened in his chair. "Rough sex," he blurted. He reached for his cards and cleared his throat.

"What?" Simon asked. "Rough sex? What d'ya mean?"

"My wife was talking to Martha," the blond man said.

"Martha?" Jonah asked. He laughed. "What's she got to do with this?"

The blond man looked at Jonah. "She told my wife to ask for rough sex."

Simon and Jonah looked at each other—eyes wide in amazement. "What?" they said in unison.

"Yeah, my wife says that Martha told her sex is better that way."

"What are we talking—rape?" asked Simon.

The blond man cleared his throat again. "Sort of," he said.

"That doesn't sound like Martha," Jonah advised. "I don't think she'd say something like that." Jonah pushed a bet into the pot. "I'm raising and calling."

"Well, my wife came to get me *after* talking to Martha," the blond man replied.

The card players studied their hands. More betting, and then a final call. They showed their hands, and this time Jonah took the pot. He turned to the blond man next to him.

"I think something got misinterpreted," he said. "Martha wouldn't advise a wife to ask her husband to rape her."

"But she did—" said the blond man.

Jonah interrupted him. "Oh, c'mon—get serious." Jonah leaned closer. "I think you have issues, pal."

The men laughed. The blond man did not.

"I'm telling you the truth." The blond man's voice rose. "Martha told my wife that I should force her to have sex with me."

"You should force Martha to have sex with you?" a voice asked from behind the man.

The card players turned. Brad was standing near the table. He stood with his legs apart, and his arms folded across his chest. He was smiling a crooked smile.

"Uh—no," stammered the blond man. "Not Martha—my wife."

"I'm not sure I get what you're saying."

"My wife told me that Martha said that forced sex is good."

Brad raised his eyebrows. "Really? She said that?"

The blond man nodded—vigorously.

"So, you are supposed to grab her. Then what? Throw her to the floor?"

"No, Martha told her to make me mad enough first. To make me want to do it."

Brad's smile widened. "Oh." He dropped his arms, and turned away.

The card players watched Brad join Vince at a far table. They watched him sit down. Vince looked up as Brad began to speak. Jonah glanced at Simon. Neither said anything. They returned to their card game.

□□□

"THAT'S NOT what I said, Josef. You know it's not." Martha's face glowed with embarrassment, and her breath came fast.

"Well, you said something to make them believe that you have condoned rape between a husband and wife."

"That's not what I said, Josef. Dammit!" Martha slammed down into a chair across from him. Their kitchen table moved a few inches from the force of her action. "It was girl-talk. Between the girl and me. That's all. She was feeling bad about herself. I just wanted her to know she wasn't alone."

"You keep doing this, Martha. Can't you be more careful? Stop blabbing off the top of your head. Think about the consequences." Josef's face had darkened. "This is NOT your compound. And you are NOT well-liked. Why must you give them a reason to criticize you?" Josef raised his hands, palms upwards, in defeat. "I give up."

"But, Josef... "

Josef stood and went to the gun chest. "I have to coach at the gun range." He pulled out several handguns. He turned to Martha. "Are you coming?"

Martha stared back at him. "Why do you always take their side?"

"I'm not taking their side, Martha. I'm on YOUR side. But you just aren't getting it."

Josef laid the guns on the table. He cinched his gun belt around his waist. He slipped the Smith and Wesson into the holster.

"Are you coming?"

Martha refused to speak. She was standing now, hands on her hips. Her embarrassment had evolved; it was now all-out wild fury.

How dare he treat her like this? He knew exactly what she was talking about. It had been a part of their love life for years. Now he was acting as if he was a stranger to the concept.

"Okay," Josef said. "You don't want to come—suit yourself. You deal with Matthew—I've had enough."

He grabbed a canvas bag, and loaded it with the guns. Then he added three boxes of ammunition. He headed for the door.

At the door, Josef paused. He looked back at his wife and shook his head. He sighed. "What do you want me to tell Matthew this time?"

"Tell him to go to Hell," Martha hissed.

Josef shook his head again. He turned and left the cabin.

Martha trembled with rage. At that moment, she hated everyone. The stupid girl. Matthew. Her husband—especially her husband. She glowered at the closed door. She willed Josef to come back.

To say he was sorry.

To stand up for her.
To protect her.
To love her.
The door remained closed.

□□□

A LOUD KNOCKING roused Martha from her nap. She had lain down on the bed, for just a moment. She looked at her watch—that was two hours ago. The knocking came again. This time even louder.

"What?"

Martha heard the door open and someone came into the cabin.

"Mom?" Ruth called. "Mom?"

"I'm in here." Martha swung her legs over the edge of the bed and groaned. She was groggy and her leg had stiffened. The healed knife wound still caused her pain.

"Mom?" Ruth swung around the corner. "What the heck have you been telling people?"

Martha groaned again. *Oh, damn.* "Ruth, it's not what you think." Martha stood—a little unsteadily.

"So, what am I supposed to think?"

"Just not what you're thinking," Martha said.

Ruth growled in frustration. "Matthew wants to see you." She paused. "No, make that he *demands* to see you."

Martha ran her hands through her hair. "Of course he does. Why doesn't that surprise me?" She looked in the mirror, and studied her face. "I look old."

"He said NOW!"

"You know what? I don't give a flying f—" she edited the dirty word before it left her mouth, "—fig about what Matthew wants." She looked back at her daughter.

Ruth huffed. "Fine," she said. "You're going to get yourself kicked out of here. And guess what? We aren't going with you."

She stomped out of the cabin.

Martha winced as the door slammed shut. She looked into the mirror again. She didn't just look old—she felt old.

Martha pulled her t-shirt over her head and chucked the shirt into a corner. She went to a big trunk on the other side of the room. She flipped up the clasps, and opened the lid. She drew her fingers lovingly across the fabrics.

Tonight is for me, she thought. *I am so sick of living for everybody else. Tonight... is for me.*

Martha pulled a soft white dress from the trunk. She loved the dress with its long scalloped sleeves, scooped neck, and wide skirt. She felt around and smiled when her fingers closed on something beneath the pile of clothes. She pulled it out. It was a small velveteen bag. She opened it and dumped the contents on top of the clothing. Crystals glittered as they caught the light of her lantern.

She picked up a necklace and clasped it around her neck. A pair of earrings followed. She selected a couple of rings—a large sapphire surrounded in diamonds, and a gold band encrusted in pink diamonds. Scavenging jewelry stores didn't usually net any treasures, but she had found the rings squirreled away in a desk drawer, in an office marked, 'Manager.' The rings had probably been put on hold or layaway for a customer—they fit Martha perfectly. She placed them on her ring fingers on either hand. She lifted her hands and admired the fire bursting from the stones as they caught the light. She smiled.

A knock on the door. The sharp sound made Martha jump. She scrambled to her feet, tore off her jeans, and pulled the dress over her head. She ran her fingers through her hair. She grabbed an eye pencil and ran a black bead along her inner eyelids; then she plumped her eyelashes with a bit of mascara from a green tube. Finally, she added a touch of light blush to her cheeks. The knocking came again.

Martha opened a box near the bed. She rummaged through and finally recovered a pair of short-heeled shoes. She slipped them on and secured the straps. She hadn't worn the shoes in a very long time—they felt odd. She took a last look in the mirror. The knocking came again. Much louder this time.

Martha walked to the door. She opened it. Her eyes widened in surprise.

It wasn't Matthew.

□□□

The Clarification

"LOVE IS overrated," The Man said.

"You've never loved anyone? Not your father? Not your mother?"

"Sure. But they're gone."

"How can you live like that?"

"*Exactly the way I am living.*" *The Man turned to the woman sharing his bed.* "*Now—shut up.*"

The brunette pulled back. "*What about if other people love you?*"

He shrugged his shoulders. "*That's their problem. Doesn't mean a thing to me.*" *He reached for the pistol lying on a side table near the bed.* "*I thought I told you to shut up?*"

The woman stared at the gun. "*I love you.*"

The Man turned. He leveled the gun at the woman's breast. "*I don't love you.*"

"*I know,*" *she said.* "*Thanks for reminding me. Those words hurt worse than any bullet ever could.*"

"*I know,*" *he said. He moved in close to the woman, and ran the barrel of the gun down the side of her face.*

The woman sat unmoving, her brown eyes shimmering in the candlelight.

"*I know,*" *he repeated.*

The Man's smile dissolved as he moved on top of her.

Chapter Twelve

The Ally

THE WOMEN standing at the door stared back at Martha—there were six of them. Martha recognized them as mothers with older teenage daughters. One of the women standing nearest to Martha spoke up.

"We'd like to talk to you." The woman motioned over her shoulder. "At the Meeting House."

Martha stared ahead—she said nothing.

"We *really* would like to talk to you," said another woman—she was chubby, with dyed auburn hair; Martha could see the dark roots.

"Sure you do," Martha said. Her words rolled off her tongue—slowly and carefully. "Let me get my coat."

Martha turned and reached for her coat hanging on its hook. She caught sight of her white sleeve. She hesitated—a moment passed. Then, she grabbed her coat and turned back to the women; they were watching her. They stepped aside as she left the cabin, pulling the door shut behind her.

Martha stared across the compound toward the Meeting House. Its small, four-paned window glowed with a soft orange light. She saw silhouettes moving back and forth.

How many people wanted to talk to her?

A cold rain had fallen during the day, and now the compound was dotted in small muddy pools. She raised her dress and sidestepped a small puddle of muck. The chilly November night air made her shiver—she pulled her coat close. She felt anxious, but her step was firm.

Martha made her way up the Meeting House steps. The gaggle of women followed.

Cows, Martha thought. *Stupid cows.*

She opened the door and stepped inside. The room was warm—too warm. She let her eyes adjust to the dimness.

Six people sat near the front of the room. She realized that all of them were men—and all were members of the Discipline Committee. They watched in silence as Martha approached.

Martha stopped. Suddenly. Her face twisted into a wicked grin when the women behind her collided into one another like fat geese on ice. Her eyes swept over the men in front of her. They came to rest on one man: Brad.

"What the hell do you want?" she asked.

"Don't swear, Martha," Brad said. "A lady shouldn't swear."

"The *fuck*, you say," Martha countered.

"You shouldn't swear," Vince said, his voice squeaking with excitement. "Didn't you hear what Brad just said?" He strutted forward, his chest and belly pushed out in a feigned attempt at bravado.

"You little toadie!" Martha laughed.

Vince made a move toward Martha, his face ruddy with anger. Brad held out a restraining arm.

"Easy, Vince. We'll deal with that issue later. Right now, I believe these ladies have something to say." Brad motioned with his arm to a chair. His eyes locked on Martha's, as he spoke: "Won't you have a seat, Martha?"

"Thanks—but no." Martha crossed her arms over her chest. Behind her, the other women obediently took a seat. Martha glanced back. She made a sound in her throat. "Get on with it, Brad. I haven't got all night."

"Apparently, you've been teaching again. Without parental permission." Brad nodded toward one of the women. "You gave some rather interesting marital advice to her daughter today."

Martha glanced at the woman. "Oh, for crying out loud—that's what this is about?" She whirled back to Brad. "Her daughter's a married adult," she said to him. "So, what's the big deal?" She watched as the mother rose from her chair.

"You think you can just tell our kids anything you want!" The woman shook her finger at Martha.

Martha rolled her eyes. "Oh, please. If you had the balls to talk to your own daughter about sex, she wouldn't need to come to me. Now would she?"

The woman sputtered. She looked at Brad. "What are you going to do about this?" The other women chimed in.

Martha eyed them like a cat watching a trapped mouse run around inside a deep sink. She wanted to laugh. So—she did.

"You think this is funny?" asked the outraged mother.

Brad held up a hand, silencing the women. "The committee will make a decision on this—I promise you. But we should hear her out first." He nodded to Martha. "Go ahead. We're waiting."

"What is it that you'd like me to explain, Brad?" Martha asked, an acidic sweetness coating her words. "Would you like me to describe the sex act to you? How men and women get it on?"

"No," Brad said. "Not how the rest of us do it. Just how *you* do it."

The women murmured behind Martha. Brad held up his hand. They quieted. Martha gave her head a slow shake.

Cows.

Martha clasped her hands together. She pointed her index fingers to the ceiling. She tapped them together and then rested them under her chin, in her most contrived angelic and prayerful look. She sighed. "Well, Brad. It goes like this... " She paused.

Martha glanced back at the women; they were leaning forward in their chairs. She looked back at the men. Brad and the rest of the Discipline Committee sat quietly. All eyes were on Martha.

"A beating is usually a good idea," she began. "But not one that leaves bruises. You know the kind... " Martha peered at Brad. "... and then the man should take what he wants." The women gasped behind her. "You know—whatever he wants." Martha studied Brad's eyes as she spoke. "And... well... any way he wants it."

Brad's eyes glittered with interest. "The woman should just accept it?" Brad asked.

"Oh, yes," Martha said.

One of the mothers screeched. "You're telling our daughters that?"

"Oh, sure," Martha said. "And much worse things, too."

Several of the women screeched this time.

"Worse things?" asked the chubby woman. Then to Brad, "See, what did we tell you?"

Brad hadn't taken his eyes off Martha. "Please, go on," he said, his tone low.

"Well... " Martha said. She stopped. She was sure Brad hadn't blinked. She could hear Vince's raspy breathing. The sound made her want to gag.

"And..." Brad prompted.

"You are truly sick, Brad. So sick. And so are the rest of you." Martha shook her head in disgust. "I'm outta here."

As Martha turned to leave, Vince leapt forward and grabbed her arm. Her voice came slow and measured, "I told you—I would make you hurt if you ever touched me again." Martha raised her arm.

She brought her hand down, hard, on the bridge of his nose. Vince screamed, grabbed his nose, and fell to his knees. Blood poured through his fingers. The women screamed, too; the men, except for Brad, jumped to Vince's aid.

"Maybe—" she said, shaking out her hand, "—you'll believe me now."

Brad's arms were crossed, and his eyes remained steady. Martha met his stare, making her challenge clear. She turned and began to walk away. She stopped near the women who cowered back from her.

"You idiots. I never said those things. Just so you know." Martha motioned toward the mother whose daughter she had counseled earlier. "Why don't you ask your daughter what I told her?" She tugged her coat closed and headed for the door.

Brad's voice cut across the room—clear and cold. Martha felt the hairs rise on the back of her neck. "You're not leaving, Martha."

"*Excuse me?*" Martha said, without turning around.

"You might have just left before—but now that you've attacked a compound member... " Brad clicked his tongue, and added, "Well, you leave us no choice. As the Discipline Committee, we have the duty and the right to decide what to do about this matter."

Martha still didn't turn around, but she knew Brad was coming up behind her. Adrenaline flooded her and her head began to buzz.

"And... we've decided—" Brad added.

Martha turned and watched as the men sprinted across the room, overturning chairs in their haste. The women screamed again. Martha's mouth went dry, and she tried to swallow. Fear suffused her, temporarily clouding her thinking. Her mind scrambled for a plan, but her brain refused to cooperate. Brad got to her first. He grabbed her arm and twisted it up behind her back.

"Bitch," he whispered in her ear.

Martha gasped—both from the pain and from the shock of Brad's voice in her ear. The word, the sound, the inflection—all bore a vague familiarity. She tried to pull free, but Brad's grip was iron. In a moment, other hands were holding her, too.

"Stop it!" Martha cried.

The mob pressed in and pushed Martha toward the door. Someone opened it. In a moment, she was outside. She looked up. The moon glowed above the compound like a luminescent coin. The mud puddles shimmered in its light.

"Stop it! Let go of me!"

"What's going on?" a man's voice called from across the compound.

"It's nothing," Brad said. "A little matter for the Discipline Committee."

"Really?" asked a different voice, as another man emerged into the light. "I'm on that committee. Why wasn't I notified?"

"Josef!" Martha called. The hands that had imprisoned her, now released her. She made her way down the steps and ran across the yard. "Oh, thank God you're here," she said, as she buried herself against his chest. "They're all nuts." Josef closed his free arm around his wife.

"What's going on?" Josef asked Martha. Before she could answer, Brad called out:

"It would be a conflict of interest, Josef." Brad stood on the top step. Vince stood near him, still clutching his bleeding nose. "She attacked a compound member," he said, motioning to Vince. "He's hurt pretty bad. You know the rules about that."

Josef glanced down at Martha. His eyes filled with questions. "What have you done?" His voice sounded incredulous.

Martha pulled away. "Why do you assume that I've done anything?" The anger that had built inside her while in Brad's grasp now switched focus. "Why don't you join your buddies—over there?" She tilted her chin in the mob's direction.

Josef took a step back. Martha glared at him; tears filled her eyes. Before a single tear could fall, she clutched her coat tight to her chest and stomped across the compound. She felt eyes following her, but no one dared stop her.

Martha fought against the emotions that swept through her. She bit her lip. She refused to cry. She quickened her pace.

I'm leaving. I hate this place. I hate these people.

Loneliness blanketed her heart like a grave cloth—gray and thick. She sobbed, but stifled the sound with her hand. Nobody. Not a soul would ever see her cry.

I don't need these people. I hate them.

She walked forward, barely aware of where she was going. So she didn't see him, but she sensed him. She looked up. He stood—a tall and formidable figure by the light of the moon. A new wave of anger crested, and with it came a fresh supply of tears. Martha stopped. She searched side-to-side like a rabbit trapped in a fenced run.

Damn him. Tears spilled down her cheeks. *Damn him.*

"Martha?" Matthew asked. He stood a few feet from her cabin door. He stood as though braced for a fight; his feet planted firmly apart, his shotgun rested in the crook of one elbow.

Martha waited. If she spoke, she risked sobbing. That thought was too humiliating. She turned her head away. She swiped at the tears dribbling down her face, hoping it was too dark for Matthew to see. She bit her lip again, nearly drawing blood this time, but the pain stopped the tears.

"Martha?" Matthew asked again, his voice soft and low. He took a step toward her. "What's going on?"

Martha didn't answer. She stood in silence, a lonely figure in a pool of light. Her coat had fallen open. Her white dress shone silvery in the moonlight. Her crystal necklace and earrings sparked with fire. Matthew came closer.

"Why are you wearing a dress? And such fancy jewelry?" Matthew asked.

"Oh." It was a breathy sound. Matthew was close enough for Martha to see the bemused and perplexed look on his face. An immediate rush of humiliation forged its way through her—she had forgotten what she was wearing.

I look like a fool.

She covered her face with her hands.

Matthew reached out and touched her forearm. Martha shuddered. His touch was so unlike Brad's. So unlike Vince's. So unlike Josef's. She shrank away, pulling her coat closed across her chest. "Don't touch me."

"Martha? What's wrong?"

Martha looked up. She met Matthew's eyes. She saw something in his eyes that she hadn't seen before.

A softness? Something more?

She felt it, more than she could see it. Then she knew. For the first time that night, she was looking into eyes that weren't accusatory. There was no condemnation in Matthew's eyes.

"Mathew?" Martha asked softly, tentatively—not wanting to break the spell. "I didn't say those things. I didn't. And I hit Vince, but only after he grabbed me."

Matthew said nothing. He continued looking at her. Martha's eyes stared into his, pleading for a break. Pleading for an ally. Just one.

Matthew opened his mouth, as if to speak, and then shut it. The mob had reached them. He pushed Martha behind him.

"What's this all about?" Matthew demanded. "Somebody tell me what's going on." He scanned the crowd.

Brad began to speak, but Matthew silenced him. "No—not you. Where's Josef?"

"Right here," Josef said. He walked up to Matthew. "I was just coming in from the gun range. And I ran into this." He swept an arm across the assembly. "So, I have only a vague idea of what's going on."

Everyone began to speak at once. Matthew held up his hand again. "To the Meeting House," he said.

Brad and Vince smiled. Two of the mothers exchanged smirks, too.

Martha cringed. She hung her head. The one place she didn't want to go. She let the tears drip.

It doesn't matter. Let them do whatever they want. I'm leaving in the morning.

She began to walk toward the Meeting House. A hand on her shoulder stopped her. She turned. The kindness was still there—in his eyes.

"No, Martha," Matthew said. "You go home." He squeezed her shoulder. "I'll take care of this."

"LOOK AT what she did to Vince," Brad said. "Look at his face." The men muttered their support.

Matthew looked at Vince's mashed nose; the man's eyes had begun to blacken. Matthew cleared his throat and stared down at his boots. Only Josef saw the smile.

Matthew looked up. "Look, there are extenuating circumstances here. Martha didn't come looking to hammer Vince. It sounds to me like it was self defense." He looked around the table at the men seated there. "Wouldn't you agree?"

A murmur rose among the men, and then Brad spoke out: "I wonder if I would've been given the same leniency if I had smashed Martha's face because she grabbed my arm."

Matthew stared back at Brad. "You want to be judged as a woman, Brad?"

"I never said that."

"No, but a man grabbing a woman is by far more threatening than a woman grabbing a man. Wouldn't you say?" Matthew waited.

Brad didn't answer.

"Good, then I'll interpret your silence as agreement."

"I didn't agree, Matthew." Brad leaned forward to emphasize his point. "I'm merely saying that there seems to be a lot of favoritism here." He paused, and then added, "As a leader, you might want to give that some thought."

Another low mutter rumbled around the room.

Matthew stood quietly. "I don't think there's anything more to discuss." He reached for his shotgun. "That's it, guys."

"That's it?" squeaked Vince. "What about the other thing we told you about?"

Matthew leaned over and picked up his shotgun. "Vince, I wouldn't expect you to know this, but what a husband and wife want to do in their own bed is entirely up to them. And talking about it has never been a crime. Not before. And certainly—not now."

Brad and Vince said nothing as they exchanged glances and slight nods. The seated men rose, chairs scraped the wooden floor, and they made their way out of the building.

Matthew stood beside Josef. "I wonder what that look was about."

Josef nodded. "Nothing good, I'll bet." He picked up his canvas bag. "Thanks, Matthew." He extended his hand to his friend. Matthew switched the gun to his other hand, and shook hands with Josef. He smiled—a crooked grin.

"She did quite a number on his nose, didn't she?" The two men burst out laughing. They made their way out of the building. Two men stood in the shadows near the stairs.

"Matthew?" asked one. It was Simon.

Matthew turned. "Yes?"

"We think Brad and Vince are planning something."

"Why?" Matthew asked.

"We overheard them talking when they got out here. We didn't hear everything, but we definitely heard Martha's name," Simon said. Jonah nodded.

Josef and Matthew exchanged concerned looks. "What do we do?" Josef asked.

Matthew pressed his lips together. "I don't think they'll do anything tonight. So, let's keep an eye on them. And whatever happens, keep them away from Martha." He paused. "And keep Martha away from them."

□□□

JOSEF ENTERED the cabin. It was dark. A very faint light glowed from the bedroom. Martha was nowhere in sight. He removed his boots and tiptoed into the bedroom. A camp lantern was on in the corner—the batteries were weak so the light was very faint. He picked it up and swung it toward the bed. "Martha?"

He stopped. The bed was empty. He checked his watch—it was nearly midnight. He walked into the front room. He lifted the lantern again. Martha's jacket was not on its hook. Hanging in its place was her white dress.

Josef pulled on his boots and grabbed his gun. He headed out of the cabin.

□□□

The Drugs

"WHERE ARE the drugs coming from?" The Man asked. He stared pointedly at the burly biker in front of his desk. The biker grabbed nervously at his chin, and then pushed his glasses up his nose.

"Grow-ops—here—right here in the city."

"I don't want drugs fucking up our operations."

"I know. That's why I'm telling you about them."

"So, must I repeat myself? I said—anyone caught with drugs is to be executed—on the spot." He paused, and leaned forward. "Was some part of that unclear?"

"Yes, sir. I understand, but I thought you might like to talk to these guys first."

The Man sat back in his leather chair. He rolled a cigar in his thick fingers, took a puff, and blew the smoke into the air. "Bring them."

The biker walked out the door, and hollered down the hall. In a few moments, a small group of older teen boys shuffled in; they were herded by two more armed bikers.

"Sir, these boys have something to tell you," the first biker said.

The Man moved forward in his chair, planting his feet firmly on the floor in front of him. He placed his massive hands palms down on the desk in front of him, his cigar pointed upwards like a fiery beacon. "What's up, boys?"

The boys stood mutely. The biker assisted. "Ask them about the garden they have growing in their house."

"Garden?" The Man queried softly. "What garden?"

"Uh—"one of the boys began. "We, uh—"

"What garden?" The Man asked, his voice rising slightly in volume.

The terrified boys stood frozen. Again, the biker assisted. "Marijuana," he said. "Marijuana."

"What?"

"They're growing marijuana plants in a backroom in their house."

The Man didn't speak. He sat quietly, almost sullenly. He turned in his chair and stared at his large Persian cat; it was giving itself a tongue bath. The cat paused, and glanced up.

The boys waited in their death row silence. They watched as The Man's chair turned slowly back in their direction. Suddenly, his hands came down in a solid resounding whack on the desk in front of him. The boys jumped and stepped backwards. A choked, squealing sound came from two of them. One of the boys began to whimper.

"Drugs?" The Man asked rhetorically. "Drugs? You're growing drugs?"

The biggest of the boys stammered in reply. "I— we— uh—a guy from—uh— we were just keeping them for him."

The Man's face darkened. "The only thing I hate worse than drugs—is lying." He began to rise from his chair. The offending boy tripped as he stepped backwards. He righted himself, and sought safety behind the other boys.

The Man struck a threatening pose. "I want the truth. I want it now. Who would like to start?"

A blond boy with full biceps stepped up to the plate. "Sir," he began. "It seemed like a good idea. A guy from California gave us the plants. He said we could get some great stuff if we had weed to trade." Sweat beaded on the boy's brow. He swallowed hard.

128

The Man's eyebrows lowered; he secured his cigar on the edge of a thick amber-colored glass ashtray; then he picked up the pistol lying near his right hand. He aimed it at the boy who had spoken. The boy fell down in a faint. His companions made no move to help him.

"Get them out of here. Make an example of them."

The bikers herded the mewling boys back out of the room. Two of them bent and grabbed the boy who had passed out. The first biker watched the boys leave and then turned back to The Man.

"What do you want done with the grow-op?"

"Find some gardeners. Check among the women. Put them into the house." The Man smiled and placed his pistol back on the desk. "I understand that weed has great medicinal value."

He picked up his cigar, leaned back in his chair, and took a long drag. Smoke swirled upward from his mouth, a thick slow curl—like a halo—in the space above his head.

Chapter Thirteen

The Newcomers

MARTHA RACED across the compound, her bootlaces whipping through the mud. There hadn't been time to do them up. The redhead had been frantic, and very convincing in her hysteria. Martha buttoned her shirt as she ran.

The full autumn moon doused Martha with its soft fairy light. She splashed through puddles—polished steel mirrors in its glow—unmindful of the mud splattering her pant legs. The Women's Bunkhouse was only a few more feet away. She heard the muffled screams. She ran up the steps, tripped on her laces, and smashed into the wooden door. She steadied herself and turned the door handle. She burst into the room.

Three girls stared at her, their faces filled with dread. One of them was on the bed, her face mottled and blotchy; her eyes were puffy and red. It was the little blonde with the big breasts: Cindy, as Martha had come to know her. She cried out when she saw Martha.

"I think I'm having the baby," she said. Her words were thick with tears.

"Okay, I'm here now. Stop crying," Martha said. She threw off her coat, and walked to the bed.

Cindy pulled herself up against the pillows stacked behind her. Her voice hitched, as she spoke. "It... really... hurts, Martha."

"Yes, I'm sure it does. But you'll survive."

Martha sat next to the girl and motioned for her to pull up her shirt. The girl was still wearing her underwear. Martha glanced at the underpants and said, "You can't have a baby with your panties on. Get 'em off." The girl obliged. She made a small attempt to cover herself. Martha noticed.

"Girl, I am going to see a whole lot more of you than that by the time this night is over."

Cindy giggled and blushed. "Oh, yeah—I guess you're right," she said. She winced as another pain gripped her belly. She started to cry out.

"Stop that," Martha said. "You aren't close to the screaming part *yet*." The girl shut up, but she continued to grimace. Martha waited for the contraction to pass.

"It makes me feel like I have to poop," the blond girl said, blushing again.

"Yes," Martha said. "And you probably will. So don't worry about it." She reached over and gently touched the girl's rounded belly. Her fingers spider-walked around, becoming more forceful in their search for familiar knobs and bumps. Martha pressed her lips together. "Hmm—"

"What's wrong?"

"I think he's coming breech."

"What?" Cindy began to cry again.

"I told you to stop that," Martha reminded the girl. The girl obeyed and sucked back her sobs.

Martha continued to massage the girl's belly. Her fingers located tiny closed fists. And a round form.

But was it the head? Or was it the butt?

The baby's head should have been down and filling the girl's cervix. Martha felt the round form again. It seemed to swivel free. She frowned. This baby was in the wrong position. Its head was still floating around at the top of the womb; that meant the feet could be coming first. It was the very thing Martha had not wanted to experience.

"Damn," she said softly. Martha stood up. She looked down at the mother-to-be. The girl stared up at her, eyes wide. But trusting.

The girl's birthing buddy, the tall redhead who had fetched Martha, stood near her. The buddy wasn't being very helpful. She stood there twisting her hands, and grimacing every time Cindy moaned. Martha turned to the redhead.

"When did the pains start?"

The redhead stood in silence.

"Hey! How long have the pains been coming?"

"Uh, I'm not sure. Um—maybe a few hours." The redhead raised her hands, palms turned upward. "I really don't know."

Martha took a deep breath. "Has anyone seen Anna?"

Martha turned away from the bed. Two girls were standing near the doorway. They glanced back and forth at one another.

"Well? Have you?" Martha asked impatiently.

"Um—not tonight." The girls' nervousness made Martha squint at them. "But we could find her," the girl offered. The taller girl elbowed the one who spoke. She shot her a warning look.

Martha looked back and forth between the girls. As she did, her crystal earrings swung against her cheek, reminding her that in her haste to leave the cabin, she had forgotten to remove them. She had had just enough time to change out of her dress, and into her jeans and shirt. The redhead had been at her door within moments of Martha reaching the cabin. Now, she took off her earrings and shoved them into the pocket of her jeans.

"What's with you two?" she asked.

The girls shuffled and glanced around the room. Finally, the shorter girl spoke again. "S-s-she's probably at Matthew's place."

An icy wind careened through Martha, sending sleet through her veins, and a hammer to her stomach.

At Matthew's?

Martha wondered if she had heard correctly. She pinned the shorter girl with a hard stare. "Matthew's?" she asked.

The girl swallowed hard. "Uh—yeah. She could be there." The girl licked her lips. "S-s-she's not always there. But sometimes she goes to his place." The taller girl widened her eyes again and glared at her friend.

At that moment, Cindy gave a yowl. Martha turned back to the girl. She rolled up the sleeves of her flannel over-shirt, and tried to remember what she had read about turning breeched babies. She glanced at the redhead.

"Give me some of that hand gel. I need to disinfect my hands."

The redhead's eyes opened wide.

"Hurry up!" Martha said.

The redhead grabbed a bottle from the bedside table. She squirted the gel into Martha's open hands. Martha rubbed the gel around. The blond girl whimpered again. She began to cry.

Martha took a deep breath. "You've got to calm down. If you don't calm down, you can't open up." Martha paused, and added, "And that's gonna make things very difficult."

Cindy began to screech again. Martha looked over at the useless redhead. "Go and get Ruth!" The redhead didn't move. "Now!"

The girl jumped and fled the room.

Martha turned back to the two girls. "Get over here."

The girls obeyed.

Martha waited for the labor pain to crest and then subside.

"Okay," she said to the girls, "I want you to stand on either side of the bed. Let her grab your hands." She shook her head, "No, better still—sit on the bed—beside her."

The two girls obeyed again.

Martha studied the sobbing blonde.

"Listen to me! You've got to take control. No more screaming. You're going to have the entire camp outside the door. When the next pain comes, I want you to ride it through. Focus over there." Martha pointed to a camp lantern sitting on a small table. "Focus on the lantern and try to enter into the pain." She paused and swallowed. "And NO pushing."

Cindy eyed Martha with suspicion, but she quieted down. "What are you going to do?"

"I think your baby is coming breech. I think you're full term, though, so it'll be safe to turn him. But it's better if he turns on his own. That will take some time. So, you can't push. Not unless I say so. You've got to labor for at least an hour with NO pushing."

Cindy nodded her head in quick agreement.

"Grab their hands."

Cindy's face began to twist. She grabbed the girls' hands.

Martha watched as the girl's naked abdomen tightened. She glanced up.

"Do as I say," she said to Cindy. "Look at the lamp. And breathe. Breathe deeply. Like this." Martha began to breathe in deep, slow breaths. The girl watched through squinted eyes, and began to mimic her. Martha nodded her approval as the girl strangled a small scream that rose in her throat. "Good for you. Now keep that up."

Martha waited until the contraction stopped.

"Okay," Martha said. "Scootch down here—to the end of the bed. Spread your legs—I need to check how dilated you are."

With the help of the two girls, Cindy complied. Martha examined the girl's vagina. Her vaginal opening had stretched, but she was very small. Martha pulled a small flashlight from her jeans pocket and peered inside the girl's vagina. No tiny feet were showing. At least not yet.

Please, God, Martha prayed. *Please, let it be a Frank breech. Not a Kneeling breech.*

Martha remembered that a Frank breech, with the baby's bottom coming first and its legs wrapped up near its ears, was the easiest of the breech deliveries, and was very similar to a head-first delivery. Babies, delivered bum first, usually survived. Kneeling breeches were much tougher. It would be better if the baby was turned. Martha shuddered. She studied her own hand. The girl was very small. The thought of reaching in and turning the baby made Martha dizzy.

Should she just let nature take its course? Should she wait it out? She clenched her hands. *What do I do?*

She heard the outer door open and slam shut. *Oh, good*, Martha thought, *Ruth is here.* Maybe Ruth had some idea of what would work. Martha waited.

Cindy muffled another scream as a ring of pain clamped around her belly. Martha cringed—she remembered the feeling.

"Can I help?" At the sound of the voice, Martha turned. It wasn't Ruth; it was Anna. Martha stared for a moment, and then she nodded toward the bed.

"I think her baby's coming breech. She's pretty small."

Anna moved next to Martha and knelt down. "I know about turning breeched animals," she said. "We usually don't reach inside though. That's a last resort."

Martha grinned. "You can't know how happy I am to hear that."

"Repositioning the mother helps. She should get up and move around," Anna added.

Martha had forgotten that. Yes, the laboring woman should be active. The idea of a mother-to-be lying flat on her back on a bed was an antiquated concept used only by hospitals, and male doctors—not by Mother Nature. Martha looked at Anna.

"Wait a minute. You made the animals get up and walk around?"

Anna smiled. "No—they usually got up and moved around on their own. I was talking about women." She paused. "I saw three of my sister's kids get birthed. The midwives let me help on the third one." She shrugged.

Martha gave a small nod—Anna was a constant source of surprises. Cindy gave another groan. Martha watched as the girl attempted the breathing exercise. She wasn't as successful and a small squeal erupted from her.

"You're doing great," Martha said. "Hang in there."

Anna reached for the disinfectant gel. She squirted a large dollop into her palms. She massaged the gel into her hands as she listened to Martha.

"I'm hoping it's a Frank breech," Martha said. "I think I felt the baby's head at the top. I can't say for sure where the feet are though." She took a breath. "If we can help her get her vagina stretched, she might do okay."

Anna nodded. "Where's the olive oil?"

Martha motioned to a bottle sitting in a pot of water on the bedside table. Anna walked over and dipped her fingers into the water. "It's cold." She looked at the girl closest to her. "Get some hot water."

The girl lifted herself clumsily from the bed, walked to the far side of the room, and poured water from a large thermal jug into a pot. She turned the knob on a small propane stove and set the pot on an element.

"Not hot," Anna advised. "Just warm."

Martha began to explain to Cindy whose face was stretched into a silent scream again. She waited for the pain to pass, and for the girl to fall back on the pillows.

"Okay, here's what we're going to do. I suspect you are delivering your baby by his bum first. That's not so bad. Anna and I are going to give you a massage. It'll help stretch your vagina. Remember, I told you before that we'll be using warm olive oil to do that?"

Cindy nodded weakly.

Anna lowered the bottle of olive oil into the warm water. A few minutes later, she twisted the top, and poured a drop onto her wrist. "It's good," she said.

She brought the bottle to the bed. Martha held out her hands.

"Wait." Anna grabbed a large bath towel. She tossed it to one of the girls. "Put this under her butt," she said. She drizzled the oil down onto the girl's vagina and over Martha's hands.

Sometime later, Martha flopped down into a chair. She was exhausted. Cindy still hadn't given birth, but she was close. She was proving to be made of tougher mettle than Martha had initially believed. She had stopped her wild screaming, and had begun to work with them.

She got up and walked around between pains. She tried different positions. Her labor seemed to be progressing well, but the baby's position hadn't changed. In spite of that, Martha and Anna decided not to intervene and attempt to turn the baby from the outside. Both feared rupturing the placenta—or worse. And, neither of them was willing to try a turn from the inside. So, they waited.

Ruth had shown up halfway through. She was coaching Cindy in soft, low tones. Martha listened to Ruth speak. Her daughter had done this before—she was good at it.

"Mom?"

"What...?" Martha rubbed her eyes. She had fallen asleep.

"I think she's close, Mom." Ruth was gently massaging the girl's belly with olive oil. "The baby seems to have moved down. And he's quiet now."

Martha knew that babies tended to quiet down just prior to delivery. The news was good. And the girl had gone more than an hour without being allowed to push, exactly as the books had advised.

"She should get into a birthing position then."

"You can deliver on your hands and knees," Ruth told the girl. "That's the best position. You can rock with the pains."

Cindy turned over, and pushed her face into the pillows. She had become much more vocal. She grabbed the sheets, and groaned. "Make it stop," she begged. She pounded the bed. "It hurts so much." The redhead reached over and touched her back. Cindy swore and swiped at the girl's hand.

Martha glanced at Ruth; they exchanged a smile. When Ruth was ready to deliver her babies, she got very loud—and very nasty. Cindy's actions fit the profile.

"Okay," Martha said, "you've done really well. It's time to push. But you've got to push at the right time—when your contraction is the strongest. And... you have to *think* your baby out." Martha stooped at the side of the bed and looked into the girl's eyes. "Do you think you can do that?"

Cindy nodded.

"Okay," Martha said. She nodded at Anna. "Let's get that baby out of there."

Cindy screamed with the pains. Martha was sure her howls would wake the entire compound. At one point, when the baby got hooked on the lip of its mother's cervix, Anna reached in and pushed the cervix to the side. Martha watched as the girl worked instinctively. Quickly and surely.

The baby's bum crowned, and then slipped back inside. Martha and Anna did nothing to hurry things along. Martha touched the baby as little as possible, but she did use one finger to ensure that the umbilical cord had not wrapped around the baby's neck; it hadn't.

"You're doing great," Martha said. "I know it hurts like hell, but everything seems to be fine." She gave a quick nod of encouragement. "Just a little longer now—so, give it all you've got."

All the females in the room now cheered Cindy on. Her screams had become growls—deep and intense, rich with determination. The girl was no longer a victim, but rather a willing participant in the birth of her baby. Martha smiled.

Anna anointed the girl's vagina with more oil and continued her gentle massage. They watched as the butt emerged, slipped back, and then finally pushed its way out. Cindy screamed, but she never gave up.

"Push," the women said in unison. "Push!"

One of the baby's arms slipped free.

"Push!"

Cindy's body clenched, and with one last howl and a tremendous push, the baby was born. The woman groaned with relief. She began to laugh. And then to cry.

"I did it!" she exclaimed between sobs. "I did it."

"Yes, you did," Ruth said, stroking the girl's back. "But there's more. You're going to feel some cramping when the afterbirth is delivered."

"I want to see my baby."

"You will," said Martha. "Just give us a second." Martha examined the girl's vaginal area, as she spoke. The second arm had been born along with the head. It was a tight squeeze and, in spite of the olive oil, Cindy had torn slightly. *A skid mark*, Martha thought. *Not a big deal.* The girl's body would take care of that. She was little, but she was strong.

Cindy turned over and relaxed back on the bed, panting. She smiled when she saw her baby. She pulled back her shirt. Anna laid the baby on her naked chest, and announced, "It's a boy."

"You should try to get the baby to nurse right away," Ruth said. "The sucking will cause contractions. It helps your body push the afterbirth out." Cindy wasn't listening. She was too busy falling in love. Ruth smiled.

"Um—Anna," Martha said. "Come here."

Anna came around and looked where Martha was pointing.

"Oh," Anna said.

Cindy groaned. Martha looked up. "You've got a little more work to do, sweetheart." The girl groaned again.

Ruth understood, and grabbed the baby.

The women watched as Cindy got back on her hands and knees. She growled, clenched her body, and pushed. Fascinated, the women watched as another baby appeared—head-down—in perfect position. Two more pushes, and another little boy arrived.

It was during the birth of the second baby that the door to the bunkhouse opened. Josef stormed in. Matthew was on his heels. The men stopped.

Josef recognized the scene; he had attended his grandchildren's births. Matthew could only stare—his eyes wide. His face reddened, and his eyes dropped to the floor. Josef watched his friend, amused by his discomfort. He laughed and clapped Matthew's back.

"It's just a baby."

"Make that *two* babies," Ruth said from the bedside. She still held the first little boy; Anna now held the second.

Anna wiped the baby down, cooing to him, and then wrapped him in a small blanket. Like his brother, his umbilical cord was still attached.

"Wait for the cords to stop pulsing," Martha said, "and then we'll clip them." She looked around. "Do we have clips here?"

"Yes," Anna said. "Right there on the table—beside you."

Cindy lay back on the bed, exhausted. Ruth snuggled the first baby back down on her chest. The new mother wrapped her arms around the tiny child, and smiled.

After a few minutes, both baby's cords were cut and secured with small plastic clips. Anna motioned for the mother's permission to take her second son over to meet Josef and Matthew. Cindy smiled sleepily, and nodded.

Anna walked over with the baby. She pulled back the blanket. The little boy was smeared in blood and his head was covered in a cheesy white film.

"He looks like a monkey," said Matthew. "What's that white stuff?"

"It's normal," Josef said. "It's called vernix."

"Would you like to hold him, Matthew?"Anna asked.

Matthew blanched and took a step backwards. "No."

Josef reached across his friend. "I'll hold him," he said. "I like holding them when they're tiny like this." The little bundle nearly disappeared in his big arms.

Martha joined them.

"I'm beat," she said. She looked at the baby in Josef's arms. The baby's eyes were open, and he regarded her in silence. "You and your brother really gave us a run for our money, little one."

Anna stood near Matthew as he peered at the baby. "Ever think you might want one of your own?" she asked.

The question caught Martha's attention.

"No," Matthew said. His response sounded curt, in its quickness.

Martha watched as a shadow passed over Anna's face.

Hurt? Was Anna hurt by his answer?

Martha's eyes dropped to Anna's belly. Then she looked back to Matthew's face.

Whose baby? His? But Anna had said it was rape.

Martha roused from her thoughts when Josef leaned over and kissed her. "I thought you were gone," he said.

"Gone?" Martha asked. "Where would I have gone?" She smiled. "Without you?"

"You aren't mad at me anymore?"

"Mad?" Then it came back to her. She looked at Matthew. Then back at Josef. "What did they decide?"

"You're in the clear," Josef said. He nodded toward Matthew. "He made sure of it."

Martha left Josef's side and stood in front of Matthew. "Thank you," she said.

"Stay away from them," Matthew said. "I don't know what they're capable of, but they don't like you."

Martha nodded. She touched Matthew's arm lightly. "Thanks, again." Martha studied his eyes. It was gone now—the kindness she had seen earlier. She looked away. Perhaps she had only imagined it. She glanced over at Anna. Anna was watching them.

Exactly what had gone on between these two?

One of the newcomers began to wail. Martha turned to see Ruth instructing the new mother in nursing technique. Martha wondered about getting compresses ready. In twenty-four hours, Cindy would be in desperate pain—her breasts would swell horribly when her milk came in.

She was going to produce enough milk to feed a dozen babies—it was a good thing she had birthed twins.

Martha walked back to the bed. The afterbirths hadn't shown yet—she stooped down. Anna stooped down beside her.

"Shouldn't be too much longer," Anna said. "Here we go," she said, as she pulled gently on the mass exiting Cindy's body. Martha helped. She plopped the placenta into a rectangular, metal baking pan.

"So, when are you due, Anna?"

"I'm not sure."

"Well, when were you raped?"

Anna's eyes flickered in surprise.

Anna said nothing.

□□□

The Gatekeeper's Buddy

"WE'VE TAKEN care of one of the women who killed our guy outside the church. But the old bitch kept insisting they never killed him."

"Oh—he just ended up getting shot through the head by magic?"

The biker laughed. "Yeah. I guess."

"Any idea who the other women were? Where they are?"

"Nope."

"Couldn't make her talk?"

"No."

"Dead?"

"Yes."

"Okay." The Man wiped his fingers on a paper napkin, crumpled it, and tossed it onto a plate of chicken bones sitting in front of him. "Good." He pushed the plate to one side. "Good riddance to both of them. Any guy that lets himself get taken out by a woman—well, he deserves to be dead."

"Yeah—my thoughts exactly."

The Man pushed back in his chair, and clamped his hands behind his head. "Has any headway been made on the diner?"

"Diner?"

The Man stared at him.

"Oh, at the north side clubhouse—I got you. Yeah, not bad. Got a couple of chefs to work it. But they want supplies."

"Like what?"

"Seasonings. Lard. Flour. Rice. Meat—lots of meat."

"Okay, so?"

"We've had a little trouble getting the food supplies up here from the Calgary area. Small gangs from some of the towns are interfering with the shipments."

"Okay, so let's re-route some of our boys down south—let them take care of the problem."

"Already done, but that's leaving us a little weak up here."

The Man rubbed his chin. "I've got a guy—military background— I'll ask him for his take on this." He opened a desk drawer and pulled out a logbook.

"You mean The Gatekeeper's old buddy?"

"Yeah. Him."

The biker eyed the plate of chicken bones. He licked his lips. "Got any of that chicken left?"

"No."

Chapter Fourteen

The Wind Technician

THE BESPECTACLED man gave Matthew a hard look. "No," he said, a nasal pompousness edging his voice. "My wife and I don't use guns. We're pacifists."

"Gre-a-a-at," Matthew responded with mock enthusiasm. "Then you can die non-violently while the Crazies shoot you. As for the rest of us—we're survivalists."

The man gave his wire-rimmed eyeglasses a quick push up his nose. "I told you—"

Matthew cut him off. "If you expect to live here with us, you will live by our rules. Every man and every *woman* learns to use guns. Every man is responsible for the safekeeping of his own household. Once he's done that—then he's responsible for the safekeeping of another man's household.

"In this compound, we *are* our brother's keeper. And when the Crazies come, it takes a gun to do that." Matthew paused. "Now—are you in? Or out?"

A woman standing next to the man nudged his ribs. The man shot her a look of irritation. "We've got to stay here," she said in a husky whisper. "We're out of food." The baby in her arms whined in agreement.

The man turned a sullen look on Matthew. "Yeah—okay—we're in."

Matthew raised his eyebrows and bent to his paperwork. "Names?"

Martha stood quietly near Matthew. He had invited her to watch the processing of new members. She was to remain quiet. However, something about the baby bothered her. She had to speak.

"Matthew?" Martha asked.

"Names?" Matthew asked the couple again.

"Matthew?" Martha repeated, in a hurried whisper. "Wouldn't it be a good idea to give them a bit of a physical examination, first?"

Matthew sat back in his chair. "Why?"

"It's winter." Martha glanced up at the trio; the woman eyed her suspiciously. "We should be careful about bringing in any communicable diseases. We got off easy with the measles scare." She motioned toward the baby with a lift of her chin. "This little one looks feverish."

The woman piped up. She had been listening. "He's just teething. It's no big deal."

Martha turned back to Matthew. "Well?"

Matthew laid his pen down on the book. "Martha's right," he said. "Let her examine the baby."

"Nobody's touching my kid," the father blurted.

The outburst made Matthew frown. He straightened in his chair. His hand dropped to his hip. Jonah and Simon moved in. Their hands dropped to their hips, too.

"Easy," Matthew said. "Martha's very good with kids. So, if you want to be admitted here —" He shrugged. "Best to let her take a look."

The woman glanced at her husband. The baby began to squall, pitching himself back and forth in her arms. The woman struggled to keep him still. "Len?" she whispered. "What do you want to do?"

Finally, the man nodded his brusque consent. Martha walked around the desk. She pumped disinfectant gel onto her hands from a bottle sitting on the corner of Matthew's desk. She approached the mother. The baby watched her and then clutched his mother. His wails made Martha's ears ring.

Martha motioned for the mother to sit. The woman perched herself on a camp chair near the window. Martha turned the baby's face toward her. His skin was hot. He tried to pull his head away, but Martha held it tight. He gave an indignant screech. Martha clicked on her small flashlight. The child howled again.

Martha steeled herself against the sound, and scanned the boy's open mouth. She saw small white blisters. She stepped back. "Let me see his hands," she said. The mother held up one of her son's hands. Tiny red blisters dotted the child's fingers and the top of his palm. Martha nodded to the mother, "I suspect I'll find these on his feet, too."

The mother nodded, sheepishly.

"Hand, foot, and mouth disease," Martha said.

"Contagious?" Matthew asked.

"Very."

"Cure?"

"Not really. It just has to run its course."

"Please don't turn us away," the woman begged. She grabbed Martha's arm. Martha shook off her hand. "We're out of food."

"Do you have mouth sores, too?" Martha asked. The woman shook her head. Martha walked back to Matthew's desk. She pumped disinfectant into her hands again.

"So?" Matthew asked. "What should we do?"

"There's good news. And there's bad news. This kid could remain contagious for a long time, and we'd never know it. But he's the most contagious for the next week."

"The good news?"

Martha shrugged. "Well, the disease isn't fatal. If the other kids get this, they'll be immune the next time it—or something else like it—comes around. But it'll mean a lot of nursing care."

"I don't know," Matthew said. "Sounds like too much trouble." He tipped his head back and regarded Martha. "What do you think?"

"Quarantine all three of them for two weeks."

"That's fine with us," the woman called out. She stood and rushed to the desk, shouldering her husband out of the way. She gave him a warning look. "We accept," she said.

Matthew studied the woman and the child. He looked at Martha. He shook his head. "No—we need our manpower."

The mother shrieked. "But we'll starve. We have no food."

"It's always been my policy to take the healthy only. Your baby isn't healthy."

The woman began to cry. "Please..." she begged. She leaned over the desk.

Matthew motioned for her to stand back. He reached for the hand gel and pumped a small puddle into his hands. Martha suppressed a smug grin. It was at her insistence that all common areas be equipped with hand sanitizers. Matthew had indulged her—but only after initially rejecting the idea.

Matthew shook his head again. He motioned to Jonah. "Show them out." Jonah nodded in return. Matthew shut his logbook. The woman gave another small cry.

"Matthew—" Martha said. "Food—they need food."

"Of course," Matthew said. Give them enough food for a couple of weeks."

"Wait," the woman cried. She stared at her husband. "Tell him. Tell him!" She paused. "Do you want our baby to die?"

Her husband's face clouded with concern. He looked from his wife to Matthew. He cleared his throat.

Matthew waited. "Well?"

"I'm a specialist—in wind power," he said. "I worked for the government. I designed wind machines for the province's experimental farms." He paused. "I'm a *wind technician*."

Martha raised her eyebrows. "Wind technician?" she asked. She glanced at Matthew.

Matthew said nothing.

"I'm not just a mechanic," he added. "I'm an engineer."

Matthew pushed his lower lip upwards in consideration of the new information. Then he leaned forward, picked up his pen, and opened his logbook. "Names?"

"Where will we put them?" Martha asked. She didn't need to be told how valuable this man was to the compound; Matthew's silence had done that.

"There's the small cabin just near here," Matthew said. "No one's using it right now, except the guards. It's got a furnace and there's plenty of wood. We can put in an extra camp cot."

"Will we get food?" the woman asked.

"Yes, of course," Martha said. "We're not in the habit of starving our people." She looked at the baby who had fallen asleep on his mother's shoulder. "But first, you and I are going to figure out a way to rinse his mouth with salt water—and not drown him in the process," she added, with a good-natured laugh.

The woman smiled broadly.

Matthew jotted the new family's information in his logbook. He looked up and motioned to Jonah again. Jonah walked over and dipped his head near Matthew's mouth. Martha was near enough to hear what he said. "Watch him."

"Why?" whispered Jonah. "He's a pacifist."

"Exactly why I want him watched. Pacifists have a boiling point, too. I suspect this guy is close to his."

Jonah nodded and backed away. Martha gave Matthew a questioning glance, but she said nothing.

□□□

THE WIND technician became a hot topic around the camp. Lenny, as the young men called him, was an old-fashioned geek when it came to engineering and electronics. Before the Change, he would have been ridiculed, but in this new world, he was revered and admired.

"He's become the camp rock star," Martha said. Matthew and Josef nodded.

They were having dinner together in Martha and Josef's cabin. The cabin was warm and scented with the sweet smell of cooking meat. Martha was proud of her fried steak—slightly rare—and well seasoned—heavy on sautéed garlic: *Steak Tuscany*, she called it. Matthew enjoyed not having to cook for himself. So, Josef's invitations to supper were readily accepted.

"Really good," Matthew said, not looking up, as he cut another piece of steak and forked it into his mouth.

"What—that Lenny's a rock star?" Martha asked.

Matthew looked up, caught her grin, and ignored the question. He went back to eating. He chewed, swallowed, took a long drink of water, and then relaxed back in his chair. "It's time we went scavenging again."

Josef looked up. "Where to? Edmonton and the bedroom communities are really slim pickings, right now."

"It's time to go farther," Matthew said. "Lenny says there's a compound on the way to Hinton. Lots of turbine equipment." He paused. "We need to do a fuel run, anyway."

Matthew pulled a small spiral notebook from his chest pocket. He flipped it open. Martha saw a list of scrawled items. Her eye caught a few: safety harnesses, torque wrenches, lube tools, propellers, pumps, chains, brakes, batteries, capacitors... The list was long. She looked at Matthew.

"Even if we find it, how do we get all that stuff back here?" Martha asked. "We don't have any big moving trucks."

"No," Matthew said. "But the Hutterites do. I think they'll be more than happy to help us get this equipment."

"When do you want to go?" Josef asked.

Matthew looked out the window. "Tomorrow. We've been lucky so far. The snow's been light. I suspect the highways are blown clear by the wind."

"It's a big chance," said Josef. "This is Alberta. And it is the middle of December."

"We'll put a crew together. Lenny—and twenty of our strongest guys. I'll go, too." He stared at Josef. "You can handle things here, right?"

Josef looked surprised. "Uh, sure," he said. "Does that mean Jonah and Simon are going, too?"

"No," Matthew said. "They're better off staying here. They're two of my most-trusted soldiers. You'll need them."

"What about Brad and Vince?" Josef asked.

"Humph," Matthew mumbled. He reached for the small plate Martha handed to him. It was laden with a tall piece of apple pie. The crust was lightly browned and wispy flakes had fallen to the plate. Sticky liquid, the color of butterscotch, had oozed into a shiny crescent puddle on the plate. Matthew sniffed and smiled. "Umm, cinnamon." He put a forkful of pie into his mouth, chewed, and swallowed. "I'll take them with me."

Martha placed a piece of pie in front of Josef. He looked up at her, and smiled. He, too, sniffed the air above the pie, gave a sigh of contentment, and picked up his fork.

Martha took her seat. She sat quietly; her pie remained untouched.

"Matthew?" Martha said suddenly. Her eyes were bright as she stared at the man next to her.

Josef glanced up. He looked first at his wife, and then across the table at Matthew. Matthew's head was bent over his pie. He looked up.

"Yes."

"We need more supplies," Martha said. "Of all kinds. Especially baby goods. The stores around here have been scavenged bare." She took a quick breath, and pressed on, "But there's a Walmart in Hinton. Maybe it's far enough out that not too many people have been there."

Martha was itching to get off the compound. The winter routine had become dull; she needed an adventure—desperately. A scavenging road trip would be perfect.

Matthew put down his fork, and looked directly at Martha. "What about the pregnant girls?"

Martha expelled her breath, "Oh, Matthew. Ruth and Anna have deliveries down to an art. And besides, I'm guessing the last six girls aren't due for several weeks."

Eight more babies had joined the November twins. Some of the girls' labors had been long and very hard, but there had been no serious complications. Apart from the many tears shed by the girls as they gave birth and then experienced—firsthand—the pain of nursing a new baby, there were few problems.

Warm compresses, breast swaddling, self-expressing milk to ease the pressure, and nursing their babies in spite of chapped and bleeding nipples—were lessons each new mother had been forced to learn. The girls soon realized that—like labor—the pain was relatively short-lived. They endured. And their babies thrived.

"Just give me a list, Martha," Matthew said, "and I'll do what I can."

"No!" Martha's voice rose, sharp and petulant.

Matthew's eyebrows shot up in surprise. "The camp is better off with you here," he said.

Martha gave her pie plate a rough shove. Josef's eyes widened. He watched for Matthew's reaction. Matthew said nothing. A heavy silence filled the cabin.

Martha stood up. "I've been cooped up here for months." She faced Matthew; her look was stern and resolute. "I'm going." She turned and stomped to the sink. "And that's—that," she said, under her breath.

Matthew cleared his throat.

Martha turned back to face the men who were exchanging looks. She took a deep breath and decided to try again. She softened her tone.

"It's less than four hours from here, Matthew. If the roads are good. And even if they aren't, I'm a damn good driver in snow." She paused and waited for Matthew's response.

Matthew rose from his chair.

"Okay, I'll take the damn gun," Martha blurted. "Just get me the hell out of here." Martha cast her husband a glance—a frantic look. Josef's eyes were filled with compassion and understanding, but he said nothing.

Matthew took his coat from a wall hook near the door. "Thank you for supper, Martha. Terrific, as always." He reached for the doorknob and hesitated. "I'm set on this, Martha. Stay here. Give us a list. We'll get the things you need."

Martha turned her back to him. She felt her blood rise along with the hairs on the back of her neck. Her breath quickened, but she remained quiet.

How dare he tell her she couldn't go? This was not a prison. He was not the warden.

Her hands shook, as she placed the dirty dishes into the small washbasin in the sink.

And—he's NOT my husband.

Matthew pulled on his gloves, waved to Josef, opened the door, and left the cabin. A chilly breeze swept in; it did nothing to cool Martha's temper.

"Martha?" Josef asked gently. He was standing next to her now. He slipped a pie plate into the basin, and reached a hand toward her chin. He tried to tip her face toward him, but she wrenched her chin out of his hand.

"You could have said something," Martha said. Her voice cracked with bitterness.

"I could have, but it wouldn't do any good." Josef shrugged. "He's right. He depends on you here. All of us do." Josef tried to catch Martha's eyes. "What's so wrong about that?"

"I *need* a break."

"I know, but can't you wait? Just till the spring?"

"No." She slammed a freshly washed plate into the waiting dish drainer. "I need to get out of here." She turned and faced Josef. "And I'll go by myself, if I have to."

"That's a bad idea, Martha," Joseph said, sternly. "And you know it."

Martha went silent.

▢▢▢

MATTHEW PIERCED Simon with a hard stare. "What do you mean she took the truck?"

"She said she was running over to the Hutterites." Simon shrugged. "I had no reason not to believe her, Matthew."

"Dammit!" Matthew looked toward the Gatehouse. "Are the trucks ready to go?"

"Yes. Your army truck, too. We've loaded them with all the jerry cans we could find."

"And the team? Where's the team?"

Simon motioned to the side of the Gatehouse. "There. Waiting for you."

Matthew glanced over. Men, all shapes and sizes, dressed in full military winter gear milled around outside the Gatehouse. Brad and Vince were with them. Matthew checked his watch. "How long ago did she leave?"

Simon checked his own watch. "Approximately—28 minutes ago."

"Okay. Get the team moving."

Simon trotted toward the men. Matthew watched him give the order, and the men separated into smaller groups. Soon the small caravan of half-ton trucks, jeeps, 4X4s, and a hauling van were rumbling down the road. Matthew led the pack in his own vehicle: a two-and-a-half-ton military truck he had bought at auction. Lenny rode shotgun beside him.

"Nice vehicle," Lenny said. "Jeep? Caterpillar engine? What's it weigh? 10-thousand pounds?"

"Thirteen," Matthew said. The American military truck belonged to Matthew long before the Change. He found it on the *Steel Soldiers* website. He bought it and refurbished it. It had not been a practical purchase—the machine drank oil by the gallons instead of quarts—but he liked it. It had handily taken him over much rough terrain and primitive roadways; he wasn't ready to give it up.

Matthew touched the gas pedal; the big vehicle rumbled forward. He pulled earmuffs out from under the seat. He handed a pair to Lenny. "You'll want to wear these."

Except for the noise from the engine, they rode in silence. Lenny had busied himself with making notes in a full-sized, thick notebook. He closed the book and looked up. "So, where does Martha fit into all this?"

Matthew stared at Lenny. "What?"

"Martha?" Lenny repeated, louder. "For a tough guy, you sure let her get away with a lot."

Matthew turned and studied the road. "She knows a lot. I give her leeway."

"Leeway?" Lenny gave a short laugh—it was an unpleasant sound— like a choked chicken might make. "Is that what you call it? When she takes off with one of your trucks?"

Matthew's hands tightened on the wheel. "Look, I'm sure you're one hell of a *wind technician*, but when it comes to how I run this compound— it's best if you keep your opinions to yourself." Matthew glanced at Lenny, who was staring back at him—a bemused expression on his face. "We'll get along better that way," he advised.

Lenny looked out the window. Matthew returned his attentions to the road. "Damn her," he muttered softly.

Lenny hid a wide smile.

THE TRUCK was easy to handle. It responded well to Martha's pressure on the gas pedal. The highway was clear of snow and black ice. The sun, entering in through the back window, warmed her neck. Martha pressed the window switch. Fresh, crisp air, chilled with snow, and slightly scented with the forest that lined the road, swept into the truck. It felt good, and Martha took a deep breath. For a second she was free—there was no compound, no troubles, and especially—no Matthew. In the next second, a fist of guilt slammed into her stomach, and she winced.

God, he was going to be mad.

A deer trotted onto the highway and skidded to a halt in the middle of her lane. Martha touched the brakes, and neatly veered around it. She saw three more deer approaching from the right, and she slowed the truck; hitting a deer was not in her plans.

Soon, an entire herd of deer had made their way onto the highway. The hapless deer weren't used to running away from vehicles anymore; they stood and looked at her. She tried to edge through the herd, but the bodies were too thick. She shrugged her shoulders.

"Oh, what the hell."

She stopped the truck, and turned off the ignition.

The deer wandered over and studied the stranger in the truck. One of them pushed its nose through the open window. Martha sighed softly. "Oh," she breathed. She reached out and tentatively touched the velvety muzzle. The deer jumped back, its large brown eyes confused and suspicious.

Martha leaned back against the headrest and watched as the deer ambled around the truck. They looked healthy. The Change had been good for deer, she surmised. Suddenly, the herd froze. Their ears went up and their noses lifted in the air. Martha wondered what had put them on alert. She looked around.

A movement from the corner of her eye caught her attention. A flash of black. One of the smaller deer leapt up, its forelegs momentarily suspended in mid-air, and then it dashed across the road. The black shape ran after it. Into the ditch and up the other side, it ran. The rest of the deer scattered and stampeded every which way. Martha sat stunned. She watched as the black shape... *a dog?—no, not a dog—a wolf*—she corrected herself... leapt at the deer. The deer fell to its front knees, struggled upwards, and fled into the woods. The wolf followed.

Martha glanced around. Wolves hunted in packs. *Were there more of them?* As she looked out the back window, her stomach twisted, and she panicked. A line of trucks was coming down the highway. She reached for the key in the ignition, thought better of it, and dropped her hand into her lap. She knew he would catch up to her, so she waited.

Martha stared straight ahead, as the military truck pulled up beside her.

"Hi, Martha," Lenny said brightly, through his open window. Martha turned her head.

Asshole.

She saw Matthew in the driver's seat. He wasn't looking at her. She watched as he put the truck into park and turned off the ignition. He opened his driver's door and stepped out. Lenny smirked. Martha bit her lip.

Martha didn't look over as the passenger door on her truck swung open. Matthew got in. He sat down. "Engine trouble?" he asked.

"Matthew, I-I... " Matthew held up a gloved hand. Martha stopped talking. She stared at his glove. It was grease-stained and some of the stitching had pulled away.

He needs new gloves, she thought.

"Get out," Matthew said.

"I-I-I... "

"Get out. *Now*." Matthew stared at her. His eyes were dark and hard.

Martha lifted her door handle. She slid down from the seat, and stepped onto the pavement. To her left, she saw the line of trucks. All of them had stopped. The men had gotten out. They were walking toward her. Brad was in the lead. She could see his crooked smile. "Oh, God," she muttered. "Oh, God." She swallowed hard.

Matthew came around to her side of the truck. Martha looked up at him, her eyes pleading. His eyes remained cold. He said nothing. Brad reached them.

"So, what do we have here?" Brad asked.

Matthew held up his hand. Brad shut up, but he continued to smile. Martha flushed, and her heart pounded in her chest.

"You know I can't let this go by, Martha," Matthew said, his tone low and flat. "I told you that I can't have compound members disobeying me."

He looked at Lenny who was leaning out the truck window, and said, "Get out." Matthew nodded toward the truck Martha had been driving. "Take this truck." Lenny got out.

Martha stepped aside as Lenny pulled open the driver's door. He got in. Matthew motioned for Martha to take Lenny's place. She complied, but with some difficulty. Like a monkey, she clambered into the big truck's cab. It was the first time she had been in this truck, and the seat surprised her. It was covered in thick pads of folded bubble wrap that had been duct-taped to the upholstery. She screwed up her face in question, but sat down.

Once inside, Martha stared forward through the truck's window. She could hear Matthew and Brad in debate through the open side window. "Later," she heard Matthew say. "Right now, we've got a job to do."

Martha risked a sideways glance. Matthew had gone toward the other men. She watched as he spoke to them. In a moment, they turned and headed back to their trucks. Matthew turned, too. He stared at her. Martha's mouth went dry.

Oh shit, she thought, helplessly. *Oh, shit.*

Matthew opened the truck's door and slid in. He started the engine. His jaw was set. He didn't say a word. He threw a pair of earmuffs at her. She caught them in her lap. He pulled on his own earmuffs, put the truck into gear, and pressed down on the accelerator. Martha sat quietly, her hands twisted together in her lap. She struggled for something to say. No words came.

She soon comprehended the reason for the earmuffs.

And... the bubble wrap.

□□□

The Shortage

THE MAN relaxed back on the dark leather couch. He watched as his bodyguards played a game of pool. The room was cool, but a generator attached to a construction heater was keeping the chill away.

"A little short-sighted on your part," the tall man said. He blew a stream of cigar smoke into the atmosphere. He was in a private meeting with The Man in the second west side clubhouse—a small bar in a neighborhood strip mall, near the Whitemud Freeway.

The Man shot him a questioning look, but the tall man didn't react—one way or the other.

"How's that?" The Man asked.

"It's easy to amass an army, but an army runs on its stomach. Haven't you ever heard that saying before?"

"Sure."

"Guns and ammunition is one thing. But if you don't have the men to use them—you won't have an army." He took a drag, making the end of his cigar glow brightly in the low light of the clubhouse. He held the smoke in his lungs briefly and then expelled it into the air. "Better get your boys some food."

"What's on your mind?"

"A raid. You're having trouble getting food supplies from the south. Well… we know there are small survival camps a few hundred miles from here—in Saskatchewan. Not well defended—according to my sources. Lots of food. The roads aren't bad. A couple of days. You could be set for the rest of the winter."

"You're going to head up the team?"

"Sure."

The Man leaned forward, his elbows resting on his knees. "You still haven't taken our colors."

"Nope. And I'm not going to."

"That might cause you a little trouble among the boys."

"I've already proven myself to you. I don't have any old gang tattoos to burn off. And… any trouble I might run into… Well—"

The Man went silent. His own cigar sat smoldering in a nearby brass ashtray. With his finger and his thumb, he stroked the sides of his mouth. The sharp clacks of colliding pool balls echoed around the room.

Moments passed.

The tall man moved. He leaned forward. With his cigar in his mouth, he pulled off his jacket and rolled up his shirtsleeve. He puffed on his cigar again—and again—making its end burn brightly. He tapped its lit end into an ashtray piled high with circular gray ashes. He blew on the end of the cigar making it glow even brighter. Then he pushed the lit end into his forearm. The air filled with the stench of scorched flesh and singed hair. He pulled the cigar away, and put it back into his mouth. He took a long drag, blew out the smoke, and then spoke:

"Now— I have your colors."

The Man dipped his head in acknowledgment. He picked up his own cigar. He took a drag, and then exhaled—slowly. A thick plume of white smoke curled into the air.

The pool balls clacked again.

Chapter Fifteen

The Crappy Day

THE RIDE WAS grueling. Martha's back hurt from being jolted up and down. She was grateful for the layers of bubble wrap duct-taped across the bench, but it was still a Spartan military truck. Only a ride on a steel tractor seat, over a freshly ploughed field, would have been worse. The truck's engine was horribly loud, and the earmuffs Matthew had given her kept slipping. Martha was miserable—the outing was definitely not living up to her expectations.

Even the scenery began to bore her. Field after barren field. Forest after forest. Snow bank after snow bank. Martha rubbed her neck. The crick she had gotten from staring out the side window was elevating her level of irritation. She stole a glance at Matthew.

Matthew sat ramrod straight, face forward, his jaw clenched. His left hand gripped the steering wheel; the other clutched the tall gearshift. His gloves were off and lay on the bench seat between them. Matthew hadn't said a word since putting the truck into gear. Martha squirmed in her seat. The bubble wrap squeaked. She ached to make him speak to her, but she couldn't find the words.

Martha returned her gaze to the scenery. They passed by a large farm. Modern metal silos and small red sheds stood proudly amongst sagging wooden houses, maybe a hundred years old. The buildings sat hunched in the snow, their wooden boards now weathered and grey. *Pioneers*, Martha thought.

Martha marveled at the stamina of her forebears—she was a third generation Canadian. She had heard stories about what her grandparents' and her great-grandparents' lives had been like. So many disappointments. Yet, they had pressed on—in the face of disease, crop failure, and starvation. The pioneers had faced so much, with so little.

How had they managed? And not just to survive? But to thrive. We've got it so easy, she thought. *Warm cabins. Lots of food. Medical supplies. Trucks. Fuel. Guns—*

"Martha!" Matthew yelled above the sound of the engine. His voice startled her and she jumped. She turned to face him. He was looking at her.

"Wh— what?"

"When we get back, you're going before the Discipline Committee," Matthew said. "You've given me no choice." He looked back at the road.

A shockwave of terror roared through her, and Martha cringed. She couldn't speak.

"I've tried to explain to you—but I can't seem to make you understand." Matthew shrugged. "You keep disobeying me."

Disobeying. There was that word again.

Martha sank down into her seat. She crossed her arms tightly across her chest in an attempt to squash the fear and the hot anger that flared inside her.

"You're very valuable to the compound—there's no question," Matthew added. "But you don't follow orders. That makes you a detriment."

Detriment? That was a new one.

Martha slunk lower in her seat.

"I'm not sure what the punishment will be," Matthew said, "but there will be punishment." He glanced at Martha. "I wanted you to be aware of that."

Punishment? Pun-ish-ment?

Martha swallowed hard. She knew there had been whippings on the compound. A boy had been whipped for stealing from the cabins.

Is that what he was saying—Brad and Vince would finally get their chance? Indignant anger flickered hot inside her. *That was NOT going to happen.*

"I'll kill myself first before I'll ever let Brad touch me," she muttered.

Matthew glanced at her. "That's not what I had in mind."

Martha eyes widened. An icy chill rippled through her veins, and her chest tightened.

What was he saying? That HE would do the whipping? She blanched. *He can't mean that.* She clenched her hands; her nails dug into her palms. *He just can't.* She struggled to speak.

"Wh-wh-what are you saying?" Utter disbelief colored her voice. "That you... *you* are going to... to *whip* me?" The words squeaked through her constricted throat. Her face flushed red.

Matthew shook his head. "No, Martha. I don't think a whipping would make much of an impression on you. There're better ways to correct your behaviour. Ways that'll make you think the next time you decide to disobey."

Martha stared at Matthew. She could barely breathe.

Better ways? What the hell was he talking about?

"Matthew, I—" she began, but he interrupted her.

"I think you need some time away."

Hurt squeezed Martha's heart.

Time away? From the compound? From Josef? From her grandchildren?

Then another thought.

From you? YOU?

Acid pain slashed through her, and she struggled not to cry. She forced herself to speak—in her defense.

"I had to go, Matthew. I just had to. I needed to get away. Can't you understand that? I was going crazy cooped up on the compound."

Matthew turned to her, his face still hard, but his eyes had softened, "I told you before—if you get away with questioning my authority, then why shouldn't everyone test it? I can't run the camp that way."

Martha turned her face toward the window. The scenery blurred. She swiped at her tears. As she did, another farm came into view.

Martha bolted upright. Something had caught her eye.

"Matthew! Stop!"

Matthew turned. Martha was pointing out the window. "There. In that farmyard. Gas drums."

Matthew craned his neck. He slowed the truck and pulled over.

"Are you sure?" he asked.

"Yes." Martha nodded. She swiped at the dampness on her cheeks. "They're uprights. They're hidden behind the silos." She continued to point.

Martha watched as Matthew got out of the truck. He waited for the rest of the convoy to stop. He walked back and had a hurried conversation with a few of the men. He returned to the truck, started the engine, pulled forward, and turned around. "Did you see a road leading in?"

"No," Martha said. "But try the mile road over there." She pointed. "The farm's driveway might lead off of it."

Matthew nodded. He drove back to the crossroad, and turned left. The rest of the vehicles followed.

About a quarter mile down the road, Martha spotted a mailbox. "Try here," she said.

Matthew turned left. The lane was thick with snow. The truck tires crunched as they rolled along.

"No tire marks," Matthew observed.

Martha nodded. She breathed a sigh of relief. He sounded like the old Matthew. A weight lifted from her heart.

They pulled into a large U-shaped yard. A massive ranch-style farmhouse sat off to the left. To the right, the yard was dotted with assorted tractors, mowers, field machinery, buckets, tools, and buildings.

"Pretty quiet," Matthew said. "Looks deserted."

Martha nodded her agreement.

A large barn sat directly ahead; there were no signs of any animals. Not even a dog. Matthew pulled over and stopped the truck. "Where did you see the gas tanks?"

"Back there," Martha said. She opened her door and began to step out.

Matthew reached over and grasped her arm. "Stay here. I'll go." His look and the pressure of his fingers on her arm made clear the intensity of his command.

Martha closed her door.

"Here—" he repeated. "—IN the truck."

She nodded her understanding, and Matthew released her arm.

Matthew opened his door and jumped out. Martha watched as men from the other vehicles swarmed up to join him. Several were carrying red, plastic gas cans; the rest carried weapons. Matthew pointed to a spot behind the silos. Half the men headed off, gas cans swinging from their hands. The other half waited for Matthew's instructions. Martha waited, too. Matthew pointed to his right and to his left. The men obeyed.

A feeling of well-being swept over Martha and she sighed. These men were *protectors—MY protectors,* she thought. Tears pricked her eyes. *I could lose all this.* Suddenly, that seemed like much too much to risk.

An apology.

She searched for Matthew. She would apologize to him. That would make things right. She looked around. Matthew was gone from sight.

In a few moments, all the men had disappeared. Martha rolled down her window. The sun felt good on her face. Sunlight glanced off the snow bank near the barn, forming a fire-spray of crystals.

How pretty.

A gentle wind touched her face. A Chinook? It was too early, but some weather anomaly was making the mid-December day feel more like spring. She looked toward the house.

Water dripped lazily down thickly ridged icicles hanging from the eaves. The front door beckoned to her. Martha desperately wanted to get out of the truck.

Probably good things to scavenge.

Her hand went to the door handle, but a ruckus to her right caught her attention. She turned her head toward a copse of spruce trees.

Martha watched as two large ravens fought over territory on a high branch. One muscled the other out of the way, and then cawed its victory loudly through the trees. The victor sat, preening his dark feathers. Martha watched as something white dropped from his behind. She screwed up her face in disgust, and said aloud, "I'm watching a bird crap." She laughed.

Martha glanced around. Matthew was still nowhere to be seen. She looked back at the house. Her fingers itched to open her door, but the memory of Matthew's eyes and his words came back to her. Crystal clear. She sighed. She took her hand off the door handle and placed it in her lap.

This time, she would do as she was told.

This time, she would stay put.

Martha nestled back against the seat.

She closed her eyes.

☐☐☐

MARTHA JOLTED awake at the sounds. The voices were unfamiliar.

How long have I been asleep?

She lifted her head and looked around her. She was lying across the bench seat, her face near the steering wheel. She raised herself, turned, and peeked through the back window. She saw a group of men, maybe a dozen—all strangers. They were investigating the vehicles. She saw their guns: *Big guns. Many guns.* Martha shrank down on the seat. Her mind raced with indecision.

What do I do?

She glanced at the truck's instrument panel. She had never driven Matthew's truck. She looked at the pedals. Matthew's legs were so long. Her legs were short. Then there was the gearshift. It had been a while since she had driven a vehicle with a clutch and a gearshift. The voices came closer. Her heart beat faster as she began to panic.

Think, Martha. Think!

She had to get out of the truck.

Now.

Martha peered out the back window again. The men had their backs turned.

Where would she go? Into the house? They would see her getting out of the truck. Could she stay hidden in the truck? Where was Matthew?

The voices were much clearer now. Martha listened intently. Panic coursed through her, making her feel light-headed. She knew the men would investigate the cab. When they did, they would find her. Blood pounded in her ears.

Martha's hand strayed inside her parka. She touched the gun. Her Browning was tucked into her shoulder holster. Not even Matthew knew she was armed. However, the men would know—because when they found her, they would search her. And take it away from her.

Better not to have the gun.

She pulled the pistol from its holster. She found a lifted edge on the duct tape. She pulled at it. She opened a small slit, wide enough for the gun. She shoved it between the seat and the pile of bubble wrap. She pushed the duct tape back down. She crouched on the floor.

She closed her eyes.

Please, God.

The first shot made Martha gasp. More shots. Then more. Bullets zinged and ricocheted off the truck cab. She didn't dare look up, but she heard running feet, and men's shouts.

She felt the truck tremble slightly as though a body had slammed into it. Another shot, and a soft grunt came up through the open window. Something scuffled outside the door.

No, she pleaded. NO!

Someone scrabbled at the door handle. Martha reached over and grabbed it. She held it against the outside pressure.

Don't look in. Don't look in.

More shots. More grunts. The pressure on the door handle ceased. Martha let go. Her palms were slick with sweat; she wiped them on her jeans. She heard men calling, but she couldn't identify any voices. The truck trembled again. Voices rose up through the open window.

"You okay?"

"Yeah."

"Who *are* these guys?" The man sounded amazed.

"How the hell should I know?" the second man said. "But they're armed better than most of the people who show up here."

"Can you tell how many?"

"No. They must have split up before we saw them."

Bullets zinged again.

"Damn. I thought you guys ambushed all of them."

"Well, they must have missed some—either that, or our people are shooting at us," the other man said drily. "Wanna try getting into the truck?"

"I don't want to take a bullet in the back."

"I'll cover you."

"Can you drive this tank?"

"Duh."

More gunfire. Martha covered her ears. She waited for one of the bullets to find her. None did.

"Uhh... " grunted a voice. "Shit—I'm hit."

"Get into the truck."

Martha had no time to grab the handle. The door yanked open. A man leapt in. He threw himself across the seat. The door slammed shut behind him. His eyes widened when he saw Martha hunched on the floor.

The man leveled his pistol at her head. "Don't. Or I'll kill you, right now."

Martha remained frozen. Her world went into slow motion. She studied the man. Handsome. Dark. Salt and pepper beard. Piercing blue eyes. *Paul Newman eyes*, she thought idly. More gunfire. The man's eyes never strayed.

"You're bleeding," she said.

"I know."

"Who are you?"

"Shut up."

Martha felt the familiar ire rise inside of her. "Don't tell me to shut up."

"Shut up—or I'll shoot you." The man shifted and winced.

Blood soaked his right pant leg.

"I'm a medic," she said.

"I'll still shoot you."

"Then you'll bleed to death."

The man gave a sharp grunt of pain as he repositioned his leg. He raised his pistol and aimed it at her head again.

Martha wanted to laugh. The surreal nature of her predicament was suddenly very funny. A gun battle was going on only inches from her, in front of her a man was bleeding to death, and all she could think about was how beautiful his eyes were.

"You have beautiful eyes," she said.

The man made a derisive sound through his nose. "Are you crazy?" He waved the pistol at her. "Do you see this gun?"

"Yes."

"Then shut the fuck up!"

It was too much. The stress, the adrenaline, Matthew, this man—everything—it was all too much. Martha clamped her hand over her mouth and she began to laugh. The man glared at her, but she couldn't stop. The gun had ceased to exist. The world had ceased to exist. In that moment, she had the craziest desire to kiss him. The thought made her laughter worse.

The blow came too fast.

She had no way to escape it.

Her world went dark.

□□□

The Santa

THE MAN TURNED *from the window. "Christmas?"*

"Yeah. The guys want to have a Christmas party. You know—with a tree, and presents, and colored lights—"

"—Candy canes, gingerbread men, plum pudding—Yeah, yeah," The Man replied.

"The old ladies are up for it. They said they'd decorate. And cook." The biker smiled encouragingly.

The Man put his hand up to his face—he scraped his fingers through the bristles. He scratched. "Sure, what the hell—why not?"

The biker brightened. "It'll be nice to hear Christmas carols again," he said.

The Man laughed. "Yeah, can't get enough of that old classic where somebody's grandma gets her lights punched out by reindeer." He sneered. "Use the north side clubhouse."

The biker smiled. "Hey, how about if you play Santa?"

The Man picked up the pistol lying next to his hand.

The biker disappeared through the door.

Chapter Sixteen

It's My Truck

"WAKE UP."

Martha groaned. One of her arms was twisted painfully under her body. She moved sluggishly—her head was pounding. "Uhhh..." she groaned again, "My head." She wrenched her arm out from under her. "Ow." The pain in her arm matched the throbbing in her head.

Martha tried to focus her eyes in the dim light. Somebody was lying next to her.

Where was she? Was she on a bed? Much too hard to be a bed.

She rose up, and tried to control her head. It felt too heavy for her neck and it lolled sideways. She reached up and touched the left side, feeling a large patch of matted hair. Then she remembered the truck, the man, her laughter, and his gun.

He must have knocked me out. Damn, where am I?

Martha's eyes adjusted. She made out a large picture window and heavy drapery. *Was that a TV to the right?* Shelves stuffed with videos, DVDs, and books came into focus. *Somebody's living room?*

She looked down. She was lying on a dining room table. She shivered. Her parka was gone. So was her shoulder holster.

"Hello." It was a man's voice.

Martha gasped. She turned to her right and gave the speaker a bleary stare. "Who are you?"

"A friend."

"The same friend who hit me?"

"No, a different friend."

"Where am I?"

"In my house."

"How'd I get here?" Martha asked.

"I brought you."

"Oh."

Martha reached over and felt for the body next to her. It was there. It was breathing. She swiveled her head to the left. At first, she had no idea who the person was lying alongside her. Then it came back to her—it was the man with the beautiful blue eyes.

"What's he doing here?" Martha asked. She made the painful swivel with her head again so she could see the stranger standing near her. "And who the hell are you?"

"I found you two in the military truck. You were both passed out."

"Yeah, he hit me."

"Why?"

"'Cause I was laughing."

"Sounds like something he'd do."

"You know him?"

"Yep. He's my nephew."

Martha studied the man. He resembled an old prospector, complete with long scraggly grey hair and a thin wispy beard. She began to shiver.

"I'm f-f-freezing," she said.

The man reached under the table and brought up her parka. "Here," he said, with an apologetic smile.

Martha accepted the jacket and pulled it on. She closed the parka tightly. "Y-y-you said this is your house?"

"Well, it is for now. I mean it wasn't mine to begin with. We... took it."

"Where are the real owners?"

"Dead."

"You killed them?"

"No—some of the guys outside did," the man said, pointing toward the window.

Martha blinked. She had stopped chattering. The old man's eyes were also blue, and they were making her feel very uncomfortable. Very... naked. She desperately wanted to be away from this man—his nephew—and... this table. She changed the subject.

"He was shot, you know," she said, motioning to the man lying beside her. "Did you stop the bleeding?"

"Yeah, he'll be fine."

"What about the bullet?" Martha asked.

"Went right through. Clean as a whistle. Didn't hit anything important. I patched him up."

Martha paused. She hesitated asking the next question. "Where are the men I came with?"

The old man motioned toward the window again. "Out there."

"Out there, where?"

"The barn."

"Would you take me to them?" Martha asked.

"Not right now."

The man beside Martha began to stir. Martha rubbed her head.

The old man handed her a small item. "Here," he said. "This'll help."

Martha held out her hand and took the item. It was an instant cold pack—the kind you crack. It was already cold. She pressed it to her head. "Are the guys okay?"

"They were when I last looked."

Something in the man's eyes troubled Martha. She felt a hitch in her spirit, and her desire to get away from him quadrupled. "I've really got to pee," she said.

She moved to get off the table. A strange clinking sound made her check her ankle. Chain links. They snaked around her right ankle and down under the table. *From the frying pan into the fire.* She had heard the saying a thousand times before—but now she understood its meaning.

Martha's heart began to pound.

"Let me help you," the old man said. Martha flinched back, but he grabbed her by the shoulders and pulled her forward. Her head banged with pain as her feet hit the floor. The man motioned to a hallway. "The can is down there."

Martha stood, her mouth hanging open. She could only point to the dog chain hanging around her ankle.

"It's long enough," the old man said. Martha's situation began to truly dawn on her, and she felt faint. She swayed, but the man steadied her. "C'mon. I'll take you."

He escorted her down the hallway; he pushed open a door to the right—it was a bathroom. He walked her in. Martha gaped at him.

"Do you need help with your pants?" he asked.

Martha shook her head. "I'm fine. Thanks."

"Well, get on with it then."

"I'd like some privacy."

"No," he said. "You just go ahead."

Martha's head swam with confusion.

Had she awakened in some sort of strange parallel universe? Or was this all a crazy dream?

She pinched her arm. It hurt. She widened her eyes at the realization.

The old man stood in front of her, his eyes willing her to let him help her. Martha's stomach convulsed and she felt a thickness in her throat.

I'm going to throw up.

She leaned over, and unloaded her breakfast on his shoes.

"Aw, dammit," he said. "Look what you've done." Martha couldn't look—she was still retching. The man left the room. Martha heard him muttering in the distance.

When her stomach stopped heaving, she dropped to her knees, and pulled at the chain. She examined the links. A small lock, like a suitcase lock, was all that was holding her captive. She had picked these locks open many times in the past after losing suitcase keys. She stood up and scanned the bathroom for something that would act as a pick.

There was nothing on the counter. Nothing on the back of the toilet. A medicine chest hung over the sink; she pulled it open: Pill bottles, cough medicine, perfume, hair spray, but nothing that would pick a lock. She closed the door. She could still hear the old man mumbling in the other room.

She grabbed a towel from a stack against the wall, and wiped her mouth. The vomit was acidic. She wanted water, but she didn't trust the tap water. *Mouthwash*, she thought. She dropped the towel.

She looked behind her. She saw a tall white cupboard—its doors closed. She turned and pulled the double doors open. Cleaning tools, cleaning products, toilet paper rolls, toothpaste, sanitary napkins, and a wicker basket; it was filled with hair elastics, curlers, hairbrushes, little girl's barrettes, and plastic combs. A bottle of Listerine caught her eye, and she grabbed it. As she lifted the bottle, she saw it—an old-fashioned hairpin—the kind she had once used when she had long hair. She grabbed it and shoved it into her jeans. Small packs of tissues sat neatly piled on the left side of the cabinet. She grabbed several. As she did, the right door of the cabinet slammed shut. She jumped. The old man was standing there. He was not amused.

Martha held up the Listerine and the tissues. "Mouthwash," she said. She opened the bottle, took a swig, swished, turned, and spit it into the sink. She capped the bottle and returned it to the cabinet. She motioned to the toilet. "I still have to go," she said. The man remained. "I still feel kind of sick," Martha advised. He turned and walked out.

Martha used the toilet as quickly as she could. She did not relish the idea of the man walking in on her with her pants only half way up; she didn't flush. She glanced around the bathroom again to see if there was anything else she could take—anything she could use as a weapon. She went to the window.

Martha swept aside a lacy curtain to reveal a jar filled with combs. She rifled through them. Something metallic glinted in the sunlight.

Barber scissors.

Martha grabbed them. She shoved them up her parka sleeve, sharp tips down. She turned, and flushed the toilet. She waited. The old man reappeared within seconds.

"I'm done," Martha said. The man motioned her out of the bathroom. She walked back into the living room, the chain dragging ominously behind her. Her 'friend' was still lying on the table. He hadn't moved. The old man offered her a seat on the couch. Martha sat. The tips of the scissors dug into her wrist, and she winced. The old man noticed. "My head," she said, and then, "Sorry about your shoes."

"I rinsed them in the kitchen," he said.

"You have drinking water?" Martha asked. "I'm so thirsty."

"Sure." The old man rose and went to the kitchen. He returned with a bottle of water. Martha took it and drank. She capped the bottle. She looked up at him.

"Why am I chained?" she asked.

"I'd like to keep you," the old man said, simply.

Martha froze. Fear stabbed her, but she remained composed. "Why me?"

"I lost my wife two years ago—I'm lonely," the old man said. "The young guys get around, so they get their fill of women." He sat down beside her. "I don't." He smiled at her, and reached for her hand.

Martha gave him an incredulous look. "You're kidnapping me?"

"No," he said. "Just borrowing you."

"I'm married," she said.

"That doesn't bother me." His fingers closed over her hand—they began a slow caress. Martha felt her stomach twitch again.

"Well, it bothers me," she said. She pulled her hand from his grasp.

The man grabbed her arm. "I'm going to keep you," he growled. Then his eyes softened. "I'll let you go after a while."

Martha felt the blood rush from her head, and she felt dizzy again. "You can't do this." She tried to pull away, but his hand held her fast. He moved in. Martha could feel his breath and his wiry whiskers on her cheek. Her stomach rolled.

Martha let the scissors slip down her coat sleeve, down her wrist, and into her waiting hand. Something cool—like emotional hoarfrost—erupted inside her, and as it did, her breathing slowed, and her stomach settled. Her hand stopped its trembling. She gripped the scissors—more like a caress, almost sensuous. Then she tightened her fingers.

She became aware of the heartbeat in her ears, a steady thrum—slow and rhythmic—a battle drum. Coolness infused her, spreading like spidery cracks on a frozen pond. Like a dark ballerina, it beckoned to her—enticing her, cajoling her, inviting her to join its fearless dance—just as it had—once before.

Martha caressed the smooth metal in her hand.

She knew she was about to dance again.

She turned to face the old man. Their eyes met. She saw the craziness there. Then the memory came—of another set of eyes. Crazy eyes.

She drove the point of the scissors into the side of his neck. He screamed, and pitched forward. She kicked at him, and he stumbled and fell.

Martha stood—frozen in place—and stared at the man writhing on the floor. Bleeding on the floor. Dying on the floor.

I've killed... Again.

The thought came to her from far away, as sharply as the wail of wind through a tunnel.

Killed... Again.

She cocked her head and for the moment, she watched—coldly and dispassionately—but completely absorbed as the old man's movements slowly ceased, and his sounds diminished. Finally, he lay still. His blood oozed, forming a shimmering pool of dark color around his head.

Martha felt nothing as she stared—not fear, not pity, not remorse. Just a deadness—the same stark deadness she had felt before when staring down at another man.

The sounds of gunfire outside roused her. She stepped back, away from the body, and turned. Martha ran to the table. She put her foot on a dining chair, and reached for the hairpin in her pants pocket. She slipped an end into the tiny lock, and twisted. The lock refused to budge. She tried again. The hairs on the back of her neck rose in prickly succession. Sweat poured into her eyes.

Please, God. Please.

She tried again. This time the little lock popped open. She pulled it off, and the chain fell from her ankle.

She ran to the front door. She thought better of it, and ran through the house in search of a back door. She found it. She turned the deadbolt and opened the door. She tried to push her way through a screen door, but it held fast. She found the little switch in the handle, flipped it, and ran from the house. She saw a row of naked, spindly lilac bushes. She ran. She reached the bushes, and ducked behind. She stooped down. She gasped for breath; her heart pounded like bongo drums in her ears. She waited. She touched the side of her chest.

My gun. I've got to get my gun.

THE YARD was silent. All the vehicles were still where they had been parked. Martha judged the distance to Matthew's truck. No one was in sight. She sprinted across the yard. She made it to the truck, she swung open the driver's door, and clambered in. She closed the door behind her. She lay on the seat, willing her heart to slow down. A moment passed, and when no one pursued her, she got down on the floor. A puddle of dark blood was on the seat; blood now coated her jeans and her jacket. She dug under the bubble wrap—she sighed when her fingers touched the gun. She pulled it out. She had no holster—the old man had taken it—so she stuck the gun in the front of her blue jeans. It was an uncomfortable fit, but she angled it, and hooked the butt end on her waistband.

She glanced out the window—nobody around. She opened the passenger door, and slid to the ground. The old man had said the men were in the barn. That's where she was going.

Martha raced across the yard, keeping to the shadows. The sun had fallen low. She guessed it was about 4 o'clock. It would be dark soon. She reached the barn. She tried to look in through one of the windows, but they were coated in a grimy film. She sprinted toward the back of the barn. As she neared the back entrance, she heard voices. She slowed her steps.

"The old man says to keep them alive."

"Why? We've got others. We don't need this many."

"I don't know. I'd rather just shoot 'em, too."

Martha crouched near the wall in the shadow of some hay bales. She rested her head on a bale. Her mind wandered for the moment. She wondered what Josef was doing. A man coughed, bringing her back to the present.

"Did we get all of them?"

"I don't know. No way to tell."

The men continued speaking, but their voices drifted away. Martha used the opportunity to walk farther. She reached the back of the barn. She stared. Her mouth open.

Behind the barn were three roads, all cleared of snow. And all leading into the distance. *That explains the lack of tracks on the main driveway*, she thought.

Adrenaline pushed her now, and the knowledge that it would be dark soon.

Where were the men? Where was Matthew? A sudden pang in her heart made her wince. *Was he okay? Or was he lying dead somewhere?*

Martha attempted to push the powerful emotions away; she was unsuccessful. She noticed the big barn door—it was open a crack. She risked peering in. Late afternoon sunshine radiated through a skylight. She gasped. Several men were lying on the barn floor, trussed up like roped calves, while others hung by their bound wrists from hooks. Martha listened. There didn't seem to be any guards around. She heard a few of the men groan.

They're alive.

She heard voices coming up behind her. The two men were coming back. She had no choice. She pushed the barn door open, and she slipped inside. She saw hay bales piled off to her left. She launched herself over a small iron railing and scrambled over the bales. She nestled herself near the wall, and waited.

The barn door opened. Six men walked in. They were dragging another man between them. Martha tried to identify him, but the barn was too dim. The men dropped the man. He hit the floor with a grunt. His body rolled into a pool of sunlight. Martha stifled a scream.

It was Matthew. His face was bloodied.

Martha waited.

Matthew's eyes flickered open. Martha breathed a sigh of relief.

"So, now what?" asked one of the men.

A commotion at the door drew their attention.

"Hey," another man called from the doorway, "the old man's been stabbed."

"What?" The men rushed to the man standing at the door.

"The broad we found in the truck," he continued, "she stabbed him with a pair of scissors. He's dead."

"Did you check?"

"I saw him lying on the floor—scissors sticking out of the side of his neck."

"But are you sure he was dead?"

"Uh—no."

"Why didn't you check, you idiot?" said one of the men. "Let's go."

Martha listened as the men left the barn. She heard their voices trail off. Now was her chance. She clambered across the bales.

"Matthew," she whispered. "Matthew." He turned his head. One eye was swollen shut, and his lips were bloody.

"I thought I told you not to get out of the truck," he mumbled.

"Yeah, right."

Martha helped him sit up. He winced. "Can you walk?" she asked.

"I think so."

"I need your knife." Martha reached to Matthew's waistband and flipped open the black pouch hanging from his belt. She pulled out his switchblade. She ran to the men and began slicing the ropes. One by one, the men were freed.

Two of them ran to Matthew. They put his arms around their shoulders and helped him to the door. The rest of the men followed.

In a few moments, the group had gathered outside, on the far side of the barn. They found an old tool shed, and they ducked in there. Martha counted—some of the men from the compound were missing. She looked at Matthew; he was now standing on his own. "Where—?" she began.

He shook his head. "Six," he said.

Martha nodded, a lump forming in her throat. "And their guys?"

"Not sure. About the same, I think." Matthew groaned.

"How did this happen?" Martha asked.

"Long story, but Lenny is gone."

"Lenny? What did he do?"

"I'll tell you later," Matthew said.

"Are you shot?" Martha asked.

"No, just got the hell beaten out of me."

"Anything broken?"

"Don't think so." He took a breath and glanced around. "They took all the guns."

Martha smiled. "No, they didn't." She reached into the front of her pants and pulled out the Browning.

"So, you did bring it," Matthew said. He grinned, and then grimaced at the pain the movement caused.

Martha offered him the gun. He waved it back to her. "I can barely see," he said. "You'd better keep it."

Martha nodded, and returned the gun to her jeans. She was about to speak, when one of the men came up to Matthew.

"What do we do now?" he asked. The man was beaten, too, but not as badly as Matthew was. He kept dabbing at a cut on his forehead. "Should we look for the rest of the guys?"

Martha spoke up. She motioned to the window. "It's going to be dark soon. We'd best get to the trucks." Voices came from outside. They froze.

"Where do you think they went?" asked a man.

"Their trucks are still here. I'll bet they went back by the silos."

"Shit," the other man said. "Blood bath back there."

Martha watched as three of the men with her held a whispered conversation. The trio moved to the door, listened, and slipped out. Martha heard grunts, the sounds of a struggle, strangled cries, and then the men were back inside.

Both had guns.

"Let's go," they said.

Two of the men rushed to Matthew, but he motioned them away. "I'm okay," he said. "Just let's get out of here." The men nodded and followed the others.

Martha looked at Matthew and smiled. "Well, you can't make me go away," Martha said. She slipped Matthew's arm around her neck, and her arm around his waist. "C'mon."

They inched their way along between small sheds, a chicken coop, and the barn. The sun had dropped, but Martha could still see through the dusk.

Ahead of them, the vehicles sat along the driveway. The lead men, with the guns, motioned several of the men to make the sprint to the trucks. Martha knew that as soon as the engines started, their group would draw fire. She looked at Matthew. He was having a hard time walking; he wouldn't be able to run.

"Let me get the truck," she said. "I'll pick you up." Matthew's face was pale, and his eyes dull. Martha wondered how serious his injuries were. She suspected internal bleeding. She helped Matthew lean against one of the tool sheds. "Stay here. I'll be back for you."

He nodded.

The two men with the guns ran forward, slipped off to the side into the shadows, and motioned again for everyone to run.

They ran.

Martha ran, too. Straight for the truck—the one she had driven—a million years ago—that very morning—when she escaped the compound.

She reached the truck, opened the passenger door, and climbed into the cab. The familiar surroundings made her feel safe. She slid over to the driver's side, and checked the ignition. The keys hung just where they were supposed to be. It was policy to leave keys in the ignitions of all compound vehicles. Another of Matthew's laws; Martha was glad Lenny had heeded it.

She turned the key. The engine roared. She put the truck into gear, and she pulled around Matthew's military truck parked in front of her. She made her way toward the barn. Three men with long guns were coming up the path. Martha peered through the gloom.

Were they her people? She couldn't tell. It was too dark.

She drove forward, slowly, and ready to duck down behind the dashboard. Suddenly, from the corner of her eye, she saw two more men appear; these men had guns, too. Martha sighed with relief. These men were her people. They leveled their guns at the other three men. There was an exchange. The three men dropped their guns and raised their hands. The two compound men marched them toward the back of the barn. One stooped and picked up the discarded guns from the ground.

Martha watched as the five men disappeared around the corner. She began to drive forward when her passenger door was yanked open. A man jumped in. She recognized him instantly—it was the man with the blue eyes. His pistol was pointed directly at her. Martha froze—her mouth hung open.

"You killed my uncle," the blue-eyed man said, and then he added, "But I didn't much like him anyway." He smiled—a long slow smile. "But YOU, I like." He motioned with his gun. "Now get out."

Martha felt the emotional steel that had flooded her before—it rose up inside her now; she welcomed its familiar frigid fingers. Her world suddenly became bright, and very clear. A vision of Matthew slumped against the shed wall filled her mind. He would die there if she couldn't reach him. But she was going to reach him.

Martha braked the truck and shoved the gearshift into PARK. Her gun pressed uncomfortably into her stomach. She faced the man with the blue eyes. She smiled. It was a sweet smile.

It happened so fast, the man had no time to react. Martha glanced past him, and nodded at a person—outside the truck—behind him. The man turned—there was no person behind him. Martha pulled her gun, and swung the butt into his temple. The man grunted, and dropped his pistol. He sagged against the door. He was stunned, but she hadn't knocked him out. She grinned—this time, it was a wicked grin.

"How do you like them apples?" she asked. The man groaned.

Martha reached behind the man, pushed him forward, and lifted the door handle. The door opened. Just enough. Martha leaned back. She lifted her feet above the seat and kicked at the man with both feet.

"Get... the fuck... out of... my... truck," she said. Martha grinned at her rhyme, punctuated with final kicks.

The man rolled off the seat and out the open door. Martha heard him grunt as he hit the ground. She climbed across the seat, reached out, and grabbed the door handle. She caught the man's eye, and she hesitated. "My truck," she said. She slammed the door.

Martha retrieved the blue-eyed man's pistol from the floor. She laid it on the dash. She smiled at it. She started the truck's engine, turned on the headlights, and headed in Matthew's direction.

□□□

The Renegade

THE SNOWMOBILES sat silently in the Quonset hut—neatly aligned by brand: Arctic Cat, Yamaha, Polaris, Ski-Doo. Another wall was adorned with simple shelves made of hollow construction bricks and long boards; the shelves were piled with cans of motor oil. Red plastic fuel jugs sat like soldiers—obediently lined up and ready for action.

The Man surveyed the machines. He followed a man dressed in a green snowmobile suit and high black snow boots. The man stopped near the Ski-Doos, and pointed to a yellow machine.

"Renegade. Four-stroke engine. It's lighter, too," said the suited man—he was the official keeper of the power toboggans and he took great pride in his collection. "Won't drag as much through powder when you're breaking trail."

The Man climbed aboard the yellow machine and gripped the handlebars. "I like it. Keep this one aside for me," he said.

"You got it."

The Man got off the machine. "I mean it," he said. "No one drives this one—except me."

"Check. Nobody but you," the snowmobile keeper assured him.

They turned toward the door where an argument had erupted between a man and a woman.

"Why do you call me his old lady?" The small woman had her hands on her hips and she leaned forward in emphasis. "Do I look OLD to you?"

"Sorry," a man dressed in full camouflage gear said. "It's just a saying. Don't get so hot over it."

"Well, I don't like it. So stop calling me that." The woman turned and stomped into the storage hut. She began examining the machines.

The Man walked over to her. "Take a look at the yellow one over there. It's mine."

The woman followed his finger. She walked over and admired the power toboggan. "Very nice," she said. "Can I have one, too?"

"What do you need one for?" The Man asked.

"I like snowmobiles, too," she said.

"Then pick one."

"I want a Renegade, too."

"Do you have another Renegade?" asked The Man.

"I don't think so, but let me take another look." The man in the green snowmobile suit searched the rows. "No, but give me a couple of days—I can probably come up with another one." He gave The Man a serious look. "If anyone can find another one of these beauties, I can," he said, hooking a thumb back at his chest. "They're getting a little hard to come by—seems other people are going after them, too."

The Man grasped the woman by the elbow. "Come on. There's a shipment of guns coming in. I want you to help me check them over."

She smiled. "From the base?"

"No. We're still waiting for those military guys to come through. This is a shipment coming up from the States."

"Ammunition, too? Or just guns?"

The Man shrugged. "Let's find out, shall we?"

He led the way out of the domed hut back to a waiting truck. He turned. "You drive," he said. "You might as well get used to it. It's yours now."

The woman gave him a surprised look. "Why?"

"You know guns. You drive a truck well. And nobody will suspect you."

"Suspect me of what?" she asked—a perplexed expression on her face.

"Being a courier of guns."

"Courier of guns?"

"Yes. I need someone to run guns between the clubs. You're perfect for the job."

"That's kind of dangerous," she said with a tiny grimace.

"Maybe, but you'll do it, won't you?"

The woman simply stared, her mouth open.

The Man reached for her chin, grasping it firmly between his gloved fingers. He forcefully tipped her chin up and down in mimed consent. "Yes, sir. Of course, I will," he said in a falsetto voice.

The woman pulled her chin out of his hands. She walked around to the driver's side, opened the door, clambered in, and slammed the door shut. She started the engine. She waited, staring forward.

Chapter Seventeen

Switching Sides

MARTHA JUMPED out of the truck. She walked alongside the barn—it was too dark to run. She couldn't remember where she had left Matthew. She called out.

"Matthew?"

"I'm over here," Matthew said, his voice gravelly and low.

Martha ran to the sound of Matthew's voice. He was sitting on the ground, his body tilted to one side. She pulled his arm around her shoulders, grasped his wrist, wrapped her other arm around his waist, and dragged him to his feet. She nearly collapsed under his weight, but she held up. *He needs a hospital,* she thought.

"C'mon, Matthew. The truck is only a few feet from here."

They made it to the truck. Martha was struggling to get Matthew into the cab when three other men arrived. Without a word, they grabbed Matthew and lifted him into the cab. Martha ran around to the driver's side. She jumped in. The passenger door was still open. Matthew and the men were talking.

"I think we've gathered everyone that we can," said one of the men. Matthew nodded. "We got gas. Quite a bit. I sent three trucks back to the compound." Matthew nodded again. He slumped back against the seat. Martha leaned across Matthew.

"I've got to get him back to the camp," Martha said.

The man nodded. "I'm going to take your truck, Matthew. Okay?"

"Just leave it," Matthew said. "Damn thing is too hard on oil anyway."

"Can't leave it," the man said. "We've stacked the dead in the back." The three of them went silent.

Finally, Matthew waved his hand. "Go," he said.

Martha nodded a good-bye to the men. She shoved the truck into gear and turned it around. The wheels churned up snow and spit gravel as she raced by the house; she avoided looking at it. The truck's headlights illuminated the narrow driveway. She observed the tire tracks left behind by the other trucks. She felt her truck skid slightly, and she slowed down.

She glanced over at Matthew; he had fallen asleep. Either that or he was unconscious. She reached to touch his face, and then stopped. *No sense waking him,* she thought. He muttered in his sleep. Martha stared into the gloom.

The night was very dark, but the moon was bright. Even so, the monotony of the passing white lines was lulling her to sleep. Martha's eyes began to grow heavy. She shook her head—bad idea. For the first time in hours, she realized her head still hurt. She hadn't even checked the condition of her own wound. She flipped on the interior light. She glanced into the rearview mirror.

The woman staring back at her was a stranger. And yet—not. On one side of her head, the hair was matted with dried blood; her eyes were underscored with dark smoky circles; her face was drawn and pale, like an overly processed photograph. The eyes were familiar. "I look awful," she said aloud.

"You look pretty good to me."

Martha jumped. She glanced over at Matthew. "You're awake," she said. She turned off the cab light.

He groaned as he switched positions. "Yeah—but I wish I wasn't."

Martha smiled. "Sorry to hear that, but I'm glad you're awake. I was falling asleep."

"You're tired?" Matthew gave a small laugh. "Why ever would you be tired?"

She laughed, too. "No, I'm fine," she said. "My head hurts though."

"Yeah, I've been meaning to ask you about that. How did that happen?"

"I was in the truck, waiting for you to come back. Then I heard gunshots, so I ducked down. Men were trying to get into the truck, but I held the door handle. I let it go. Then this guy throws himself into the truck. He was shot. He told me he would shoot me. I don't know what happened, but everything seemed so weird. And so funny. I laughed at him. He got mad and hit me."

Matthew laughed out loud. "Well, that's one way to make you shut up." He grabbed his ribs. "Ow, it hurts to laugh."

"Very funny, Matthew." Martha's smile was genuine. It was so good to be bantering with Matthew. To have him sitting next to her. Alive. She glanced at him. He was still slouched against the seat, but his eyes were open. Slowly, he leaned forward. He picked up the pistol laying on the dash. He examined it.

"A Colt .45. One of theirs?" he asked.

"Yeah. The guy who hit me."

"That would have hurt. Where is he now?"

"I don't know." Martha said. "The last time I saw him was when I booted him out of the truck."

Matthew grunted as he leaned over and put the gun on the floor. He pushed it under the seat. "Was he still alive?"

"I think so," Martha said.

"You didn't shoot him?"

"No." Her tone was flat and final. They sat in silence for a few moments.

"You done good," Matthew said.

Martha looked over at him. "What?" She wrinkled her forehead at him. "I got a bunch of our guys killed today."

"No—we're alive, at least most of us, because of you." Matthew was looking at her. "You were a soldier today."

Martha smiled at the warmth that suffused her. "I stayed in the truck, Matthew. I never left." She turned her eyes back to the road, and then added, "It was the old man who took me out of the truck."

"The old man?" Matthew asked. He paused. "Wait a minute. The farm guys were talking about an old man with scissors in his neck." His voice rose slightly, "That was you?"

"Yeah. I found them in the bathroom. He—uh—well... he wanted to... keep me."

"Keep you?"

"I woke up in the house. I was lying on a table. He had a dog chain around my leg. I picked the lock."

"What?" Matthew studied her intently. "Did he do anything else to you?"

Martha turned back to Matthew and smiled. "Nope—he never got the chance." A memory of the old man screaming, and stumbling, and bleeding flashed across her mind. She shoved the image away. "What happened with Lenny?" she asked quickly, as she turned her eyes back to the road.

Matthew sighed. "He's dead." He shifted his legs and groaned again. "The gas tanks were an ambush, Martha. They were waiting for us."

Martha turned to him.

Matthew breathed a heavy sigh. "I thought the place was abandoned because there were no tire tracks in the snow." He paused. "I should have known better."

"They were using back roads," Martha said, "behind the barn. You couldn't have known."

"I should have known."

"Matthew—?"

He held up his hand to shush her. "Our men didn't have a chance," Matthew said.

Martha squeezed her eyebrows together. "*What?* I don't get it. They all had guns."

"There was no warning," Matthew said. He shrugged. "And there was no reason for us to be on hyper-alert—the place looked deserted."

"Then—why aren't you all dead?"

"Martha, they didn't want us dead." Matthew paused for effect. "They wanted us as *quarry.*"

Martha opened her mouth. Matthew held up his hand.

"I was coming down the path behind the tractor shed when I saw the farm guys attack. It happened so fast. One minute everything was quiet—the next they were attacking. Like a pack of crazy apes. No guns. They just started to beat on the guys. Hammers... chains... metal pipes... "

"What?" Martha asked, her voice rising in pitch. "Our men didn't get off a single shot?"

Irritation laced Matthew's voice. "They had men hiding in a lean-to near the tanks. They had it camouflaged with straw. More of them were hiding in the sheds."

Martha shook her head. "This sounds nuts—like some crazy movie."

"It's a game to them," Matthew explained. "One of them bragged to me about it. He told me they got bored with hunting deer. So, now they hunt people."

Martha's mouth hung open. Her mind flashed back to the old man. Revulsion filled her. "Hunt *people*?"

"Yes," Matthew said.

Martha expelled a small breathy sound from her throat. "But I don't get it. Why didn't our guys shoot?"

"They couldn't," Matthew said. "And don't look at me like that." His eyes hardened. "One second they were filling gas cans. The next, they were on the ground. They never had a chance." He took a breath and shook his head. "And I couldn't fire. Too much commotion. I couldn't tell where our men were."

"But I heard gunfire. When I was in the truck."

"The guys on watch," he said gravely. He shook his head. "They're in the back of my truck now."

"Oh," Martha said, softly.

They sat quietly for a few moments. Matthew stretched his legs and tried to find a comfortable position. He grunted and gave up.

Finally, she asked, "So what happened to Lenny?"

"I saw Lenny come out of a small building. He saw me, too. He was so close to one of their guys, he could have touched him. I pointed to my gun. The dumb bastard shook his head." Matthew took a long breath. "Then he did a Lenny thing—he walked out with his hands raised—with this sort of holy expression on his face. He went straight over to a guy holding a metal pipe. The guy looked at him, said something I couldn't hear, and then he whacked him across the head. Lenny went down. The guy whacked him a few more times. Gave him a kick. Lenny had to be dead after that."

"Where are Brad and Vince?" Martha asked. She was surprised at the tiny shot of joy she felt at the thought of Brad and Vince lying dead somewhere. She glanced at Matthew. "Are they dead, too?"

"I have no idea," Matthew said. His eyes closed. "I'm not sure who we lost today—" He shifted around again. Martha glanced at his bruised and bloodied face. She was stabbed by a pang of compassion. And regret.

A suffocating sense of responsibility exploded inside Martha. If she hadn't have left the compound, she wouldn't have been with Matthew, and he never would have known about the gas tanks. He wouldn't be hurt now. And the other men wouldn't be dead. Her throat constricted, and tears filled her eyes.

They're dead because of me, she thought. *Not you, Matthew. Me.*

She tried to make her voice steady as she spoke, "I'm sorry, Matthew."

Matthew said nothing.

Martha glanced over. He had fallen back to sleep.

□□□

THE FLICKERING light ahead made Martha slow down. She didn't have a walkie-talkie, so she had no idea where the rest of the trucks were. She supposed they were half way back to the compound. She was wrong.

As she got closer, she realized the trucks were parked at a trucker's rest stop on the side of the highway. A bonfire was blazing; silhouettes of men walked in its light. She slowed their truck and pulled in behind the last vehicle. She turned off the ignition.

Matthew awoke and grunted. He looked around, bewildered, and then asked, "Why are we stopping?"

"They're here," Martha said. She pointed out the window. "They've built a fire."

Matthew sat up. "Oh, they decided to stop and eat," he said. "Sounds like a good idea."

"Uh, Matthew—" Martha said. "You're badly injured. I think that maybe we should keep going. I can patch you up in the Medical Building—better than I can do it here."

"I'll be alright. I need to talk to them. Find out who survived." He clutched the door handle and pulled. The exertion made him grab his side and cry out in pain.

"Oh, for heaven's sakes—hold on, Matthew." Martha jumped out of the cab and went around to Matthew's door. She opened it and helped him to the ground. He winced when she brushed his side. "I'm thinking cracked ribs," she said softly.

Matthew righted himself. He swayed, and Martha reached to steady him, but he brushed her hand aside. He hobbled away, toward the fire. Martha watched him go. The hurt of rejection was acute—but she understood.

"Hey, it's Matthew," Martha heard some of the men call out. She smiled. They loved him. He was their leader. To them, he was flawless—perfect—in every way. Martha followed him.

A short way from the fire, Martha stopped. She stooped down and gazed at herself in one of the truck's side view mirrors. She touched her head. The blood had hardened her hair into a scabby mass. Intense blue eyes appeared in her memory. *Humph.* She turned around and walked toward the men.

The sound of an engine came from behind her. Matthew's military truck pulled up. *Dead bodies,* she thought. She wondered if Brad and Vince were part of the pile. Maybe somebody at the fire would know. She turned around and began to walk again. The sound of another vehicle coming up the road caught her attention and she turned back. She couldn't remember seeing another of their vehicles left behind on the farm. She squinted.

The truck pulled up—she didn't recognize it. The men behind her had seen it, too. They quieted. The man who had driven Matthew's truck was now standing in front of it. Martha saw the gun in his hand. She slipped behind the truck nearest to her, and squatted down.

She heard the sounds of men talking, but she couldn't make out the words. Truck doors slammed, and feet crunched through the snow. She shrugged. *No gunshots.* She stood up. She stepped out just as the men reached her truck. She looked up. Her eyes went wide. The man's grin was wider.

"Hi," he said.

"What the *fuck* are you doing here?" She took a small step back.

The blue-eyed man winked. "I'm one of you now." He pointed behind him. "He and I came to an agreement."

Martha watched as the other man came into view.

It was Brad!

He smiled a thin, challenging smile as he brushed by her.

Martha stood, her hands clenched at her sides. *Matthew would not stand for this,* she thought. *Matthew would throw them both out.* She stomped after the men.

She didn't want to miss the fireworks.

MARTHA SEARCHED for Matthew; he wasn't near the fire. Several men sat on logs. Others sat on small collapsible campstools farther back from the heat of the blaze. Some stood in small groups, and stared into the flames. The mood was somber as the men passed around plates filled with cooked bacon and home-baked beans, and loaves of rye bread spread with butter and honey. One of the men was passing around a large plastic container of jam-jam cookies. Martha accepted one. The heavy oatmeal cookie was thick and sweet, and the raspberry jam slathered in its middle was tart and delicious. They drank water from canteens. Some of the men were sipping coffee from enamel cups. Martha saw aluminum coffee pots steaming on small wire grates. The scent was inviting. Again, she scanned the crowd for Matthew.

Finally, Martha spotted him—he was sitting in a large camp chair about fifty feet from the fire. Several men had joined him. Their chairs sat together in a semi-circle. They were obviously holding some sort of meeting. Martha got up and walked over. She stood close enough to overhear the conversation.

"I think he showed good will, Matthew. That should count for something."

Another man nodded his assent. "He showed Brad where all the guns were. He could have just killed him."

Several of the men nodded and agreed.

"Brad says he helped to fill more gas cans, too," said another man.

A man to Matthew's right held up a few boxes of ammunition. "He turned over at least two dozen boxes."

Matthew touched his swollen face. He winced. "So, we're agreed then?"

The men nodded their approval. Matthew motioned, and one of the men got up. Martha watched as the man went over to Brad and the blue-eyed man. He said something. Both men followed him; the blue-eyed man was limping. They stopped in front of Matthew.

"We've agreed to let you stay," Matthew said. He held out his hand and offered it to the blue-eyed man. Martha's mouth hung open in shock.

What was he doing?

She wanted to rush in to the group and exclaim her disapproval, but something held her back.

"I appreciate it," the blue-eyed man said. He shook Matthew's hand.

Matthew turned to Brad. "Sorry about Vince," he said.

Brad mumbled something. Then he and the blue-eyed man made their way to a picnic table situated not far from Martha. Someone offered them plates of food. They accepted.

Martha watched them dig in. They chatted in between mouthfuls. Every so often, the blue-eyed man would look up and glance around as though searching for someone. Finally, he caught Martha's eye. Martha glared at him. He turned back to his food.

A few minutes later, he got up. He limped toward her. She saw the bloodstains on his jeans. Pity welled inside her, and she quashed it.

Why the hell am I feeling sorry for him?

"Aren't you going to congratulate me?" he asked.

"You son-of-a-bitch," Martha said. She began to walk away, but the man caught hold of her elbow.

"Let go of me." She yanked her arm away, sending the blue-eyed man off balance. He took a step backward, stumbled, and fought to regain his footing.

"Ow... " He held his own arms up in surrender. "Just being friendly," he said, his face twisted in pain.

"Why are you here?" Martha asked.

"I joined your group."

"Why?"

The man smiled. "Because I like you."

"Oh, bull," she said. "You tried to kill me."

"No, I didn't. I just hit you in the face with my gun."

"Why did you leave the farm?"

The man shrugged. "Nothing left there," he said. "Your guys killed most of the farm guys."

"That doesn't seem to bother you," she said.

"It does— And it doesn't. They were all kind of short on smarts."

"And you? Are you short on smarts, too?"

The man pressed in closer to her. "You know I'm not," he said. Martha looked into his blue eyes. They sparkled in the firelight.

"Then what in hell were you doing with them? They hunt people!" Martha lifted her eyebrows. "That's sick."

The man shrugged. "They were bored."

"It's cold-blooded," Martha said.

"I wasn't really into it," he said. "I liked the ladies."

Martha gave a small scornful snort. "A chip off the old block, hey?"

He gave her a puzzled look, and then, "Oh, that block—you mean my uncle. He's not really my uncle," he added quickly.

"Oh—that makes it okay then that he chained me like a dog."

"He had his issues."

"Issues?" Martha's voice rose. "Is that what you call it?"

"Well—he *had* issues," the man said. "Scissors in the neck kind of put a stop to them." His grin was slow and wide. "You remember that, don't you?"

Martha grimaced. She looked away in an effort to push the memory from her mind. "I don't trust you," she said.

He turned to her and smiled. "C'mon, give your old truck buddy a break." He nudged her. "I mean—look how much we have in common." He tapped his damaged head. "See?"

Martha's eyebrows went up. She felt a smile coming on. She struggled to hide it.

"Look," he said. "I played straight with your guys. I showed them where the guns were. I helped them carry away more fuel. And— I let Brad drive my truck," he said. The latter was said with mock enthusiasm. He glanced down at his leg. "And I did all that... wounded," he said, with a dramatic flourish of his hand.

Martha burst out laughing. She stopped and gave him a serious look. "Is it okay if I laugh?" she asked. "Or are you going to hit me again?"

The blue-eyed man smiled at her—it was a warm smile. "Look, I'm not armed," he said. "See for yourself." He held his coat open and he turned around, limping on his wounded leg.

The light caught the matted mess of blood and hair on the side of his head. Martha felt a twinge of satisfaction. "Does your head hurt?"

"Yeah—some bitch nailed me."

"Good for her," Martha said.

They both laughed.

Martha stared into the fire for a moment and then looked back at the man. "Give me your word that you won't harm me or anyone else in my group."

The blue-eyed man held up his hand. "I do so solemnly swear," he said. The smile on his face grew wider. "You have my word."

Martha gave him a half grin. She believed him. "Okay," she said.

"Thanks," he said.

"You're welcome."

Martha spotted an empty log near the fire. She went over and sat down. The blue-eyed man joined her. She watched as he lowered himself into a sitting position, his injured leg stretched out in front of him.

"What's your name?" he asked.

"Martha. And yours?"

"Meteor," he said. He had picked up a stick and was drawing it idly through the dirt.

"Pardon?"

"Meteor," he repeated. "As in shooting stars."

Martha laughed. "Really?"

"Yes," he said. "Really." He tossed the stick aside.

"Meteor?" Martha asked again. She paused. "You mean some woman pushed you out of her vagina, and then named you Meteor?" Martha began to laugh again.

"Yep."

"Oh, okay," she said. She rolled her eyes. "It's a stupid name."

"I like yours just fine," he said. "I actually knew what it was before I asked you." He smiled. "Brad told me."

Martha glared. "You talked to Brad about me?"

"Oh, yes," he said. "And it was all good."

"Bullshit."

He laughed. "I think he's hot for you."

Martha groaned. "Oh, for God's sakes."

"Brad's a great guy." Meteor laughed again. "And he *likes* my name."

Martha gave him a wicked grin. "A self-fulfilling prophecy, perhaps?"

"What do you mean?"

"Your name," she said. "Is it representative of your sexual ability?"

What am I saying? He's a total stranger. He tried to kill me. But the joking came easily, like she had known him her whole life.

"You mean hot and hard?" Meteor asked.

Martha laughed. "No, I meant that it looks good fired up, but it burns out pretty fast."

Meteor grinned. "Wanna give it a try?"

Martha smirked. "No, thanks. I'll pass." She paused for emphasis. "I hate disappointment."

Meteor reached over and cupped Martha's knee in his hand—he squeezed gently. His hand was warm. Martha gave him a warning look, but she didn't push his hand away. He leaned closer to her—his mouth next to her ear.

"I promise you," he said, "you won't be disappointed."

Martha shivered. She turned to face him. Their eyes met. "I'll take a rain check," she said. "I'm not in the mood to buy."

She lifted his hand from her knee, and dropped it into his lap. She rose from the log. "Besides," she said, "I'm married."

Meteor stared up at her. "But, I wasn't asking you to *marry me*, Martha."

"I know *exactly* what you were asking me, Meteor," Martha replied. She held her lips tight, and let her eyes do the smiling. She turned and walked away.

Martha stopped and turned back. "By the way, I have your gun," she said. "I kind of like it. I think I'll keep it."

Meteor smiled. "What are you offering in trade, Martha?"

"I promise not to hit you with it."

Meteor's eyes held hers. "That's nice of you," he said. "But I was really hoping for something a little more—um—sweaty."

Martha smiled. She turned her back on him, and walked away.

She had walked only a few feet when suddenly Brad was blocking her way. She eyed him. He was smiling. "What do you want?" she asked.

"I wonder what Josef will say?"

"None of your business."

"Oh— But it is," Brad said.

Martha shoved him out of the way. "Stay away from me." She paused. "Or I will hurt you."

"Scissors?"

Meteor had told him.

"Leave—me—alone." Martha walked away.

Josef.

"Oh, damn," she said, running her hands through her hair—the strands that weren't matted to the side of her head.

So much explaining to do.

Martha suddenly felt very tired.

□□□

The Winter Plans

"WHAT ARE your plans for next winter?" the tall man asked. He was leaning against a wall—inside a massive concrete warehouse—his booted feet crossed at the ankles. Many trucks were parked, their boxes filled with supplies from the last scavenging trips. One truck had just arrived; its box was loaded with guns. The tall man pointed at it. "Again, I see all these guns, but how are you going to feed the men who are going to fire them?"

The Man lifted two rifles from the back of the truck. "Some of these look like garbage," he said. He handed the long guns to a captain standing near him. "Where did this crap come from? These guns are in terrible condition." He reached deeper and pulled out two smaller hard black plastic boxes. "Are these locked?" He handed them off to the same captain. "Open these."

Two bikers jumped into the truck box. They began pawing through the weapons. "Some of these don't look too bad," one of them said, holding up two Colt .44 Magnum pistols. "They look almost new."

The Man took one of the handguns; he turned it over and examined it. "That's great. Two decent pistols out of a truckload of guns. We need new guns—guns that have been taken care of."

The Man turned back to the captain. "What happened to those military guys who promised us weapons from the base?"

"Haven't talked to them in a while."

"Well, find them. I want to know the status on those guns."

"I'll do that— right away, sir."

"Not right away," The Man said. "The day BEFORE right away."

"Yes, sir." The captain left.

The tall man cleared his throat. "You still haven't answered my question."

The Man stopped looking through the weapons, and stepped up to the tall man leaning against the wall. "So, what's on your mind?"

"The Gatekeeper."

"The Gatekeeper?"

"Yeah—Matthew's been storing goods for years. And from what I hear, his camp is always well-stocked for the winter."

The Man gave the tall man a smug grin. "You were his buddy once, huh?"

"Things change."

"Yeah. They certainly do."

Chapter Eighteen

The Homecoming

MARTHA GLIMPSED the lights of the compound—bright and inviting. She fought an urge to drive right by and, instead, turned the truck to the right. "We're almost there," she said.

Matthew stirred and looked out the window. "What time is it?"

"Nearly midnight," Martha replied.

"Long day," Matthew said. He pulled himself up in the seat.

"Are you feeling any better?"

"Some." He touched his side and winced. "And you? How's your head?"

"Aching, but I'll live." Martha pulled the truck into the compound's vehicle lot. She parked it, and turned off the ignition and the headlights. She turned to Matthew. "I didn't get my shopping done." She smiled.

Matthew smiled back. "Next week." He put his hand on the door handle. "Right now—I need to get to bed."

"Maybe you should go to the Medical Building."

"No. Just my own bed."

"Want some help?" Martha asked. She remembered him shaking off her hand back at the trucker's stop.

Matthew looked at her. "Yeah," he said. "That would be good."

Martha got out and made her way around to Matthew's door. The night had gotten colder, and she shivered—she needed sleep, too. She opened the door, and helped Matthew to the ground.

"God, I'm stiff," he said. He put his arm around her neck. She slipped her arm around his waist. They stood that way as they watched more trucks arrive.

A few men came over. "We'll take him, Martha." She released her grip on Matthew's waist and let the men take him.

"Good night, Matthew," Martha said. "I'll check on you in the morning."

She watched as the men helped Matthew to the gate. Heaviness hung in her chest. Something had changed in her world. Shifted. She knew the change was permanent. A tear made its way down her cheek and she wiped it away. Another fell, and another. She let them fall—hot rivulets down her face.

What did it matter? She didn't want to go forward; she only wanted to go back. The heaviness in her heart became an anvil.

Josef. What is he going to say? I ran out without a word. What will he say?

"You had better change your clothes."

Martha swung around at the sound of the man's voice. Meteor stood there, his arms folded across his broad chest, standing crookedly, favoring his sore leg.

"What?" she asked.

He pointed at her bloodstained jeans and parka, and then at her head. "Your husband is going to think someone tried to kill you." He winked.

"Oh, ha-ha-ha," Martha said. "Very funny."

Brad walked by and Meteor followed him. "Bye, Martha," Meteor called over his shoulder.

Martha stared after the men. She guessed that Brad was taking Meteor to the Men's Bunkhouse. She knew the blue-eyed man would be instantly popular. She gave a long sigh.

Meteor—what am I going to do with you? She smiled. She noticed that her spirit felt lighter.

Martha took a deep breath—she gave one last look at the open road, and then began the trek through the gate and across the compound to her cabin—where Josef would be waiting.

Martha walked several feet, paused, and then turned back. She sprinted to the truck, opened the passenger door, bent over, and reached under the seat. His Colt was still there. She picked it up, her hand closing over the butt; she enjoyed the feel of the textured grip and the way it fit her hand.

Mine, she thought. Nobody needed to know she had it, except for Meteor. She doubted he would ever mention it again. She checked the safety, and then tucked the gun into the front of her jeans.

Mine.

□□□

The Photograph

THE MAN left the bed and went to a chest of drawers on the far side of the room. He pulled on a drawer—it slid open with a squeak. He reached in and pulled out a brown leather case. He took it to a small table. He turned up a propane camp lantern. He opened the case.

He took out a thick pack of photographs. He smiled as he began to file through the images.

An old barn, frosted trees, autumn leaves, glass bulbs with tiny orbs of bokeh light, rusted machinery, wrecked cars—squashed and rusted with weeds growing all around, a black dog—running with a ball in its mouth, targets with neat holes—in and all around the bull's eye, candles, a field of red flowers, a fox, a feather...

"Are these your photographs?"

The Man turned with a start. The small woman was standing next to him. She was naked except for a thin gold chain around her waist. "Yeah." He stacked the photographs and began to stuff them back into the case.

The woman put a soft hand onto his. "Wait— I want to see them."

The Man let the photographs fall to the table. The woman scooped a few into her hands. "These are very beautiful." She picked up one—a Christmas scene—a house with colored lights and puffy white snow banks. "The colors are so vivid."

"HDR," he said.

"What?"

"High dynamic resolution. I'd take three or five pictures at different exposures and then combine them. That way I'd get all the detail in the shadows, the highlights, and the midtones. That's why the color is so intense."

"Oh." *She picked up another image. It was of a woman—a blonde with a wide smile filled with perfect white teeth. Next to her sat a little boy, also blond, also with a big smile.* "Who're these people?"

The Man grabbed the image from her hands. He put it back with the rest of the photographs, gave them a tap on the table to align them, and shoved the pack into the leather case.

"Nobody," *he said.*

Chapter Nineteen

Home Again

MARTHA REACHED the cabin and turned the handle. The door swung open. Josef was there. He scooped her into his arms.

"I was so worried," he said. Martha slumped into his arms. She tried to hug him back, but her strength had left her.

"I'm so tired, Josef."

He drew back, and pulled her inside. He reached behind her, pushed the door shut, and hugged her again. "I missed you." Josef pulled back and he looked at her. He touched her matted hair. His face darkened into a scowl. "What happened to you?"

Martha touched her head. "It's nothing. I'm okay."

He surveyed her clothing. "What happened?" he asked gruffly.

"It's not my blood," Martha said. "Would you heat some water? I really need to wash."

"Sure." He let her go. Martha saw the hurt in his eyes, and she gave him a tiny smile. She walked into the bedroom. She went directly to her trunk. She opened it. She pulled out her white dress and laid it on the floor. She pulled Meteor's pistol from her jeans, laid it on the dress, and rolled it up. She put the package at the bottom of the chest.

"Martha?"

She looked up. Josef was standing at the doorway. She closed the trunk. "I'll be right there."

"I just wondered if you wanted something to eat or drink."

"Tea would be nice. With honey. We stopped on the road. I had something to eat. But tea would be nice." She smiled.

Josef smiled, too. He walked back into kitchen.

Martha stared at the empty doorway. I'm so tired, she thought. She unzipped her parka and dropped it to the floor. It landed with a loud thump. She remembered her Browning was in the pocket. She picked up the coat, removed the gun, and dropped the coat back to the floor.

She stared at the gun by the light of the lamp. She hadn't noticed earlier, but she noticed now—blood stains on the handle.

His blood.

She laid the pistol on a small table, and removed her bloody jeans. Her mind wandered.

"Martha," Josef called.

Her mind tottered back. She pulled off her shirt, dropped it to the floor, and then removed her sport bra. She looked down at her underwear. They were bloodstained, too. She pulled them down, and stepped out of them. She kicked them away. She stood, naked, by the light of the lamp, her arms hanging at her sides. Tired. So very tired. She looked at her hands. They were dirty.

Martha shivered. She swayed.

I'm dizzy.

One of Josef's flannel shirts was lying on the bed. Martha scooped it up. She put it on. She pulled back the bedclothes. She crawled into the bed. Her world tilted again. She shut her eyes to stop the swirling.

Lie down and sleep. Forget. Just sleep.

Martha didn't hear Josef come into the room. She didn't know when he pulled the covers over her. She didn't feel his kiss on her forehead. She didn't know about the look in his eyes. She didn't know.

She slept.

□□□

THE DREAMS came one after the other. *So much shooting. So much blood. A man's hand. A man's face. A river. Trees. A forest filled with light. She was running. Something ran behind her. A cabin up ahead. She pounded on the door. Something came closer. She was running again. A man's hand in front of her face. A gun. The sound of a shot.*

Martha awoke with a start. She was sweating. Her heart pounded like an insane thing. Her hands seized the bed covers. She released them. The lamp was out. The room was dark except for the moonlight that spilled in through the window, showering the bed with light. She saw the dim outline of Josef's body next to her. His chest rose and fell with his soft snores. Martha watched him. Her head throbbed.

Josef stirred. He opened his eyes. He laid his arm across her pillow. Martha lay back down and snuggled in beside her husband. He drew her in, and she cuddled on his chest. He was warm.

Martha murmured and closed her eyes. The dream images came, but she willed them away.

A man's hand.

A man's face.

A face with blue eyes.

Martha squeezed her eyes shut.

No. Go away.

Please. Go away.

□□□

The Camera

THE MAN returned the leather case to the dresser drawer. He was about to close it, when he changed his mind. He reached further into the drawer and removed a camera. It was large, with a heavy lens attached. The woman came up behind him.

"Your camera?"

"Yeah. A Nikon."

"Oh. My sister had a big camera, too, but it was a Canon."

The Man made a derisive sound. "People who want to be photographers use Canons. But people who are photographers—they use Nikons."

"Really," the woman said. "My sister took some pretty nice shots." She reached out and touched the camera. "Sounds a lot like Ford versus Chevy to me," she said. "Aren't all cameras sort of the same?"*

"No." He removed the lens cap. "Go back to the bed," he said. "I'll take your picture."

The woman stopped and retrieved a nightshirt from the floor. She began to pull it on.

"You don't need that."

The woman turned—she held the shirt in front of her. "Uh—I'd rather not."

"I wasn't asking what you wanted." He twisted a dial on the camera body, walked over to the lantern, examined the camera, and made a few more adjustments. He walked around the room, turning on more lanterns. Then he walked toward the woman. "Get up on the bed."

The woman clutched the shirt to her chest. "I really don't want to."

"Trust me," he said. "I'm good at this. Women used to pay me to take their pictures—"

The woman took a small step backwards. The Man wrenched the shirt from her hands. "Without their clothes—"

The woman gave him a bewildered look.

He aimed the camera.

The shutter clicked.

And clicked.

And clicked.

Chapter Twenty

Stinky Boys

SNOW FELL. More snow fell. One grey day merged into the next grey day. Children got sick; they got well again. New babies arrived. People quarreled; they made up. Romances blossomed: some thrived; some died. Meals were made, and dishes got washed. Life went on.

Martha's appointment with the Discipline Committee never came to be; the subject didn't come up. There was always the sickly knowing smile when they passed on the compound—but otherwise, Brad left Martha alone.

Meteor had all but disappeared. The gregarious man became popular, quickly—an instant romantic hit with the females, and a fun-loving pal for the guys. Other than a wink or two, Meteor and Martha had limited interaction.

Martha's meetings with Matthew had become perfunctory at best. Business only—the intimacy was gone. It was as though the night at the farm had ceased to exist. At least, in Matthew's mind. Martha went to his cabin the morning after they had gotten back from the farm to check up on him, and then for a few mornings after that. But one morning, on her way to see him, they passed on the compound, and Matthew gave her only the briefest of greetings; Martha stopped checking up on him.

Martha attended gun practice without being asked, or being reminded. She took any gun handed to her, loaded it, and fired it. She ran into trouble only once. Matthew had ordered that all the women attend a new class: gun cleaning and assembly. Brad was one of the instructors...

"DON'T JUST tell me to do something—tell me why I should do it!" Martha's face flushed red. "Do I look like some sort of monkey to you?" She glared up at Brad. "I can think. And I do that a hell of a lot better than you."

Martha's tolerance level was reaching meltdown. Brad was exacerbating the situation with his condescending tone, not to mention the arrogant tip to his head. Martha hated him before; now she hated him more. She felt a pressure headache form—a dark thundercloud inside her skull.

"Leave it. I can do it," she warned Brad, as he tried to take the gun from her. Martha fumbled with the metal puzzle in front of her. She finally managed to get it apart. She took a tiny, white cotton patch, squirted on a bit of gun oil, and began to clean the gun parts.

"You don't use oil until after it's cleaned, dear," Brad said.

Martha turned hard eyes on him. "Back off. I've seen my husband do this a thousand times. Go help somebody else."

"Well, you're putting oil on top of dirty parts."

"I'll do it my way. You do it your way. Now get lost."

"My, my—we do have an anger issues, don't we."

"Get the hell away from me."

Brad smiled a saccharine smile and said, "Yes, dear. Of course. Do calm yourself." Again, he reached to take the gun.

Martha whacked his hand—with her fist, not the gun, although she had itched to hit him with it. Brad winced and made a swift motion toward Martha. She brought her hands up to protect her face. Another man's hand entered the combat zone. It was Matthew's.

"No," Matthew said, as he stopped Brad's fist from making contact.

"Leave her alone," he said quietly. "There are plenty of other women here who need your help." Matthew motioned to a table down the way.

Brad glared at him, but he dropped his hands to his sides. Matthew pointed to the group of giggling girls who were fussing with their weapons in a fruitless effort to get the handguns apart. Brad turned and walked toward the girls.

Matthew turned back to Martha. His look was tired. "Martha, can't you just give it a rest?"

"I hate that word."

"Which word?"

"Just."

Matthew laughed, and then sighed heavily. He slid in next to her. He picked up the barrel and held it up to his eye. "Hmm, look at that rifling. Not a scratch. Josef takes good care of this gun."

Martha sat back and watched as Matthew deftly wiped, oiled, and quickly reassembled the gun.

"I thought I was supposed to do that," she said.

"Are you thirsty?" Matthew asked, ignoring her question, as he handed the gun to her.

Martha nodded.

He pulled a can of Pepsi from his coat pocket and gave it to her. "We found a Pepsi truck on one of the last runs. They're a little flat, but not too bad."

Martha popped the tab; a small hiss escaped. She drank. "How're your ribs?" she asked.

"A little sore, but the pain doesn't knock the wind out of me anymore." Matthew said nothing more. He rose and walked away.

Martha watched as he wended his way across the room. He stopped near Brad. He leaned down to Brad's ear and said something. Brad scowled and said something back. Matthew shook his head, and then he turned away. Martha saw Brad's look: *Dark. Angry. Threatening.*

Suddenly, Brad called out, his voice loud enough to draw attention from everyone in the room, "She gets away with everything, Matthew."

Matthew turned around. "Don't," he said. "I run this camp. Not you. You got that?"

"Sure, Matthew, sure." Brad raised his hands in mock surrender. "I got it."

"Good," Matthew said. He turned.

Martha watched as Brad scanned the room. He caught her eye. He made a gun shape out his forefinger and thumb. He fired it. Then he smiled—a humorless grin. He turned his attention back to the giggling girls.

Martha stared at the pistol in her hand. Josef would want it back. He was going on patrol in an hour. Martha rose, nodded to some of the other women, and walked out the door.

That happened weeks ago—she hadn't interacted with Brad since. And... she was glad of it.

☐☐☐

MARTHA STARED out the kitchen window. She groaned. Twenty-eight days—to the day. Her head ached and her lower abdomen felt like it had been beaten with a cudgel. She winced as another cramp took hold. The pain of this one was staggering, and she had to sit down. Her mind drifted. She longed to stand in a shower under a stream of hot water that ran forever. It would feel so good on her aching back. She got up and looked out the window again.

One of the Gatehouse guards was heading her way. *Trouble,* she wondered. *Or, was it a medical issue?* She was on medical duty; she was always on medical duty. Martha never knew when a person would show up. And they did—at all times of the day and night—and with all kinds of complaints.

The guard reached the cabin and knocked.

"Come on in," Martha called.

A young man stepped in. "Hi," he said. "Matthew said I should come and see you." He lifted his boot. "Got a problem with my foot."

Martha motioned to the chair she had been sitting on. "Go ahead. Take a seat."

Martha studied the boy—dark-haired and very good-looking. As he shrugged off his coat, she wrinkled her nose. The boy stank. He removed his boot and sock. The smell was terrible.

"You need a bath," she said, as she examined his foot.

Foot fungus.

"No time," he said.

"Nonsense. It's all about priorities. You can make time to take a bath."

"Maybe on Sunday," he said.

Martha shook her head. "Listen, buddy. I can hardly bear being next to you. You really smell. I can't imagine a girl wanting to be near you."

"I have lots of girlfriends," he said.

"Really? And they don't mind the way you smell?"

"Guess not."

Martha shook her head. "Well, you are going to have to take better care of your hygiene. That's what this foot fungus is all about."

"So, what're you going to do about it?"

"You mean what are YOU going to do about it."

The boy guffawed. "Yeah, sure," he said.

Martha sat back. As cute as the boy was, he was annoying her with his flippant attitude. "Look," she said. "Don't expect me to take care of you, if you won't take care of yourself."

The boy glowered at her, but he remained silent.

"You need to heat water and wash your feet. EVERY night. Change your socks. Keep your feet dry in your boots." Martha took a breath. "The Supplies Building has hundreds of pairs of good socks. Ask Matthew to hand them out."

The boy still sat in silence. His arms were crossed.

"I'll give you something for the fungus. But you have to start taking better care of your feet," Martha repeated. "And the rest of you—for that matter." Martha went to a shelf. "Here," she said.

"What is it?"

"An antifungal cream. Just read the directions. And follow them." She took a bottle of apple cider vinegar from the shelf. She put it on the table. The boy laughed.

"What? You want me to pickle my feet?"

Martha gave him a tired look. "Yeah, sure, that's what I had in mind." She sighed. "Mix a cup of vinegar with a cup of hot water and soak your feet. Every night for 20 minutes. But wash your feet first. With soap. And then wash them after, too. Make sure they are perfectly dry before putting your socks back on."

The boy pulled on his sock and boot, and tied the laces. He shrugged on his jacket and stood. He took the tube of cream and the bottle of vinegar. He smiled at Martha. "The guys told me you'd try to boss me around."

"I'm not trying to boss you around, you dolt. I'm telling you something for your own good." She glared at him. "Girls don't like stinky guys."

He laughed and headed for the door. "They seem to like me just fine."

"We'll see about that," mumbled Martha, as the boy closed the door behind him. "We'll just see about that."

A cramp forced her to sit down again.

□□□

MARTHA LADLED stew onto their plates. The beef chunks were thick and fell apart with just a touch of a fork. Large cubes of potatoes and carrots sat in a puddle of rich, brown gravy. An aroma of garlic, rosemary, oregano, and onions filled the air. Josef leaned in and sniffed.

"I'm starving," he said. "It smells delicious."

Martha sat down across from him. They began to eat. She pushed a plate of thickly sliced sourdough bread toward him. A small dish of yellow butter sat nearby. Josef reached for both. He spread butter on his bread and took a bite. Martha watched as he chewed.

"Josef?"

"Umm... " he said.

"The boys stink."

"Huh?"

Martha put her fork down. She took a piece of bread, and spread it with butter. "They don't bathe enough."

"So— Do something about it," Josef said. He continued stuffing food into his mouth.

"Like what?"

"Uh... " Josef said. He took a long breath and then looked up at Martha. "Motivate them."

"With what?" Martha asked.

"There are two very powerful motivators for young men—" Josef said, a smile forming on his lips. "Food— and sex."

Martha laughed. "So, how do you propose I use those things to get the boys to take a bath more often?"

"I don't know. You figure it out," Josef turned his attention back to his plate. "You're good at that."

□□□

MARTHA CORRALLED the girls, the sexually active ones, and the good cooks. They had gathered in the Meeting House for a very secret meeting, as Martha had called it. She called the meeting to order.

"Do you girls like the way the boys smell?"

"Hell, no," said a buxom blond-haired woman with dual nose rings. "Paul makes me want to gag sometimes. But—well, you know... " she trailed off as the other girls roared with laughter. They knew. Paul was a catch, even if he did stink.

"Okay," Martha said, holding her hand up to quell the laughter. "But maybe there's a way to get the guys to bathe more often."

The girls eyed Martha suspiciously. One spoke: "What did you have in mind?"

"This can only work if we do this as a group. A united front," Martha said. "You understand?"

The girls nodded in unison.

Martha unfurled her plan.

☐☐☐

A WEEK later, a knock came on the cabin door. Martha rose, and opened it. Matthew was standing there.

"Hi," she said. Matthew didn't greet her.

"What's this the boys are telling me? You've told the girls not to cook for them? Or to have sex with them?"

"They shouldn't be having sex anyway," Martha said. "They aren't married."

"That's not for you to decide," Matthew said. "So what's going on?"

Martha pulled the door wider, and smiled. "Won't you come in, Matthew? I'll be happy to explain."

Matthew strode into the room. Josef glanced up from his Bible, and grinned. The two men acknowledged each other with a nod. Matthew stood near the sink, his arms crossed.

"So?" Matthew asked.

"Matthew, the boys stink. They don't bathe enough."

"They don't have a whole lot of time for baths, Martha."

"Everyone has time for a bath. The girls don't like how they smell. So we decided to do something about it."

Matthew's eyebrows dipped. "Those boys are some of my best fighters. I expect them to get what they need—whatever those needs are."

Martha pulled out a chair and set herself down. She motioned to another chair. Matthew shook his head. He waited.

"Matthew, you and I have talked about the overall good of the compound before. The smelly boys are a health hazard—foot fungus, infections, and who knows what other bacterial issues they carry. A regular bath will take care of all that." She wrinkled her nose. "Not to mention the smell."

Martha reached for a teapot, pulled a cup toward her, and poured tea. Matthew continued to glower. "Want some?" she asked.

"I'm still waiting," he said.

"I merely told the girls that if they wanted to get the boys to bathe regularly, they should withhold their favors. Like cooking. And sex." Martha smiled sweetly. "I think it'll work, don't you?"

Matthew glanced at Josef who was watching him intently. Josef gave a small smirk.

Matthew uncrossed his arms. He pulled off his cap and scratched the top of his head. He laughed. "Okay, you might have something there." Then with a lift of his chin in Josef's direction, "You in on this?"

Josef gave Matthew a wide smile and returned to his Bible.

Matthew pulled out a chair and sat down. "I'll have some of that tea," he said, with a smile. Martha poured. She pushed the honey jar toward him. He took a spoonful of the dark amber liquid and stirred it into his tea. He sipped. He smiled again.

"Come to think of it," Matthew said. "The guys have smelled a whole lot better over the past few days."

Martha raised her teacup in salute. Josef said nothing.

They sipped their tea in silence, and then Martha spoke:

"I want to go out, Matthew. We never made it to Hinton. You promised me that we'd go later. That was weeks ago."

Matthew drew back in his chair. He eyed Martha. He said nothing. Martha waited.

He who speaks first...

Matthew picked up his cup. He continued to drink his tea. He put his cup down and pushed back from the table. "Okay," he said. "Day after tomorrow."

Martha smiled.

A commotion outside the cabin door drew their attention. Martha and Matthew got up. He opened the cabin door. Several of the girls stood there.

"Anna's in trouble—" a dark-haired girl said. "She needs you."

Martha glanced at Matthew. She couldn't read his expression. She brushed by him, grabbed her coat from its hook, and her birthing bag. She shoved her feet into her boots. When she looked up, Matthew was already gone.

□□□

The Smart Woman

"SHE'S UP TO her old tricks again."

"What now?"

"She told all the girls to stop cooking for the boys. And to stop having sex with them."

The Man laughed—a low short sound. "Why?"

"She said the boys were unhealthy. They weren't taking enough baths—smelled bad."

"I can see her point there. Some of the guys around here could use a bath, too." The Man tapped his cigar ashes into a nearby ashtray. "Did it work?"

"What?"

"Did it work? Did the boys start taking baths?"

He gave The Man a perplexed, bemused look. "Uh—yeah—it did, actually."

"Smart woman."

"You think she's smart?"

"Not smarter than me. Certainly not smarter than you. But yes—she's smart."

"Never thought I'd hear you say that... about a woman."

"You ever sleep with a woman?" The Man asked.

"Sure."

"No, I mean **sleep** with a woman. Put your head down on the pillow and go beddy-bye."

"Yeah—sometimes."

A biker walked into the back room where the pair were seated.

"Hi, Brad," he said. Brad held up a hand in greeting. The Man motioned for the biker to wait. He continued:

"Then you had better realize that some women are smart—very smart. And you better not underestimate them." He paused. "Or, you could end up getting knifed in your sleep." The Man pulled his jacket aside and lifted his shirt to reveal a ragged scar across his ribs.

"Oh," Brad said. "I guess she is smart, now that I think about it. She should have gone before the Discipline Committee, but she got out of it."

"Discipline Committee? That sounds like fun."

"Used to be—until she arrived."

The Man gave his attention to the messenger waiting by the doorway. "What?"

"Carbines came in the last load," the biker said.

"Great," The Man answered. "Ammo, too?"

"No."

"See—that's the problem. Lots of guns, but no ammo." The Man stubbed out his cigar. "Let's go take a look." He walked toward the door, and then turned. "You coming? Or do you need more time to ponder smart women?"

"Nah—I'm coming."

"By the way, "Where's Vince?"

"Dead."

"Dead? What happened?"

"Some wacko guys on a farm near Edson. Back in December. A really crazy bunch—they hunt people for sport."

"Hunt people for sport?" The Man echoed. "Huh—never thought of that before. A big waste of time, but exciting, I'll bet."

Brad followed The Man out of the room.

Chapter Twenty-One

Father and Son

ANNA WAS CRYING, but her sobs were weak. Martha could see the girl was exhausted. Ruth stood near her; she looked grim.

"Nothing seems to be working, Mom," Ruth said. She had a wet washcloth and she wiped Anna's face with it, as she spoke. "She's been in labor for so long."

"How long is long?" Martha asked.

"Hard labor—maybe a couple of hours. But she started mild labor yesterday—about this time. She never called anybody for help—until just a little while ago."

"Is the baby in position?"

"Yes, but he's not moving down. And he went quiet." Ruth said.

"Is she dilated?"

"Yes, but every time I think the head is coming down—it stops."

"Hung up on the cervix?"

"Could be."

"Have you tried her in different positions?"

Ruth nodded.

"And you can't see the head?" asked Martha.

Ruth nodded again. "What do you want to do?"

Martha went over and sat down next to Anna. The girl's face contorted as her belly stiffened and she entered into another hard contraction. Martha breathed along with her. The contraction let up and Anna fell back on the bed. Martha marveled at the girl's fortitude.

"Anna?" Martha pushed sticky hair from the girl's forehead. "Anna?"

"I can't do it anymore," Anna squeaked. "I'm so tired." Tears rolled down her face.

"Anna, if you can't push your baby out... " Martha paused and took a breath. "I could try doing a caesarean. But you know what that would mean." Martha's voice was low and steady. "You'll have to make a decision. If I am to save your baby, I've got to do it soon."

Anna shook with sobs, and her face contorted again as another contraction gripped her. She stifled a scream. She rode the contraction, and fell exhausted to the bed. Her breathing was shallow, and her face was ashen.

"Anna... " Martha said. "Anna?" The girl opened her eyes.

"Take the baby," Anna said, her voice a low raspy whisper.

"You know what you're agreeing to, Anna? You know we don't have the proper equipment."

"Yes," Anna said. "Take the baby. It's okay."

Martha motioned to Ruth. "I put together a kit for this—you know where it is."

Ruth nodded. She grabbed her coat and ran from the room.

Martha turned back to Anna. She wiped the girl's face with a washcloth. "You're one of the bravest people I've ever met," she said. "I just think you should know that." Her eyes warmed with a soft smile.

Anna went through several more contractions, each one sapping her strength. Finally, the door to the bunkhouse burst open. Martha turned. Ruth came rushing in. Matthew was right behind her.

"Mom," Ruth said. "Matthew wants to talk to you before you do the operation."

Martha looked at Matthew. The expression on his face surprised her. "What is it, Matthew?"

"My mother had a hard time giving birth to me. My sister-in-law had a hard time giving birth to her son, too. He paused, and then added, "Apparently—large heads run in our family."

Martha's eyes widened. "What're you saying?"

"It's mine, Martha—the baby's mine."

He was the father—Matthew was the father!

A shock like a shard of ice shot through Martha. It settled into the pit of her stomach. Questions tumbled through her mind, but she didn't ask them.

Anna had begun to cry softly.

"It was a one-time thing," Matthew said, hurriedly. He turned his head from side-to-side as though he were trying to escape the truth. "I met her months ago—well, nine months ago, while scavenging in Edmonton. One thing led to another, and... " He thrust his hands into his jacket pockets.

"So, why are you telling me this now?" Martha asked.

"Because I know my mother and my sister-in-law managed to give birth without a caesarean— Maybe Anna can, too."

"She's exhausted, Matthew."

"Give her a chance," he said.

Martha turned to Anna. "That's up to her."

Anna was going through another contraction. She could barely rise up from the bed. Martha watched the girl's face contort with the pain. Suddenly...

"That's it," Martha said. She clapped her hands. "Anna. Look at me. We're going to get this baby out of you. And you're going to help me." Martha waved to Ruth.

"No caesarean. C'mon, let's get her into a better position. On her side. One of you— Hold her leg up."

Martha grabbed the bottle of disinfectant and squirted the gel into her hands. She got on her knees in front of Anna.

"Okay, Anna, this is going to hurt. But you can do this. On your next contraction, I'll push your cervix aside, and I want you to push. With everything you've got, Anna." Martha looked at her. "Everything, Anna!"

Anna nodded. The contraction came. She screamed as she bore down. Martha cried out.

"That was good, Anna! You did good. His head moved. Harder on the next one." Anna fell back on the bed.

Martha glanced back at Matthew. He was white, but he had remained. She motioned to him. "Sit behind her on the bed," she said. "Let her rest against you. And then when the contractions start, let her push up against you."

Anna moaned.

Matthew kicked off his boots and climbed onto the bed. Anna's belly tightened, but she lay still. For a moment, Martha thought she might not be able to go through with the contraction. Suddenly, a growl erupted from the girl, and she sat up. She gripped her knees. Matthew pushed up behind her. Anna's face was set, and she leaned into the contraction. Martha reached for the lip of the cervix, and pulled it out of the way.

Anna screamed.

Martha let out a whoop of joy—the baby's head was coming through. "You did it, Anna. You did it. Just a few more pushes now."

The contractions came, and Anna pushed. Soft dark hair atop a small orb presented itself, and then drew back.

"Okay, "Martha said, "On your next contraction, you might feel the ring of fire. You know what to do, Anna. You've told a dozen other girls what to do. Don't push through. Hold back just a bit. Let your tissues relax." She turned to Ruth. "A little more oil."

Ruth nodded, as she poured a thin stream of warm oil from the bottle.

The next contraction hit. Anna screamed and struggled. The baby's head appeared, but didn't push through.

"Good girl," Martha said. "Now go for it. *Think* your baby out."

Anna needed no encouragement on the next contraction. With a tremendous growl—primal and determined—she bore down. The baby's head erupted. Martha checked for the cord. It was fine. A couple minutes later, the baby spurted out in a splash of water, and flopped into Martha's waiting hands.

"You have a son," Martha said, with a quick glance up at Matthew. Martha touched the umbilical cord; it was still pulsing. But the baby wasn't stirring.

She held one of its tiny feet and flicked it. Nothing. She flicked it again. "A towel," she said. "Quick." She laid the baby on the bed and began a massage. "Come on, little one," she prayed. "Come on." The baby remained quiet.

God, please help me.

Martha studied the tiny face. She gently squeezed the baby's nostrils to rid them of any mucous. "Come on, little guy. Your Momma worked really hard to get you here. Breathe."

Martha took the towel and swabbed inside the baby's mouth. Then she bent over him and covered his mouth and nose with her mouth. She breathed five soft puffs of air into the infant. His chest rose and fell with the breaths. She pulled back. Then she heard Ruth cry out.

"He's breathing, Mom! He's breathing."

Martha breathed, too—a huge sigh of relief. She wrapped the little boy in a towel, and handed him to Ruth. "Take care of the cord," she said.

Martha moved off the bed. She knew Ruth would be able to care for Anna now. She glanced up at Matthew. He still sat behind Anna who was now holding her baby. Matthew reached over and touched the baby's open palm with his finger. The baby reflexively grabbed tight. Matthew gave a start. Then he smiled.

Martha reached over, stroked the baby's head, and kissed Anna on the forehead. Anna looked up and smiled. "Thank you, Martha."

Martha smiled. "Oh, no—dear one—nothing to thank me for. You did all the work—I just did the catching."

Anna smiled again. The baby began to cry.

Martha looked away from the baby and back to Matthew. He was looking at her. Their eyes met and held.

He nodded to her.

Martha nodded back.

□□□

The Visitor

BRAD STOOD patiently in front of The Man's desk. He had just been summoned. He had come at once. Now he waited.

"So, what's happening over at Matthew's place?"

"Lots of new people arriving," Brad said. "Plenty of babies, too."

"Any problems?"

"No—the camp's got midwives."

The Man gave him a pained look. "I meant with the camp."

"Oh." He scratched his head. "Not really—Matthew has us training all the women in firearms. Some of them are really good."

"And your personal favorite?"

"Who?" Brad looked blank for a moment, and then scowled. "Oh, you mean Martha. Yeah—her, too."

The Man stroked the Persian cat curled in his lap. "If you dislike like her so much, do something about her."

"I can't—she's got the guys wrapped around her little finger. Matthew lets her get away with everything."

The Man laughed. "I really must meet this Martha some day."

A biker came to the door. He caught The Man's eye. "Sir?"

"In a minute," The Man said.

"So, what's next on your agenda?" Brad asked.

The Man's eyes flickered up—he studied Brad for a moment, before answering. "More arms coming in. The last truckload that came across the border was a bunch of junk. But we should be getting some from the military base—if those guys ever come through."

The tall man entered the room. The Man gave him a nod. A petite brunette came in next; she turned to the biker who was fidgeting as he waited for The Man's attention.

"I'll tell him," the woman said. The biker left the room.

"Tell me what?" The Man asked, his tone sharp as he addressed the woman.

"You have a visitor," she said simply.

"Who?"

"A woman—she says she knows you."

The Man stood abruptly. The cat leapt from his lap. He glanced at the tall man who was now lounging up against a far cabinet.

"Go," The Man said to Brad.

Brad turned and left the room.

The Man addressed the woman. "Tell her to come in."

The woman didn't leave immediately. Instead, she gave The Man a searching look.

"Go!" he said. The woman left. He turned to the tall man. "You leaving?"

"Who is she?"

The Man stared briefly. "My sister," he said.

"Your sister?"

"Not my blood sister—kind of adopted."

"Kind of adopted?"

"Yeah. We met online. Years ago," The Man said flatly.

"Your sister—"

"Hello, little brother."

The tall man turned. A slender blond woman stood in the doorway. She was smiling. He appraised her—long legs encased in tight blue jeans, full chest enhanced by a v-necked blue sweater, slender arms and neck, and thick honey-colored hair caught up in a ponytail. He turned back to The Man. "Your sister?"

"Yes." The Man gave him a hard look of finality.

The tall man gave the woman a small bow as he passed her. The woman raised her eyebrows slightly. She smiled again.

"Who is that?"

"Don't pay any attention to him," The Man advised.

"Why?" the woman asked. "He's got a really interesting face."

"Steer clear of him."

"We'll see," she said.

The Man caught her eye with his. "You'll regret it," he said. Then, "Why are you here?"

"You mean I can't come to say, hi?"

"Sure, but I know you better than that? What do you want?"

"I'm bored."

"Bored?"

"Yeah. I'm thinking I would like to get involved."

"Involved? You mean here?"

"Yes. Why not?"

"Women don't get involved here."

"Really? What about the sweet little thing outside?"

"She's different."

"Oh." She walked to the desk, reached over, and pulled the lid off the candy jar. She took a small handful, popped the colored sweets into her mouth, and chewed. She swallowed. "So—tell me—who's the tall drink of water that just left?"

"An ex-buddy of the Gatekeeper."

"Really? An old friend of Matthew's. Well, that makes him even more interesting."

"You're pissing me off now."

"You're very easy to piss off," she said. "Don't be so cranky."

"Don't tell me how to be."

The woman walked around to the other side of the desk. She walked behind The Man's chair; she ran her long arms down his chest, and kissed the top of his head. "Take it easy," she said. "Don't get so upset."

The Man swiveled his chair. He put his hands on her waist. The two exchanged a look.

"Uh-uh," she said. "We've talked about this before. Sister status only."

"And what if I decide to change that?"

*"Then—" she cocked her head, "—you might have my body, but you would lose me **forever**." She caressed his face with soft fingers. "And then where would you be?"*

A man clearing his throat caught her attention. She looked up. The tall man was lounging against the doorjamb.

The woman dropped her hands to her waist; she pushed The Man's hands away from her. She took a small step backwards. The Man swiveled his chair to face the door.

"Hi," she said, as she directed a small smile filled with promise at the man near the door; it lit up her green eyes. "My name's Marion. What's yours?"

"Virgil." He bowed slightly. "Nice to make your acquaintance."

"Yours, too," she said. She ran a hand along the side of her face as she spoke, pushing a few stray hairs back behind her ear.

The Man glowered at Virgil. He moved his head from side-to-side, and mouthed the word, "No."

Virgil smiled.

Marion smiled, too.

Chapter Twenty-Two

The Angry Dad

"THE BABY is in great shape," Martha said, as she hung her parka on the nearest coat peg. "He's so cute—and so much hair."

"How's Anna?" Josef asked.

"Oh, she's pretty sore. But she's tough," Martha replied. "She'll live to push out another baby."

"By the way, I asked one of the new boys to come and see you," Josef said. "City kid. No more sense than I once had." Josef picked up a handgun and began disassembling it. "He literally doesn't know how to break an egg."

"Oh, joy—" Martha said. "Why me?"

"Matthew suggested you." Martha gave Josef a disdainful look, but his attention was back on his gun.

"Thanks—I guess," she said. Then, "I'm going with Matthew today. He said we're leaving close to noon."

"I know," Josef said. "He told me. I'm taking over the compound while you're gone." He examined a gun barrel. "Think you can stay out of trouble, this time?"

"I'll be fine, Josef." She walked over and kissed him on the head—on the balding patch that he insisted wasn't there.

"Wear your vest," he said.

"Okay."

THE MORNING dragged on. Martha scanned the yard outside her kitchen window; bright spring sunshine had turned dirty grey snow into dirty grey puddles. The kids were having a ball. Stomping, and splashing, and slipping. Some were covered from head to toe with mud. Martha smiled. There would be some mad moms tonight, but the days when she might have cared were long behind her now. Martha heard a knock and she turned.

"Come in."

A boy with red hair, the color of carrots, walked in. His face was sprinkled with freckles, and when he smiled, broad white teeth loomed from his mouth. Martha tried not to giggle, but a MAD comic book came to mind.

"Hi. Josef sent me."

"Of course, he did," Martha said. "But why are you here?"

"Cookin'," the boy said.

"Oh," Martha said. "Do you like eggs?"

"Yup. I like scrambled eggs."

"Okay then—come over here and help me break the eggs," Martha told the boy.

"I don't do no cookin'. That's woman's work."

"Well, on this compound if you want to eat, you'll have to break a few eggs," Martha said. An edge rose in her voice.

Obstinate little shit. She wanted to break something all right. She looked at her watch. *Would noon never come?*

She stared at the boy. "C'mon."

The boy resisted, but he joined her near the sink. "So what do I do?"

"You've never cracked an egg before?" Martha asked.

"Nope."

"Never?" she asked incredulously.

"Nope. I told you—it's woman's work."

Martha gave him a surprised look. "Most of the best chefs in the world are men," she said. "How can cooking be woman's work?"

"Probably all fags," was his curt response.

Martha barely suppressed the chuckle that erupted from her. She cleared her throat.

"Hmm, that's not true—but think what you like." Martha knew how difficult it was to turn a mind that had been set like concrete toward certain ideas. And she didn't have the patience to try. "Okay, take the egg and crack it on the edge of the bowl."

The boy did so, mashing the egg horribly and mixing shell with white and yolk. "Yuck!" He dropped the crushed egg into the slop pail near his leg, studied the goo on his hand, looked around, and then wiped the mess on his pant leg.

"That was too hard," Martha scolded. "Like this," she said, giving an egg a quick, sharp tap on the edge of the ceramic bowl. She divided the resulting two halves and plopped the egg into the bowl. "See, it's really quite easy. Try it again."

The boy picked up another egg. This time he struck concisely, then separated the two halves as he had seen Martha do, and dropped the egg into the bowl.

"You're a fast learner," Martha said with surprise. She wasn't sure, but she thought she saw pride wash over his funny face.

"I'm a PK," he said. "Home-schooled—we tend to be smart."

Martha hid another grin. "P-K?"

"Preacher's kid," he said.

"Oh," Martha said. "Here's another." She handed the boy an egg still warm from the chicken coop.

He cracked the egg and began dropping its contents into the bowl. "Yuck! What's that?" he said, pointing to a tiny red droplet in the egg.

"Oh, that's no big deal," Martha said. "It's just blood. It means the egg has been fertilized."

"Fertilized?" The boy looked stricken. "I ain't eating no egg that's been fertilized. That's like being a cannibal."

Martha couldn't hold back—she burst out laughing. "No, you'd have to be another chicken eating a chicken to be cannibalistic. And even then, only humans who eat other humans can be cannibals."

"Well, I'm still not eating blood. The Bible's against it. Just ask my Dad."

"Ah," Martha sighed.

No, dear boy. I don't really want to ask your dad—anything.

She had known many men like his father—too many—insecure men who hammered their beliefs into their children's heads—both the important beliefs—and the petty ones—especially the petty ones.

Martha reached for a small bowl and scooped up the offending egg from the rest. "No problem," she said. "But you should know that people once paid extra money for fertilized eggs."

"Don't care—I'm not stupid like them." The boy turned, walked over to the kitchen table, and sat down. Martha gave him a corrective look.

"Where are you going? You think these eggs are going to cook themselves?"

The boy got up and came over to the hotplate; Martha handed him a skillet. "There's the butter," she said. The boy placed the pan on the burner and turned on the propane. He reached for the butter when a pounding on the door caused both of them to jump and turn.

"Hey," a masculine voice called, "I know you're in there."

Martha gave the boy a questioning glance. The boy looked sheepish, maybe even a little afraid.

"My Pa," he said. "I gotta go."

The door burst open. A tall man with hair as red as his son's stormed into the room. The boy rushed to pull on his jacket. "Coming, Pa," he said. He tried to duck by his father, but the man caught him by one sleeve.

"What're you doing here, kid? You missed your Bible studies."

Martha stood with her mouth open.

"Matthew—uh—Josef... told me to come here."

"Is he your father now?" the man demanded.

"No, sir. But he said I needed to learn how to cook." The boy winced slightly. "So that I could go out on guard duty."

"Cook? That's women's work." The man clenched a fistful of the boy's jacket and drew him up close to his face. "You do as I say. You got that?"

The boy turned pale under his freckles. Martha watched as he struggled for words—the right words that would appease his father. Nothing came out of his mouth.

"That's enough," Martha said. "Let the boy go. He did nothing wrong."

The boy's father raised his head and leveled a stare at Martha. "Stay out of our business," he said.

"This *is* my business," Martha retorted. She took a step toward the man.

He shoved the boy aside. "Get home," he said. "Your mother is waiting for you."

The boy scurried out the door. The father drew the door shut, and he turned. Martha watched as he crossed the room to her. He stopped barely inches away from her face. He put both hands on the counter on either side of her, and he leaned in.

"I know all about you," he said. "And I don't like you." The man was so close that Martha could see his nostril hairs. "I don't want you teaching my boy your whoring ways."

Martha pulled back in shock, and her mouth went dry. Fear stirred in her belly, but she continued to stare back at the man. She raised her hands to push him away, but he grabbed her wrist and twisted it back.

"Ow," she cried. "Stop it."

The man smiled—the same awful smile she had seen before. On the face of another man—a dead man. Familiar cold steel rose up inside her.

"STOP it," Martha growled. The man increased his pressure. "STOP! You're going to break my wrist." She tried to pull away, but she only succeeded in encouraging the man to twist her wrist tighter. She screamed.

"Shut up," he said.

In an instant, Martha brought up her knee directly into the man's groin. He grunted, and let her go. Martha tried to run for the door. The man grabbed her by the shirt and wrenched her back. She saw his fist come up, and she ducked to the side. It whizzed past her.

"What the hell is wrong with you?" Martha yelled. "Are you nuts?" The fist was coming at her again. This time she launched herself forward, pushing the man into the kitchen table. As he hit the table, he grabbed Martha's arm. He pulled her to him, and then righted himself. He raised his hand again, but a sound from the door stopped him.

"No!"

The man looked up.

"I wouldn't do that if I were you."

Martha gasped, and whirled around at the sound of the voice.

It was Meteor.

Meteor strode over to the man—he took him by the upper arm. "We can do this nicely," he said, "or we can do this the hard way. You pick."

The man glowered at Meteor, but he shook his arm out of Meteor's hand, tugged at his lapels to straighten his coat, and went to the door. He turned, and shook his finger at Martha. "You watch your step around my boy," he said.

Meteor was at him in an instant. He grabbed the man's finger and bent it back into an unnatural position. "Let me tell you something—this woman is a friend of mine." Meteor gave the man's finger an extra push. "Don't threaten my friends." He gave the finger another push, causing the man to let out a yelp. "Do we have an understanding?"

The man nodded, vigorously. Meteor released his finger and the man fled from the cabin. Meteor watched him go, and then he turned back to Martha.

"Now—" he said, "I believe you and I—my dear—have a date." He smiled, and his blue eyes lit up with mischief.

Martha smiled, too. With relief, and something else. Something warm. Something welcome.

"Yes," Martha said. She glanced at her watch—it was noon. "We do."

She went to the chest, searched around, and pulled out her vest. She found the extra protection pads and slipped them inside the vest. She pulled it on, and did up the Velcro straps. Meteor watched her actions with great interest, but he said nothing. He stood with his arms folded across his chest. When Martha had finished, she turned to him. He was smiling.

"Why that's a fine ensemble," he said. "And just what shoes and accessories go with that sporty little number?"

Martha laughed. "I just need my parka. Thanks."

Meteor lifted a parka from a hook on the wall beside him. "This one?" he asked.

"Yes." Martha took it from him.

"Nice," he said. "We'll try to keep this one clean." Martha studied him for a moment.

"Clean?" she asked.

"Yes—no bloodstains," he added. Martha grinned. He opened the door. "C'mon, Matthew is waiting."

"Wait a minute—you're going, too? To Hinton?"

"Wouldn't miss it," Meteor said.

Martha hid her smile.

She followed him out the door.

□□□

The Kidnapping

"IT'S TIME."

"Are you certain?" The Man studied the book on his desk—he didn't look up. He made some notations.

"Matthew's taking the women scavenging all the way up to Hinton. Josef's been left in charge."

"Good. I'll finally get a chance to meet the husband of the famous Martha." The Man flipped a page in his journal. "You got a hate on for him, too?"

"He's not one of my favorite people," Brad said, "but he's okay."

"So, you'll find it hard to kill him then?"

"Why will I have to kill him?"

"Because I'll ask you to," The Man said. He looked up. "You got a problem with that?"

"No—not at all."

"Good." The Man looked back down as he spoke. "What about Cindy?"

"What about her?"

"You fond of her?"

"Sure—sort of."

"We won't need her any more after tonight. Kill her."

"Is that really necessary?"

"You want her blabbing about you after Joseph is gone?"

"No, I guess not." Brad turned to leave.

"Wait a minute—did you say Hinton?" asked The Man.

"Yeah," Brad said.

"Some friends of mine are heading down through there. They're supposed to attend the captains' meet-up. One of them is my cousin."

Chapter Twenty-Three

The Attitude Adjustment

METEOR LOPED across the yard ahead of her. "Hey," Martha called. "Wait up." Her vest, with its heavy inserts, made jogging difficult. She continued to walk.

Meteor headed for the small group of men standing near the Gatehouse. Martha watched him join Matthew and Josef. Jonah and Simon stood nearby, attentive—their hands resting on their hip holsters. She couldn't hear them, but she watched a hurried exchange take place. Matthew and Josef looked past Meteor to her, and then back to Meteor. Heads nodded and the men moved in unison. They strode across the compound. Josef broke from the pack and ran up to Martha.

"Are you okay?" he asked.

"Yeah, I'm fine. Where are you guys going?"

"We're booting the guy."

"Really? I'm coming, too."

"No, you're not," Josef said, putting a hand on her shoulder. "Stay here, Martha." His look was firm.

"Okay," she said. Martha stepped back.

Josef turned and ran to join the other men. Martha watched the men make their way down the corridor of cabins. They turned right and disappeared down the path leading to the RVs at the back of the compound. "Posse," she thought, with a half grin.

"What's going on?" Ruth asked. She was coming from the Women's Bunkhouse; little Mary was attached to her hand. Martha told her:

"You know the kid with the bright red hair?"

"Yeah."

"I think Matthew's booting his dad off the compound, right now."

"Why?"

"He attacked me in the cabin."

"Attacked you? The kid? Or his dad?"

"His dad. Matthew sent the kid over to get some cooking lessons and his dad freaked. Didn't want me teaching his kid."

Both women turned to the sounds of men yelling. Martha held her breath and waited for the sound of gunshots. None came. More shouting. A woman screaming. Both women hurried toward the sound. A woman crying. More shouting. A man's voice. Angry.

As they neared the path the men had taken, Martha saw Matthew and his posse returning. The kid's father was between them. He was shouting. Profane things. Martha raised her eyebrows. As they got closer, she saw that the shouting man's hands were bound in front of him—white electrical ties. Jonah and Simon walked alongside, each gripping one of the man's forearms. The man continued to curse.

"Keep shouting like that," Matthew said, "and we'll gag you, too."

"What about the Discipline Committee?" the man demanded.

"We're all members of the committee," Josef said. "You have our decision."

"That's not the way it's done," the man roared. He balked, and planted his feet like a stubborn pony, but Simon and Jonah dragged him forward. The man shot Josef a look. "She's a whore, ya know. Your precious wife. Just ask Brad."

Martha felt the blood rush from her face—her eyes widened.

Oh, God, don't let him say anything more.

Panic enveloped her like a choking grey cloud. She held her breath. The man was staring at Josef.

Josef raised his hand like a general halting his troops. The men stopped walking. He moved in front of the shouting man, balled his fist, and swung. The man's head snapped back and then it flopped forward. Jonah and Simon struggled to support the sudden dead weight.

"Prick." Josef shook out his fist.

Matthew's mouth hung open.

Meteor laughed. "That oughta shut him up for a while."

"Damn," Josef said. "I haven't cold-cocked someone in a long time." He rubbed his hand. "Hurts."

Meteor grinned. "Yes—I'm sure our friend would agree with you." The men laughed. They continued up the path to where Martha and Ruth stood.

Martha let out a ragged breath.

Would he stay unconscious?

She had no idea what Brad had told him, but anything Brad might have said would be designed to make her life miserable.

Please let him stay unconscious, God. Please. Just until he's away from here.

"What're you doing, Dad?" Ruth asked.

"He's been exiled," Josef replied. "We knew he was a loose cannon when he first arrived. He just proved that this morning when he attacked your mother."

"No committee meeting?" Ruth leveled her gaze on Matthew.

"Meteor saw him attack her," said Matthew. "That's good enough for us. Unprovoked attacks by a man on a woman on this compound... " He shook his head. "Not acceptable." He looked at Martha and pointed toward the Gatehouse. "We're leaving right now. You ready to go?"

"Sure," Martha said. "What're you doing with him?"

"He's coming with us," Matthew said. "Taking him to Hinton. Let him cool off there. Give him a chance for an attitude adjustment."

"If he survives," Meteor added with a wide grin.

□□□

THE CAVALCADE motored westward along the highway. Dirty grey mounds of rotted snow peppered the road, but otherwise the highway was passable. And, other than a few stops to remove broken branches that had been torn from trees during winter storms, the trip went smoothly.

Martha was riding shotgun beside Matthew. Meteor and another man were in a big GMC truck just behind them. The bound redheaded man was in Meteor's back seat. Four other trucks followed behind, each carrying two men and one woman. The women were Martha's suggestion. *Better shoppers*, she had said with a grin. Matthew had agreed.

Matthew's military vehicle was back on the compound. Too hard a ride on the backside, he had said, and they weren't expecting any rough roads—so the massive vehicle was unnecessary. Martha had been very relieved.

Empty jerry cans and siphoning hoses rattled around in the trucks' cargo areas; the men expected to find abandoned vehicles along the way—maybe some still had fuel.

Matthew's truck carried extra supplies: guns and ammunition, tents, sleeping bags, water, and food. All drivers and their sidekicks carried walkie-talkies that squawked regularly.

Martha glanced at Matthew. At the last minute, he had invited another man to ride with them, putting an end to Martha's plans for conversation. She listened as the two men droned on about guns, ammunition, and truck engines. She leaned up against the window and fell asleep.

□□□

THE WALMART was easy to spot, just off Highway 16. It sat on one end of a large enclosed shopping complex; a Safeway grocery store anchored the other end. Cars and trucks of all sorts littered the parking lot, looking very much like their owners were just inside the store.

Matthew slowed. He scanned the lot for movement. After a short conversation on his radio, the trucks split up—their drivers began a creeping prowl of the parking lot. Things seemed very quiet.

Martha twisted impatiently in her seat. She wanted to dash from the truck. She laughed inwardly at herself. Before the Change, Josef joked she could find a Walmart anywhere. And she could. But what he didn't find funny was how much time she could spend in one. Ambling. Browsing. Josef just wanted to get in, and get out. But not Martha—shopping and browsing to her was like sipping fine wine. It had to be done slowly—and with great attention.

The old excitement grew inside her. Scavenging was as much fun as shopping. *No—it was better*, she thought—no infuriating line-ups at the cash registers and no aggravating cashiers with dull eyes, and even duller attitudes. She willed Matthew to hurry and park the truck.

Martha reached under the seat and pulled out several scavenging sacks—neatly folded giant blue Ziploc bags. As she bent, a memory surfaced. This was the same truck she had driven away from the farm—the very same one out of which she had kicked Meteor. She couldn't resist a broad smile. His gun was still wrapped in her dress back home—she hadn't touched it since.

Martha fingered her shoulder holster—her Browning was there. She grimaced and tugged at the heavy vest strapped to her back and chest. She considered taking it off and leaving it in the truck. She began fiddling with the straps.

"Don't even consider it, Martha," Matthew said. He wasn't looking at her. Martha's mouth hung open in a half smile of surprise, her eyebrows lifted. She let the vest be.

Matthew pulled onto the sidewalk several feet back from the store's front entrance. Martha began a mental inventory—the first place she would hit with her team of shoppers: the pharmacy. Diapers and menstrual pads topped her list. However, medical supplies, sunscreen, herbal supplements, and socks were just as important. She looked at Matthew. He nodded his approval, and she jumped from the cab.

Meteor had pulled up behind them. He left his truck and came over to Matthew's window.

"What do you want to do with our foul friend?"

"Is he conscious?"

"Oh, yeah," Meteor said with a grin. "Not for the whole trip," he added with a wink. "But he's awake now."

Matthew's lips curled into a quick smile. "Keep him under truck arrest until we're finished. We'll drop him off when we leave."

"Where?"

"I think we'll just leave him here."

Meteor nodded. He returned to his truck. He gave instructions to the armed man who had been riding with him. The man nodded back.

"Son-of-a-bitch," the bound man yelled through the driver's open window. "Let me out of here." The armed man glanced back at the irate man, and then leapt out of the truck. He closed the door and stood nearby—gun drawn. The man finally quieted. He glared at his captor from where he sat imprisoned in the truck's cramped back seat.

The women ran up to join Martha. All were carrying the same collapsed plastic bags. Matthew stopped them. "Show me," he said. They proved to him they were armed. He nodded.

"Get these trucks around to the back," Matthew said. "No sense advertising our presence." Drivers jumped back into the cabs, and the trucks began to move.

Four men stood near Matthew; he split the group, motioning to one of the men to join him. The men stepped inside the store's smashed front doors—the five women followed.

Huge puddles of dirty water, illuminated by a long sheet of sunlight, lay where piles of snow had once been. Except for the entry area, the store was very dark. The men snapped on their headlamps. Martha had discovered the tiny lamps in a sporting goods store—months back—before she joined Matthew's group. He had nodded and smiled when she presented him with the box containing dozens of the lamps and their elasticized head belts. Now, all scavengers carried one as part of their standard equipment.

Martha pushed the switch on her own headlamp—both tiny bulbs lit up. *Batteries*, she thought. She would look for some after scavenging the pharmacy. She waited. Matthew gave the thumbs-up signal, and the women walked farther into the store.

Martha glanced from side to side; she finally located the pharmacy, off to her left. She waved the women in close to her. They giggled. For most of them, it was their first scavenging mission, and they were excited. She shushed them. She pointed toward the men as they disappeared into the gloom. Her eyes sought and found Matthew. He motioned his okay again.

"C'mon," Martha said. She sprinted through the dark toward the pharmacy, the other women close behind her—whispering excitedly. She turned and shushed them again. Properly chagrined, they quieted.

The pharmacy aisles had been ravaged. Debris was scattered everywhere, as if a bomb had exploded. Vitamin bottles littered the aisle, cast away as having no immediate value. Martha mentally noted them; she would check them later. She had already established a good supply of multi-vitamins and chewable Vitamin C at the compound, but the stocks needed replenishing.

Reading glasses were strewn across the floor, too, their lenses cracked from the weight of booted feet. Empty boxes, that had once held protein bars, sat squashed up against the bottom edges of shelves—their bars long vanished into some desperate mouth.

Sticky puddles of goo pockmarked the floor—vestiges of cough medicine, soda pop, protein drinks, and baby lotion—according to the bottles that Martha and the women kicked out of their way, as they explored.

Martha set two of the women to gathering goods from the shelves. "You'll get a chance to scavenge just for fun later, but first we get the serious work done," she said. "Stuff your bags full. Get the bags out to the trucks. And don't mess around."

"Aw," said one older woman. "I wanted to get some new clothes for my kids." Martha shot her a look.

"I told all of you before you left that you'd do as I told you to do. If you have a problem with that—" She stared at the offending woman, as she spoke. "—then get back to the truck. Otherwise, do as I say."

The woman lowered her eyes. She shook out one of her blue sacks and began to fill it. Martha gave her a last look and then continued to assign tasks to the other two women.

Martha crooked her head at the youngest woman, a heavyset girl with wide shoulders and a thick waist, indicating she join her. The pair went behind the pharmacy counter—the place where druggists once doled out their magic pills. It was a worse mess than the outer area.

Martha found a few drugs she recognized as being helpful—painkillers and penicillin—she put those into her plastic sack. She found a pharmaceutical reference manual on a bottom shelf and stuffed that into her bag, too.

She noticed a door off to the rear of the cubicle. *Receiving door*, she thought. She wound her way through the garbage on the floor and pushed her way past stacked cardboard boxes of medical supplies. The room on the other side of the doorway was more like a hallway—it was even darker than the store. Martha suspected there had to be an outside entry door. She looked at the full bags in her hands. *No sense dragging these around back there*, she thought.

Martha left the drug area; she handed her full bags to the older woman—the one she had scolded earlier. "Take these to the truck. At the back," she said, as she pointed. The woman accepted the bags and left without a word. Martha turned and noticed another woman stuffing her bag with large tins.

"What the hell are you doing?" Martha whispered gruffly, grabbing the woman's arm. The woman's hand held a round tin of baby formula. "Put that junk down."

"It's for the baby," the woman said. She swept her arm over the shelf, "Look—lots of cans."

"And then what?" Martha asked.

The woman looked confused and hurt. She pointed to her belly. Martha knew she was expecting her first baby.

"What will the baby drink after you run out of formula?" Martha asked—her voice low and accusatory.

"But I don't get it—" the woman said, irritation tinting her voice. "Won't all this formula be good to have?"

Martha huffed. "I don't have time for this," she said. She turned away, and then turned back again. She spoke in a husky whisper "Look—if a baby is allowed to nurse naturally from its mother, its suckling will generate all the milk it'll need. As it gets bigger and needs more milk, it will suck more. If you supplement... " she paused, "... if you give the baby canned formula, it doesn't suck as much, making the mother's milk production go down. If the baby is fed enough formula from a bottle, the mother's milk will dry up completely." Martha stopped and studied the woman's face to see if anything was registering with her.

The woman stared up at her, blankly, and then, "Oh, I get it now. When the formula runs out, and if my milk is gone, the baby will have nothing to eat."

"Bingo," Martha said.

No kidding. Idiot. Glad you figured it out.

Martha stooped down and eyed the back of a middle shelf. She reached in and dragged out two packs of disposable diapers for newborns. "Take these instead," she said as she tossed the packages to the floor in front of the woman. Cans fell and rolled as the woman unloaded the offending formula from her hands.

"And this, too." Martha grabbed a lone plastic box of wet wipes and dropped it into the woman's now-empty hands. She turned. "I'm going to look for more medical supplies."

"Okay," the woman said. In the next second, her eyes grew wide.

The growls of engines—motorcycle engines—made both women freeze.

□□□

The Rats

THE CAPTAINS pulled into Edmonton from across the province. Many were die-hard fans of The Man's quest for domination, having attended the Vulcan gathering, but many—the new and uninformed—were not. They saw his plan as a potentially flawed concept that would ultimately lead to their enslavement... or their deaths. They wanted to believe, but they were a cautious breed—and they weren't buying.

Many of the smaller groups of Crazies—the more successful of the self-governed bikers—were content to continue marauding, thieving, raping, and killing—where and when it suited their purposes. Planning long-term for their survival proved more of an annoyance than a practical idea. They wanted what they wanted—NOW. They had made it clear that they objected to The Man's plans. And especially, to his control. Their allegiance was not forthcoming. Not without a very good sales pitch.

"How are you going to handle their resistance?" Virgil asked. He and The Man were once more meeting in a secluded back room of the bar in the west side clubhouse.

"It's not going to be easy, but we've got our operations up and running—province-wide. And we've got powerful allied chapters of Crazies to the west and to the east. The top men are spread out evenly, and as long as they're offered their own fiefdom—their own feudal lord identity—complete with women—I think we can maintain their loyalty. It's in their own best interests to protect their territories and keep the peace. I think that in itself will quell any resistance."

Virgil nodded.

The Man watched the scotch swirl silkily around the inside of his glass. He took a swallow. "I've been thinking about putting some new members into leadership. I think Brad might make a good sergeant-at-arms. What do you think?"

Virgil studied his hands for a moment, and then clapped them down onto his kneecaps. "Sure, why not? He's got drive, determination, and hate—plenty of hate. He might make an excellent choice."

"Glad you agree, because when I have the president captains assembled, I'm going to make him my sergeant-at-arms."

"You know he's got his sights set on Matthew's compound, right?"

"Yes, I know that. But isn't that something you'd like control of?"

"Maybe there was a time— But not anymore. Give it to Brad—with my blessings. I'll stick with battle. That's more my style." Virgil picked up his glass and raised it in the air. He watched as the rich, amber liquid caught the light. "When's the meeting?"

"A few weeks. We haven't reached all the captains. They'll need time to get here."

Where's it going to be held?"

The Man reached over and clinked glasses. "Right here." He took a drink. "By the way, I'd prefer if you'd stay quiet that night—a best kept secret, as it were."

"You mean stay away from the clubhouse?"

"Yes—I'll get together with you after the meeting. Brief you then."

"Sure." Virgil shrugged.

"Good. Oh, and another thing—we're planting the information about Brad being promoted. It might draw some fire, but that way we can see who is trustworthy among the newer captains. Jealousy has a way of flushing out the rats.

Virgil raised his glass in salute. "Here's to flushing out the rats," he said.

The Man eyed him and lifted his own glass in response.

"Yes." The Man said. "The rats."

Chapter Twenty-Four

The Shopping Adventure

THE WOMAN dropped the wet wipes as her hand went to the gun on her hip. The noise of engines grew louder. Martha laid a hand on the woman's arm. She gave the woman a warning look.

Martha was sure the bikes were just outside—behind the door she had noticed a few minutes before. Deep rumbles made the floor tremble beneath her feet. Her breath came quickly, and her palms became sticky with sweat. Suddenly, the engines shut down. She heard voices—men's voices, but she couldn't make out what they were saying.

The other woman backed toward her, holding her gun. Its dark metal barrel was pointed toward the sound. Martha heard a sharp metallic click as the woman pulled the gun's hammer back.

"Wait," Martha whispered.

The other two women crept over and crowded next to her. Their eyes were wide with terror. The heavy girl's forehead was damp with sweat. Dread filled Martha, too.

Where are the men? Where's the gunfire?

Then she remembered—she was at the front of the store; the trucks were now at the back. Martha touched her chest. She felt the hardness of the vest beneath her fingers. She thought of Josef. Then, she heard the screech of a door being opened. Adrenaline flooded her veins, and her heart hammered.

They're coming in!

Martha ushered the women out of the pharmacy area and back into the store. She scanned the darkness—her headlamp's beam jerked erratically as she looked for cover.

Someone had pulled several clothing racks filled with women's dresses into the middle of the main aisle. The women followed Martha as she scurried over, hunkering down inside the clothing. Martha snapped off her headlamp and motioned for the women to do the same. They held their breath as the bikers entered the back of the pharmacy. Flashlight beams cut the darkness.

Where is Matthew? Where is Meteor? Hadn't they heard the engines?

The guttural guffaws of men echoed down the darkened aisles as they stomped through the pharmacy and into the store.

"What are we supposed to get?" one of them asked.

"Stuff for girls."

"Stuff for girls? Like what?"

"I don't know—perfume and shit, I guess."

Martha heard the men shuffling around—muttering, rummaging through products, and dropping things to the floor. She tried to estimate how many men had entered the store—she guessed two or three.

"Whoa, yeah," one yelled. "Jackpot."

"What did you find?"

"Tampons."

"Tampons?" There was a pause. "Yeah, I guess that's a good idea."

Another man called from farther down in the store. "Hey, how about sexy stuff?"

"Check the women's clothing," said one of the men. "There's some dresses over there." His flashlight shone in Martha's direction. The women shrank back between the clothing racks.

Martha's eyes had become accustomed to the darkness; she peered through the clothing, and up one of the aisles. The shadowy figure of a man made her gasp. He came closer. He was tall, heavy-set, and his beard was long and unkempt. His hair was shoved up beneath a leather cowboy hat; greasy tendrils swung loosely near his face. Martha bit her lip. She knew these men were Crazies, but how many of them were there? And where were the rest of them?

Like playing chess in the dark, she thought.

"I'm gonna check the pharmacy to see if there's any good shit left," the cowboy said.

Martha heard him tromp away. Moments later, she heard pills spilling onto the counter; empty pill bottles clattered to the floor. *Asshole*, she thought. She wished she had gotten to the pills first.

Martha searched the gloom for Matthew and the other men. Instead of seeing one of the compound men, she saw another biker coming down the aisle. The light from his flashlight bounced rhythmically, as he walked.

He's going to see us.

"We've got to get out of here," Martha hissed to the women crouched near her.

"There's nowhere to go," one woman whispered back. She pointed. Another dark figure was moving up the aisle.

"Not much here," called the cowboy from the pharmacy.

The women jumped as one of the other bikers answered back. He was on the other side of the clothing racks. They were trapped. They looked at each other—their eyes wild with fear.

What now? Run? Fight?

Martha fought the panic rising in her chest. The women began a slow retreat through the clothing racks. Their guns were out and aimed forward.

"Hey, we've got enough," called the cowboy. "Let's get out of here."

The man in the aisle next to the women spoke. "I want a gun magazine... The Man likes them... it'll be a present."

"Get serious," the cowboy shouted back. "The Man doesn't need presents from you. He's got plenty of magazines for his guns. Besides, you're not gonna find gun magazines in a Walmart."

Martha heard the man nearest to them grunt. "I meant a book, ya dumb fuck. You know—a paper magazine."

"Come on—let's go," called another biker. His words were mumbled. "I found a box of potato chips over here," he added. "They're good."

"I'll damn well look if I want to," the biker nearest Martha, retorted. "The Man likes presents. My brother told me." He paused and then added, "The Man's my cousin, ya know?"

The man? The man?

Martha looked at the other women, her eyebrows raised in question. One of the women mouthed, *"Who's the man?"* Martha shrugged her shoulders. She stared ahead into the darkness.

Martha heard the heavy, nasal breathing of the biker nearest them. A memory flashed through her mind of the old man's face—too close to hers—the sound of his breath in her ears. Her fingers tightened on her pistol as a familiar coldness suffused her.

Martha's heart thrummed in her ears. She had stopped creeping backward, unsure of what to do next. A sound drew her attention. She turned.

A muffled cry, a small scuffle, a soft thud, and then the sound of something heavy hitting the floor.

The younger woman had disappeared. Martha strained to hear anything that would tell her what had happened to the woman. Suddenly, the woman was behind her. She grabbed Martha's arm and motioned off to her left to a darkened doorway with double swinging doors— about 100 feet away. Martha looked. They would have to run for it.

Martha hooked a thumb in the direction of the biker on the other side of the aisle. *"What about him?"* she mouthed. The woman drew an index finger across her throat. Martha's eyes widened. *"You?"* she mouthed.

The woman drew her eyebrows together and shook her head vigorously. *"No,"* she mouthed back.

"C'mon," said the cowboy. "We've still got 4 hours to ride." He paused. No answer. "Come... on," he said again—louder. "You're not going to find a gun magazine here anyway. If you gotta have one—we'll hit a bookstore in Edmonton. But I'm telling you— The Man ain't gonna give a rat's ass about your damn present."

Martha heard the cowboy shuffle around—pill bottles rattled and cracked beneath his feet as he walked into the main store, away from the pharmacy, toward the front door. The younger woman pulled on Martha's arm and pointed. The women peered out from between the racks. They watched as the cowboy disappeared up the aisle. The man searching for the gun magazine was nowhere in sight.

Please, Lord. Please, Martha prayed. They waited.

A few minutes later, Martha heard the sound of hangers being shifted back and forth; she realized the dresses were being examined. One by one, dresses dropped to the floor. She covered her mouth. She had to make a decision, and make it soon, or they would die.

Where was Matthew?

Martha glanced back to the double doors—they were barely visible in the darkness. She tugged on the heavy girl's shirt. Martha stabbed with her finger in the direction of the doors. The women nodded their understanding. Martha knew that one of them could get shot, but she had to take the chance. She held up her hand and counted down, using her fingers. When her hand became a fist, the women crept out of the clothing racks, one-by-one. Keeping their bodies low—they followed Martha.

It took a lifetime, but the women reached the double doors. In a moment, they pushed their way through. Martha scanned the gloomy area; it was illuminated slightly by light entering through the crack beneath a heavy metal door off to her right. She ran to the door. The women followed. Martha turned the handle, but it wouldn't budge.

"*Key,*" she mouthed. Her eyes searched the wall.

Wouldn't they keep a door key nearby? For deliveries?

A commotion inside the store made the hairs rise on the back of Martha's neck, and her stomach grew sick with fear. The other women's eyes were saucer-wide with terror. They all turned and stared at the double doors. That's when Martha noticed the pharmaceutical supplies—boxes and boxes—still sheathed in protective, thin plastic wrap.

"What the hell?" Martha heard one of the bikers exclaim. She could only guess at what he had found. The youngest woman, once again, pulled a finger across her throat. Martha screwed up her face in question, but a second voice drew her attention.

"*What - the - hell?*" It was the cowboy's voice this time—a pointed and vicious sound. She understood that sound—it meant violence. Martha felt her skin crawl and her tongue tasted a metallic tang.

Martha motioned to the women and mimed twisting a key in a lock. She pointed to the nearby wall and then to a large desk. The women moved quickly, feeling along dusty side shelves. The women gasped when the cowboy's angry yell cut through the darkness again.

"Somebody killed Curt." A pause. "His throat is cut." Another pause. "When I find the guy who did this—"

Martha envisioned a smile spreading like thick oil across the man's face—a terrible, slow smile dotted with dark teeth. She could almost smell the evil.

Then something caught her eye; she breathed a sigh of relief.

Their salvation hung from a wide blue lanyard imprinted with the name of a drug company. She hissed at the women, pointed, and grabbed the key. She ran to the door, fumbled, missed the keyhole, and tried again. The angry voices rose and fell in volume.

Martha tried again, inserted the key, and turned it. She turned the door handle, and nearly vomited when the door hinges squeaked. She and the rest of the women bolted through the opening. Martha closed the door behind them.

She looked around. Huge Harley-Davidson motorbikes, their wheels coated in mud, were parked several yards away. Near the pharmacy door, she guessed. Four bikes. That meant four riders. She mentally calculated the voices she had heard inside the store. Four. Now there were—three. Good, she thought.

"Stupid Crazies," the heavy girl said.

The women turned right and fled along the front of the store.

□□□

MATTHEW WATCHED as the man crept towards him—he recognized him as one of his own. The man was breathing hard.

"Did you see the women?" Matthew asked.

"No," the man whispered. He held up a knife close to his eyes, and examined it—dark patterns covered its blade. He had a small t-shirt in his other hand. He scrubbed at the blade with the shirt, turned the knife over, examined it again, and then shoved it back into its sheath on his belt. "But I think they know we're here," he added, as he tossed the shirt to the floor.

"What does that mean?" whispered Matthew.

The man shot him a knowing look. Matthew gave a small low sound of understanding.

"Nobody's shooting," the man whispered back. "Where are the other guys?"

"Meteor is going around to the front," Matthew said, his voice low. "Half the guys are still out back with the trucks. The rest of us are scattered around the store. There's four bikers." He glanced at the stained shirt on the floor. "I guess there's three now."

"I turned around—" the man explained. "He was right there. He saw me. I had to take him out." He paused. "I slit his throat."

"Great—I guess you didn't hear me about not killing any of them." Matthew stared into the darkness. "Wish I knew where the women are."

"I somehow think they're fine," the man whispered. "They're with Martha."

"Yeah."

A man's yell broke the silence. Both men jumped.

"I think they just found their dead friend," Matthew said. "Let's go."

"Where?"

"Pharmacy," Matthew said. "Other side of the store."

The pair followed the sound of the man's rantings. Their eyes had grown accustomed to the gloom, and they slipped soundlessly through shelving and clothing racks. Matthew looked up an aisle where a large dark form lay in a heap—it wasn't moving. He held up his hand. He heard the angry biker swearing farther down the aisle, closer to the front entrance.

"He could get himself killed making all that noise," the man whispered to Matthew. Matthew nodded. He tried to catch any sign of the women. No movement.

Suddenly, two bikers loomed in the aisle directly in front of them. Matthew glanced at the man next to him. He nodded. They launched themselves.

They each hit a man, knocking them to the floor. The men went down with loud grunts. They tried to roll away, but found their movements blocked. Matthew knelt near the man he had taken down. He pulled his pistol and pressed it deeply into the flesh under the biker's bearded chin.

"Shut up, or you die," Matthew said, his voice low, but crystal clear. He looked over. The other biker was frozen, too, a pistol pressed to his cheek. In one smooth move, Matthew felt for the man's gun belt, and pulled a pistol from its holster. The other man did the same. They both rose to their feet. Matthew dropped the biker's pistol into the canvas sack slung over his shoulder. He took the other biker's gun, and put that into his sack, too.

"Get up," Matthew said. "Slowly." His pistol was steady, aimed directly between the biker's eyes. "Say one word—and we will shoot you." The bikers got up. They eyed Matthew, but they didn't speak. "Move," Matthew said. They began to walk—in the direction of the angry biker at the front of the store.

The irate cowboy turned, and recognized his friends. "Hey—" He stopped when he caught sight of Matthew and the other man. And their pistols. He dropped his hand to his holster.

"Don't," Matthew said. "Just don't." He motioned toward the front doors. "Turn around. Walk." The cowboy hesitated. Dark figures moved in from the side aisles.

"Want some help?"

Matthew glanced over. Meteor and two other men joined them. "Get his gun," Matthew said. "This is all of them. Another one is dead back there." He motioned with his free hand. "We haven't frisked the other two."

"We've got it," Meteor said. He and two other men moved forward and patted the bikers down. "Hey, boys, got some nice junk on you?" He used electrical ties to secure the men's hands. Meteor gave them a push. "Party's over." He smiled. "Actually another one is just about to start."

"Where are the women?" Matthew asked.

"They're just fine," Meteor said over his shoulder. "Outside—waiting for you." Meteor smiled. "You didn't think Martha would let anything happen to them, did you?" Meteor began to sing—a sixties tune: "Born to be wild... " as he pushed the men toward the door.

Matthew grinned.

Outside the store, several men rushed over when they recognized Matthew. The women stood clustered on the sidewalk. They watched as the men escorted the three bikers out of the store. Martha studied Matthew— *No blood*, she thought. *Good.*

Martha caught Meteor's eye—he was watching her. Martha smirked. He blew her a kiss. She slapped the airy gift out of the air. They both laughed.

She motioned to the rest of the women. They followed her as she marched up to Matthew.

"Shit, that took you long enough," she said. Her eyes sparkled and her lips pulled into a soft grin. Matthew grinned back. She waved the women forward.

"Where are you off to?" Matthew asked.

Martha looked back over her shoulder. "I came to shop—I'm going shopping." She stopped. "If you can spare a few of these guys, I could use their help." She thought a moment. "Send them to the side door with a truck. We'll let them in—there's a ton of medical supplies back there."

Matthew motioned to two of the men. "Give her a hand." To another group he said, "You guys get the gas cans and..." he waved toward the vehicles in the parking lot, "... start siphoning." And then, "Keep the diesel fuel separate. Somebody screwed up, last time." He paused. "And get those trucks back up here."

Martha was at the store's front doors when she stopped and turned. "By the way, you might want to ask these guys about somebody they call— 'The Man,'" Martha added.

"The man?" Matthew asked. He looked at the three captives, and then back at Martha.

"Ask them," she said. "I'm going shopping."

Matthew turned and motioned to Meteor.

"Yeah, boss?"

"Pick one. Let's take him for a walk."

"For a little chat?" Meteor asked, grinning.

"Yeah—a chat."

Meteor walked up to the three men. Their sullen eyes studied him as he circled them. He eyed the cowboy and a tall skinny man with bleached blond hair and a full beard. He grinned as he reached past the pair to another man standing just back of the other two.

"C'mon, my friend," he said. "You got some 'splaining to do." He grabbed the shorter man by the shoulder of his leather jacket. The man resisted, and pulled back.

"I'm not your best choice for this," the biker advised. "I'm really not all that talkative."

Meteor hauled the man forward and planted his face a few inches from the biker's nose. "Let me be the judge of that," Meteor said. "Walk." He gave the biker a hard push and the man stumbled forward.

"Who in hell are you guys anyway?" asked the cowboy.

Meteor stopped and turned. "You speaking to me?"

"When The Man finds out— You assholes are dead." The cowboy shook his head slowly and seriously. "That's his cousin lying in there." He indicated the store with his chin.

"Oh, how rude of me," Meteor said. He walked over to the cowboy. "Allow me to introduce myself." He drew back his knee, and drove it into the side of the man's thigh. The man grunted as his leg gave way, and he fell to the pavement. Meteor bent over him.

"My name is Meteor. So pleased to make your acquaintance. Now— shut the fuck up. I'll let you know when we want you to talk."

Meteor straightened and walked back to Matthew. He paused and turned. "By the way, this—" He pointed at Matthew, "—is Matthew. People call him the *Gatekeeper*."

"You're the 'Gatekeeper?'" The skinny biker's eyes widened.

"The Man wants you dead," groaned the cowboy.

"Me?" Meteor asked.

The injured cowboy was still on his knees, but he lifted his head and spoke, "No," he said. He lifted a finger and pointed at Matthew. "Him."

Meteor made a move toward the two bikers, but Matthew laid a restraining hand on his arm. "Never mind. Let's talk with this guy."

Meteor grabbed the third biker's arm. He smiled—a wide smile that made his eyes sparkle. He began to sing again, the same sixties tune he had been singing before: "Born to be..." He followed Matthew across the parking lot.

The Distraction

"EXPECTING COMPANY tonight?"

"Yeah... sounds like it," said The Man. "This might be a good time to take over the entire compound," he mused.

"We're not ready for that. When we go for it—I want to know we're taking it for sure. Not hit and miss. We're still not certain how strong Matthew's army is." Virgil took a breath. "We've got new recruits coming in from Manitoba today—some of them are military." Virgil leaned back and stretched his legs out in front of him. "How about if I round up a few of the more trained guys and build a special ops force?"

The Man looked up. His smile was bright. "I like that idea. Very much." And then, "How much time will you need?"

"Depends—a few weeks... maybe a month." Virgil sneered. "But we'll need better weapons."

"I'm working on that," The Man said. "Sending in my own secret weapons."

"The women?"

"Yep—CFB Namao is dry, you might say. But the men there don't want to part with the goods. So, I'm arranging a little distraction. I think we can make them look away—at least for an hour, or so," said The Man. He raised his arms above his head, and stretched. "But first—a meeting with Josef."

"Why him?" Virgil asked. "What's so important about him?"

"Apparently—he's become Matthew's closest and most trusted friend." The Man paused and watched the tall man's face for a response. When he saw none he continued, "Sorry—didn't mean to bring up old memories."

"You didn't," was the gruff reply.

Silence hung in the air between them. The Man continued:

"So—as his good friend—I suspect Josef will have been privy to all of Matthew's secrets... his strategies. With the right pressure, Josef might be willing to share his confidences." He leaned forward. "Brad's mentioned a second camp—wouldn't you like to know about that? I would."

"Matthew was always keen on setting up several camps—not just one."

"You knew?" The Man gave him a hard look.

"No—just something he used to talk about." Virgil gave his head a slow shake. *"I don't think this is your best move. I mean—why rile up Matthew? What's the point?"*

"To send a message of strength."

"I told you, we aren't that strong—at least not yet."

"But in war—what is truth and what is presented as truth—they're never the same things." The Man cocked his head. *"Haven't you heard that before?"*

The tall man gave no response. He stood up.

"Well?"

"So, you're going to keep Josef a prisoner? Or kill him?"

"We're sending a message," The Man said with a small sneer. *"What do you think?"*

Virgil breathed out a heavy sigh. *"I'll see you later tonight, but—I'm going on record—I have strong reservations about this. It's too early."* He retrieved his jacket and pulled it on.

"If things go well, and Josef talks, we'll have all the intelligence we need to make our next move. This Josef isn't military—he'll be easy to break. And then we'll move on to the Gatekeeper's camp."

"You're short-selling Matthew," Virgil said with another shake of his head.

"Defending your old pal?"

"No," Virgil responded, his voice edged in irritation. *"I'm watching out for your ass. And mine. He's a good strategist."*

"That remains to be seen."

"I wouldn't do this," Virgil repeated, as he turned and left the room.

The Man smiled and spoke softly to himself, *"But I would."*

Chapter Twenty-Five

The Double Agent

A YOUNG MAN dressed in military fatigues ran up. "Matthew? What are we supposed to do with the guy in the truck?" Matthew stopped and turned.

"We're leaving him behind. Just keep him there for now." The young man nodded and jogged away. "Wait," Matthew called. The man stopped and turned back. "Tell someone to load these bikes," he said, pointing to the Harleys.

"Yes, sir." The young man ran off.

Matthew looked ahead to see Meteor give the biker a hard push to his shoulder. The biker stumbled, righted himself, and then walked on. Matthew hurried to catch up.

"Hey," Matthew called out. "This will do," he said, nodding toward a cluster of cars out front of the Safeway store. Meteor grabbed the biker's jacket and swung him toward the cars. They stopped near a grey minivan. Meteor shoved the biker against the van's side door.

The biker was sullen. Fear lit his eyes when he saw Meteor produce a set of brass knuckles. "Found these on you guys," Meteor said. "I wonder how they work." Meteor laughed out loud at his own joke.

Matthew's mouth twisted into a grin.

"I've never used a set of those... personally," the biker answered. "But I believe they're applied to the lower jaw with force."

Meteor gave the biker a questioning look. Then he threw his head back and laughed.

"So, who's 'the man?'" Matthew asked. He stood in front of the biker, his legs apart, his arms crossed. "And what's his real name?"

"That is his name."

"Does he have some sort of God complex?" Meteor asked.

"Maybe. I don't even know his real name. Everyone just calls him, 'The Man.'"

"So tell us about his plans to kill me," Matthew said. The biker stared back at him, his lips closed in dogged silence. "Fine with me," Matthew said. He nodded at Meteor. "But you know how we guys are with new toys. Meteor, want to give those knuckles a go?"

Meteor raised his brass-wrapped fingers. "Sure," he said with a wide grin. "Love to. Whereabouts? Teeth?" He shook his head. "Naw, too messy. Side of the head?" He shook his head again. "Naw. That'd put him out cold." Meteor pressed an index finger to his lips. "Oh, wait. I know." He gave the biker a humorless grin. "The family jewels," he said slowly. He drew back his fist.

"Wait," the biker cried. His face showed true alarm. Meteor relaxed his arm. "Now that you put it that way... "

"Talk away," Meteor said.

"We're headed to a meet-up—a big one—in Edmonton. Captains from across the western provinces, but mostly from Alberta. The Man is pulling the Crazies together into an army. He's going to take over new territory— Like your camp."

The biker relaxed a bit when Meteor leaned against a small Toyota sedan. Meteor crossed one foot over the other, propping it on the toe of his thick, black boot. He folded his arms across his chest. "Go on. We're all ears."

The biker talked. He didn't stop talking. He talked about The Man and his plans. He talked for a long time. Matthew and Meteor looked at each other.

"What do you want to do?" Meteor asked.

Matthew stared at the biker. He pushed back his cap and scratched his head. "I'm going to give you a choice."

The biker held up his bound hands in surrender. "Okay, what?"

"We can kill you. Right now. Or, you can work with us."

The biker gave a wry smile. "Gee, let me think."

"Don't be smart," Meteor said. He raised the fist wearing the knuckles.

"Okay. Okay," the biker said. "Take it easy. Look, if I switch sides, I'm dead. If I don't switch sides, I'm dead."

"Sounds like a win-win situation to me," Meteor said.

The biker gave Meteor a sour look. Then he brightened. "Do you have lots of chicks in your camp?"

Matthew squeezed his eyebrows together. "What?"

"I really need a woman." He gave a small laugh. "I mean—" He paused. "Not a lot of them this far north." Pause. "I really need one."

"Good thing you decided to talk before I hit you," Meteor said, with a wicked grin.

"Yeah," the biker said. He returned the grin.

"What's your name?" Matthew asked.

"Trojan." The biker made a small awkward gesture. "Well, actually it's Harvey. But the guys call me that. It stuck." He shrugged. "I like it."

"Okay," Meteor said. "I gotta ask. How'd you get the nickname?"

Trojan shrugged again. "Ah, you know—I like the ladies." He gave a half grin. "A lot."

Meteor laughed out loud. "So, the skirts have you by the balls."

The biker looked sheepish. "So— You got some to spare?"

"Balls? Or women?" Meteor asked.

Trojan grimaced at him.

"We've got more females than we know what to do with," Matthew said.

"Speak for yourself, Matthew," Meteor said, with another laugh.

"So? What's your answer?" Matthew asked.

Trojan thought a moment. "I'm in."

"Besides banging the ladies, you got the balls to do some double agent work?" Matthew asked.

Trojan studied Matthew, his face serious. "If I get caught, they won't just kill me," he said. "They'll—"

"Then don't get caught," Meteor said.

Trojan squinted. "Thanks. Great advice."

Matthew exchanged a look with Meteor.

Meteor walked over, and pulled out his knife. Trojan's eyes went wide. "Relax," Meteor said as he slit the electrical tie on the biker's wrists. "You're one of us now."

Trojan rubbed his wrists. "Thanks."

Meteor stared into the man's face. "Don't screw with us."

"I won't," Trojan replied. He smiled. "So, how soon do I get to meet those ladies?"

"Never mind that," Matthew said. "What about your friends? Will they turn?"

Trojan rubbed two fingers across his upper lip. "Hmm, not sure."

"Can you convince them?" Meteor asked. "Because if you can't—"

"Yeah, I get it," Trojan replied. "I can try—"

"Wait a minute," Matthew said. "Put a tie back on him."

"What—?" Trojan looked stricken.

"Play the part," Matthew said. "We'll keep you guys together. Prisoners. Then we'll arrange a fake escape."

"They'll never believe me," Trojan said. "You guys didn't even beat on me."

"That's easily fixed," Meteor said. He removed the metal knuckles, drew back his bare fist, and hammered Trojan in the mouth. Blood appeared on the man's lips, and he slumped to the ground.

"Shit," Trojan mumbled. "You knocked one of my teeth loose."

Meteor leaned over and pulled Trojan to his feet. "Just be grateful I didn't hit you in the nose. Might have broken it. And then you'd have bone shards in your brain." He admired his work. "Besides, ya big baby, I took off the knuckle dusters."

Trojan groaned. He dabbed at his mouth with his imprisoned hands. "Not sure I'm gonna like you."

"That's okay," Meteor said. "Don't like you much either. Just stay focused on those ladies." He smiled. "C'mon. Let's go."

☐☐☐

The Assignment

"DO YOU know what to do?"

"I think I can handle this. It won't take much brain power to seduce a bunch of randy soldiers, you know." The woman cast him a how-stupid-do-you-think-I-am glance.

"Your truck will be the only one bringing back the weapons. So when it's loaded—get in and drive away."

"What about the other women?"

"They'll ride back with the guys who drop them off."

"The women are just agreeing to this—to be whores?"

"Yes—as a matter of fact—they are. Why are you so surprised? You understand the commerce of sex."

"Yeah, sure."

"And even if they didn't agree, it's cold outside. A night or two with nowhere to sleep, nothing to eat—they'd soon see the light. Don't you agree?"

"Sure."

"Good." He reached over and gave the woman's butt a whack. *"Now hustle that little ass out of here. Go get me some guns. Big guns. And make sure you get the ammo, too."*

She stood rubbing her rear. *"I've asked you before not to do that."* Her eyes were bright with anger.

"Yes, I know you have." The Man walked over and pulled the woman into his arms. He gave her a full kiss, bending her back against his encircling arm. He pulled away. *"But we both know you don't really mean it."*

The woman pushed him away. She straightened her jacket, smoothed her hair, and took a breath. *"When do I get to carry a gun?"*

"When I trust you to carry a gun."

"I'm coming back with a truckload of guns. Maybe I'll just help myself to one of those."

The slap came so fast, she had no time to duck. She stumbled backwards as her hand flew up to her face to protect it from a second blow. No further blow came.

The Man reached for her and yanked her back into his arms. He pulled her hand away from her cheek, now a bright red. He kissed the redness, and then kissed each of her eyelids. He kissed her mouth, softly. Then he put his hands on her shoulders, turned her away from him, and gave her a push toward the door. *"Hurry back. I'll be waiting."*

The woman left the room.

She didn't look back.

Chapter Twenty-Six

The Traitor

JOSEF WATCHED the vehicles pull away. The late morning sun was warm, and he shrugged off his outer jacket. He turned. Simon and Jonah stood nearby.

"Okay, boys... they've gone shopping. Let's do our jobs. And make sure we've got everything covered." He motioned to the Gatehouse, and the three of them entered the building. Josef went to Matthew's desk and sat down.

"I sent the relief patrols to the Hutterites about an hour ago," Jonah said.

"You're handling the perimeter scheduling really well," Josef said, with a quick smile.

"The compound perimeter guards are good for another three hours," Simon added, a hopeful smile creasing his face. "The relief guards are visiting at the Women's Bunkhouse."

"I'm sure they are," Josef said. He laughed. "What else is on for today?"

"The usual," Jonah said. "The girls have target practice tonight." Josef looked up. His look was questioning.

"Haven't you two picked a woman yet?"

Jonah and Simon exchanged glances and grinned.

"We're not really looking for anything permanent," Simon said, with a shrug. "Besides, we're doing okay—the girls like us."

"And we don't smell bad like some of the guys," Jonah added.

"Hmm," Josef said. "You might like having a wife. Give it some thought." He bent his head to the papers in front of him.

"Yeah, sure, Josef," Simon said. "We can hardly wait to have a wife. Just like... Martha." The boys began to laugh.

Josef looked up. He gave them a corrective glower. "Martha's a great wife," he said. "We've been together a long time. She's everything to me." The boys looked sheepish.

"We know," Simon said—his voice soft and placating. "We like her, too. But she's so... bossy."

Josef regarded the boys for another moment. "Get out of here."

Jonah and Simon turned and went to the door. As they reached it, somebody knocked. Simon turned the handle. He opened the door. Anna stood on the other side.

"Hi," she said. "I need to see Josef."

"Hi," Simon said, a blush creeping up his neck.

"C'mon in, Anna," Josef said. He smiled as the girl entered the room. Her baby boy was swaddled in a small hammock hanging from her shoulders. Josef got up. He walked around to Anna and pulled the hammock's fabric aside. He stared into the infant's face. The baby was asleep. "He's cute." Josef ran a finger down the baby's cheek. The little boy stirred. "What did you call him?"

"Gordon. After my dad," Anna said.

Josef looked up. "What can I do for you?"

"I need to talk to you about one of the girls." Anna took a quick breath. "I think she's a traitor."

"Oh?" Josef's eyebrows shot up. Jonah and Simon were about to leave. "Hold it, boys," Josef said. He waved them back to the desk. "Let's hear this." Josef sat on a corner of the desk.

"Here, Anna," Josef said, motioning to a chair. "Have a seat." Anna sat down. She hoisted the baby into a more comfortable position, and readjusted the strap of material across her shoulder.

"It's Cindy," she said. Jonah and Simon exchanged glances, and small grins.

"Yes?" Josef said.

"I haven't known her for as long as I've known some of the other girls—" Anna hesitated. "She joined us in kind of a strange way. One day, she just showed up." Anna took a breath. "She wasn't with anybody. I mean, she wasn't anybody's old lady. She just showed up."

Josef frowned. "So?"

"Well," Anna went on, "have you ever heard of someone they call, 'The Man?'"

Josef shook his head. "No."

"He's this big biker leader. I think he might be from the States, but he knows Alberta really well." The baby made a sound and Anna glanced down—he was still sleeping. She looked back at Matthew. "The guys—the Crazies—talk about him. They're all pretty scared of him."

"Why haven't you mentioned him before?" Josef asked.

"I didn't see any reason to say anything. Until now."

"Now?"

"Yeah— Cindy," she said, "I think she's friends with him." The baby squirmed again. Anna repositioned him.

"I see," Josef said, "but I still don't understand why you think she's a traitor."

"She leaves the compound at night," Anna said.

Josef was taken aback. "Leaves the compound?"

"Yeah. She goes with... Brad."

"What? Brad? You must be kidding."

"We thought she was meeting an old boyfriend, or something. But I saw both of them last night coming up between the RVs in the back."

"Well," Josef said, "that doesn't prove anything."

"I know," Anna said, "but I followed them. And I overheard some of what they were saying."

"And...?"

"I think they're planning to... kill Matthew."

"What?" Josef's eyes were wide. "Okay, what did they say? Exactly?"

Anna leaned forward. "Cindy said something about what it would be like after Brad was running the compound. After Matthew was dead."

Josef sat back in his chair. He glanced up at Jonah and Simon. Their faces were grim. He stared at them for a moment, and then looked back at Anna.

"That still doesn't prove anything, Anna. We all know that Brad has big aspirations. Maybe they were just shooting the breeze."

"No. I don't think so, because they mentioned The Man."

"Tell me more about The Man. Did you ever meet him?"

"Just once. At a Crazies' party. It was just after my dad was killed. I was sitting in a corner and this strange man came over to me. He sat down beside me and started to ask me about myself. He seemed nice enough.

And he was really nice to talk to. But he creeped me out when he asked me if I wanted to go upstairs with him. I told him I didn't. That I was pregnant. He kind of smiled. Then he just walked away."

Josef looked at her expectantly. "Is there more?"

"After that, I was put into a house with the other girls. We were all pregnant. We were together that way for a few weeks. Then Cindy showed up. Just out of the blue. None of us knew her—but The Man did. She talked about him sometimes. We sort of got the idea that he was the father of her babies. But she never said so."

Josef leaned forward. "And..."

"We all thought it was strange that she was dumped here along with the rest of us. We sort of got the idea that she was...well, special to The Man." Anna shrugged. "Once we got here, we forgot about it. She never mentioned him, so... But now... " Anna paused and added, "I suspect she and Brad go into Edmonton at night to meet with him. At least, that's what it sounded like from what they were saying."

Josef nodded again. "Do you think they have plans to get together tonight?"

Anna nodded. "They get together nearly every night. I help babysit the twins when Cindy leaves." Anna paused, and added, "Cindy stays out quite late sometimes— We have to wet nurse her babies."

Josef folded his hands, and rested his elbows on the desk. He sat quietly for the moment. "Okay," he said. "Thanks, Anna." He smiled at her. "We'll... uh, we'll check into this."

Anna stood. "Thanks, Josef." She turned and smiled at Jonah and Simon. Both smiled back. Jonah hurried over to the door, and opened it for her. "Bye," she said, as she turned and left. Jonah closed the door and returned to the desk.

"What do you want us to do?" Simon asked.

"Can you shadow them?" Josef asked. "Find out what they're up to when they leave the compound?" Both boys nodded vigorously.

"Sure, Josef, but you'll have to replace us on the first shift tonight," Jonah said.

"Done," Josef said. "And I know I don't have to tell you this... but be careful. Both of you." He smiled. "I like you guys."

"Don't worry, Josef. We'll get it done," Jonah said. The boys turned in unison and headed to the door. Jonah turned back. "Should we detain them if we find something out?"

"No," Josef said. "We'll wait till Matthew gets back. That's something he needs to be a part of."

The boys nodded and left the Gatehouse.

Josef stared at the closed door. "Traitors? Traitors?" he said aloud. He pulled his gun from his hip holster and turned it over in his hands. He pushed the release and popped the cylinder; it was fully loaded. He snapped the cylinder back in and put the gun back into its holster.

He rose and left the Gatehouse, too.

□□□

JOSEF TURNED on one of the propane lamps in the kitchen. The day had wound down uneventfully—everything was quiet on the compound. He made himself a quick supper of scrambled eggs and fried onions, and then he settled down to read.

He yawned and stretched. He looked toward the door and spotted a pair of Martha's shoes—sturdy hiking boots; they were covered with dried mud, bits of sticks and leaves. He smiled.

Josef pulled out his little blue Bible, adjusted the lantern so he could see better, and began to read. He read for about 20 minutes before somebody knocked on the cabin door. He rose and opened the door. Anna was there. "Come in."

Anna walked in and closed the door behind her. "They're gone," she said.

"Who? Brad and Cindy?"

"Yeah." She took a seat at the kitchen table.

"Any idea if Jonah and Simon were able to follow them?"

"Yes, I saw them go."

"How long ago?"

"About 10 minutes."

"Did Cindy say anything to you?"

"No. She just asked us to watch her kids again."

Josef nodded. "What time does Cindy get back here?"

Anna pursed her lips and thought. "Um—maybe after 1."

"Pretty late." Josef checked his watch. It was 10:30. "Okay, I'll stay awake and wait for Jonah and Simon to get back." He smiled at her. "Where's your baby?"

"With one of the girls. I told her I'd be right back."

"Then get out of here. Go get some sleep yourself. We've got this under control."

Anna smiled, rose, and left the cabin.

Josef stared at his open Bible, inserted the ribbon bookmark, and closed the book. He pushed it into the center of the table, and got up. He pulled his jacket from the hook. He threw it over a chair. He went to the chest, and selected one of the Kevlar vests. He slipped it over his head, and secured the Velcro straps. He picked up the steel plate and shoved it into the inner pocket. He slipped his arms into his jacket, and grabbed a flashlight. He patted the pistol on his hip and reached for his long gun. Then he turned down the lamp, and left the cabin.

Josef strode across the compound; he checked the Gatehouse. It was dark and silent. He nodded at the two sentries on the gate. "Everything okay?" he asked.

The two men gave him a thumbs-up.

"I'm going to check the perimeter guards," he said. "Jonah and Simon had something else to do tonight. I think I'll see how their replacements are doing." He waved to the men, and walked off.

Josef aimed his flashlight into the darkness. The moon was bright, but dense fir trees blocked its light, making walking without a flashlight very difficult. He heard a sound in the bushes to his left, and he played the light over the foliage. Nothing. He continued to walk forward.

The perimeter guards had a set pattern they were to follow, so he knew they should have been coming around near the back of the compound about then. He headed in their direction. He heard another sound, deeper in the woods, and he stopped. He again swept the light across the darkness, but saw nothing. He began to walk again.

Voices. Somewhere in the distance.

Josef craned his neck and tried to hear what they were saying. One of the voices was female. He quickened his pace. The voices got louder. Ahead, he could see the bright flicker of firelight. He turned off his flashlight. He grunted. *A party*, he thought. He made his way between the RVs.

As he neared the fire, he could make out several people—all young men and women from the compound. Somebody noticed him, and motioned. The rest quieted when they realized who he was.

"Hi kids. What're you up to?"

"It was such a nice night, we thought we'd have a party," said a tall girl, with flowing long hair.

"I see," Josef said. "Are any of you supposed to be working?"

"Just us." Josef turned to his right. Jonah and Simon were coming toward him.

"Anna told me you guys were going somewhere."

"We did," Jonah said. "Now we're back."

"And?"

"Nothing to report," Simon said, "unless you want to hear about Brad's love life."

"What?"

"Yeah," Jonah said. "We followed them and watched them. Until they started getting it on."

Josef frowned. "Why would they leave the compound just to have sex?"

Jonah shrugged. "Beats us. But that's what they were up to."

"Where are they now?" Josef asked.

"Still there. Probably," Jonah said.

"Where is 'there'?"

"About a half mile from here—near the highway."

Josef thought a moment. "Are you sure they didn't see you following them?"

"We don't think so. But we can't guarantee it."

"You mean to say they walked a half mile, and then they lay down in the dirt to have sex?"

Jonah shrugged again. "Yeah."

Josef shook his head. "Something doesn't sound right." He motioned to the two boys. "Are you staying here?"

"Yeah, if it's okay with you."

"It's fine. Do me a favor. If you see either one of them, come tell me." The boys agreed. Josef turned. "I'm going to the Girl's Bunkhouse—to see if Cindy's back yet." Josef walked off.

Josef made his way down the path toward the main area of the compound. He flicked on his flashlight and played the light across the path in front of him. He decided he could see well enough without it, so he turned it off, and dropped it into his pocket. He shook his head.

Not right, he thought. *Something wasn't right.*

"Josef," a man's voice said. Josef jumped. He turned. Two men were standing in the shadows.

"Brad?" he asked.

Brad stepped forward. "Yeah." His gun was pointed at Josef's face. "Sorry, old man," he said.

Josef raised his rifle.

"Don't do that," Brad said. A second man, a stranger, went to Josef and took the rifle from his hands.

"What're you doing?" Josef asked. He backed away.

"We're going to take a trip," Brad said. "There's somebody who wants to meet you. Actually, he's wanted to meet you for some time now." Brad used the gun to usher Josef down the path toward the back of the compound. Josef could hear the partiers again—they were laughing. Loudly. He doubted they would hear a shout over their revelry.

"What's this all about?" Josef asked.

"Oh—" Brad said. "Let's just say I work for someone else now."

"The Man?" Josef asked.

"Oh, you've heard of him, have you?" Brad asked.

"Only in passing."

"He's quite the guy—but you're going to find that out first hand."

"So, you knew you were being followed tonight?"

Brad laughed. "Oh, you mean by your two private dicks." He laughed again. "Idiots."

"Where's Cindy?" Josef asked.

"Back at the bunkhouse, I guess. Why?"

Josef shut up. He surmised that Brad knew nothing about Anna. Any further questions about Cindy might get Anna in trouble.

They walked to the far corner of the compound and then made their way through the fencing. It had been cut and pulled to one side. They walked into the forest on the other side. Brad and the other man pulled out flashlights. Josef thought about his gun, but Brad had a pistol aimed at his head, and the other man carried his rifle.

They walked for another fifteen minutes and came to a clearing, near a gravel road. A truck, with a full back seat, sat on the side of the road. The man with Brad motioned and ran around to the driver's side. He jumped in and started the engine. Brad prodded Josef with his gun. Josef opened the backseat passenger door and got in. Brad followed him.

Josef felt the weight of his own pistol on his hip. It was covered by his long jacket.

Maybe that's why they hadn't taken it. They didn't know he had it.

He let his hand slide across his hip. He knew he couldn't reach his gun and draw it without getting shot. He sat quietly. He stared ahead into the gloom now lit by bright, blue instrument panel lights.

The trio rode in silence up the dark highway.

Behind them, another truck followed.
It held two idiots.

□□□

The Mutiny

VIRGIL CAME *into the room.*

"They've got him," said The Man.

"Now what?"

"We wait."

"I'd rather not be a part of this," Virgil said.

"Why?"

"No reason. I just don't want to be there—if it's all the same to you."

"It's not all the same to me," said The Man.

Virgil crossed his arms. "This time—I'm turning you down. I don't see the purpose in this. It does nothing to further your cause."

"You'll be there."

Virgil turned. He reached the doorway, but stopped when he heard a sharp click. "Don't do that," he said very quietly, but loud enough for The Man to hear. He paused for another second and then he walked out the door.

The Man stared out the small window. He flicked the top of the steel lighter in his hand—up and down—again.

The sound echoed through the empty room.

Chapter Twenty-Seven

A Meeting by Moonlight

"CAN WE AT least know what you're going to do with us?" the cowboy asked from the back seat.

Martha turned and studied the man. He gave her an evil glare. Martha raised her eyebrows slightly, but she said nothing. The armed man beside the biker poked him with a pistol.

"I told you once already to shut up," the man with the gun said. "Watch the scenery."

Matthew was driving and he continued to stare ahead at the road. Martha glanced at him, willing him to look her way. She wanted to know what his plans were for the bikers, too. She glanced back at the cowboy behind them. His face was stony. He glared at her again. Martha turned her attention back to Matthew.

"Matthew?" Martha asked. He didn't respond. "Matthew?" She reached over and touched his forearm.

"Huh?" Matthew seemed startled. "What?"

"I'm just wondering what your plans are—it's getting kind of late."

"Oh. We're stopping at a provincial park near Evansburg."

"You mean the Pembina River Park?"

"Yep."

"Just to eat?"

"Nope. We'll stay the night," Matthew said.

Martha bowed her head to hide a creeping smile. She couldn't hide it, so she looked out the side window and stared at the scenery long enough for the smile to abate.

Overnight. A campfire.

The smile returned. She let it.

Matthew's caravan pulled left off Highway 16 toward Evansburg. They traveled toward a stop sign and then turned right into the town. They drove past a sign announcing Evansburg as "Home of the Grouch." Another sign—looking very homemade—proclaimed the town to be a "thriving village with clean air, fresh water, and friendly people."

Farther up, they passed a small strip mall, a Racetrac gas station with huge storage tanks (those made Matthew do a double take), a Super Foods store, and across from it, a CN caboose parked out front of a tourism information center. Next to it, sat a Rona lumberyard proclaiming to be "Proudly Canadian." Matthew followed the highway out of town where it curved around for the next three kilometers. The road leading to the park appeared on the left.

Matthew turned and crossed over a long bridge spanning the Pembina River. Another left turn took them to the park's entrance. Past the campsite registration building, a chained iron gate barred their passage. One of the men jumped out with bolt cutters. In less than a minute, the double gate was open.

One truck after the other, the drivers wound their way down the gravel road to a large group-use area. Matthew had decided it was easier to guard an area with only one access road, so they avoided the main camping area.

The trucks pulled over, and the passengers jumped out. Some of the men grabbed tenting gear and began setting up. Other men gathered kindling and started small cooking fires in iron fire pits near the picnic shelter. The women wrestled the cooking gear and the food supplies out of the truck boxes. Soon, tripod grills and large pots sat over blazing fires.

Martha organized a garbage crew to clean the immediate area cluttered with debris: torn sleeping bags, empty food boxes, bottles, newspapers, empty tin cans, cooking utensils, condom wrappers, cigarette packages, and broken campstools. Several abandoned cars, their doors hanging ajar, were now homes to birds and small woodland creatures. Some of the younger men took cans and siphoning hoses and went to check the abandoned vehicles for fuel.

"Matthew?" Meteor stood beside him. Matthew was busy under the hood of his truck.

"Yeah?"

"Trojan and the other two bikers? What do you want done with them?"

Matthew sighed. "I'm still not sure about Trojan. If we let him go, he'll probably just switch right back." Matthew studied the oil dipstick in his hand. "That is—if he ever actually switched in the first place." He replaced the dipstick into its reservoir.

"I vote for trusting him," Meteor said. "What choice does he have? I suspect the guy is just a good old boy looking for a home-cooked meal."

"And a piece of tail," Matthew said. Meteor laughed.

"Yeah, that, too," Meteor said. "Several pieces." The two men laughed together.

Meteor motioned to the road. "I'm grabbing some of the guys—we're gonna head back into Evansburg—do some scavenging."

"Sounds good. How long?"

"Two hours?"

"Okay, we'll watch for you. By the way, there's an RCMP detachment somewhere off the main street. Check it out."

"Gotcha," Meteor said. "Should I take Martha?"

"No, leave her here. She's running the cooking crew."

"Okay," Meteor said. He turned and walked away. He stopped and called back over his shoulder. "Can I pick up anything for you while I'm in town, dear?"

Matthew laughed. "Get the hell out of here." They both looked up as a lop-sided V-formation of Canada geese honked their way across the sky.

TWO HOURS later, nearly to the minute, an RCMP truck rolled down the road and into the campsite. Everyone stopped to watch. Matthew eyed the truck. Martha did, too. The perimeter guards hadn't stopped it. *Why not,* she thought. Her question was answered when the door to the cab opened, and Meteor leapt out. He walked over to Matthew.

"Hey," Meteor said. He smiled. "Look what I found." He swept his arm toward the truck emblazoned with the RCMP logo. Matthew nodded. The pair walked back to the truck.

"Nice—" Matthew said, as he bent near the front of the truck. "Hmm, winch, too." He straightened. "Find any guns and ammunition to go along with it?"

"Some," Meteor said. "But look at the back seat." Meteor opened the back door. Matthew nodded. All the windows were covered in black metal bars.

"Nice—" Matthew said. "A jail on wheels."

"Won't our bikers be pleased," Meteor said, with another smile. He fished around on the floor. He came up with his hands full of blue items. "And look at these," he said, handing them to Matthew. "Flak vests. Small sizes. For the ladies."

Matthew took one. He turned it over in his hands. He made a dismissive sound through his nose. "Well, they'll stop a knife. Maybe a small caliber handgun. But not much else."

"Better than nothing," Meteor said. "I found a dozen of them."

"Give them to Martha," Matthew said. "Tell her to distribute them."

Meteor smiled. "Will do."

□□□

MATTHEW SAT by the fire; he was alone. He gazed into the flames, stirring the remnants of the food on his plate with his fork.

"You done?" Martha asked. Matthew looked up.

"Yeah." Martha offered to take his plate. Matthew handed it to her. "Thanks."

Martha took his plate to the woman washing dishes and then she walked back to Matthew. He was still sitting alone, still staring into the flames. Martha screwed up her face in puzzlement and then took a deep breath. She sat down near him. She struggled to speak, to engage him, to bring him back.

"Got a lot on your mind?"

Oh, geez. How insipid. Martha rolled her eyes at her own stupid question.

"Yeah."

Great. One word answers.

Matthew made a move to leave. Martha touched his arm to draw his attention back to her. "Have you decided what to do with the bikers?"

"Nope," Matthew said. "Not yet."

"It might help to talk it through," Martha suggested. "I'm happy to listen."

Matthew turned to face her. Martha searched his eyes for the kindness she had seen before. It wasn't there. Matthew wasn't there, either. Only the Gatekeeper was there. Martha felt her heart squeeze. She hid a wince.

"No, Martha. It's fine," Matthew said. "As soon as I decide, I'll let you know. But for now, they're safely locked up in the back of Meteor's new ride."

Martha smiled. "He's really happy with that truck."

"Did you pass out the flak vests?"

"Yes."

"Not much protection. But they're better than nothing," Matthew said, repeating Meteor's earlier words.

"They're actually designed for women," Martha said. "The girls like them."

"It's getting late," Matthew said. He rose to his feet. "I've got a meeting with some of the captains." He gave Martha a half smile. "I'll see you in the morning. Good night."

An invisible hand grasped Martha's heart again. Hurt radiated out like a mushroom cloud. She mustered up enough breath to respond. "Okay." She gave a quick nod of her head in agreement.

Matthew turned and walked away.

Don't go. Don't go. I need— What?— What do I need?

Anger flared inside her.

Damn him. Damn...him.

Martha clenched her hands and pulled them in tight to her chest. The nails felt good biting into her palms. She squeezed tighter. She opened her hands, and gazed at the tiny crescent moon shapes dotting her palms. Her wedding ring glistened in the firelight. She twisted it round her finger with her other hand.

Josef.

Emotions collided inside her heart—they wrestled for position like ungainly bumper cars at a fair.

You are a married woman.

She sighed heavily.

Why, God? Why? Why do you allow this?

She rested her elbows on her knees, and clasped her hands beneath her chin. She knew she loved Josef, more than anything—but she also knew there was a part of her that needed Matthew—an emptiness inside her that only Matthew could fill.

Please. Please.

The craving receded, but like a crouching thing in the dark—Martha felt its presence—quivering and alive. Waiting...

Help me make it stop. God... help me!

She squeezed her eyes shut tighter. *Stop it.* The crouching thing only smiled.

"Son-of-a-bitch." She kicked at the ground with the toe of her boot. "Damn you, Matthew," she muttered. "Damn you."

The sound of a guitar being strummed made Martha look up. She looked across the way where several men and women sat around a large bonfire. One of the men was playing accompaniment on a harmonica. Somebody was singing. Martha recognized the lyrics from an old Bob Dylan tune. "... *She takes just like a woman...* "

"Oh, crap... very funny," she said to the fire. She stood and walked over to the group.

Two of the older men were making the music. Heads and shoulders, silhouetted against the fire, rocked to the tune. Those who knew the words (the majority knew the chorus) sang along—some pleasantly, some horribly off-key. No one seemed to mind.

Martha sat down at a wooden picnic table near the fire; its flames were dancing high into the air. The wooden seat was damp. Condensation soaked into her jeans. The air was chilly away from the fire, and she shivered. She jumped when she heard a voice close to her ear.

"... *introduced as friends...* " a deep voice sang.

"Meteor," she said. "You scared me."

He slid his arm around her shoulders and pulled her close to him. He continued to sing. "... *Ah, you fake...*"

Martha grimaced at him as he sang. His warm breath in her ear made Martha shiver again. A tiny thread of excitement zipped through her stomach, and she sucked in a breath. Martha tried to elbow the big man away, but he didn't move—not his arm from her shoulders—or his mouth from her ear. He still sang.

"Stop it," she said. He reached the line in the song about breaking like a little girl, and Martha elbowed him again.

"Meteor! Stop it." Martha turned to face him. She placed her hands on his chest and pushed. He didn't move. He smiled and it made his blue eyes sparkle. She saw the look in his eyes. Another tendril of excitement lanced through her belly, and she swallowed hard.

"Meteor... " Martha warned. Her voice was low. She pushed on his chest again. This time he moved back, and took his arm from around her shoulders.

"Okay," Meteor said. He leaned back against the table and spread his arm along the top. He stretched out his long legs in front of him and crossed them at the ankles. "But you know what, Martha?— I've been hit in the head by you... kicked out of a truck by you... " He turned to face her and grinned. "You have more strength than that."

Martha's face flamed with a sudden blush. She slid down the bench seat away from Meteor—but only a few inches. She stared back at him.

"Behave yourself," Martha said. "Or I will use *all* my strength. And in a way you won't like."

Meteor lifted his hand from the table behind her back; he drew his fingers along her collar allowing them to tickle the back of her neck.

Martha pulled away. "Stop!"

Meteor studied her, his blue eyes bright in the ambient light.

Get up. Go away.

Martha willed her body to obey, but it remained sitting, while her conscience continued its mantra.

Get up. Go. Now.

Her hands clung to the edge of the bench seat. Meteor reached over and grasped her wrist. "C'mon."

Martha's world tilted. As though swaddled in soft cotton, the sounds of the people singing and the crackling and spitting of the flames grew muffled and distant. Her inner voice had quieted, too. Suddenly, nothing else existed, nothing except the man before her. And his intoxicating eyes. The pressure of Meteor's hand on her wrist was firm, but not unpleasant. She didn't pull away.

Meteor stood and as he did, he pulled Martha to her feet. "C'mon." Martha fought against a burst of dizziness. She resisted his grip. Meteor studied her. He nodded, gave a half smile, and dropped her wrist. He turned and walked away. Martha watched him as he headed back toward the fire.

"Wait—" Martha called out, her voice a husky whisper. Meteor turned back. He held out his hand. She caught up and took it.

What the hell am I doing?

He led her away from the fire. Into the darkness. Into the night.

Martha's feet moved forward of their own accord. Her mind had resumed its rant, but she shushed it.

Meteor led her behind the cookhouse. He pointed to a winding path leading down the bank. "Let's go to the river. More privacy there."

Martha felt a punch of fear mixed with wild excitement.

Turn around. Go back.

Her feet continued forward, crunching on the gravel. They had headlamps with them, but the moon was full. Meteor's hand gripped hers, warm and possessive. They didn't speak.

They walked down the path. Martha could make out the river as it rippled by them, a wide silver ribbon snaking its way into the distance. She heard its music as it burbled over rocks near the shore. She stopped. Meteor tugged on her hand again. "Over here."

Martha turned. One of the compound's tents was pitched in a raised clearing. A pool of moonlight highlighted its sharp angles. *'X' marks the spot*, she thought. She hesitated and turned to Meteor, "You planned this."

Meteor turned to her and pulled her to him. "Of course." He lifted his hands to her face, cupping it. "I've been planning this ever since you kicked me out of your truck." He smiled.

Martha gave a small nervous laugh. She closed her eyes.

I can still go. Nothing has happened yet. Go.

But the wild thing inside her stirred. She couldn't leave. Martha opened her eyes. Meteor was staring at her. She felt her resistance drain as she yielded to the intensity in his eyes, the warmth of his hands on her face, and the sound of his voice in her ears. She stood—mesmerized, compliant, and afraid.

Now. Go now.

The warning voice was now pale and weak. When Meteor tipped her face up to his, she was ready. She parted her lips in silent invitation. He took it.

His kiss made her gasp. Rough. Demanding. Searching. Unlike Josef's kisses. The wild thing inside her twitched—she felt her body respond, and yield. A small sound erupted from deep inside her throat. She reached up and pulled Meteor's head toward hers. She opened her mouth wider and kissed him back. No longer a recipient, but an active participant, she moved her mouth over his. Meteor groaned. He reached around and gripped her butt, pulling her against him. Martha felt his hardened desire, and she gave a small cry, but Meteor's mouth blocked its escape.

Their kiss intensified, their tongues darting and searching in a feverish exploration of newness. Waves of emotion swept through Martha, carrying her like an autumn leaf on the wind, so that when Meteor stopped kissing her, she staggered back in surprise. Meteor caught her—and pulled her to him.

Meteor's hands fumbled with her parka zipper. He finally found the tab, and pulled it down. Martha stood quietly, her hands at her sides, waiting for him to touch her. Meteor pushed her jacket open, grabbed her shirt, and pulled it free from her jeans. In an impatient move, his hands pushed the fabric up. Martha moaned when his hands closed on her naked flesh—seeking and possessive. She willed him to take more of her, and she arched her neck—head back, and mouth open. She cried out as his hand slipped inside her bra and found her breast.

Meteor kissed her again, one hand gripping the back of her head, the other massaging a breast, his thumb grazing her nipple. Martha clung to him. He suddenly pulled away again. "Let's lie down." His voice was a gruff whisper. He grasped her wrist again, tighter this time. Insistent. Hurting. He tugged Martha toward the tent. She allowed him to pull her along behind him.

Too late. Too late. Oh, God. Too late.

Meteor pulled back the tent flap. He reached in and retrieved a small battery-powered lantern. He flipped a switch. The tent filled with a soft light. They crawled in and fell onto unrolled, piled sleeping bags. A thick foam pad, peeking out from beneath the bags, softened their fall. Meteor rose up on his knees. Martha watched him.

Meteor's eyes held hers as he undid his jacket and pulled it off. He unbuttoned his shirt, pulled it off, and threw it on top of the jacket. He pulled his turtleneck sweater and undershirt over his head in a single move. They joined the shirt and jacket. He remained poised over Martha. He reached for his buckle, but Martha cried out in alarm. "No," she said.

Meteor looked puzzled, but he stopped. Instead, he knelt over her and began to unbutton her shirt. Martha pressed her hand over his in an attempt to stop him. He shook it off. Panic swept over her, and she began to protest. Meteor pulled her up, and pushed her shirt down over her arms. Martha pulled her arms free. She still wore her black sport bra. Meteor eyed it.

"Take it off.

Martha obeyed.

She grasped her shoulder straps, slid them down off her arms, and then she lifted the bra over her head. Meteor was resting back on his calves. He looked at her. Martha crossed her arms across her chest. Meteor smiled and shook his head. "Arms down." Martha slowly complied, her eyes locked on his. "Lie down," he said.

Martha lay back. She began to shiver. "I'm cold."

"You'll be plenty warm in just a few minutes," Meteor said. He got on top of her. His chest touched hers, and she moaned. Her hands reached around and clutched his naked back. He sought her mouth and kissed her again. Hard. Harder than before. The force bruised her lips. Martha cried out again; Meteor's mouth hushed the sound.

He rolled to his side and began to explore her naked chest. When he bent his head to take her nipple in his mouth, she pulled back in shock. "No, I... "

"You're not backing out on me now, are you?" Meteor was propped up on one elbow and staring into her face. "Not now, Martha." He smiled. "We've come way too far." She shook her head. He moved his hand across her breasts. She cried out again as his hand traveled down her belly. His fingers crept under her waistband, but she caught his wrist.

"No—"

Meteor brought his hand back up to her face. He held her chin between his fingers and turned her face toward him. Martha closed her eyes.

"Look at me," he said.

She opened her eyes.

"Let's finish what we've begun, Martha."

Meteor's words traveled through her—like a diver slicing through blue water, they penetrated deeply. Martha felt herself grow wet. Then a sudden gush.

Oh, damn.

She remembered. She sat up.

"No— Wait." Martha pushed Meteor's hands aside. "I can't," she said more firmly.

"An attack of conscience?" Meteor asked.

"No." Martha said. She reached for her discarded clothing.

"It's a little late." Meteor said. He ran his hand up her thigh.

"No!" Martha cried. She shoved his hand away. "I can't. I-I-I... I'm having my period." Heat flooded her face as she spoke the words. Meteor reached over and turned her face toward him.

"That doesn't bother me," he said. Martha pulled her face from his hand.

"But it bothers me," she said. She pulled her bra over her head. She grabbed her shirt and her parka, and got to her knees.

Meteor flopped back on the sleeping bags. He folded his arms behind his head and gave a deep sigh.

Martha crawled out of the tent.

□□□

MARTHA ran up the path.

"Thank you. Oh, thank you," she muttered under her breath as she climbed the stony path.

She shivered again, but this time from relief.

Stupid, she thought. *So, stupid. What if something had happened?*

She congratulated herself for having put on a pad—as a security measure—that morning, when she had first felt the mild twinges of cramps. At least she wouldn't be washing her pants in the middle of the night, she thought. Her mind flipped back to Meteor and she flushed with embarrassment.

Thank you. Oh, thank you.

Gratitude poured from her soul as she thanked God, as never before, for the blessing of her monthly cycle.

□□□

The Grace

"HELLO, JOSEF. The name is Josef, right?" The Man asked.

"Yes—it is," Brad said. He gave Josef a rough shove.

Josef stumbled toward a leather couch. They were in a backroom of the clubhouse. Several men were in the room, including Virgil; he stood near the doorway, his arms crossed, and his lean face dark with anger.

Brad gave Josef another push and he fell to the couch. Josef's hand went to the gun on his hip. Brad smiled and he held his own pistol to Josef's temple. "Uh-uh," he said. "I'll take that." Brad pulled the revolver from Josef's holster. He opened the cylinder. Spun it. "Good." He stuck the gun into the front of his jeans. He turned back to The Man. "He's all yours."

The Man strode over. He sat in a chair next to the couch. "We can do this the easy way—or the hard way. It's up to you."

Josef said nothing.

"I want information on the camp."

Josef sighed. "Hasn't Brad provided you with enough information?"

"He's given us great information. Several nice night-time tours of the camp, too."

"So, it was you guys."

The Man laughed. "I guess you and your wife took a beating on one of those outings." His laugh stopped abruptly. "How is she—your wife? Martha, right?"

"Fine."

The Man chortled—a forced unpleasant sound. "Tough keeping her at home, huh? One of those run-around types?"

"No— But she's none of your business."

"Sure she is. I'm looking forward to the day I meet her. And it should be soon, too."

Josef's face hardened. The voice that came from him was deep and guttural. "Leave my wife alone."

"Your wife... She's some wife—according to Brad. Sounds like you two have a very interesting sex life."

"Brad's full of shit. He doesn't know what he's talking about."

"So, then you tell me. Amuse me."

"I have nothing to tell you."

"Not even about a secret location? Another camp with underground oil tanks?"

"No."

"Have it your way." The Man looked up.

Several more men had entered the room. They were armed with short lengths of thick chain, baseball bats, and brass knuckles. He turned back to Josef. "You're sure you don't want to reconsider? 'Cause this is going to hurt."

"I told you, 'No.'"

"I believe you," The Man said.

Josef whispered softly. "Be with me, Lord."

"He will be. You won't have long to wait. But according to what my daddy used to tell me—only if you have been really good. Have you been really good, Josef?"

"Your daddy was wrong—that's not the way salvation works. Grace isn't earned—the Lord's grace is free. You only have to confess and believe."

"Well, MY grace is tough to earn—and you've done nothing to earn it. And just for the record—my daddy was never wrong."

The Man rose and swung his fist into the side of Josef's face. Blood welled up as Josef's lip split. Josef raised his hands in protection, but The Man had turned away.

The Man pointed a finger at the mob of armed men. "Do what you want to him, but don't mess up his face. I want Matthew to recognize him. And—don't kill him. That's Brad's job."

The Man looked across the room to where Virgil stood. "You want second blood?"

Virgil glared back at him and left the room.

"Let me," Brad said.

The Man stepped aside and with a wave of his arm, he granted Brad's request.

"GOOD MORNING, Martha."

Martha turned. Meteor was standing behind her, a plate filled with bacon and eggs, and sourdough toast. She felt her face flush. She turned back and bent her head over her own plate.

"Hi," she mumbled. She poked at her eggs.

"Have a nice sleep?"

"Yeah. Fine."

"What's the matter? Not talking to me this morning?"

"Go away."

Meteor leaned down and whispered in her ear. "Don't worry. It's our secret. Yours and mine." He gave her ear a slight nuzzle. Martha pulled away. "But I'm taking a rain check," Meteor said as he straightened. He turned and walked away.

Martha watched him join a group of people who were chatting and laughing loudly, as they ate. Soon, she could hear his laughter above the rest. Martha bent her head back to her plate. She shoved her scrambled eggs around with her fork. Her appetite was gone.

THE TRUCKS were packed and the people climbed into their respective rides.

"Who are you riding with, Martha?" Matthew asked, as he threw gear into the truck box.

Martha eyed him. "You, I thought."

"Oh." He rearranged some loose tools. "I thought you might be riding with Meteor."

"Why would I do that?"

"Things happen."

"What things?"

"You know what I'm talking about, Martha. Hell—half the camp is talking about it."

"Dammit, Matthew—*nothing* happened." *But it nearly did,* she reminded herself, *it nearly did.* "We didn't do anything."

"Really—" said Matthew. "That's not how it looked. Not to me...or to anyone else watching, for that matter."

Martha searched his face, tried to read his expression, but it revealed nothing behind the coldness.

"*Nothing happened,*" she repeated. *But...nearly.* Guilt suffused her, and anger filled with self-recrimination, grew hot inside her.

"Uh-huh," Matthew said.

Her creeping anger needed an outlet. She exploded on Matthew.

"You smug, self-righteous son-of-a-bitch," she said. Martha faced him, her hands clenched at her sides. Frustration brought hot tears to her eyes. "I went with him because he wanted me to. He *wanted* my company. He *wanted* to talk to me. Unlike YOU." She nearly spat the last word at him.

"So, it's my fault that you're fucking around on your husband?"

Matthew's words stunned her. Martha stepped back, her eyes wide. She swallowed, and her face flushed with heat. "*We—didn't—do—anything,*" she repeated.

Matthew's eyes were dark and hard. He shrugged. "Ah, doesn't make any difference to me, one way or the other. I was only thinking about Josef." He turned his back on her and walked around to the driver's side.

Sudden pain—acute and suffocating—sucked the breath out of her. Martha gripped the truck's door handle for support. Tears threatened, but she bit her tongue until it hurt. She would do anything to keep those teardrops from falling. Suddenly, the idea of riding with Matthew was repulsive. She grabbed her gear, and went to find another truck.

Many of the trucks were already pulling out. She saw Meteor hop into his RCMP truck. He waved to her and closed his door. He started the engine and drove off. Martha looked around but couldn't see another option for a ride home. She turned and walked back to Matthew's truck.

She yanked the door open and climbed into the seat. She slammed the door. She looked straight ahead.

"So... "

"Don't talk to me," Martha said.

"Have it your way."

"Shut up, Matthew." Martha shot him a warning glance. She folded her arms and slumped down into her seat.

Matthew started the truck and pulled onto the road leading up to the highway.

Martha heard him exhale heavily, but he said nothing more.

Chapter Twenty-Eight
A Price to be Paid

MARTHA WATCHED rain drizzle down the truck's side window, rivulets in constant slippery motion. Down. Down. Down. Her chin rested in her hand. They were nearly back at the compound. She sighed inwardly. She would be glad when this trip was over. Matthew hadn't uttered a single word. His silence—although she had demanded it—hurt her. It was like having a window slammed down onto her fingers by someone she trusted. Now—she wasn't so sure about telling him to shut up.

"Ready to talk?"

Martha looked up in stunned surprise. "What?"

"You ready to talk?"

"I'm always ready to talk, Matthew."

"Good," he said. "What happened back there between you and Meteor?" The question caught Martha off guard.

"Uh, I told you—nothing." Guilt stomped back into her heart. She tried desperately to quell its booming echo.

Matthew sighed. "A woman does not walk into the woods with a man who isn't her husband... and then nothing happens," he said.

"It's not what you think." Martha put her hand to her forehead in exasperation. "Sure, something *could* have happened. But it didn't." She stared at Matthew. "Okay?" And then, "Can we drop it now?"

"I'm not worried about *me* dropping it," he replied. "What about all the other people who saw you walk off with him? Hand in hand."

"Oh—" Martha breathed out an angry whoosh of air. "Let them think what they want—Josef won't listen to them. I've been with him for nearly thirty years. He knows me."

"He might have known you before, but does he know the Martha that's here now?"

Martha cocked her head. "The Martha that's *here now?*"

"Yeah, that one."

Martha faced forward and watched as Matthew made a turn off the highway. They would be at the compound in a few minutes. "I'm not sure what you mean, Matthew."

"I think you do," he said.

"Then think what you like," Martha responded curtly. "You'll forever judge me no matter what I do. No reason you should change now."

"And what about your judgment of me?"

"What?"

When had she judged him? Martha was very confused. *What was he talking about?*

"You heard me," Matthew said, as he drove up the lane. The Gatehouse lay ahead. Martha saw several people milling around. They looked excited about something. "You've misjudged me," he said, as he turned into the parking lot.

He put the truck into park, and turned off the ignition. He turned and faced her. "I care about what happens to you. And to Josef."

Martha stared back at him. She searched his eyes, desperate to see it. *Was it back? Was the kindness back in his eyes?*

Matthew turned away, distracted by the crowd of people who were rushing to his truck. He opened his door and stepped to the ground. Martha did the same.

Everyone was talking at once. Matthew held up his hand. "One at a time, please. What's going on?"

One man spoke. "It's Josef," he said.

Martha felt a terrible chill; it coursed through her like an ice fog—its frozen fingers tapping out tiny darts of pain.

Another heart attack?

She rushed forward to the man. "What's wrong with Josef?"

The man looked at her, and then back at Matthew. "He's missing."

"What?" Dread suffused her.

"He's been missing since last night," said the man. "We've been looking for him." He paused. "Simon and Jonah are gone, too. So is one of the trucks."

"Does anyone know what might have happened to him?" Matthew asked. His eyes swept the people assembled in front of him. They landed on Anna. She stood to the side, grief clearly present on her face. "How about you, Anna?"

Anna glanced around. She pushed her way through the people until she was standing in front of Matthew. She nodded at Martha who stood next to him.

"Well?" Matthew asked.

"He... I told him about Cindy... and Brad... "

"Cindy? Brad? What are you talking about?" Martha interrupted. Matthew shushed her and motioned for Anna to continue her story.

"I told him that Brad and Cindy were secretly meeting. I thought they were planning to... " She hesitated, and added, "to... kill you." Matthew's eyes widened. "Cindy is friends with a guy called The Man. He leads a big group of bikers. He's—"

Matthew held up his hand. "I've heard of The Man. What else?"

"Simon told me that Josef asked them to follow Brad and Cindy last night. To find out what they were up to. Cindy left. I saw Simon and Jonah follow her. I told Josef they went." She licked her lips. "He must have gone after them."

"Where's Brad?" Matthew asked. Anna shrugged. "And Cindy? Where's she?" Anna shrugged again.

"We haven't seen her since last night," Anna said. "Not Brad either."

Matthew looked at the men who had gathered around him. He nodded to one of the captains. "Get a team together."

The man nodded. He began motioning and calling names.

Another truck was coming up the road. Matthew looked up. It was Meteor.

Meteor stopped the truck and jumped out. The three captive bikers sat in the back seat. He waved to the armed guard who had ridden with him. The guard nodded back. Meteor rushed toward Matthew. "What's going on?"

"Josef's gone."

"What?"

"Jonah and Simon, too. We're putting together a team to search for them."

"I'm in," Meteor said.

Matthew nodded toward the truck. "Let's lock those guys up in the Gatehouse cell. We might need the truck."

"Right away," Meteor said.

"Uh—wait. Let's have another chat with Trojan."

"You got it, Matthew."

Meteor bounded back to the truck. He opened the backseat door and grabbed Trojan, who sat nearest the door. He yanked the surprised biker out of the truck and pushed him forward.

Matthew nodded toward the Gatehouse. "There," he said. "I'll be with you in a minute."

Martha stood dumbly. She watched as activity unfolded around her. Like characters in a slow motion movie, she saw Matthew put his hand on Anna's shoulder and take her off to one side. He spoke to her. Anna nodded her head in agreement. They glanced over at Martha, looked away, and spoke some more. Anna nodded again. Matthew smiled. He gave the girl's shoulder a quick squeeze and with one concerned glance back at Martha, he turned toward the Gatehouse. Martha watched as he entered the building, closing the door behind him.

A deadly calm infused Martha—as thick and as still as a shrouded corpse. Her thoughts swirled—all of them were about Josef.

Where are you?

A scream rose up inside her.

Oh, God. No. No. Please no. Don't make me pay. Please don't make me pay. I'll never do it again. Never. Please, God. Please.

She was unaware that she had clenched her hands together in a prayerful clutch. The skin on the backs of her hands whitened from the force of her fingers. She jumped when she felt a touch on her arm. It was Anna.

"Let's go to the cabin and wait there," Anna said. Her eyes were soft, tender. "C'mon, Martha." She tried to take Martha's arm, but Martha wrenched it away. She tried again, but Martha stepped back.

"I'm going with them," Martha said.

"Matthew figured you'd say that, but he said you can't go," Anna said, with a delicate shake of her head.

"I will go," Martha said firmly.

Anna shook her head again. "Matthew asked me to take care of you. And make sure you don't leave the compound, Martha."

"He can't stop me."

"No, Martha. He's not trying to stop you. He thinks it's better that if Josef comes back when the search party is gone, you'll be here for him."

Martha relaxed. "Oh."

"C'mon," Anna said again, with a tiny smile. "I'll make you some tea."

The women had begun to walk away when the Gatehouse door burst open. Matthew called to the men waiting. He had a hurried conversation with them; they split into smaller groups, and headed to the trucks.

An assembly line formed as the men began to unload supplies from the truck boxes: the Walmart bags filled with the goods that Martha and the women had collected, the boxes of medical supplies, cans of fuel, and white metal bottles of propane they had found in Evansburg. The four Harleys were off-loaded, too. Soon the trucks were empty, except for their onboard fuel storage tanks.

The men again split into smaller groups and filled the trucks. Matthew jumped into his own truck. He turned the key and threw the truck into gear. He backed out, turned the truck around, and was about to head down the road. Someone ran up to the side of the truck; it was Meteor. Matthew stopped and rolled down the window.

"Wait," Meteor said. He pointed up the road. "Someone's coming."

Matthew watched as a truck came into view. It was the missing truck. As it came closer, a huge cheer went up. Jonah and Simon were sitting in the front seat. The truck pulled up and stopped.

Matthew killed his engine, and jumped out. He didn't bother to close the door and instead ran toward Jonah and Simon. They were out of their truck. People were crowding around them with greetings. And with questions. Matthew broke through the crowd and finally stood in front of the two boys. Anna and Martha had run up, too. They now stood next to Matthew. Meteor and Trojan stood behind them.

"Where's Josef?" Matthew asked.

Martha held her breath.

Please be lying in the back seat. Be hurt—it's okay. But please be there. Please, God. Please.

The boys stuttered, and their eyes darted from Matthew to Martha, and then back again. Finally, Jonah spoke:

"I'm sorry—so sorry." Tears welled in his eyes. "We did our best." He reached into his coat and pulled out a gun. Martha choked out a strangled cry, as Jonah handed Josef's pistol to Matthew. "Really sorry," he said. He began cry.

"No! Not Josef! Not Josef!"

Martha felt the earth shift under her feet. The tilt came so fast. The ground rose up and engulfed her. She slid into its sucking embrace. Meteor caught her as she fell.

□□□

MARTHA AWOKE. She was lying on her bed. Through bleary eyes, she looked around and struggled to make sense of her world. Like thick molasses, reality oozed across her mind—sticky and dark.

Josef. Josef.

Martha began to keen. She clamped both hands over her mouth. Her wail receded inside her, and she screamed soundlessly into her hands.

Anna stood near the bed. She watched Martha, her own face twisted and wet with emotion. Meteor stood quietly to the side of the bed. He glanced up at Anna, pursed his lips, and nodded his head in firm agreement to a private thought. He charged out of the cabin. Anna jumped, as the door slammed. Martha continued her silent scream.

MATTHEW WAS coming across the compound toward Martha's cabin. Meteor rushed toward him.

"Hey...how's she—" Matthew blocked Meteor's path and grabbed at the big man's arm as he tried to rush by him. Meteor turned. His eyes blazed. "Hey—" Matthew said again, louder.

"I'm going to kill Brad," Meteor said, his voice low and raspy.

"I know," Matthew said. "Hang on." He stood his ground in front of Meteor as the man tried to go around him. "Stop!" It was a command.

Meteor stopped. His eyes reflected his emotions; an ice blue inferno of hatred and rage.

"You run off like this," Matthew said, "and you're dead, too." He paused. "And then what will become of Martha?" He paused again. "Losing two men that she cares for. In a single day."

Meteor growled low in his throat. But he remained still. Matthew studied the man's livid face. "We'll do this together, okay?"

Meteor stared back at Matthew. He said nothing.

Matthew gazed at a spot in the infinite distance just past Meteor's shoulder. "He was my friend." His voice caught, and he cleared his throat. "C'mon."

Matthew turned back toward the Gatehouse. Meteor stalled. "C'mon," Matthew said again. Meteor finally relented and walked alongside Matthew. "How's she doing?"

"Not good," Meteor said. "Not good."

"Do you love her?"

The suddenness of Matthew's question made Meteor jerk his head around in surprise. "What?"

"Do you love her?"

Meteor squinted at Matthew. He shook his head. "No," he said slowly, "but I sure like her."

The men continued to walk.

"Yeah—me, too," Matthew said. He sighed heavily. "Me, too."

"Which one?" Meteor asked.

"What?"

"Which one? Love or like?"

Matthew said nothing. They entered the Gatehouse. Trojan was waiting for them.

"You guys all set?"

□□□

MATTHEW STEERED his truck up the road. The boys' story echoed inside his head, inciting a burst of hot anger. He tightened his grip on the steering wheel. He hoped Josef knew how much he had liked him. His throat grew thick, but he pushed the strong emotions away. A thought of Brad made his anger blaze anew. He let Simon's telling of the event roll through his mind...

"WE KNEW something was wrong, so we went to check the place we'd last seen Brad and Cindy," Simon told them after Martha had collapsed. "We found Brad all right—he and another guy were forcing Josef into a truck. At gunpoint. It was too dark to take a shot, so we figured we'd follow them. We ran like hell, got a truck, and sure enough—in a few miles—we saw them heading into the city."

"Brad was in on it for a long time," Jonah added.

Meteor looked up from where he knelt, his arms cradling Martha's unconscious body. "How do you know?" he asked.

"We overheard them talking," Jonah said. "About a guy called The Man, about taking the camp—about everything."

"We know where The Man's clubhouse is," Simon added.

"Yeah," Jonah said. He had stopped crying and he wiped his nose on his sleeve. "We followed all the way. No headlights—we followed their taillights. They finally pulled over at a warehouse on the edge of Edmonton."

"We stopped way back of them though," Simon said. "They never saw us. But we watched them. They took Josef into the building."

Matthew looked perplexed. "How did you get Josef's gun?"

Jonah covered his face with his hands. "Oh, God," he mumbled. Simon looked away.

"What?" Matthew asked.

Meteor stared up from his position on the ground. "Tell us—"

Simon swallowed and continued. "We get out of our truck—sneak around the building. We look for a way in. The entrance is too heavily guarded. So, we can't go that way. We look for another way, but we don't find one. So we wait near the parking lot." Jonah picked up the story:

"We waited for hours." Jonah said. "We were lucky not to get caught—" He took a ragged breath. "—Lucky they didn't have guard dogs. Finally... it was already light out... we saw some men come out of the clubhouse. They were dragging a man. We knew it had to be Josef." He swallowed and looked at Simon. "I can't tell it," he said. "You tell it." Simon continued the story:

"We were hiding in the bushes near where they parked their truck. They dragged Josef over. They stopped by the truck and dropped him on the ground. One man was walking behind them. Then... we heard Brad's voice. He asked the man walking behind them what he wanted them to do. The guy said, 'Send the Gatekeeper a message— From The Man.'

"Then the guy walked over to Josef, looked down at him on the ground—and kicked him. We heard Josef make a sound. 'You should have told us,' the guy said. 'Would have saved you a lot of pain.' Then he laughed and he said, 'We'll still get Matthew's camp.'

"He started to walk away, but Brad asked, 'What do you want us to do?' The Man said, 'Kill him. *You* kill him.' And Brad said, 'Yes, sir.'

"We tried to figure out a way to attack them, but there were eight guys, and they all had machine guns. So, we held our position. We could only watch." Simon took a breath and went silent.

"So, get on with it—what happened?" Meteor asked.

"Brad told one of the guys to take Josef's jacket off. And his shirt. 'Kevlar vest,' Brad said. He told them to take that off, too. They did. And Brad took it. He said it would fit him perfectly. Then Brad held up a gun. It was Josef's. Brad laughed and he said, 'You're such a sap, Josef. Could have pulled it on me.' He cocked the hammer. He aimed it at Josef's chest." Simon took a breath. "He said, 'This heart attack will be your last, Josef.' And he fired. Point blank. Into Josef's heart. Then he dropped the gun on the ground beside Josef. He said, 'Here's your gun back, Josef. May it protect you well.' The guys standing around, just laughed—" Simon went silent again.

The crowd of onlookers gasped. Some of them began to cry. Some for a second time. Jonah was crying again, too. "We couldn't do anything, Matthew," he sobbed. "Nothing."

"There's more," Simon said. He took another breath. "Brad said— " He hesitated. "He said... 'I'm going after Martha, Josef.' He said he was gonna teach her how to be a proper wife. 'Cause Josef couldn't do it. The guys laughed at that, too."

Anna gave a small cry. She glanced at Martha, who still lay unconscious in Meteor's lap. Matthew and Meteor said nothing; their eyes were on Simon. Simon continued:

"We waited. They just left Josef lying there. We snuck out after about an hour and checked him." He shook his head. "But he was dead. So, we grabbed the gun. And ran. And came right back here."

Matthew looked at the crowd. His eyes scanned the assembled people, right and left. He motioned to Martha.

"Nobody, and I mean NOBODY tells Martha what happened." His eyes scanned the people again. "Understand?" The people muttered their corporate agreement. Matthew's voice went low—a threat for disobedience vibrated through his words. "NOBODY!"

Meteor rose when Matthew finished speaking. He lifted Martha with him. "I'm taking her to the cabin," he said, his voice edged with cold rage. "After that—I have business to attend to."

"Meteor," Matthew said, his tone was stern. "We'll do it as a team."

Meteor said nothing. He turned and walked across the compound.

MATTHEW STARED at the road ahead. His truck was leading a small convoy of trucks, all headed for The Man's clubhouse. He knew they had no chance of taking on and defeating The Man's forces. Not today. Not yet. But they weren't about to leave Josef's body lying in the dirt. He glanced over at Simon. The kid looked stricken, but he was tough—he hadn't cried.

"You know that all we're going to do is get Josef's body, right?" Matthew asked.

Simon nodded. He stared ahead. Then he pointed. "There's Meteor."

Matthew sped up. Meteor slowed, allowing them to overtake his vehicle. Matthew nodded as he passed him, sending Meteor's truck into second position.

"What about Meteor?" Simon asked. Everyone had overheard Meteor swear he would kill Brad, just before he grabbed Trojan and tossed him into the cab of his truck.

"He's a wild card," Matthew said, "but he can take care of himself. I'm hoping he won't do anything stupid. But he might. Whatever happens, I want you to stay next to me. You understand?"

"Yes, sir."

"Good."

They drove on. Except for Simon's directions, they didn't speak further.

□□□

JOSEF'S BODY lay where Simon and Jonah had said it would be. Matthew's men had approached the clubhouse from a side street—parked their vehicles, and then ran on foot. The area was very quiet: no guards in sight, no bikers in the parking lot.

Matthew crouched near Josef's body; the eyes were closed, the mouth was slightly ajar. A trickle of blood had scabbed along a cut leading from Josef's eye down to his jaw. His face was bruised. One eye was puffy. Blood encrusted his lips, too. His naked chest was covered in blood. Matthew looked away.

He motioned to two of the men. They had a collapsible litter. Four of them loaded Josef's body. Then they raced back to the waiting trucks. The men piled in. They made their way back to the compound.

About a mile from the camp, Matthew stopped his truck. The rest of the drivers followed his lead. He had pulled over near a small creek.

"What's up?" Simon asked.

"We can't take Josef back looking like that," Matthew said. "Let's clean him up first."

Simon nodded.

The litter bearers unloaded Josef's body near the creek bed. They bent to assist Matthew, but he waved everyone away—back to the trucks. He held a small cloth in his hand. "I'll do it," he said.

The men clambered up through the ditch to the trucks parked on the shoulder of the highway. They stood and watched as Matthew washed

Josef's body. No one spoke when Matthew stopped his washing, when he sat hunkered down near his dead friend, his head bowed, and his shoulders shaking. He sat that way for a long while.

No one looked at Matthew's eyes when he came up and instructed the men to fetch Josef's body. No one said anything about his private time at the creek.

They were getting back into the trucks when Matthew called out to one of the men. "Where's Meteor?"

The man shrugged his shoulders. He shot Matthew a guilty look.

"Where in hell is Trojan?" Matthew asked.

The man shrugged again. "He told me to take his truck, Matthew," the man said, thumbing toward the RCMP truck. "I thought you knew. He stayed behind. He kept Trojan with him."

"When?"

"Before we left the clubhouse."

"Aw, shit," Matthew said. "Goddamn him. I told him to wait."

"What do you want us to do?" the man asked.

"Damn him," Matthew said again. He covered his own mouth with his hand and breathed heavily through his fingers. He thought for a moment, and then he shook his head. "I told him," he said. He flipped his fingers upwards in a gesture of dismissal. "He's on his own."

The men looked puzzled.

"Let's go," Matthew said. "We have a friend to bury."

□□□

The Body Pick-up

"THE BODY'S gone," the biker said.

"Good," said The Man. "Didn't take them long—"

"Just as you instructed," Brad said. "Executed with his own gun."

"Nice touch," said The Man.

"I still think killing Josef was a mistake," Virgil said. He shook his head, "More like the actions of a Crazy."

The Man grew very silent. When he spoke, his tone was encrusted with bitterness and a dark warning: "What did you say?"

"Look—killing Josef might have started something—too soon. Something we're not ready for—that's all I'm saying." Virgil's hands were raised in a gesture of placation.

"Just make sure your force is ready—I'll take care of the rest of the business. We've got the captains' meet coming up soon. We'll be inducting new probates. And announcing a new sergeant-at-arms."

The Man nodded in Brad's direction.

Brad smiled.

Chapter Twenty-Nine

The Spoils of War

THE TWO MEN hunkered down in the weeds near the clubhouse. They were arguing.

"I don't care," Meteor said. He used a gray linen handkerchief to wipe sweat from his eyes. He shoved it into a back pocket.

"But they'll kill you," Trojan said. The two of them were crouched several hundred yards to the right of The Man's clubhouse. They noticed several armed guards—the guards had appeared just shortly after Matthew and the other men left with Josef's body.

"They know you, right?" Meteor whispered.

"Kind of—I've only been around a couple of times."

"And it's not unusual to bring new recruits?"

"No. We do it all the time."

"So, why should they kill me?"

"You have a look, Meteor," Trojan advised.

"A look?"

"The Man is pretty up on himself, okay? Thinks the sun rises and sets... You have a way of... " He paused and thought, "...acting like you don't care. You know... respect."

"Oh, that," Meteor whispered. "Just get me inside. I'll figure it out from there."

"So, how do you want to work this?" Trojan asked.

"You tell me."

"Well, they're gonna wonder where my bike is. And where my buddies are."

Meteor thought a moment. "That could work in our favor. Just tell them that you and your boys were attacked on a farm when you stopped to siphon gas. Men attacked you, you fought them off, but they killed your three friends. You ran and left the bikes behind. I came along and picked you up."

Trojan looked skeptical. "This is going to get us both killed, you know."

"Ah, come on," Meteor said. "With that fat lip I gave you, you already look like you've been beaten up."

Trojan grimaced as he touched his mouth. "Still hurts," he said. "And my tooth is loose."

"I could give you another good whack. A black eye, maybe. Make it look really good." Meteor grinned.

Trojan frowned. He shook his head. "What about that Brad-guy? What's he going to say when he sees you?"

"I hope I'll be the last thing he sees."

"You think you'll get a chance to kill him when we get inside?" Trojan frowned. "Not gonna happen. The first thing they'll do, when we walk in—is take our weapons."

"There are other ways to kill someone."

"So— You are planning to get us killed." Trojan said. He stared at Meteor. "I don't think you've thought this through." He paused and shook his head. "I'm not willing to give up my life just yet."

Meteor stared at Trojan. He breathed deeply. "So, do we wait out here to ambush Brad?"

"I doubt he'll be alone. There's no telling how many guys he'll be with."

"I need to send a message back to The Man from the Gatekeeper."

"Okay, I get that—but there's got to be a better way than walking through those front doors on a suicide mission." Trojan paused. He shot Meteor a questioning look. "How are we getting home?"

Meteor pointed toward the parking area filled with bikes and trucks. "We steal a ride," he said.

Trojan sighed. "Oh, joy—I've allied with a nut. I'm in for such fun."

A commotion at the front door drew their attention. Several bikers were leaving the clubhouse. They were laughing and teasing each other, poking fun with ribald comments about each other's sexual prowess.

Meteor studied the men. "These will do," he said.

"What?"

"Let's leave The Man a message."

Trojan grabbed his arm. "I don't have a weapon," he hissed. "You took them."

"What's your choice? Knife or gun?"

Trojan made a face. "Gun, thanks."

Meteor reached down and pulled up his pant leg. He took a pistol from a holster on his leg.

"Here," he said, handing it to Trojan. "The sight's a little off. Shoot high." He reached into his coat pocket. "Extra ammo."

Trojan took the gun and the bullets. "So, what's the plan?"

"Let's see where these guys are headed." They watched the men. There were six of them. None of them was Brad.

"I gotta take a leak," said one of the men—a tall thin biker in a checkered flannel shirt and dark vest. He made his way to the side of the building and down into a small alleyway.

"I'll be right back," Meteor said. He slipped out of their hiding place and ran toward the building. Trojan gripped his pistol and watched him go. Meteor was soon out of sight.

Five minutes went by. Trojan looked through the weeds. There was no sign of Meteor. He gasped when the big man pushed in beside him."

That's one," Meteor said. "Five to go."

"What d'ya do?"

"Quick kill. Nothing messy. Broke his neck."

"Oh," Trojan sighed. "Only five more necks to break." He sighed again.

The pair continued to watch the five men. Soon the bikers were glancing around for their friend.

"Hey!" one of them said. He was a man of medium-build with long blond hair pulled into a ponytail. "That's the longest whizz ever. You coming back?" The man stared at the area where his friend had disappeared.

"Can you use a knife?" Meteor asked.

"Of course— Why?"

"We can't risk gunfire. Let's take out four more, and save one. For questioning." Meteor reached to his waist belt. He pulled the snap on his knife sheath. "Take this." He handed Trojan a serrated fishing knife with a wickedly curved blade. "This'll do some fast damage." Trojan took the knife. He turned it over in his hands.

"How are we going to split them up?" Trojan asked.

"You are."

"Me?"

"Yeah, you look like one of them."

Trojan scowled. "Am I gonna like this idea?"

"Wait," Meteor whispered. "Listen."

Three of the men, who had been smoking, stubbed out their cigarettes and turned back to the clubhouse. "I'm not waiting for him," said one of the men. He was short and chubby and dressed in a long brown leather jacket that came almost to his knees. "He's probably taking a crap." The five men laughed again. The trio nodded to the guards at the door and went inside.

"—and that leaves two," Meteor said.

"Great—" Trojan said. "You can do subtraction. Now what?"

"Do you think you can convince those two guys that you need some help with your bike?"

"What bike? You took my bike."

Meteor stifled a small laugh. "You idiot. Just pretend."

"Oh." Trojan thought about it. "You really are trying to get me killed."

Meteor smiled.

"There *are ladies* waiting at the end of this craziness, right?" Trojan asked.

"Sure. If we get out of this alive," Meteor advised.

Trojan sighed again—this time it was a drawn-out, deep, breathy sound.

The two bikers began a slow amble toward the street. Meteor elbowed Trojan. "Wait till they get out of sight of the guards," he said. "Then we'll take them from behind."

Trojan looked puzzled. "Kill 'em both?" he whispered. "I thought you wanted one for questioning."

"I do, but we'll see what happens," Meteor whispered back.

They watched as the men turned up the street toward them. In a few minutes, the two bikers were strolling by their hiding place. Meteor could see they were heavily armed. Any move he made would have to be fast, silent.

The bikers moved off down the street. Meteor glanced back at the guards. They were standing, booted feet apart, and staring toward the street. They would notice their movement. A man came out of the building. The guards turned to talk to him.

"Now," Meteor whispered.

Trojan followed Meteor as they crept from their hiding place. The bikers were now about 100 yards away. They would have to sprint to catch up. Suddenly, Meteor grabbed Trojan's arm. They were near a massive corporate lawn sign. Meteor pulled Trojan in behind it as a large black F-350 Ford truck careened around the corner. The two bikers stopped and waited.

The truck pulled up alongside the bikers. It jolted to a stop. A small woman leapt out of the driver's side. She called out a welcome and walked around to the men. They greeted her with smiles and hugs. She pointed to the back of the truck. The men followed her.

"Our ride," Meteor whispered.

"Yeah, but now there's three," Trojan hissed back.

"Yeah, but one's a woman," Meteor said, with a sly grin. "Kind of cute, too."

Trojan scowled. "Remember our deal," he hissed. "I get first dibs."

The two bikers and the woman smiled and laughed as they gazed into the truck box.

"They sure like what they're seeing," Trojan observed.

"Now," Meteor said.

"Now what?" Trojan asked. But Meteor was already sprinting toward the truck, his gun drawn. Trojan followed.

They made the short run without being noticed. They huddled near the truck's grill, and waited.

Meteor heard the two men coming back along the passenger side. The woman was coming along the driver's side. He nudged Trojan. "You take the woman," he said. "I'll take care of the guys."

Meteor stood up. "Hi, gents," he said. The men jumped back in surprise. They both stared silently at the gun pointed at them. Meteor put a finger to his lips. "Sh—" he said. He motioned with the gun. "If you want to live, move back."

The men backed up, their eyes wide.

"Turn around," Meteor said.

"You know you're dead if you fire that," the taller biker said, as he turned.

"Yeah, Einstein—but you'll be dead first." Meteor poked him with the gun. "Move."

Both men moved forward.

The shorter man went down like a sack of bricks when Meteor hit him. The taller man turned back with a start. "You want it, too?" Meteor asked. The man shook his head and turned around.

Trojan came around to the back of the truck. He had the woman with him. Her eyes were wide. Her full mouth was open, showing bright white teeth, but she didn't say anything. She faltered and winced when Trojan gave the arm he had twisted up behind her back an extra twist. Meteor pulled electrical ties from his jacket pocket. Trojan took them. He quickly secured the girl's wrists.

"Better gag her," Meteor said. He pulled out his gray handkerchief.

"No, please," the girl said as she eyed the grimy cloth. "I'll be quiet."

Trojan bent his mouth to her ear. "Make a sound, and I will break your neck. Be good, and I will treat you fine." The girl jerked her head away. She shot Trojan a hateful look. He smiled back.

"Hey!" Meteor said, at a volume designed to capture Trojan's attention. Meteor motioned to the man in front of him. "Tie him..."

Trojan shoved the girl up against the truck, gave her a warning look, and walked toward the tall biker. He wrenched the man's hands behind his back, and secured his wrists with a large white tie. The band made a zipping sound as he pulled it tight.

Meteor grabbed the man by his crooked elbow and pushed him toward the front of the truck. Meteor stopped, yanked the handkerchief out of his pocket, balled it up, and shoved it into the man's mouth. He opened the back door and pushed the man toward the seat. "Lie down," he said. The man climbed in and lay down. Meteor shut the door. He motioned to Trojan, but Trojan was staring intently into the truck box.

Trojan let out a low whistle. "We won't be going back empty-handed." He looked up. "Wait till Matthew sees this."

Meteor walked around and looked. "Holy shit!" They stared into the truck box for another long moment. The woman began to protest, but she quieted when Meteor turned his eyes on her.

Meteor handed Trojan another tie. "Take care of this guy." He nudged the unconscious man on the ground with the toe of his boot. "I'll take her."

Trojan scowled again.

Meteor laughed. "Easy. Just putting her in the truck." Meteor grabbed the woman's arm, and pulled her toward the truck. He opened the front door and shoved her in. She began to protest again. "Don't test me," he said. "I will shoot you. Not a sound."

Meteor watched as Trojan pulled the unconscious man off the street and dragged him back behind some tall evergreen trees. He turned back to the truck, but then he stopped. He dropped to his knees, did something with his hands, and then got back to his feet.

Trojan returned to the truck. Meteor indicated the passenger seat. Trojan got in. Meteor ran around to the driver's side, opened the door, and jumped in. He smiled at the woman perched on the console between them. "You're going to like us," he said. Meteor nodded toward Trojan. "Especially him," he said. "You are really gonna like him."

"I doubt that," the woman said.

Meteor smiled and turned the key. He put the truck into gear. "His name is Trojan, you know."

"Oh, ooh, wow—" the woman said, "—now I am impressed. Does he come with his own supply of penicillin?"

Meteor laughed and turned the wheel. He touched the gas.

Trojan turned. He smiled. He raised his arm and slid it around the woman's shoulders. She gasped and tried to pull away, but he held her fast.

They were blocks away when Meteor finally turned to Trojan. "What were you doing back there?"

Trojan faced him and smiled. "Leaving a message from the Gatekeeper," he said.

Meteor nodded. "Did you wipe my knife off?"

"Yeah, sure," Trojan said. He bent his head to the woman and nuzzled her cheek. "You smell great." The woman squirmed. She twisted and glared at Trojan.

"You are so dead," she said. "I belong to The Man. Just wait'll he finds out." Meteor glanced over.

Trojan had raised his eyebrows and widened his eyes in pretended terror. "Oh yes—I'll wait. Look, I'm holding my breath." He did so.

Meteor burst out laughing.

The woman shook her head. "Assholes," she said.

"Be nice," Meteor said. He reached over and squeezed her knee. With her bound hands, she shoved his hand away.

MATTHEW LOOKED up from his paperwork. He placed his pen carefully on the desk, folded his arms across his chest, and sat back in his chair. Meteor stood in front of him. Neither man smiled.

"I gave you an order—" Matthew said. "You disobeyed."

"You aren't going to be so pissed at me when you see what I've got," Meteor said. He pointed over his shoulder at the Gatehouse door. "Outside in the truck. A new truck," he added.

Matthew sat silently. He shifted his position, making the chair creak. He leaned forward, "Meteor, I like you. I would trust you with my life. But I gotta be able to rely on you." He paused. "With Josef dead, I need a second-in-command. You up to it?"

Meteor took a moment, and then answered, "Uh, Matthew... I'm not such a good choice for that."

"Why not?"

"Uh... I gotta say, 'no,' Matthew. There are better guys here for that job."

"No... not better," Matthew said. "Just more willing." He got up. "Show me," he said. The men walked out of the Gatehouse to the truck.

"Nice," Matthew said. "It's your week for picking up new wheels. Nice," he said again, as he moved around to the truck bed. He peered in. He nodded his head, and looked up. "VERY nice." Matthew smiled.

"I told you," Meteor said. He undid the tailgate and dropped it down. Two sturdy chains stopped its fall. The men gazed at the assorted weaponry that lay before them: rocket launchers, sub machine guns, hand grenades, and ammunition—cases and cases of ammunition."

Matthew turned to Meteor. "The Man is going to be pissed."

"Uh—that's not all he's going to be pissed about," Meteor said. He pointed to a table near the parking lot. Trojan and his new female friend were seated there. The woman's wrists were still bound.

Matthew frowned. "Who's that?"

"A little something that belongs to the man," Meteor replied.

"Oh, great. Just what we need. Another of his females."

"Speaking of which," Meteor said, "ever find out where Cindy got to?"

"Yeah, a patrol found her body— in a ditch off the back mile."

"Looks like Brad was trying to tie up loose ends. Any word from him?"

"Aren't you the one to answer that question?" Matthew asked.

"I can't. But I brought along someone who might be helpful." Meteor pointed into the truck's backseat. Matthew peered in through the side window. He saw a bound man lying there.

"Who's that?"

"A prisoner of war," Meteor said. "We picked him up just outside The Man's clubhouse."

Matthew shook his head. "We're gonna have to build a cell house with all the prisoners we're collecting."

"Do you want to interrogate him now?" asked Meteor.

Matthew shook his head. "In a minute." He turned. "Introduce me to that lady over there."

The pair walked to the table. Trojan was busy teasing his captive. Matthew watched. The woman didn't seem to be minding his attentions.

"What's your name?" he asked.

"Who wants to know?" came her reply. Her eyes were round and a deep rich brown with flecks of gold. Her lashes were dark. But it was her mouth that was the most fetching: full thick lips, red and pouty. Matthew spoke again:

"I asked you your name." Trojan began to speak, but Matthew held up his hand. "She knows her own name," he said.

"Cammy. My name is Cammy. Want to know my shoe size, too? How about my bra size?" Matthew's eyes flickered over her chest.

Trojan laughed. "She's got spunk," he said. He stood up. "Since we're keeping her as a prisoner, I'm volunteering to keep an eye on her." It was Matthew's turn to laugh. Meteor joined him.

"We did promise you a woman, didn't we?" Matthew caught Cammy's eyes. "How would you feel about that? Stay with Trojan? Or... you could share a cell with a couple of bikers."

Cammy smiled—a crooked grin. It was not wasted on Matthew. He caught the subtle message, and he smiled back at her.

"What's it gonna be?"

Cammy looked to Meteor. She raised her bound hands, lifted her two index fingers, and brushed stray auburn hairs from her face. She drew her fingers across her cheek, and then down her jaw to the curve of her neck—slowly and with great intent. She lifted her chin. As she did so, she motioned to Trojan. "Is he any good?" Her voice slipped through her lips like silken fire

Meteor gave a short laugh. "How the hell am I supposed to know?" He smiled. "Why don't you find out and then you can tell us."

Cammy looked back at Matthew. "You still haven't introduced yourself."

"I'm Matthew. They call me the *Gatekeeper*."

"Ah," Cammy said. "The 'Gatekeeper.' I've heard of you." She dipped her head, and smiled again—slow and deliberate—like a cat licking its fur. "The Man has spoken of you often."

"All good, I hope," Matthew said.

"Oh, yes. Of course. Very good."

Matthew studied the woman for another moment. "She's yours, Trojan. Since she passed on the chance to make the decision for herself, I'll make it for her." Matthew eyed Cammy as he spoke, "Keep her jailed, though. I suspect this one will run at the first chance."

Matthew turned away. He took a step and then turned back. He looked at Cammy. "By the way, just so you know. If you run, and we catch you, your next home will be a twelve-by-twelve cell with two bikers. And no private toilet facilities." He paused and waited for his words to sink in. "You got that?"

Cammy nodded. "Yes, I got that—*Matthew*."

Matthew turned to Meteor. "Check with Mar..." he caught himself. "Check with Anna... she'll know where to put Trojan and..." he motioned to Cammy, "... his new missus." Cammy regarded Matthew—a hard glint in her eyes.

"When The Man finds out I'm gone, he'll come after me. And he will *kill* you."

Matthew nodded. "I'm sure he will." He raised his eyebrows. "I'd come after you, too, if I were him." Cammy looked mildly taken aback.

Trojan got up and grabbed Cammy by the arm. Without effort, he lifted her to her feet. "C'mon, sweetheart," he said. "Let's go home."

Cammy resisted and said, "Wherever we're going, there'd better be food—I'm starving."

Trojan smiled. "Food? That'll be the last thing on your mind." He grabbed her elbow and escorted her away from the table.

Meteor and Matthew watched the couple walk in the direction of the Women's Bunkhouse. Meteor crossed his arms.

"Humph," he said. "That was easy." He turned to Matthew. "How come you did that? Both of them are from the other side. What if they turn on us?"

Matthew looked up. "Don't you trust him?"

"Yeah—I do."

"That's good enough for me." Matthew paused. He thought a moment, and then said, "You sure you don't want that position?"

Meteor shook his head. "No, my friend—I do much better as a foot soldier. Give someone else the headache of running things. I'd rather—" Matthew interrupted him.

"—do as you please?"

Meteor laughed. The two men turned and walked back to the truck holding the prisoner.

Matthew signaled to one of the guards. "I need a brigade," he said. "We've got some heavy off-loading to do. We'll meet at the Munitions Storehouse." The man nodded. Matthew checked his watch. "In 15 minutes." The man nodded again.

Meteor glanced into the backseat. Their newest prisoner had fallen asleep. "What do you want to do with him?"

"Let's lock him in the RCMP truck for now. At least until we interrogate him."

Meteor banged on the truck's back door. "Hey, buddy. Wake up." The man sat up. He looked confused. Reality set in, and his eyes hardened. Meteor opened the door, and the man got out. "We're taking you to new digs," he said.

After the man was secured in the RCMP truck, Meteor returned to Matthew. Matthew was giving instructions to one of the men for off-loading. He turned as Meteor approached. "I'm going with them so I can log this stuff. Are you coming?" Meteor shook his head.

"I'm pretty damn tired," he said. "Besides, I want to check on Martha." Matthew nodded his head and smiled.

"Okay. Give her my best," Matthew said, as he jumped into the truck. "Let's get together later. My cabin. Debriefing. I want to hear all the details."

"You're on," Meteor said. He saluted as Matthew pulled away. Then he turned and started across the compound.

Toward Martha's cabin.

□□□

The Message

THE BIKER returned to the room. "Sir?"

"What?"

"Something went down about a block from here."

"What?"

"One of our men was found dead, neck broken, and another one is alive—but he was tortured."

"Explain," The Man said to the biker at the door.

"Somebody carved a gate into the guy's chest."

Virgil gave a small whistle through his teeth. "And so it begins," he said.

The Man shot him a sinister look.

"There's something else, sir."

The Man turned and glowered at the speaker.

"Cammy left with the guns from the base hours ago. She should have been here by now." He faltered. "One of the guys says they saw your truck about an hour ago. Heading away from the clubhouse."

Virgil studied his fingernails. He said nothing.

Chapter Thirty

A Parting of Ways

METEOR BENT down to the girl. Anna looked up. Her eyes were puffy and dark. She was perched in a chair beside Martha's bed, her feet drawn up, and her knees beneath her chin. "How is she?" he whispered.

"Not so good, but at least she's sleeping."

Meteor nodded. "You really are a good friend to her," he said. "She's lucky to have you." He patted her shoulder.

Meteor fetched a chair from the kitchen, brought it into the bedroom, and sat down next to Anna. "You look like you could use a break," he said. "Who's taking care of your little guy?"

"I ran out an hour ago and nursed him. So, he's okay. One of the other girls will nurse him if he wakes up." Meteor touched her forearm.

"What about you? When are you going to get some rest?"

"I can't leave her," Anna said. "She wakes up every once in a while— Screaming. I calm her down. And she falls back to sleep." She opened her mouth in a deep, wide yawn. "I've got to be here for her."

"I'll stay, Anna," Meteor said. Anna's eyes flickered up to meet his.

"I'm not so sure that's a good idea."

"Trust me," Meteor said. "I won't leave her." He gave her arm a squeeze. "Go, get some rest. I'll stay with her." Anna looked skeptical. "Really," Meteor said, with a smile. "It's okay. Go."

Anna smiled and rose from her chair. "She hasn't had anything to eat or drink. I have everything ready for tea, for when she wakes up."

Meteor smiled. He nodded. "I can make tea," he said. "Go."

Anna stooped over the bed, and brushed hair from Martha's forehead. She leaned down and kissed Martha's cheek. "Okay. I'll be back in a couple of hours."

She turned and left the cabin.

□□□

MATTHEW DROPPED the logbook to his desk. There was going to be hell to pay for Meteor's opportunistic acquisition—but the munitions were a welcome addition, especially the rocket launchers. He sat down and pulled a large hardbound book toward him. He flipped it open. It was Matthew's registry of all compound occupants; it included the date they arrived, and the date they departed.

Matthew turned pages until he found what he was looking for. He sat quietly staring at the entries. There they were; Martha and Josef's name, as he had entered them last fall. He picked up his pen. He located the column under "Departed," ran his finger down to Josef's name, and entered the date in the empty box. He lay his pen down on the desk, gently closed the book, and pushed it away from him. He leaned on his elbows with his forehead in his hands. He stayed that way until he heard a knock on the door.

Matthew looked up. "Come," he said.

Simon and Jonah walked in. They strode to the desk.

"We came to see if there is anything we can do," Jonah said.

Matthew stared at the boys. "You guys look awful. Have you gotten any sleep?"

"Yeah, some," Simon said. "But it's hard to stay asleep."

Jonah nodded. "We're happier doing something."

Matthew nodded. "I get that."

"Can we do anything for the funeral?" Simon asked. Matthew listened, but he remained quiet. "We'd like to help."

"He was a Christian. Can either of you do something Christian?"

Jonah nodded. "I can— I'm a believer."

"Well, then, you go ahead and put a service together." Matthew looked at Simon. "Can you make a wooden grave marker?"

Simon nodded his head. "The very best," he said.

"Josef really liked you guys. He would want to know that you two were handling these things." Matthew smiled warmly. "Go. We'll hold the funeral after supper tonight. I'll assign somebody to dig his grave." The boys nodded and turned toward the door. As they did so, they heard a knock.

Matthew nodded toward the door. Jonah opened it. Trojan stood there. Cammy was with him.

"Oh, sorry," Trojan said. "Just came over to ask a question."

Jonah and Simon exchanged looks and then looked back at Matthew.

Matthew nodded. "Trojan and Cammy have joined us," he said. He motioned toward the boys, "This is Simon and Jonah." He waved. "Come in."

Trojan took Cammy's arm and they stepped into the room. The boys pushed by and left the Gatehouse, closing the door behind them. Trojan walked to the desk. Matthew waited.

"I need something to do here," Trojan said. "I also need some weapons. Meteor loaned me some, but he took them back." Trojan shrugged. "I won't be much good to you without a weapon."

Matthew nodded. "I hear you. And I agree. And we'll get that taken care of. But in the meantime, I have another job for you." He nodded to Cammy. "She can help, too— It'll be kind of fitting."

"We'll see," Cammy said.

"It wasn't a request." Matthew's tone was stern, and final. "It was an order."

"Oh," Cammy said, tempting a response. "An order..."

Trojan shot Cammy a warning look. Then he looked back at Matthew. "What do you want us to do?" he asked.

"We're burying Josef tonight. I need a grave dug. Can you do that?"

Trojan nodded. "Sure. No problem. Just tell me where to find the shovels."

Cammy regarded Matthew coolly, her lips curled into the tiniest hint of a smirk. Matthew studied her for a moment, and then he looked back to Trojan.

"I want you to know something—you wouldn't be here if it weren't for Meteor. It's because he trusts you that you aren't back in a jail cell with your other two buddies."

"What's gonna happen to them, anyway?" Trojan asked. Matthew shook his head.

"I'm getting to them—tomorrow—and to the new prisoner. Right now— I want to get Josef buried."

Matthew pulled the logbook toward him. He flipped it open. He selected a page and picked up his pen. He held the pen poised over the page. "Trojan or Harvey?"

□□□

MARTHA STIRRED and moaned in her sleep. Meteor jumped up and leaned over her. He stared at her for a moment. He called her name.

"Martha? Martha?" Martha murmured, and shifted her position. "Martha?" Her eyes flickered open. She stared at him. She closed her eyes and opened them again. "Can I get you some tea?" he asked.

Martha fought her way through the fog. It hung over her consciousness like a downy grey quilt, all thick and soothing. She kept slipping back into its embrace.

Tea? Someone was asking her for tea? What day was it? What time was it? Where's Josef? Was he on patrol? Josef?

A memory began to surface. Martha whimpered and squirmed. Like oily cement, the memory oozed across Martha's mind. It slid through her like a frosted pane of glass, sheer and sharp. It entered her chest, and sat upon her heart, suffocating it. She struggled for breath. As she did so, a small cry rose up from her throat. She squeezed her eyes shut tight. She felt someone touch her hand. Her eyes flew open.

Josef? Josef?

Reality hit her—as clear and as cold as a mountain stream.

Josef was dead. Dead. He was dead. Her husband was dead. But who was this? Who was here? Beside her? Beside their bed? Who was standing in his place?

Martha willed her eyes to focus on the man standing near her. She looked into his face. His blue eyes.

Blue eyes.

Another memory surfaced. Of moonlight—a tent—a touch—a kiss... his kiss. Her hand shot to her mouth.

Meteor.

"No," Martha cried. "No."

Meteor touched her arm, and she flinched away. "Martha?" He touched her again and she wrenched away, rolling with the covers to the other side of the bed. She sat up, clutching the blankets to her chest. She stared at him. Meteor walked around to the other side of the bed.

"Martha," he said. "It's okay." Meteor sat down next to her and put his arm around her. She pulled away, but he held fast. He wrapped his other arm around her and drew her into his embrace. She struggled, but he didn't let her go. "I'm sorry," he whispered. "So sorry."

"Get away from me," she moaned, her voice muffled against his chest. "Get away." She began to weep, her body shaking with the sobs.

"Sh..." Meteor held her, and stroked her hair. He continued to shush her. She continued to cry. After a while, she quieted. Her breathing became rhythmic and heavy. Meteor held her while she slept.

□□□

METEOR GLANCED toward the window. The light had changed—the rays were now long and golden. He had fallen asleep, too. He eased Martha out of his arms and down onto a pillow. He checked his watch: Five o'clock. Josef's funeral would be soon. He glanced at Martha. She was awake. She was staring at him.

"Get away from me."

Meteor frowned. "Why?" His tone was soft and puzzled. He reached for her, but she pushed his hand away. "Martha—" he said.

"Get out." Martha's voice grew deeper, as the wild thing inside her turned on itself. Its teeth sank into her, ripping at her soul, tearing at her heart, making her blood run like ice fire through her veins. She jolted upright. She moved away from Meteor to the other side of the bed. "Go away."

Meteor swung his legs off the bed. He stood. He walked around to the other side of the bed and sat down in the chair he had occupied earlier. "I'm staying with you till Anna gets back," he said.

Martha watched Meteor. He sat silhouetted with the window at his back; soft gilded light framed him in an ethereal way. For the moment, Martha envisioned Josef. Her heart wrenched inside her. With it came a stream of emotion, an avalanche of shame: red and raw, and accusatory. She had been with him—with this man—with Meteor. While Josef was being murdered. Feelings of revulsion birthed inside her. Like deadly mushrooms, the feelings sprouted in the darkness of her soul.

"Get out of here." Martha took a slow ragged breath. "I can't stand the sight of you."

Meteor's mouth hung open in surprise. He stood and walked to the edge of the bed. He held Martha by her shoulders and stared into her eyes. "What happened between us had nothing to do with Josef being killed. If you must hate someone, hate the people who killed him. Hate Brad," he said.

"Brad?" Martha asked. She shook her head. "What are you talking about?" Meteor relaxed his grip on her shoulders and let his arms drop to his sides.

"Brad killed Josef."

Martha's eyes grew wide.

"What happened?"

Meteor held up a hand. "That's all I can tell you. But we know for a fact that Brad killed him." Meteor paused. "I thought I could catch up to Brad. But I couldn't find him." He paused again. "I'm sorry, Martha. I truly am."

"Tell me what happened," Martha said.

"I can't," Meteor said.

"Tell me," Martha said. "Tell... me." She pleaded with her eyes. "I need to know."

Meteor shook his head. "Not now, Martha. You don't want to hear about it."

"You know me, Meteor," Martha said. "If you care for me at all... tell me."

Meteor studied her. He turned back to his chair, and sat down.

He took a breath.

"Brad and another man abducted Josef while he was on patrol. They took him to the man's clubhouse. Simon and Jonah followed them. The place was too heavily guarded, so all they could do was watch. They saw Brad and some other bikers come out of the clubhouse. They had Josef with them." Meteor paused. "He was badly beaten, Martha."

A soft moan escaped Martha's lips and she covered her mouth.

"You still want me to go on?"

Martha nodded.

"Brad told the guys to remove Josef's jacket—and shirt." Meteor winced. "They took off his vest, Martha."

Martha's eyes widened. A strange choking sound erupted from her, but she stifled it behind her hands, clutching and white-knuckled.

"Then Brad took Josef's gun and shot him."

Martha sat, frozen, her mouth open.

"Martha?"

Meteor jumped at the sound that came from her throat.

Martha's thin, reedy cry rose up, curling and snaking through the air like tendrils of some deadly vine, creeping and reaching, climbing ever higher. Like a rogue wave, it exploded through the walls of the cabin, ripping through the calm of the evening.

Meteor jumped from his chair. He reached to comfort her, but Martha collapsed on the bed and drew herself into a tight fetal ball. She screamed into the bedding, but her terrible wail spiraled high and piercing, reverberating through the tiny cabin.

"I'll get Anna," Meteor said.

Meteor ran across the compound. Behind him, Martha's screams continued. Anna was already running to meet him.

□□□

MATTHEW GLARED at Meteor; his eyes were dark and cold. The two men were standing near the vehicle lot. "What did I say?"

"I know what you said," Meteor said. He stood eye-to-eye with Matthew. "But she's one of us. We wouldn't withhold that information from one of the men."

"You crossed me again, Meteor. I warned you before." Matthew went silent.

"She needed to know."

"I gave a direct order—that no one was to tell her. And you went against my orders."

"You weren't in the room with her, Matthew. You would have agreed with me. She needed to know." Meteor's voice was now edged and brittle.

"Yeah," Matthew said. "It sure sounded like she needed to know."

"Dammit, Matthew. I'm telling you, she wanted to know. She begged to know."

"You know I like you, Meteor. I told you that. But I can't run this compound if my men won't obey an order." Matthew's voice went low. "You leave me no choice."

Meteor held up his hand. "I know. I get it."

"Do you?" Matthew took a breath. "Only one man on this compound has veto power over my decisions. That's my second-in-command. Take the position, or... "

"Or what?"

"Or leave."

Meteor's face darkened. He shook his head. "I can't, Matthew. I just can't." He took a deep breath and shook his head again. "I'll leave."

Matthew remained silent.

"I'll take one of the Harleys. I'll leave after the funeral."

"It's better if you don't attend the funeral," Matthew said.

Meteor swallowed hard. "Okay." He extended his hand to Matthew. Matthew shook it.

Meteor turned and began to walk away. He paused and turned back. "You haven't seen the last of me, Matthew."

"Stay safe."

Meteor walked away.

Matthew watched him go.

☐☐☐

The Secret Meeting

"HE'S NOT going to like this," she said.

"Who's going to tell him? Certainly not me," Virgil said, with a smile.

They were meeting in a small city playground—near Marion's home—a mansion The Man had commandeered for her, several months prior. He had set her up with generators and supplies.

Earlier that day, Virgil had stood outside The Man's office waiting for Marion to leave. On her way out, she stopped and gave him her address and a smile—Virgil accepted both.

Now they shared a park bench. The late day sunshine was warm on their faces. Virgil slipped an arm along the back of the bench—his fingers just barely touching her shoulder.

"Things are really edgy right now," he said. "Might as well throw this into the mix, too." He dropped his hand to her shoulder. She moved closer to him.

"I told you that I'm not his." She gave Virgil an earnest look. "I care about him, but only the way a sister would care for a brother."

Virgil gave her a warm smile. "That's good, but some brothers can be very possessive of their sisters. Very protective."

"Yeah. But what he doesn't know—won't hurt him." She snuggled closer.

Virgil's hand moved up her shoulder to Marion's cheek; his thumb absently stroked the soft flesh. Marion murmured her contentment.

A squirrel scampered across the lawn—it hesitated for a moment and studied the pair. Marion laughed. The sound caused the squirrel to bolt away.

The rumble of bikes in the distance caught their attention. Marion sat up as Virgil stiffened.

"This might not be such a good place to meet," Virgil said. "Is there somewhere more—private?"

"Oh, yes." Marion stood up and held out her hand to him. "Way more private," she said with a soft smile.

Chapter Thirty-One

The Bible

MARTHA CREPT to the edge of the bed. She sat up. "Uhhh," she said, as her hands flew to her head.

She leaned her elbows into her knees and raised her fingers to her temples. Her head throbbed with an intensity that made her stomach pitch. She massaged two tiny sore spots, and then looked up at the window. The brightness of the light (morning, she guessed) made her wince, and new pain lanced through her temples. She squinted. Under the window, she noticed a dark shape curled up on a sleeping bag on the floor. The shape shifted, and a face appeared. Then a small smile.

"You're awake," Anna said softly. She pushed back the sleeping bag and she stretched.

"Did you sleep there all night?" Martha asked.

"Yeah." Anna yawned.

"Where's Josef—" Martha caught herself. She had a sudden urge to cry, but no tears came. She closed her eyes and rocked back and forth, her fingers still holding her aching temples.

"How about some tea?" Anna asked.

"Sure," Martha replied. Then slowly, "Where's Josef's body?"

Anna stopped. "You don't remember?"

"Remember what?"

"His funeral was last night. You were there. Remember?" Martha looked up at Anna. The girl's expression was guarded and nervous.

"No, I don't—" Martha said. She caught her breath as a gray shadow entered into her consciousness. A dark hole, a pile of brown earth, a wooden cross, somebody reading words from the Bible, a large shape wrapped round in cloth, somebody crying, many people crying, and then nothing. "Oh," she said.

Anna got up and sat beside her. She put her arm around her shoulders. "It was pretty hard on you," she said. "You fainted. Matthew brought you back here."

"Matthew? Where's Meteor?"

Anna pulled away and stood up.

"Uh—he and Matthew had a falling out." Anna paused. "He—he left."

Martha winced and grabbed her temples again.

"Left? For where?"

"I don't know. Matthew let him take one of the Harleys and he left before the funeral. Matthew told everyone he was gone just before we buried Josef."

Martha processed the information. She knew she should feel something, she wanted to feel something, but the numbness over her heart and soul was dense and all-inclusive.

Meteor. Meteor. She cast the thought away.

Martha lifted herself from the bed, but the pain rocketed through her head, and she staggered. Anna grabbed her elbow. "I'm okay," Martha said. "I'm okay." She turned and shambled toward the cabin's front room. She rounded the corner and grabbed a kitchen chair; she turned it away from the table, and sat down, heavily. She winced again.

Anna followed Martha, went to the hotplate, and prepared the tea. Martha turned and leaned on the table. She held her head and stared through her fingers. Josef's Bible lay within reach. Without looking up, she stretched out one hand and laid it softy on the battered blue cover. She marveled at her expectations—she expected the cover to feel warm; it was. She pulled the book toward her.

"We should have buried this with him," she mumbled.

"What?" Anna asked. She brought two cups to the table. "Oh, you mean the Bible?"

"Yes... I think Josef would have wanted it with him." Martha gave a choked laugh. "God knows, only He and Josef could ever read Josef's handwriting."

"Matthew said it would be better for you to have it," Anna said. She turned back to the hotplate.

"Oh, he did. Good for Matthew." Martha sat quietly for a moment. "Where's Gordon?"

"He's fine. One of the newer moms is nursing him."

"Yeah, but what about your milk? You'll interfere—"

"No, no. I still got over there a couple of times." Anna brought the teapot and the honey jar. She poured the tea and sat down across from Martha.

Martha stared at the pot. She watched the reflections change on its portly ceramic body. Pregnant, she thought. Her eyebrows drew together in question.

"Is Matthew really Gordon's father? Or were you raped?"

"I was raped, but I'm pretty sure Matthew is Gordon's dad," Anna said. "I was raped after I was with Matthew. I had already missed a period."

"How did it happen—I mean with Matthew?" Martha asked.

"One night stand."

"Where?"

"Near West Edmonton Mall—" Anna said. She stirred honey into her tea, and told Martha the story...

MATTHEW AND Anna had met during a scavenging mission on the city's west side. West Edmonton Mall was a favorite place for scavengers, but the Zellers store hadn't been completely plundered. Matthew had run into Anna in the linens aisle.

She froze when she caught sight of Matthew, and grasped the bedding she was holding, clutching it tightly to her chest. She backed into the shelves as he advanced up the aisle.

"I won't hurt you," Matthew said. He stopped in front of the girl. "It's not smart for you to be here, you know? Are you with somebody?"

Anna shook her head. "No, just me."

Matthew studied her, and smiled. "Stay with us then. At least until we're finished in the store." He held out his hand. "The name is Matthew. Yours?"

"Anna," the girl said, placing a small hand into his. They shook quickly.

"Are you finished here?" he asked.

Anna nodded and motioned to the bedding in her hands. "I have this."

"C'mon, then." Matthew motioned, with a tilt of his head toward the end of the aisle. He began to walk. Anna followed.

Anna stayed with the group for the rest of the day and into the night. They had taken over a few rooms in a motel near the mall, with plans to continue scavenging the next day. She and Matthew sat and talked together in the hotel lobby. When he invited her back to his room, she didn't resist.

"THAT'S REALLY all there is to it," Anna concluded.

"Are you still... together?"

"No," Anna said. "But we're really good friends. And he is such a great dad."

Martha nodded. She held her cup with both hands, and stared at the Bible. *Josef had been a great dad, too*, she thought. "Have you seen my kids?"

"Ruth has been here on and off. So have the other two. Mary came by. She's so cute."

Martha smiled a tiny, weak smile. "Yes— I adore that little mouse." She sipped her tea. "Where did you say Meteor went?"

"I didn't. Nobody knows."

"Oh," Martha said as she sipped her tea again. She set down the cup and looked up at Anna. "You can go," she said with a smile. "I'll be okay. Go take care of little Gordon."

Anna reached across the table and touched Martha's hand. "Are you sure?"

"Yes." Martha paused. "You've been wonderful."

Anna smiled. "Matthew has been a wonderful friend to you, too."

Martha put her face into her palms, and gave her temples another light massage. "I'm sure he is," she murmured. Anna took another drink of her tea and then rose.

"I'll check in on you later." She walked over to Martha and kissed her cheek. "Bye."

Martha reached up her hand and stroked Anna's cheek. "Bye, sweetheart."

Martha's eyes followed Anna to the door. She watched the door open and close. She looked back at the table. At Josef's Bible. At his jacket hanging on the hook. At his shoes tumbled near the door.

Hysteria rose inside her and she gasped for breath. As though drowning, she sucked quick breaths into her lungs in short ragged bursts. She was crying again, but she was unaware of the wet sticky trails coursing down her cheeks. With the back of her hand, she swiped at the mucous dripping from the tip of her nose.

I am alone. Alone. Alone. So alone.

Hysteria switched to anger, and Martha clutched the Bible, cursing it, the walls, the world, and God—especially God. She cursed without words. She cursed from her broken heart. Fuelled by a pain so acute and so deadly in its intensity, Martha clutched at her breast. Then with a wild strangled cry, she heaved Josef's beloved Bible at the far wall. It fell with a small thud.

Martha swung her head, glancing from left to right, like an animal seeking escape from a cage. Terror swept over her, enveloping her, cloaking her. Like the wings of a dark and mighty specter, panic wrapped around her heart, closing in, squeezing, and trapping her in its sucking grip.

Alone, it whispered. *Alone.*

Martha sobbed and reached out—for what, she didn't know. The world swayed, the chair tilted, and she slipped to the floor. She fell with a thud that no one heard, because no one was there to hear.

Not even God, she had thought. *Not even God.*

□□□

MARTHA AWOKE on the floor with a pain in her side, and the back of her head throbbing. She had fallen off the chair in a faint and knocked her head on the floor. She touched her skull, withdrew her fingers, examined them, but not finding blood—she sat up.

Was it a dream? Hallucination?

She willed her lips to move, her tongue to speak his name. "Josef?" she cried softly. "Josef?"

Even as she spoke his name, Martha knew the truth. Josef was dead; it wasn't a dream. She lay back on the floor and curled herself into a fetal position. She cradled her head on her arms, and willed herself back into unconsciousness. To forget. To die.

Martha heard a knock on the door—a tiny soft rap. "Nana?"

It was Mary.

Martha pulled herself up and walked to the door. She opened it. Mary stood there, one small fist clutching a spray of pussy willows.

"I got something for you," she said, with a wide smile. "Look, pussies on a stick." Martha smiled, and knelt down. She took the twigs, and then drew the little girl into an embrace.

"Thank you, Mary." Martha pulled back and smiled. There was at least one thing left to live for. She hugged the little girl again. Mary threw both arms around Martha's neck and hugged her back.

"I miss Papa," Mary whispered into Martha's ear. Martha winced, and squeezed her eyes shut against the tears.

"I know," Martha said. "I miss him, too." She patted the little girl's behind. "Why don't you run and play now. Nana has a bad headache." Mary smiled up at her; she turned, and skipped off across the compound, braids flipping against her shoulders.

Martha closed the door and walked to the table. She picked up the teacups and shuffled over to the sink. She moved slowly, sluggishly, like a time traveler pushing her way through wall after thick wall of what had gone before. Her foot hit a small mass. She bent to look; it was Josef's Bible. She retrieved the book, and attempted to straighten the pages that had bent over. She tried to iron out the crease with her fingers, but it remained—a testament to her fury from when she had sent the Bible flying.

I'm sorry. I'm so sorry.

To whom she was apologizing, she didn't know. She just knew she had to apologize. She stroked the Bible's worn cover. She brought it up and rubbed it against her cheek, still sticky from her morning tears. The sensation brought back a memory of Josef's warm fingers trailing down her face, something he had done regularly when she needed comfort. Her already heavy heart grew even more leaden at the thought. She walked to the table and carefully laid the Bible down. She turned back to the bedroom.

She needed a bath. *But would it be worth the effort?* She sighed.

Another knock on the door.

Martha walked over and opened the door. Matthew stood there.

"Hi," he said. "How are you?"

"Fine."

"Can I come in?"

"Suit yourself." Matthew gave Martha a puzzled look as he stepped inside the cabin. She motioned to a chair. "Have a seat."

He sat.

"Do you need anything?" he asked.

"From you?"

"Yeah."

Martha sat down across from Matthew. She bent her head into her hands, and rubbed her forehead. Her head still throbbed. "No, I don't need anything from you, Matthew. But thanks for asking." Silence.

Matthew stood. "I'll be going then." He got up and left the cabin.

Martha shoved aside a thin shadow of regret as it tried to wedge its way into her heart. She reached across the table and once more pulled Josef's Bible toward her. She clutched it to her chest. She wept.

□□□

DAYS BECAME weeks, but the sorrow didn't fade away. Instead, it transmuted into a dull ache—an ache that rose in the morning with the sun, getting stronger as the day progressed, but unlike the sun—it never set. There was no escape. Not even in dreams. Awake or asleep—she missed Josef.

Spring demanded that Martha pay attention. More babies—both humans and animals—were being born. Gardens needed prepping and tilling. Seeds needed sprouting. Early crops needed planting.

Some, not so educated in the ways of the Alberta climate, decided to risk the potential of a Victoria Day snowstorm and final frost, and plant seedlings early. Martha acquiesced, but as the middle May holiday drew near she took a stand and organized a frost brigade—hundreds of hands that would cover all the tender plants with yards and yards of light, white airy fabric. The snow came, but thanks to her foresight, the plants survived. But not her heart.

The heaviness dragged her down, and with it came a profound depression—one so great that she could barely get out of bed in the morning. She plodded through her day like an old gray mare. One foot in front of the other—just to get where she was going.

I must be a terrible disappointment to You, God.

Something had to change; she knew it, but she had no idea what would pull her out of her deep depression.

She never suspected a murderer would be the tonic she needed. The perfect tonic.

The Switch

THE TWO MEN leaned over the high table. They were in the second clubhouse. They held beers that had been taken from a bar, in a small town, on a recent scavenging mission.

"It's all bullshit, Brad. You know how things go."

"Thought you had it bad for Martha?"

"I did. But once I had her— You know the story."

Brad laughed. He took a deep drink from his beer. "Did Josef ever find out?"

Meteor made a derisive sound through his nose. "Nah. Dumb fuck." He laughed again. "Thanks for not telling him."

"What happened to him?" Brad asked.

Meteor shrugged. "One of the man's people took him out."

"How'd you find out?"

"A couple of the guards on patrol saw a truck leave the compound. They followed it. They watched Josef take a bullet. Then they high-tailed it back to the compound."

"Did they see who killed him?"

Meteor pushed up his lower lip in a semi-frown. "Nope. No idea." He took a long drink from his beer can—burped and wiped his mouth with the back of his hand. "Matthew had a bunch of us go to the clubhouse and pick up Josef's body." He paused. "Man, he was a sorry mess."

Brad smiled, and took a slow drink. He twirled his can between his fingers. "So—uh—what happened between you and Matthew?"

"I was in the way."

"Of what?"

"Ah, c'mon, Brad—you know Matthew has a thing for Martha."

"Of course, I knew that. Why else would she have gotten away with all the shit she pulled?"

"With Josef dead—" He shrugged. "But Martha still wanted me. It's Matthew's compound—I'm the newcomer—I got tossed."

"Why didn't Matthew just kill you?"

"Good question. But you know he and I were pretty good friends. I don't think he wants me dead. He just wanted me gone."

"So, you're switching sides? Just like that?"

"I don't usually pick sides, but in this case—I'd rather be with the winners—Matthew's gonna lose." Meteor paused and gave Brad a wide grin. "I mean— hey—why am I telling you this? You figured that out months ago."

"Yeah, I did figure that out, didn't I?" Brad tipped his beer can, swallowed beer in great gulps, squashed the can, and chucked it over his shoulder into a big blue barrel to his right. The can made a soft metallic sound as it hit other similarly squashed beer cans in the barrel. He took a fresh beer, and popped the tab. "So, you think The Man is just going to let you join us?"

Meteor looked at Brad. He grimaced as he spoke. "No—I suspect he has his rituals. Can't say I'm looking forward to them."

Brad took a long drink. Then he pushed up his t-shirt sleeve revealing a large, round scar. "You're gonna love this one."

"What is that?"

Brad smiled and raised his beer in salute. "You'll find out." He drank, burped, and squashed the can.

"It's time," he said. "Let's go."

Chapter Thirty-Two

Eleven Kittens and a Leader

MARTHA AWOKE. She had no idea what time it was other than it was daytime; she could tell that from the honeyed light-spray pouring in through her bedroom window. Her head throbbed, and her eyes stung. She heard voices outside, but not words. A dog barked, and an ATV zipped by.

Gunfire. However, it was rhythmic. *Target practice,* she thought.

Martha ran her hand through her hair; it was sticky with sweat. She needed to go to the bathroom, and she needed a bath. She rose from the bed and stood on trembling legs. Weakness overtook her and she sat back down, heavily. She put her hands over her face.

How many days was it now? How many hours? How many minutes? How long?

She allowed a memory of Josef smiling at her to float around in her mind. Like a toy boat on a lake, the memory bobbed—she waited for the tears to start again, but none came. She stood. This time she made her way into the front room. She poured water into a kettle, turned on the small propane burner, and set the kettle on an element.

A half hour later, Martha was dressed in fresh clothes. A sponge bath and a hair wash made her feel a little better, but nothing could wash away the heaviness choking her heart; like a mummified hand, its grasp was cold and sure. Martha took a deep breath, more of a ragged sigh. She looked around the front room. Josef's heavy jacket, his winter boots, one of his many canvas bags, all sat exactly where he had left them. Awaiting his return.

Gone. Really gone.

She sat down in the kitchen chair. And she waited.

Martha had no idea of the passing of time. She had no idea if a minute or an hour had passed. If she had slept or if she had simply stared into space. What she did know was that there was a soft rapping at the door.

"Nana?" said a tiny voice. "Nana?" Martha shook her head and rose. She walked to the cabin door, and opened it.

"Hi, Mary."

"Hi, Nana." The little girl smiled. "I brought you flowers," she said, as she handed over a fistful of yellow dandelions.

"Thank you, Mary," Martha said. She forced a mechanical smile to her lips.

"Can we go for a walk? Mom said I should ask if you want to go for a walk."

Martha stared at the little girl. "Uh—Nana isn't feeling very well, Mary. Maybe another time."

"But Mom said—"

"I know," Martha said. "But I don't want to go right now."

"I want you to come." As the little girl spoke, Martha looked across the courtyard. Anna was headed their way. In a moment, she had joined them.

"Hi," Anna said. "How are you?"

"Better," Martha said.

"I checked on you a few times, but you were sleeping so hard, that I thought it best to just leave you alone."

"Thanks, Anna," Martha said. Anna smiled.

"I need to talk to you about something. I know it's a bad time, but I'm hoping you can help."

Martha sighed. "Sure. Come on in." She pushed the cabin door wider and invited Anna and Mary in with a wave of her hand. The three sat at the kitchen table.

"What is it?"

"There's a new medical person that just joined the camp. I think he got here a week ago, but I've only really become aware of him in the past couple of days." She paused. "He's an abortionist, Martha."

Martha stared mutely.

328

"He says he can perform abortions." Anna paused. "And many of the pregnant women are talking about getting abortions. Does that sound like a good idea to you?"

Abortions? Didn't those go the way of the Big Mac when the world changed?

Martha spoke, "That's really up to them, I guess."

"That's how you feel?" Anna asked incredulously.

"Anna, I don't know how I feel. I don't think I really care. All I know is that I miss Josef."

"What's 'bortion?"

Martha and Anna glanced toward Mary. They had forgotten the little girl was there. There—and listening. With both her ears.

"Uh— You should ask your Mom that, okay?" Anna said.

Martha added, "It's a way somebody kills little babies before they're born."

"Before they're *borned*?" Mary asked. "How?"

"Mary," Anna said, "Why don't you run outside and play with the kids?"

Mary's face was firm. "No, I came to take Nana for a walk."

Martha gave the little girl a small smile. "Yes, she did." She nodded to Anna. "Can we talk about this later?"

"Sure, but not too much later. The camp is meeting tonight to decide if he should be allowed to go ahead."

Martha nodded. "Okay. I'll think about it." She stood. "C'mon, Mary. A walk sounds like a great idea."

"Okay," Mary said. She slipped off the chair and headed for the door.

"Hold it," Martha said. "Where's your hat?"

Mary reached for a pink baseball cap lying near the door. "I'll wear yours," she said.

"Come here," Martha said. "Let me make it the right size for you."

"I can do that by myself," Mary responded.

"Okay, then do it yourself."

Mary adjusted the cap's band, and then shoved the cap onto her head with the brim facing backwards. It still didn't fit right, but it was a little tighter. Martha knew better than to say anything. Mary was content.

□□□

THEY WALKED up the path that ran alongside the compound's vegetable gardens. The musty and cloying smell of the earth, as it sat baking in the sunshine, reached Martha's nose, and she breathed deeply. The scent of fresh bread made her look across the compound, to the camp cookhouse, where women, teen girls, and teen boys scurried to and fro.

Martha smiled at a memory...

THE BOY with the orange hair, the one she had tried to teach to cook eggs, before his dad had so rudely interrupted them, had been assigned to the cookhouse. He had shown up, complete with his orange hair, his freckles, and... his daddy's bad attitude.

"Hi, kid," one of the young women said when she saw the boy. "There's a ton of pots over there. Get to it."

"I don't wash pots," the boy replied, a stubborn set to his chin.

"Why not?"

"It's women's work."

"Really?" the woman replied. "Well, guess what? Here... in this kitchen... in this camp... washing the pots is men's work, too." She grabbed the boy by the shoulder and gave him a good-natured push. "So, get to it."

The boy grabbed her hand and gave her arm a hard twist. The woman cried out. Her scream attracted the other people. In a few minutes, the boy found himself standing in front of Matthew.

"What's your story, kid?" Matthew asked.

"She pushed me."

Matthew looked at the women standing nearby; one of them was Martha; she shook her head.

"Kid, you should apologize," Matthew advised.

The boy gave Matthew a fierce look. "For what?"

"For hurting her," Matthew said, pointing to the offended woman.

"I don't apologize to no woman who tries to push me around."

"Then I'll have no choice but to discipline you." Matthew paused. "And you know what that means..."

The women watched the boy, their faces intent.

"Just like you did to my dad," the boy blurted. "No Discipline Committee. You just decide?"

"Pardon me?" Matthew gave the boy a stern look. "If you don't want to end up like your dad— Apologize."

The boy remained silent for a few moments, and then he looked down at his boots. "Sorry," he had muttered.

MARTHA REALIZED she hadn't seen much of the boy with the orange hair since; she wondered, idly, what had happened to him.

Martha walked on, lost in her thoughts. She suddenly realized that Mary wasn't with her.

"Mary?" she called. "Mary? Answer me." Martha listened for a moment and then added, "Answer me. NOW." She heard a soft squeak deep in the woods off to her right.

What was that child up to?

"Mary?"

"Nana!" Mary was running toward her. She had something clasped to her chest. "Nana, look what I found." Mary stopped short, her face beaming with excitement. She held a tiny animal up for inspection. A mouse? Martha thought. She had backed up slightly, but then recognized the tiny gray clump as a kitten—a very new kitten. Its eyes were tiny slits, having just begun to open.

"Oh, Mary," Martha said. "It's so tiny. You have to take it back to its mother."

Mary clutched the animal to her chest. "No, I want to keep him."

Martha's heart grew soft as she remembered the little girl's grief over the loss of her cat, Wilbert, two months before. The kitten might be a good thing, but it was newly born.

"Mary," Martha said, "That little guy needs his mother. He needs to drink milk from her— Or he'll die. You don't want that, do you?"

Mary considered her advice. "But there're lots of them. The mother cat won't care. And then I can call him, Wilbert."

"That's not the point, Mary. You can't take this kitten until it gets older." Martha put her hand on the little girl's shoulder. "C'mon now, let's take it back."

Mary pouted, but she obeyed, and led Martha back into the forest to a pile of discarded wood. Inside an overhang, Martha saw a mass of soft writhing bodies. The tiny creatures were mewling and squirming about in their blindness; the mother cat was nowhere in sight.

"Hmm," Martha said. "I wonder where their mom is. She must be getting food. Let's put that kitten back before she gets back here." Martha attempted to take the kitten, but Mary held fast. "Mar-r-r-y," she said. "Put it back. Now."

Mary stood her ground for another moment—then she bent suddenly and stuffed the kitten back into the squirming pile of soft bodies. She stood up. "When can I take Wilbert?"

Martha smiled. "We'll keep an eye on the kittens, and when they are running around, you can take him."

"When will that be?" Mary asked.

"In about six weeks," Martha replied.

"Is that a long time?"

"Not really. You'll see. Now come on, Mary."

As they walked back toward the path, Martha noted the position of the cat's nest; it had troubled her not to see the mother cat.

"Can I take Wilbert for a walk?" Mary asked.

"Mary, what did I tell you? Leave the kitten where he is. Until he's older. Putting your human smell all over him is not a good idea."

"Why?"

"Because the mother cat will reject him when she gets back."

"What?"

"She won't want him because of your smell on him. She won't let him eat—and he'll starve to death."

"Maybe I should go back and get him."

Martha gave an exasperated sigh. "Mary, no— Let him be. I'll check on him later."

Mary pushed out her lower lip, but she marched alongside Martha.

☐☐☐

"SHE WAS RAPED," the dark-haired girl said. "She should have an abortion." The Meeting House was crammed with compound members of all ages and sexes.

"Abortion is murder," retorted a younger girl, her long blond hair twisted into tight French braids.

"Only to you," the dark-haired girl replied. She turned as Martha reached them. "What do you think, Martha? Shouldn't she have an abortion?"

Martha stared at the girls. She had just come into the room where the abortion debate was already in full swing. "It's not a baby, right?" asked the girl. "It's just a mass of tissue."

A small redheaded girl had joined the argument. "It is so," she said. "I know. I saw pictures on the Internet—it showed a tiny, tiny baby. And you could see its arms, and its legs, and its fingers, and its eyes."

"My Mom had an abortion when I was about five years old," said a thin girl at the other end of the table. "She says she wishes she'd never done it. But I told her it was okay since she already had four kids."

"How would you feel if it had been you she aborted?" the blond girl asked.

"It wouldn't have mattered," said the thin girl, with a grin. "I would have been dead."

The red-haired girl piped up, "Aborting babies is like the way the Nazis killed all the Jews, you know."

"It is not," said a heavy girl with wheat-colored hair. "The Jews were adults and kids. They had already been born. They were alive. They were..." she searched for the word.

"Viable?" Martha asked.

"Yeah, viable," the girl agreed.

"Do you know what that means?" Martha asked.

"I'm not exactly sure, but I think it means they can breathe on their own."

"Yes—kind of," Martha said.

"But they killed big babies, too," said the redhead. "Not just teeny ones."

Martha sighed. She had heard it all before. Many times. From both sides. She had seen the pictures. She had heard the pros and cons. However, as a twenty-year-old carrying an unplanned baby, there had been only one option.

Martha allowed herself to drift back—back to a place she usually tried to avoid. She remembered the smell of the clinic. She remembered the muted sounds of people moving around as she lay in her bed, waiting. She remembered the pain. She remembered the emptiness. And she remembered the regret. Always the regret.

"You're so stupid," said the dark-haired girl. "A fetus is just a fetus. It's not a person. It's different if the baby is born. You can't kill it then. Because then it's human."

"Nana?" Martha spun around.

"Hi, Mary," she said. "What are you doing here?"

"Did you check on Wilbert yet?"

Oh damn, Martha thought. *The kittens.* She had completely forgotten about them. Mary's eyes were bright with expectation.

"Can we go see them?"

"I think it's best if I go and check the kittens by myself, Mary. You stay here."

Mary began to argue, but Martha shushed her. Martha feared finding a nest of dead cats. Mary didn't need to see any more dead cats.

"You go back home. I'll go check the kittens. And then I'll come and tell you, okay?"

"Now?"

Martha checked her watch. It had been hours since they'd found the kittens. She looked over at the quarreling girls. The real meeting hadn't begun yet. The captains hadn't arrived. There was time to check on the kittens.

"Okay. I'll go now. Run home," Martha said.

MARTHA PICKED her way through the brush toward the deadfall of wood. She listened, but she heard nothing except for the call of a raven high in the branches above. She knelt down near the overhang and peered into the darkness. The kittens were there, but they were very still. Their piteous mewling was so weak that Martha could barely hear it. She knew the mother cat had not returned— The kittens were dying.

How am I going to tell Mary?

Martha's mind went back to the girls in the Meeting House and their abortion debate.

What's another dead kitten?

Martha froze. She thought for a moment, and then she took off her jacket and laid it on the ground. She scooped up one tiny body after the other. Eleven in all. They wriggled and mewled with the strength they had left. Martha cradled them in her arms. She shook her head. She wondered what Matthew would say when he found out. She remembered his last lecture about preaching at the camp members. But she didn't care—she was willing to risk his wrath. Life was far too precious to be killing babies in the womb. Josef came to her mind; there had been enough death, she decided. If Matthew wasn't willing to do something, then she would.

□□□

MATTHEW LOOKED up as the Gatehouse door opened. Cammy entered. Trojan wasn't with her.

"Where's Trojan?" Matthew asked. "And, for the record, knock next time."

"Which one?'

"Which one, what?

"Which question would you like answered first?"

"I only asked one question."

"No," Cammy said. Her sultry smile would have melted cast iron. "You asked two questions. The second one was whether I would obey you, or not. So, which one?"

"The second one," he said.

"Yes," Cammy said. She walked across the room.

Matthew pushed back in his chair as Cammy came toward the desk. He eyed her as he leaned back, placing his hands behind his head. His cap moved forward slightly as he did so, shading his eyes. "And the first one?" he asked.

"I'm not sure. Eating maybe."

"He lets you off on your own now?"

Cammy was standing at the desk to Matthew's right. He watched her. She ran a long slender finger along the desk's edge.

"Yes. I keep him satisfied. And, well, when you keep a man satisfied..." Her smile grew bigger.

Matthew laughed; it was a short blast of sound. "I see," he said.

"Trojan may claim he owns me," Cammy said. Her eyes were wide and their soft brown depths focused on Matthew. "But, I prefer... Leaders." Another smile. Smaller and sweeter than the last.

Matthew sat forward in an abrupt movement that made Cammy jump. "There's a meeting I've got to attend."

"Really?"

"Yeah. Abortion. The camp's going to decide if abortion will be allowed here." He waved his hand through the air. "Doesn't really make any difference to me—one way, or the other. But it will make a big difference to some other people."

"Like Martha?"

"Yes, like Martha. And a lot of others," Matthew said, a lazy aloofness coloring his tone.

"Well, from what I know of Martha—I suspect she'll handle the meeting just fine."

"I don't know if she'll be there." Matthew gazed out from under his cap. "She's still getting over losing Josef."

Cammy smiled again. She took a step closer to Matthew. "Is that a good thing? Or a bad thing?"

Matthew's eyes hardened. "What do you mean?"

"That Martha is still getting over Josef. She won't really have time for you."

Matthew said nothing.

Cammy moved closer. Her eyes held his, a velvet grip. She stood near him, and reached out a hand. Matthew pulled back slightly, but allowed her to touch him. She slid her fingers down his cheek. Over his lips. Across the scar above his lip. Then back up his cheek.

Matthew gave a slight shiver.

"A good thing? Or a bad thing?" Cammy repeated.

Matthew reached up and caught her hand. "Josef was my friend," he said, as he pushed Cammy's hand away from his face and back down to her side. "Why are you here?"

Cammy leaned back against the desk, her arms behind her, and her weight resting on her knuckles. "I want something to do. I'm bored," she said.

"What are you good at?"

"Many things," she said.

"Like?"

"Hunting. Engine repair. Guns."

"That's it?"

"No," Cammy said, as she pulled herself erect. "There is something else." She leaned forward over Matthew and placed her hands on the armrests of his chair. She climbed into his lap, straddling his body with her legs, her knees on either side of his thighs.

Matthew did nothing.

Cammy bent her face to his and touched his lips with hers. Softly. Then with insistence. Her tongue began its search.

Matthew groaned.

Cammy squirmed in closer.

Matthew's hands closed on her shoulders and, for a moment, Cammy drew back. Her eyes met his. His fingers tightened on her shoulders, and she winced. Her breath flew out of her as he shoved her backwards to the desk. His mouth covered hers. Cammy clutched his head, her mouth moving against his. She pushed her body into his.

A knock on the door startled them. They both looked toward the door. Matthew lifted Cammy from his lap and set her on the floor. She stumbled and righted herself. She moved around to the other side of the desk, straightened her shirt, and smoothed her hair.

"Come in," Matthew said. The door opened. It was Simon.

"Hi Matthew." Then with a nod in Cammy's direction, "Hi."

"Hi, yourself," Cammy said. Simon blushed.

"Uh— Just reminding you about tonight's meeting. Are you coming?"

"Not sure." He glanced at Cammy. She was examining her fingers. "If I don't make it, will you keep an eye on things for me?"

"Sure, I'll bring you a full report, Matthew." Simon gave a slight salute, a small bow in Cammy's direction, and then he left the Gatehouse.

Matthew sat forward in his chair. He piled some papers, opened a desk drawer, searched around, nodded, and then closed the drawer. He looked up. Cammy stood quietly, arms folded, and legs slightly apart. She lifted her head. A slow smile like liquid fire tipped one corner of her mouth.

Matthew rose from his chair, and pulled his jacket from a hook on the wall. He looked back at her. "You know where my cabin is, don't you?" he asked.

"You expect me to just wait around there for you?"

He stared for a moment. "Yes," he said.

Cammy's mouth fell open, but she closed it. She stepped out in front of Matthew, blocking his exit. "I know what I want," she said. "But know this— I *won't* let you treat me like shit. Not you. Not *anybody—*"

Matthew regarded her, dispassionately.

Cammy continued, "Keep me waiting too long, and I promise you the offer will be withdrawn."

Matthew reached up and grabbed her chin. "And what a loss that would be," he said. He dropped his hand to her shoulder and firmly pushed her toward the door. He closed the door behind them and turned in the direction of the Meeting House.

Matthew had walked several yards across the compound when the sounds of ATV engines caught his attention. He turned around. Cammy was still near the Gatehouse, watching him, her fingers curled into small fists at her sides. Her eyes followed his gaze toward the main road.

"Matthew, wait up," a voice called. It was Jonah. He leapt from his ATV and loped toward Matthew.

"What's going on?" Matthew asked.

"I think we have a chance to get Brad."

The Request

"ANY WORD on Cammy?"

"No. Sorry."

The Man shoved the cat from his lap. The cat stood for a moment, eyed the man, gave a flick of its tail, and then sauntered away. The Man abruptly rose from his chair. "Bitch," he said. "I wonder how long she was planning to leave me."

"Leave you?" the biker asked. "I don't think she left you—at least not voluntarily. She was taken."

The Man stopped to think. "What's Meteor's take on this? Where is he anyway?"

The biker shrugged. "I think he spends most of his time with Brad."

"Is he healed?"

"Yeah— As far as I know."

"He's interesting—we really worked him over." The Man stood near the small window, lifted the venetian blinds, and looked out. "I didn't think he had really switched his allegiances, but—"

"He took your colors," the biker prompted. "Why would anyone do that if they hadn't really switched sides? Too damn painful." The biker pulled back his t-shirt and looked at the ruddy oval scar on his own biceps. "Hurt like fuckin' hell—" He huffed. "— And took so damn long to heal. The infection— Damn—" He gave a small dismissive laugh. "Just glad it's over."

The Man stood quietly, thinking. He drew his eyebrows together. "Things are really different now. Took years to get into a club before the Change." He shook his head. "Took me a long time before I could ride as a full-patched Angel—"

The biker smiled and nodded. "Yeah, me too— Rock Machine."

The Man snorted. "Our enemies— In Quebec." He glanced out the window again. "Those were the days," he mused, almost dreamily.

He turned back to the biker. "Meteor said he was the one who took Cammy. Maybe he should be the one who brings her back." The Man turned back to the window. "Get him."

The biker left the room. The Man walked over to a large safe in a corner. He twirled the combination, pulled on the heavy steel door, and reached inside. He found what he was looking for: a book. He quickly flipped a few pages, grabbed a pen from the desk, and made a notation. He closed the book and returned it to the safe. He closed the door, and twirled the lock. A noise behind him drew his attention. He turned.

"You wanted to talk to me?" Meteor asked; he stood near the doorway.

"Yeah. Have a seat."

"No, thanks. I'll stand. I was just heading out. The guys are waiting for me. What's on your mind?"

"Cammy— Do you think she's still a prisoner? Or is she staying with Matthew's camp of her own accord?"

Meteor smiled. "Hard to say—I wasn't around long enough after she was captured." He shrugged. "But then—who knows? Maybe she's just biding her time—waiting for a chance to do something that'll help you. She's a smart girl."

The Man put his hand up to his chin and stroked it. "You might have something there." He paused. "What about those guns?"

Meteor laughed outright, causing The Man to stare at him. "You aren't going to get those guns back—I can guarantee that. It was love at first sight when Matthew saw them."

"That pisses me off," The Man said. "Those guns were hard to come by." He paused. "I want them back." Pause. "Cammy, too. But I still suspect that bitch has deserted."

"Don't be too sure," Meteor said. "She might have a plan. Give her the benefit of the doubt."

"Meteor—you still coming?" A short biker in a deep green hunting jacket and a John Deere ball cap was leaning through the doorway.

"I'm nearly finished with him," The Man said.

The biker grunted. "We're waiting at the end of the lot."

"Okay," Meteor said. The biker left. "Anything else?" Meteor asked.

"Yeah. I figure since you took Cammy, you should be the one to bring her back." The Man went silent, waiting for Meteor to respond.

Meteor rubbed his arm. "Sounds fair," he said. "I'll see what I can do. Is that it?"

"No. We're going to make Brad my sergeant-at-arms."

"Yeah. I heard something about that. When?"

"Tonight. The ceremony will be at the second clubhouse. Be there."

"But I'm not a captain."

"Come anyway."

"I will."

"In the meantime, see if you can figure out some way to get Cammy back."

Meteor gave a crooked smile. "And if I do that? What's in it for me?"

"What do you want?"

"To be a captain, of course. To have my own land—my own territory."

"Really—you didn't strike me as the type of guy that wanted to be managing anything."

"Getting old," Meteor said. "Maybe it's time to settle down."

The Man laughed. "With the little woman?" A shadow passed over Meteor's face. The Man watched it go. "Do you have a woman?"

"Sure. Lots of them." Meteor looked down at his boots for a moment and then glanced up. "I gotta go. I'll do what I can to find out about Cammy."

"Wait a minute—" The Man said. "There is a woman. Who is she?"

"No— There's nobody. At least—not anymore. There was someone— But that's over."

"Interesting." The Man sat down and motioned toward the door. "Okay— Go. Let me know what you find out."

Meteor gave a small dip of his head, but he didn't smile.

He left the room.

The Man's eyes followed him.

Chapter Thirty-Three

Killing Time

MARTHA HEARD the raised voices long before she reached the Meeting House. She checked her watch. She was a few minutes late. She climbed the steps and opened the door. She walked to an old oak table set at the front of the room. To her right was a chalkboard scrawled with notes, dusty reminders of the last security meeting. She slid the cardboard box she had been carrying onto the tabletop. A soft rustling came from within. Something batted up against the side of the box.

Martha stood quietly, searching the assembled faces for Matthew. She didn't see him. However, she did see several of the compound's captains—and their wives.

"Who's running the meeting?" Martha asked. The arguing stopped as all eyes turned to her. A woman to her left held up her hand.

"I am," the woman said. She was tall, with short dark hair, and an angular face.

Martha glanced at the woman. "I'm taking over for a few minutes." The tall woman began to protest, but Martha ignored her and looked across the room.

Two boys came in carrying four pails of water. Another boy followed with small, plastic handled buckets. She motioned for the boys to bring everything to the front. Water sloshed from the pails as they walked. She indicated that the smaller buckets needed water. The boys filled them.

Anna was seated near the front; her eyes were filled with questions. Simon sat next to Anna.

Martha had just begun to speak when the door opened. One of Matthew's most trusted captains, the captain's wife, and two other armed men came into the room. Another man trailed them—Martha had never seen him before. She looked over at Anna who had glanced back and was now nodding.

The abortionist, Martha guessed.

He was tall, well built, tanned, and handsome—his silver hair clipped into a brush cut, and his outfit was trim and neat—designer safari clothing. His countenance was expressionless, as he scanned the room, finally coming to rest on Martha. He took a position near the far wall, arms crossed, waiting.

Martha took a breath. "Let's conduct an experiment."

"An experiment?" one pimply-faced boy scoffed.

"Yes," Martha replied. "It'll help make a point." She motioned forward. "Some of you have buckets of water in front of you. In a moment, I'll give you something to put into those buckets. You might want to roll up your sleeves."

Martha lifted a pink blanket from the box on the table; she tossed it to one side. It slipped from the table's edge, dropping to the floor. A soft sweet sound rose from the cardboard walls. She reached in and brought out a tiny, grey kitten, its eyes still tightly shut.

An "*Awww*," went up in the room.

"Lots of stray cats around," she said. "Kittens everywhere. Way too many for us to feed. The humane thing for us to do is to get rid of them."

She picked up several more wriggling bodies and walked toward the tables. She placed a kitten into the hands of anyone near a bucket. Then she returned to the front.

"There's been talk about abortion around the camp recently—"

A murmur went through the room. The abortionist shifted his weight from one foot to another.

"Like an unwanted child, these kittens serve no useful purpose." Martha shrugged. "The mother has deserted them, and they can't survive on their own. And they'll put a burden on us if we keep them." Martha paused, and then added, "In other words—they aren't *viable*."

She pointed to the buckets on the table. "I would like you to drown the kitten you're holding."

A series of exclamations of "gross" and "that's sick" emanated from the crowd.

"Don't worry," Martha added, "unlike abortion—drowning is a quick and painless death." She stared pointedly at the abortionist. He ignored her.

Martha continued, "Drowning the kitten isn't much different than killing an unborn child with a saline solution." She motioned with her hands. "Go ahead."

Martha walked forward and stopped in front of a young woman. The woman cradled an orange and white kitten in her cupped hands. She was cooing to it as she brushed it up against her face. She gave Martha a fierce look.

"You might want to stand up to do this," Martha said, "because the kitten will put up quite a struggle as it dies." The woman turned white and burst into tears.

Martha stopped near a young man. "There's a pair of scissors in the box over there—in case you'd prefer to stab it in the head and pull out its brains. That's what's done during a partial birth abortion." The boy looked at her, his eyes dull and uncomprehending. "The pain is short-lived. Or so I've been told," Martha added. She glanced across the room at the abortionist. This time, the man stared back at her. He spoke:

"Nice. What's next?"

Martha ignored him and moved on to an older man sitting near the back. His beret was grimy with sweat and dust. His military green t-shirt was sweat-stained. He, too, held a kitten.

"You might want to try a limb removal," she said. "That's another form of abortion. It's done when the baby's too big—" Martha went on, "Just pull its legs off. Then its head, too."

The man smirked. To the horror of everyone watching, he began to do just that.

Two girls, sitting nearby, vomited. Martha's eyes widened, but she said nothing. Blood spewed and smeared on his hands. The man sat holding the torn limbs as though awaiting a critique on his technique. One girl near the back fell to the floor in a faint. Two others rushed to her side and began to fan her.

Martha turned away. Around the room—sounds of retching, more crying, and exclamations of disgust.

"You are a monster," said a middle-aged woman from off to the left. She was struggling to hold back tears. "How could you suggest we do this to helpless kittens? You're sick." Martha turned to face her.

"Abortion of an unborn fetus is very similar to what I've suggested here. With one difference—a fetus is human. These kittens are animals. Do you still think we should be aborting unwanted babies?"

The woman's mouth gaped wide. She said nothing more.

Martha walked to the front of the room where she retrieved the cardboard box and the pink blanket; she made her way back through the tables. She tossed the blanket into a side cupboard.

"Unless you have plans to adopt the kitten you're holding, please return it to the box— They must be destroyed." Martha held out the box as she walked to the door.

She stared at the captain as she brushed by him. His eyes, unlike the eyes of his wife, were dry. Martha knew he would be reporting everything to Matthew. The look in his eyes confirmed what she already knew: she would be in trouble. Again.

The abortionist glared at her. Martha stopped. She glared back. "Are you him, then?"

The man nodded.

"Are you completely nuts? We have lost hundreds of thousands of people. Do you honestly think we can afford to kill babies?"

"Babies need to be fed," he said. "What about that?"

"You're a fool," Martha retorted. "Babies need nothing more than their mother's milk for the first year of their life."

The man rolled his eyes. His face darkened and he took a step forward, but Simon, who had trailed behind Martha, stepped in between them.

"Easy, guy," Simon said. He smiled and added, "You don't want to tangle with Martha."

Martha turned away. She stomped out of the room, slamming the door behind her. Outside, she leaned against the doorjamb and breathed heavily. She dropped the cardboard box near the steps; it was empty.

She knew her point had been made.

But to what end?

The horror of what had just happened would race around the camp. Then there was Matthew.

What was he going to say?

Martha began to walk. She would deal with that tomorrow.

Tonight, she had something more important to do.

□□□

MATTHEW'S MEN crouched near the trucks and watched the door through binoculars. Four heavily armed men in leather jackets and jeans stood guard at the entrance. Behind them, windows covered in graffiti shone with reflected sunlight. Nothing could be seen through the windows because they had been blacked out.

"This is nuts," Trojan whispered. "Look—you guys haven't known me very long, but I'm telling you that what you've heard is bullshit. The Man wants you dead. They fed you the information— It's a trap." Matthew stared forward, but then he turned to Trojan.

"We're far enough away. Even if they did spot us, it would take too many men to surround us. I don't think they have the manpower to take us out."

Trojan sighed. "The Man has lots of manpower. I'm telling you— This is NUTS." Trojan shook his head again. "You're as cracked as Meteor."

Matthew spoke again, "We're doing this." He tipped his head toward the rear. "You did your job. You got us here," he said. "Go back."

Trojan looked surprised, but then he grinned. "What? And miss all the fun hanging out with you fucking wackos?"

Matthew's face creased into a smile.

They were a long city block away from another clubhouse, not the one where Josef was killed. This one was a large bar, in a strip mall, also on Edmonton's west side. A grassy field across the street was littered with motorcycles. Men wandered around, chatting, wiping chrome, and laughing. Early evening had come and the sunlight was low and golden.

An informant, a Crazy, who some of Matthew's scouts had befriended, had told them that The Man was installing a new sergeant-at-arms that night. The informant, who knew Brad from other meet-ups, said he was sure it would be Brad. The location was no secret among members. A time had been set: 9:00. Matthew glanced at his watch; it was 8:45.

Matthew looked down the street; the compound's trucks dotted either side. His men weren't visible, but he knew they were there. Nearly four dozen of them, all heavily armed. He had pulled men from the Hutterite patrol force, and he had called off-duty men to assist, too.

"Trojan," Matthew said. "I mean it. You've done your job. You're more valuable to us alive, than dead. Take a vehicle, and go back to the compound." Trojan looked puzzled. Matthew smiled. "Really, it's all good. Go."

Trojan nodded and backed away. He made his way down the block to one of the last trucks. None of Matthew's men was nearby. He got in. He started the engine and backed up. He drove down the block and up another block closer to the bar, and then he stopped. He parked the truck, and cut the engine. He checked his gun, the extra ammunition hanging off his belt, and the rearview mirror. He jumped out of the truck.

Matthew watched Trojan leave, but a fight that broke out in the field, between two bikers, drew his attention. A small crowd circled the pair—applauding and egging them on. Matthew swung the binoculars across to the other side of the street and studied the bar's entrance. The armed guards showed interest in the fight, but they didn't leave their posts. He leaned over to one of his captains.

"What do you think? Should we try a back door?" The captain, a middle-aged man with a thin moustache, regarded Matthew carefully.

"We could probably get into the place, but what if that meeting is already in progress? What if Trojan is right? And it is a trap? They'd kill a lot of us— Fast."

Matthew nodded. "So... wait here in ambush?"

The captain nodded.

"That could be all night," Matthew said.

The captain nodded again.

The fight across the street had escalated and they listened as the hollers and the laughter grew louder. Matthew sighed. A sound off to his right made both of them rise to attention.

Three large motorcycles pulled into view, Harleys, beautifully painted, and well maintained. Matthew studied the riders through his binoculars. The captain next to him had his binoculars trained on the bikers, too. He and Matthew lowered their binoculars at the same time.

"There he is," the captain said. "Now what?"

"Now we wait," Matthew said.

□□□

MARTHA FLUNG open the door to her cabin. She grabbed a bottle of cow's milk from the cooler and pulled a small pot from the cupboard. She flipped the switch on the propane stovetop, lit the burner, poured some milk into the pot, and began to heat it.

She crossed the room and retrieved the tiny doll's bottle she had found in the toy box in the Meeting House. It wasn't perfect, but it would do the trick.

She returned to the pot, dabbed her finger into the milk, and tested it on the inside of her wrist. She felt nothing. *Perfect temperature*, she thought. She took the pot off the stove, and turned off the burner. She uncapped the bottle, and filled it with milk.

She rummaged in a trunk on the floor near the door. She found one of Josef's old wool socks. She rolled it back onto itself, so it was half its size. Then she went to the corner of the room and stooped down.

"Hey, little one," she said. "Are you ready for something to eat?"

She reached down and picked up a tiny kitten. Wilbert's tiny body was limp, but he was alive. The milk she had fed him earlier had worked its magic. She tucked him into the sock. Martha held the plastic nipple to his mouth and squeezed out a droplet of milk. "Hey, Wilbert, it's time to eat." She waited. In a moment, the kitten responded and Wilbert began to drink. Martha stroked the soft grey head.

Thank you for keeping him alive, God.

She thought of how happy Mary would be when she found out, and she smiled. Then her stomach clenched as she thought about what the morning would bring: a camp filled with bitter gossip, evil sidelong glances, rude words, and an angry Matthew. But with no Josef to soften the blows.

Martha focused on the greedy little kitten in her hands; its eyes were still tightly closed. She knew that when they opened, they would be blue for the first few weeks. A vision came to her. Of another set of blue eyes.

Meteor.

Her stomach clenched once more. A pain began in her heart—its dull throb spread across her chest, and entered her spirit. It stole her breath as it passed. She swallowed hard and fought against the tears.

Gone.

She had sent him away. And he had gone. He was gone. The hurt intensified.

Anger rose up inside her. Like a crawling dark shadow, it confronted her pain and twisted it back into submission.

He would have stayed if he had really cared.

Martha wiped away a single tear that had fallen on the kitten's forehead. Another shimmering orb fell to replace it. Then another. And another.

MATTHEW WAVED to the captains down the line. They had silenced their walkie-talkies and had gone to hand signals. The captains left their positions and moved up to Matthew's truck. They gathered back of the tailgate.

"What's the plan?" one asked.

"Brad's in there now. Since we don't know how long the ceremony will go on, we'll wait it out."

"What about trying to get access through a back door?" asked a captain with long dark hair and a black skullcap.

"We discussed that, but there's no way to tell how many are inside or how many weapons they have."

"Yeah," said the man, "but we have the element of surprise. We could do a lot of damage."

"No. We don't want an all-out war. Not right now. We just want Brad." Matthew nodded toward the bar's entrance. "He went in, and as far as we know, he's gotta come out." He shifted his weight. "We'll be here when he does."

"He'll get right back on his bike," said another captain. "Do you want us to send out two sniper teams? They can wait about a block up, in either direction, and take him down when he leaves here."

Matthew thought a moment. "No— Stay here." The captain ducked his head and crept back along the line of trucks.

"Do you know that Trojan left with one of our trucks?" another captain asked.

"Yes—" Matthew said. "I told him to go."

"Ah," said the man. He turned and joined the rest of the captains as they made their way back down the line of trucks. In a few minutes, two of the rear trucks had pulled away; they went down to a cross street where one headed left; the other headed right.

Matthew sat on the truck fender. He yawned. He pushed his cap back and massaged his forehead.

"You good, boss?" Matthew looked up at the captain speaking, and he nodded. The men returned to their crouched positions, and their binoculars.

Across the street, several bikers continued to mill around. Somebody started a bonfire; small cinders jumped and danced upwards like fireflies into the twilight, only to be extinguished in an instant. Several men were busy tearing boards from a nearby shed. One had a chainsaw and he zipped through dead tree limbs that had been piled in the middle of the field. Another was tossing the cut wood onto the fire.

A collection of women, all shapes and sizes, sat cross-legged on the ground in a kind of hen party, chatting and laughing. Matthew fought another yawn.

A shoving match near the bar's entrance made the women turn. They stared and then rose to their feet. Matthew watched as they crossed the street—like a gang of dark squirrels with their teased hair, dark leather clothing, and their chattering. They gathered near the front of the bar and waited, some kicking at the pavement with their pointed high-heeled boots. Matthew cocked his head.

"Hey," he said, as he nudged the captain next to him. The captain grunted. "Look." Matthew pointed. "I don't think the women are armed." The captain studied the women through his binoculars.

"Their clothes are pretty tight, and I don't see any gun belts." The captain lowered his binoculars. "Why wouldn't they be armed?"

Matthew shrugged. "Cammy knows guns. I can't imagine her not being armed."

"Maybe The Man doesn't allow his women to carry guns?"

"That can't be," Matthew said. "When Meteor and Trojan took Cammy, she had a truckload of weapons.

"Doesn't mean she was personally allowed to carry guns," the captain responded.

Matthew scratched his head. He made a small derisive sound. "Not arming his women—"

The captain glanced up. "—a fatal flaw?"

Matthew continued to stare at the women. "I wonder how hard they'd be to interrogate."

"Not bloody hard, I'd guess," the captain said.

"Yeah," Matthew said. "Not bloody hard at all."

The two put their binoculars back up to their eyes and watched as the women began a slow amble down to the other end of the strip mall, away from the bar. Matthew swung his binoculars to follow them. He saw a convenience store. He nudged the captain again. "What do you think?"

"I'm thinking— Yes."

"Move," Matthew commanded. The captain gave a quick nod and hurried back alongside the trucks, silently gathering men as he went.

Matthew watched the men disappear into the shadows, as they made their way down the street toward the back of the store. He smiled.

The Sergeant-at-Arms

THE PARTY was in full swing. Brad's ceremony was nearly over, as he accepted his new role as The Man's new sergeant-at-arms. The old one had disappeared several weeks before; it was assumed he was dead.

"You know what we used to do when someone was inducted or got a new position—I mean before the Change?" asked one of the chapter presidents who was watching the proceedings.

"No." The biker next to him raised a bottle to his lips. He took a swig of the clear liquid and then handed the bottle to his companion. "What?"

The other man shook his head. "Vodka makes me sick. I'll stick to rum."

A shout drew their attention. Brad had just been made a sergeant-at-arms. Men—all full-patched members—stood around Brad, glad-handing him and slapping him on the back.

"What? What did you do?"

"Oh—we'd pour oil—motor oil—all over the dumb bastard."

The other man grunted. "Like The Man would let you get away with that now."

The biker agreed. They continued watching the rowdy celebration.

Chapter Thirty-Four

A Fair Trade

MATTHEW STARED through his binoculars. The light was fading, and it was getting harder to see, but the women had not come out of the convenience store. No alarm had gone up. The men with the machine guns, in front of the bar, were still in position; one lit a cigarette and blew a plume of smoke into the air above his head; the other three chatted and joked together.

The bonfire across the street had grown larger; orange flames snaked upwards, licking the deepening darkness, casting fiery light on the men who were walking and lounging on the ground, nearby. Matthew switched his view to the back of the store, but the shadows were too deep. He couldn't make out any details.

"Can you see anything?" asked the captain who had remained with him; he had a long ponytail and dark eyes.

"No," Matthew said. "It's getting too dark."

The pony-tailed captain made a soft sound through his teeth. "Look."

Matthew swung his binoculars in the direction the captain was pointing, just to the right of the convenience store and slightly down the street. Figures were moving, many figures—more figures than had originally left them a few minutes earlier.

"Looks like they did it," Matthew mused.

The pair watched as the crowd of dusky figures came toward them. The captain, who had been in charge of the mission, ran up to them; he was breathing hard.

"We got them, Matthew—" he said. He panted for a moment. "It wasn't too tough. The back door was hanging open, so we didn't have to break in. We waited and took them, one by one. No screams."

"Where are they now?" Matthew asked.

The captain motioned toward the end of the street. "Down there."

Matthew and the pony-tailed captain quickened their pace. The men stepped aside, revealing a small group of women, all bound and gagged. The women stared at Matthew—their eyes watchful and fearful. Matthew singled out one of the men.

"Any idea which one we should interrogate?"

The man nodded toward a short woman with long, coal black hair, and heavy eye make-up. "Try that one," he said. "Just a feeling."

Matthew nodded toward two of the men, and then toward the woman. They cut her from the group, slipping a hand into the crooks of her arms. Matthew motioned toward one of the trucks with a large back seat. "There," he said.

Matthew and the pony-tailed captain sat in the front seat. The other two men pushed in on either side of the woman in the backseat. They closed the doors. Matthew switched on his headlamp, but held it in his hands, shielding its harsh light. He tilted his chin toward the woman, "Take it off." The man on her right removed the tape across her mouth. The woman winced as the duct tape came free, but she said nothing. Her breathing was shallow and her eyes were wide.

"Who are you?" the captain asked.

"None of your fucking business," the woman responded.

"What's your name?" Matthew asked.

"None of your FUCKING business," she said again. She winced and cried out as the man on her right grabbed the soft flesh of her underarm between his thumb and finger, and twisted.

"Ow!" she said. Tears now shone in her eyes. "Victoria."

"Who's in the bar?" Matthew asked.

The woman pursed her lips, but she cried out again when Matthew nodded to the man at her side. "Okay! Okay! All full-patched members."

"What does that mean?"

"Pull up my sleeve," she said. The man to her left, did so. Scarred flesh, in an oval pattern, adorned her forearm. "This is the new patch."

"That's a burn?" asked the captain.

"Yeah. The Man makes us burn off our old club tattoos—" She grimaced. "—with hot spoons."

The men looked back and forth at one another. Matthew nodded.

"That must have hurt," the captain added.

"You think?" she said, her voice laced with sarcasm.

"So, tell us more," the pony-tailed captain said. When she didn't respond, he allowed his gaze to drift to Matthew. Victoria pressed her arm in close to her side and glared. "Well?" the captain asked.

"The Man is there. Chapter presidents. And a new guy—he's going to be made a sergeant-at-arms."

"Brad?" Matthew asked.

"Yes," she replied.

"Why are you women here? Who do you belong to?" the captain asked.

"The Man," she said. Matthew and the captain exchanged looks.

"Are women allowed at these meetings?" Matthew asked.

"Some of us are... special," Victoria said, with a shrug. "We get to go to these things."

"How special?" the pony-tailed captain asked.

"Very special. So special that you are in for trouble— Big trouble— when The Man finds out." She took a breath. "Who are you guys, anyway?"

The captain responded. "That's not something you need to worry about."

Matthew asked, "How many men are inside?"

"Lots."

Matthew nodded to the man beside her. He grabbed her arm, and she squawked. "Stop it."

"Then quit messing with us and answer the question," the captain said.

"Maybe two dozen. I don't know for sure," she said.

Matthew studied the woman and then asked, "If we kill you, would he miss you?"

Victoria's face registered shock. She gasped and struggled for words. "Yes— We're the inner circle." Her eyes shone with fear and her words tumbled forth. "He chooses us. We're special to him."

"Do you know someone named Cammy?" Matthew asked.

The woman's face darkened. "Yes," she said. "She was kidnapped weeks ago. The Man was pretty pissed." She brightened. "But that was good for some of us. Since she always spent so much time with Him."

"How much would he care if all of you disappeared?"

The woman looked shocked again. "Very much. He'd care very much," she blurted.

"Yeah," the captain said, "but women like you are easily come by."

"No," she said. "We're clean."

"Clean?" the captain asked.

"I suspect she means no diseases," Matthew said.

The woman nodded her agreement, eagerly.

"Okay," said the captain. He turned and faced Matthew. "You were right. They have trading value. How do you want this to play out?"

Matthew pushed back his cap and ran his hand over his face. "Kill this one," he said. "We'll dump her body as a message. The Man will have to respond."

"No-o-o-o," the woman cried out. Tears glistened in her eyes again, but this time they poured down her cheeks. "Please," she sobbed. "Please don't."

Matthew glanced at the captain. They exchanged crooked grins. "So, make it worth our while to keep you alive," Matthew said.

Victoria began to talk.

A CAPTAIN ran up and knocked on the truck's side window. Matthew opened the door. "What?"

"People are leaving the bar," the man said. "We think Brad might be with them, but it's too dark to tell. What do you want us to do?"

Matthew glanced back at Victoria. "Is The Man going to leave? Or will he stay here?"

"I don't know," she said—her eyes wide and earnest. "He didn't say. He just told us to wait—till they were done."

"If that's so, then he is going to start looking for these girls," said the man standing at the window.

"Get the women into trucks," Matthew said. "Send one man with each truck and tell them to rendezvous about a mile outside of the city—near Winterburn. Tell them to stay in radio contact, and they'll receive further orders." The men in the backseat began to leave, the man on the right dragging the woman with him. "No," Matthew said, as he held up his hand. "Leave her here. We'll use her." The man nodded. "But gag her," Matthew said.

The man on her left tore a piece of duct tape off a roll he had in his pocket, and placed it over the woman's mouth. He examined her wrists and then nodded as he confirmed that the electrical tie was still snug.

Victoria glared at him.

Matthew ordered the woman out of the truck. She hitched herself across the seat and jumped out. Her high-heeled boots hit the ground, and she cried out as her right ankle twisted. The man next to her grabbed her elbow and steadied her. She yanked her arm out of his grip.

"Over here," Matthew said. Victoria obliged and hobbled toward him. Her truck seatmates now flanked her, each with a hand holding her arms. Matthew picked up his walkie-talkie and began to issue commands. He turned and watched as four trucks pulled away into the darkness— without their headlights. Matthew knew they would creep along until it was safe to turn the headlights on. He turned back to the men in front of him. "It's time to make a trade," he said.

"What's the plan?" the pony-tailed captain asked.

"I can't go— The Man wants me too much. You'll go," Matthew said, motioning to the pony-tailed captain. "We'll send five guys with you. But I'm taking twelve others around back. If The Man's soldiers retreat, we'll take them down inside. And if The Man hangs back, we'll take him down, too."

"So, what do we do with her?" the captain asked, pointing to Victoria.

Matthew nodded to the men holding her arms. "Bring her up just far enough for his guys to see. When they do see her, tell them we're interested in a trade. Thirteen for one. All we want is Brad. And they get their "clean" ladies back. If not, threaten that we'll radio our men to kill them. Emphasize that all we want is Brad. Got it?"

The pony-tailed captain nodded. "I think we can handle that," he said. "And if they agree?"

"Tell them we'll meet near the TV station on Stony Plain Road to make the exchange."

"And if they don't agree?"

"Then I have misjudged the value of those women, and you'd better start ducking and firing."

The pony-tailed captain didn't smile. "I think I understand," he said. He made a hand motion, and another man ran back along the trucks. The man soon returned with five other men—burly men, all heavily armed. The captain quickly relayed the plan.

"Listen," Matthew said. "Give me about ten minutes to get into position around back. I'll signal you on the radio."

The captain nodded. He waved to the two men with the woman, and they began their trek up the street toward the strip mall. They paused about fifty feet away, and waited. The captain tapped his wrist.

Matthew nodded.

Another captain now stood in wait with eleven men in high anticipation near him. All had drawn their weapons, and their eyes glittered.

Matthew smiled. He was secretly glad these men were on his side. He hadn't hesitated when the men, their wives, and their children had shown up at the gate—three months back. They were family men, and they were hungry. However, they didn't show up empty-handed. They arrived with the kind of knowledge very few men had; all were highly skilled combat soldiers. Matthew doubted that The Man had anything comparable. Matthew checked his own handgun, his extra ammunition, his gear, and then he waved to the men to follow him.

They took the same path used by the men who had abducted the women earlier. They made their way around back of the strip mall and down toward the bar. A door was visible in the dim light. Two armed men stood near the door. They were lounging, not guarding. Matthew motioned for two of his men to break away and circle around in order to surprise the guards from the opposite side. As Matthew watched, the door opened and the guards disappeared into the building.

"What now?" the pony-tailed captain hissed into Matthew's ear. "Knock and say, 'Avon Calling?'"

Matthew chuckled. "Give it a second," he said. He held up his walkie-talkie. The captain leaned in. They listened. No sound. Matthew studied the long building; no back entry doors hung open. He looked up at the roof. He shook his head.

"What now?" the captain whispered.

"Do you feel lucky?" Matthew asked.

"What?"

"Take a couple of the guys, stand to the side, and knock on the door. Wait for someone to open it. But don't rush in. Let them come out to us." The captain nodded and beckoned to a younger man kneeling a few feet away. The young man crept over, knelt, and listened.

"Hey!" a man yelled from several feet away. Matthew and the captain turned toward the sound.

Matthew recognized the voice as belonging to one of the men he had sent off a few moments earlier. He saw a small scuffle in the shadows. In a moment, the two men emerged with a third man between them. They were coming back through some brush behind a garbage dumpster. Matthew squinted. The men came closer. The third man wore a big grin.

"Trojan," Matthew said, with an exasperated sigh. "I thought I told you to go back to the camp."

"Yeah—whatever." Trojan shrugged. "I figured you guys were going to try something like this, so I stuck around."

Matthew sighed.

"Besides, I've been here once before," Trojan said. "A president of one of our northern chapters was invited here. I was with him." Trojan shook his head. "Nasty ceremony. They burned his old tattoo off with a heated spoon—smelled like hell."

Matthew nodded, "Yeah— We know all about it."

"You do?" Trojan asked.

"One of The Man's women told us."

"A woman? You talked—" Matthew interrupted him.

"Look, we've got to get into a better position," Matthew said. "The front door team is waiting for my signal. Any ideas?"

"Front door team?" Trojan asked.

"Never mind that— What do you know about this back entrance?"

Trojan shook his head. "You can't go through that door," he said. "You'd be dead in a second. That door leads into a room with couches and pool tables. Lots of guys hang out there during The Man's meetings." He brightened, "But there's another way in."

"Why didn't you say something before?"

"You never asked."

"Oh." Matthew grinned. "So?"

Trojan pointed to a closed door two units down from the bar. "If you can get in through there—they've cut mouseholes between the stores."

"Mouseholes?"

"Yeah, that's what one of the guys called it."

"But aren't those guarded, too?"

"Maybe. But they weren't before."

The captain had been listening. "Sounds better than our first plan," he said. He glanced down at his walkie-talkie. "Let's get inside and then signal them."

Matthew nodded to the captain, but then he hesitated. He caught Trojan's eye. "Why should I trust you? You didn't go back as I told you to. What if this is just a way to gain points with The Man?"

Trojan laughed—a short laugh. "If I had wanted to get back here, and make points with The Man, I would have left your camp long ago. And taken Cammy with me. From what she's told me, The Man would have been very happy to have her back." He stopped speaking and waited.

Matthew went silent, as he thought. The captain nudged him. "I say we trust him."

Matthew gave a nod. "Okay," he said to Trojan. "Lead the way." As Trojan turned, Matthew grabbed his arm. "I'm not a forgiving man," Matthew said.

Trojan stared at the big hand on his forearm. "I am," he said, shaking Matthew's hand from his arm. Then he hunkered down and ran across the pavement toward the door.

Matthew glanced over at the bar's back door—it was still closed. The guards had not reappeared. He waved the men forward.

□□□

The Daddy

"I CAN'T stay long," Virgil said. "He's expecting to meet with me after Brad's ceremony."

"I know. Just a little longer," Marion mumbled.

"Do you think he suspects anything?"

"No. And even if he did, I told you—he doesn't own me."

"He thinks he does."

"Well, he doesn't."

"How did you get to become his sister anyway?"

"He tells people that we met online, but that's not true. I was friends with his sister—when we were teens. Before she died, I mean."

"She died?"

"Uh—well, she was killed."

"By who?"

"Not sure. But people suspect that his crazy dad killed her."

"Crazy dad?"

"Yeah— One of those redneck preacher types. He had his own church—a small congregation. They believed in picking up rattlesnakes. You know the type."

"Oh, yeah. I do. Really screwy bunch."

"Yeah, well—I didn't like going to their house. The old man kept plastic tubs with rattlers for his church services. He'd force his kids to hold them— My girlfriend used to tell me about that. She told me about other stuff, too. That's why it's not hard to believe that her father might have killed her. He used to beat on her horribly. She'd come to school with thick purple welts, the width of a leather belt, all over her arms and legs."

"Did he beat The Man, too?" Virgil asked.

"Yeah. From what I could tell. Anyway, after my friend died, I lost contact with the family. And then one day, I was cruising around Facebook, and I found The Man. Well, I found him by his real name." She laughed. "Funny how nicknames catch on. Want to know what his real name is?"

"Sure."

"Hezekiah. It means 'the Lord has strengthened'— His dad chose his name."

"Oh— His mother had no say in his name?"

"Oh, boy— You have no idea. His mother had no say in anything. She was a miserable mouse of a woman. A black eye or bruises on her face were normal. And she wore long sleeves and long dresses—often. Even when it was boiling outside. I was visiting at their house once and I walked by her bedroom. She was dressing. She never saw me, but I saw huge bruises on her arms. And on her back. My girlfriend said she was always getting punched by their dad. I mean their—'daddy'—the kids always called him by that name."

"I think men like that should be executed. On the spot," Virgil said.

"Sure— We can do that now. But not then. Those kids and their mom had to live through some horrible stuff. That's why I care about him— He's got a lot of problems. His mind is crawling with spiders and snakes. So, I guess I kind of love him—in a way. But he's a hard one to love. I don't think he's ever loved anyone. Except for maybe... Cammy. He was attached to her."

"Yeah. He's really upset she's gone. He thinks she planned to desert him. He's told one of the ex-members of Matthew's camp to bring her back."

"Who's that?"

"A guy called Meteor."

"Meteor? That sounds familiar to me. Does he have blue eyes?"

"Yeah, he does. Why?"

"I know him. Nice guy, actually. Well, at least he's nice to the ladies. He's a loner though." She wrinkled her brow. *"He's joined The Man?"*

"So it seems." Virgil curled his arm around Marion's neck and checked his watch. *"I've gotta go."*

Marion rose up and pushed him back against the pillow. *"No-o-o,"* she whispered. *"Just another few minutes."* She kissed him and climbed on top of him. *"Just a few minutes,"* she cooed.

Virgil groaned. *"You're gonna get me in such trouble."*

"Yes, but I'm so worth it."

Chapter Thirty-Five
Matthew and The Man

THE DOOR was not locked; it opened easily and soundlessly. The room was pitch black. The men switched on their headlamps, but carried them shielded in their hands. They followed Trojan through a maze of tables and chairs, large cardboard boxes–their sides stamped with FRAGILE and FLOWERS, tall rectangular glass coolers, and piles of plastic buckets. Matthew guessed the store had been a flower shop.

Trojan gripped one of the coolers against the far wall and shoved it aside. It screeched along the cement floor as he pushed. Matthew grimaced, but the sound was short-lived. Behind it was a full sheet of drywall leaning on an angle against the wall. Two men went forward and lifted it aside. Trojan gestured with a sweep of his arm. "See?"

There it was, just as Trojan had said it would be—a mousehole. It was an oval opening about the width of a big man, and the height of a dwarf. They saw a room on the other side of the hole; it was inky dark, too. Matthew motioned the captain forward. He, Trojan, and the rest of his men followed.

Once through the mousehole, Trojan pointed across the room. A quick sweep with their headlamps showed the place to have been a dry-cleaning outlet. Clothing still hung neatly in long cellophane sleeves from a U-shaped rod running along the ceiling. A steam table anchored the area toward the front of the room; to their left, washing machines flanked an entire wall.

The men followed Trojan's soundless lead and picked their way across the room. He stopped and pointed to another sheet of drywall. He put a finger to his lips and then pointed to an area on the wall, up and off to the right. Matthew's eyes followed. He could just make out a dark rectangle. A piece of fabric hung from the wall. It appeared to be concealing something. "It's a speakeasy," Trojan whispered.

The captain heard and eased over to the wall. He lifted an edge of the cloth, and peered through a small hole. The men waited. The captain waved a hand to Matthew, indicating he should look, too.

Matthew peered under the cloth. He saw another room, a storage room filled with stacked tables and chairs, old signage, drink coolers, and cardboard liquor boxes piled precariously to the ceiling. The space was slightly illuminated by light coming from an open door on the other side of the room. The room seemed deserted. Matthew backed away. He nodded to the captain.

Two men grabbed the sheet of drywall and lifted it away from the second mousehole. The men, led by the captain, filed in, with short delays to ensure they weren't heading into an ambush.

One after the other, they entered until all the men were in the bar's storage room. They kept to the shadows and waited. Matthew and the captain crept up to the open doorway through which the light was coming. They could see a large pool table and several couches. They couldn't see the guards, but they could hear voices. The conversation was too low to understand.

Matthew and the captain crept back to the rest of the men. "We've got one chance to get this right," Matthew whispered. "Take three of the military guys."

"Quick and painless," the captain assured Matthew. "Well— Almost painless." He waved to the men.

Matthew watched as they slipped through the doorway. In moments, they were back.

"Done," the captain whispered. "Four." He clutched his throat. "We broke their necks," he said. "No mess."

Matthew motioned for the rest of the men to head through the doorway; the men obeyed. Trojan was still at his side as they ran into the room. To his right, he saw the back door, the one that had blocked their entry before. Behind one couch lay the bodies of four men. He motioned, and again the men jumped to action. They pulled the bodies into the storage room and out through the mousehole, depositing them in the dry-cleaning store.

Matthew crouched with the captain and Trojan nearby.

"Now what?" the captain asked.

Matthew lifted the walkie-talkie. He pressed the transmit button three times. "Okay," he said. "The front team has been given the go-ahead. Let's see how far we can get in here." He turned to Trojan.

Trojan pointed toward the door to their left. "Through there—" he said. "That's the bar. The door leads up a hallway by the bathrooms."

Matthew nodded. He looked at the captain who nodded back.

"It's now or never," the captain whispered.

"Go," Matthew said. "See if you can find out what we're dealing with." The captain obeyed.

They waited.

A few minutes passed, and then the captain and the three men were back.

"There's a meeting going on alright. Lots of guys—two, maybe three dozen. The place is too tight for a shoot-up. We'd get a lot of our own men killed."

Matthew nodded his understanding. "Any ideas?" He looked at the captain. Then at Trojan.

"Use me—" Trojan said.

"What?"

"Use me. I doubt anyone really remembers me. I'll run in and tell them there's something happening out back. That should draw a few of them. You can take those out."

Matthew and the captain looked at each other. "It sounds like our best bet," the captain said with a shrug.

Matthew began to nod and then he said, "What about Brad? If Brad is in there, will he recognize you?"

"I've never met Brad," Trojan said. "He won't have a clue who I am." He paused, and added, "I won't know who he is either."

"Wait," the captain said. "We've got a couple new guys with us—guys Brad has never met. Why not send them in, too?"

Matthew nodded. "Good idea. Do they look like Crazies?"

The captain pointed at two men crouched a few feet away and motioned for them to come forward; they did. Matthew studied their scraggly beards, their long, unkempt hair, and their jackets. He shook his head. "The jackets will never pass. Anyone got a vest?" Two other men slipped out of their jackets, and pulled off leather vests. The two bearded men were soon wearing leather vests; they had been briefed on their roles. Matthew smiled at Trojan. "Okay, you're on." He grabbed Trojan's arm. "Don't get killed."

"Thanks," Trojan said. He stood and then looked back over his shoulder at Matthew. "If I don't make it, you'll take care of Cammy for me?" Matthew grinned. Trojan led the men toward the lit doorway. They disappeared through the opening. A slight lull, and then a burst of voices.

Matthew and the captain exchanged glances. "They're in trouble," the captain said. "Let's go."

Matthew stood, but at that moment, shadows filled the doorway. Matthew and the rest of the men crouched back into their hiding places. The silhouettes turned out to be Trojan who was nattering excitedly to three strangers. The two bearded men Matthew had sent with Trojan were nowhere in sight. Matthew watched as one of the men behind Trojan pulled a pistol. The captain saw the movement, too, and hissed at two men hunkered down in the shadows near him. They attacked.

The three strangers gave a shout of surprise, but the sound was quick. Soon there were no sounds. The men had been dealt with, and their bodies dragged into the storage room. Trojan slipped in beside the captain and Matthew.

"They were going to kill you," Matthew whispered.

"Yeah— I thought so."

"Where're the other two?"

Trojan shook his head. "The Man told them to stay. I think they're in deep shit."

"How many are left?" the captain asked. His agitation at the possible loss of good men made his whisper gruff.

"There's a lot of yelling outside the front door," Trojan said. "About a half dozen left while we were there. I think they suspect something."

"Did you recognize anyone?"

"No."

The captain spoke again, his voice still thick with irritation. "I'm not letting our guys die in there. Not without a fight."

Matthew held up his hand. They heard voices coming from the front of the bar. He held up his walkie-talkie and pointed toward the mousehole. "Hold your positions. I want to listen in. I'll be right back."

Matthew sprinted toward the storage room. Once inside, he knelt in the dark, flicked on his headlamp, shielded the light, and turned up the volume on the walkie-talkie. It had been pre-arranged that as soon as he sent his go-ahead signal, the pony-tailed captain would keep his radio transmitting. Matthew listened. One voice boomed above the rest.

"The Man doesn't negotiate." And then, "He's on his way out here."

Matthew twisted the volume down low, and crept back into the room. He crawled up beside the captain. "The Man is going outside."

The captain raised his eyebrows. "What about Brad? Any word about him?"

"No— The only thing I heard was that there'd be no negotiating."

The captain nodded. "I want to get in there," he said. "I think we can take them."

They watched as figures moved into the open doorway. Three men emerged. "Not ours," the captain hissed. They watched the men stride into the darkened room, directly to the back door. They opened it and stepped outside. Three of Matthew's men followed. A moment later, they returned, one of them drew the door closed behind them. "That's three more," the captain said. He stared at Matthew, "Now?"

Matthew nodded. "Go."

The captain waved his men forward; they moved soundlessly toward the doorway. Trojan followed. Matthew stopped two of the rear men, indicating they should stay back with him. "I can't go in," he said. The men nodded. He motioned toward the back door. "We'll go around the side."

Matthew and the two men waited. They heard sounds of a fight coming from the bar, but no gunshots. They hurried to the back door.

"Hold it," a man's voice called out. Matthew froze as a man came up behind him. His stomach sank as a muzzle ground into his neck. The other two men had guns pressed to their necks, too. Matthew turned.

A second man came forward out of the shadows. Matthew clenched his jaw as he recognized the face: *Brad.*

"An old friend of mine," Brad drawled. He waved at the man holding the gun to Matthew's neck. "Don't kill him." Then to Matthew he said, "The Man was right. He said you'd come." Brad smiled. Matthew's face was stony. "Drop the gun," Brad said. "You won't need it."

Brad looked at Matthew's men. He nodded at his men holding them at gunpoint. "They're not important," he said. "Do what you want with them." He turned back to Matthew.

"Why?" Matthew asked. "Why did you turn? Why did you kill him?"

Brad waved away the man with the pistol and held his own gun up to Matthew's face. "There just wasn't much of a future with you, Matthew. I was looking forward to being your second-in-command, but then Josef showed up. And you two got real tight—left me out in the cold." He laughed. "And then there's darling Martha."

"What about Martha?"

"I got sick of watching her run you—run the compound. Women like her need shutting up, not indulging."

"Jealousy?" Matthew asked. "You were jealous?" Brad's fist caught him on the mouth, causing Matthew's head to snap back, his cap to fly off, and blood to spurt from his lip.

"No— Not jealousy," Brad said, as he shook out his fist and rubbed it with his other hand. "—Ambition. I just got made The Man's sergeant-at-arms." He smiled and watched Matthew wipe the blood from his face with the back of his hand. "How's that for climbing the corporate ladder?"

Matthew straightened up. "You don't have the stuff that leaders are made of, Brad. People don't respect you— They fear you. You're a lousy leader. The Man will learn that."

Brad laughed again—a thin, caustic sound that echoed up against the blackness of the room. "What do I care? Guess who takes over leadership of your compound when The Man takes it?" He peered into Matthew's face. "Guess who gets to be the almighty Gatekeeper? And guess who gets to teach Martha a lesson or two?"

Matthew's eyes flickered, but he didn't speak.

"Me," Brad answered. He gave Matthew's chest a hard shove. "Let's go," he said.

Matthew stood his ground and stared at Brad. "You'd better kill me, Brad, because... " he shook his head slowly back and forth, "... when I get the chance... I am going to kill you. What you did to Josef—"

Brad threw back his head and laughed again. For the first time, it sounded mirthful. "Sure you will, Matthew. Sure you will." Brad grabbed Matthew's arm and shoved him back toward the door leading to the bar.

Another man joined Brad. Brad nodded at him and the man walked behind Matthew, wrenching both of his arms behind his back. He secured Matthew's wrists with an electrical tie.

Brad spoke again, "You have an appointment with The Man, Matthew. And I guarantee you won't be killing anybody after that." He gave Matthew's shoulder another sharp push.

Matthew stumbled, caught himself, and turned back to the doorway. His companions watched, but said nothing. Matthew wondered what had happened out front. He and Brad moved through the doorway and into the hallway. The bar looked deserted.

Brad pushed Matthew forward and then motioned to a room off to the side. It was a smaller room filled with casino machines and two large regulation-sized pool tables. Two men lay on the tables—their arms and legs splayed wide. Their limbs were secured with ropes to the legs of the pool tables. The light was low; Matthew noted that it was coming from several camp lanterns that had been placed in an orderly fashion around the room. In this dim light, he could see that the men had been beaten, but their eyes and their mouths still moved; they were alive.

"We've got him," Brad said to the shadows. Matthew waited. Brad gave him another shove forward. Matthew saw a figure seated in a large chair in the shadows at the back of the room. Two armed men stood to either side of the chair.

"Bring him here," the figure said. Brad gave Matthew another shove. Matthew stiffened and walked forward, choosing his steps carefully. He was about twenty feet from the chair when the figure leaned into the light. "That's far enough."

Brad and the other man stepped back leaving Matthew standing alone. Matthew stared at the face, at the eyes of the man leaning toward him—the eyes were cold and gray, like a shark's eyes. But unlike a shark's eyes, they glittered with interest.

"So, you're the *Gatekeeper*," The Man said.

Matthew echoed back, "So, you're *The Man*." He grinned in spite of the pain from his cracked lip. "So— How did you know?"

"Know? You mean that you would come here tonight?" The Man smiled slowly, and stood. He was taller than Matthew was, and a little broader. Matthew could see they were about the same age. The Man walked toward him. The armed men followed, but The Man stopped them with an upheld palm. "Do you think you got wind of tonight's ceremony by accident?"

Matthew felt surprise, but he kept it concealed. He spoke, "Clever— A very clever move." He shook his head. "But your decision to put this asshole into any position of authority— Not so clever." Brad made a move toward Matthew, but The Man stopped him.

"Really," said The Man. "Then we are both fools. As I understand it, you put Brad into a position of authority, too." Matthew said nothing. "I think he will do very well here. He was a kind of a square peg in a round hole on your compound." The Man smiled at Brad.

Matthew snorted with disgust. "I'm not sure how much you know," he said. "But we're holding a number of your women hostage."

"Ah, yes," The Man said. "I heard about that." He walked over to Matthew. His bodyguards slipped in behind him—mute like cobras, silent and deadly. The Man took Matthew's forearm, not violently, but firmly. He propelled him forward toward the bar's entrance. They stepped through the doorway.

The night was black, but the bonfire still blazed across the street. Matthew's eyes adjusted to the dark. Ahead of him, on the parking lot, stood two groups. The larger group was nearest him. It was composed of several bikers—all men. All had weapons drawn. He recognized the second group as his own men. They had their guns drawn, too.

"Mexican stand-off," Matthew muttered.

Victoria stood with his men; still bound and gagged. Matthew winced. He had walked them all into a trap. Just like Trojan had said. Matthew looked around.

Where was Trojan? And the captain? And the special forces soldiers? They were not part of the group.

The realization gave him a faint rush of hope. The Man was now out in the open. As was Brad. Matthew held his breath, waiting for the attack to come.

But it didn't come.

The Man spoke. "I understand you wanted to make a trade," he said.

The pony-tailed captain at the front of Matthew's group of men spoke up. "Yes, but now it'll be thirteen for two."

"Ah-ha," The Man said, simply. He drew Matthew along with him. They now stood parallel with the group of bikers. "I see one woman," he said. "Where are the others?"

"We're holding them. But one word from me, and they'll be killed."

"Just like that?" The Man asked.

"Just like that."

"What makes you think that I would care about a bunch of women?" The Man asked.

"They're 'clean,'" the pony-tailed captain retorted.

The Man stood quietly for a moment and then continued. "Ah, I see Victoria has been talking to you." He motioned with his hand, as though removing something from across his mouth. "Would you mind allowing her to speak?"

The captain obliged and pulled the gaffing tape from the woman's mouth. Victoria cried out as the tape ripped at her skin.

"Do they really have the other women?" The Man asked.

Victoria nodded through her tears. "Yes," she said, her voice quaking. Terror made her eyes grow large.

The Man spoke again, "And what of the other one?"

"What other one?" the pony-tailed captain called out.

"I believe you have another of my women—" The Man said, his voice edged with menace. He turned and faced Matthew squarely. "Cammy."

Matthew stared back, but said nothing.

The Man grinned. "By your silence—I know that you know who I'm talking about." He paused, and then added, "And then there is that little matter of a truck full of weapons."

Matthew grinned this time. "Yes," he said. "A nice bonanza. Thank you."

Matthew didn't see the blow coming, but he doubled over as The Man's heavy fist slammed into his belly. He staggered and fell to his knees. He gasped for breath.

"I am also a little pissed that you took out some of my best men tonight," The Man said, as he kicked Matthew in the thigh, sending him into a heap on his side.

"I want my weapons *and* Cammy— Back." The Man kicked him again, a more vicious kick to the ribs. Matthew grunted. "Do you think you can oblige me?"

"Matthew—" the pony-tailed captain called out. "Say the word."

Matthew struggled for breath. "No—" he gasped, as he got to his knees. "We'll make the trade."

"Good," said The Man. He leaned over, grabbed Matthew by the arm, and pulled him to his feet. "Now it's just a matter of ironing out the details." The Man addressed the captain. "We're going to keep your commander—for safekeeping. I promise that no harm will come to him. You go—fetch our weapons—and Cammy. Bring them here, and we'll make the exchange."

"Agreed—" said the captain, "—except for one thing. The exchange doesn't take place here. We'll make the exchange at another location."

"What did you have in mind?"

"The TV station on Stony Plain Road."

"I know the place," The Man said. "Okay— Agreed." He checked his watch. "Let's say in six hours from now. The light will just be coming up."

As he spoke, Victoria wrenched herself free from the men holding her. She ran across the parking lot toward The Man. He reached to his hip, pulled his pistol, and fired. The woman sank to the pavement.

"Loose lips," he said, as he returned his gun to its holster.

Matthew stared at the dead woman and then back at The Man. His silence asked the question.

The Man smiled and breathed in deeply through his nose. "She was never one of my favorites."

Men on both sides murmured at the murder they had just seen. The Man turned to the bikers. "Keep an eye on things until they're gone, won't you?" Several of the bikers nodded their assent—somewhat dumbly, their eyes glazed with shock.

The Man took Matthew's arm again. His bodyguards shielded his back as he pulled Matthew back to the bar. Brad followed. The Man, Matthew, Brad, and the bodyguards stepped back inside the bar.

Once inside, they walked back to the room with the pool tables. The Man pulled up short. "Where are they?" he said, his voice tinged with intense irritation.

Matthew gazed across at the pool tables where his men had been tied down; both tables were now bare. Matthew hid a satisfied smile. His men *were* here. And they had been busy.

The Man motioned to the door. "Get six guys and a driver. We're going to move him."

One of the bodyguards bounded out the front door; in less than a minute, he returned with the requested men. "They're here," the bodyguard said. "The trucks are coming around back."

The Man was brief. He motioned to Matthew. "Take him to the main clubhouse. I'll meet you there."

"Do you want me to go, too?" Brad asked. Matthew heard eager, almost childlike anticipation in Brad's voice.

"No," The Man said. "Run things here. I've got some business to attend to."

"You aren't really including me in the exchange, are you?" Brad asked.

The Man smiled. "We must—at least—make it look like you are part of the exchange. I'll get word to you."

Brad gave Matthew a look of self-satisfaction. "I'll be here," he said.

Matthew was hustled out the back door. He looked around, but there was no sign of his men: not living, not dead. *That was good*, he thought. A sudden fatigue took hold, and his legs turned to cement. He began to fall, but one of his captors grabbed him and hauled him toward the waiting truck. A door swung open, and he was pushed inside. Two men got in on either side of him. Another one hopped into the front seat. Three more men hopped into a separate truck that pulled in behind the first. The engines roared to life.

Matthew's head hung forward, but he lifted it when the driver spoke: "How far ya going, buddy?"

The question had a sardonic and familiar ring to it. Matthew stared at the driver looking back at him in the rearview mirror.

Meteor.

Chapter Thirty-Six

Martha and Cammy

MARTHA LOOKED up from her medical textbook. She was tired, but she couldn't sleep. The abortion meeting weighed heavily on her mind. She glanced through the kitchen window into the darkness. Lantern lights glowed in the distance. She looked toward the door. She was half-expecting to hear someone banging on it— Someone like Matthew. She sighed. She got up from the table and went to the window. Lights were on in the Gatehouse.

Why put it off any longer?

She turned, pulled a jacket from the wall hook, slipped on her boots, and opened the door.

The compound was so still. Even the dogs were silent. Martha reached the Gatehouse. She knocked. The door swung open. It was Simon.

"Hi," he said.

"Hi. Is Matthew here?"

"No," Simon said. "He left ages ago."

"He left?"

"You didn't hear?"

"Didn't hear what?"

"He took a team into Edmonton. They went after Brad."

Martha felt her heart close and her mind darken. *Brad.* She remembered Meteor's words as he told the story of Josef's death. *Brad.*

Martha gritted her teeth. "I hope Matthew finds him. And when he does… " She paused. "I hope he makes him hurt."

"Most of us feel that way," Simon assured her. "Want to come in?"

"No," Martha said. "But will you tell me when Matthew gets back?"

Simon's face grew serious. "Yeah, but there's no telling when that will be. They went to war, you know. He took the special forces guys with him."

Martha stood silently. She looked at her watch. It was 11:30. "How long ago did he leave?"

"Before the abortion meeting started. Jonah said Matthew was on his way over there when he told him what he had heard about Brad."

"What did he hear?"

"Jonah knows some street boys in Edmonton. Some of them hang out with the Crazies. One of them told Jonah that Brad was to be made The Man's sergeant-at-arms tonight."

"How did Matthew know where to go?"

"Trojan."

"Oh," Martha said with a quick tilt of her chin. "Where's Cammy?"

Simon looked down at his shoes. "Don't know," he said.

Martha stepped away from the door. "Let me know when Matthew gets back, okay? I don't care how late it is."

"Sure," Simon said, with a small smile. "I'll do that." He disappeared back into the Gatehouse, closing the door behind him.

Martha looked across the way toward Matthew's cabin. A soft glow came from his kitchen window.

Was he back already?

She walked toward the light.

Martha reached Matthew's cabin. She knocked on the door. She heard a small movement from inside, and then the door swung open.

"*You?*" Martha stared in amazement. "What are you doing here?"

Cammy looked stunned, too, but her look of surprise eased into a honeyed smile. "Matthew asked me to meet him here."

"He did?"

"Yes." Cammy's eyes remained steady.

"He's not here," Martha said.

"I know," Cammy said flatly.

"I mean he left the compound."

"Where did he go?"

"He's gone to kill somebody."

"Who?"

"You don't know him."

Cammy shrugged. "Who is it?"

"A guy who used to be with our camp. The guy who killed my husband."

"Oh, you mean—Brad."

Martha stared at Cammy. "You know him?"

"Yeah."

"Since when?"

"Ever since he started hanging around The Man."

"When was that?"

"Maybe about a year ago."

"You've been with The Man that long?"

"Longer than that— More like two years."

"Why?"

"Why—what?"

"Why did you choose to stay with The Man?"

"He liked me. He offered me protection. He let me come and go as I pleased. He gave me responsibilities."

"Gun-running?"

"Yeah...that was one of my duties."

"Let me guess the other ones," Martha said. Her sarcastic tone had its intended effect.

"I wasn't his whore, if that's what you mean," Cammy retorted.

"You never slept with him?"

"It's none of your business, but, yes—I did."

Martha couldn't resist. "Any good?"

"He had his ways," Cammy said. She spoke slowly, "He was... different."

"Different bad? Or different good?"

Cammy smiled. "No complaints."

Martha stood quietly for a moment and then said, "Matthew won't be home for a while. You should go back to your own cabin."

Cammy's smile slipped back to her lips, a slow undulating movement like that of a cat's writhing tail. "Matthew told me to wait." Her smile disappeared. "Some of us do as we've been told." She reached to close the door, but Martha stopped it with her foot.

"I told you to go back to your own cabin." Martha said. She felt her face grow hard. "Now."

Cammy reached to pull the door shut again. But again, Martha held it open.

"I... said... now."

Cammy's eyes widened.

"I'm low on patience. Go."

Cammy stepped back inside. She sat on a chair, and pulled on her boots. She stood, grabbed her jacket, and shoved her arms into the sleeves. "I'll be sure to tell Matthew why I wasn't here when he got back," Cammy said, as she elbowed Martha out of her way.

"You do that," Martha said, her voice low. "You just do that."

"I will," Cammy called back over her shoulder. "You can be sure of it."

Martha closed the door with a sharp bang. She was breathing fast. Dark anger zipped through her veins like acid fireworks.

Bitch.

She reached her own cabin, yanked the door open, and walked in. She kicked her boots into a corner, and wrenched off her coat. She let it fall to the floor. She went into the bedroom and threw herself down on the bed. She gripped her pillow and pressed her face into it. Memories of Josef's death came whirling back. It was all wrong—everything was wrong.

Brad! Matthew! Cammy! Everything was wrong! So mixed up.

The monster inside her growled. Like the shadow of a killer, it loomed over her soul. She screamed her rage into the cotton and feathers. But her anger was too large.

It pounded at the cage.

It had to get out.

Martha sat up. She flung the pillow aside. She jumped up, and strode back into the kitchen. She opened Josef's chest. She removed her gun and holster and set them on the table. She found her flak jacket and secured it around her chest. With the gun and holster buckled firmly beneath her arm, she went to the ammunition box and removed several magazines and boxes. She sat at the table, loaded the magazines, and cursed when the bullets jammed or slipped from her fingers.

She grabbed a notepad and pen and scrawled a note: "*Gone to find Matthew. Feed Wilbert. Every 4 hours.*"

She pulled on her boots and did up the laces. She snatched her jacket from the floor. She checked her watch; it was after midnight.

Martha turned off the lantern and left the cabin. She sprinted across the compound to the vehicle lot. Her favorite truck was still there. She yanked the door open and slid onto the seat.

She caught a glimpse of her eyes in the rearview mirror—they belonged to a stranger. A feeling flared inside her, razor-sharp and unstoppable, like lava erupting through a long dormant cone.

Brad!

She took a slow breath and closed her eyes as she immersed herself into a womb of wildness—a swirling ecstasy that flushed her face and fed her soul.

Josef was my husband. Brad killed him. I will kill Brad.

The monster smiled.

Brad was going to die.

Martha turned the key. Out of the corner of her eye, she saw Simon emerge from the Gatehouse, but she was well on her way up the road before he could stop her.

Adrenaline coursed through her like an intoxicating drug and she welcomed its familiar caress.

Brad. Yes—the honor of killing you will be all mine.

Something occurred to her. She slammed on the brakes. She didn't have a clue where she was going. She needed a guide. And—she knew exactly the right person.

Martha drove to the end of the driveway, pulled over, and parked the truck. She jumped out, and ran back to the compound, but not up the main road. Instead, she took a path through the woods. She arrived at the cabin. She twisted the doorknob, opened the door, and stormed in.

Cammy gave a little shriek. "What are you doing here?"

"You're coming with me."

"What?"

"I want to find Brad. I need you to help me find him. So, you're coming with me."

"Now?"

"Yes— Right now."

Cammy's eyes questioned Martha, but she obeyed. She gathered her coat and her boots, and left the cabin. Martha led her back up the path through the woods. They reached the truck and got in.

"What exactly are you hoping to do?" Cammy asked, as Martha shoved the truck into gear.

"Just tell me where to find him." Martha said. She looked over at Cammy, "I know you know."

Cammy smiled. "Then you also know that I won't be coming back."

"Sweetheart... " Martha drawled, "I'm counting on it."

Martha pressed down on the accelerator and the truck roared up the highway.

□□□

The Strategy

"DID THEY buy it?" Virgil asked as he stared out the window into the darkness.

"Swallowed it— Hook, line and sinker. They arrived in force. And right on time, too."

"Those street kids are reliable. And Brad—did he buy it, too?"

The Man laughed. "Especially Brad," he said. He sat down. "He's such a putz, but he's useful." The Man waved to his bodyguards to take a seat on a long, dark leather couch toward the far end of the room. "And you wouldn't believe the bonus we got."

"Bonus?" asked Virgil, still standing at the window.

"We have the Gatekeeper."

"Get the fuck out of here." Virgil turned from the window and sat in a club chair across from The Man. "So, you got Matthew." He reached for a dark wooden humidor that sat at one end of the low table, flipped it open, and removed a fat cigar. He ran the cigar back and forth across his tongue, took a small bite off the end, spat it to the floor, and then using a disposable lighter he had in his front shirt pocket, he lit it. The air above his head filled with thick clouds of smoke. "Didn't think he'd give himself up that easily. Must be slipping in his old age. Did you kill him?"

"No, I had him taken to the main clubhouse. We'll deal with him later." The Man waved the smoke away from his face. He sat back into his chair. "Those things are going to kill you."

Virgil laughed. "Ah, you like them, too. Besides, I suspect a bullet will do that long before these things will." He held the lit cigar out at arm's length and admired it. "Matthew always liked cigars," he said. "I wonder if he still does."

"Would you like to find out?" The Man asked.

"That sounds like a splendid idea," the tall man responded. He took another long pull on his cigar, and blew a slow, curling plume of white smoke into the air.

The Man leaned forward, his elbows resting on his knees. "I think Matthew has padded out his team. I think I saw the work of special ops tonight. They took out quite a few of our men. Fast and quiet, too."

Virgil stopped studying his cigar and looked over at The Man. "Humph," he said, his eyes scornful. "I don't think he's got anything to match my boys."

"How's that team coming? Is it ready?"

Virgil stared across the narrow table between them. "They've been trained to kill. And to take orders. And they're loyal to me. They'd kill each other if I commanded it," he said with a self-satisfied grin.

The Man grinned back. "Well, Virgil... the time has come to test your boys. It's come sooner than expected, but we'll do this." He stood. "We'll take out Matthew's men. And then we'll take his camp. They'll never see it coming." He smiled again. "And they've made it easy for us."

"How's that?" Virgil asked.

"We've got a meeting time set for..." The Man glanced down at his watch, "...Five hours from now." He looked up. "Get ready. I want a perfect ambush. No errors. Anyone who makes an error and survives the battle— They won't survive me." The Man's face was hard, his eyes narrow and dark. "Tell them that."

Virgil held up his hand, two fingers extended upwards in support of his cigar. "Absolutely. But what's this about a meeting?"

"They took a dozen of our clean women. They've bargained to trade for Matthew. And for Brad."

Virgil laughed out loud. "A dozen bitches for Brad? And Matthew? Hardly sounds like a fair exchange."

The Man gave Virgil a long, patient stare. "Our stolen arms and ammunition are part of the deal."

"Now you're talking," Virgil said, as he took another draw on his cigar. He coughed, and then spat on the floor. "Full force?"

"They need the exercise. Full force," The Man said.

"What if the women get in the way?"

"Take them out. We've got plenty more coming up in the house."

"That—we do." Virgil paused and thought quietly for a moment. "It's hard to stay away from some of those young ones. They're starting to look pretty damn good."

The Man gave him a hard look. "Don't touch them."

"I know. I know." Virgil said. His hands rose in mock submission.

"And another thing—" The Man said, *"They're supposed to be bringing Cammy back, too. I don't want anything happening to her."*

Virgil nodded again. "Can't guarantee her safety. But we'll do our best." He sat back, dragged on the cigar, and then leaned forward. "She's caught your eye pretty good."

The Man frowned.

Virgil shoved his cigar between his teeth. He chose a pad of lined white paper from a dusty stack of notepads beneath the table. He picked up a blue pen from a box of pens lying open near the notepaper, and clicked it. "Let's get started. What's the plan?"

"TV Station on Stony Plain Road... big field behind..." The Man began.

Chapter Thirty-Seven

The Get-Together

BRAD WATCHED the front door of the bar close. He stood alone. He glanced at the empty pool tables. He swung his head from side to side in a quick, hawk-like gesture, and then he backed up. He turned and followed The Man out the door.

From his hiding place in the back room, Trojan watched Brad leave. He shook his head and clucked his tongue. The captain held a warning finger to his lips. The two injured men moaned softly in the darkness. Their wounds had been cleaned and dressed by the team's medic, but the pain medication was only beginning to take effect. The sounds of bikes firing up, and then roaring off, reverberated through the empty bar.

They waited quietly for a few more minutes. The captain motioned for the men to come out of hiding. They moved quickly through the bar's storage room and back through the mouseholes to the flower shop, carrying the wounded men with them. Once outside, they sprinted toward the vehicles.

Many of the trucks were gone, but a few still sat where they had been parked hours before. The men gathered near the captain and awaited his instructions.

"Take only two trucks," the captain said. "We should leave a couple behind. Just in case."

"I have a truck parked a little way from here, too," Trojan said.

The captain nodded. "Go get it," he said as he picked up his binoculars and studied the strip mall. The bonfire was still blazing. Many of the bikes that had been parked across the street were now gone.

"Should we go back and see if Brad is still there?" asked one of the men.

"He's not stupid," the captain replied. "He knew we were still around. He's long gone. And there are still too many men—with too many guns—for us to take down."

"What's the plan?" Trojan asked. "Where are we meeting up?"

The captain lowered his binoculars and turned Trojan's way. "If I send the two injured men with you, will you take them back to the compound?"

Trojan's face fell. "And miss the war?"

"Look, we really appreciate your help, but you aren't trained. Take my injured men back. If you don't, they'll die here. And they don't deserve that."

Trojan shrugged. "Sure, when you put it that way." He pointed up the street. "Give me a couple of minutes. I'll bring the truck back here."

The captain nodded again.

Trojan returned in a few minutes. He jumped out of the truck. "You've lost two," he said, shaking his head. "The ones who went out the back door with Matthew. I found their bodies on the street just back of the bar."

The captain looked alarmed. "And Matthew? Any sign of him?"

Trojan shook his head. "No, just the two guys." He paused. "I checked them for weapons, but they'd been cleaned out."

The captain gave an order and the wounded men were loaded into the back seat of Trojan's truck. The other eight men got into two of the compound trucks. Two compound vehicles remained on the street.

TROJAN SPED up the city streets as fast as was possible—without his truck's headlights. He wound his way around side streets, finally turned on his headlights, and drove out of the city and up the main highway toward the compound.

He was just past the city limits when he noticed another vehicle heading toward him.

MARTHA AND Cammy rode silently up the highway. Martha had risked full headlights since the night was so dark. She made a small questioning sound when the first three trucks whisked by them in the direction of the camp, but she didn't stop.

Matthew? Had they found Brad? Was it all over? But there weren't enough trucks. Where were the rest of the trucks? Simon had said "war." There would be many more trucks coming back.

Something inside of Martha told her to press on and she pushed hard on the accelerator, causing Cammy to stare at her.

"Take it easy. I'd like to arrive there alive."

"Where is *there*?" Martha asked, her voice clipped and impatient.

"I'm thinking we should go to the main clubhouse. The same place Trojan and Meteor found me."

"You're going in as my prisoner when we get there," Martha said.

"Sure," Cammy said. "Whatever you say, Martha." She turned her face away as a slow grin curled her lips.

Martha stared ahead into the darkness. Without a full moon, the night was black as tar. Driving at night, after the Change, was a challenge. It took extreme concentration to follow the highway without any guiding lights. Martha drove for a few more minutes; from the odometer reading, she knew they were within a few miles of the city limits. Suddenly, up ahead, twin beams cut through the blackness. Something made her hesitate this time. She took her foot from the accelerator, and then braked to a stop. She waited. The other vehicle—a truck, shot by. Martha watched its red taillights grow faint in her rearview mirror.

She was about to drive off when she realized that the truck taillights were getting bigger; the driver was backing up. She waited. Cammy stared out the back window.

"Who do you think it is?"

"I don't know, but I know it's one of our trucks," Martha said, with solid surety in her tone. She smiled as she spoke. Matthew had had the uncanny good sense to mark their vehicles with luminescent paint. They could always be identified—even in the dark. Martha had seen the illuminated mark as the truck passed by.

The driver backed up until he was directly across from Martha. He rolled down his window and peered out.

"Trojan!" Martha said, as she rolled down the window.

Cammy pressed in to see, too. "Hi," she called, with a small wave of her hand.

Trojan gave a quick look of surprise. Then he opened the door and jumped out of his truck. He leaned in to Martha's driver's side window. "What in hell are you two doing?"

"We're going for a drive," Martha said. "What are you doing? And where is everyone?"

"Long story," Trojan said. "But you should turn around."

"Why?"

"War," he said.

"Hey," he said to Cammy. "They're going to be looking for you."

"Why?" Cammy asked.

"You're part of a deal."

"I am?"

"Yep— The Man insisted on it. You—the guns—and the other women. In exchange for Brad... And for Matthew."

Martha sputtered, "Whoa, back up. Matthew? What are you talking about?"

Trojan explained what he and the other men had seen and had overheard back at the bar.

"I'm sorry, Martha," he said. "I don't think Matthew has much of a chance. They killed the two guys that went with him." He shook his head. "The Man has no intention of going through with any deal." He gave her a solemn look. "He's going to kill him— If he hasn't already."

Martha felt the blood drain from her face. Her jaw went tight, and she clenched her hands into fists, so tightly that her nails cut into the flesh of her palms. "Not if I have anything to say about it," she said. Her voice had taken on a deep timbre, almost a husky growl as she spoke through a throat swollen with anger. Martha reached for the gearshift.

"Wait," Trojan said. "What are you doing?"

"I'm going to get Matthew out of there." She glanced at Cammy. "And you're going to help me."

"Wait, Martha," Trojan said. "I can help you, but I've got two injured guys in the truck. I have to take them back to the camp. Will you wait long enough for me to do that? Then I'll go with you." Trojan gave Martha a sincere look— His eyes were wide and hopeful.

Cammy remained silent.

Martha checked her watch. She knew Trojan would be an asset.

Could she stand waiting the 20 minutes for him to make the round trip?

She checked her watch again. "Can one of the injured guys drive your truck?"

Trojan pressed his lower lip up in an unsure gesture. "I'll find out."

Trojan returned to his truck and opened the door. A brief conversation took place. Martha watched as he opened the back door, helped a man out, and then helped the obviously distressed man into the driver's seat. Another brief conversation—between the men.

Martha watched as the injured man handed weapons and ammunition through the truck's window. Finally, Trojan turned to Martha with his hands full of guns, magazines, and a couple of knives—their curved and serrated blades gleaming wickedly in the ambient light.

Trojan climbed into the backseat of her truck. Martha pushed the truck into gear, and slammed her foot onto the accelerator making the truck wheels screech and skid. Too much time had already been wasted.

Trojan reached forward from the backseat and ran his fingers along the back of Cammy's neck. She shuddered and pulled away. "Not now," she said.

Trojan reached further, and grasped Cammy's shoulder. "I don't need your permission," he said. "You're still mine." He looked into the rearview mirror. Martha was staring at him. "I'm not giving her up," Trojan said.

Martha smiled, but it was a smile of challenge. "We'll see how things go," she said. "I want Matthew back, and if that means trading her—that's what's going to happen."

Trojan's eyes glinted in the dashboard light. He opened his mouth to speak, and then closed it again. He squeezed Cammy's shoulder.

They reached the city. "Where do I turn?" Martha asked.

"Two streets up," Trojan said.

Martha stomped on the gas pedal, and slowed just enough to take the corner. Trojan was thrown to the other side of the backseat.

"Whoa—" he said. "Slow down."

Martha ignored him, and the truck sped up. Trojan clutched the backseat with both hands.

"You drive more like a man, than a man, Martha."

The Question

THE MAN and Virgil sent the trucks and the troops ahead. They took a few minutes to gather their own gear. They had gotten word that everything was ready for them. Including the Gatekeeper.

"Will it be nice to see your old buddy again?" The Man asked.

"I don't know—" Virgil said. "Maybe."

"You still hate him?"

"Never stopped."

"What happened between you two?"

"A woman."

"Ah."

Virgil brushed by and bent to retrieve his overcoat from the floor. The Man gave him a queer look.

"Hey, speaking of women—you sure smell nice. Managed to squeeze in a little face time, so to speak?"

Virgil grunted a response.

"Who is she?"

"Nobody important."

"Uh-huh. I know most of the women around the clubhouses. Is she new?"

"Yeah— New." Virgil buckled his gun belt around his waist.

The Man gave Virgil a wry smile. "Be sure to invite her over next Sunday—for dinner, okay? I'd love to meet her. She smells great."

"Let's go," Virgil said. "Don't want to keep the Gatekeeper waiting."

Chapter Thirty-Eight

An Early Morning Battle Plan

MARTHA EASED the truck up the city street. "How much farther?" she asked.

"Another block and a half or so," Cammy replied.

Martha pulled the truck over and parked.

"Why are you stopping?" Cammy asked.

"This is enemy territory," Martha said. "I've learned enough from my time in this crazy world to know better than to pull up in plain view." She glanced back at Trojan. "Tie her wrists."

Cammy's eyes went wide. "Please don't," she said.

"Shut up," Martha said. "Tie her wrists," she repeated, staring at Trojan in the rearview mirror. "I mean it." Martha reached into her jacket and pulled out her small pistol. "Or I'll kill her, right now."

Trojan held up a hand in submission. "Okay, take it easy, Martha."

He opened his door, jumped out, and opened Cammy's door. She tried to slip by him, but he caught her and yanked her arms behind her back. He took an electrical tie from his jacket pocket and cinched it around Cammy's wrists.

"Ow—" she said. "You don't have to be so mean."

Trojan turned the woman to face him. "Trust me," he said, "If I wanted to hurt you—I would." Cammy looked away. He grabbed her chin and turned her face toward him. "Look at me. I like you and I won't let anything happen to you." He glanced over Cammy's shoulder at Martha.

"But she's right—if Matthew is in there, we gotta go get him. And you're part of the deal. So, behave." She stood silently at his side. He closed his hand around her arm. "C'mon."

Martha got out of the truck. She pulled her headlamp out of her pocket. She held it cradled in her hand; it illuminated a small area just a few feet in front of her. She walked around to Trojan and Cammy. "Where's yours?" she asked.

Trojan reached into his coat pocket and pulled out his own headlamp. He snapped it on. He, too, kept it in his hand instead of slipping it onto his head. He looked at Martha. "What's the plan?"

THE PONY-TAILED captain reached the camp. He raced from his truck and pounded on the Gatehouse door. Simon opened it and he stepped outside.

"What's going on? Is it over?"

"Is Matthew here?"

Simon shook his head. "No. Why would he be here? He left with you guys. The only person I've seen tonight is Martha. And she took off."

"Took off?"

"Yeah, she took one of the trucks. She's long gone."

A man standing behind the captain spoke, "Hey, we passed her on the road about 20 minutes ago."

The captain nodded. "Did she say where she was going?"

Simon shook his head again. "Nope. I tried to stop her, but she was too fast." He paused. "I'm not sure. I'll bet she's going to try and find Matthew."

"How is she going to do that?"

Simon shrugged. "Hell, if I know. I don't even think she knows where to go."

"Where's Cammy?"

Simon shrugged again. "I don't know. She was in Matthew's cabin earlier."

"Matthew's cabin?"

Simon grinned. "Yeah."

The captain waved at two of his men. "Get Cammy. One of you try Matthew's cabin. And, you—" he said, motioning to the second man, "—try her cabin." The men nodded and ran across the compound. The captain turned back to Simon. "We need more men," he said. "Get them."

Simon called out to one of the guards. The man came over, listened, and then ran off.

"We'll need lots of firepower," the captain said. "I'm going to the Munitions Storehouse. Tell the men to meet me there."

"Will do." As Simon spoke, the captain's radio crackled.

"She's not here. Over." It was the man who had run to Matthew's cabin. The radio in the captain's hand crackled again.

"Not in her cabin."

"Copy that. Meet us at the Munitions Storehouse." The captain addressed Simon, "Do you think she left with Martha?"

Simon thought for a moment, and then he brightened. "That's what happened," he said, with a snap of his fingers. "I thought I heard her truck stop. She must have pulled over, and run back here to get Cammy." He paused. "Of, course! She needed Cammy to help her find Matthew."

"Yeah—" the captain said. "Except we need Cammy. And the guns."

"Why?"

"Part of the exchange."

"What exchange?"

"They have Matthew. The exchange is set up for a few hours from now—at the TV station on the edge of the city." The captain glanced at his watch. "We've got to get our team in there while it's still dark."

Simon looked grave. "I'm going with you," he said. "I'll get a replacement for me."

"Fine," the captain said.

The captain turned to go. Simon followed him, closing the Gatehouse door behind him.

"Get your replacement," the pony-tailed captain said. "Meet me in 10 minutes. In the parking lot."

A woman's voice called out to them.

"What's going on?" Anna asked.

Simon walked up to her. "It's Matthew," he said. "The Man has him. We're going to rescue him."

"What?" Anna looked shocked. "When did all this happen? How did this happen? Is he okay?'

Simon shrugged. "We don't know, but they want Cammy and the guns in exchange for Matthew. And for Brad. The captain is taking more men and going back to the city. I'm going, too."

Anna's eyes filled with concern. "I don't like the sound of this," she said. And then, "Do you have to go?"

"I want to go." He touched her face. "I'll be back though. I promise," he said with a smile.

"Should I tell Martha what's going on?"

Simon gave a short laugh. "Martha's long gone. She took Cammy with her."

Anna looked perplexed. Then she shook her head. "Of course, she's gone. Crazy woman."

The sound of a truck coming up the drive drew their attention. It was moving slowly, weaving up the road, and then it lurched to a halt. Anna gave Simon another puzzled look, and then the pair ran toward the truck. A man was struggling to get out of the driver's seat.

"Easy there, guy," Simon said. The man began to fall; Simon caught him. The man groaned. Anna came to his side.

"He's really hurt," she said. "But he's been bandaged." She examined the man's face. "What happened?" she asked.

"The Man," he muttered. "Trojan. Gone with Martha," he gasped.

"Where did they go?" Simon asked. He struggled to hold the heavy man up. Anna slid to the man's other side, and gently pulled his arm around her neck. The man cried out with pain.

"Sorry," she said.

The man winced as he tried to straighten up. He hooked a thumb toward the backseat. Simon peered through the window.

"There's another guy back here," he said. "He's hurt, too."

Simon pulled the door open. He pulled the man out; he was barely conscious. Simon called out to two boys who had run toward them. "Take them to the Medical Building," he said. He nodded at Anna, "I'll leave them in your very competent hands." He smiled.

Anna smiled back.

MARTHA AND Trojan crouched behind bushes about 100 yards from the clubhouse entrance. Cammy was nestled between them. She had been warned to remain quiet. Gaffing tape was offered as an option, but she promised silence. So far, she had kept that promise.

"Do you think Matthew is in there?" Martha whispered to Trojan.

Trojan shrugged. "Maybe. But that's just a guess." He looked at his watch. "We've got to make a decision, Martha. We hang out here and wait, or we go to the TV station. But I'll tell you this—there's no way I'm messing with those guys," he said, motioning to the dark figures of the men gathered on the parking lot.

"I'm with you on that," Martha said.

THE TRUCKS left the compound laden with men, guns, and ammunition. Like dark armored beetles, they slipped into the night. Simon and the pony-tailed captain were in the lead truck; Simon was driving.

"Do you want to try their main clubhouse first?" Simon asked. "Or are we off to the TV station?"

The captain took a deep breath. "You know the clubhouse area, don't you?"

"Yes."

"Let's go there. But we'll park several blocks away and walk in."

"I've got the perfect place in mind," Simon said. "It's a semi dealership. There's a huge parking lot around the back. Room for all the trucks and they'll be hidden there, even when the sun comes up."

The captain gave his assent, and Simon sped up.

MARTHA HEARD the rumble of engines—many engines. Men jumped from the trucks, but they didn't go inside. They stood near vehicles, stiffly like wooden soldiers, weapons hanging at their sides, flashlights, and headlamps winking up and down. There was something different about these men, Martha thought. Very different. They looked too... professional. They still looked like dirty bikers, but there was a seriousness about them— a deadly seriousness. She shivered.

Six more trucks pulled into the lot. Martha watched as some of the men hauled generators out of the truck beds. They set them around the lot and connected tall pole lamps. Soon, bright light washed over the parking lot and the front of the clubhouse.

"Well, that makes it a whole lot easier to see the enemy," Trojan mused. "Wonder why—oh—," he said, as he saw the items being unloaded from two of the trucks. Men rushed up, took the guns—carbines—and the ammo boxes being handed to them, and then hurried back to another vehicle waiting farther down the line.

Another truck pulled up. The men in the parking lot came to attention, as two men got out. The pair nodded to the bikers, and continued into the clubhouse.

"The Man—" Cammy said, "—and Virgil."

"Who?" Trojan asked.

"Virgil. He's The Man's closest friend. Very few members have met Virgil, even the full-patched ones."

"But you have?"

"Well, of course."

"And?" Martha asked.

"And," Cammy continued, "He's not to be messed with. He is one of the most dangerous men I've ever met."

"More dangerous than The Man?" Martha asked.

"Maybe—but The Man is pretty nasty, too." Cammy paused and then added, "Just not to me."

Trojan made a sound through his nose. "I'll just bet," he said.

Cammy glared at him.

METEOR STARED across the room at Matthew. They were alone. Matthew sat on a leather couch. His feet were bound at the ankles, his hands secured behind his back. He was leaning to one side. His face was bruised, and his mouth was bleeding. Meteor walked closer to the couch. He sat down in an armless chair nearby. Lantern light illuminated the room.

"You sure get yourself into some pickles, don't you?" Meteor asked.

Matthew raised his eyebrows. His eyes flickered toward the door, and then back to Meteor. "Why doesn't it surprise me to see you here?"

"Well, the party was over at your place. You threw me out, remember?" Meteor winked.

"That's what it's all about, isn't it, Meteor? Always looking for a better party."

Meteor leaned forward, "How's Martha?"

"Same," Matthew said.

"You two get together yet?"

"No. Why would we?"

Meteor shrugged and smiled. "No reason. Just asking."

Matthew's eyes turned back to the doorway. Three bikers entered the room. The tallest one strode over, his eyes fixed on Matthew. Matthew stared back.

The biker stopped near Meteor and clapped a large sinewy hand on his shoulder. He spoke, his voice low and level like the growl of an armored tank, "Hey, Matthew. Nice to see you again."

"Virgil," Matthew drawled. "Can't say I've missed you."

THE CAPTAIN pounded on the dash.

Simon jumped. "What?" he asked, his face showing surprise and concern.

"It's a set-up," the captain said. "It's a goddamned set-up."

"What do you mean?"

"Their fort—" the captain said. "The whole city is their fort. Or at least the west side." He pounded the dash again. "Son-of-a-bitch," he said. "They know exactly what we're doing. They just need to watch the main highway with binoculars." He glanced back. "Stop the truck."

Simon did as he was told. The line of ghostly vehicles drew slowly to a halt behind them. They were still several miles away from the city.

The captain turned to Simon. His look was serious and kindly at the same time. "Kid," he said, "I'm going to send you into hell. Are you up for it?"

Simon gave his superior a beaming smile. "You know I am."

"Good."

The pair left the truck.

□□□

The Doubt

"HAVE YOU seen Marion today?" The Man asked. He was standing behind his desk.

"No, sir."

"You sure? She didn't come by here while I was away?"

"Uh—nope. Pretty sure."

"What about Virgil? Was he here? This afternoon?"

The biker shook his head. "No—but he's here now. Not earlier—I don't think." The biker paused. "Do you want me to ask around?"

"Never mind."

Chapter Thirty-Nine

Taking Out the Trucks

METEOR WATCHED the interchange between the two men. Virgil and Matthew stared back at one another—neither saying a word. Meteor broke the silence.

"Hey, Virgil," he said, with a bright grin. He looked toward the door. "Where is he?"

"He's here."

"Did he say what his plans are for the Gatekeeper?"

"Nope. But I'm sure he's got something in mind."

Virgil sat down in a wide leather armchair across from Matthew. "So-o-o, Matthew... "

"Slumming now, Virgil?" Matthew asked. He grinned, but his eyes weren't smiling. "This all seems a bit beneath you."

Virgil laughed. "You don't look comfortable," he said. "Here, let me help you." He kicked at Matthew's feet, making Matthew lose his balance and tip over on his side.

"Thanks," Matthew mumbled, drily. "That's much better."

Virgil laughed again. "Matthew and I had a parting of the ways." He glanced back at Meteor. "That means you and I have something in common," he said.

"I see," Meteor said, with a small nod. "What happened?"

Virgil opened his mouth to speak again when a man yelled from the doorway. The three men turned their heads. A young biker, in a hunter's camouflage cap, burst through the door. "They're all here, Virgil."

"Okay, give me a few minutes," Virgil said. He held out a hand to Matthew, as though to shake. "Oh, sorry, I guess you're a little tied up."

Matthew sneered. "Always the asshole."

Virgil laughed—a sarcastic hollow sound. He dropped his hand to his side. "It's been a real pleasure, Gatekeeper." He paused. "But I guess that won't be true much longer. We're looking forward to taking over the camp. Nice place. I got a look at it once. Brad invited me." He gave another short, humorless laugh. "But we ran into this crazy woman— Martha. Know her? Feisty thing. I'm looking forward to getting to know her better."

Virgil leaned in closer to Matthew. He smiled—a wide white-toothed smile filled with lightly veiled intentions, "I'll be sure to give her your regards—your warmest regards. And mine— too."

It was Matthew's turn to laugh. "You don't know Martha."

Meteor laughed out loud—a genuine sound of deep pleasure. Virgil whipped around, a warning look in his eyes.

"You coming, Meteor?"

"Not yet—" Meteor said, as he rose from the chair. "I haven't gotten my orders. I'm sure I'll see you later, though. Are you headed over to the TV station now?"

"Yeah. Moving out the new team today."

"I thought they weren't ready," Meteor said. Virgil arched his back and stretched his arms over his head.

"Oh—they're ready." Virgil looked back at Matthew. "Your guys are in for a real treat."

Matthew smiled. "So are yours."

Virgil turned away. He and the bikers left the room.

Meteor and Matthew were alone again.

THE PONY-TAILED captain and Simon waited at the side of the highway; it took a few minutes for the men to gather. He called them to order. A sea of eager faces watched and waited. This captain was a favorite among them. Well-respected. Well-liked. He had their attention even before he asked for it.

"Switching tracks," the captain said. They leaned in as he told them his new battle plan.

METEOR CHECKED the door. No one was coming. He looked back at Matthew. "So, Virgil was a friend of yours?" Meteor asked.

"Yeah— But things change," Matthew said. "Didn't help that there was a woman in the middle of it."

Meteor laughed. "Say no more. I get it."

Meteor stood up and walked to the couch. He grabbed Matthew by the lapels and pulled him into a sitting position. As he did, he whispered, "Listen, buddy. This isn't the real war—that one's still coming. The man's people are all over the province. But you can take them— If you move now. Before they get too powerful." He shook his head. "I'm not so sure about later."

Matthew nodded. "You coming back?"

Meteor shook his head again. "I'm more valuable to you on the inside. I'll try and stay in. If you survive this, you'll need the intelligence I can pull from the other strongholds." He shrugged. "I mean—I've already paid the price of admission." Meteor pulled back his jacket, and lifted his shirtsleeve. Matthew stared at the large angry oblong scar; he had seen it before. It had shocked him then; it shocked him now.

Meteor glanced back to the door again. He continued to whisper, "Right now, we've gotta get you out of here. But if you don't make it, don't worry about Martha. I'll take care of her— I promise."

Matthew sat quietly. Then he smiled and nodded. "Thank you."

At the sound of approaching voices, Meteor straightened and returned to his chair. They both looked toward the door. The young man in the hunter's cap came back into the room. Another man was with him.

It wasn't Virgil.

SIMON LED the line of trucks into the night. They took the Devon highway turn-off. They raced up the road, careening around abandoned cars, trucks, and RVs as they drove. He knew the detour would add time, so he pressed down on the accelerator. The side road he had been looking for appeared, and he turned left. The rest of the trucks followed.

They made their way up the bumpy gravel road, past a casino, and soon reached the Anthony Henday ring road. He sped across the roadway, and continued up the Whitemud Freeway. At the 178 Street turnoff, he yanked the wheel right, and continued up the exit ramp. The line of trucks followed obediently; then they turned left.

Past the big mall, back over Stony Plain Road, a quick right through the car dealerships, and forward for a few more blocks. The semi dealership wasn't far away. The trucks rolled in and parked. The men jumped out and assembled.

"Two blocks—" Simon said. "Follow me."

THE CAPTAIN circled off the main highway. He led his forces away from the main roads, the ones he was sure were being watched. They slipped into the city from the north, and used side streets to reach the TV station. A scout was sent forward to meet with the men who were holding The Man's abducted women. The scout returned with his report. The men were there. The women were there. But the Man's army was nowhere in sight. The captain grinned broadly. So far, so good.

THE MAN strode into the room. He looked at Meteor, but tipped his head toward Matthew. "Is he behaving himself?"

Meteor gave a small nod. "Perfectly."

More men came through the doorway. One of them was Virgil. He stood beside The Man.

"You ready?" Virgil asked.

"In a minute." The Man turned and addressed Matthew. "We'll be going soon, but there's something I need to know first."

"What's that?" Matthew asked.

"I need to know if our pal here—" he thumbed at Meteor, "—has really switched his allegiances."

Matthew glanced at Meteor, but Meteor's face was cool, expressionless.

Meteor looked at The Man. "What did you have in mind?" he asked.

"Break his fingers," The Man said, tipping his head toward Matthew once again.

"A gun guy with broken fingers," Virgil said. "This should be interesting, Matthew."

"Sure," Meteor said. "But wouldn't you like to give this honor to Brad?" He paused. "Where the fuck is he anyway?"

"I told him to wait for us back at the bar," The Man replied. "So, that means you get the honor, Meteor." He gestured toward Matthew again.

THE PONY-TAILED captain directed his troops; like a maestro of a symphony, he placed trucks and men strategically up Stony Plain Road, nearby in the fields, and down the street that ran past the TV station. The ammunition was divvied up, and the big guns were positioned. The captain smiled.

The Man's women were now safely secured many blocks away. Nothing would happen to them. The captain liked clean women, too. He thought for a moment, checked his watch, and then he picked up his walkie-talkie. He clicked the send button three times.

"That does it," the captain said to the young man with him. "Now, let's see if Simon gets his part right."

The young man smiled. "Yeah— The Man isn't going to know what hit him."

SIMON'S MEN ran soundlessly through the dark. Simon led them back toward the place he had seen Josef die. He held up a hand as they neared the clubhouse; they were still a block away. He held his fingers to his lips, and pointed. Peering through the darkness, they saw long lines of trucks and dozens of armed men. Somebody had set up generators and large lights, so the entire front of the clubhouse and the parking lot were illuminated.

The man next to Simon spoke. "The signal came in." He held up his radio. Simon took the walkie-talkie. He smiled and pressed the send button.

He spoke.

MARTHA THOUGHT another moment. "Back to the truck," she said.

Cammy resisted when Martha and Trojan grabbed her arms, but their grips were firm. She relented and trotted along in their grasps. As they neared the truck, the radio tucked under the seat began to crackle.

"Crap—" Trojan said. "It's too loud. They'll hear it." He ran to the truck, wrenched open the door, and grabbed for the radio.

MATTHEW WATCHED Meteor rise from his chair. The big man moved across the floor. Matthew held his breath, waiting. At that moment, the walkie-talkie hanging from Matthew's belt began to squawk. Everyone in the room stared at it.

"En route to the TV station," a young man's voice said. "We should be in position in about 20 minutes. Will rendezvous with you there. Over."

"Damn it," an older man's voice responded. "I said I wanted radio silence. What in hell is wrong with you, Skippy?"

"Sorry, sir," came back the humble reply. The radio went dead.

The Man turned to Virgil. "Hook, line, and sinker—" He laughed. "Keeping his radio on was a nice touch."

Virgil glanced at his watch. "They're a little sooner than expected. But we're ready to roll." He clapped The Man on the back.

Matthew and Meteor exchanged a look. Meteor added a slow wink. Matthew returned a tiny nod. Meteor settled back in his chair.

MARTHA STARED at the radio in Trojan's hand.

A young man's voice came through the speaker. A pause.

"Damn it," an older man's voice responded. "I said I wanted radio silence. What in hell is wrong with you, Skippy?"

Martha and Trojan exchanged glances. "Skippy?" Martha said.

The voice belonged to *Simon*.

FIVE DÉCOY trucks took to the highway. As ordered, the five drivers wended their way forward toward Edmonton.

Men with binoculars, searching for headlights, radioed the information back to The Man.

MARTHA SMILED. "I get it. They're coming here," she said.

Trojan nodded.

They had dropped Cammy's arms. Finding herself free, she took the opportunity to bolt. Martha gave Trojan a stern look. "Catch her."

Trojan hesitated.

"Catch her— Or we're both dead."

Trojan sprinted up the street, his long legs closing the distance between himself and Cammy. Martha watched as he reached the woman, and tackled her. Cammy screamed out.

"Shit," Martha said. "Shit." She regretted not using the duct tape. It was only a matter of time now.

Trojan had a grip on Cammy, one arm and one hand was clasped firmly around her torso; the other hand was clamped over her mouth. She struggled uselessly. Martha had retrieved the gaffing tape from the truck, and had a piece waiting. She slapped it over Cammy's mouth.

"We've got to get out of here," Martha said. "There's no way they didn't hear her scream." She glared at Cammy. Cammy's eyes twinkled back at her.

"They're probably on their way," Trojan said. "Do we try to outrun them in the truck? Or hide here?"

"Truck," Martha replied.

ANOTHER BIKER ran into the room. "We've got activity a couple blocks up," he said. "A man and two women— Guys just left to go after them."

The Man smiled a thin smile. "Somebody looking for you, Matthew?" Matthew shrugged.

The Man thought a moment, and then he turned back to the messenger. "Tell whoever's gone after them to keep them alive. I'd like to *speak* to them." The messenger nodded and left the room.

The Man turned back to Matthew. Matthew was scowling, but he said nothing. The Man turned to Virgil.

"What do you say, Virgil? Could be entertaining, don't you think?" The Man's grin was cold.

"Yeah." Virgil said. He was looking at Matthew. "We'll give you a front seat for the event, Matthew."

"This is what you've come to, Virgil?" Matthew asked, with a sneer. "Torturing women?"

Virgil returned the sneer. "Yeah, Matthew. Especially *your* women."

Matthew laughed. "I pity you guys if it turns out to be Martha."

Meteor suppressed a smile.

"I'm hoping it turns out to be the famous Martha," The Man said. "From what I've heard, she'll be worth talking to." He paused. "For a few minutes, anyway." He turned. Virgil followed him.

The pair left the room.

MARTHA AND Trojan wrestled Cammy into the back seat. She fell over on her side. They jumped in; Trojan was in the driver's seat. He started the engine and raced forward, finally turning the truck in a wide circle, and back up the street. They hadn't gone far when they saw two trucks pull crosswise across their path.

"Oh, shit," Martha said. "Shit."

"What now?" Trojan said. "Go back?"

"No—" Martha said. "We still have a bargaining chip." She glanced toward Cammy who lay prone across the back seat. Cammy's eyes glittered brightly with anger. "Time to earn your keep," Martha said.

Trojan stopped the truck. They both got out. Trojan pulled Cammy out and set her on her feet. "Behave," he said.

Martha grabbed the woman, resting the barrel of her pistol against Cammy's right temple. "Walk," she said.

Cammy obeyed.

THE MAN and Virgil were bent over a map of the city spread open across The Man's desk.

"I was kind of hoping to see what he was going to do," Virgil said.

The Man answered. "Who?"

"Meteor. I wanted to see if he really would break Matthew's fingers."

"Sure you did." The Man continued to study the map.

"We'd know for sure we could trust him," Virgil advised.

"Trust— Yeah. Trust is important, isn't it?" The Man glanced up from the map. "We put him through hell—" The Man said. "I trust him." He repositioned the map and traced a roadway. "Besides—" he said, as he made another mark with the pen, "—I like him."

"Why are we keeping Matthew alive?" Virgil asked. "He's really only good to us dead." The Man pressed his palms flat to the table. He raised his head and looked at Virgil.

"A popular and well-liked *dead* leader can stir up a whole lot of courage among his followers—even the pacifists. And a whole lot of trouble for us," The Man said. He shook his head, "No, we'll keep him alive. Until I have a change of heart."

"Okay, but—" Virgil began. A young biker entered the room. The men turned.

"Confirmed," the biker said. "Five trucks on their way up the main highway."

Virgil burst out laughing. "*Five* trucks? Five? This won't take long," he said. "Let me take care of this." He checked his pistol.

"Hurry back," The Man said.

Virgil slammed his pistol back into its holster. He grabbed some boxes of bullets from a side shelf, and then he looked up. "I'll be back. With your women," he said, grinning.

"Don't forget my guns."

Virgil left the room. The Man bent back over his desk.

He studied the map. He took a red felt marker and made some marks. He tapped a spot, circled it, and then set the pen aside. He walked to the far wall, moved aside several large cardboard boxes, and revealed a gun safe. He twirled the combination and opened the heavy steel door. He removed a pistol, a holster, and several boxes of ammunition. He stroked the gun—an absent gesture, more than one of fondness.

He walked to the desk, laid the gun down, and then buckled the holster around his waist. He retrieved the felt pen, and returned to the gun safe. He rummaged around and pulled out a large hardbound notebook. He opened it.

Inside the book were organizational trees with the names of individuals. Several had red diagonal slashes through them; some had question marks; some had exclamation marks; some were circled—but all had a notation, of some kind.

The Man flipped a few pages and stopped. He ran his finger across the diagram until it came to rest on a name—it already had several question marks beside it. The Man added another question mark.

Meteor????

The Man closed the book, thought better of it, and re-opened it. He picked up his pen, found the page with Meteor's name, and added another name just below it.

Virgil?

VIRGIL GAVE an order to a guard standing near the clubhouse door. The biker ran off. In less than a minute, trucks of all shapes and sizes, loaded with soldiers, rumbled out of the parking lot.

Virgil stood and watched as the trucks, with their deadly cargo of men and weapons, moved forward. Like a dark snake, they wound their way up the deserted street, their taillights winking in the darkness as the drivers turned left, a few streets up. The TV station was only minutes away.

Virgil turned and looked up the block in the opposite direction. He shook his head.

"What are you looking for?" his companion asked.

"A woman."

"You want a woman... now?" The man laughed.

"No," Virgil said gruffly. "One particular woman."

"Don't we all?" the man replied.

"Never mind. They'll find her."

The man gave Virgil a puzzled look.

"C'mon. Let's go."

Virgil and the man jumped into a waiting truck. They sped off in the direction of the departing trucks.

THE SOUNDS of many truck engines firing up behind her caused Martha to turn her head. Trucks filed into the street; they drove away in the opposite direction. Martha breathed a quick sigh of relief.

Martha pulled Cammy in close to her. She called out to the men near the trucks parked in front of them. "Move those damn trucks out of our way. Or I'll kill her."

Silence.

"This is Cammy," she called out. "The Man is not going to be happy if something happens to her." Martha could feel Trojan close behind her. "Can you take them out?" she asked, her voice a low whisper.

"Not sure. I can't see how many there are."

"At least two—" a male voice said. "Right behind you."

Martha turned with a gasp. She watched as Trojan took a fist to his face. He dropped like a sack of flour. Martha looked down; Trojan was out cold. She grabbed Cammy.

"I *will* kill her," she said to the two men holding guns. She backed away, as she spoke, toward the truck. She wanted the truck's protection behind her. The men smiled. They lowered their guns.

"Let her go," another man said, from directly behind her.

THE PONY-TAILED captain gripped his laser light, his finger ready to send the signal. He was positioned several blocks down from the TV station. As he had guessed, the trucks were coming from the north, neatly in single file; like lemmings, they obediently meandered after one another. He counted as the parade of trucks rolled by.

"Now?" the man next to him asked.

"No—" The captain smiled. "I want all the fish in the net," he said.

The last truck passed by. The captain studied the road. No more trucks were coming. He raised his hand and clicked the laser light twice. He watched as another light clicked twice about a half block away. He smiled again. He knew the light was leapfrogging along—exactly as planned. He held his breath.

SIMON AND his men continued to watch the front of the clubhouse. He saw the trucks leave the lot. They would make their move soon. One of his scouts ran up.

"Trouble up the street," the scout said, gasping for breath. "I think it's Martha and Trojan. They're surrounded."

"Let's go," Simon said. "Take sharpshooters." Simon backed out of his hiding spot, and ran after him.

MARTHA JUMPED at the sound of the man's voice behind her. She released Cammy and the woman ran from her. Martha turned to see another man emerge from behind her truck. His gun was unusually large and it was pointed at her. She wondered absently if she would even feel the shot. She imagined her guts blown all over the men standing behind her. All over Trojan's face. *But he wouldn't know,* she thought.

She lowered her pistol and stepped sideways. The man who had hit Trojan blocked her path. She swung around. She could see Cammy still running toward the clubhouse.

Good riddance.

She turned back and stared at the man with the big gun.

"Drop it," he said.

Martha shrugged her shoulders. Faces flashed through her mind. One stuck. *Matthew.* Martha sighed. She dropped her pistol to the ground. The man with the large gun smiled. She stood meekly. There was nowhere to run.

What a day to die. Soon, Josef. Soon. I hope this doesn't hurt.

Martha winced at the thought.

She closed her eyes and waited.

Chapter Forty

Giving Back the Weapons

A GUNSHOT.

Martha jumped. She gave a small screech, and opened her eyes. Something soft hit her face as it burst from the man in front of her. A large red hole appeared on his forehead with fissures snaking out like the rays in a child's drawing of a sun. Something oozed slug-like from the cracks. His big gun clattered to the pavement. He slumped to the street. Martha touched the goo on her face; she pulled her fingers away.

Brains, she thought dreamily. So... this is what they look like.

More gunshots.

Martha reeled around and watched as her other captors fell to the ground, blood spurting from fresh bullet wounds. Martha's mouth fell open and her arms hung at her sides. She stiffened as she watched dark figures rush toward her. Many dark figures. She couldn't identify them, but she guessed them to be friendly; they hadn't shot her.

She hurriedly wiped her hands on her jeans. She looked back at the man lying on the ground, and the dark blood pooling slowly around his head. She watched as the puddle widened, slick and shiny in the low light of headlamps and flashlights. She clamped her hand over her mouth as her stomach revolted.

An individual broke out of the pack and raced toward her. Relief flooded over Martha when she recognized the young face.

"Simon," Martha cried. She felt her legs go weak. She sank to the ground.

"Are you hurt?" Simon asked, as he reached her side. He touched her face and drew back fingers covered in blood.

"No," Martha said.

Simon nudged Trojan with his boot. "Is he dead?"

"No." Martha mumbled. She stared into the darkness. "He's napping."

Deep booming sounds came from the distance.

"What the hell?" Martha said. She clambered to her feet. Orange light slashed across the murky, early morning sky. Like sheet lighting, the sky brightened and then darkened at regular intervals.

"Yes!" Simon exclaimed, with raised arms. "It worked. He got 'em."

He swung his binoculars up to his eyes. He waved to more of the dark figures coming out of the shadows. Martha watched as man after man regrouped on the far side of the street.

VIRGIL slammed on the brakes, sending the soldier with him into the windshield. The man sat mutely, staring through the glass, his hand rubbing his forehead, as the sky burst into flames. Virgil threw the truck into reverse, pressed down on the accelerator, and raced backwards. A block away, he stopped the truck, swung it around, and headed back in the direction of the clubhouse.

"Those sons-of-bitches," he said.

THE PONY-TAILED captain shielded his eyes as the trucks exploded. His face creased into a smile of deep satisfaction. The bazookas had done their jobs. One by one, the trucks burst into flames.

"Wow," said the man next to the captain. "Listen to those fuckers blow."

"We'll have to thank The Man for his contribution to the cause," the captain said. They watched and listened as more trucks exploded while the blasts of the rocket launchers echoed between the buildings.

"Look." The young man had turned and was pointing down the road. The captain followed his finger. He saw a truck in the distance. It was going in reverse.

"Damn," the captain said. "We missed one." He started his truck's engine. "Let's get him."

BRAD SAW the sky light up. He slowed his bike. The bikers with him slowed down, too. The motorcycles came to a stop, their motors rumbling. Brad and the rest of the bikers—those that had been at the bar—were on their way to the TV station. Now, they stared ahead and watched as the sky continued to explode in color.

"Damn," one of the bikers muttered. "What d'ya think is happening?"

"No way to tell who's getting hit," Brad answered. "But those explosions look like the work of bazookas... bazookas we don't have anymore."

"What should we do?"

Brad studied the blazing sky. "Not sure," he said. "But I know we're not going there."

He circled his bike around and fled back up the street. The rest of the bikers followed him.

MATTHEW AND Meteor exchanged looks when the explosions began.

"I've got to get out of here," Matthew said. "Can you find out what's happening out there?"

Meteor went to the door, looked around, nodded to the guards standing just outside, and then made his way out of the clubhouse. For a moment, he studied the sky. He glanced around the parking lot, and then he went back inside.

He nodded to the guards again as he passed through the doorway into the back room. He walked over to Matthew.

"Virgil's trucks and his soldiers are gone," he said. "Lots of explosions happening to the west. I'm guessing the TV station. I can't tell who's doing what to who. We'll have to wait and see."

"You got a plan?" Matthew asked

Meteor grimaced. "A half-baked one."

"That's good enough for me," Matthew said.

"THAT'S ONE way to give the weapons back," Simon said, dryly.

Simon and Martha watched as fireballs rose into the sky; the horizon changed color with each explosion. Martha stood mesmerized. She murmured her agreement.

Behind them, Trojan moaned and moved. He sat up, rubbing his jaw. "Crap," he said. "Sucker-punched. That really hurt."

"Get up," Simon said, a complete lack of empathy in his voice.

Trojan groaned. He got on his knees, and then stood up. He looked at the sky. "What the hell's going on?"

"Exactly as we planned," Simon said. "We're taking out The Man."

"Oh," Trojan said. "He's not going to like that."

THE PONY-TAILED captain chased after the retreating truck. He sped along the street and followed a curve to the right. He watched as the truck made its way up the street. Suddenly, its brake lights came on and the driver zipped into the parking lot. The captain slowed, pulled over and parked, and turned off the headlights. He raised his binoculars.

SIMON LOOKED over at Martha. He called her name. She turned away from the fireworks.

"Can you leave this with us now?" He grinned, hopefully. "Please?"

Martha began to object. Simon stopped her. "We could end up with a lot of injuries. Your medical knowledge..."

Martha gave a small smile. "Okay," she said. She bent and picked her pistol up from the ground. "Go— I'll wait here."

Simon looked relieved. He waved at his men, and they rushed off. Trojan loped along behind them.

EARLY MORNING light had begun to break, but the parking lot was still brightly lit by the pole lamps. The captain watched as the truck came to a halt and two men jumped out. They raced into the building.

MARTHA WATCHED Simon and his men disappear into the shadows. She looked around. She looked down at the dead bodies at her feet. She looked up at the empty trucks still crisscrossed on the road. She looked back at the sky still exploding in vibrant color. She suddenly felt alone and left out. She didn't like the feeling. She began to walk. Then to run.

VIRGIL BURST into the clubhouse. The Man was still in his office.

"We gotta go," Virgil said. "Or we'll get trapped here."

The Man looked up. "What's going on?"

"Can't you hear the explosions? They took out my men. It was an ambush." Virgil paused. "They outsmarted us." His voice was low and bitter. "And they used your weapons to do it."

"My weapons?" The Man said slowly, responding to the accusation.

"*Your* weapons have gotten *my* men killed."

"The rocket launchers?"

"Yeah. The damn rocket launchers."

The Man grabbed the gun lying on the desk, and put it into his holster. "Let's go."

"They'll be here soon. If they aren't already," Virgil added. "I've given the order to prepare for a fight, but we're short on men." He paused. "What do we do about Matthew?"

MOVEMENT FAR up the street caught the pony-tailed captain's eye. He watched as dozens of dark shapes advanced on the building. They were coming in from the east side. He smiled. "Our guys," he said, and pointed. He reached for the door handle. "Let's go." He stopped and raised his binoculars. He watched as a single person ran toward the building. He lowered his binoculars.

"By God," he said. "It's Martha."

He raised his binoculars again.

VIRGIL AND The Man stormed into the back room. Matthew was still seated on the couch, his feet still bound, and his body leaning to one side. Meteor jumped up when he saw the expressions on the men's faces.

"What's going on?" Meteor asked, positioning himself between Matthew and Virgil.

"They tricked us," Virgil said. He raised his pistol, and pointed it past Meteor toward Matthew's head.

"Wait," The Man said. "I want to talk to him first."

"Lucky you," Virgil said to Matthew, and he lowered his gun.

Meteor let out his breath; his gun hand slid back down his hip.

"What happened?" Meteor asked, his eyebrows drawn together over his bright, blue eyes.

A sound came from outside. The men turned. Cammy burst through the door. Her hands were still bound behind her. Gaffing tape still closed her lips. The Man turned to her as she ran up to him. He pulled the tape from her mouth.

"Where did you come from?" he asked.

"Long story," Cammy said. "I'm here now." She turned. "Get this off me." The Man used his knife to cut the cable on her wrists. Cammy swung her arms forward and rubbed her wrists as she grimaced. Then she brightened.

"Oh— Hi, Matthew."

"Hello, Cammy." Matthew smiled. "You here to continue our date?"
The Man's eyes grew dark.

MARTHA SLOWED her pace. She had watched as a sole truck returned to the clubhouse and screeched to a halt. Two men had jumped out. They ran into the clubhouse.

She looked around; very few vehicles remained on the lot. A few men with guns roamed the perimeter. Martha studied the clubhouse's front door. No guards were in sight. No one coming; no one going.

Maybe they've gone inside to get Matthew.

She inched closer to the building, but she remained hidden in the shadows cast by the trucks. She wished the pole lights weren't so bright. It was going to be tough running across the lot to the doors. She looked around her.

Where the heck are Simon and Trojan?

CAMMY TOUCHED The Man's arm. "Nothing happened," Cammy said, her face turned up to his. "He's just trying to make you mad." She spoke quickly. She reached up a hand to touch The Man's face, but he grabbed her by the wrist and forced her hand away. She winced.

The Man strode up and stood over Matthew. "You knew there was never going to be an exchange for your ass, right? Besides, you've lost your value now. Those bazookas were hard to come by."

"Bazookas?" Matthew gasped, eyes widening in feigned surprise. "They used *bazookas*?" Matthew smiled. He stared up at The Man. "So, now what?"

"How many men are out there?" The Man asked.

"How the hell should I know? Ask Virgil."

The sounds of a commotion could be heard from somewhere outside the clubhouse.

"We're running out of time," Virgil warned.

"I'm thinking," The Man said.

"Not a whole lot of time for that," Matthew said with a smirk. The Man looked at Cammy and then back to Virgil.

"Okay, we leave him here." The Man turned to Cammy. He handed her a radio. "We might still need him," he said, motioning to Matthew. "I'll call you. If we don't need him, he's all yours," he said.

"You mean kill him?"

"No, I meant... fuck him." The Man gave her a venomous look. "Yes, *kill* him."

Cammy drew back as though she had been struck, and blushed. "Um— I don't have a weapon."

"Take his." The Man pointed at Meteor. Meteor moved his hand over his pistol's grip.

"I don't think so..." Meteor said. His eyes held The Man's in challenge. "You either trust me... or you don't."

Virgil's hand moved to his gun.

"Don't," Meteor warned. "I'm faster than you."

Virgil relaxed and let his arm fall to his side.

More sounds from outside.

The Man spoke to the guards behind him. "Gather the men we have left. Regroup at the northern clubhouse. We'll make our move from there."

They nodded and left the room.

Cammy stood quietly, expectantly. "And me?" she asked. "What happens to me?"

"Finish up here. I'll leave a couple of guys and a truck for you," The Man said. "They'll be waiting outside the door."

"A gun?"

The Man motioned to one of the bodyguards still standing near the door. One of them unholstered his gun and handed it to her, butt first.

Cammy took the gun. She hefted it and smiled. She knew it was loaded and ready to fire. No bodyguard of The Man's walked around with a pistol, with its safety on. "Okay," she said.

"Give me about 10 minutes." The Man looked back at the bodyguard and said, "Give her your radio." He turned back to Cammy. "If we can get out of here without any trouble, I'll call you. Then do what you have to do."

"Why don't you kill me, yourself?" Matthew asked. Meteor gave Matthew a warning look. The Man flicked his eyes over Matthew.

"I have people for that," The Man said, his words firing out from between his gritted teeth—wood chips from a chainsaw.

"Hey, that makes you his go-boy, Virgil," Matthew said with a derisive snort. "How does that sit with you?"

Virgil growled and made a move in Matthew's direction. Meteor's hand crept back to his pistol.

"Easy, buddy," The Man said, as he grabbed Virgil's arm. Virgil stopped moving. The Man smiled. "You really want to do him damage?"

Virgil stared without speaking.

"Find Martha."

Virgil still stared ahead at Matthew.

"Do to her... what you want to do to him—" The Man turned back to Matthew and added, "—In front of him."

"Let her be," Matthew said.

The Man regarded Matthew with cold, dark eyes. "We'll get her, Matthew. Maybe not now. But we'll get her. I promise you. Right, Virgil?"

Virgil let out his breath, but his hands remained clenched at his sides.

The Man turned, and flanked by his bodyguards, he headed toward the doorway. He nodded his head at Meteor. "Let's go."

Meteor gave Matthew a furtive glance; he followed The Man to the door.

"You, too, Meteor?" Matthew called. "You guys don't have a full set between the three of you." Matthew laughed—a sound of contempt, not an expression of humor.

The Man turned back, gave Matthew a hard stare, and then he looked at Cammy. "Turn it on."

"I did," Cammy said, holding up the radio. "I'm not stupid."

"That remains to be seen, doesn't it?" The Man said. He turned and left the room.

Cammy watched the men leave and then she turned back to Matthew. Her eyes shone with hurt and anger. She paced back and forth in front of him. She checked her watch.

"We treated you well," Matthew said. "You were one of us."

"Shut-up, Matthew."

"C'mon, Cammy. We didn't harm you." The sounds of people came from the front room. "Besides Trojan really likes you. And I think you like him, too."

Cammy gave a nervous laugh. She glanced back at the doorway, down at her watch again, and then back up at Matthew. She took a step closer to him. She aimed the pistol at his head.

"How about if I do you a favor?" she asked.

Chapter Forty-One

The Escape

A MAN ran into the building. He wore a biker's jean jacket and a wool cap. He came to a halt in front of The Man and Virgil as they came away from the back room. Meteor had hung back, but he listened to their conversation. The biker was agitated.

"Sir," he said. "Men are headed this way. Lots of them. There's already been some gun action up the street on the east side." He shook his head and added, "Not sure we can hold them."

The Man thought a moment. "We might need him after all," he said to Virgil. They returned to the backroom. Meteor and the bodyguards followed them.

Cammy jumped and turned. Her gun was still raised. Now it was pointed at them.

"Lower that," Virgil warned. Cammy obeyed. Immediately.

"Hey," Matthew said when he saw the men return. "Ya miss me?"

The Man strode up to Matthew. The biker in the wool cap rushed up beside him. "What do you want us to do, sir?"

The Man held up his hand in a gesture of silence. The biker obeyed, but in his urgency, he shifted from one foot to the other. Meteor moved in near the couch. His hand rested on the butt of his gun. The Man continued his silent pondering.

"Tough times, buddy?" Matthew asked, with a huge grin. Meteor gave him a concerned look, but Matthew ignored it. "My men will take you down. And you know it. Even if I'm dead."

The Man lifted his head—like dark, curling smoke—he raised his face and gazed at Matthew. His eyes glittered with malice. "Get up," he said.

Matthew struggled to his feet, in spite of his bound ankles. "Okay," he said, "I'm up. Now what?"

More commotion from outside.

The Man turned toward the biker in the wool cap. "We're leaving. Kill as many as you can. And then get out of here." The biker nodded and ran out of the room. The Man turned back to Virgil. "Bring him."

Virgil moved toward Matthew, but Meteor was standing in his way. "What the fuck are you still doing here?" Virgil asked, glaring at Meteor.

"Same as you," Meteor replied. His face was blank, but like the blade of a cutlass—his voice was dangerously edged.

"Let's go," Virgil said. He pulled Matthew roughly, making him stumble into Cammy, who was still standing near the couch. She jumped back, her eyes wild with questions.

"Hey," Matthew said, "I'll be able to walk a whole lot faster if I can move my feet." Virgil grabbed a knife from his belt and cut the cable tied around Matthew's ankles.

Cammy went up to The Man.

"What about me?"

"What about you?" The Man said, his tone nitrogen cold. "You've been gone for a long time." He raised his eyebrows. "No chance for escape—in all that time?"

Cammy stepped back as though punched in the gut. "I was their prisoner," she exclaimed.

The Man reached for her chin. He grabbed it cruelly, and Cammy cried out. He pushed her face from his hand so hard that she fell backwards. "Sure you were," he said.

Once more, Cammy's eyes registered confusion and hurt.

The Man turned back to Meteor. "Outside," he said. Meteor nodded. The Man turned and headed for the door. "Let's go," he said to the rest of the men. Meteor lagged behind. He waited for the men to leave the room, taking Matthew with them.

Cammy raised the pistol. In the next instant, Meteor was at her side. "Don't—" He bent to her ear and added softly, "You might miss."

Cammy lowered the pistol. She turned to Meteor. "What—?"

Meteor smiled and placed his arm around her shoulder. "Cammy... I think it's best if you find yourself a nice quiet spot to hide in. Just for a while, okay?"

SEVERAL ARMED men emerged from the clubhouse. The pony-tailed captain watched them scramble over one another as they broke into smaller groups and fled to either side of the building. Small bursts of gunfire echoed in the distance.

He trained his binoculars on Martha. She was hunkered down near a small cluster of vehicles. She had her hands clapped over her ears. He watched as she crept into the shadows.

"Damn. Too many trucks in the way to see where she went." He studied the scene. "She's gonna get shot."

"Should we go and help her?" asked the young man at his side.

"I don't know what she's doing."

"Where is she now?"

"I lost her," the captain began, and then, "Wait a minute. There she is."

Martha had slipped around a large truck. It sat only a few feet from the truck that the captain had chased up the road. The captain could just make her out, crouched, her arms extended.

"Who the heck is she planning to shoot?" he wondered aloud.

The young man next to him shook his head.

THE MAN stopped on his way out of the clubhouse. He waved to one of the armed guards.

"Kill her," he said.

The guard looked puzzled. "Who?"

"Cammy. She's the reason our trucks are blown to pieces."

"What?"

"Kill her. Dammit!"

THE PONY-TAILED captain watched as three more men walked out of the clubhouse.

"It's The Man," the captain said. "He's with two other guys." He paused. "And there's Matthew."

"Is he okay?" the young man asked.

"I think so. He seems to be walking on his own."

Another man came out of the clubhouse.

"Damn," the captain said. "This just keeps getting better."

"What?"

"It's *Meteor*."

MARTHA PUSHED herself up against the side of a truck and tried to calm her pounding heart. She took a quick peek around the front of the truck when she heard the sound of voices. She saw three figures coming toward her.

Crap. Now what?

Martha risked another glance. She couldn't quite tell who the men were, but one seemed familiar. Martha watched as the two men shoved the third man along in front of them—his hands were tied.

Matthew?

The men neared the truck just off to her side; Martha heard their hurried conversation.

"You ordered her execution, huh?" a tall man asked. "I thought she was special to you."

"Not any more. She was doing Matthew. She's damaged goods now," the shorter man answered. Martha gasped and clapped her hand over her mouth.

Cammy? Were they talking about Cammy? Was this The Man? The same man who ordered Josef's death?

Martha remembered Meteor's story of Josef's execution. Rage filled her and with it came the familiar, cold calm. Her hand tightened on her gun.

I want to kill him.

The thought surprised her, but it didn't bother her; instead, she embraced it, rolled it around in her brain. She estimated the distance. The Man was about twenty-five feet away. Martha had managed shots at that distance in target practice, many times.

But a killing shot? Could she do it?

"Maybe she didn't," Virgil replied. They stopped when a man back at the clubhouse called out to them. Martha recognized the voice and she took another peek.

Meteor! She stifled another sound of surprise. *What was he doing here?*

A new excitement filled her as she strained to hear the sound of Meteor's voice. She couldn't quite make out what he was saying— something about Matthew.

She watched as The Man came closer.

METEOR RAN toward the truck. "Where are you taking him?" he called. More gunfire off to the left drew everyone's attention. "Hey—" he called again.

The Man stopped. "What?"

"Wouldn't it make more sense for me to drive? Leave Virgil here to command the men who are left?" Virgil shot him a hateful look. Meteor shrugged, his face appropriately masked with deep concern. "I'm no general—but I can drive a truck."

The Man thought. "Okay." He turned to Virgil, whose face was stony with suppressed anger, and said, "Stay. Let Meteor drive."

Virgil glowered. "I don't trust this guy." He still had Matthew by the arm.

"Get Matthew into the truck," The Man said. "You stay here. Meet me later on the north side." The Man moved around to the other side of the truck.

MARTHA RAISED her pistol—she grimaced. So small. She steadied it on her opposite forearm, looked down the barrel, and set the sight on The Man's chest.

She pulled the trigger.

She watched as The Man toppled backwards—his hand flew to his shoulder. She flattened herself back against the truck.

Virgil released Matthew's arm. He raised his weapon, glancing around him, as he ran to The Man. He dragged him into the shadows of the truck, and waited. Virgil stared as blood seeped through The Man's jacket.

Martha felt her energy drain, and she slumped down. She was suddenly very tired. She knew she hadn't killed The Man. And now, a second shot wasn't possible. She took a deep breath and leaned her head back against the truck.

She thought about Josef.

Sorry.

MATTHEW HAD begun a slow retreat, but Meteor came up behind him and blocked his path.

"Hold it Matthew," Meteor said. His gun was pointed at Matthew.

THE PONY-TAILED captain whistled through his teeth. "She took a shot," he said.

"She did?"

"Yeah. She hit The Man. She didn't kill him, but she nailed him."

"No kidding? Where is she now?"

"Can't see her." He paused. "Damn, what's this?"

"What?"

"Meteor's holding a gun on Matthew." The captain started the engine. "Let's go," he said.

MARTHA PEERED around the truck again. She gasped. Meteor was holding Matthew at gunpoint. *He really has switched sides*, she thought, as a new confusion formed in her heart.

Meteor motioned Matthew toward the truck. He opened the backdoor and Matthew got in. Meteor shut the door. He jumped into the driver's seat. Martha considered another shot, but Meteor sat directly in front of Matthew. She could easily miss, hitting Matthew, instead. She heard Meteor call out to the men on the ground, near the truck.

"Hurry up, Virgil," Meteor said, as he pushed open the passenger door from the inside. "Get him in here." More gunfire—this time much closer.

The Man shook Virgil's hands away and got into the truck by himself, one hand pressed against his bullet wound. "Go—" he said to Virgil. "Handle this *fucking* mess."

Virgil nodded and ran back in the direction of the clubhouse.

"Drive," The Man said to Meteor. Meteor hesitated. They both jumped when a tap came on the window. It was Cammy.

"Wait," she said. She ran around to the other side and jumped into the backseat beside Matthew. She was panting. "Guys are coming in through the back of the clubhouse," she said. "Go!"

BEHIND THE truck, Martha took a deep breath.

I have led a charmed life.

She closed her eyes. If she didn't go now, they would drive off with Matthew. And her chance to save him would be gone. He would probably be dead by morning. She had to go.

She took another breath. A vision of her holding a gun on Meteor and pulling the trigger made her heart ache. But she had no choice—it was now, or never.

Martha left her hiding place, but the truck and its occupants had already begun to move. She stood helplessly as the truck tore out of the parking lot and onto the street.

METEOR GAVE the wheel a hard turn to the right. Another truck pulled directly across his path. He slammed on the brakes. The Man slid forward on the seat. So did Matthew and Cammy.

Two men jumped from the truck, guns in hand. They pointed their weapons, motioning for Meteor and The Man to get out. Meteor shook his head.

"Don't shoot! Matthew's in that truck," the pony-tailed captain said. "Keep them covered." He ran around to the passenger side of Meteor's truck. The young man continued aiming his gun at the two men in the front seat.

METEOR WATCHED as the pony-tailed captain came around to the passenger side of the truck. The back door was yanked open. Meteor jolted and turned when he felt the gun barrel in his ribs.

"Just to keep you honest," The Man said softly. Meteor's eyes flickered with surprise, but he said nothing. "Get me the hell out of here."

Meteor glanced into the backseat. The pony-tailed captain had pulled Matthew out. The captain motioned Cammy out, too. She slid across and joined Matthew outside the truck.

Meteor watched the captain raise his pistol—his intent was clear. In a smooth move, Meteor threw the truck into reverse; the open back door knocked the captain to the ground. Meteor sped backwards down the street.

A few blocks away, Meteor swung the truck around and headed forward. He turned his head toward The Man.

"Get the damn gun out of my side."

The Man lowered his pistol.

"Don't do that again," Meteor warned.

"Just drive the fucking truck."

THE YOUNG man standing in front of Meteor's truck was taken by surprise. He recovered and swung his gun to follow the truck, but Matthew shouted out. "Don't shoot. Let him go." The captain got up from the ground and gave Matthew a puzzled look.

Matthew shook his head. "I'll explain later."

MARTHA SIGHED. Matthew was safe. Sounds to her right caused her to turn. Trojan and several of Simon's men were headed across the lot toward her.

"Simon's been shot," Trojan called out when he saw Martha. Martha ran toward him. He motioned back at the clubhouse. "He's in there." Martha ran by him, while Trojan and the men continued forward.

Another truck roared away from the far end of the parking lot. It was gone before anyone could react. Trojan stared after the retreating vehicle. "Damn," he said. "I thought we got all of them."

The men with Trojan gathered around Matthew and the pony-tailed captain. Someone cut the electrical tie around Matthew's wrists.

"Well, it's damn well about time," Matthew said. He smiled and shook the pony-tailed captain's hand. "I've got to hand it to you." He laughed. "Skippy..."

The captain smiled, and clapped Matthew on the back. "You're looking not-too-shabby," he said. "Few cuts and bruises." He laughed.

Matthew laughed along with him. Then his voice took on a serious note. "How many guys did we lose?"

Trojan answered. "Maybe 10—maybe 11—if Simon doesn't make it."

"Simon's hurt?"

"Yeah, he caught a bullet in the leg. Martha's with him now."

"Martha?" Matthew pursed his lips. "So, she is here."

"Yeah, she came with me and Cammy," Trojan said. "Right, Cammy?"

Cammy glared at him. "You were really mean to me."

"Ah, I didn't have any choice. You know that. Martha made me do it."

"Martha made you do what?" Matthew asked.

"She sort of kidnapped Cammy. So that she could find you. And then she found me. And then we came here. And she was going to use Cammy to get by the guys that blocked our way. And Cammy ran off. And—" He paused. "—It's a long story."

Matthew looked at the pony-tailed captain. "And on your end?" he asked.

"Not sure. But I suspect no casualties. We took out their trucks, one after the other—before they could fire any shots."

Matthew looked around. "I wonder what happened to Virgil."

"Who's Virgil?" the captain asked.

"Old friend. Not a friend now."

Trojan spoke up. "Another truck left. I think it was him."

"Too bad," Matthew said. "Virgil is probably more dangerous than The Man."

"Uh... speaking of which—" interrupted the captain, "—why did we let him and Meteor go? Why didn't you let us shoot?"

Matthew was silent for a moment. He took a breath, "Because you would have killed our ally."

"Our ally?"

"Yeah—" Matthew said. "Meteor."

Chapter Forty-Two

A Matthew Dilemma

THE CHILD SWUNG back and forth, her wispy hair flipping up and down with the motion of the swing. It was mid-July—the lilacs had long since bloomed and were now sad brown memories of their former splendor. Peony bushes hung pregnant with giant, luscious blooms: some white, some deep pink, some scarlet, some mauve.

Matthew was gone. Again. Without a word to her.

Martha winced at the thought as it evoked a tiny sting in her spirit. A tiny clutch in her stomach. A tiny pain in her heart. She made a weak sound at the back of her throat, and gave her head a sharp shake in an attempt to dislodge the thought and the feelings, but mostly to clear the image of Matthew's broad back and his tanned face from her mind.

Dammit! Stop it. Don't waste a second thinking about him.

Martha gritted her teeth.

Stop it. Stop it.

She shook her head and then concentrated on her granddaughter swinging in front of her.

They were in the compound's new play-park. Simon, Jonah, and some of the other young men in the camp had decided to do something nice for the children. But Martha suspected they were bored, and missing the excitement of battle. *Like I am*, she thought.

Mary was singing something about clouds and cats. Martha noticed that the swing had slowed. She walked over and began to push the little girl.

"Hey, Nana. You want to play I spy my little eye?"

Martha sighed. "No, I don't think so, honey—Nana has things on her mind."

Things. Yes. Things. Matthew kind of things.

She suppressed the growl of annoyance that rose in her throat.

"Nana? Please push me again. Really high."

Martha obliged, and gave the swing a firm push."How's that? Is that high enough? Pump your legs now. It'll make you go higher."

"Yes, but sometimes I get scared and cry. I'm afraid of heights." Martha eased off on the pushing and stood watching as the child flew back and forth in the air. Mary began to prattle again.

"I am a captain of an airplane. All day long." Mary said the words, again and again. Martha smiled. The swing's metal chains creaked and groaned in a strange sort of harmony to the little girl's rhyme.

Matthew. The chains had begun to speak. Matthew, they said. *Matthew.*

Oh, good God! Stop it!

Martha tipped her face toward the blue sky. The sun felt warm and it was so very welcome after the late arrival of summer. The province's last snowstorm had happened only two months ago, in mid-May. Martha breathed deeply, her face upturned and seeking. For the moment, things felt right, but the moment was short-lived. She remembered...

Matthew had become withdrawn following the battle with The Man. He was complimentary the day they returned to the camp, but not effusive. He had lacked the enthusiasm he had shown her the morning after their encounter with the men at the farm. Martha felt as though she had done something wrong, but she couldn't put her finger on what her error had been—how she had displeased him. He kept to himself, and she was left to handle her own responsibilities.

It didn't stop her from missing him.

"Push me, Nana! Remember, I like going very high."

"You just said you were afraid of heights," Martha reminded the child, as she pushed the swing.

"No, that was only one time," Mary said, with a wild giggle.

Martha smiled again, and gave the swing a mighty push. She pushed again. And again. The swing. The thoughts. The feelings. The man. He had no right being inside her head. But worse, she could feel him creeping around inside her soul.

Damn him!

She pushed the swing and watched it arc into the sky. The child laughed and called out, "I'm not afraid of heights," Mary sang. "I'm not afraid of heights."

I am, Martha thought. *I am*. The throb inside her was as hot as the overhead sun.

When would he be back? What did he say? What if—? No, couldn't think that. Can't think that. Must not think that!

Martha pushed the swing again. Harder. The child and swing flew up into the blue sky. "Pump your legs, Mary. Pump your legs."

Don't think. Just be. Just let it be.

Martha swallowed and willed the gnawing ache to go away. But with each push of the swing, the hollow feeling returned, stronger than before. Anger rose up inside her, and she pushed the swing again.

"Nana!" Mary screamed. "Too hard! You're pushing too hard."

Martha grabbed the swing to slow it down. The swing stopped, but the child continued forward, falling in a heap onto the sand. A short pause, as if to evaluate her situation, and Mary began to cry.

Martha knelt beside her and gathered the little girl into her lap. "Sh..." she said. "You're okay." Mary's crying subsided and then she turned a damp face upwards.

"Sing me a song."

"Which one?"

"You know which one, Nana. About sunshine on my shoulders. It makes me happy." Mary grinned.

Martha smiled down at the little face staring up at her. The old John Denver tune had always been one of her favorite songs, and now it was her granddaughter's most requested song. Martha cradled the little girl to her, stroking her hair, and she sang.

For the moment—Matthew did not exist.

□□□

SIMON BEAMED at Martha when she stopped by the Gatehouse.

"Hi, Martha," he said. He was visiting with Jonah. Matthew was nowhere in sight.

"Hi, you— How's the leg?"

Simon lifted his leg. "Coming along—just fine. Thanks to you," he said, with another broad smile.

"Hey, did you hear?" Jonah asked.

"Hear what?"

"Simon and Anna?"

"What about them?" Martha looked to Simon for an answer. He was still smiling.

"They're gonna be moving-in."

"What? Really? When?"

"As soon as we can."

Martha smiled. She reached up and took Simon's happy face between her palms. She kissed his forehead. "You, dear Simon, have my most sincere blessings. I think you and Anna will make a wonderful couple."

Simon blushed.

"So, when's the big day?" Actual marriages didn't happen anymore; people called it 'moving-in'.

"Before the celebration bonfire, I think," Simon said.

"*Celebration* bonfire? What celebration bonfire?"

"Matthew said he's treating the camp to a big outing near Edmonton."

"Oh, did he? When?"

"Next week."

"It's the first I've heard about it," Martha said.

"Should be fun," Jonah said. "He says things have calmed down enough—no attacks. He thinks it'll be safe."

Somebody knocked on the door. Jonah rose, walked over, and opened it. It was Anna. She had Gordon on her hip. She rushed in and went straight to Simon. She kissed him warmly, and then turned to Martha.

"Hi, Martha. Did you hear?"

"About you and Simon?"

Anna looked puzzled. Then she smiled. "No, I meant about the twins that Ruth and I just delivered this morning."

"No," Martha said. "Congratulations. You two are very adept at birthing babies." She laughed, a small laugh. "I don't even get bothered anymore."

Anna looked sheepish. "We don't mean to shut you out."

Martha shushed her. "I have plenty of work to keep me busy. I'm glad you two have become the camp midwives. You should be very proud of yourselves." She motioned to Simon. "Now tell me about your plans for this guy."

□□□

SIMON AND ANNA'S impromptu moving-in day didn't seem to surprise any member of the compound. People were hooting, cheering, and backslapping. "Well, it's about time, you two," was perhaps the most common comment. And, "What took you so long?" was the other.

Simon and Anna couldn't stop smiling. Martha smiled, too. She held Gordon on her knee while she admired his mother; Anna was so pretty in a simple white gown they had scavenged from a pricey dress shop in the mall. In her hair was a handmade band of woven daisies that Ruth had crafted. *So pretty*, Martha thought.

I was a pretty bride once. Josef... I miss you.

Martha fought back tears. She buried her face in Gordon's little neck, as she held him close and inhaled his wonderful baby fragrance. He squirmed and began to whine. She set him on her knee and began to bounce him, making him laugh with each unexpected, sharp jounce.

She looked up. Matthew was standing several feet away. He was chatting with Trojan and Cammy; they were holding hands.

Trojan's forgiveness of Cammy seemed to be limitless, and he had claimed her as his again—without reservations. Cammy had shown genuine hurt and then revulsion after Martha told her about the conversation she had overheard going on between Virgil and The Man. She looked happy now.

Matthew finished a sentence and looked in Martha's direction. He caught Martha's eye and immediately looked away. Martha felt a twinge of pain—so severe it made her catch her breath.

What was his problem?

Ruth came over and sat down next to Martha. She held a plate with a giant piece of chocolate cake. She waved it under Martha's nose. "Want some?" she asked.

Martha breathed in the delicious scent. She pushed Gordon toward Ruth. "Here, I'll trade you."

Ruth set the plate on the table and took the baby. She stood and carried him off.

Martha turned to the cake. She picked up a fork, scooped up a large chunk of the glistening richness, and put it into her mouth. The silky smooth feel of the chocolate icing in her mouth was wonderful, and she closed her eyes as she savored the experience.

"Looks good."

Martha jumped and opened her eyes.

Matthew.

"Uh—you want it?" Martha pushed the plate at him. She handed him her fork. Matthew took both. He cut into the cake and put a large portion into his mouth. Martha watched him chew.

"This is really good," he said.

"Finish it," Martha said. "I've had all I want." Matthew accepted and in a few moments, the plate was bare.

"Would you like to go for a walk?" Matthew asked.

"A w-w-walk?" Martha stammered.

Matthew studied her for a moment. "You don't want to?"

She gave him a quick smile. "I'd love to."

"C'mon." Martha hid a look of extreme curiosity as she rose to follow Matthew.

A walk? Where did this come from?

He had barely spoken five words to her in the past few weeks.

Matthew led her away from the camp, toward the far woods. The air was sweet with the perfume of scented evening stalk. Martha heard frog song off to the right where a small pond played host to hundreds of the spotted amphibians. Matthew placed a hand on her shoulder and then pointed to a tree.

"Look up there," he said. "It's an owl." Martha drew a quick breath at the touch of his hand on her bare shoulder. She tried to hide a little shiver, but she failed. She looked for the owl. Matthew kept his hand on her shoulder. She couldn't see the owl.

"I don't see it," she said.

"There... it's right there," Matthew said. Martha tried to see it, but still couldn't. Suddenly, looking for an owl seemed horribly trivial. She turned to face Matthew.

"Why have you been avoiding me?" she demanded.

Matthew drew back. He looked stunned. "What? I haven't been," he said.

"Yes, you have," Martha accused him, her voice rising in pitch.

"I've been busy," he said.

"Oh, sure you have, Matthew. Sure you have."

"Martha," he said, his voice taking on an edge. "I was busy. I wasn't ignoring you. I had things to do." Matthew had withdrawn his hand from her shoulder. His eyes were fixed on hers.

"You take off without telling me where you're going." Matthew remained quiet and let her rant. "I get worried about you. I wonder if maybe you've gotten yourself killed."

"Don't yell at me," Matthew said.

"I'm not yelling."

"You are. Stop it."

Martha tried to lower her voice, but her anger got the better of her. "You treat me like crap, you know that?" She stared at him. "Would it have killed you to tell me about the celebration bonfire?"

Matthew didn't respond. Martha watched as a small tick began in his cheek. A little shock went through her—*he's furious*, she thought. She waited. His silence became unbearable and she willed him to speak.

"It's always about you, isn't it, Martha? It couldn't possibly be that I have a couple thousand people to care for. That I am the go-to guy for nearly all the problems here—that I am worried about the next attack by the Crazies—the next attack by The Man—where we get more ammunition—keeping good relations with the Hutterites—keeping our people safe." He took a fast, deep breath. "No— That's not enough for you. I'm supposed to be reporting my every move to you? Like some sort of child."

"I care for them, too!" she said hotly. "I take care of problems, too." She fought with a sudden rush of tears.

Don't cry, stupid. Don't cry.

Like an unexpected blast of wind, his tone took her by surprise. "You know, I thought it might be nice to spend a little time with you, but now... " his voice trailed off.

Martha felt her heart clutch with pain, and her spirit sink. "Matthew, I—"

"I'm tired, Martha. Has it ever occurred to you that I'm tired?" His voice slid through tightened lips like a sheet of cool steel, iced with a bitter chill and a resolute inflexibility that Martha had never heard before.

"I—" she began again.

"Are you so wrapped up in yourself that you can't see that I might have my own problems? And that I don't need you harping at me?"

Martha flushed with embarrassment.

Is that what he sees? Is that what he thinks of me? Some sort of a fishwife?

She sucked in a short breath, and stepped backwards—away from his anger. Fear pooled in the pit of her stomach. Words tumbled about inside her brain, urgently seeking a way out, but there was no escape, because her tongue lay like a dead thing frozen inside her mouth.

Nothing, she thought, helplessly. *Nothing.* She felt trapped and afraid. She panicked.

"I just care about you," she blurted. "I worry—"

"Don't bother," he said. Matthew's face was devoid of the gentleness she had seen only moments before. "If that's how you care—don't bother. I don't need a warden... I need a friend." He paused. "And you obviously don't know how to be that."

"Matthew, I never—"

"Good night, Martha." Matthew turned and walked off.

Martha wrung her hands together.

Can't I learn? What's wrong with me? Can't I ever learn?

She let the tears come.

□□□

The New Gatekeeper

"I UNDERESTIMATED him," Virgil said. *"He's got good men. Damn good men. And they are bloody loyal to him."*

"You had good men, too."

"Yeah. Had."

"You did it once," The Man said. *"You can do it again."*

"Yeah, but it'll take time."

"How long?"

"Two, maybe three months."

"Then do it."

"That'll take us into the fall."

"Nice time to take over Matthew's place. Just think—all the storehouses will be full. You told me that."

"That's true."

"You want to really rub Matthew's nose in it?" The Man asked.

Virgil waited.

"Let's put Brad in charge when we take the compound."

Virgil laughed. "Yeah, that'll do it."

"Especially if we tell Brad he can do whatever he wants with Martha." The Man rubbed his shoulder. It was still very sore. *"Bitch,"* he muttered. *"She deserves him."*

"Brad will like that—the new Gatekeeper."

"You're sure you don't want the honor?"

"Nope."

The two men settled back into their leather cowhide chairs, and picked up their crystal highball glasses. They swirled the amber hues of eighteen-year-old single malt Glenfiddich Scotch whiskey, stuffed fat cigars into their mouths, and toasted to their plan.

Their glasses clinked and echoed in the darkened room of the north side clubhouse.

Chapter Forty-Three

The Gathering

THE PEOPLE were gathered in a field on the western edge of Edmonton. It had been several weeks since the battle, and it was time to celebrate. A large bonfire lit up the sky, but several smaller campfires dotted the barren ground, too. Children ran with glowing sticks, writing in the air, while their parents lounged on campstools and logs nearby, correcting them when their play took them too close to the flames. Matthew chose this spot because it was easily defended, and it had plenty of resources nearby: restaurants, shops, hotels and motels—all were easy to scavenge and most yielded up some treasure, something practical or some comfort item: blankets, pillows, candles, matches, candy, pens, paper, and the highly coveted—toilet paper.

The compound dwellers embraced the outing; so did Martha. It was like the shopping trips she had taken before the Change, when they would make the two-hour drive into Edmonton, stay in a motel near the big mall, go shopping during the day, and then see a movie or go to a restaurant with friends at night. Now, it was a welcome break from camp life, and a welcome break from the memories of the battle with the Man.

Martha looked around. She saw the pony-tailed captain surrounded by his men. He roared at something one of them said. Martha smiled, too.

The captain had taken on hero status in the camp, as had Simon. Both of them basked in their newfound positions of glory, and especially in the admiration of the women. And there were plenty of women in the camp; The Man's clean women had been given the chance to join the compound, or to be driven up to the mountains, where they would be left to fend for themselves. A few opted for the mountains, but the majority chose Matthew's camp. Their numbers necessitated the building of a second women's bunkhouse...

"CAN I SUGGEST something?" Trojan had asked, as he watched the walls go up. "I'm no construction guy, but wouldn't it be a good idea to have an alternate way in and out of our big buildings? Like The Man's mouseholes? Secret ways, just in case we're under attack?"

Matthew had weighed the idea and then presented it to the builders. They had bent over their graph paper with their carpentry pencils in hand. Now, the new bunkhouse had its own Nancy Drew secret doorway. The children loved it; they used it often.

While the new building went up, other camp tasks continued. Everyone was expected to pitch in and do their part: gather and prepare vegetables, pick fruit and berries, glean the Hutterites' grain fields, and preserve the meat brought in daily by the hunters. New people had joined the camp, under Matthew's watchful eye. With so many more mouths to feed, the workload had tripled, and Martha wasn't about to let anyone sit around. If they did, one word from Martha, and Matthew would show them the gate. Few chose the gate...

TONIGHT—the daily grind was forgotten. The Gatekeeper's people were relaxed and happy.

For the most part.

Martha sat alone at one of the small campfires. She poked at a burning log with a long stick, sending up sparks into the darkness. Mary had run off to play, and Ruth was chatting with her friends. Martha looked across the way where Anna and Simon sat together, holding hands, and laughing. Gordon sat on a blanket on the ground at his mother's feet. Somebody had given him a set of plastic rings and some foam blocks; he was busy piling them, knocking them over, and then giggling. Martha smiled, but the loneliness in her heart kept her smile tiny.

Martha looked into the distance where the trucks were parked. She saw many of the compound men in lively conversation; Matthew was with them. She felt a tug on her heart, but she quelled it.

Matthew had barely spoken to her since Anna and Simon's moving-in night. She craved his attention, a soft word, a tender look like the one he had given her, in the moonlight, so many months ago. But she had to content herself with perfunctory, get-the-business-done conversations. And she had—but not easily. She felt her heart squeeze with pain again. And she thought of Josef.

Josef had been dead for months. Martha missed him horribly, but he was fading away. She twisted the wedding band that she still wore on her finger. She sighed.

The sound of a motorcycle coming up the side road caught her ear, and she looked up. She watched as a big Harley rumbled into view. She couldn't see the driver, but she could see the welcome he was getting.

A cheer went up among the captains gathered near the trucks. She watched as Matthew stepped out of the group and strode over to the biker. He clapped him on the back, and shook his hand. The man still hadn't removed his helmet. Whoever it was, he was very well liked. And very welcome. The man pulled off his helmet and turned in Martha's direction.

Meteor.

Martha's spirit did a leap and she gasped. Until that moment, she hadn't realized how much she missed Meteor. With a small twinge of guilt, she remembered their last time together—just after Josef's death—and how cold she had been to him. She sank inside herself.

Martha watched Meteor join the group of men with handshakes and laughter. She willed him to see her, to recognize her, to come to her—but he didn't. The lonely feeling intensified; like a thick velvet glove, emotions closed around her heart, choking it, and she felt tears come to her eyes. She was glad no one was around to see her cry.

Stop it. Stop it.

She chided herself for being weak. For wanting. For desiring. For being wrong. Anger rose—just as it always did when she felt stupid. Like a hunting knife, she felt its blade: sharp and mean and hurtful. But instead of turning it on herself, she turned it outwards.

At Matthew.

And at Meteor.

To hell with you. To hell with all of you. I'll do just fine. By myself.

Martha turned her attention back to the fire and allowed its heat to dry her tears as they trickled down her face.

"Hi—" a voice said.

Martha looked up, startled. It was Jonah. "Hi." She smiled. "Are you having a good time?"

Jonah nodded. His eyes glowed with excitement. "Did you see him? Meteor's here."

Martha nodded, but said nothing.

"He came as a surprise for us. Matthew invited him."

Martha nodded again, and gave Jonah a weak smile. "Glad he's still on our side," she said.

She remembered seeing Meteor drive off the night of the battle with The Man. Matthew had explained to her later that Meteor was remaining undercover in The Man's camp, that he had always been undercover, and that his loyalties had always been with the compound. The thought brought Martha comfort, but no joy.

And she needed joy.

"Martha?"

Martha hadn't realized that Jonah was still talking to her. "Oh, sorry," she said. "What'd you say?"

"Are you coming over to see him?'

Martha shook her head. "No, later," she said.

"Okay," Jonah said. He leaned over and kissed her cheek. "Why don't you come where the guys are? They like you. Besides, you're our hero. You were the only one of us to actually get The Man."

"Yeah, but I was a lousy shot." Martha gave Jonah another small smile.

Jonah smiled back. He rose and walked back to the men near the trucks. Martha returned her gaze to the fire.

She longed to join them, to be a part of their group, to partake in their easy camaraderie, but she didn't feel like she belonged. Even now. In spite of everything. She didn't know where she belonged. Now that Josef was gone. And Matthew didn't want her.

Protective anger bloomed inside her again. She welcomed its familiar poison—so much easier to take than the pain—the damn, suffocating pain. She let the anger infuse her—allowed it to cloak her wretchedness. Embalm it. Disguise it. Hold it at bay.

So she could breathe again.

Matthew.

So she could survive.

Matthew.

The *Disagreement*

"I THINK he suspects something's going on between us," Virgil said. He sipped the coffee Marion handed to him. "Hey, this is good."

"Why?"

"Why? — Things he says. I think he recognized your perfume on me once."

"Yeah, but he doesn't own me. He's just going to have to get used to that idea."

"Uh, I don't see that happening. Especially since he doesn't have Cammy anymore. He took that pretty hard."

"I know." She reached across the table and ran her fingers down Virgil's arm. "But in the meantime, let's just relax."

"That's tempting, but it might be exactly the wrong thing to do. His temper is so bad. We're playing with fire."

Marion sighed. "I know. But I like this fire."

Virgil smiled. "Me, too. But not enough to die for it."

Marion pulled her hand back. "What does that mean?"

"It means that we've got to cool it, and keep an eye on him."

"I don't want to cool it."

"Doesn't really matter what you want. Or what I want—for that matter. The Man has a short fuse. He'll kill us both. Or have us killed." Virgil rose from his chair. "No woman is worth dying for—no matter how hot she is."

Marion went very quiet.

Virgil bent at the door and retrieved his boots. He pulled them on, and opened the door. He checked around, and then walked out. In a moment, the sound of an engine—his Harley.

Marion didn't move.

Chapter Forty-Four

Rain-checked

"RAIN CHECK," a deep, familiar voice said in her ear. Martha jumped and grabbed her chest. She turned to the man who had come up behind her.

"Fuck you," she said.

"Exactly," he said. "Shove over."

"I could have shot you that night, you know?" Martha said, angrily.

"Ah, yeah, but you didn't." Meteor took a seat beside her. He pushed in close to her, but she elbowed him away.

"I nearly did," she added.

Meteor shrugged.

"It would have been nice to know the truth," she said.

"You know it now." Meteor bent forward and looked up into Martha's face. Like an expectant puppy, his eyes questioned her.

Martha pretended to ignore him, but finally, she laughed.

Meteor smiled, too—a wide, bright badge of conquest. He held a long-necked bottle in his hand. Someone had brought several cases of beer to the gathering. He offered it to her.

"Is it still fizzy?" she asked.

"Yeah, it's pretty good," he said. "Have some."

Martha accepted the bottle and drank. She handed the bottle back to Meteor. She tried to squelch a burp but it only made her eyes water. Meteor laughed. He finished the beer and tossed the bottle.

"Strange," Martha said. "I know it doesn't matter anymore, but chucking bottles still bothers me." She sighed.

"Why didn't you come over and join us?" Meteor asked. He reached over and placed his hand on the back of her neck. She shivered under the touch of his fingers. She turned. His eyes were brilliant in the firelight.

"Thanks." She shook her head. "But—no." She turned back to the fire.

"Hey, what's the matter?" Meteor reached over and tipped her face back to his. "You done good— The man is still recovering from your bullet." He smiled again, and added, "You should be celebrating."

Martha stared back at him, but said nothing.

"Feel like celebrating?" he asked, trailing his fingers up her cheek.

Martha felt herself drawn once more to the blue eyes that had bewitched her so many months before. The wild thing inside her stirred. Like a feral cat, it rose up. With it, came an intense desire. She smiled.

"Where?" she asked.

Meteor pointed up the street. "Lots of motels up that way." He stood and held his hand out to her. She accepted it and he pulled her to her feet. He slid his arm around her waist and they walked away from the fire.

As they made their way toward the street, Meteor snatched a lantern, a bag of cookies, and a jug of water that were sitting on a collapsible camp table. "Picnic," he said with a crooked grin.

Martha laughed.

THEIR MOUTHS collided, and their tongues fought for position. Martha's heart thumped loudly as blood pounded in her ears. Its racket got in the way of any clear thinking. She knew her other reality existed, but it didn't exist now. Not here. Not in this room. She needed him. She wanted him. She would have him.

She gasped as Meteor's hands slid up her back, under her shirt, warm and seeking. She pressed into him, her arms around his neck, drawing him in closer to her, willing him to kiss her deeper, harder.

Meteor did just that.

It took only moments, and their clothes lay discarded on the floor. They were on the bed, their naked skin touching, and hungry. Martha ran her hands over his chest and his arms. Her fingers found the corded scars. *So many of them*, she thought. She knew how he had gotten them; Matthew had told her.

"Do they still hurt?" she asked.

"Sometimes," he said. He held up his arm and showed her an oddly shaped patch with purplish red skin. "This one still hurts. This is where they burned me. It took the longest time to heal."

"Why? Why did you let them do this?"

"I had to make them believe me," he said. Martha gave him a questioning look.

"When you left the camp that day, did you know where you were going?"

"Yeah— I had a pretty good idea," Meteor said. "I figured I'd be more help to Matthew as his confederate. He offered me his second-in-command, you know. But I turned him down."

"Uh-huh," Martha said softly, as she traced his scar. "Are you coming back to the camp?"

"No— I can't."

"Why not?"

"Things," he said. "Things, I gotta do."

"Like what— What things?" Then she added, "I never did understand why you stayed with The Man."

"Matthew and I felt it would be better if I stayed. Get more inside info on the man's strength around the province. He's got a lot of people. But I'm wearing out my welcome." He paused. "The man is getting suspicious of me, even though I've played his game. And Virgil— He hates me. He wants me dead."

"So, come back to us."

"Martha, I never much liked taking sides before. I'm better off being on my own."

"Oh— I see," Martha said. *You, too*, she thought. She sat up and stared across the room. She made a move to get off the bed.

"No—you don't see," Meteor said softly, as he pulled her back down to him. "But you will after a while." He looked into her face. "Trust me, okay?"

She bent her head and kissed the burned skin. She looked up with a mischievous grin. "Does that feel better?"

"Not quite," Meteor said, as he pushed her back on the bed. He kissed her again.

Fire flooded Martha, and she pulled him in closer to her. She murmured her pleasure against his lips.

Meteor rose and positioned himself atop her. Martha drew her knees up and apart—but at his first contact, she responded as though stung. She squirmed back into the bed.

"Oh, damn—" Martha covered her face with her hands. "I can't." She was panting.

Meteor drew back. Martha looked at him through her splayed fingers. His blue eyes were filled with questions.

"Not *again*..." His tone was perturbed.

"Oh God— I'm so sorry, Meteor." Martha pushed him away.

Meteor groaned. He sat up.

"I'm really sorry," Martha said as she rolled off the bed, and began to search the floor for her clothing.

Meteor ran his hand through his hair. "Dammit, it's a good thing I like you, Martha, because you're starting to piss me off." He laughed and shook his head, "So, what's the problem this time— Your period again?"

Martha blushed and shook her head. "You know it's not," she said. She continued to dress.

Meteor went on, "So, you aren't having your period. You aren't married any more... " He paused. "Is it me?"

"Oh no." Martha laughed. "Oh no, Meteor. There's nothing wrong with you. I want you. Big time." She gave a crooked grin and shrugged. "But... " her voice trailed off.

"But what?" Meteor stared at her.

"I need stability," she said.

"I'm stable."

"Oh, sure. Like a tom cat," Martha said with a chuckle, her eyes sparkling. She pulled on her boots and began to lace them up.

"Wait a minute," Meteor said. Martha paused and looked up. "The first time you stopped us—it wasn't because of your period. And it wasn't because of Josef, either." It was his turn to laugh. "Does he know?"

"Does *who* know *what*?"

"Does he know you love him?"

Martha blushed and stood up. "I don't know what you're talking about."

"You do, too." Meteor reached over and grabbed her hand. "You love Matthew." He looked faintly surprised as he moved his head slowly back and forth and mused, "You always have— Even when Josef was alive."

Martha pulled her hand away. "That's not true."

"It is so," Meteor said. He sighed loudly. "And he loves you, too."

"No, he doesn't."

"Yeah—he does."

Martha looked at him, her mouth pursed, and her face showing surrender.

Meteor stared for a moment. "Let's make a pact," he said.

"To do what?"

"Some day, when you don't need stability, you aren't in love with Matthew, and..." he paused for effect, "... you aren't having your period... " They both laughed. "...Come and find me. And we'll finish what we've begun."

Martha smiled. "I've heard that somewhere before." She leaned over and kissed him. On the lips. A lingering kiss. One that he returned. She drew back. "It's a deal."

Meteor grabbed her hand. "We could be good together, you know?"

Martha shook her head. "I don't think so. Good in the trenches, but not good on the home hearth."

"We could give it a try."

"Meteor," she said gently, "I need somebody to hold me when I need to be held." She added, "You can't be that somebody." She gave him a small, sweet smile—one tinged with sadness. "You and I both know that."

Meteor gave a small nod. "Another rain check," he muttered. He jumped out of the bed and collected his own clothing.

Martha watched him as he dressed by the light of the small camp lantern. She studied the welted scars on his chest and arms, the ones she had touched earlier. She wondered at how much pain he had gone through to get them. Warmth flooded her heart for him. *Agony*, she thought.

She smiled when he offered her his arm. She took it and they made their way back outside. A few minutes of walking and they were back at the gathering.

MATTHEW WAS seated near the central bonfire. He was involved in a loud conversation with some of the captains. They all looked up as Martha and Meteor got closer. Martha caught the look of condemnation in Matthew's eyes. She dropped her hand from Meteor's arm. She knew what Matthew was thinking, and he would have been right.

But he wasn't right.

She tried to ignore his stare. But his eyes remained locked upon her—accusatory and cold. Righteous anger roared through her, prickling her scalp, as it passed. She strode over to him, leaving Meteor behind.

"Matthew," she said. "Can I speak to you privately for a minute?"

"What about?"

"Privately." She looked at the men sitting with Matthew. The captains nodded and rose, leaving an empty spot on the log for Martha to take. She sat.

Matthew watched her—his eyes were dark, his scowl unforgiving.

"Don't look at me that way," she said. "It's not what you think. And even if it was—I'm not married anymore."

"No—" Matthew said curtly. "Just newly widowed."

Martha felt her anger rise and her eyes became dark slits. "*Nothing* happened."

"You mean the same *nothing* that didn't happen before?"

"You are so self-righteous, Matthew. What about Anna? What about Cammy?"

"At least I wasn't married."

"Well, who the hell would have you, anyway?"

Matthew made a sound of disgust. He rose from the log. Martha watched as he headed toward another group of men. They welcomed him with warm greetings, and hands clapped to his back. She felt her heart sink, and tears filled her eyes. She swiped them away.

Fuck you, Matthew. Think whatever you want. What does it matter? Nothing matters now.

Martha stared into the flames. She kicked at the ground, and then she got up. She wasn't sure where she was going, but she knew she needed to be away from there. Away from him. Away from *Matthew.*

She looked beyond the bonfire. Meteor was still standing where she had left him. He was looking at her. He lifted his arms away from his body in a gesture of embrace. He smiled. Softly. Welcoming. For a moment, Martha wanted to run to him.

To feel his arms around her, his hands on her skin.

To feel his lips.

To feel him.

To finish what they had begun.

But she fought against the temptation. Instead, she smiled back at him and shook her head.

Then she turned away.

The Replacement

"WE NEED a replacement—a new informant inside his camp since we no longer have Brad on the inside," Virgil said.

The Man pushed the food around on his plate. They were in the new clubhouse diner. "We need beef, too— I'm tired of chicken."

Virgil continued. "I think I'll send a couple of guys in. See what they can find out."

"Easier to send in a woman," The Man countered. He picked up a thick piece of rye bread spread with butter, and took a bite.

"A woman?"

"Sure," The Man mumbled around his half-chewed bread.

"Like who?"

"Oh, someone smart. Someone pretty. Someone with the goods." The Man shoved his plate away, and sat back. "Someone who might be able to turn old Matthew's head."

Virgil eyed The Man. "You sound like you have someone in mind for this job."

"I do— I think you know her."

"Who?" Virgil asked impatiently.

"Marion, of course. She'd be perfect—don't you think?" The Man took a swallow of red wine from a tall long-stemmed glass.

"What's she going to do?" Virgil asked. "Just walk up to the gate?"

"No. We'll get a couple of the guys to mess her up first. Then we'll dump her there. You know—play on Matthew's sympathies." The Man studied Virgil's face, as he spoke.

"Why would Marion consent to that?"

"Because she likes her nice big house. She likes having protection. And she likes not having to work for it."

The Man motioned to one of the women across the room. She grabbed a small plate bearing a large wedge of pie and scurried over, fork in hand.

"But she's your... sister. Why would you do that to your sister?"

"Adopted sister—" The Man corrected him. He took the fork and began to eat, the piecrust crumbled under his pressure and red berry syrup oozed out the edges. "You havin' some of this?"

"No—Thanks." Virgil's forehead creased into a frown. "But still— You can't mean that." He looked down at his plate.

"Oh— But I do. I do."

The Man scooped up a last forkful of pie, shoved it into his mouth, dropped the fork to the plate, and sat back in his chair. He eyed Virgil, as he spoke:

"And the sooner, the better."

Virgil didn't look up.

Chapter Forty-Five

A Joy Ride

MARTHA'S LIFE had become dull, and her day-to-day schedule with its farm-life routine was taking its toll. She ached for excitement, anything that would give her respite from the drudgery. But none came.

There was little or no threat from roving marauders. Since the battle, The Man and the rest of the Crazies had quieted down. It was rare to hear of a skirmish between Matthew's men and the bikers.

Morning dragged into mid-day, mid-day into evening, and evening into the next day. Martha fought a yearning to be on the road, to be exploring. To be fighting. She desperately craved the adrenaline rush that only fear could bring. Nevertheless, her daily duties continued. And she plodded on.

The crops were lush. "Probably a sign of another long cold winter," Martha had mused, as she assigned tasks to other camp members: canning fruits and vegetables; pickling cucumbers, beets, and mustard beans; picking potatoes, yams, and squash; gleaning the berry and the apple trees, smoking meat, harvesting grain for flour, making candles, and chopping firewood. There was always plenty to do.

Then there was Matthew.

Since the night of the celebration bonfire, he had kept to himself, distracted and lost in his thoughts. He spent more and more of his time away from the compound. When he was in camp, Martha would see him at meetings, or crossing the compound, or jumping into one of the trucks—

but they rarely spoke. When they did encounter one another, their conversation was mechanical. No wasted words. No wasted smiles.

She toyed with the idea of telling Matthew the truth about the night of the bonfire, but every time she worked her courage up to do so, she remembered his coldness and rejection of her. Then the pain would resurface—a dark and creeping fist that would grab her heart and squeeze until she wanted to cry out.

Some days, the depression was so intense that it took an effort just to breathe. That's when Martha's mind would wander in search of something—anything that would give her the desire to go on. That's when she would remember him. His grin. His blue eyes.

She missed Meteor. She thought about going off on her own in search of him, but she had no idea where to look. He had disappeared after the bonfire. She regretted her decision to turn him away.

Martha looked up from the pea patch. Children were running and laughing in the new playground. She smiled. It was good to see children playing like children again instead of sitting in front of computers. Sweat poured from beneath her straw hat. She shoved it back and wiped her brow.

You are a sad mess of a woman. A sorry, sad mess.

She needed to escape. She needed an outing. Desperately.

She watched as men moved back and forth near the Gatehouse. She sighed.

To be one of them. To be a man. Would that be better?

She heard Mary's voice. The little girl was bossing around her friends, instructing them in their play. Martha smiled. *No, then she wouldn't have Mary.*

But right now, Mary wasn't enough.

I'll go insane if I don't get the hell out of here.

Martha pulled off her work gloves, and her hat; she pushed the gloves inside her hat, and walked out of the garden. She placed her plastic bucket loaded with fat pea pods near the tool shed. She dropped her hat and gloves on top of the peas. She straightened up, and arched her back, stretching out her stiffened muscles. She ran her hand through her hair— it was sticky with sweat. She desperately wanted a shower. Maybe a swim.

A swim. Great idea.

Martha went to her cabin. Her bathing suit was hanging from a hook. She grabbed it, took a large bath towel from a shelf, and slipped into a pair of sandals. She stopped in front of a mirror. Her face was very tanned. A few wrinkles, laugh lines—and frown lines—but her eyes were bright with good health. She smiled. The Change had been good for well-being—less junk food, more fresh air, and lots of physical exercise.

Martha left the cabin. She made her way to the Gatehouse. Several people were standing around. They were dressed in various versions of shorts and t-shirts; some of the girls were in bathing suits—the skimpiest kind that only a younger woman can wear—without a cover shirt. Martha smiled at the increasing crowd of appreciative males; Jonah was among them.

"Going swimming?" Martha asked.

"Yes," Jonah replied. He gave Martha a quick smile and then turned his attentions back to the girls.

"Not us," said one of the older men. It was Thomas; he was the husband of a woman Martha had been teaching to bake. "We're going to do a perimeter check."

Martha smiled at him. "It's a lovely day for a perimeter check. Can I come, too?"

Thomas gave a small shrug. "I don't see why not." He gestured to the people in swimsuits. "But wouldn't you rather go swimming?"

"I'll go later," Martha replied.

"Okay. Want to ride with me?"

"Sure."

□□□

THE LOW BUSHES obscured the car. They had come across it as they drove down one of the lesser-used gravel roads. A glint had caught Martha's eye, and she demanded that Thomas stop the truck. The two trucks following them stopped, too. Clouds of dust wafted up into the summer sky as the drivers applied the brakes. Everyone jumped out.

Martha stroked the smooth, shiny finish of the car's hood. It was hot to the touch. "Oh, I'd like to own this," she said.

"Doesn't look abandoned," Thomas said. "Look around for the owner first."

Martha smiled and walked around the vehicle—a Dodge Magnum—sleek and black. She bet it had a hemi. How wonderful it would be to drive. She stopped by the driver's door and looked inside. The keys were still in the ignition. A purse lay on the passenger seat.

"Hey, I think we found the driver," someone shouted. "She's over here."

"Don't touch her," Martha said. She walked over. The body lay in a crumpled heap. Flies buzzed around Martha's head; they landed on the woman's body, and then flitted away. Martha examined the area. There were no signs of vomit or diarrhea. But the smell was bad.

"Doesn't look like she had a stomach ailment. I'd guess a heart attack," Martha said.

She pushed the body over with her foot to get a better look at the face. The woman was older, maybe in her sixties. That's when Martha saw the blood. "Um—not a heart attack," she said. "She's been shot."

It wasn't the first dead person Martha had seen. Nor was it her first gunshot wound. Still she hurriedly stepped back from the body. "Get some shovels over here. Let's get her buried."

Shovels were retrieved from the trucks, and after tamping about for soft earth, they started to dig. In about twenty minutes, they had finished the grave. A man grabbed a blue plastic tarp from his truck. He laid it on the ground, and they rolled the woman's body into it. They dragged the tarp-covered body to the grave; each man grabbed an end and they swung the body into the open hole. They shoved earth back into the grave. Martha nodded her approval. Then she went back to the car.

She opened the Magnum's door and got in. The interior was stifling hot, but the leather-covered bucket seat was luxurious and inviting. She picked up the purse, opened it, and looked for ID. A burgundy credit card holder turned up cards in the name of Diana Baker. In a windowed compartment of a blue wallet, Martha found a driver's license with the likeness of the woman they had just buried. Martha smiled.

"So?" Martha jumped from the sudden intrusion. Thomas stood at the car window. Martha held up the driver's license.

"That's her, alright," he said. "Guess the car's yours."

Martha reached for the key. The engine turned over with no hesitation. Martha tapped the accelerator. A powerful throb reached her ears. It was too much to resist. "Can I take it for a drive while you guys finish up?"

Thomas shrugged his shoulders. "I guess—but don't go too far." He thumbed in the direction of the fresh grave. "Don't know who shot her. Don't want you getting shot, too." He looked at his watch. "Matthew doesn't like us splitting up. 10 minutes, okay? Then we'll go back to the camp."

"Okay," Martha said. She pushed the stick shift into DRIVE. She tapped the gas pedal. The car responded. Martha pressed harder. Small, sharp rocks ricocheted like bullets off the satiny finish of the paint as she sped up the road. She smiled at the thought of the previous owner and the look of horror that would have spread across her face.

Nope, Diana wouldn't have liked this—she wouldn't have liked this at all.

But Martha liked it a great deal.

The speedometer needle climbed.

Not since she was thirteen in her mother's 1965 Corvair had she driven with such abandon. Martha remembered sneaking the joy ride in the small blue car. The car had overheated and stalled about three miles from her home. Luckily, a neighbor had come to the rescue. Her mother never found out.

Martha reached the main highway. She turned left. She checked ahead. The road was clear. She studied the car's instrument panel. The fuel gauge indicator rested on half, and Martha's foot felt heavy. She pressed down on the accelerator. Like a cat on its haunches, she felt the car lift.

"*Don't go too far,*" Thomas had said. Martha heard his words like a chant in her head. But the power of the car, the smoothness of the ride, and the trees whipping by her were so exhilarating.

Who cares—this feels too good. I'll go back when I'm ready.

The Magnum rocketed onward.

□□□

MARTHA HAD been back in her cabin for about an hour when she heard the knock on the door. She opened it. It was Simon.

"Matthew wants to see you," Simon said.

"He can wait," she said. "I'm busy."

"Uh—I don't think so," Simon advised. "You'd better go now."

Martha grumbled, but she went to the Meeting House. Matthew was seated at a side table. Two of the men she had been with on patrol that afternoon, were with him. Thomas was there, too.

Oh God, she thought. *What a bunch of whiny tattletales.*

Matthew looked up. "What is wrong with you, Martha?"

"What do you mean?" she asked, with as much innocence as she could muster.

"Where's the car?"

"With the rest of the vehicles," she replied.

"You were told not to go far, but you didn't come back to the group for nearly an hour."

"Yeah, so?"

"You put everyone in jeopardy—including yourself," Matthew said. "What if the car had broken down? Or what if the rest of the group had been attacked while waiting for you? That woman had been shot!"

"I know," Martha said. "But it was just a car ride, okay. I came back and we're all here. So what's the big deal?"

"It's about listening to authority and listening to those people I've put in charge."

"You mean the MEN you put in charge, don't you?" Martha asked.

"I told you when you got here that men were in charge. You agreed you could live with that. Remember?"

"Oh, for heaven's sakes." Martha said, her face twisting into a sneer. "C'mon, Matthew. It's not that big a deal. I took a ride."

Matthew stood and strode toward her. She winced as he grabbed her forearm, squeezing it so tightly that her hand began to swell with trapped blood.

"It is that big of a deal," he said. His face was dark with fury.

"Okay, fine— I'm sorry." Martha tried to pull her arm from his grasp, but he held fast. She struggled for something to say. "I have to go," she said. "I just heard that one of the kids in the far cabin is sick. I have to check on her." It wasn't exactly true, but it was true enough. She had actually visited the child the night before. Martha waited.

Matthew's eyes glinted with a ferocity Martha had seen before—but not often. And not directed at her.

"Don't," he said, through clenched teeth. "Don't do it again." Matthew released her arm, and Martha backed away from him.

"Sure, Matthew." She turned and walked to the door.

She stopped when she heard Matthew's voice again, thick with warning, "Don't question my authority again."

Martha stormed out of the Meeting House, slamming into Simon as she left.

"Whoa," he said. "Is Matthew still in there?"

"Oh, yeah— He's in there." Martha stopped and watched as Simon raced into the building. She heard him call out.

"Matthew! The supplies are here."

Supplies? What supplies?

Martha turned around and marched back into the Meeting House. The men looked up.

"What supplies?" she demanded. She confronted Matthew. "Or is that none of my business, too?"

Matthew shook his head.

"Sit down, Martha." The angry man she had seen earlier was gone; this man looked tired—almost beaten. "It's time you knew about this."

Martha sat.

"Knew about what?"

"I've built a second camp."

□□□

The Secret

"I'M WORRIED," Virgil said. "I think he might try to harm you."

"Never. He's known me for years," Marion said. "He's bluffing. He won't hurt me."

"And what if he's not bluffing?"

"I'm a big girl. I can take care of myself."

"Famous last words," he said.

"I'll be fine. Really."

Virgil thought a moment. "I think we'll be moving on Matthew's camp soon. The Man's gotten wind of a second camp."

"A second camp?"

"Yeah. Apparently there's oil hidden under the ground in this one."

"Really?"

"He's never mentioned this to you?" Virgil asked.

"No."

"Be sure not to let it slip, or he'll know for sure that it came from me."

Marion smiled. "My lips are sealed."

Chapter Forty-Six

The New Gloves

THE CHILDREN hooted and applauded when Martha announced plans to visit the Hutterite colony, the *Bruderhof*. Since the Change, the Germanic people had insisted visitors refer to their collective farms by their correct German name. The kindly Hutterites were always good to the kids, and the kids loved their odd accents—not to mention their thick honeycomb dripping with golden honey.

Now the children crowded in close as a Hutterite woman, in a printed headscarf, pulled up a large rectangular screen covered in tiny hexagons of wax, oozing honey. Martha felt saliva burst in her mouth as she watched. She knew the taste well—the honey was almost tangy in its intense sweetness.

"Me first," Samuel said. He gave Mary a shove. The Hutterite woman broke off a piece of the gooey sweetness and held it out. She held it up and to the right of Samuel, and deposited the honeycomb into Mary's hands.

"For the little one," she said with a wide smile. Mary beamed and shoved the mess into her mouth. Honey dripped from her fingers. She licked them.

"You look like a big cow," Samuel said, his words tainted with disgruntlement. Mary shook her head and continued to chew. The Hutterite woman cut another piece, raised it into the air, and gave it to a little boy to Samuel's right. Samuel frowned and mumbled. Martha suppressed a chuckle as the drama unfolded.

"Maybe you should try the polite way," Martha suggested. "Let everyone else go first."

Samuel scuffed at the floor with a dirty boot. "I don't like waiting."

"Well, neither do I, but sometimes we have to."

Whether we like it or not.

Martha had waited a long time for Matthew to give her more details on the second camp. He hadn't wanted too many people to know about the camp while it was under construction, so he had kept it secret from most people in the compound, including Martha. She had felt hurt—she still felt hurt—that he had kept it from her, too.

"Who are you allying with?" Martha had asked him.

"Sandy Beach. The townspeople are really dug in and they're used to making-do, and doing without. They're low on firepower, and they're getting attacked more often—the Crazies like the place because of the big lake and the cabins—instant vacation accommodations."

Now many more of the Gatekeeper's people knew the camp existed. In fact, the parents of the children Martha was shepherding that day were working at the second camp.

"Thanks," Martha heard Samuel say. He and Mary were in her care today, too. Ruth was busy birthing another baby. Samuel wasn't smiling as he took the tiny piece of honeycomb proffered to him by the woman. The woman's face showed nothing, but Martha sensed her thoughts. She nearly laughed out loud, but she cleared her throat instead. The two women exchanged warm smiles.

"I would love a bucket of honey," she said to the woman. "Buckwheat, if you have it."

The Hutterite woman led Martha to a small side room. Dozens of plastic pails, in all shapes and sizes, sat in neat vertical piles against one wall. On the tops of several of the larger buckets, Martha could make out the word, Buckwheat, written in thick black felt pen. The woman motioned to the wall.

"Help yourself. Take whatever you need. You've got good credit here."

Martha took a yellow bucket from the top. She grunted as she lifted it. She tested the weight. *I can carry two,* she thought. *The other camp will need one. She took a second pail.*

Martha watched as the Hutterite woman bent over a pockmarked wooden table; it was laden with dusty notebooks, lethal-looking knives, and empty jars. The woman pulled a huge hardbound journal from the top of one pile of books, and flipped it open to a partially filled page; Matthew's name was at the top. Martha saw many other farm products itemized in fine cursive writing in the book: butter, milk, eggs, flour, chickens, pigs, oats, cheese, rabbits, apples, chokecherries, Saskatoon berries, raspberries, potatoes, quilts, down-filled pillows, leather gloves, candles, and soap. On an empty line beneath Matthew's name, the woman added, "Honey," and "2 pails" in parallel columns.

Martha's eyes roved beyond the woman's bent head to the upper wall. Two long white papers hung there. Martha saw they were fruits and vegetables itemized under the months of the year. Corn was available July through September. Her mouth watered with the thought of sweet Peaches and Cream corn, dripping with fresh butter, and sprinkled with coarse salt and cracked pepper.

"Your corn is so good," Martha said. "Even better than ours."

"I have something else you might like."

Martha watched as the woman opened an upper cupboard; it was lined with jars of preserves. The woman reached for one of the jars.

"Wait—" Martha said. "What are those?" She pointed to a lower shelf.

The woman hesitated and then drew out a pair of leather gloves. Martha took the gloves. Man-sized. She turned them in her hands. The deerskin chamois was lightly colored and softer than a baby's cheek.

"These are very handsome."

"You would like them?" The woman bent and picked up her pen.

"No, wait," Martha said. "I'd like to give them as a surprise. As a gift. I'd like to— um— earn them myself. Can I do that?"

The woman laid the pen back on the open book. She thought a moment, and then said, "How are you at plucking chickens?"

Martha beamed. "I'm an expert. I'm an ex-farm girl."

"How about drawing them?"

"I haven't done it in a while, but I know how. And I'm not squeamish about it—if that's what you mean."

The woman smiled. She handed Martha the gloves. "Then it's a deal. We're killing 300 young hens the end of next month. We shall expect you then."

Three hundred chickens? Three hundred? I am in for one mighty sore back.

Martha rubbed her fingers across the gloves. *It might be worth it,* she thought. Matthew's gloves were looking very worn. A new pair might be just the thing to win him over—to make peace with him. Especially when he discovered how hard she had worked for them.

□□□

THE END of August came quickly. The sky was clear and blue with just a hint of puffy cumulus clouds sailing high above. Martha packed a canvas bag with her sunhat, sunscreen, bottled water, bread and cheese, and a large chunk of lemon square she had baked the night before. It was still slightly warm, and very aromatic. She resisted having a chunk for breakfast and opted for a bowl of oatmeal with dried cranberries instead.

Martha pulled on her leather hiking boots. She had taken a pair of Josef's thick wool socks. She would be on her feet for hours, and she needed the padding, and the support. She thought about her dead husband briefly as she pulled on his socks. She tried to see his face in her mind's eye. She couldn't.

She stepped out of the cabin and raised her face to the sun. She sniffed the air. Birds squawked and twittered in the forest to her right.

Boy, will I sweat today. I need another shirt to change into.

She walked back to the cabin, but was stopped by the sound of her name. It was Matthew. She turned.

"Yes?"

"Watch the younger kids today. I'm taking a group of parents to the new camp again. We're going to clear more of the land. Get it ready for more cabins."

Martha choked. "I-I can't, Matthew."

"What?"

"I can't. I made a commitment to do something else today. Ask Ruth. I'm sure she'll do it."

Matthew's eyes darkened. "Break your date, Martha. You have a job to do here. Or are you no longer part of this camp?"

"I am, Matthew. I'd do it in a second, but I can't. I promised to—uh—help someone today."

This was not going at all well. This was not what Martha had envisioned their next conversation would be. The new gloves flashed into her mind.

Should I show them to him now? Then explain?

"You're telling me you can't do this?"

"Uh—yes. Sorry, but yes—I mean—no, I can't."

Matthew's eyes turned cold. "We'll talk later." He walked away.

Martha stood trembling.

What am I doing? As if he's even going to care when I give him the damn gloves.

She played with the idea of getting the gloves and throwing them into his face.

She went into the cabin and retrieved a package wrapped in brown paper, from a shelf. She turned it over in her hand, and then with a huff, she tossed it on the bed. She grabbed another t-shirt and left the room.

She made her way across the compound. She passed through the gate with a nod toward the armed men standing there.

□□□

THE DAY had gone well. The Hutterites were pleased with Martha's work. She had had only a couple of mishaps. She hadn't scalded a chicken long enough to loosen the feathers, and she ended up ripping the skin; and a medium-sized nick with the butcher knife had set her back for a few minutes, while she stopped the blood flow. However, in spite of that, Martha had kept up pace with the adept farm women.

As she was leaving, the Hutterite woman, whom she had begun to call Sarah, presented Martha with a thick pillow—amply stuffed with soft goose down. Martha refused, but Sarah insisted, so Martha thanked her, and accepted the gift.

Martha made her way up the small path toward the compound. A feeling of dread had bubbled up about midway through the afternoon. Martha worked harder and faster in hopes of pushing the feeling away. It never left, and now it was stronger than ever.

The bread and cheese she had had hours ago sat heavily in the pit of her stomach, and slight nausea overtook her. She swayed and fell. She tried to get back up, but the dizziness was too much.

Nuts. Too much sun.

She was trembling and sweating. She scrabbled in her canvas bag for her water bottle. Sarah had refilled it with cool, sweet well water before Martha left; she opened it and drank deeply.

Martha crawled under a sturdy evergreen tree, plumped up her brand new pillow, relaxed back into it, and breathed a sigh of relief. The cool shade felt so good. She watched a couple of brown squirrels scamper along the ground, their bushy tails flipping impishly. They stopped, studied the new forest resident briefly, and then scurried on. It was the last thing Martha saw before she fell asleep.

☐☐☐

SHE AWOKE with a start. It was dark, but the moon was high. Martha glanced at her wristwatch, as she pressed a button to illuminate the watch's face; she had slept for several hours. Matthew would be wondering where she was.

He was going to be angry. Again.

She raced up the path toward the camp.

The guards nodded as she approached. The tallest guard shook his head with ominous slowness.

"He's been asking about you."

"You are in big trouble," the other guard said. "Big trouble."

"Yeah— What else is new?" Martha said, as she passed through the gates.

Maybe for the last time she thought. The last damn time.

Her cabin was dark; its coolness enveloped her as she entered. She was so tired. She kicked off her boots, tossed her clothing to the floor, and pulled on a light cotton gown. She threw her new pillow on the bed, climbed between the sheets, and allowed her exhausted body to relax. Her mind to drift.

I'll be on my way—tomorrow... and I'm taking MY car.

She kicked at the packet that lay near her feet.

Martha closed her eyes and she slept.

☐☐☐

Zero Tolerance

"CHURCH" WAS in full session. The Man and Virgil stood at the front of the room. Regional chapter presidents had gathered from all parts of the province, and from the flanking provinces of Saskatchewan and British Columbia, too. No prospects, probates, or 'friendlies' were in attendance at this meeting—this meeting was for club captains and presidents only; it was a strategy session:

The Man was going to war— Matthew's camp was at the top of the hit list.

The Man called the bikers to order. He didn't raise his voice; he didn't demand silence. The Man merely looked up, raised his hand, and let his eyes wander over the faces.

He waved a hand behind him, and Virgil took a step forward. "You all know Virgil?" The assembled men murmured. "He'll explain the plan—but first I want to go over some old business."

The Man bent over a book in front of him. He looked up. "Is the president of the Medicine Hat chapter here?"

A man wearing a black kerchief tied over gnarled dark curls strode forward. He was wearing a black leather vest over a blue jean jacket. "Here," he said.

The Man studied him for a moment. "We have a zero tolerance policy in this army. I've made that clear to all of you. Haven't I?" he asked, looking out across the room.

Again, the men nodded and murmured their assent.

"Without clear rules and a strict adherence to those rules, we can't build strength. Without strength, we can't achieve power. Without power, we can't achieve dominance." He paused. "And isn't that what we want?" Then louder, "Isn't it?"

The men exploded into hurrahs filled with expletives. Their fists pumped the air, and their boots made the small room shake as they stomped their approval of The Man's words. Silence came quickly as they watched The Man pick up a pistol lying on the table next to him. He rested the gun's barrel gently across his opposite hand.

"I said that all actions must be approved by me, did I not?" The men agreed. The chapter president standing in front of The Man mumbled something as he shifted from one foot to another. "That's what I thought," The Man said. He turned his eyes on the biker standing in front of him.

"Didn't I also say that One-percenters would be dealt with?" The Man motioned with his pistol towards the biker. "You attacked Brooks. Under your leadership, your men destroyed property, and killed people—property and people we could have put to good use. You attacked the town like Crazies—without a good reason. And without my permission." He paused, and the room grew deathly silent.

"Zero tolerance," The Man repeated. He nodded toward the back of the room. Four guards walked up. Two of them grabbed the president's arms and led him out the door, while the other two followed behind. The Man motioned for the rest of the gathered men to follow.

The president stood in the parking lot, a sole figure, with his arms hanging at his side. His face was frozen in the knowledge that he was about to die. He made no effort to escape as the mob advanced.

Five minutes later, the mob retreated and moved back into the clubhouse. Two young men, in hunter's caps, bent over the crumpled body; they dragged it toward a waiting truck. They dumped the heavy load over the side of the truck box, wiped their hands on their pants, and picked up beers sitting on the pavement near the truck. They drank.

Inside the clubhouse, The Man resumed his meeting.

Chapter Forty-Seven

A Truck Ride

MATTHEW OPENED the cabin door and ran into the kitchen. No one had answered his knock, so he called out, "Martha? Martha, I want to speak to you."

She wasn't in the kitchen; he walked into the bedroom. It was empty, too. He saw a gift-wrapped, bulky packet lying on the bed. He noticed a label bearing his name stuck to the package. He shrugged his shoulders and picked up the packet. With one tear, he removed the paper. A pair of chamois deerskin gloves fell to the bed.

Matthew leaned over and retrieved them; he stroked the leather between his fingers. Then he dropped the gloves on the bed, and headed to the doorway. He paused and returned to the bed. He picked up the gloves and the wrapping. He raced out of the cabin.

"Where is she?" he called, as he neared the gate. The armed man leaning against a doorjamb jumped to attention.

"Who, sir?"

"You know who I mean... Martha."

The man tried to disguise a smile, but it erupted in a twisted grin. "She just left, sir. She took the *car.*"

"Not sure how long I'll be gone. Tell Thomas to take care of things," Matthew called over his shoulder. He headed for the vehicle lot. He hopped into a nearby truck, turned the key, and roared off; the truck's tires churned up water and mud as he drove up the road to the main highway.

Matthew had driven for about five minutes when he saw the black Magnum ahead of him. He leaned on the horn. The Magnum continued its steady pace. He punched the horn again. This time he saw the brake lights come on.

Martha pounded the wheel. "Damn it, can't he leave me alone?"

She had seen the truck a short way back, but decided to press on. She suspected Matthew was at the wheel; it was even more reason not to stop. However, the persistent honking had the desired effect; she tapped the brakes and stopped the car. Martha turned the key, wrenched open the door, and got out. She waited.

The truck sprayed gravel as Matthew pulled it to the side and stopped behind her. He leapt out. Martha marched up to meet him.

"I've had it, Matthew. I'm always in trouble with you. I'm sick of it. The camp is in good shape. You have medical people. You don't need me anymore. I'm leaving."

Matthew stood in front of her, but didn't say a word. Martha was trembling, and her voice shook with rage.

"What is it? What do you *want*, Matthew?"

He still didn't speak, but merely looked at her. She drew a quick ragged breath.

"You win. Are you happy now? You win." Martha felt tears rise in her eyes and she turned away to hide her face from him. She wouldn't let him see her cry.

"Nice day for a drive, isn't it?" Matthew said.

"What?" Martha turned back to him. Her fingers flew to her eyes and she flipped tears away.

Matthew was studying the sky—his eyebrows dipped together in concentration. One hand shaded his eyes.

Like some damned birdwatcher, she thought.

"I said it looks like a nice day for a drive. Can I join you?"

Martha stood dumbly.

"I've got an idea. There's a nice pond near here, but your car is too low-slung to handle the roads. Let's take the truck."

Your, she thought. *YOUR car?*

She stood silently, watching him.

"C'mon." He held out a hand to her.

She stared at Matthew's hand—the details stood out sharply and defined as though under the brightest light: deeply tanned, the wrinkles, its dark wiry hairs, its age spots, its thick fingers, and its dirty fingernails.

His hand.

Matthew's voice drew her out of her reverie. She looked up. Their eyes met.

"Shall we?" he asked. There was gentleness in his tone that made Martha's breath catch in her throat. Her eyes narrowed suspiciously.

What was this? What did he want?

Martha raised her hand slowly and placed it into Matthew's hand. Fiery warmth shot up her arm. Its intensity made her flinch. She tried to withdraw her hand, but Matthew held it fast. He gently pulled her toward the truck.

He opened the passenger door and waited for her to climb in. He closed the door and walked around the front of the truck. That's when Martha saw the package. Her heart began to beat hard.

The gloves? What were the gloves doing here?

The driver's door screeched open and Matthew jumped in. Martha stared ahead. Waiting. She gritted her teeth. *He had tricked her and she had fallen for it. Idiot*, she thought. And he had made her leave her beautiful car behind, too. *Idiot.* She reached for the door handle, but a movement caught her eye.

She watched as Matthew picked up the gloves. He pulled them on, one at a time. He held up his hands, turning them over, admiring the gloves. She watched him warily, like a starving animal eager for the food, but not trusting the hand. He placed his gloved hands on the wheel, and turned.

"Thank you, Martha," he said. "I think these are the nicest gloves I've ever owned." He smiled. "The Hutterites make such fine gloves, don't they?" He gave her a warm smile.

Martha's mouth hung open in surprise. A wave of something washed over her. She wanted to smile, but couldn't. She stared as Matthew reached up to the visor; it was the place he usually kept gloves while he was driving. His old pair was there. He pulled them out.

"I guess I won't be needing these," he said. He tossed them out the open window. He started the engine, placed his hands on the wheel, and pulled the truck onto the road. Martha's own hand dropped from the door handle into her lap.

The truck sped up the highway. A few miles up the road, Matthew slowed down. He cranked the wheel to the right, pulling the vehicle into a rough-hewn driveway, one Martha had never seen before. He maneuvered the truck slowly over the rutted lane, sending muddy water spraying.

"How far is it?" she asked.

"Not far," Matthew replied. "About a half mile, or so."

Martha pressed the window button on her door, and the window zoomed down. She leaned out, luxuriating in the warm breeze on her face, as it lifted her hair. Matthew spoke.

"What?" she asked.

"Where were you going?"

Martha shrugged. "I don't know."

"I understand The Man could use a good medical officer. He's still fighting with that bullet you put into his shoulder."

Martha shot Matthew a look. "Yeah—right. That would be the first place I'd go."

Matthew smiled.

Martha raised her eyebrows. "And how would you know about that, anyway?"

"I have my sources."

"Oh, you mean Meteor."

Matthew nodded.

"How is he?" she asked.

"Good. I just saw him yesterday." Matthew pulled the truck off to the right, into a clearing. Birds broke from the trees and soared into the air, disturbed by the unnatural sound. Matthew turned to Martha. "He's always got something to tell me."

"Oh," she said. Matthew's face wore an enigmatic expression. Martha studied it for a moment. It was the first time in weeks that the subject of Meteor had come up in a conversation of theirs; it surprised her that Matthew didn't seem vexed by the topic.

Matthew stopped the truck, and turned off the engine. He removed his gloves and tucked them neatly above the visor. He hopped out and went to Martha's side.

"C'mon," he said. Martha had already opened the door and was stepping down. He offered his hand in assistance, and she took it. It was warm.

"Where are we going?"

"I'll show you."

Matthew led Martha out of the sunlit glade and into the cool of the woods. They followed a trail through the trees. The air was sweet—an intoxicating scent of tree sap and damp earth. A bird that Martha couldn't identify sang somewhere high above. Its trill was answered by another, and then another.

Martha stumbled on a tree root as they rounded the trail, and Matthew turned back to catch her. "You okay?"

"Yes— No problem," she assured him.

Martha followed him through a large opening, a natural archway made by tree boughs intersecting one another, their huge branches linked in a feathery handshake. Ahead lay a marsh, its water bright with reflected sunlight. The honking call of Canada geese caught Martha's attention, and she turned to see a large group take to the air, their long necks stretched out before them. Ahead of her, on the pond, sat many more.

"Look," Matthew said, pointing to a pair of geese near the water's edge. They floated, easy and unconcerned, golden in the glow of the mid-morning sun, and framed in ripples.

"They're so beautiful," she said. She turned and smiled at Matthew.

"I'll be right back," Matthew said.

Martha stood unmoving. She watched as the secret world unfolded. Birds sang out from the treetops, squirrels chattered, and the geese continued to honk. The sun was warm and Martha pulled off her jacket. She threw it to the ground, and sat down.

Matthew appeared again. He stopped several feet away from her. He held a shotgun in his hand. "Supper," he said with a smile, as he pointed to the geese overhead.

He pulled shells from his shirt pocket, and loaded the gun. He raised it to his shoulder, tucking the thick butt firmly into the indentation between his chest wall and his arm. He squinted. He swung the gun in an arc, panning it in tandem with the flying geese. "I want them to fall in the woods," he said.

Martha stood up. "Please don't," she said. "Don't."

Matthew stared at her briefly, and then lowered the gun. He cracked it open, and removed the shells from the barrel. He dropped them back into his shirt pocket. Martha walked over to him.

They stood together, silently, as the music of the morning filled the air. Soft splashes of leaping fish drew their attention, as telltale concentric circles dotted the pond. The angry chatter of a squirrel high in an evergreen tree and the return squawk of a large black raven made them both laugh.

"I'm really hungry," Matthew said, suddenly. "I kind of left without eating breakfast."

"Me, too."

"I don't think I have anything to eat in the truck. Do you have anything?"

Martha remembered her canvas bag; it was still hanging on the hook back in the cabin. She shook her head. "I wasn't planning on a picnic," she said with a smile.

Matthew made a small sound of assent. Suddenly, he looked back at her and said, "Let's go shopping."

"What? You mean scavenging? Where?"

"Town."

Martha studied him for a moment. "Okay. Let's go."

Matthew grabbed Martha's hand. She tripped and fell against him, and he steadied her. Their eyes met. Martha recognized the intent in his eyes. She had seen that smoky look before—in other men's eyes. Josef's eyes. Meteor's eyes. And now, in his eyes. Her heart pounded as she waited.

The sound of cracking branches startled them. Matthew bent and grabbed Martha's jacket. He thrust it at her.

"C'mon," he said, glancing into the woods. He pushed Martha forward onto the path. More cracking off to the right made them hurry.

They both breathed a sigh of relief when a doe stepped out. Her large brown eyes regarded them briefly, before she leapt back into the bushes.

"Oh," Martha said, softly. "Her eyes are so pretty."

"So are yours."

Martha was shocked. She turned slowly to face Matthew. "What did you say?"

Matthew looked down at her. "I said you have pretty eyes, too." He reached toward her and gently pushed her bangs away from her eyes.

Martha gave a little start at the touch of his fingers on her skin. Matthew opened his hand and cupped her face. She leaned her cheek into his hand; he didn't pull away. A fleeting memory of Josef's hand touching her face played across her mind, but she caught Matthew's eyes, and the vision faded.

Matthew took her face between both of his hands and moved closer to her. She held her breath and waited. He drew her face close, and gazed into her eyes, and then, finally, he lowered his face and kissed her. On the lips. Gently. Softly. Slowly.

Martha sighed and leaned into him.

Matthew stopped kissing her and pulled her tight to his body. She laid her head on his chest and listened to the beat of his heart; it was rapid and it thrummed loudly. His jacket hung open, and she reached up and placed her hands on his shirt. She hooked the fingers of one hand into the opening of his shirt between two buttons, so she could feel his skin. Matthew stroked her hair and the back of her neck with one hand, while his other hand held her clasped to him. They stood that way for a few minutes, without speaking. Matthew broke the silence.

"This might sound awful..." he said. "But there's a motel not far from here."

Martha smiled softly as the wild thing came alive again. "Doesn't sound awful at all," she replied. She pulled away and looked up at him. "I'm too old to be frolicking on the hard ground in pine needles with voyeuristic squirrels chattering at me." She grinned. "And a truck cab with a stick shift is not my idea of a good time." She took his hand. "Take me there."

Matthew bent and kissed her again. This time the kiss was much harder, much more demanding, much more promising. This time, Martha parted her lips and participated in the kiss. Fully. Its intensity took her by surprise, and she clung to him.

Matthew drew back. He widened his eyes slightly and raised his eyebrows. "Enough of that— Or we will end up entertaining the squirrels." He smiled.

Martha gave him a small, crooked answering grin.

They made their way back to the truck and got in. Matthew backed out and drove the truck up the lane.

Martha touched her cheek; it was hot. She touched her lips. They felt bruised.

Did Matthew really kiss me? Were the last few minutes really real? Am I going to a motel with Matthew?

Martha blushed. She wanted to giggle, but instead she stole a look at him. He was concentrating on turning the truck onto the highway.

They drove along for a few minutes in silence.

"So?" he said.

"What?" Martha asked, jolted back from her thoughts.

"Why are you sitting way over there?" Matthew patted the seat next to him.

Martha's blush deepened. She shook her head. Then she laughed. "I haven't sat next to a guy while he was driving since I was a teenager."

"Then maybe it's about time." Matthew patted the seat again. "C'mon."

Martha hesitated as she fought with a sudden and unexpected shyness.

Matthew grinned. "What're you afraid of? That you'll get a ticket for not wearing your seatbelt?"

Martha burst out laughing. She pushed the wrapping paper that had held his gloves to the floor, slid across the seat, and eased into his outstretched arm. She fit perfectly, her shoulder tucked close to his side, and her head against his chest. She reached up and grasped the hand cupping her shoulder. She drew it close to her face.

Drive, Matthew. I don't care about the motel. I don't care about the camp. Just this. Only this.

This I want.

This I need.

Forever.

□□□

The Trick

"I DON'T TRUST her," The Man said. The meeting of the captains was over. He and Virgil were relaxing in the clubhouse's backroom.

"I don't see any reason not to trust her," Virgil said. "She's done nothing to earn your distrust."

"Nevertheless, I don't trust her." The Man thought briefly. "I think it's time we had a talk with her. Can't risk another turncoat like Cammy." The Man stubbed out his cigar. "Go and pick her up."

Virgil rose. "Okay, whatever you say. But I still don't think you have anything to worry about." He turned and walked toward the door.

"Uh, Virgil—" The Man called after him. "Don't you want to ask me for her address?"

Virgil turned back to The Man. Silence passed between them.

"When were you planning to tell me?" The Man asked.

Virgil returned to his chair and sat down. "What do you want to know?"

"Finally—"

Chapter Forty-Eight

A Secret Place

MATTHEW AND Martha rode along in silence, each lost in thought. There was nothing to say. Their togetherness had been a long time in coming, and now they relaxed into it, and soaked in the calm that the unleashing of their deep feelings had created.

"I want to show you something," Matthew said suddenly. Martha lifted her head, roused from her quietude.

"What?"

"A special place."

"Will there be food?"

"Uh-huh."

"Okay." She looked at him and smiled. "No motel then?"

Matthew gave a small chuckle. "Don't worry—you won't be disappointed."

"I wasn't worried about being disappointed. I was worried about something else," she said, with a grin.

The hand on her shoulder tightened, and Martha rested her head against Matthew's chest again.

They had traveled for about 10 minutes more when Martha saw Matthew press the truck's turn signal arm. She nearly laughed—old habits were hard to break—signal lights just weren't necessary anymore. Nevertheless, Matthew had pushed the signal arm down before he slowed the truck. He turned left. Martha sat up.

"Where are we going?"

"You'll see," he said.

They were on a side road, rutted and very dusty, in spite of the mud puddles. A perfect row of giant spruce trees ran along one side; on the other side stretched endless fields, some black, some covered in plants—mostly weeds, Martha suspected. Others were dotted with large circular hay bales. *Moldy now*, she thought; they would make livestock sick. She looked around. The area was deserted save for the many ravens that had claimed the hay bales as their own.

They drove along for a few more minutes before Matthew slowed the truck once more. This time he turned right onto a small lane—barely a path cut deeply with old tire tracks—that led into a field. The road paralleled a windbreak of willow trees. Martha bounced and jounced as Matthew followed the furrowed, hard-packed trail.

Martha saw a farmhouse. There were barns, sheds, and upright gas tanks. Farm machinery sat in a neat row in front of an open equipment shed. There was no sign of occupation: no trucks, no cars, no barking dogs.

"Whose place is this?"

Matthew pulled in behind one of the barns. He stopped the truck, pushed the gearshift into park, and turned. "Mine," he said. Martha looked stunned.

"Yours?" Martha's voice rose in pitched surprise.

"Yep. I'm going to open the barn. Drive the truck in, okay?"

Martha slid into the driver's seat. She could barely touch the pedals because the seat was adjusted for Matthew's long legs. Like she had once done as a child, when driving her father's car, she wriggled down and stretched her foot toward the pedal. She waited for Matthew to open the barn door, and she drove in. She turned off the truck, and jumped out.

The barn was fragrant with special scents that only a barn can have: hay, grain, wood, and—sunshine. Dust motes cavorted in the light rays that speared the floor, as sunbeams broke through cracks and holes in the wooden walls and ceiling.

Martha smiled.

I'm home.

The thought surprised her, and yet it didn't. The barn felt like home, a place she had known her whole young life. Moreover, she and Matthew belonged here. Together. She smiled again and ran her hand through a sunbeam, disrupting the silent dust ballet. "I love it here."

"Farm girl."

"Yeah." She laughed. "Wait a minute." She gave Matthew a stern look. "Is this supposed to take the place of a motel with a nice bed? I'm not into thistles and slivers either, you know."

"No." Matthew took her hand. He led her to a side room. It had a small cot, some gardening tools, a workbench, and a few hooks on the wall, filled with men's clothing and horse tack: bridles, halters, and braided ropes.

"Kind of small," Martha said, with a grimace when she noticed the small bed. She waited for Matthew's response. When he didn't reply, she gave him a questioning look.

Matthew went to the cot, grabbed its edge, and pulled it up onto its side. Beneath it, Martha saw a sheet of plywood. Matthew lifted the board, revealing a small trap door in the floor. He reached down, grabbed the small door by an iron ring, and wrenched it upwards. Tiny specks flew crazily in the soft golden light that bathed the room.

"A trap door?" Martha asked. "In a barn?" She thought for a second. "They're usually up in the hay loft. Why do you have this here?"

Matthew dropped to his knees and looked down. He reached in and pulled out a small camp lantern. He turned it on and then reached back inside the hole. The opening lit up and Martha saw a set of steps leading into the darkness. "Wow," she said, softly.

"C'mon," Matthew said, as he descended into the hole.

Martha followed.

MATTHEW TURNED on another camp lantern. He used it to light their way through the tunnel. "Watch your step here," he said. "Broken glass. Haven't had a chance to clean it up."

Martha looked down and picked her way through glass shards. She pushed larger pieces to the side with her booted foot. "Who built this?" she asked, as she hurried after Matthew.

"My father."

"Your father?"

"Yes."

"Where is he?"

"He's dead."

"Oh, I'm sorry."

"Don't be. He died many years ago."

"Oh," she said. "Where's your Mom?"

"She died, too."

"Your brothers and sisters? I know you have a sister."

"Two brothers, both younger. Don't know what happened to them. But they were both living in Vancouver during the Change. No idea what's happened to my sister, either."

Martha could see they were nearing the end of the tunnel. "Where does this lead?"

"Up into the house."

Matthew stopped at a simple wooden ladder. Martha could make out the shadowy outline of another trapdoor in the tunnel's low ceiling. Matthew hung the lantern on a large iron hook on the tunnel wall. He climbed the ladder, and paused. He held a finger to his lips and pressed an ear to the door. He listened, and then he shoved the door upwards.

The small square door creaked, and then fell heavily on the floorboards above their heads. Dust rained down into Martha's eyes. "Oh, damn," she said, and rubbed at her eyes. When she finally looked up, Matthew was already up the ladder. She grabbed onto a rung and climbed up, too.

Martha emerged into a room—not a kitchen, not a living room, not a bedroom, not even a closet—but rather—a war room. "What is all this?" she asked, as she spun around.

"My work room," Matthew said. He had lit another camp lantern. Now, he went to the edge of the room, and turned a crank. Two vents opened; light poured in. Martha gave a small breathy gasp.

Huge maps covered the walls, colored tacks dotted the maps, and notes—so many notes—hung from the tacks. Her first thought was of a movie she had seen with Russell Crowe, where he played a schizophrenic man. Such intricate detail, she thought. However, Martha knew Matthew wasn't mentally ill; Matthew was a brilliant strategist. She was only beginning to appreciate that fact.

Martha continued to explore the room with her eyes. Cardboard boxes sat piled in one corner; they were labeled with years; some were more than three decades old. Plywood sheets acting as desks lined the walls. The makeshift desks were piled with papers of all shapes, sizes and colors, newspaper clippings, textbooks, journals, and more maps—still neatly folded. Martha walked over and sorted through the stack of journals. She picked up one toward the bottom of the pile. She recognized Matthew's handwriting on the front cover: *September 23, 1990*. She opened the book.

Martha read a few pages. She soon realized what she was reading. "You began planning the survival camp that long ago?"

Matthew nodded. He took the journal from her and returned it to the pile. "My dad and I, actually. We thought we were making provisions for the year, 2000. When that turned out to be a joke, I decided to just keep going."

Martha turned around. The wall behind her was lined with filing cabinets and shelving. "What's in the cabinets?" she asked.

"Reference materials. Everything from how to treat a snake bite to how to build a jerry can bomb."

Martha saw a secretarial chair. She pulled it out and sat down. "I had no idea, Matthew."

"Nobody does." Matthew rolled out a second chair and sat next to her. "My dad and I kept it that way. For a long time. After he died, I took on some partners, and they helped me. We did a lot together, but the Crazies killed them. So, that left only me."

She took his hand. "And now— Me." Martha smiled.

Matthew smiled back. "Want to see the rest of the house?" he asked.

Martha looked around. "How do we get out of here?"

Matthew rose and walked over to the far wall where a large corkboard hung; it was heavily covered in notes and tacks. He lifted it from the wall and set it to the side. He felt with his fingers along a thin break in the drywall. Martha heard a small click, and then she watched as a rectangular section of the wall opened.

"This is awesome, Matthew," she said, her eyes sparkling with delight. "It's like Nancy Drew." She jumped off the chair and headed toward the opening.

"Hold it," he said, in a hushed whisper. "Check first. If you come here by yourself, always remember to check for sound first, okay? Make sure there's no sound," he emphasized. "This room is soundproofed, but once the door's opened, someone in the house would be able to hear you."

Martha nodded. Matthew crept from the room. Martha followed him. They were in a larger room, like a closet, or an old-fashioned pantry. *That was it*, Martha decided, when her eyes became accustomed to the low light. Dusty cereal boxes and a few jars of peanut butter sat on the shelves. Matthew crept up to the door, leaned his ear against it, and listened. Martha held her breath.

Matthew reached up to a hook near the door. A slender string, with a fender washer attached to the end, was wound around the hook. He pulled on the string. Martha heard a small sound, and the door popped open. Matthew pulled it aside and they walked into the room beyond.

"The kitchen," Matthew said.

The floor was strewn with debris—broken glass, food wrappings, dry leaves, and dirt; dishes, stacked in a topsy-turvy pile, filled the sink, and mouse droppings dotted the kitchen countertop. The kitchen's bay window had been smashed; someone—she presumed it had been Matthew—had covered the hole with cardboard and duct tape. The tape had lost some of its stickiness and hung limply from one side of the cardboard.

Martha tiptoed through the mess on the floor. She followed Matthew as he crunched his way into another room. She gave a wary glance upward, as she stepped through the doorway crisscrossed with dust-enrobed spider webbing. She was in a dining room.

In the middle of the room, sat a formal dining table with eight straight-backed chairs. To the side, she saw a sideboard—its façade a mosaic of intricately detailed carvings. One of its small doors had been broken off its hinges, and it lay on the floor. Pretty china teacups lay in pieces nearby.

"Royal Albert," Martha said. She picked up a large piece. "Old Country Roses." She smiled as an image of her late grandmother came to mind. *Gramma.* She turned. Matthew was gone. She walked to a doorway at the far end of the room. She looked out.

Matthew was standing near a large fireplace. He turned. He held something in his hands. "One of my trophies," he said. "I was a pretty good hockey player once." He placed the trophy back on the mantle. Martha came closer. "*MVP*," it read.

"Come on," Matthew said. "I'll show you upstairs. My old bedroom is up there."

Martha turned and gave him a cheeky grin. "Oh, I don't know about that," she said. "My Mom told me to *never* go into a boy's bedroom." Her grin deepened. "No matter how nicely he asked me."

Matthew returned to Martha. He took her face in his hands and kissed her—an unhurried kiss, soft and undemanding. He pulled away. "There's a nice bed up there," he said, smiling.

"Oh, well then—that makes all the difference..." Martha said with feigned seriousness. "Mom always said that as long as the boy had a nice bed... "

Matthew laughed. "C'mon."

Martha followed Matthew up the wooden stairs. Several creaked loudly under their weight. Matthew stopped, and pressed his foot up and down on one particularly noisy board. "I always had to avoid this board when I snuck out at night," he said.

"Oh, Matthew. You were bad," Martha said, her voice once more feigning a serious tone. "And why, pray tell, were you sneaking out of your house in the middle of the night?"

"Tailgate parties," he said. "Lots of trucks, lots of beer, lots of music, and lots of girls." He looked at her. "You never went to a tailgate party?"

"Who—me? Oh, never," Martha said, with a sarcastic grin. They had reached the top of the stairs. She followed Matthew down the hallway. He spoke as he walked.

"That's Mom and Dad's room, that's my sister's room, that's the bathroom, that's my brothers' room. And this... " He turned the doorknob and pushed the door open "...this is my room."

Martha stopped at the doorway and peered into the room. It was a typical teenaged boy's room: sport posters on the wall, a few movie stars, a calendar—she couldn't see the year—sport pennants, a shelf with more hockey trophies, another shelf laden with books—pulp novels, mostly—a tall dresser—with its drawers open and clothes hanging out, and a bed.

The bed had a large rounded iron frame headboard and footboard. What surprised Martha the most was that the bed was neatly made, complete with a heavy duvet and pillows. A thin sheet of plastic was atop the bed covers. It was dusty. She looked up at Matthew. "You sleep here often?"

"When I need to—" he said. "This is where I come when I need to escape— The compound, other people's problems, and annoying, bossy women— " He turned and smiled at Martha as he spoke. She punched him lightly in the arm.

"I am not bossy. Annoying, maybe—but never bossy." She grinned at her own joke.

Matthew laughed.

"Help me," he said. He motioned to the other side of the bed. Between them, they folded the plastic sheeting onto itself and laid it on the floor at the foot of the bed.

Matthew left the room and came back with folded pillowcases in his hands. "Here," he said. "I can never put these things on right." Martha accepted the cases. She grabbed the pillows, removed the old pillowcases, and quickly replaced them with the clean ones. She stepped back.

She looked up. Matthew was staring at her. Suddenly, the room felt too close. Her heart began to pound inside her ears, and she felt too hot. She turned and walked to a window. Simple green cotton curtains hung on either side. "Can we open this?" she asked.

Matthew came to the window. He reached above the sash and turned a latch. He slid the window up into the frame. A warm breeze wafted through the opening, moving the curtains as it did.

Martha looked out across the yard. Everything was so silent. So deserted. So strange.

She heard the bikes before she saw them. Instant fear shot up inside her. She drew away from the window and backed into Matthew, up against his hard body. She continued to peer out from behind the curtain. A half dozen big bikes—Harleys, she guessed—roared up the mile road that fronted the farm's property. Matthew put his arms over her shoulders.

"It's okay," he said. "Just a small group. They live around here somewhere. I've seen them before."

Matthew's words, instead of bringing Martha comfort, produced extreme angst in her spirit. Matthew's closeness, his protective arms, made her feel something she had resolved not to feel—weak, vulnerable. She fought with her confused emotions as they tumbled around inside her, each gaining a foothold, and then like a line of retreating soldiers, they fell back. Waiting. For another push forward.

Her desire to be submissive and soft was inhibiting the hardness in her soul—the same hardness that had equipped her to fight off the old man back at the farm, strike Vince, stand up to Brad, and to shoot The Man. She winced. All of her wanted to relax, to rely on Matthew, to let this man take care of her, to protect her. But a part of her—more primal than the emotions of her heart—screamed in protest. To be soft, to be feminine meant losing her edge—her ability to think—to plan—to react under pressure. And to fight.

A new emotion joined in: depression. And on its heels—profound loneliness.

She had lost one man.

How soon before I lose another one? How soon?

Martha turned. Matthew pulled her into his arms. She went into them and snuggled up against his chest. He tightened his arms around her. She breathed in his scent. She wrapped her arms around his waist and hugged him closer.

For a moment, if only for a moment, she would indulge her softer side.

"Hold me, Matthew," she whispered. "Just hold me."

□□□

The Bargain

"LOOK, it just happened." Virgil said. "You said she was your sister. It wasn't like I was stealing your wife or girlfriend."

"But you agree it was stealing?" The Man asked.

"No, I don't. Marion doesn't belong to you."

"But I told you she wasn't available."

"And I heard you. But one thing led to another—it couldn't be helped."

"I disagree with you. And I could shoot you right now for going against my wishes."

"And what good would that do you, huh? What good? We're gearing up to hit Matthew. And you're going to take out your lead man— over a woman? Who isn't even your wife?" Virgil gave The Man a disbelieving look. "Give your head a shake."

The Man sat in sullen silence.

"You've got dozens of women," Virgil continued, "Why is this one so important to you?"

"She just is."

Virgil shook his head in a slow motion of denial. "This is crazy." He slapped his hands down on the armrests of his chair. "Fine," he said. "I'll stay away from her."

The Man drew his hand over his own face, massaging his cheeks as he did. "That's right— You'll stay away from her."

The room was electric with energy as the two men stared at one another.

"Okay," The Man said, breaking the silence. "I'll tell you what. You take down Matthew, get control of his compound, and Marion will be my gift to you." The Man paused. "A carrot on the end of a stick—a little something to encourage your success. What do you say?"

"I think you are comparing me to a donkey. And I don't like it."

"That's not at all what I meant," The Man said, with a flip of his hand in the air. "Get that thought out of your head." He placed his hands *palm down on his knees, and he leaned forward.* "C'mon, what do you say?"

"What's the opposite side of the coin?"

"You mean if you don't take down Matthew and get his compound?"

"Yeah?"

"A bullet to the brain. Does that sound fair?"

"Whose brain?"

"That, my friend, remains to be seen."

Virgil rose. "Don't worry. Matthew is going down. I'll be back for Marion."

Chapter Forty-Nine
The New Outlaws

METEOR LOOKED around the campground. He stood near the picnic shelter; it was just up from the path that led down to the river. The deciduous trees had begun to turn color, as summer rusted silently into fall.

A large flock of Canada geese flew overhead in a ragged V-formation. Meteor watched as the first feathered leader fell behind and a new leader flew into position. He looked toward the riverbank. He hadn't been back to the campground since the night he and Martha had first gotten together. He smiled at the memory.

The sound of bikes roused him and he looked to his left. He checked his watch—right on time. Very few people were aware of the impromptu meeting, but those who knew were eager to hear what he would have to say. And he had a lot to say.

Things had changed between Meteor and The Man. Meteor had managed to maintain his undercover status. His charm had kept The Man believing in his loyalty, but Virgil was an obstacle to any long-term security. Virgil had never believed that Meteor had switched sides. And Virgil had become very dangerous.

Meteor had watched as Virgil drew men to him—men trained in combat and killing. Meteor knew luck was running out—for himself, and for Matthew. As he thought about the compound and Matthew's men, he realized that the Gatekeeper would soon be outgunned; Matthew was going to need help.

Meteor made a decision. He went off on his own—but not completely on his own—he still had friends. Like the ones pulling into the campground.

The bikes filed in, one after the other. Unlike The Man's gang, these motorcyclists were not festooned in colors. Some had patches, like the Christian bikers, but most wore ordinary clothes— hunting jackets and hiking boots.

Meteor stood and waved as the bikes rumbled in. In a few minutes, the large picnic area was covered in motorcycles and their riders. Maybe a hundred of them.

Meteor smiled.

Meteor took a position on top of one of the central picnic tables. Men clustered around. Many were familiar to him; many were not, but all had one thing in common—they were their own men—with their own stubbornly held beliefs, and one of those beliefs was that The Man's army was not for them. These men kept to themselves and only ventured out from their secret homes and hideaways at the behest of another independent biker's call for assistance. These men were the new outlaws. It was a coveted status—one they would fight to keep.

"What's up, Meteor?" called a tall man. He was native with ebony hair braided neatly into a single braid that hung down his back. The First Nations people, with their mineral resources, had often had skirmishes with The Man. They had succeeded in holding him off, but each attack was getting harder to repel.

"Hey, Richard," Meteor said. "How they hanging?"

Richard laughed. "Just fine."

The last engine was shut off, and the men assembled in front of Meteor.

"Okay," shouted a man. "What's this about?"

Meteor drew a long breath. "Here's how I see things working. The Gatekeeper did a great job of taking down the man a few months back. Destroyed a lot of his trucks and killed many of his men. The man took a bullet, too, thanks to a friend of mine." He paused. "But the man's forces are back up in strength—in fact, they're stronger than ever. The general in charge is a guy named Virgil. He used to be buddies with Matthew. They had a falling out and Virgil has had it in for Matthew ever since.

"I've been a full-patched member—undercover—in the man's army for several months. I got out of there before Virgil killed me. I'm still connected to some of the gang's friendlies—so I'm still getting inside information. Part of that information is that the man is planning to attack the Gatekeeper— Soon.

"You guys all know of Matthew— You know he's always been fair to you. I don't think he has the muscle to protect his people. He maintains a patrol on the Hutterites' land, and his main camp is always guarded, but he's got a second camp now— His forces will be very thin once they're split up." He caught a quick breath.

"The Man knows about the second camp. What's worse is that he knows that Matthew has oil in underground tanks in the second camp. You know oil will be more valuable than gold since every engine needs oil. Matthew has been stockpiling oil for years. The second campsite is sitting on black gold— Pardon the expression. Now the man wants it." He paused again.

"You know you'll be needing oil, too. Getting it from Matthew will be a damn sight easier than getting the man to share. So, how about it? Are you guys ready to help Matthew?"

"You're talking war, Meteor," Richard said. "We—" he waved his arm around, "—we've been trying to avoid war."

"I know. But it's necessary. If the man isn't stopped—and he takes Matthew's camps—he'll also gain control of the Hutterites' farm." He paused and gave the men a searching look. "How many of you depend upon the Hutterites for food?"

The men murmured. Meteor continued.

"So, what do you say?"

"War means organization and leaders. Who's going to lead us, Meteor?" asked a blond man with a full long beard, complete with bushy muttonchops.

Meteor straightened up. "I will."

"Since when is Meteor an army general?" Richard asked. "I've known you for a long time. You've never wanted to lead anything."

"This time is different. I've got knowledge about the man. And Matthew's camp, too."

"This wouldn't have anything to do with a woman, would it?" Richard asked.

"What if it did?"

Richard laughed. "Ah—it does have something to do with a woman." His fist shot up into the air. "I'm in. I'll fight with any guy who's putting his life on the line for a woman." The men laughed.

Meteor gave a quick grin and then he became serious again. "By a show of hands, will you accept me as your leader?" He waited.

A man standing near Meteor broke the silence. "Okay, so maybe you'll lead us—but what do we do about guns and ammunition? We don't have any extra lying around."

"Good question," Meteor said. "Matthew has a well-stocked weapons storehouse. We'll get the ammunition from him."

"And fuel?" asked another man.

Meteor nodded. "Yes, fuel, too."

Another man spoke.

"How many of us do you see here, Meteor? And how many guys does The Man have?" The speaker was an older man, well respected among them. He drew his arm across the crowd. "We're all worried about The Man too, but if we go off half-cocked, we'll just wind up turning our own women into widows." He folded his arms across his chest, as he finished speaking.

"A pocket of resistance," Meteor said. "Not a full army. A special force. We come in behind Matthew's troops. As a back-up. A surprise attack. No one will be expecting us. That gives us strength." He gave the men an earnest look. "It's been done in history. It can be done again."

"A lot of dead bodies in history," the older man replied.

"A lot of enslavement, too," Meteor said. "How long before The Man takes over your world, takes your women, takes your freedom?" He paused. "If we don't unite and do something about him—now, before his forces get too large—we're sunk. It'll only be a matter of time."

The older man unfolded his arms. He gave a small nod. "Okay," he said. "I'm in."

"And the rest of you?" Meteor asked.

All the hands went up.

Meteor studied the men standing in front of him. He waited. No one else asked anything further.

"Okay," he said. "Here's the plan."

The Dead Mentor

THE MAN pulled the large book from the shelf. A photo fell to the floor; he picked it up and carried it, with the book, back to his desk. He sat, leaned forward, and flipped the book open. It fell open easily. He read:

"The psyche of the broad masses does not respond to anything weak or halfway. Like a woman, whose spiritual sensitiveness is determined less by abstract reason than by an indefinable emotional longing for fulfilling power and who, for that reason, prefers to submit to the strong rather than the weakling—the mass, too, prefers the ruler to a pleader."

Parts of the passage had been underlined: <u>anything weak</u>; <u>Like a woman</u>; <u>fulfilling power</u>; <u>submit to the strong</u>; <u>prefers the ruler.</u>

The Man ran his finger down the rippled page as he read, then he closed the book; he trailed his fingers down its cover, now ravaged by years of ownership and reading. Voracious reading. Part of the book jacket had torn away: "...ein Kampf," it read.

Beneath the title, was written, in perfect cursive handwriting: "<u>MY</u> Struggle." He opened the book to the inside page. A short essay, written in pencil, and in the same handwriting, ran the length of the white space.

"Possession, ownership, and control," it read. "Trust others at your peril. Never let the left hand know what the right hand is capable of." The text continued, never wavering from the fine, cursive penmanship. "A secret will only ever be safe with one man, and one man only."

The Man reached for the photo lying next to his hand. He picked up the black and white image, and studied it. He reached for his steel pocket lighter.

"Fool," he said. "Weak. You could have had it all. You didn't know how to keep a secret. You deserved to die."

The Man flipped the lighter's lid. Holding the photograph by one corner, he lit an opposite corner. He watched as a tiny flame licked upward, toward the face of a man—a man infamous for the murder of millions of innocents. The photograph disintegrated into delicate gray cinders.

The Man dropped a smoldering bit into a large glass ashtray. Then he opened a desk drawer. He drew out a large, clear plastic container filled with small brightly colored items. He pulled back its tight, red lid. He reached in and picked up one of the items ...and then another...and another. Children's toys...

Mickey Mouse with a bugle in his hand.

Mickey Mouse with his thick, white-gloved hands raised in welcome.

Mickey Mouse with a top hat.

A sound from the hallway drew The Man's attention. He swept the figurines off his desktop and back into their container, closed the lid, and shoved the box into the drawer.

"What?" he said, as he slammed the drawer shut.

"A messenger from the South Camps to see you," was a man's reply.

"Send him in."

"It's a her."

"Send HER in."

The messenger backed out the door.

In a moment, a woman entered the room. Raven black hair, blue eyes, and soft lips. She was in her mid forties—she would have been attractive except for the wide, ragged, red scar that cut a swath across the left side of her face, ending at her jaw-line.

The Man spoke quickly. "What are you doing here?"

"He wants to meet with you." *The Man held a finger to his lips and motioned for the woman to close the door. She closed it.*

"I told him NO communications of any kind. That I would come to him when the time was right."

"Look, don't get mad at me— I'm only his messenger," *she said, her voice husky with anger.* "You know I'd never go against you. But you left me down there."

The Man rose and walked over to the woman. She took a small step backwards, but he grabbed her arm. Her eyes never left his.

"YOU left me there—" *she blurted.* "He tells me what to do now—"

The Man glared. He spoke, his tone iced with anger.

"Go back. Tell him that he is never to do this again. I'll come there when I'm ready." *He released his grasp on her and gave her a small shove.* "You got that? When—I'm—ready..."

The woman blinked. "I have never done anything to make you distrust me—." *She paused.* "—not even when I was married to you. Don't forget that."

"Get out of here."

The woman left the room.

Chapter Fifty

A Marriage of Convenience

THEY SAT together in Matthew's old bedroom. Martha was sitting at a small metal desk. Matthew sat on the bed. They munched on nuts and chocolate chips, and drank from bottles of orange juice that Matthew had taken from a metal trunk tucked under the bed.

Noonday sun poured in through the open window, making the room oppressively hot. Martha wiped sweat from her brow. She pulled off her light over-shirt, wiped her face and her neck, and then threw it to the floor. She cupped a handful of chocolate chips and shoved them into her mouth, reveling in the silken sweetness on her tongue. She smiled. The cozy room had become a womb: safe and comforting. She felt her spirit nestle into its warmth. She took a long, slow breath.

"Tell me about the boy who occupied this room," she said.

Matthew told her more about his time in high school, his years in college, and his short time in the military.

"Where did the money come from to build the compound?" Martha asked.

Matthew sighed. "The Canadian government," he said.

"What?"

"My dad was a member of CSIS. He worked covert operations. He'd get sent to places like Bosnia, Afghanistan, Paris, Dubai. He'd be gone for weeks—sometimes months. Our family never knew what he was doing, but

we knew what he was. Mom hated it when he left, but he always returned—
Except for one time."

Martha's eyes softened. "And...?"

"It was after the Toronto debacle—after some guy found a CD with
highly secret CSIS information on it—inside a phone booth."

"A phone booth? I don't know what you're talking about."

"One of my dad's colleagues 'misplaced' the disk," he said. "She was
relocating from Ottawa to Toronto. She was carrying the disk with her
when she stopped to make a phone call. The disk apparently fell out. A
person found it. He turned it over to CSIS. Then all hell broke loose. Dad
was called in to investigate. That was back in 1996. He stayed with it, and
then toward the end of 1998, he said he'd found something out. He left. He
never came home.

"A few weeks later, Mom got a phone call. She broke down. She
cried for days. I was already handling our family's finances, so I got a shock
when I logged on to our bank account. There was a lot of money there."

"A lot?"

"Over two million dollars."

"Oh."

"Dad and I had already done so much work on the survival camp,
and the year 2000 was coming, I figured I'd put the money to good use. My
buddies and I bought supplies—guns, ammunition—and oil."

"Oil? What oil?"

"The second camp. It's full of oil. The tanks are underground, but
the oil derricks are all above ground—very visible. I'm getting nervous.
That's why I've built the living quarters. I want people there—guards living
on site."

"Oh," Martha said. The soft word was a huge understatement to
what she was actually feeling— Matthew never failed to amaze her.

Matthew rose from the bed. He walked over to Martha. He bent and
pulled her to her feet. "Can we stop talking now?"

"Just one more question."

Matthew scowled. "Okay, one more."

"Were you ever married?"

"No, but I almost was." He reached behind her and pulled opened
the desk's thin drawer. He rummaged around and withdrew a snapshot.
He handed it to her. "That's her."

Martha studied the photograph and the petite brunette woman that
smiled back at her. "She's pretty. Who's that with her?"

"Virgil."

"But they're holding hands."

"Yep— Things change," Matthew said. He took the photograph, dropped it into the drawer, and slammed it shut. "No more questions," he said.

Matthew pulled Martha to him—gently, hesitantly. She felt his warmth through the faded flannel shirt he always wore, and the outline of his muscled chest as he pressed himself to her. Heat swept over her, drawing a loud sigh from her lips. He kissed her, softly at first, and then more deeply. Martha kissed him back, moving her lips beneath his, an invitation for more.

Martha felt a familiar urgency escalate inside her, and she tried to remember the last time she had made love. She didn't resist as Matthew lowered them both to the bed. Her mind drifted as her body slipped unimpeded toward a more primal, uninhibited state of being. Matthew pulled at her tank top, pushing it up and over her head. His fingers found her bare flesh, and she moaned.

Martha thought about Josef for just a moment, but his visage was fading. She could no longer see his face as clearly as she had before. She directed her emotions to the man bent over her. She closed her eyes on the memory.

"Matthew," she whispered, as though seeking confirmation of his presence. She moved her body under his hands, willing him to touch her, more intensely, more deeply. His warm hand slid up her belly to her bra; it slipped beneath the fabric and closed on her breast—warm on warm, calloused on soft. Matthew made a sound deep in his chest. It was a good sound. Martha answered with a soft sigh.

Finally. Finally.

Martha tugged at Matthew's shirt, freeing it from the waistband of his jeans. Matthew drew back, and with one hand unfastened the buttons. One by one. Martha watched, transfixed. She had seen his naked chest before, but this... unveiling... was making her breath come in quick gasps. Heat flooded her cheeks and, for a moment, she felt foolish.

Young.

Almost virginal.

His shirt was open now, and Martha flattened her hands against his chest. Warm. So warm. A small cry rose up from the back of her throat, unbidden, and surprising. She met his eyes. He was watching her. Intently.

What was he seeing? Did he like what he was seeing?

The thought vanished as Matthew's mouth came down upon hers, hard. His tongue moved between her lips. Martha opened her mouth to receive him.

She could feel him, hard and insistent upon her thigh. She wanted to be out of her clothes. She wanted to feel his body. Feel his skin. Next to hers. Warm on hers. She wanted to feel him. Inside her. She made a soft sound and closed her eyes.

Matthew drew back. Martha opened her eyes and stared back at him. Her heart pounded its staccato tune in her ears. So loudly, that she barely heard his words.

"Let's get out of our clothes, Martha."

She sat up, and tugged at her clothing, tossing the pieces to the floor. She turned and watched as Matthew rid himself of his clothing, too. He lay back on the bed. Martha joined him.

Matthew gripped her naked body and pulled her to him. Martha felt her body respond to his hands. Her nipples hardened under his touch, and her thighs parted. She shivered as he ran his hand down her side, onto her thigh, and then between her legs. She cried out as he touched her, his fingers moving over her moistness, and then they began to probe. Martha wriggled toward Matthew, aching for him to touch her deeper.

He did.

The release came so suddenly, too suddenly. Her nails dug deeply into the flesh of his shoulders. She cried out as wave upon wave rushed through her. She shuddered.

Moments later, she opened her eyes. Matthew was looking at her. She studied his face, the lines, the crevasses, and the darkness around his eyes. Martha raised her fingers and trailed them down his cheek, tracing the line from his eye down to the corner of his mouth, and over the scar, where a small smile had begun. She smiled back. She drew him down to her and kissed him.

The kiss was long and comforting, but Matthew ended it when he pulled away. He nudged her legs apart. "My turn," he said.

Martha began positioning herself for his entry. A memory of Josef flashed into her mind—their wedding night. *Wedding.* Martha felt a hitch in her spirit, and she put a restraining hand on Matthew's chest.

"Wait, Matthew."

Matthew was breathing hard, but he pulled back in surprise. "What is it?" he asked gently.

"I - I - can't have sex with you."

Matthew looked perplexed. "What? Why not?"

Martha blushed. She held his face between her hands. "I want to. I really do. But—"

"But—what?"

"I've never had sex with a man I wasn't married to," she blurted out. She stared at him, her eyes soft and pleading.

Matthew groaned. "Martha," he said. "Why now?"

"I thought I could, Matthew. I thought I could. I really did."

Matthew rolled over on his back. He sighed. "What about Meteor?"

Martha cringed at the question, but she answered it, an edge of hardness in her voice. "I told you I never had sex with Meteor."

"Never?"

"No. Never."

"Why not?"

"I couldn't."

"Because you weren't married to him?"

"No."

"Then why?"

Martha took a long breath. "Because he wasn't—*you*."

Matthew turned to her. "Oh," he said simply. He smiled. "So, do I have to marry you to have sex with you?"

Martha nodded, apologetically. Then she brightened. "But we can do other things," she said.

"Other things?"

"Yeah—other things," Martha said with a sly smile.

"And you'd be okay with *other things*?"

"Yes." She sat up.

"You are a strange woman, Martha."

She flattened her hand against his naked chest and drew it down toward his belly. She bent and kissed his mouth. She moved lower, dropping kisses, dragging the tip of her tongue as she proceeded down his body. Matthew shuddered when she reached his navel. Her hand moved up his thigh to the soft flesh between, and finally came to rest on his hardness. She began to stroke him. He groaned.

Matthew reached down and grabbed her shoulders. "Wait," he said.

Martha looked up. Surprise and concern filled her eyes. "Why?"

"I don't want the other ways," he said.

Martha crawled up and sat beside him, with her back to the headboard. Bewilderment made her go silent.

"I meant—maybe some other time—just not now," Matthew added. Martha turned to face him.

"But, I can't, Matthew. I just can't— It doesn't feel right for me."

"Because we aren't married," he confirmed.

Martha blushed again. "Yes," she said hesitantly.

"Do you love me, Martha?"

She didn't answer.

"Do you love me?"

"Yes." Her voice was soft and low. "But... " she shook her head.

"But what?"

"You don't love me... "

"When have I ever said that?" Matthew asked. He sat up. "That I don't love you?"

"Never. But you've never said you love me, either." Martha drew her eyebrows together. She bent toward him slightly, "Do you?"

Matthew sat quietly and regarded her. Martha watched his eyes. Beautiful eyes. Dark eyes. She reached over and touched his face again, running her fingers down his cheek over his scar.

"You never did tell me how you got that," she said.

"Yes."

"Yes?"

"Yes. I love you, Martha."

Martha smiled. Her heart swelled, but a sliver of distrust poked its way into her mind. "Why did you have to think about it so long?"

"I wasn't thinking about whether I loved you—I knew I loved you. I was thinking about something else."

"What?"

"Marrying you."

"Huh?" Martha looked genuinely confused.

"Yes. Will you marry me?"

Martha smiled, wide and warm. She gave a short laugh. "How will we get married? I don't know of any pastors. And moving-in day... " She wrinkled her nose. "...it just lacks something."

Matthew was silent for a moment.

"Why can't God marry us?" he asked.

Martha sat back so hard that she hit her head on the iron headboard. "Ow," she said, as she rubbed her head.

"Why not?" Matthew asked again.

"Is this a trick?" Martha asked.

"A trick?" Matthew raised his eyebrows in surprise. Then he smiled. "Oh—you mean so that I can get you to have sex with me."

Martha nodded.

"No—it's not a trick." Matthew reached for Martha and pulled her into his arms. "If you're open to it, I'll marry you right now. Before God."

Martha snuggled into his chest. She loved the feel of his arms wrapped around her.

Marry him? Before God. Would that work? Would that be acceptable?

As if reading her thoughts, Matthew spoke again, "I mean who married Adam and Eve?" He paused. "God, right?"

Martha pulled away. She pushed herself up and looked into his face. "Then ask me properly."

Matthew waved an arm across his body. "I'm naked here, Martha."

She giggled. "Ask me."

Matthew smiled. He let go of her and got up on his knees. He took her hands in his. "Martha, before God, will you marry me?"

Martha studied the face before her, checking it for veracity, for sincerity. It was there, in his eyes. She smiled. "I love you Matthew. I've loved you for so long. Yes, I'll marry you."

"I love you, too, Martha. And I will take you as my wife. To have and to hold. In richer and in poorer." He grimaced. "Can we skip the stupid vows?"

Martha laughed. "Oh, yes— I don't think I can stomach the 'obey' part, anyway."

Matthew pulled Martha close to him. He looked up. "God, we're here. And we've agreed. So, in your sight, we are now man and wife." He waited. "I think that's it."

Martha mumbled into his chest.

"What?"

She pulled her head back. "A ring. I need a ring."

"I don't have a ring," he said. "Can we do this without a ring?"

"No, Matthew—we can't. I want a visual reminder of our union."

Matthew sighed. "Okay," he said. "I'll get you a ring— Tomorrow."

Martha smiled. "I don't like garish rings. Just a nice band with diamonds."

Matthew nodded.

"Good diamonds," she added.

"Wait a minute." Matthew jumped up. He went to a bookcase and fumbled around. He came back with a cigar box. He opened it and pulled out a ring. It was thick and wide, with a bright green stone. "My high school ring," he said. "I'll give you this—until I can get you another ring."

Martha took the ring. She moved Josef's wedding band to her right hand. Matthew's ring was far too big for her ring finger, so she pushed it onto her index finger, where it fit. She held her hand out before her and admired the ring. "I don't need another ring," she murmured. "I like this one just fine."

"So... " Matthew began, as he ran his hand along her side.

Martha laughed. "So, that *WAS* your plan."

Matthew threw back his head and laughed. He stopped laughing. "I love you, Martha. I've married you." Matthew pushed her down on the pillows. "And now—I want my wife." He kissed her gently. Then with insistence.

"Matthew, I... " Martha sat up.

"What now?"

"I'm really nervous. It's been a long time."

"Me, too," he said.

Martha looked puzzled. "Not Cammy?"

"Nope."

"Anna?"

"Nope."

"Oh."

"And..." Matthew added, "... I know about you and Meteor. He told me."

"What?" Martha asked with genuine surprise.

"He told me that you stopped him— Both times."

"He did?"

"Yeah, he did. Yesterday." He smiled. "Now can we stop talking about other people?" Matthew nuzzled her breast while he slid his hand up her leg. He pulled back and looked into her eyes. "Let's try this again."

A sharp cry escaped her, this time one of pain. She had grown tight and he was in such a hurry. Soon the fire of contact was replaced with a pulsing need. She raised her hips to meet him.

Matthew grabbed her shoulders roughly, stiffened, and then he grunted—a low rumble that erupted in force from the back of his throat.

Martha remembered the sound—the explosive kind that only a man can make. It made her own senses collide and a new wave of pleasure swept over her—more powerful, more complete than the first. She rose to accept his final thrusts. As she did so, she felt a piece of herself break away, and another part of her come to life.

"Matthew..." she said softly.

"Sh..." he whispered into her ear. "I know."

□□□

The Understanding

"HE WANTS them all dead," Virgil said. "Kill every male. But save the females—especially the little girls."

"Understood," said the captain, a burly man dressed in full military gear. The men standing near him murmured their understanding and their agreement.

"But don't kill Matthew if you come across him. Bring him back to The Man." Virgil paused, and then added, "Oh, yeah—don't kill any babies, or little boys—The Man thinks a few of those kids might be his."

Laughter echoed around the room.

Virgil waited for the laughter to die down. "All of us attack the first camp. Then you—" Virgil pointed to a group of men to his right. "—guys are going with me. We're going after the second camp. If my guess is correct— Matthew will assume the oil is our primary goal. And he'll be right, but The Man wants Matthew's compound taken first."

"You know where the second camp is now?" asked the burly captain."

"Yes," Virgil replied. "Off highway 44, on the Alexander Indian Reserve."

"Near Sandy Lake?"

"Yes."

"Lots of oil derricks there."

The men murmured.

"By the way," Virgil added, "there's a woman named Martha—the one who shot The Man." The men made derisive comments in recognition of the name. "Take her to Brad if you find her." Brad waved and smiled from where he stood in a corner of the bar. "Whatever you do, don't kill her, either. They have plans for her."

The men guffawed.

"Also—once we capture Matthew's compound—Brad becomes the new Gatekeeper." Virgil looked in Brad's direction. Brad smiled again and gave a small bow.

More murmurs of agreement, but not as many as before.

"When?" the burly captain asked. "When do we move?"

"That information will be given to you at the last second. The Man is worried about a leak in our group, so he'll give the word only minutes before we are to leave. So, stay prepared."

"Where's Meteor?" one of the men asked.

"Not sure." Virgil shrugged. "Haven't seen him in a while."

"He's been gone for a couple of days," the man advised.

Virgil glowered. "Meteor is the least of your concerns— Worry about the Gatekeeper, instead. Matthew has a strong army. And powerful weapons—thanks to Cammy. Big guns, remember? Worry about facing that action."

Once more, the men agreed.

Virgil stretched and arched his back. "We're done here."

The men filed out of the building.

A LONE BIKER left through the back of the bar. He straddled his motorcycle and roared away.

Meteor looked up as the biker approached. The biker stopped near him.

"It's not good—" the biker said. He still sat atop his bike, but he had shut down the engine. "They're ready. And they know the location of the second camp."

"Who told them?"

"Not exactly sure, but I think it's the kid that's been hanging around the clubhouse."

"The kid?"

"Yeah, the one from Matthew's camp. The kid with the orange hair."

Chapter Fifty-One

The Warning

MATTHEW TURNED the truck off the highway and onto the bumpy road where he had taken Martha a few weeks earlier. He pulled the truck into the same spot where they had parked before.

"Does Meteor already know about this place?" Martha asked.

"Yeah. We've been meeting here for months."

They waited near the pond, hand-in-hand, and then turned at the sound of a truck engine. Soon, they saw Meteor walking up the trail.

"Hi," he said. He strode up to Martha and pulled her into his arms. Martha's eyes went wide. "May I kiss the bride?"

Matthew laughed. "Have at 'er."

Meteor gave Martha a soft, warm kiss—on the forehead. Then he pushed her away from him. He stared at her. She saw something in his blue eyes—something she couldn't identify. She had seen that something before—it made her heart ache.

Meteor reached over and clasped Matthew around the shoulders. "Well, old man," he said. "It's time to get off your ass. 'Cause the man is gunnin' for it."

The trio sat down on the bank. Meteor stretched out his legs, and rubbed the one that had been shot the day he met Martha.

"Still bothers you," she observed.

"Only when I'm awake," Meteor said with an exaggerated, pained expression.

"Sorry to hear that," Martha said with a mischievous smile. "You're lucky that's the only memento you have from that day."

Meteor glanced at her, his eyes warm. "Got your car back?" he asked.

"What?"

"I understand you had to abandon it on the side of the road." Meteor's eyes sparkled.

Martha sat quietly for a moment. Suddenly, she twigged to what he was saying. She jabbed him in the ribs with her elbow. "Yes, thank you— It's safe and sound."

"So?" Matthew asked. "What's going on?"

Meteor turned to his friend.

"Virgil has another team ready, Matthew. And, according to my inside guy, they're mean. And they're ready to move." He looked across the pond while contemplating his next words. "His guys are good—really good."

"Where's Brad in all this?" Matthew asked.

"Like shit on a stick," Meteor replied. "He's tight."

Martha made a sound of dismissal. "What an asshole."

"Yeah, maybe he is, Martha, but he knows how to play his cards." Meteor turned back to Matthew. "He takes over when the man ousts you, Matthew."

"I see—"

"Virgil figured that once they take over the compound, they'll put Brad in charge. He'll continue the Hutterite patrols. Just like before. Virgil's not stupid. He's not about to kill the golden goose."

"No— Virgil is anything but stupid," Matthew agreed.

"As for your camp, the man figures this is the perfect time to hit you. Your storehouses are filled with food and supplies for the winter."

"That lazy bastard!" Martha said. "After all the work we've done, he just wants to come in and take it?"

Meteor nodded. "He also figures that clean women will be the way to go. I think he's had an STD before, so he's really careful. He plans to keep women in your camp, like... " He searched for a word, "... like puppy mills. He plans to sell them down the road."

"Prostitution?" Martha asked. "He wants to be a pimp?"

Meteor took a deep breath. "It's a little more than that. More like a sex baron. He figures pretty women—clean women—will always have value. Money doesn't have any value. Nobody gives a damn about jewels."

He glanced at Martha and smiled. "Well except for you. Nice ring," he said, indicating Matthew's ring on her hand.

"Thank you," Martha said. "Keep talking."

"He says the world is going to begin running out of the three 'F's. So, he'll trade women—for fuel, food, and firearms. He figures he can do that for many years. He doesn't care what happens after that."

Martha caught Matthew's eye. His expression was hard.

Meteor continued, "What's worse is that your compound is full of children."

Martha drew back in shock. "What?"

Meteor held up his hand. "No—I don't think the man's into kids, but he figures that the only way to guarantee a *clean* woman is to raise her up from a little girl. And the younger—the better."

"That's disgusting," Martha said. "He'll have to come through me to get to my little Mary."

Meteor made a sound—a hollow humorless laugh. "He plans to do exactly that."

"How many men?" Matthew asked.

"In the hundreds. Maybe close to a thousand."

"No, I mean the highly trained ones."

"Um—maybe fifty."

"That's a lot," Matthew mused. "A single well-trained man can do a lot of damage."

"They're promised perks, too," Meteor said. "They get to be land owners. They'll get control over the small farms, the towns, and Hutterite colonies that the man controls now. Some of them will be given a woman. Maybe even an entire harem."

Martha made a sound of disgust. "That would be the day that I would ever be part of some man's harem."

Both men looked at her with bemused smiles.

"Oh—" she said. She blushed.

Meteor threw a stone he had been holding into the pond. It made a small plunking sound as it hit the water. "He knows all about your oil. And he wants it."

"I knew that was coming," Matthew said. "How much time do you think we have?"

Meteor shook his head. "Maybe a week. Maybe a day. I don't know. Your guess is as good as mine."

"How do you know all this, Meteor?" Martha asked. "You aren't even in The Man's camp anymore."

"I know. But I have friends—and one of them likes me better than he likes the man. He keeps me posted."

"Of course, you do," Martha said, with a grin.

Matthew pushed his cap back and rubbed his forehead with his closed fist. He pulled his cap back. "Okay. I'll put the troops into position now. The guys are going to have to eat and sleep guard duty."

"There's something else," Meteor said.

"Can I take any more?"

"You'll like this—" Meteor said with a conspiratorial grin. "I've put together a little army of my own."

Martha stared at Meteor with surprise. "You've done what?"

"I have a lot of friends who aren't allied with anyone. I called them together. They've agreed to back you up. But they need weapons, ammunition, and fuel." He paused and looked at Matthew. "I told them you'd supply them."

Matthew stared at Meteor.

Meteor lowered his eyebrows. "Will that be a problem?"

Matthew began to laugh. "You wouldn't consent to being my Second, but you're okay with pulling together your own army."

"Yeah, well... "

"Gotta love ya, Meteor," Matthew said, as he clapped his friend warmly on the back. "Tell your guys to come tonight—they'll get what they need."

Meteor nodded. "Not sure how soon that'll be. Might be in the wee hours of the morning."

"Not a problem—" Matthew assured him. "We'll be ready for you."

The trio stared ahead and watched geese paddle lazily around the pond. Suddenly, Meteor slapped his thighs. "Gotta go," he said. He rose and winced when he put his weight on his leg. "Getting too old for this sitting around ponds stuff," he said.

Both Martha and Matthew laughed at his signature humor.

The three of them walked up the path to the trucks. Meteor went to his vehicle. Martha walked with him. He opened the door. He put his foot into the cab, and then turned back to her.

Our deal, he mouthed.

Martha smiled—a soft, sweet smile.

Meteor smiled back, got in, and closed the door. He rolled the window down, leaned through it, and called out, "Take care of her, Matthew—the man is gunning for her, too." He looked at Martha. "Be careful, sweetheart."

"Thank you," Martha said with a quick smile. "You too, Meteor." She waved and walked around the back of Matthew's truck. She got in and closed the door.

An uncomfortable feeling—a kind of panic—crept into her heart; Martha suddenly wished she had kissed Meteor good-bye. She wondered when she would see him again. And when she did—would he be dead or alive? She grabbed the door handle. But it was too late. Meteor had already pulled away and was heading back up the road.

A sudden wave of loneliness washed over her, and tears pricked her eyes.

Stay safe, Meteor. Please stay safe.

□□□

The Assassins

"YOU DON'T really want to go back to him, do you?" Trojan asked.

"No— But I'm really afraid now," Cammy answered. "I know him. He probably thinks I'm a traitor—that I was one right from the beginning."

"But you're safe here."

"No—" she said. She gave him a grave look. "I've got a bad feeling. I don't think I'll ever be safe again—at least until he's dead."

"Well, what if we try to kill him?"

"You say that like you're going to bake a pie. Guards and bodyguards surround him. You're not going to get to him."

"No— Maybe not. But you could."

"Are you crazy? Martha said he ordered my execution. They'd kill me on sight."

Trojan reached over and pulled Cammy in close to him. "Yeah, you're right." He hugged her and kissed her cheek. "I love you."

Cammy pulled away in surprise. "What? What did you say?" She gave a nervous laugh.

Trojan raised his eyebrows in surprise. "I love you." He gave a little nervous laugh, too. "Why is that so surprising?"

"Your timing. We were just talking about murdering a guy."

"Oh. That. Well—anyway—I love you."

"You do? Really?"

"Yeah. You're pretty easy to love."

"I am?"

"Cammy? You're kidding me, right? You knew I loved you."

Tears shone in the woman's eyes. "No—" she said, "I didn't."

"Well— I do." Trojan gave her a crooked grin.

Cammy went quiet. Then she looked up, "Let's do it," she said.

"Do what?" Trojan asked—a guarded look in his eyes.

"Let's get The Man."

"Now who's crazy?"

"We can come and go as we please. We've got a truck. We've got plenty of weapons. Let's be an army of two."

"Oh, that's a plan—" Trojan said, his voice tinged with in sarcasm.

"Why not?"

"Why not?" he echoed.

"Yeah, why not?"

Trojan paused. "I don't know." He studied Cammy's face. "Okay," he said simply. "Let's do it."

Cammy leaned into his arms and kissed him—more fully and more passionately than she ever had before.

Trojan kissed her back and then pulled away. He smiled, a wide smile that caused multiple creases to form near the corners of his eyes.

"Let's plan to kill people more often," he said.

Chapter Fifty-Two

The Taking of the Camp

THE MEETING HOUSE was crammed with noisy men. Matthew called for order. The men settled down.

"It's time," he said. "We're going into full battle mode." He handed out sheets of paper to a half dozen men standing near him. Among them were Simon, Thomas, Jonah, and the pony-tailed captain. "Here's how I've broken up the troops," Matthew said.

Each captain studied the sheet handed to him. The captains conversed, nodded, read, conversed a bit more, and then looked back at Matthew. The pony-tailed captain was the first to speak.

"How soon do we put our boys into position?"

"Right away," Matthew said. "We can't wait. Meteor said The Man is ready— His attack can come at any time." Matthew paused. "I have to risk an educated guess here. I suspect The Man will send the majority of his men to the second camp. He's hot for the oil. So, I'm going to send the strongest force and many of the weapons over there.

"We'll strengthen the guards on the Hutterites' perimeter, too. Set up some of the bigger guns. And speaking of guns—" he paused for effect, and added, "—Meteor now has his own army."

A stir went around the room as the men reacted to the unexpected news. Matthew held up his hand.

"It's true. I've promised to arm them—and give them fuel. They'll be here sometime tonight or tomorrow morning. Early."

Matthew nodded to Simon. "You're in charge of that detail. Equip our guys first, and then put someone in charge of taking care of Meteor's men when they get here."

Simon gave Matthew his most serious take-charge look. "Yes, sir. You can count on me."

The next captain to speak up was Thomas. "Um— Matthew. You've put me in charge of this camp, but you haven't left me a lot of men. That concerns me."

"I know—but the women are here," Matthew replied. "Most of them are well trained with guns. I think you and the men I've assigned to you— along with the women's assistance—should be able to hold the camp. As I said, I'm guessing that the assault on this camp will be small."

Thomas gave Matthew a long look. "Okay," he said. His voice was thick with misgiving.

"Hey, you'll have Martha," Jonah said brightly. The men roared with laughter. Thomas relaxed and laughed, too.

Matthew waited for the men to quiet before he addressed the captains again. "Get your men into shifts. Whatever you do, keep up your guard. If somebody is found sleeping on their watch—punish them." He held up his hand as the captains began to ask for clarification. "Don't ask— just make it clear that they stay awake—or they face consequences."

"Where the heck is Trojan?" the pony-tailed captain asked, glancing around the room.

"Don't know," Thomas said. "Haven't seen him or Cammy since yesterday."

"Should this concern us?" the captain asked.

Simon shook his head. "I don't think so. Trojan and Cammy have been loyal to us." He turned. "Matthew?"

"Don't worry about those two— They'll turn up." Matthew waved his hand in dismissal. He looked around the room. "I'm done," he said. "Go do your jobs."

Matthew watched as the men filed out of the Meeting House. He looked out the window. Simon was already taking charge—he motioned for some of the men to follow him to the Munitions Storehouse. Matthew slumped down into a chair. He leaned his head into his hands.

He was still sitting that way when the door opened. A figure walked into the room.

"Matthew?" Martha asked. "Are you okay?" She walked to the front of the room. She put her hand on her husband's shoulder. "You're so tired," she said. "Can you come and rest now?"

Matthew shook his head. "It's like trying to keep snakes on a table. So many details." He reached up and clasped her hand. "I've got a couple hundred men that need direction." He sighed. "Trouble never comes at a good time, does it?"

Martha gave a small laugh—more an expression of solidarity than humor. She squeezed his shoulder.

"Have you seen Trojan and Cammy today?" Matthew asked.

Martha shook her head. "Why?"

"Just wondering." He got up and stared out the window. "Just wondering."

Martha gazed out the window, too.

□□□

METEOR'S ARMY arrived just after midnight. Martha awoke from a troubled sleep as the motorcyclists drove up, picked up their supplies, and rumbled off into the night. Martha wanted to get up and see if Meteor was with them, but her eyes were heavy. She reached over—the place beside her was empty, as she expected it would be. She snuggled her pillow to her face, and fell back into a deep sleep.

□□□

MARTHA AWOKE with a start. She clutched her pillow. She reached across the bed—the place beside her was still empty. The room was dark. She grabbed a small flashlight and looked at her wristwatch—it was 5:30 in the morning. She got up and looked out the window. So dark, except for the glow from a bright harvest moon.

Why am I awake?

Everything was so still. So silent. Unmoving, as though frozen by an enchantment.

Something was wrong.

She sensed it—deep in her spirit. The quiet was too quiet.

Something was terribly wrong.

Martha spun from the window.

She discarded her sleeping clothes and pulled on underwear, jeans, and a t-shirt. A jacket lay on the foot of the bed; she snatched it, too. She ran into the kitchen, and took her gun from its holster where it was hanging on the wall. She wrenched open Josef's ammo box, and grabbed six magazines already loaded. She crammed a few more boxes of bullets into her jacket pockets. She shoved her sockless feet into a pair of boots, yanked open the cabin door, and ran into the night.

THE ATTACK came without warning. No bike motors. No truck engines. First, there was silence. Then there were screams. And the crying. Of women. And of children. Then there was the gunfire—the rapid chatter of machine guns.

Machine guns!

Martha knew Matthew had machine guns in his arsenal, but whose guns was she hearing now?

Martha stopped running—she gave her situation another quick thought, and then she changed her mind—she backed into the shadows. From there, she watched. And, she listened.

The gunfire eased up, but the screams of frightened women and children continued, echoing into the darkness. Soon, Martha heard the distinct sounds of men's voices. Orders were being given by some, and being responded to by others.

Martha looked across the compound. There were lights on in both of the women's bunkhouses. She wondered briefly if Ruth was busy with a new mother and baby. She hoped not. That's when she saw the crowd of shadowy figures—some tall, and some small—that was being herded by men with long guns toward the new Women's Bunkhouse. Martha watched in horror.

She was roused out of her shock by the sound of another voice, a voice from her past, a voice she knew well—a voice that should not have been in Matthew's camp. In her camp. Near her cabin.

It was Brad's voice.

"Her cabin is right there," Martha heard Brad say. "Be sure to get her. I have business with her. She'll be useful if we have to negotiate with Matthew."

The man with Brad grunted. "Got ya. Will do." Another man ran up.

"We've rounded up all the women," he said. "They were pretty easy to take. Especially in the bunkhouses. They were all sleeping. We're sweeping the cabins now. And the RVs."

"Good," Brad said. "What about children?"

"We've rounded up lots of kids. We're probably gonna find more. It shouldn't take long."

"Where are you keeping them?"

"In the bunkhouses— Just like you ordered. I've posted several guards outside each one. There's only one entrance, so they don't need heavy guarding."

"What about the men?"

"We've killed most of them. At least the ones we could find."

"How many would you guess?"

"Maybe three dozen or so. Hard to tell. We'll know better when it gets light out."

Martha remained hidden and still, with her hand clamped over her mouth.

Maybe three dozen? The thought horrified her. *Who was among the dead? Don't think that. Don't.*

Martha hadn't been privy to Matthew's battle plans, but she knew he had divided the captains and the top men into teams.

Where had he sent them?

Martha didn't know. She winced. Matthew had decided that the women didn't need to be put on alert till the morning.

Oh, Matthew—you made a mistake. A bad one.

Martha was near enough to her cabin to hear the noise coming from inside. A man burst out of the door. "The place is empty," he told Brad.

"Well, find her! The Man was clear about taking her prisoner. He's got a score to settle with her." Brad looked away from the cabins. "Check the bunkhouses. Maybe she's already been taken."

"Right," the man said, as he ran off. He turned back. "Wait, I don't know what she looks like."

"Oh, for cryin' out loud—just ask for Martha. There is only one of her." The man gave another grunt and left.

Brad stomped off.

TROJAN AND CAMMY heard the gunfire long before they were in range of the camp.

"What the hell—?" He glanced at Cammy. Her eyes were wide. He pulled the truck over, and they rolled down the windows.

"Oh, damn..." Trojan gripped the wheel. "This isn't good—there's shooting everywhere."

"What do you want to do?" Cammy asked.

Trojan gave a short, humorless laugh, "Exactly what we were planning to do." He turned to her. "Let's go get The Man."

"Okay, but where should we go? I-I-don't know where he is."

Trojan thought a moment. "Let's try the camp."

MARTHA HELD her hand over her mouth for fear that even a soft breath would give her away. She looked at the sky—soft pink hues, cerise, the color of summer roses, washed over thin fingers of wispy clouds. She knew the sun would be up by 7:00, but even in the hour leading up to sunrise, it would be light enough for Brad and his men to see her.

Martha panicked.

We're all going to die, she thought. After all the talk, after all the planning, after all the surviving, and for what? We're going to die.

The thought suffocated her and she wanted to drop to her knees under its weight. Then a new thought crept in:

You're a strong woman, Martha. You're smart. Do something.

Martha reined in her racing emotions.

Think. Think. What would Matthew do? What would Josef do?

Get help, she answered herself.

But how do I do that?

The second camp was miles away. *Drive to it? No*—she wouldn't be able to sneak a vehicle; Brad's men would notice. Then she remembered— *the Hutterite patrols*. She could take the back path through the woods to the Hutterites. Matthew had said something about shoring up the guards there. Martha hoped he had done as he said.

THE MAN yanked on the safe's handle. Once opened, he rammed his hand inside and grabbed a book. He took it to the desk and threw it down. He grabbed a pen and slapped pages open—one after the other. He found what he was looking for. He stabbed at the page, stroking with his pen in hurried, vicious dashes of ink.

"You son-of-a-bitch."

The Man sat heavily in his chair. The energy he had expended to stroke out the name left him drained: *Meteor*.

He sat unmoving. Staring.

Sounds from the hallway drew him out of his trance.

He slammed the book shut and returned it to the safe. He turned. Marion stood near the door.

"So, now that you know— Now what?" she asked.

MARTHA CREPT away. She stepped carefully down the pathway near the backs of the cabins, ducking down when one of Brad's men appeared. She reached the edge of the garden and thanked God, under her breath, for corn. She made her way inside the tall, reedy stalks. She crouched down, and willed her heart to slow its wild beating.

When it didn't, she ignored it, and carried on up the row of corn. She knew she would have only a short run to the woods once she reached the end. She hoped the moon wouldn't betray her. She squatted at the end of the row, and listened. No sounds came from the woods beyond. She held her breath and dashed the 50 feet to safety. She hugged a big spruce tree and gasped for breath. She waited. No one was coming.

Martha found the path— She began a slow careful jog toward the Hutterites' farm. She had no flashlight and the path wasn't as brightly lit as it had been the night she had finished plucking chickens. A thought of Matthew flashed into her mind—a memory of him admiring his new gloves caused her heart to clench. She pushed it away.

No time for that.

Martha reached the edge of the woods. The Hutterites' farmland was just ahead. She made a move to run forward, but some instinct stopped her. She waited. She watched as dark figures moved in the weeds ahead of her. She counted—six of them—all men—all holding long guns.

What am I supposed to do now?

VIRGIL'S MEN had returned to their trucks. Brad and Virgil stood near the Gatehouse.

"We're done here," Virgil said. "The camp is yours." Virgil butted his chin toward the cabins "Did you find Martha?"

"No, but we will." Brad smiled. "Don't worry— I've got things under control."

Virgil cocked his head, and said, "Alive, right? Keep her alive."

"Of course." Brad glanced down as he spoke. He looked up. "What are your plans now?"

"Some of my men are heading to the Hutterites' farm. But most of us are going after Matthew— At the second camp."

"Are you going to radio The Man?"

Virgil sneered. "And risk telling Matthew what's up? Not a chance. We want to be a complete surprise."

"Sure— But one of us has to contact him."

"You do it. But give us some time to get into position." He paused and added, "When you call, tell him to courier more weapons. We're gonna need them."

Virgil turned and strode up the road.

Brad watched him leave. He smiled.

MARTHA WEIGHED her situation. It was getting lighter out. She knew she wouldn't be able to stay hidden much longer. One small noise and she would be killed. In an instant.

Martha sat quietly and watched the men, willing them to move off. Then, as if in answer to prayer, the six men began to run. Martha had taken a few steps forward when she saw him—a lone figure. He faced forward, his long gun a shadowy silhouette in the dawn's light. Martha heard something crackle. A radio came to life.

"First camp taken. Over."

A walkie-talkie. The Man's communications.

A desire began to burn inside her. Martha had to have that radio. But not at any cost. She would deal first with the man who owned it. She looked around.

The underbrush was too noisy for her to sneak up on him. He would hear and turn on her in a second. She couldn't fire her gun—she would have the other six men on her within seconds. Then she remembered Matthew's teachings:

Make them come to you. Give them something they want. Get them when they come to you.

Martha swallowed hard. Then she summoned up her softest and most pliant feminine voice.

"Help—" she called. "Help me."

She was hidden behind a large tree; her gun barrel was in her hand, the butt facing out. She watched as the man turned. He crept cautiously toward the voice he had heard. Martha held her breath. The man came closer. She could almost smell him now. Her hand twitched with excitement.

Wait, Martha. Wait.

The man took a few more steps ahead. He was past her now. Martha moved with the speed of an alley cat trapped in a cardboard box. Adrenaline super-charged her arm and she banged the butt of her gun down on the man's skull. The man sank to the ground in a heap. Martha undid his ammo belt, cinched it around her waist, and then she pulled his radio off his belt. She patted him down for other weapons. She took a knife and its sheath from his ankle.

Martha reached into her jacket pocket; she nearly always had electrical ties, and she found one now. She rolled the man to his side, pulled his arms around to his back, and cinched his wrists. She didn't have duct tape, so she pulled off his boot and his sock, and stuffed the sock into his mouth. Time had slowed down, and her thoughts were coming quickly, and with crystal clarity. She wondered if the man had left something where he had been hiding. Martha reached down and grabbed the man's rifle, and then she crept forward. The heavy ammo belt made walking difficult, but she managed.

She reached the spot where the man had been crouching. A duffel bag lay in the grass. Martha undid the zipper and looked inside.

Hand grenades! She suppressed a giggle of delight.

She grabbed the bag and slung the shoulder strap over her head and across her chest. *Time to move*, she thought. The radio came to life.

"We're in position. Over," a voice said. Martha stared at the radio as though it were going to bite her. She waited. A voice spoke again. "You there? Over."

What now?

"I WANT HIM dead at all costs. ALL costs," yelled The Man. "I want that bastard dead."

"Who?" the guard asked as The Man stormed from his office.

"Virgil was right— Meteor never became one of us."

"Meteor? He's turned on us?"

"Turned on us!" He leveled his fury on the guard. "That son-of-a-bitch has his own goddamned army."

"What?"

"He's pulled together a bunch of farmers and cowboys."

The Man raced into the backroom. Guards ran after him.

"What are you talking about?" the first guard asked. "How do you know?"

"Marion knows Meteor. She knows his friends. They don't know she's my sister. One of them told her. She just told me."

The guards didn't say a word.

"Dammit! Where's Virgil at?" The Man demanded.

"He went after Matthew's camp. He's been gone for hours."

The Man's face darkened. "He hasn't called in. Have any of you heard from him?"

"No, I suspect he's out of radio contact. We lose the signal here pretty easily."

"Then—get to him. Tell him."

"Who should go?"

"I don't give a damn who goes! Just get to him!" The Man shouted.

The guard stood, his mouth hanging open in indecision.

"Go!"

MARTHA DECIDED to take a risk. She muffled her mouth, lowered her voice, and hoped the voices on the other end would buy it. "In position. Over." She waited.

Please God.

"Wait for our signal. Advance on the back gate. Will get back to you in about 10. Over."

Martha breathed a sigh of relief. *Ten minutes.* She had 10 minutes to make her move. The radio spoke again, but this time it was a different voice:

"The perimeter has too many guards. We need more light. A few more minutes... then we can get them. Over." Another man answered, and then the radio went silent.

They were talking about shooting her people. Fear and desolation gripped her. *Her people. Good people. They were all going to die.*

Suddenly, something shifted inside Martha. Fear fled from her as something wild took its place—something that made her blood race and her thoughts come clear again.

Martha knew where the guard checkpoints were. She knew her way around the Hutterites' perimeter; she had learned that the day she found her car.

She crouched low and ran.

THE MAN'S messenger turned the key. The truck's engine roared.

"You done back there?" he called.

"Not yet," a man answered.

The messenger looked in the rearview mirror and watched as other men loaded the truck with weapons. They slung a heavy canvas tarp over the top of the truck bed, and cinched it down.

"Okay," said the man, standing next to the window. "Brad called in a few minutes ago. He says Virgil needs more guns. Go to the first camp. Brad will meet you. He'll tell you how to find Virgil."

The messenger drove off.

TROJAN PULLED the truck into the shadows. The light was coming up, and he didn't want to risk being seen.

"What do we do?" Cammy asked.

"I don't know." He scratched his head. "I don't have a clue."

"We could wait here and see what happens," Cammy suggested.

"I suppose— Maybe that's our only choice." Trojan snorted. "Look at us—an *army of two.*"

Cammy laughed. "Can I be the general?"

Trojan pulled her in close to him. "No, I'll be the high-ranking officer." He smiled. "Because I prefer you *underneath* me."

MARTHA HURRIED in spite of the heavy belt slipping too low on her waist. She was still keeping to the shadows. She didn't have far to go—she had found the path leading to the gate behind the big barns—she knew it would have at least one guard. She hoped he had a walkie-talkie. She turned down the volume on her radio as she walked.

She saw the guard. Then she saw another one. She studied the men in the low light. *Our boys, all right*, she thought. She didn't want to alarm them, so she slipped up to the fence, and whispered.

"Hey, guys—it's me—Martha." The men looked surprised as they turned to the sound of her voice.

"Martha?" one of them whispered back. "What the hell are you doing here?"

Martha stepped forward. The men's eyes widened at the long gun and the ammo belt. "Saving your lives," she said. "Radio the rest of the guards. There's a sneak attack coming. Snipers. Tell them to get under cover."

The man stared at her.

"Now," Martha said. "You've got less than a minute."

The man did as he had been instructed to do. In a few moments, all the guards had been warned. They were on the alert now. A sniper takedown would be very difficult. The guard turned back to Martha.

"Thanks," he said. "Does Matthew know you're here?"

Martha shook her head.

The guard groaned. "Matthew will give us what for if he finds out we let you stay out here to catch a bullet. Go back to the camp."

"There is no camp to go back to," Martha replied. "Brad's there now. All the women and children are being held hostage in the bunkhouses."

"What?" one of the guards asked. Gunfire caught his attention and he turned away from Martha. He motioned with his arm for her to get down—behind him. Martha crouched and watched. She heard the cries of men as bullets found their mark. She hoped they weren't their men being hit. She knew she didn't have the medical supplies necessary to care for lots of wounded men.

Suddenly one of the bazookas fired. They watched as something exploded in the distance. Then another. Then another. Martha continued to hope that The Man was taking the beating, and not her people.

My people.

Martha's thoughts turned to the women and children trapped back on the compound. She tapped the guard on the shoulder. He turned.

"I have to go back," she said.

"What?" the guard said. "That's crazy. If Brad has the compound, you'll be killed. Stay here."

"Actually, he won't kill me. The Man has staked a claim on me. So, Brad won't kill me right off." She smiled. "Don't worry. I'll be fine. I got me this far, didn't I?"

"Stay here," the guard repeated.

Instead, Martha handed the man the rifle. "Here," she said. "Take this. It only slows me down." She unbuckled the ammo belt, and handed it to the man, too. He took both.

"Oh, here's something else." She pulled the radio off her belt. "It's one of theirs." She turned the volume button up. "I had it off so you wouldn't hear me come up." She handed him the radio.

"This is perfect," he said. "I'll let the captain know."

"Who's captaining here?"

"Jonah and one of the new military guys."

"Say hi to Jonah for me."

"I will." The guard reached up and squeezed her shoulder. "Be careful, okay?"

"I will." Martha paused. "Do you know where Matthew is?"

"Yeah. He's at the second camp."

"Have you heard anything?"

"Not for a while."

"Please—get word to him that I'm okay."

"I will."

"And send us some help."

"As soon as we can," he said.

Martha smiled and backed away. "Oh," she said, "I nearly forgot. Merry Christmas." She handed him the duffel bag.

The guard opened the bag; his eyes lit up. "Now, you're talking."

They both looked across the field, as something else blew up. Martha noticed the creeping edge of the sun, as it crested the pasture in the distance, showering the grain stubble with soft light. Without darkness, she would have a hard time making it back to the camp—unseen. But that was a chance she was willing to take.

"I'm outta here," she said. "God be with you."

"And with you as well," the guard said. He hefted the duffel bag, the gun, the ammo belt, and the radio—and walked away.

CAMMY PULLED Trojan's face toward her. "I don't want to sit here any longer. Let's do something."

"Like what?"

"Let's sneak up to the gate. Find out what's happening..."

Trojan gave her a wary look. "That could get us killed."

Cammy gave him a quick kiss. "Not if we're careful," she said, opening her door. She jumped out.

Trojan groaned.

But he followed her.

Chapter Fifty-Three

The Gatekeeper

METEOR HELD the radio up for the rest of the men to hear. They were on the rutted road, near the pond, where he and Matthew had held their previous meetings. Trucks and motorcycles lined the road, facing forward, toward the highway, in wait. At the other end of the pathway, his men had settled in—one-man tents dotted the woods and the shoreline, while small campfires smoldered in the early morning light. Meteor and a handful of men, including Richard, were gathered near his truck.

"Damn!" Meteor pounded his fist on the truck hood. "They've taken the first camp. And all the women and kids as hostages."

The men standing near him muttered their responses, as well as a variety of suggestions. Meteor stopped them. He pointed toward the rising sun. "We've gotta wait till night," he said. "Remember, the man doesn't know about us. We've got to stay a secret, or we lose our strength."

"So," asked Richard, "What should we do now?"

Meteor thought a moment. "We can't take bikes in. Too noisy. We'll have to walk in. That'll take an hour or so."

"What about the Hutterites' farm? Should we go there?" the man with the muttonchops asked. "Maybe we should contact Matthew."

Meteor shook his head. "No— Virgil might be monitoring our frequency. I don't want him finding out about us. At least not yet." He took a breath. "We'll stay focused on rescuing those women."

"And especially that one woman, right?" Richard asked. His eyes teased with false innocence.

A shadow passed over Meteor's face. He said nothing.

TROJAN GRIPPED Cammy's arm, drawing her down beside him. They were near the Gatehouse, within earshot of the guards. A truck was coming up the driveway. It pulled over, and a man jumped out. He ran up to the Gatehouse.

"Where's Virgil?" the man called out. A guard stopped him. They had a hurried conversation. The guard ran off. In a moment, he was back with Brad in tow.

"The Man has a message for Virgil. We can't reach him by radio." The messenger stopped for a breath. "It's Meteor—he has his own army now. The Man wants Virgil to know that." He paused for breath. "And I've got the extra guns..."

Cammy and Trojan exchanged a look. *Meteor's army?*

Brad was skeptical, at first, about the news, but he finally believed the messenger, and the conversation moved on.

"Virgil's expecting you," Brad said.

"Can't we just radio him from here?" the messenger asked.

"No, he wants to maintain radio silence. Besides, you have to get those weapons to him before he takes on the second camp." The messenger nodded as Brad gave the details on Virgil's location.

Cammy and Trojan exchanged another look. Then they rose, and raced back through the brush, up toward the main road.

SIMON AND the pony-tailed captain huddled up close to Matthew. Matthew's troops had lain in wait for several hours. The sun was beginning to rise.

"What's on your mind, Matthew?" the pony-tailed captain asked.

Matthew's lips were pursed in concentration. "Where are they?"

The radio on his hip crackled—it was Jonah. Matthew's face grew pale as he listened.

"Dammit!" he exclaimed. "It was the first camp all along." He rose. He shoved his radio at one of the other captains; Jonah was still talking. "Let's go."

"Wait a minute," Simon said, running after Matthew. "They've got to be listening to our transmissions. Or, at least, let's assume they are." He caught up to Matthew and walked backwards in front of him. "Let's feed them some information."

"He's right, Matthew," the pony-tailed captain said, as he hurried alongside. "It worked for us before— It could work again."

Matthew's face was grave. "We've got to tell the men." He looked down at his hands. He shook his head and closed his eyes.

"Oh, God. I made a mistake," he whispered under his breath. His right hand gripped his left, squeezing down hard on its knuckles, and turning his fingertips white with the effort.

God, if you're there—we need some help. Give me an idea. How do I get her out of there? How? Matthew gave a loud sigh.

Keep her safe. Please. Keep her safe.

MARTHA RACED back along the perimeter to the trees. She felt naked and so very alone—so very visible without the cover of night. The sun was rising fast, and soon it would be impossible to hide. She wondered if she should check on the man she had knocked out, thought better of it, and ran into the woods, several feet away from where she had left him.

MATTHEW'S MEN gathered. "We're heading back," he told them. "Brad has taken the first camp. The women and children are hostages."

Angry outbursts from the men. Panic and revulsion colored their language.

"Easy," Matthew said. "I'll get them back. I promise you."

His men were tired, and now they feared for their women and children. No one said it, but Matthew knew what the men were thinking:

He had made a terrible blunder.

Now he had to make it right.

MARTHA RAN until her lungs burned. She stopped halfway between the Hutterites' land and the camp. She sat down on the ground and tried to catch her breath. Her heart pounded in her ears. The morning sun shone like a starburst through the trees, showering Martha with warm golden light. Birds twittered, and squirrels chattered. Martha looked up. It all seemed so normal. Like nothing was amiss. But things were amiss. She remembered the shadowy figures of the women and children outside the bunkhouse.

Things were very amiss.

She stood up.

Martha realized she hadn't peed in hours—she pulled down her pants, and squatted. As she did, something on the path caught her eye. A nail. It looked very out of place, all shiny and new. She stared for a moment and then she remembered: the Women's Bunkhouse. She recalled seeing boxes and boxes of the nails when the men were building the women's new bunkhouse.

The new bunkhouse.

She stood, and did up her jeans. A plan began to form in her mind. She grabbed the nail.

It was time to go.

SIMON AND the pony-tailed captain studied their leader. They waited expectantly. "Ideas?" Matthew asked.

"Let's think this through," the pony-tailed captain said. "The Man was counting on us to protect this camp—over and above the first camp—because of the oil reserves. But he was really after our women and children—"

"Meteor mentioned that," Matthew said. He winced. "I won't go into details, but I'm not surprised."

"So, they've locked down the first camp. What's their next move?" asked the captain.

"To go after us," Simon answered. "— To make sure we can't take back the first camp."

The captain holding Matthew's radio ran up. "Sir, the patrols at the Hutterites seem to be holding their own. Jonah said they got a little unexpected help..." He caught Matthew's attention. "...Martha," he said.

"Martha?" Matthew looked stunned. "She wasn't taken prisoner with the rest of the women?"

"Don't know that, but he says she showed up at the Hutterite colony just before sunrise. No details. Sorry."

"Where is she now?"

The captain shrugged. "Sorry, Matthew— I don't know." He smiled, and added, "But he says she gave them a bag of grenades and a two-way that she got off of one of The Man's soldiers."

"I'll just bet she did," Matthew said with a satisfied grunt.

Thanks.

A moment passed. He ran a hand down his face, and grabbed his chin. "So, where were we?"

Simon continued, "If they know that we know about the women and children—then they'd be expecting us to withdraw from here and try to retake the first camp." He paused. "Why don't we tell them we're planning to do the opposite?"

"What do you mean?" Matthew asked, his voice deep and controlled.

"Let's split our forces. Leave half the men here to protect this camp—just in case we've misjudged The Man. We'll send the other half back to the first camp—by the backroads." He held up his walkie-talkie. "But our radio message will say that we're holding our position here—for the next 24 hours."

"That has some merit—" the pony-tailed captain said. "But let's split the second force in half, too. Just in case things go badly—that way we haven't put all our eggs into one basket." He looked to Matthew for input... and approval.

Matthew studied the two men before him—trusted leaders, and trusted friends. He knew they would stand by him and fight to the death; he hoped to avoid the latter.

"I think that might work," he said. "It won't screw Meteor up. He's agreed to stay off the radio—to keep his force a secret. So, we'll have to be careful not to interfere with his plans." He paused. "I'm very concerned about Martha," he said. "The Man and Virgil said something back in the clubhouse that stayed with me."

"What was that?" Simon asked.

"The Man told Virgil that the best way to harm me was to harm Martha— In front of me."

Simon and the pony-tailed captain exchanged looks.

"Sorry, Matthew," Simon said. "Anna is back at the camp, too." He went quiet.

"I'm sorry, Simon," Matthew said gently. "I forgot about that."

Matthew looked back over his shoulder. "The men are getting really agitated. Let's get this plan squared away."

CAMMY GRABBED at Trojan's arm as they ran.

"What's your plan?" she gasped.

"We've got to stop that truck."

"How?"

They were near the top of the driveway. Their truck was several hundred feet up the road.

"We can't reach our truck in time, and we don't know which way he's going to turn. We have to stop him here," Trojan said.

"Yeah— How?"

Trojan smiled.

"Oh, no—" Cammy said, as he reached for her shirt.

Cammy was already in position when the truck came up the driveway. Her shirt was torn, and a bare breast was visible. She held up her hand in a piteous gesture. The driver slammed on the brakes and the truck ground to a halt, gravel flying. The messenger opened his door. "What—?"

In an instant, Trojan was on him, and the man went down. "What's your name?" The man did not respond. Trojan ground the man's face into the gravel. Hard. "What's your name?" he repeated.

The man groaned.

"Tell me, and I won't kill you."

A few minutes later, "Trevor" was bound and gagged. Trojan and Cammy deposited him into the truck's back seat.

They were about to drive off, but Cammy held up her hand. She went to the back of the truck and lifted the tarp.

"Oh, my," she said. A huge smile lit up her face. "Trojan—you did it again."

MARTHA HAD only a foggy notion of how she was going to free the women and children—without being caught. The nail in her hand had given her an idea. She neared the edge of the woods. She hunkered down and waited. She listened. No sounds of anyone approaching.

She dashed across the opening between the woods and the cornrows. She squatted on her haunches and again listened for sounds. She reached up and broke off a piece of corn stalk. She sucked the syrupy liquid out of the shoot. It helped, but her thirst was acute.

She peered out. No one was patrolling the back of the cabins. She crept forward.

MATTHEW AND the captains hunkered down. He drew a rough map in the dirt, on the ground. "Listen. Nobody knows where I am. As far as we know, The Man thinks I'm still alive, and that makes me valuable." The captains nodded. "Why don't I act as bait? Make them come after me?"

"I don't like the sound of this," the pony-tailed captain said. Simon wagged his head in disapproval.

"Hear me out," Matthew said.

He told them the plan.

TROJAN PULLED over to the side of the road.

"Okay, we're close enough now," he said. "I don't think we've been seen."

Cammy got out of the truck and closed the door. She dropped the torn shirt, and pulled on her t-shirt. "This is a stupid idea," she said.

"Love you," Trojan said with a grin.

"Then don't hit any potholes," Cammy said.

SIMON HAD his instructions and a radio. Matthew nodded as Simon relayed the planned misinformation over the airwaves.

"Let's get these eggs split up," Matthew said to the pony-tailed captain. "Take your troops north to 650, then cut across to the east, come through Alcomdale, and then double-back south on 263. You can swing back west on 554. Toward Riviere Qui Barr. If Virgil's coming for us, he'll be on the main highway. I don't think he knows the back roads. You should be able to surprise him there." Matthew paused. "If this works, you should come up behind him.

"Then, we'll head west and come back south. That keeps us off Highway 44. We'll go back to the main camp." Matthew thought for a moment. "Oh, don't use your radio. I'll call you, if there's a change in plans."

The pony-tailed captain nodded. He held out his hand. "I've got your back." His eyes were sincere. "You know that, right?"

Matthew gave the captain's hand a firm shake. He smiled. "Go."

The captain and his men headed to the compound's vehicle lot where dozens of trucks sat parked. Matthew waited for the men to load up and drive off. He watched as they slipped out a side entrance, avoiding the main camp entrance. Soon, the trucks were out of sight.

Matthew turned. "Move out," he said.

His men ran to the lot and piled into the trucks. They traveled in single file up the camp's driveway to the main road.

Matthew gaped when he saw the sole truck coming toward them.

It wasn't theirs.

MARTHA CREPT up to the rear of one of the cabins. She slipped around to a shadowed side and then she moved forward—slowly—so she could see into the main yard. She gasped and drew back. Several dozen armed men were milling around near the Gatehouse. Others wandered around the vehicles. She remained hidden for another moment and then she risked another look—this time to see the bunkhouses. *More armed guards.*

The guards, bikers of various shapes and sizes, and in a variety of outfits from jean jackets to t-shirts with the sleeves lopped off, lounged on the steps leading up into the houses; some lay on the ground; some stood idly, their machine guns drooping by their sides. Martha wished she could get close enough to listen in on their conversations. But she nixed that idea.

Martha heard a dog bark. It made her heart leap. She hadn't considered the dangers involved should a compound dog decide to greet her. All the dogs knew her well, and they were always very friendly toward her.

Please, God. No dogs.

Martha remained squatting in the shade, but impatience got the best of her. If she could work her way around the perimeter of the camp, she might be able to maneuver herself into a place where she could hear conversations—like into a vehicle near the Gatehouse. She liked that plan, and she crept along the back of the cabins.

The Meeting House was ahead, but it was too far from the last cabin for Martha to make the sprint—safely. Another dog barked. She held her breath. She would have to go back between the RVs and then come up on the other side of the Meeting House. And continue on from there. She hoped Brad's men were ignoring the RV lot. No— She prayed they were.

She slipped back between two large fifth wheel motor homes. She was scurrying toward the rear when she heard a shout from the yard. She dashed around the side of the trailer, and leaned against its metal wall. Her heart raced.

Martha knew she couldn't stay there. Dogs barked again—this time in an excited, "what's-up" tone that could only mean bad news for her. The Meeting House was her only hope. With a quick glance around the motor home, she confirmed that men were headed her way.

Go, Martha. Go.

MATTHEW WAITED as the truck drew near and slowed down. There was a single man in the cab. He stopped the truck and got out.

"Hi," the man said.

"What the hell?" Matthew said. "Where did you come from? And how did you get that truck?"

The man laughed. "I took it. And look what else I got." He held up a two-way radio. "It's The Man's."

I ask for help—and this is what you send me?

Matthew smiled. "Trojan, it's good to see you." He glanced over Trojan's shoulder to the truck cab. "Where's Cammy?"

Trojan turned and walked to the side of the truck. He pulled back a heavy gray tarp.

The muzzle of an Uzi was pointed in Matthew's direction.

MARTHA RAN. She ducked in and out of RVs, kids' bikes, washtubs, coolers, ATVs, scooters, clotheslines, and wheelbarrows. Sweat poured down her face. She came to the last motor home. She had no choice. She would have to run for the Meeting House.

She ran.

She knew the truth even before she heard the men's shouts. She reached the building, and raced up the steps. She had her gun. Maybe she could hold them off.

She opened the door, ran in, and pushed the door closed behind her. Her heart hammered in her ears. She pulled the locking bar down. She backed away.

Please, God. Please. I need a miracle.

Boots banged up the steps. Martha knew no miracle was coming her way.

She clutched her pistol and waited.

MATTHEW STEPPED back, his eyes wide. The men at his sides raised their guns.

"Wait," Trojan said. "Look—" he said with a huge smile. He pulled back the tarp.

"Trojan's Horse."

A woman popped up. It was Cammy. She glared at Trojan. "Don't call me a horse." Trojan smiled and gripped her arm; he helped her clamber out of the truck. "I told you this was a stupid idea," she said. "They were gonna shoot me."

Trojan hugged her. "Nah," he said.

"What the hell are you guys up to?" Matthew asked, his voice incredulous.

Cammy laughed. "Thought you might need more guns." She pointed to the truck bed. The men walked over. They burst out laughing.

"I don't even want to know—" Matthew walked to the truck, and hugged Cammy. Trojan eyed him.

"Okay, so what's going on?" Matthew asked, releasing Cammy.

"They've taken the first camp, and Brad's in charge now," Trojan said. "We know where Virgil is— We can take you to him." He held up the radio, "And—we have this."

"That makes two of The Man's radios," said one of the men.

"Two?" Trojan asked.

"Yeah, Martha gave one to Jonah."

"Martha? Where's she?" Cammy asked.

Matthew shook his head. "We don't know. But she was at the Hutterites' farm for a while—early this morning."

"So they don't have her then—" Trojan said. And then, "Oh, yeah— they said something about Meteor having an army. What's that all about?"

Matthew waved the question aside. "Great, so now they know. Damn—" He gave a heavy sigh. "We had a plan to rescue the women and children, but... I think that's changed now."

"I have an idea," Trojan said.

Matthew studied Trojan briefly. "What is it?"

"It's a good one," Cammy said, not waiting for Trojan to respond. "Trojan says he'll play the part of The Man's messenger. Virgil is already expecting to see a messenger—and he's expecting more guns. That's why these are here— He ordered them."

Matthew went quiet as the pair continued unveiling their plan.

"You see?" Trojan said—his eyes bright with anticipation. "We think it'll work."

The radio crackled. A voice spoke.

It was Brad.

"GO AHEAD," The Man said.

"I think we've just found Martha..." Brad laughed. The walkie-talkie squawked, obscuring some of his words.

"Good. I want to meet her. Have a little chat. Then you can have her."

"Roger, that."

"As soon as Virgil gives me the word, I'll meet you there. Sounds like the boys were having a tough time taking the Hutterites' farm. We might have to re-route some of your men over there. What have you heard?"

"Lots of gunshots, but nobody has asked us to act as back-up." Brad said. And then, "Your messenger showed up. I sent him to Virgil."

"Roger that. I think this little war is nearly over," The Man said.

"Well, it's all done here. We've got things under control. Matthew's men are dead. And the women and kids are locked up."

"Lots of girls?"

"Lots." Brad laughed. "Josef's grandkid, too. She's cute."

"Now that is an unexpected bonus."

MATTHEW'S JAW clenched and he spoke through gritted teeth, "Let's get this plan into place."

"We've got to draw Virgil out," Simon said. "How do we do that?"

Trojan held up The Man's radio. "Why don't we use this?"

"Go on," Matthew said with an encouraging nod at Trojan.

"I'll pretend to be the messenger," Trojan continued. "I'll tell Brad that I can't find Virgil. If I yak long enough, Virgil's sure to cut in. 'Cause I heard Brad say that Virgil had ordered radio silence."

"Hmm," Matthew said. "That could work. Catch Virgil in a crossfire." He turned to Trojan. "You do *know* where he is, right?"

"Of course."

"Okay, we've got to bait Virgil into the Riviere Qui Barre area— That's where the captain's coming up."

"What do we use as bait?"

"Me," Matthew said.

"How about the guns?" Cammy asked. The men turned. They had forgotten the small woman was there.

"What do you mean?" Matthew asked.

"If Trojan can make Virgil believe that he's going to be trapped by the Gatekeeper's men, and that they'll get the weapons—" Cammy didn't have to finish her thought. The men ran with it.

Soon they had a plan and a script for Trojan to follow. Matthew held up his hand. "What about the crossfire?"

"Use the trucks," Simon said.

"What?" Matthew asked.

Simon explained. The men bobbed their heads in excitement. Trojan could barely contain himself, as he waited for Simon to finish.

"My *Trojan Horse* idea," he blurted. He looked at Cammy. She grinned while Trojan explained his addendum to their plans.

Minutes later, the men were assembled. Matthew gave last minute instructions. "Give Trojan one of our radios," Matthew said. He turned and smiled. "Cammy, thank you. I'll see you later."

"Later? Uh-uh. I'm going, too."

Cammy was already on her way back to The Man's truck before Matthew could disagree.

Trojan smiled and shrugged.

Matthew grinned.

Chapter Fifty-Four

A Meeting with Brad

MARTHA JUMPED. She knew it was coming, but still—the sound of splintering wood made her insides quake. She gripped her pistol tighter.

The door burst open. Muzzles of machine guns pointed through the entryway.

"Drop it," a voice said. Martha recognized the speaker. Cold fear raced through her, and she struggled to take a breath.

"Drop it. Or we'll shoot you. Not kill you—but it'll hurt. Count of three, Martha." The man began to count.

Martha let her pistol slip from her fingers to the floor as Brad walked into the room. Men followed behind him—men she didn't recognize. Past Brad, she saw more men in the yard—all were strangers to her. Brad spoke again:

"It's been a while since we've been here together," he said, with a wide, slow smile. He came closer, bent, and retrieved her Browning pistol from the floor. "Nice," he said, tucking the gun into his jeans.

Brad turned, "Gentlemen, I'd like you to meet Martha—" He waved a hand toward her in mock servitude. "The famous Martha." He gave a small bow, and added, "Matthew's blushing bride."

"Asshole."

Martha took a step back, but not soon enough. Brad moved swiftly and struck Martha across the face, so hard, that she fell to her knees. He advanced toward her. She saw the second blow coming and she rolled to the side. Brad's kick went wild and he fell backwards. The men laughed.

Martha got up and ran to the front of the room; she scrambled under a table. Like a trapped wild cat, she peered out at Brad. He was getting back to his feet. His face was ugly, contorted, and turkey-red with rage. Fear flashed through her like a rush of acid bubbles, foaming and popping in an exquisite kaleidoscope of crazy. She wanted to laugh, but Brad's face froze the urge in her throat.

She looked for an escape.

There was none.

A commotion outside the door drew their attention. Martha cried out when she saw the small shapes of children enter. She heard them crying. Three men with guns drawn ushered the crowd of tiny silhouettes into the Meeting House. Martha backed out from under the table and stood up.

"No!" Martha cried. "No!"

The children were all girls—*one of them was Mary.*

"A little surprise for you, Martha," Brad said—his voice silky and low. He crossed the room toward her.

She faced Brad. "Take me. Do what you want with me, but leave them alone." She was pleading now. "Do whatever you want, but let them go, Brad." She took a breath. Her voice trembled with emotion. "Even you can't be that evil."

Brad laughed. "We don't have any plans to hurt these sweet little things, Martha. At least not yet."

Brad reached out, and grabbed a handful of her hair. He yanked her head back. Tears sprang to her eyes, but she remained quiet. "We have plans for them." He yanked again. "The Man prefers *clean women.* And the only way to ensure that is to find little girls—train them to be respectful. And grateful. And obedient."

Brad yanked so hard on the last word that Martha was sure he had pulled out chunks of her scalp. Still, she kept silent.

"Not something you'd know anything about—hey, Martha?" He let go of her hair and shoved her backwards against the table. He smiled. "Let's take care of that—right now."

Martha's eyes went wide—so wide they burned.

What was he saying? What?

She shook her head and backed away.

No— Not that.

The little girls were screaming and crying. Martha glanced over.

Not in front of the children. Not in front of Mary.

"Brad... " she began.

"Lower your eyes," he said.

Martha didn't. She couldn't lower her eyes. Not for this man. Never for this man.

As she stared, a terrible calm infused her as something rose up inside her. She felt it climb out of the pit of her soul.

It was large, and lumbering.

It was angry.

The monster stood erect.

"I will *never* lower my eyes for *you*," Martha said—her voice thick and low with the ice of conviction. "*Never.*"

"Have it your way," Brad said. He reached for her, but Martha evaded his lunge. She was now up against the room's heavy oak desk. She leaned back, gripped the edge with both hands, and smiled. Brad walked toward her.

In an instant, Martha lifted both feet from the floor. Fueled by fear and her instinct to survive, she drove her feet into Brad's stomach. He went down hard. He remained on his knees and gasped for breath. Martha ran behind him.

Her hatred for Brad engulfed her—an exquisite burn, as clear and as sharp as the finest crystal. She wanted to hurt him. She needed to hurt him. She raised her foot to kick him, but an arm around her throat choked the wind from her. She was lifted off her feet.

Hands grabbed her, pinning her arms back. She tried to kick, but the arm around her neck squeezed tight—so tight that she began to lose consciousness. She heard Brad speak from somewhere down a long tube, a dark tube—a foreign place where no light existed.

"Don't knock her out," Brad said. "I want her conscious for this." He planted his fist in her stomach with such force that she doubled over, and threw up.

"Nana!" Mary screamed. "Nana!"

Brad turned to the little girls, and waved to the men. "Get them out of here," he said. The men nodded and ushered the hysterical girls out the door.

Brad turned back to Martha. She had finished vomiting and now hung quietly between the two men holding her forearms. Brad grabbed her hair and pulled her face up to meet his. "Now, you'll learn."

Martha felt her clothing being torn from her. She knew she was naked, but she had no sense of where she was. She felt the coldness of the table beneath her back. She saw the ceiling beams, but nothing was real. Brad grabbed her by the throat.

"Pay attention," he said. "You're not allowed to miss this."

Martha saw fires of hatred, hot like bubbling pitch in Brad's eyes. She squeezed her own eyes shut.

She felt her legs wrenched open wide, and she cried out as a bolt of pain lanced through her inner thighs and hips.

Please, God— Mary. Please, God— Little Mary.

Like a flaming sword, Brad ripped into her. Martha tried to scream, but the hand clamped over her mouth forced the sound back into her throat. She could only moan.

Matthew.

She heard laughter and his voice again. "Hard," Brad said. "Just the way you like it, Martha."

Tears trickled from the corners of her eyes and down her cheeks.

Please take me. Take me away. Please, God.

The pounding. The searing pain. She was aware of it, but she was no longer in her body. Martha floated away in her mind. Far away. Back.

An old song began to play in her head, a song she heard as a child in Sunday school. "*Jesus loves me, this l know... For the Bible tells me so...* "

In her mind, Martha hummed along.

Where are You, God? Don't You hear me? It's bad. Can't You see? Can't You see?

Help me.

HELP me!

Men's voices. Muffled words. Martha's stomach felt sick and she wanted to vomit. More shoving. Talking. Laughter. Pain. Wetness. So much wetness. Then coolness. She felt herself jostled. Her legs lifted. And then a new pain. More acute than the last. She screamed into the hand holding her mouth. Dizziness swept over her like a fuzzy blanket. And she slipped into it, willing it to suck her down. Into the void. Into death.

Please. Please. Please.

A vision came into her mind. The face of a man. It was so bright, and she felt drawn toward it.

Comforted.

There was no pain, no fear, in the presence of this man. There was only peace. And a sense of hope. He was speaking.

Martha smiled and leaned in to his words.

"I am with you. I will never leave you, nor forsake you."

The pain, the horror, and the thoughts that she could no longer bear to think retreated into the hazy mist that swirled around the face of the man—the man with the kindly eyes and the soft mouth. Martha reached to touch his cheek. As she did so, her hand disappeared into the mist.

Like a child lost in a fairy tale, she followed blindly, allowing the mist to gently enfold her in its cloak. Martha yielded to the welcome tenderness—as sweet and as perfect as the reflection in a dewdrop.

She lay back as it rose up to claim her—to swallow her in its thick, grey tsunami of warmth.

It carried her away.

MATTHEW REACHED the highway as planned—the highway that would take him back to the main camp. Back to Martha. He turned right. A string of trucks followed behind him.

The two-way radio sat on the seat next to him. He knew it would remain quiet. Until the time was right.

He pulled to the side of the road and waited.

He listened.

Click. Click.

Matthew put the truck into gear and drove forward. He drove within a quarter mile of Riviere Qui Barre. In the middle of the highway, he stopped the truck. He checked the rearview mirror. Trucks trailed behind him.

He nodded.

MARTHA AWOKE. She was shivering where she lay curled in a fetal position on the wooden floor. She was naked. Her stomach hurt and she tried to remember. Then she did remember. Pain—so much pain.

She moved her legs, and strangled a cry. She hurt so much. She began to shake uncontrollably. She opened her eyes and looked around. Late afternoon sunshine poured through the window, gilding the wooden floorboards. Her teeth began to chatter.

Shock. I'm in shock. Must get warm.

She struggled to sit up, and managed, but just barely. Her head spun, and she closed her eyes to stop the swirling. Her stomach felt sick. She resisted the urge to vomit.

My clothes, she thought.

When she couldn't see them, she pulled herself along the floor into the pool of sunlight. She collapsed and lay in its warmth—willing it to fill her broken body, to heal her, to give her strength. She felt herself begin to drift, but a memory caused her eyes to pop open.

Mary. Where was she? Had they hurt her, too?

The thought was so painful and so intense that Martha cringed. She pulled herself tightly into a ball in an attempt to protect herself from the agony of the thought. However, the thought wouldn't go away.

She forced herself to sit up. She looked around the room. She scanned the wall hooks for a leftover coat, a sweater—anything that would cover her nakedness. But there was nothing.

She tried to push herself to her knees, stifling a scream as her thighs rubbed together. She could feel the wetness between them, and she dared not look—but then she did.

Blood. Blood was smeared down her legs. Fresh blood leaked from her vagina and fell as crimson droplets to the floor. Her stomach lurched. Her teeth had stopped chattering, but she was still shivering. She looked around the room again.

She pushed herself up to one knee. Then—slowly—she stood. She wavered and nearly fell, but she steadied herself. Blood flowed freely down her legs. She watched as dark rivulets wound their way down her thighs and then down her calves to her ankles.

Internal injuries, she thought. She began to shake again.

She took a step toward the door. And then another. Then another.

Step.

Step.

Step.

Pain shot through her, but she didn't cry out.

Breathe through it. Just like birth. Just breathe through it.

More blood dripped to the floorboards.

Blood.

A sudden flashback and Martha remembered the abortion meeting with the kittens—and the man who had torn the kitten he was holding into pieces. Martha swayed and nearly fell, but she kept herself erect.

Then she remembered:

The pink blanket. Was it still here? In the side cupboard?

VIRGIL HEARD the radio on his belt squawk. He glared at it.

"I need Virgil's location," a man's muffled voice said. "Hello...?"

"Are you nuts?" It was Brad's voice. "Virgil's gonna have your balls. He wanted radio silence. I told you that."

"I know," said the voice, "but I think I'm trapped. I'm just off Highway 44. Where's Virgil?"

Virgil cut in. "Get over here, you idiot!"

"That you, Virgil?" the voice asked.

"Where are those damn guns?" Virgil growled.

"I got 'em, but I'm gonna get hedged in. About a dozen trucks coming up the highway. I'm guessing it's the Gatekeeper. I've got one chance to get out of here. I'm near Riviere Qui Barre. Can you meet me there?"

"Damn it. I'm not moving from here," Virgil responded.

"Sorry, you're breaking up. I'm on my way. See you there."

The radio went silent.

MARTHA MOVED slowly toward the wall with the bank of pinewood cupboards. She reached it and began opening doors. Books, notepads, chalk, brushes, paper, crayons, pencils, scissors. She pulled another door open.

"Oh..." she breathed, when she saw the baby pink color. She reached in and took the blanket. It was no larger than a big bath towel, but it was enough. She wrapped it around her torso. She turned and walked slowly to the door.

The sound of voices and scuffling boots caught her attention. The men were coming back.

Martha stuffed the blanket back onto a shelf and rushed back to the spot where she had awakened earlier—slipping in her own blood as she ran. She lay down. She prayed they would be content with what they saw, and not come near her. She tried to quell her panting.

The door screeched opened.

Please, God. Please.

"She's right where we left her," she heard a man say. "I think she's still out cold."

"What if she's dead? Should we check?" asked a second man.

Martha thought quickly—she moved slightly and gave a soft moan.

"She's alive."

"What are we supposed to do with her?"

"Nothing. The Man is coming. So for now, she stays here," the first man said.

"She looks cold."

"Brad wants it that way."

"Does he want us to stay here and guard her?"

The first man laughed—it was a sour sound of contempt. "Look at her—where in hell do you think she's going? Especially without any clothes?"

"Oh, I see your point," the second man said. He gave a short conspiratorial laugh.

"C'mon. We'll check on her again in a few hours. I'm hungry."

The men left, drawing the door shut behind them.

METEOR'S MEN shuffled in excited anticipation. Their gear was on their backs, and they were heavily armed—Matthew had provided them with ample firepower.

"Let's go—while there's still enough light to see through the bushes," Richard said.

"You all know the plan?" Meteor asked.

The men shouted their corporate agreement.

"Women and kids, first. Then we take back the camp."

The men shouted again.

"Let's go," Meteor said.

He led the way.

MATTHEW LIFTED his binoculars. He watched as the trucks approached. Like hapless krill in a humpback's bubble net, they rolled into the trap. Matthew gripped the wheel and closed his eyes. He knew what was coming.

Let this work. Please let this work.

Matthew opened his eyes. He watched as another truck pulled onto the highway. It passed the other trucks and came alongside the lead truck. Matthew watched as the driver motioned toward the back of his vehicle. The lead truck slowed as the passenger rolled down his window.

Virgil. Matthew breathed a sigh of relief. *So far, so good.*

Virgil shouted something, and then the truck sped up. The second truck slipped in behind the lead truck.

Matthew gripped the wheel. It was time. He pushed his truck into gear, and inched the vehicle forward.

MARTHA WAITED. The men's voices died away. She listened. She willed her world to change—her men to come for her.

Matthew. Meteor. Where are you?

Tears began, but she gritted her teeth and she shoved them away.

She rose and scuttled back to the shelf where she had left the blanket. She grabbed it and wrapped it around her shivering body once more. She went to the door.

She opened it and peeked out; the compound was quiet. Not even the dogs were barking. Small campfires burned off to her left; she could see the silhouettes of men. No one was near the Meeting House. No one was looking her way.

She stepped outside.

VIRGIL'S TRUCKS roared forward. Matthew gave a panicked look and braked his truck. They had seen him. He closed his eyes, and waited.

Don't shoot. Please don't shoot.

Men soon surrounded his truck; the muzzles of many machine guns pointed his way. He couldn't resist a smile. *Overkill*, he thought.

Someone yanked open his door, and motioned him out. Matthew got out. One man took his pistol.

"Hello, Matthew," a man's voice called out.

Matthew looked toward the sound. Virgil was coming toward him, a radio in his hand. He waved it in the air.

"Not this time, Gatekeeper. Not this time." Matthew stood quietly. He held his breath.

Hang tight, guys. Hang tight.

Virgil now stood in front of him. "Figured this would come in handy." He waved the radio again. "Recognize it? It's one of yours." He smiled as he spoke.

Matthew's eyes remained fixed on Virgil. He said nothing.

"Bring him," Virgil said.

Two men grabbed Matthew. Matthew could see many more trucks in the distance. He studied the men surrounding him. *Less than a dozen*, he calculated. They walked him back to Virgil's truck. The messenger stood a few feet behind Virgil's vehicle; Matthew suppressed a smile.

"Gee, all for me, Virg?" Matthew indicated the armed men. Virgil smirked. He leaned back against the truck's cab. He held up a cigar and rolled it between his fingers, studying it. He put it in his mouth, and took a long slow drag. In a moment, a thick white trail of smoke curled upwards from both sides of his mouth.

"So, I take it you were headed back to your first camp? You know Brad's in command over there now?" Virgil paused. "And last I heard, they found somebody named—Martha." Virgil took another drag on his cigar. "Would that be *your* Martha?" Smoke trailed from his lips again.

"Let's finish this, Virgil," Matthew said. "Just you and me. Man to man."

Virgil laughed. "We will—I assure you, Matthew. But first there's something I want you to see."

Matthew winced inwardly. "Don't, Virgil," he said. He knew where this was going. "We were friends once. Try to remember that."

"Once," Virgil said. He drew on the cigar again, a long leisurely pull. "But that was so long ago." He walked up to Matthew. "Fair is fair," he said. "Woman for woman."

"She's never done anything to you."

"Maybe not, but The Man has a bone to pick with her, too." Virgil paused for effect. "She's pretty tough—it'll be interesting to see what it'll take to keep her down."

Matthew lunged at Virgil, but the armed men pulled him back. Virgil gave him a bemused smile. "Virgil, I swear to you—" Then he sensed it—a new presence—something was coming.

Virgil sensed it, too. He flicked his eyes back and forth across the horizon. He looked back at Matthew.

Matthew was smiling.

Virgil struck him.

Matthew slumped to the ground.

MARTHA CROUCHED low as she eased her way down the steps. Walking was difficult, but she tried to hurry. She stayed to the shadows as she made her way back to her cabin. She opened the door, walked in, and pushed the door shut behind her.

Tears sprang to her eyes, as a mad feeling burst inside her chest, suffocating her with its intensity. She leaned into the door, hard, as though willing it to embrace her, take her, claim her. She sank to the floor, clutching the pink blanket to her chest. She leaned her face into her hands, and she began to cry—huge sobs that shook her body.

She felt sick again, and she crawled across the kitchen floor to the slop bucket. She leaned over it, and retched, but nothing erupted. Her stomach contracted in dry heaves. They finally abated and she lay down on the floor, exhausted. The room began to spin, and she closed her eyes.

Sleep.

She wanted desperately to sleep, but memories came to her mind. She winced as she remembered Mary's screams and the hysterical cries of the other little girls.

Where were they? What had happened to them? Little Mary? Where was she? Was she okay?

Martha struggled to her feet; the pink blanket dropped away.

She went to the sink. She ladled water into a kettle from the water crock, and turned on her propane stove. In a short while, the water was boiling. She poured it into a washbasin; then she added cold water, bringing the water to an acceptable temperature. She took a rag and began to wash. The water turned pink as she rinsed.

She took a bar of soap, turned it over in her hands, thought better of it, and replaced it in its bowl. *The sting would make her cry out,* she thought. She had no time for screaming. She washed and rinsed until her body was clean.

She walked to the bedroom, and pulled a box of menstrual pads from the shelf. She retrieved a pair of cotton underpants from a dresser drawer. She removed the protective paper from the sticky underside of the pad. She stepped into her underwear and pushed the pad into the crotch of her panties. She winced when she pulled the underwear up, and the pad pushed up against the raw tears. The pad chaffed as she walked.

But at least, I won't be bleeding all over the place.

She retrieved a pair of jeans from another drawer, and pulled those on. She found a sport bra, and a t-shirt. She put those on, too. She looked in the mirror. Her eyes were dark and sunken, and her face was bruised. She ran her hands through her hair. She walked out of the bedroom.

She went back to the washbasin and dumped the pink water into the slop bucket. She leaned over the sink, and took fresh cold water and splashed it onto her face. The cold made her gasp, but it was refreshing; she did it again. She dried her face on a small hand towel, and then turned.

She went to Josef's trunk. As she opened it, she touched her chest. She remembered. Her holster and her gun were gone; Brad had taken them. She rummaged around until she found Josef's gun belt and his Smith and Wesson. She buckled the gun belt around her waist. She checked the cylinder; it was fully loaded. She snapped it closed. She shut the chest.

After grabbing several boxes of bullets from the ammunition box, Martha took a jacket from the hook and pulled it on. She pushed her feet into a pair of slip-on sport shoes.

She glanced through the window—the shadows had deepened. It would be very dark soon. She sat down at the table. She reviewed her plan. She was ready.

METEOR HELD up his hand and his men halted.

"We're close enough," he whispered. "Now we wait."

"How long?" Richard asked.

"Let's give it a couple of hours. Till it's really dark."

"Why not send in a scout?"

"Great idea. Any volunteers?"

"I'll go," Richard said.

Meteor clapped him on the back. "Stay low, buddy." Meteor pointed. "Just follow that path. It'll take you up to the compound."

A MAN ran down the highway. Virgil stood silently waiting for the man to reach him.

"Sir—" the runner said. "Their trucks... they're *empty*! No drivers."

Virgil growled—a low, threatening sound. Gunfire coming from behind made him jump. He turned.

Armed men swarmed out of the ditches, firing machine guns.

"Oh, shit—crossfire." Virgil ducked down. Matthew's unconscious body lay a few feet away. "Damn you, Matthew."

Virgil's men drew close. "What now? We're trapped."

"No, we're not—" Virgil said. "We have a hostage. We have a truck full of weapons. And we have one of their radios."

MARTHA SLIPPED into the night. Like a wraith, she crept silently in and around buildings, moving with the confidence of a seasoned hunter. The night was dark, but the moon was bright. Small campfires crackled around the compound. She sniffed the wood smoke in the air as she listened to the sounds of men talking and laughing.

Out front of the bunkhouses, men sat near campfires, too. Martha watched as they tipped bottles, steel flasks, and leather wineskins back and forth from their mouths.

Good, she thought. Drink up, boys.

Martha sprinted behind the new Women's Bunkhouse. She pulled the shrubbery aside and located the hidden entrance.

Thank you, Trojan.

With great care, Martha opened the door; she slipped inside.

The women sitting nearby gave a little shriek when she entered. She gave them a warning look and held her finger to her lips.

"Where are Ruth and Anna? Are they here?" The women nodded and pointed across the room. Anna was already headed her way.

"Oh, my God, Martha—you're here." Anna's young face showed stress; her eyes were bright with fear. "They're looking everywhere for you."

Ruth ran up. "Mom? What are you doing here?"

"Came to rescue you."

"We were planning to try an escape when it got dark enough," Anna said.

"No—" Martha said. She lifted her chin toward the front of the bunkhouse. "Wait till they've had more time to get drunk."

"Okay," Anna agreed.

"Oh my God, Mom—" Ruth said, her eyes filled with shock. "What happened to your face?"

"It's nothing— Don't worry about it." Martha put her hand to her cheek. "I'll come back for you in a few hours. Make sure that everyone is ready to go. Talk to the kids. Make them understand they need to keep quiet."

"I'll make a game of it," Ruth said.

"Nana!" Mary cried out, as she rushed across the room. "Are you okay? Did those bad men hurt you?" Martha grabbed the little girl.

"Shush!"

"What?" Anna asked.

"Not now," Martha said.

"Nana—I was so scared," Mary said, her voice hushed.

"Sh..." Martha said. "You can't yell like that, Mary. You have to be quiet—like a mouse."

"Okay, Nana," Mary said, her eyes filled with an earnest regard. She reached up and touched her grandmother's face.

Martha smiled and stroked Mary's hair. "Mary, you're going to have to do something very brave. You're going to have to walk in the dark. And you can't talk."

"Not a word?"

"Not a word. Will you do that for Nana?"

"Can I take Wilbert?"

"No, Mary. Wilbert has to stay here." Tears began to well in the little girl's eyes.

"No crying, Mary. Wilbert will be fine. I promise. Okay?" Mary sniffed and gave a little nod of her head.

"Good girl." Martha set the child away from her.

She looked at Ruth and Anna. "The women must be ready. They'll have only a few minutes to make it to the back garden—and then into the woods." Martha gave the women a stern look. "They must stay quiet."

Martha walked to the hidden doorway. She waved for Anna to follow her. Anna did so.

"Here," Martha said. Anna fumbled as she took the items Martha handed to her.

"But... they're yours—"

Martha didn't hear her—she had already disappeared through the doorway.

METEOR WATCHED as the bushes parted. He smiled when Richard's face appeared. "How did it go?" he asked. The men crowded in as Richard spoke.

"Lots of perimeter guards," he said. "And I mean—lots. Heavily armed, too. Machine guns."

"We'll have to break up into smaller groups and launch sneak attacks," Meteor said. The men agreed.

"I couldn't see much around the compound," Richard said, "but it looks like there's a lot of small campfires—like the guys have settled in for the night."

"Any sign of the women and children?" Meteor asked.

Richard shook his head.

"How about Matthew's men?"

Richard shook his head again. "I'm guessing... but... all the men I saw are The Man's people."

Meteor took a long breath. He turned to the men. "Look, you know yourselves best. Break up into teams. Make sure that at least one of you knows how to use a knife. And isn't afraid to use it. We've got to do this quietly— No gunshots. At least, not until later. Okay?"

As ordered, the men formed their groups. Richard stayed with Meteor.

"Let's give the guards some time to get sleepy," Richard said. "Then we'll attack."

Meteor agreed. Then he pulled out a pad of writing paper and a thick carpenter's pencil. "I should have done this sooner, but better late than never."

He began to draw a map of the camp, complete with all the buildings. He labeled the drawing and passed it to Richard. He began a second drawing. Within twenty minutes, he had made a half dozen maps.

The men studied them by the light of their headlamps.

"Once we take out the perimeter guards, we advance on the camp. We'll take out the interior guards, and then begin a search of the buildings."

Meteor took one of the maps; he portioned the camp into small rectangles. Then he assigned a section to each group. He assigned the women's bunkhouses to his own group.

"Everybody ready?"

The men nodded.

"One hour," Meteor said.

VIRGIL PRESSED the send button and spoke into the radio. "Cease fire or we'll kill him."

It took a few seconds, but the chatter of machine gun fire quieted.

"Let's get the hell out of here," Virgil said. He turned back to the messenger who had crouched low near the weapons truck. "Let's go."

The messenger stood and smiled as he spoke:

"I don't think so Virgil—" He reached over and drew back the tarp.

"My name is Trojan and this... is my horse."

Virgil went pale as armed men rose up and leapt from the truck bed. Virgil raised his hands in submission. He turned back to Matthew, who had regained consciousness. He was being helped to his feet by one of his men.

"You got me," Virgil said, as men took his weapons. His arms dropped to his sides in defeat.

"Yeah, we did—didn't we?" Matthew said. He smiled at Trojan. "Nice job."

"Kill me—" Virgil said. "I'm dead, one way or the other."

Trojan raised his pistol. "Let me."

"No—" Matthew said.

He walked over and took Trojan's gun. He turned back to Virgil. He leveled the pistol on Virgil's left eye.

"For Martha—" he said.

Chapter Fifty-Five

A White Dress

MARTHA OPENED the trunk in her bedroom. She moved several items aside. She sighed with relief when she saw it. She hadn't touched it since the day she put it there. She reached for the white packet. She picked it up—it was heavy. She placed it on the bed. She pulled out her jewelry bag and laid that on the bed, too.

She lifted the package, and unwound her white dress from around Meteor's gun. She checked—the gun was loaded. She shook out the dress and laid it across the bed. She smoothed out the creases in the bodice. She frowned at the grease stains.

She turned and studied herself in the mirror. The lantern light barely softened the dark bruising on her face. Nothing she could do about it, she decided. She doubted that anyone would care. She touched her cheek and winced.

She opened a drawer and pulled out a small pouch of make-up supplies. She dabbed a bit of blush onto her cheeks. She selected a black eyeliner pencil and drew a dark, smoky line along the inside of her lower eyelids, and a shorter one on her top lids, ending in a slightly curved corner. She picked up a tube of mascara and stroked the wand through her lashes. She studied her reflection again.

She tried a smile.

It had to look good. It had to be believable.

She tried another.

She ran her hands through her hair. She winced again, this time when her fingers touched the spots where Brad had yanked her hair. Her hair hung limply. It was dirty, but there was no time to wash it.

She took off her t-shirt, and pulled off her jeans and her socks. She turned back to the bed. She stared at the dress lying across the coverlet. She remembered the last time she had worn it, in the moonlight, in front of Matthew.

Matthew.

She wondered where her husband was. She wondered if he was dead or alive. She wondered how he would react when he found out.

She bent to pick up the dress, and her head swam.

Blood loss, she thought.

She checked her pad. It was stained with dark blood, old blood. *Good*, she thought—the bleeding had subsided. She exchanged the bloody pad for a fresh one.

She reached for the dress again, and began to draw it over her head. She stopped. She left the bedroom and went to Josef's trunk. She rummaged around, found what she was looking for, and closed the chest.

A few minutes later, Martha stood in front of her bedroom mirror. She ran her fingers down the front of her dress. She frowned again at the greasy smears. She reached up and touched the crystal earrings hanging from her ears, and then she adjusted the heavy crystal necklace hanging around her throat. The stones sparked fire in the lantern light. She took a long, deep breath and tilted her chin upwards. She turned to the bed and picked up Meteor's gun. She left the bedroom.

Martha sat down at the kitchen table and studied the items she had put there earlier. She pulled Josef's Bible toward her. She picked it up and cuddled it to her face. A memory of his warm fingers on her cheek yielded a soft smile. She kissed it and laid it gently down.

Matthew's flannel shirt lay near the Bible. She gathered the shirt to her face and breathed in his scent. She laid it on the table, too. Then with deliberate strokes, she smoothed and folded it. She carefully placed it next to Josef's Bible.

Martha stared at her hands.

She wore only two rings—a wedding band on the ring finger of her right hand, and Matthew's high school ring on her left hand. She pulled off one, then the other. She laid her old wedding band atop the Bible; she put the ring Matthew had given to her on top of his shirt. She drew back her hands and placed them in her lap. She clenched her fingers into fists.

Tears began at the back of her eyes, but she refused them by squeezing her eyes tight.

I mustn't cry. I mustn't feel. There mustn't be anything there.

She rose from the chair.

She reached for Meteor's pistol. Her hand closed over the grip. It felt familiar.

Comforting.

Martha stopped by the front door. She slipped her feet into a pair of open-heeled shoes. When she raised her head, she saw one of Matthew's jackets hanging from a hook. Josef's grey canvas bag hung next to it. She reached out, and touched the bag—tentatively. She moved her hand to Matthew's jacket. Her fingers trailed down a sleeve, and then she clutched a handful of the fabric. She pressed her face into the cloth. Pain squeezed her heart, and she cried.

I can't do this. Help me, Matthew. Help me, Josef. Help me. Somebody. Help me.

She pulled back. She swiped the tears from her face.

Stop it. Stop it. You were born to do this. You can do this.

She stood.

Unflinching.

A soldier in white.

Martha reached for the door—she turned the handle, and began to step outside. She hesitated and turned back to the coat hooks. She grabbed Matthew's jacket, and shoved her arms into the sleeves. She leaned against a wall, and hugged herself. Moments later, she stood erect.

She took a deep breath.

She walked into the night.

SMALL CAMPFIRES sparked and flared in the darkness; a large bonfire burned in a far corner of the compound. Martha heard the voices of men, many men, joking and laughing; some were singing. They were very loud. She guessed they were also very drunk. She suspected that Brad would be there. She had to go to him, but first—the women.

Martha turned toward the new Women's Bunkhouse. She slipped into the shadows and made her way around to the rear. She noticed the armed men out front of the building; they seemed unconcerned. Her thoughts strayed to Trojan once more, as she located the hidden entrance and knocked softly.

She wondered if he was one of the unlucky camp guards lying dead in a heap somewhere. She hoped not—she truly hoped not. As for Cammy, she suspected the feisty woman was in the other Women's Bunkhouse. Martha grimaced—she couldn't do anything for the women imprisoned there.

Martha tapped on the door again. Anna opened it.

"Are you all ready?" Martha whispered.

"Yes," Anna replied. "There are more of us than there were before," she said.

"Where's little Gordon?"

"He's here."

"Good." Martha looked past Anna into the room. The women were standing in small clusters. Reggie clung to Hannah's hand. Ruth came over and joined them. She hunkered down beside Anna.

"Why are you dressed that way?" Ruth asked sharply.

"Long story—" Martha said. "I'll tell you later." Ruth gave her mother a suspicious stare, but she didn't press the question.

"You know the plan?" Martha asked. "You remember how to get there?"

"Yes," Ruth whispered. "Mom, this is crazy. What if they catch us?" She paused. "And what about you? What will they do to you?"

"It's the only way. I'll be fine." Martha smiled and touched her daughter's face. "Just do as we planned, okay? Get Mary to safety. I couldn't bear it if something happened to her."

She looked over her shoulder. "The men sound really drunk now." She looked back. "Be careful."

Anna and Ruth's eyes confirmed their understanding of the danger.

"Okay, it's time," Martha said. "Keep those little ones quiet. As soon as you're on your way, I'll do something to distract the men— It'll gain you some time."

Within a few moments, the women and children began to leave. They followed Ruth into the garden, and finally—into the woods. They scurried up a hard-trodden path lit now by silvery moonlight. Short, tall, and tiny—like figures out of a fantasy novel, or a fairytale—Martha watched them slip into the night.

"Martha?" She turned to see Anna. Little Gordon was in her arms. Tears filled Anna's eyes. "I—"

"Sh..." Martha said, as she touched the young woman's cheek. "It's okay. I'll be fine."

"I love you," Anna said.

"I love you, too," Martha said with a warm smile. "Like my own blood." Anna pulled a small toque onto Gordon's head; he promptly pulled it off. Both women grinned.

Martha touched the baby's face. "He looks a little like Matthew, doesn't he?" She gave Anna a tender look. "Take care of him. Now go."

Anna left.

Martha stared after them until she couldn't see them anymore. Still she waited. She wanted to give the escaping women a good start.

She peered around the front of the building. The guards were resting on the ground, leaning back on their elbows. Two men smoked cigars, large white clouds of thick smoke swirled above their heads. Others drank from steel flasks.

Martha looked toward the woods. *No movement.* She looked up at the moon. It stared back at her—its countenance stern and dispassionate. The moon knew—Martha knew that the moon knew.

She touched her leg. Meteor's gun sat firmly in a thigh holster she had manufactured from a Velcro strap.

She pulled herself erect and took a deep breath. Like a cool midnight mist, she glided into the light.

The guards leapt up in confusion. "Hey," one of them said. "How did you get out?"

Martha looked at him and smiled—her sweet, practiced smile. "I was never in there." She moved closer to the man. "Take me to Brad, please." She stood passively, feigning her best rendition of cowed and obedient. "He'll be expecting me."

"Are you one of his women?"

"Yes— One of his *special* women." Martha winked. The men exchanged looks—pasty thick with unmerciful judgment.

The men glanced back and forth at one another. The first guard shrugged his shoulders. "I'll take you to him," he said.

"Thank you," Martha said. She smiled again, a soft sensuous smile— cool and sultry—powered by the light of the moon. "Once he's done with me, should I come back to you?"

The men grinned and pounded the first man in the shoulder. "Yeah," they joked. "Maybe she should come back."

The first guard reddened. "Let's go," he said. He took Martha by the arm and walked her across the compound.

The moon followed their movements; Martha could feel it tracking her. The air was chilly. She shivered and pulled Matthew's jacket close to her. Then she stopped. The guard wasn't leading her to the bonfire; instead, he wound his way through the buildings to the other side of the camp.

"Why are you stopping?" the man asked.

"I don't want to disturb him," she said. "Would you please tell him that I'm waiting for him?" Another sweet smile. "I'll wait right here." The guard shrugged his shoulders and walked away.

Martha looked up into the sky. She let Matthew's jacket slide down her arms to the ground. She smiled a tiny smile, and raised her arms to become one with the moon.

Like a luminescent ghost, she stood bathed in the lunar light. She closed her eyes as she sank under the enchantment of its silken sheen, allowing it to baptize and sheath her with its immortal steel—its ethereal calm.

Men's voices. Martha stepped into the shadows.

"Who is she?" Martha heard Brad ask. She watched as Brad and two men appeared in the clearing.

"I don't know," said the guard who had escorted her earlier. "She said you were expecting her."

"So— Where is she?"

"She was right here. Here's her jacket."

Brad stooped and picked up the coat. "I know this jacket," he said. He dropped it to the ground. He looked around. "Martha?"

Martha stepped into the moonlight. Her chest expanded in exhilaration as the lunar light penetrated her spirit, infusing her with the determination of an ancient warrior.

She stood resolute and strong—no longer a woman; and yet, more a woman than she had ever been. She held Meteor's gun close to her side.

"What the hell?" Brad said.

Martha waited. She wanted Brad close—so close, she could touch him. Then she could do what she needed to do.

The bunkhouse guard that had taken Martha across the compound lost interest, and walked off. Brad and the other man walked toward her.

Martha set her jaw. Like the belle of the ball, her dress swishing gracefully around her ankles, she stepped forward. Gunfire rattled in the distance. Martha was startled, but she remained calm. Excited voices came from the direction of the Women's Bunkhouse.

Brad stopped walking. More gunfire. This time closer.

Martha clutched the pistol hidden in the folds of her dress. She wanted to raise it, but Brad wasn't close enough. She wanted her aim to be true.

Brad stared at her, his eyes hard. "What the hell are you doing here?" More gunfire. He sneered at her, "You looking for more of the same?"

"I wanted to speak to you," Martha said, her voice a soft purr.

Brad grunted, and spoke to the man with him, "I don't have time for this bullshit. She belongs with the rest of the women. Get her over there." As he spoke, the bunkhouse guard came running back across the compound.

"They're gone!" he shouted. "They're gone."

Brad and the man with him turned away from Martha. Martha dashed in behind Brad. She pushed Meteor's pistol into the side of his neck.

"I will shoot you dead, you *son-of-a-bitch*," she hissed into Brad's ear. "Tell him to shut up."

Brad gasped.

"Do exactly as I say," she said. With a lick of her lips, she jabbed the gun into his neck as though it were a knife.

The other man turned back; his eyes widened in surprise when he saw the gun pressed to Brad's neck. He reached for his gun.

"Don't," Martha called out. "I will kill him. I have absolutely *nothing* to lose." Martha pushed the gun into Brad's neck again. "Tell him, you filthy bastard." Her voice was hard and as steady as an anvil. "*Tell him.*"

"Don't," Brad said. "She means it."

The shouting man ran up. He stopped short. "What the fuck?" His eyes darted between Martha and Brad.

"Tell him to drop his gun," Martha said. She jabbed Brad again— harder. "Now."

"Drop your gun," Brad called.

The man obeyed.

"Walk," Martha said. "The Women's Bunkhouse." She sensed that Brad was going to turn on her. She pushed the barrel into his neck so hard, that he winced. "I'll kill you before you can blink," she reminded him. He walked forward.

Time. They need time. Think, Martha. Think.

The other guards that Martha had charmed earlier came to immediate attention as she and Brad came closer.

"What the hell?" one of them exclaimed.

"Don't," Martha said. "I will shoot him. Drop your guns. And get into the bunkhouse. All of you. Now!" The perplexed guards dropped their guns and filed up the bunkhouse steps. The door was ajar.

The gun battle was very close—Martha heard men's shouts, and the screams of those taking bullets. She jabbed Brad. "Lock them in," she said.

Brad moved up the steps, slowly, with Meteor's pistol at his neck. He closed the hasp, and snapped a padlock on the door. Martha motioned him to the top of the steps. As he turned, she gave him a powerful shove, sending him toppling backwards down the stairs. He grunted when he hit the ground.

Brad lay sprawled, face down—he groaned and rolled over. He looked up at Martha. The moon illuminated his eyes, and they glittered at her. Blood streamed from his nose—burgundy rivulets in the moonlight.

Martha smiled. Hatred rushed through her—a fiery tidal wave of pitch crashed across her mind. Martha's breath came slow and shallow. She steadied Meteor's pistol and aimed at Brad's chest.

Always aim for the chest, Martha. Josef's voice rang out like Christmas bells inside her head. *Shoot to kill.*

"You killed my Josef," she said. "Now I'm going to kill you."

As her finger closed over the trigger, a memory came again—a vision of a man's head, a hole running with blood, and her own hand, her own gun—splattered in crimson. She faltered.

Can I do this thing?

Then another voice rose up, deep inside her soul.

Thou shall not kill, Martha.

Martha felt her arms droop as her moon steel slipped away—running from her like mercury down a crack. With it, went her rage, her hatred, and... her desire to kill.

To murder.

Thou shall not...

Brad watched her. A moment of eternity passed between them.

Suddenly, he rolled to the side, and jumped up. Martha saw the flash of metal in the moonlight.

A vague notion that she should have taken Brad's gun flitted through her mind. The thought was replaced by another—an oddly happy thought.

I'm going to see Josef.

Bye, Matthew.

She smiled a strange smile as a soft peace washed over her.

"Stupid bitch," Brad sneered. "You should have shot me."

He fired.

Martha flew backwards. Against the door. She slid down and collapsed on the landing.

Brad ran up the stairs. He stared at the locked door and at the woman lying in front of it. He swiped at the blood running from his nose. Then he looked over his shoulder where the gun battle had intensified. Men's voices called out to fallen comrades. Men's voices shouted out commands.

Brad stared down at the woman. She was moaning.

Men's voices came closer.

More gunfire.

He glanced into the night.

He raised his pistol.

He fired again.

□□□

MEN RUSHED into the camp. They spread out. They began to search cabins, the Gatehouse, the Meeting House, and the bunkhouses. One man broke from the pack—a large man. He ran up to the new Women's Bunkhouse. He paused and looked up—he loped up the steps.

On the landing, he dropped to his knees.

The man bent low. He scooped the woman into his arms. Her white dress, now stained a dark crimson, shimmered in the moonlight. He drew her to his chest. He rocked her.

Then, like a lone wolf in a feral salute to the moon, he raised his face to the sky. But, unlike a wolf, the cry that rose from his throat never pierced the darkness.

It remained locked, muffled, mute—deep inside the caverns of his heart.

Silent.

Soundless.

Secret.

For it had to be.

Epilogue

Martha's Vine

THE SOUND of gunshots reverberated through the trees. The woman stopped walking. The child whined and squirmed—she repositioned his weight on her hip. Ahead of her, the women and children disappeared into the darkness—different shapes and sizes, twisting and turning as they wound their way through the moon-drenched forest.

Like a trailing vine, she thought.

Martha's vine.

The woman glanced back the way they had come. More shots echoed through the gloom. She stood still for a long time. Under the moonlight. Thinking. Something tugged at her. She wrestled with it.

With a final glance up the path that the women and children had taken, she turned. The gun slapped heavily against her thigh.

"*Take this,*" Martha had whispered. "*Josef would have wanted you to have it.*"

The woman stared at the Smith and Wesson revolver. She grasped the pistol's butt. It filled her hand—and her chest—with a strange sense of... what was it?

Comfort? Power? Bravado?

Whatever it was—it surged through her. Like a potent drug—it infused her. She smiled.

She heard gunfire again. Louder.

The woman began to run.

Back to the place where she knew she belonged.

HE JUDGED the distance from the bunkhouse to the concealing security of the cornrows. Gunfire had continued on the perimeter.

Could he risk getting seen? Getting shot?

He looked down at the woman in his arms. So much blood. Her face shone white in the moonlight. He gathered her into his arms. He stood.

He scrambled down the steps and hurried around the side of the building. He leaned against the wall, obscured by inky shadows. Gunfire erupted off to his right. He heard cries of pain. And shouts of alarm. He waited for a lull. When it finally came—he bolted.

He laid the woman on the ground between the cornrows. His jacket was smeared with her blood. A sound of something or someone scrabbling through the corn caught his attention—he turned. He sank low and aimed his pistol in the direction of the disturbance. He held his breath.

A dark silhouette—oddly shaped.

He studied it—*a woman. With a baby.*

The woman saw him and stifled a scream. He lowered the gun.

"You—" she said. Then, "Oh—no, oh—no, oh—no-o-o—" She got down on her knees. "Is she dead?"

"No."

"How bad is she hurt?"

"I can't tell. I can feel her pulse. It's weak— But it's there."

The woman handed the baby to the man. She unbuttoned the white dress. She pulled it open. She fumbled with the Velcro straps and pulled the vest aside. She gave a little gasp.

"Oh... look at that—" she said. She glanced back at the man. They shared a brief smile.

"I've heard about that happening..." he said, "...but I've never seen it before."

"Help me get this off," she said.

Loud gunfire nearby made them look up.

"No— Do it later," he said, as he gathered the unconscious woman to him. "Right now, we've got to get her out of here."

"And go where?"

"Into the woods. You and the baby will be safer there, too."

"But then where do we go?"

"I know a place," he said.

REVIEW, COMMENTS, QUESTIONS? Submit to marthasvine@shaw.ca   MARTHA'S VINE: The Sequel **Coming Soon! Summer 2011**

558

On Sexuality in Martha's Vine

I FOLLOW A WILD God, a passionate God—a God who responds in an extreme and passionate way. I worship a God who embraces the coming together of men and women, and a God who embraces the notion of sex. Heck, he created it (have you read Genesis?).

I am a Christian—born again, and adult-baptized. I am also a passionate woman, a creative writer, and—as an ex-crime reporter and mystery theatre producer—I am an ardent fan of details—all the details. Sex is just another detail—more titillating than most, to be sure—but still, just a detail.

As one of my colleagues pointed out, I detailed everything else in this novel, from childbirth to the destruction of a kitten, so why wouldn't I detail physical expressions between a man and a woman? It naturally followed then that sex would be included as a necessary detail in my characters' lives, especially in Martha's life.

However, I must admit, the writing of the sexual content in Martha's Vine surprised me. What I thought was going to be a middle-of-the-road Christian romance novel, took a turn. I followed the bend in the road to see where it went.

Not at all, what I had initially planned. Not at all.

Something interesting happens when you write a story filled with characters rich in human emotions. If you have infused them with enough of your own life's energy, they begin to take on energies of their own; they begin to make their own decisions; they begin to tell their own story.

That is exactly what happened in Martha's Vine.

I wrestled with the sexual content in Martha's Vine; I even tried to cut some of the details, but it felt like attempted murder; I couldn't do it.

I prayed and sought the counsel of friends—both Christian and non-Christian—but the answer always came back the same:

Leave the novel as is. Don't change it. Publish it. And then leave it to God.

Nevertheless, the decision to print Martha's Vine intact with its sexuality remained a tough choice. Very tough.

Because of what people might think.

So... I continued to think it through...

Does my God embrace a wild abandonment to sexuality? No, that's why He also created love. My God hates promiscuous activity (see Sodom and Gomorrah, Genesis 19).

But He is very much a fan of the passions between a man and a woman. He could have left well enough alone when he created Adam, but he knew that man needed more—so he created Eve. To love...and to make love to Adam.

My God also knows those passions sometimes extend beyond the marriage boundaries—they have since time began. Otherwise, there would be no Seventh Commandment: You shall not commit adultery.

I could see unexpected, unplanned, incorrect loves occurring very easily in Martha's world—a world in chaos where the human instinct is to grab hold and to love—deeply and with passion, in an effort to escape the confusion. Regardless of right or wrong.

I like novels, and I have read my fair share of Christian novels, but their characters have always struck me as so contrived, so one-dimensional, so pious, and so holier-than-thou. Not like people in real life—not at all. At least not like the people, I know. That includes my saved Christian friends. I wanted the characters in Martha's Vine to be real, complete with all the gory details. So, the sexual details were a must.

As a contemporary writer, I see sex as part of life—part of my life—and certainly part of Martha's life. Therefore, it must be part of this novel.

God created sex; he included sex in the Bible. Song of Songs is one of the hottest reads in the Bible. If sex is good enough for Him, then it is good enough for me.

As to the swearing.... What?—Christians don't swear? Like heck, they don't. Especially in their minds. Just another detail.

Martha's Vine is a very violent book. Martha's Vine is a very passionate book.

But then—

So is... the Bible.

There is a favorite saying among evangelistic Christians:

Let go, and let God.

It feels like good advice.

~~Sheree~~

About the Author

SHEREE ZIELKE was born in Winnipeg, Manitoba. She spent her childhood on a farm, in the tiny hamlet of St. Ouens, located near Beausejour, Manitoba. She is a born again Christian who embraces passionate, vibrant relationships between men and women. She also teaches digital cameras and photography, her other life's passion. She currently resides in Edmonton, Alberta, with her husband, David Thiel. Martha's Vine is her first novel.

Email Sheree: **shereezielke@shaw.ca**
Martha's Vine book website: **www.marthasvine.com**

About the Artist

I MET HIM as TheWalkinMan.

Well—I have never actually "met" him. We are Flickr.com buddies, photographers, who happened across each other online and who enjoyed each other's work. We've met many times through our images, but never in person; we have never even talked on the phone. However, this is our second collaboration together.

His mundane name is Fred SanFilipo. But to me, he will forever remain... TheWalkinMan.

TheWalkinMan intrigued my imagination with his name and his images, but then he impacted my life. I learned from his work, from his attitudes, and from his extreme talent. My eye began to see things a bit differently through my camera lens; I began to process my images differently -- with more flair, with more abandon. I even got the courage to try self-portraits. I learned a great deal from TheWalkinMan.

Then, in keeping with my impetuous nature, I asked Fred if he would do the jacket art for Martha's Vine. Because we had worked so well together before, I believed that Fred would be the one to interpret my written words with a graphic image.

And he did. Admirably so.

I remember, vividly, the day I first saw Fred's interpretation of Martha's Vine...

I was sitting in the dealership where I have my Magnum serviced; I was feeling very glum, and very stuck; I was considering giving up on the novel, pitching it, and walking away. But an email came in from Fred, announcing that he had something to show me. When I opened the attachment, I nearly dropped to my knees.

It was perfect.

It was exactly what I would have asked for, if I had known what I had desired in the first place—which I didn't. The elation I felt upon looking at Fred's artwork evolved into energy—a much-needed energy that helped to fuel my remaining efforts to finish my first draft.

I am honored to have TheWalkinMan's work on my first novel, but I am more honored to call him my friend.

Fred SanFilipo is a longtime upstate New York regular. Fred closed the doors on a successful 20 year design and marketing firm a few years back in quest of the quieter pace and lifestyle of a freelance designer. He lives in the city of Rochester on Lake Ontario.

LaVergne, TN USA
09 November 2010
204059LV00002B/2/P